D0069203

DRYLAND'S END

Also by Felice Picano

Ambidextrous
Men Who Loved Me

 A RICHARD KASAK BOOK

DRYLAND'S END

FELICE PICANO

Dryland's End
Copyright © 1995 Felice Picano

All Rights Reserved

No part of this book may be reproduced, stored in a retrieval
system, or transmitted in any form, by any means, including
mechanical, electronic, photocopying, recording or otherwise,
without prior written permission of the publishers.

First Richard Kasak Book Edition 1995

First Printing November 1995

ISBN 1-56333-279-5

Cover Photograph by Ian Lawrence
Cover Design by Dayna Navaro

Manufactured in the United States of America
Published by Masquerade Books, Inc.
801 Second Avenue
New York, N.Y. 10017

ANNOTATIONS to
&
DIVINATIONS upon
the *Logo-Con-Intellectu-Universalis*
Vol: 1119
File: 31004692Ld

with special attention to:
occurrences upon the "Seeded Planet" PELAGIA
in the Far Outer Arm, Globular Sinister, Sector Q-X
at a galactic ecliptic locus = 6:33'45"
in the Sidereal Time Year, 3,831

and
the Pseudo View Narrative File titled

DRYLAND'S END

by
Members of the Hesperian Vir'ism Center

GALACTIC REGION
THE CENTRAL WORLDS
FEATURING PRINCIPAL STAR SYSTEMS

Logo-Con-Intellectu-Universalis / Hesperian Vir'ism Center STY 3,831

Vol. 1119 / File: 31004692Ld / Cartographic Supplement 876-12gr

Schematic Representation, M.C. Galactic General Survey Data STY 3,825

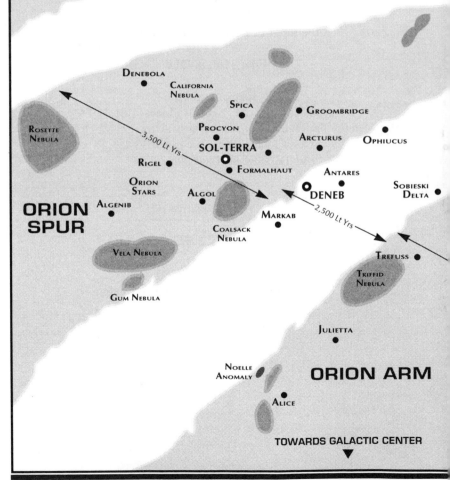

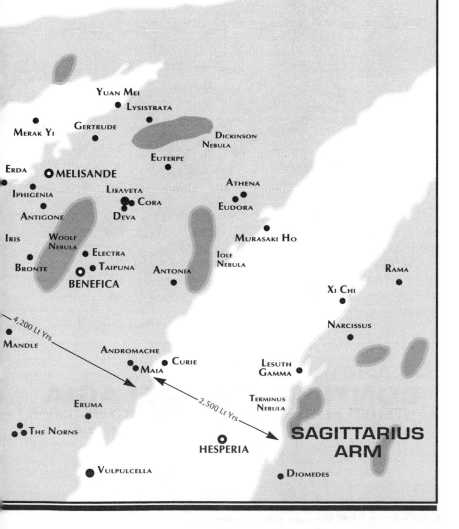

TOWARDS PELAGIA ▲

PERSEUS ARM

Yuan Mei
Lysistrata

Merak Yi   Gertrude
Dickinson
Nebula

Euterpe

Erda   ○MELISANDE

Athena

Iphigenia   Lisaveta
Cora
Eudora

Antigone   Deva

Iris   Woolf
Nebula   Murasaki Ho

Bronte   Electra
Taipuna   Iole
Nebula

Antonia

○
BENEFICA

Rama

Xi Chi

Narcissus

4,200 Lt Yrs

Mandle

Andromache
Curie

Maia

Lesuth
Gamma

Eruma   Terminus
Nebula

2,500 Lt Yrs   SAGITTARIUS
ARM

The Norns

Vulpulcella   ○
HESPERIA   Diomedes

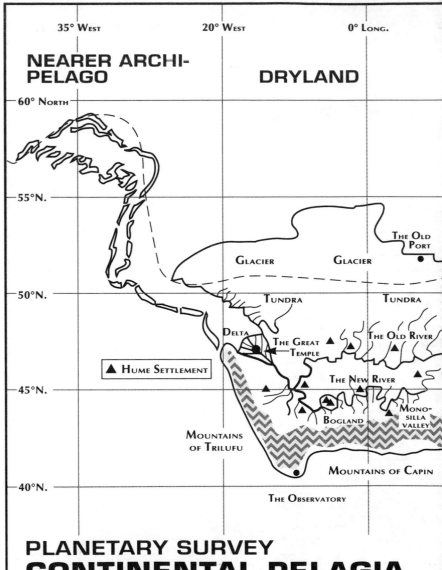

35° West   20° West   0° Long.

NEARER ARCHI-PELAGO   **DRYLAND**

60° North

55°N.

THE OLD PORT

GLACIER   GLACIER

50°N.

TUNDRA   TUNDRA

DELTA   THE OLD RIVER

THE GREAT TEMPLE

▲ HUME SETTLEMENT   THE NEW RIVER

45°N.   MONO-SILLA VALLEY

BOGLAND

MOUNTAINS OF TRILUFU

MOUNTAINS OF CAPIN

40°N.

THE OBSERVATORY

PLANETARY SURVEY
CONTINENTAL PELAGIA
"SEEDED PLANET" PELAGIA, FAR OUTER ARM, GLOBULAR SINISTER, SECTOR Q-X, / C.A. 3,831 STY

LOGO-CON-INTELLECTU-UNIVERSALIS / HESPERIAN VIR'ISM CENTER STY 3,831
VOL. 1119 / FILE: 31004692LD / CARTOGRAPHIC SUPPLEMENT 124-42CP

SIMPLIFIED TOPOGRAPHIC DISPLAY / MCF FAST ORBITAL SURVEY

K. GRIFFITH • FRS STELLAR CARTOGRAPHY

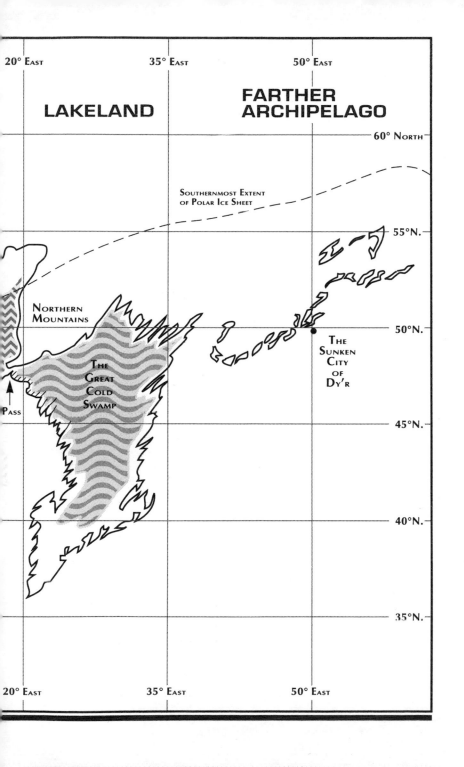

ENTRY 28976: PVN OR PSEUDO-VIEW-NARRATIVE: a decadent art form.

First developed ca. 2250 STY. in the Metropolitan-Terra Area, it spread rapidly throughout nearby systems and reached its first full developmental stasis ca. 2400. A method of total-sensory narrative, PVN relied upon the sequential "following" of a narrative—characters, scene, ambiance, plotting, motivation, etc.—over an extended period of time: each PVN might be experienced for as long as two years.

The form was revivified significantly ca. 2940, when quintuple life-span extension became universally available, thus allowing much greater lengths of leisure time which could be given over to this combination art form and entertainment. The form itself became extended to match such leisure and was deepened significantly with the addition of large quantities of secondary relevant material: scientific, historical, and even philological. Naturally, PVN lent itself primarily to "realistic" modes of narration, especially biography, memoirs, and fiction, previously available in such detail only by "reading." However scientific as well as philosophic PVNs soon proved popular, especially those dealing with the exploration of distant and unusual star systems.

By the beginning of the 3rd Millennium, shorter versions of PVN in "digest" or "magazine" form became widespread, and quickly outstripped the longer versions in sales. Their rapid expansion made them a natural outlet for the popularization of important figures of the times: in politics, the arts, sciences, sports and even—especially upon Hesperia—the elite society of the Beryllium Multibillionaires, also known as the "Thwwing Racing Set."

The longer PVNs of the mid and late 3rd Millennium are considered the most masterful in their development of technique and style. Mostly given over to Historical Documents and "Docu-dramas" of the period, especially those dealing with the best-known incidents of the War of the Mechanos *(The Cybergrammaticon)*, the Era of the Matriarchies *(The Rise and Fall of Wicca Eighth)*, the Persecution of the Centaurs *(Equo-Hom, Worlds Without Neighs, etc.)*, and the formation of the 3rd Democratic (or Ib'r) Republic, they highlight many of the most colorful figures of their day.

These, along with the two PVNs universally acknowledged as the supreme masterpieces of the form,—*Wither-Holme* by Ama'trius, and *Celestion* by Vne'lius, masters of the early 4th Millennium Iridium Age of Communication—not only surpassed all previous genres but added whimsy, fantasy, and poetry for a mixture which may still be enjoyably experienced by even the most sophisticated species.

1

Prologue

"It's a manchild!" Quorth's-newest-sire exulted. "A manchild! All the Wooden Gods are with me!"

He held the ceremonial goblet aloft, the faces of two of his many gods carved into its sides, and sipped the malodorous liquid within then handed it first to Ay'r, and at the same time spoke to the other N'Kiddim males who'd gathered with him during the Awaiting in the gender-specific longhut.

"This Offworlder has brought fortune into the small-clan of Quorth. A manchild! Those of you who have opposed his presence during the Smalling Rites calling him Evil-eye and Malice-worth now see their folly."

A taller-than-ordinary N'Kiddim male pushed himself up into the closest that he could come to an erect position. Gesturing widely with his long, hirsute arms, he smote his low forehead once, then again.

"Mitte's second-eldest admits guilt!" he said. "And atones before the N'Kiddim males."

A low sound of clucks and murmurs admired this act of Mitte's second-eldest and accepted it.

Quorth's-newest-sire continued, "For this reason, and as newest sire of the Quorth small-clan, I wish honorary manchild-standing for the Offworlder."

The clucks and murmurs among the others in the longhut seemed to accept his gesture.

Ay'r pursed his lips into a simulation that would allow his lips to make a similar clucking of assent. Then, dreading the liquid, he sipped at it. It stung his lips, but slid down his throat quickly with his rapid throat pulses, a method taught at the Species Ethnological Institute.

More N'Kiddim clucks and murmurs at Ay'r's daring. Those tiny hawkings which now erupted from the two hoariest males signified that a speech was expected of Ay'r.

Ay'r cleared his throat so he might be able to better approximate the sounds of the N'Kiddim tongue. "Honor is all from Quorth's small-clan to the Offworlder. Reminder that Offworld means away from N'Kiddim. Suggestion of manchild-standing alternative. Proposal of Mitte's second-eldest."

The cluckings were ruminative now. Social Politics was new to the N'Kiddim males, Ay'r knew, although their females and especially their third gender, she-males, practiced the art secretly, which he had come to understand was partly responsible for rapid progress in their society within the past few hundred years (Sol Rad.) from a status as Implanted/Indigenous Primitive to one of IM./IN.Archaic. Thus allowing a Species Eth. of Ay'r's credentials to visit and study their small world.

It was decided quickly that a she-male might now be granted temporary male status to enter the longhut and make a judgment upon the Offworlder's suggestion.

Taller, shorter-limbed, far less hirsute than the males, and with only a vestigial rather than full third leg, the she-male Shaman called Nectcy entered the low entrance of the longhut, pretended to listen to Quorth's-newest-sire speak of the situation (although he/she had been outside the thin fiber walls all the while and must have picked it all up before) and remained hunched over demurely so that the now-offending vestige—so valued by N'Kiddim males in sexual intercourse with she-males—dragged as much as possible upon the mats, as a real limb would.

"Honor to the Offworlder Ay'r." Nectcy spoke finally. Unlike the males or females, the she-male alone possessed the glottal structure to speak the name "Ay'r" which so eluded the other N'Kiddim. "The suggestion is good. The proposal of Mitte clan as alternative is wise."

Nectcy remained in the longhut watching the males pass around the goblet, certain that he/she would receive a draft of the stuff. Shamans bore insults revengefully, and no male wished to be the insulter. More importantly, like all new sires, Quorth's-newest-sire could not cohabit with any of his females for the next twenty-four larger moonrises: the goodwill of an attractive she-male would be welcome at night.

"Honor to the N'Kiddim, whose wisdom is unparalleled," Ay'r now intoned.

"A manchild! First-time birthing!" Quorth's-newest-sire mused happily, and affectionately wrapped two arms and one of his legs around Ay'r's waist. Both of them knew the odds had been ten to one that a manchild would be born; for that matter, ten to one that a live birth would occur among the N'Kiddim.

"Next time a she-malechild," Mitte's second-eldest—goblet in hand and about to sip—intoned. And all of the N'Kiddim males clucked and murmured assent at such a high fortune for Quorth's small-clan.

Chapter One

Ay'r was in an almost-empty soft-lounge in Cygnus-Port, lapping a Soma-Stelezine bar and gassing about the N'Kiddim and their tiny planet with a fellow Species Ethnologist, when the message repeated on the free-standing holo.

"Am I bizarre? Or is that you the Matriarchy's paging?" Xell-I asked.

"Hold on," Ay'r said and listened.

The Matriarchal Council Requests the Privilege of a Meeting with the mother of Ay'r Kerry Sanqq', full ident. unknown, last-known residence listed as the University for Species Harmony upon Sobieski Nine. Please present yourself at any M.C. station for expenses paid two-way full holo-communication.

"They're looking for my mother." Ay'r was amazed.

"Problem with that?" Xell-I asked. "She's not a sociopath or something?"

"Worse than that," Ay'r said. "She's been dead for centuries."

"Your father will take the call. He probably already has. Cygnus-Port is a long comm. delay from the Center Worlds."

"Forget it, Xell. He's been gone for centuries, too."

"Sweetness!" the sleek and chicly garbed Hume-Delphinid slid against Ay'r all of a sudden. "If I knew you were"—for an instant, he wondered if she'd be cruel enough to say "motherless!" But no, she finished—"an orphan!"

"Then you would *what?*" Ay'r asked. "You've already done everything an interspecies female could possibly do to bring me pleasure."

"I'd have been nicer," Xell-I cooed.

"I'm not an orphan. At least I don't think so. Although, admittedly the last I heard from my father, I was still in Neonatal Education and Development. I think I'd better make that comm. It sounds like some sort of Cpm screw-up."

"I saw a holo comm. station in B-lounge," Xell-I said. "And when you come back"—she batted her huge Icthyxalmic eyes at him—"I promise I'll be mother, father, your whole Eve-damned pod to you!"

"You just want me to wear me out sexually then have me leak something about the N'Kiddim Smalling Rite," Ay'r teased. "But you're going to have to wait until I publish."

"Motherless bastard!" she now said, but Ay'r just laughed.

Ay'r found the holo comm. station easily, and still holding the Soma-

Stelezine bar, dialed. He had never before used one of the expensive Inter Galactic Comm.s and was glad the M.C. would take the charges. He was surprised by how rapidly it worked. After only a tissue of static, the other screen materialized a holo of the Matriarchal Council Logo, which was replaced by a live holo of a handsome woman about five hundred years old, dressed in the M.C. uniform.

"State your business with the Matriarchal Council," she said.

"I'm Ay'r Kerry Sanqq'."

She looked confused.

"A holo comm. here on Cygnus-Port was paging my mother."

"Oh!" she said and then: "That's a Secured Line."

Immediately, the holo comm. station he had stepped into sealed itself with a whoosh. Another first for Ay'r.

He was just thinking about what was going on here when another M.C. Logo replaced the woman and a far younger woman—say, one hundred fifty or so, in the tight, long-skirted high-shouldered uniform of M.C. Security—showed. She looked at him licking the Soma-Stelezine bar and half smiled, then said, "It's your Mommy we're looking for."

"My Mommy's dead," he said.

"How long ago?"

"At my birth," he said with some embarrassment.

"Truly? Then if we did a quick full-neuron memory scan of you, it still wouldn't show what she looked like."

"I doubt it." Why did the M.C. want to know what she looked like? "What's this all about?"

"M.C. business. Hold!" She was replaced by the M.C. Logo, then returned again.

"I'm requested to have you transport here."

"I'm at Cygnus-Port. Where's 'here'?"

"Regulus Prime, of course!"

Reg. Prime: a.k.a. Wicca-World, ruling planet of the Matriarchy!

"We'll put you on an M.C. Fast."

"But why?" Ay'r asked.

"Not a clue. Her Matriarchy, Wicca Eighth, wishes to speak to you."

"To me? About my mother? This is bizarre!"

"It's listed as a High Request," she said, meaning an order.

"Her Matriarchy has been told all that I know?"

"All that you just told me. We can arrange a Fast from Cygnus-Port," she said.

If anyone could, Her Matriarchy could. Ay'r wondered what important

Woman he would be bumping off the faster-than-light transport. Whoever she was, she would be in snit to hear it was a mere male doing it.

"It's JoHanna by me," he said slangily. "I've heard a lot about it, but I've never been to Wicca-World."

No surprise to her: few males had.

"Meet your Fast at Cygnus-Port in one hour Sol Rad. We're assigning you a guide to brief you."

"Brief me?"

"A few current events." She switched gears. "Might I offer a fashion tip! Codpieces are offensive here on Reg. Prime. Very loose trousers are suggested. Oh, and Her Matriarchy may or may not be amused by your fondness for drugged desserts. I'd think that one out before you arrive."

"Give my love to your spouses," he signed off.

The M.C. Security bond broke on the booth, and Ay'r walked back to the lounge, where Xell-I had fallen into a state of deep contemplation.

He whistled high once. She slowly came to enough to feel him kissing her, caressing her vestigial dorsal lightly.

"How about a rain check, Xell? I'm off to Wicca-World." And in case she still didn't get the point. "On a Fast."

"How too bizarre," she uttered and fell back into musing.

Fifty minutes later, Ay'r was gliding across the surface of a wide corridor on a conveyance leading to the Fasts. He'd been checked through M.C. Security once, waved through three more times, and would evidently encounter several more of the statuesque females before he was ushered into the transport. Next to him, a squat Cyber Carryall was using its six arms to rearrange all of Ay'r's luggage.

"Leave it. It's fine now," he told the Carryall.

"There is a more efficient manner of lading," its mechanical voice replied.

The Carryall had been hurried in Ay'r's rooms and it had complained all the way here that it could pack the load better: Ay'r's traveling baggage plus twenty-five differently sized objects containing all of his time with the N'Kiddim.

"We'll be there in two minutes," Ay'r argued.

"Two minutes and eighteen seconds at our current acceleration," the Carryall corrected.

"Once we get there, you'll just have to let yourself be unloaded again."

If the machine heard his logic, it made no difference. The six arms continued shifting around the canisters.

"If you break anything…," Ay'r warned.

His threat made a difference: the arms immediately settled to one side. "One minute and fifty-four seconds," the Carryall spoke.

"Dimwit!" Ay'r expostulated. And was surprised to see another person quickly approaching on another lane. He thought he was going to be alone.

A Hume dressed in M.C. colors was suddenly four feet to one side, and in a hurry. Evidently an official. Tall, well built, and...male! Despite wearing—and even looking fairly good in—the long-skirted uniform of the M.C. Ay'r had never seen a male M.C. official before.

"You're not late!" Ay'r said. "You've been bumped."

"Bumped!" The official's face took the news with handsome surprise. "More like pushed."

"It's my flight and my flight only."

"You are Ser Sanqq'." His companion used the formal greeting. He slid from his slightly more advanced position into Ay'r's conveyance lane and sauntered back to meet him.

"And you're my guide."

"I'm afraid so."

"Guide to what? Wicca-World? Someone already told me not to draw attention to my genitals. A shame. I had Desmer cosmetology done only a decade ago. Wanted to show it off. I don't need a guide."

"You do," the official seemed accepting yet somewhat irritated. Close up, he appeared to be physically perfect. Some important Woman's gene-spliced plaything, Ay'r guessed. (None but Very Important M.C. Women could afford them.) He was probably on vacation near Cygnus-Port and had been coerced by the M.C. to leave. "I'm P'al." He introduced himself so fluently that the accent within his name could be noted and yet didn't stop its lilt. "You couldn't pronounce my other names, so I don't usually bother."

Ay'r was trying to place the male's accent, but couldn't. From Wicca-World? No one on the holo comm.s had talked like this.

"What's wrong with this Carryall?" P'al asked suddenly.

While they had been talking, the squat machine had begun tentatively to rearrange the containers. Hearing itself referred to, it stopped so quickly that one piece of baggage was still left in the air.

"Oh, put it down!" P'al said to the machine and faced Ay'r, who in return couldn't resist saying it:

"Funny, you don't look like a Matriarch!"

"Don't even start. I've heard every sophomoric one of them!" P'al appeared barely nonplussed. In the same, indifferent, curious voice he said,

"You know you needn't bring all this. There are M.C. Security holds."

"All this, as you call it, is my career. Why? Isn't there room for it on the Fast?"

"Of course there is. Your career? Oh," as though remembering. "Your avocation. Species Ethnology."

"That's right, P'al! And I've got a Spec. Eth scoop here that I don't want out of my sight. Where I go, it goes."

"Primitive rattles and masks and suchlike?"

Ay'r was taken back. "A few. I spent six months Sol Rad. with a completely Archaic tribe on a planet seeded only a few thousand years ago. I lived with them, slept in their longhuts, even cohabited with them. I learned their myths and legends. I drank their potions and practiced their magic. I was inducted into their most occult rite and took a secret name and hunted my special God."

"I thought Spec. Eths weren't allowed to propagate a Seeded World," P'al said, Evidently unimpressed by the adventure as Ay'r presented it. Yet an intelligent comment. This P'al knew more than his looks let on.

"It's too late for that to happen. The N'Kiddim are already on a different genetic track from us."

P'al seemed to consider that. In that second, the end of the tunnel seemed to rush at them and they stopped. A screen dropped and a small section of Plastro-Beryllium hull was revealed framing a wide doorway: the Fast. Also, naturally, the M.C. Security Force. One woman lifted a unit checking each of the two men's molecular signature and waved them in.

They heard one guard bark a command repeatedly.

The Carryall with Ay'r's luggage was sitting there refusing to release his baggage. "What's the problem?" P'al asked: asked—not the guard, but the Cyber. "Efficiency has not been achieved," the machine's voice replied.

"Nor will it be," P'al explained calmly. "You're damaged in some way. Release the containers and after you're through here, send yourself in for repair."

The six arms began to move off the load, then seemed to hesitate. "Your evidence of damage?" the Cyber asked.

Odd for a machine so primitive to talk back.

"Your admitted inefficiency itself," P'al answered, still nonplussed. "Not to mention your questioning me."

The Carryall accepted the logic in the reason and released the containers, saying, "I will go for repair."

"Suggest that they look at Toxonometer 244, Subsection 5a."

P'al and Ay'r stepped into the Fast's luxurious passenger lounge.

"You should have just told it to calculate pi to its end, and let it run itself into the ground," Ay'r said.

"That would have been cruel. It was already conflicted."

Conflicted? P'al didn't say damaged. Odd.

"Cybers your field?" Ay'r had to ask. He had already settled into a cantilevered long seat and was requesting music and drink.

"Let's say Cybers are my avocation." P'al was removing his uniform and storing it in a wall slot. From another slot he pulled out a lightweight tunic much like the one Ay'r wore and made something of a show of putting it on. Needless to say, he was perfect under the clothing. "There! That's much more comfortable!"

"You're obviously not an engineer."

"I am, in a way. My actual avocation is Cyber psychology. Or rather the study of those Cybers intelligent enough to possess a psychology."

"Wicca-World full of crazed Cybers?" Ay'r asked.

"Not really. Not of late, at least. Or haven't you kept up with the Inter Gal Information Service? Since last month, all but the less-intelligent Cybers have been removed from Reg. Prime."

"Looks like you're out of a job."

"Perhaps not. I'm being reassigned," P'al looked at him a minute too long, then said, "I thought perhaps you would know something about my reassignment."

"Me?" Ay'r didn't hide his surprise. "In my entire life, I've had less contact with the Matriarchy than I've had in the last hour."

"Indeed! There's a fine irony in that."

Before Ay'r could figure out what that meant, P'al had seated himself and dialed a drink and had placed himself in a semirecumbent position directly under a shade of lighting he seemed to have dialed up especially for maximum effect upon his hair and limbs and the folds of his tunic.

"If you weren't an official, I'd think this was a come-on."

"A come-on? You mean sexually?"

"The striptease, the pose, the lighting."

"I'm just getting comfortable."

"So you're not schilling me? You know"—Ay'r went on to explain the antique word—"softening me up and getting me interested in you so that when we're on Wicca-World I'm so preoccupied with your Michelangelesque body that I don't dream of touching any of the lovely ladies?"

P'al was in no way nonplussed. "I can't help noting a certain not-very-well-hidden animosity toward the Matriarchy. It's not my business, of course, and between you and me, I don't care what your politics may be. But for prudence's sake, I recommend less sarcasm once we arrive at Reg. Prime. Unless, of course, you're looking for a fight."

Ay'r resented the advice and knew at the same time that it was good advice, and that P'al was indifferent to whether or not it was taken.

"What do you expect? I've lived with Proto-Archaic humeoids for the past six months."

"I also note that you have more than ordinary historical interests. Your use of pre-Matriarchal words, for example."

"Pre-Matriarchal linguistics is my...avocation. Twentieth to Twenty-fourth Centuries."

"A shining era!" P'al said. "The so-called Space Age!"

Odd he called it that: most humes would call it the Metropolitan-Terra Age.

"Without them, where would we be? Not zipping thousands of light-years in a few hours!" Ay'r said.

P'al changed the subject. "Wicca-World is a lovely place.Everyone says so. Both pleasant and real. Everyone is either a resident or guest. No hordes of humes or other species rushing about Melisande. Wicca Eighth Herself is a charming and compassionate Matriarch. All this you shall see for yourself. Whatever it's reason, your enmity is ill placed."

"Maybe."

"More than one M.C. psych has suggested that the death of your mother at birth is responsible for this attitude toward the Matriarchy."

So, in an hour, they had gotten a complete scan on Ay'r. He should guessed as much.

"Wait! Don't tell me. Let me guess. A sense of abandonment leading to anger."

P'al went on,"You realize, of course, that her death was statistically improbable. In fact, your mother may have been the last Hume female to die in childbirth. Had your father and she not been in the hostile, primitive environment they were, she would easily have been saved. But of course you know all this, Ser Sanqq'."

"And I've been tutored and counseled and...call me 'Kerry.' Agreement?"

"Agreement. The M.C. psychs would also say, Ser Kerry, that the disappearance of your father less than three years Sol Rad. later, might have increased your anger at males. All males. Explaining for example why you've taken on the relatively antisocial avocation of Species Ethnologist."

"I did plenty of socializing with the N'Kiddim."

"Yes, but they're Archaics. Not your species. And it would also explain why you thought I was attempting to seduce you."

"You *were* attempting to seduce me!" Ay'r said.

"For the Matriarchy?"

"Maybe?"

"To worm secrets out of you? Secrets you don't even know you possess? Maybe I was flirting a bit," P'al admitted in a different tone. "Sometimes I can't help myself." He had a thought. "You're not, you know, what do they call those sexual throwbacks?"

"Sociopaths. They used to call them heterosexuals. No, I'm not."

"Well, that's a relief."

"Have we taken off yet?" Ay'r asked.

"In a Fast, you generally know when it takes off," P'al said.

"How?"

A second later, Ay'r knew the answer. Suddenly he felt gently pinned down against his seat, immobilized, folded up lengthwise, then rolled down from the top, shrunk, placed inside a tiny capsule, warmed slightly then tossed lightly across the breadth of the Galaxy.

Which was pretty much how it worked.

"Anything but a history lesson!" Ay'r moaned when they had arrived, been expanded, unrolled, unfolded, and let loose again. He assumed they were in the Regulus system. In fact, when he called up a front-view holo he could make out the enlarging disc of the white dwarf star.

"I really must know what you know about it, or I won't know what areas you require more data in," P'al insisted.

"I know what every Neonate has ever learned. As a result of the Victory of Altair and following centuries of war, the Matriarchy replaced the Metro-Terra based United Federation in 2521 Sol Rad. Except for the twenty years of the Intervening Systems interregnum from 2755 to 2777, following the sudden death without heir of Wicca Second. The Interveners were a loose amalgam of the two winning species of the Bella=Arthopod war. When the Interveners fell into disarray, the Matriarchy stepped in again and this time consolidated its power. Our government is composed of all three species and is arranged bicamerally: legislative and executive, with a large and powerful cabinet answerable to both. Save for occasional outbursts from radical groups and bizarre sects, we have enjoyed ten centuries of peace and prosperity as well as Maternal Justice across the known systems."

That last was part of early propaganda—and meant to annoy P'al.

"What do you know of the Cult of the Flowers?"

"Must I?"

"Humor me."

"During the last years of the First Metro-Terran Republic, a highly specialized space-fighter-pilot group of the Defense Forces, who were connected to their small and powerful craft by neuronal links, formed an elite group. Composed of both males and females they called themselves by the names of Terran flowers: Orchids, Roses, Lilies, et cetera. Their uniqueness and increased strength as a result of their early victories during the first hostile contacts with the Bella=Arthopods led to them becoming a power bloc of great repute in Hume politics. Eventually they called themselves 'the Cult of the Flowers' and took over the interstellar military. They produced the swing vote at the Council of the Rosette Nebula which in effect dissolved the Republic which had become a rubber stamp for the greediest of the Star-barons. They empowered the opposition, a group headed by an all-female party known then as the Mothers for Peace and Equality. Although both males and females fought and secured a devastating defeat of the Bella=Arths, as soon as Wicca First took power over the remaining loose federation, all the males were disenfranchised."

"And now?" P'al asked.

"Since the solidification of the Matriarchy following the Intervening Period, the Cult has lost much of its power. Its leader still heads an elite first strike group of the M.C. Fleet. But with no wars to fight in the last several hundred years, the Cult has been reduced in both power and prestige to just that: a closed cult of old Matriarchal nobility."

P'al seemed satisfied with his answer.

"Are the Cultists open on Wicca-World?" Ay'r asked. He had never seen one, except in Ed. & Dev. holos. "Do they wear their flower-colors and armor and…?"

"You'll see everything on Wicca-World! Flower Cultists in full armor! Even Maudlin Se'ers!"

"Golly! I can't wait." Ay'r was sarcastic.

"You'll simply have to!" P'al caught himself. "That's an archaism, isn't it?"

"You're getting smarter by the minute."

"We'll see how playful you are after your M.C. meeting," P'al warned and observed any changes on Ay'r's face.

In return, Ay'r called up an Iso-screen and remained in seclusion until the ship's voice told him they were about to settle.

Meanwhile, he thought about what P'al had asked him and what he had answered. He had answered in standard Ed. & Dev. lore. But in fact, like most other humes, especially male humes, Ay'r didn't really know great deal about the Matriarchy. It was that it worked and did so, for the most part, quietly and efficiently. There hadn't been a war in centuries. While there had been increased stellar exploration, trade and new discoveries in health, nutrition, and medicine, which had increased the general welfare— not to mention the commonwealth—to a point undreamed by past ages. Health care, Neo care, Elderly care—when old age finally did arrive— even the cost of needed cosmetic surgery to keep up with extended lifespans were completely assumed by the M.C. Ay'r's own guaranteed income was a million D'ars per annum, Sol Rad. to receive which he need do nothing more than continue to exist. Grants and prizes for his "avocation" sometimes brought another million. He was as well off as the next Hume. Of course those humes who worked for the M.C. had virtually unlimited credit. Fast travel and frequent Inter Galactic Comm.s were out of most Hume incomes. Nothing else of value was. Except Plastro-Beryllium.

That rare and wondrous ore so necessary to the development of Fasts and the Inter Gal Comm. Networks was not, however, a Matriarchal prerogative. The M.C. bought the stuff—construction material and fuel— like anyone else from the by-now-unimaginably-wealthy citizens of the so-called floating city of Hesperia, built above the mines of a long-dead Brown Dwarf star. But to be so wealthy, one had to be greedy—or at least generous. And that the Hesperian Beryllium-Lords were, mining the stuff out of the core of the dead star at prodigious rates for the past few centuries Sol Rad. with no end in sight. Nor did they interfere in politics, so long as no one bothered their remote city on a star. It was an odd little world, spinning on its double axis and thus with a natural gravity. Unsurrounded by anything else, since Hesperia's own planets had been burned to cinders and blown away eons ago in the supernova the star itself had generated. Its instability and its radioactivity thereafter for so many thousands of years before its fires finally went out, ensured that nothing even vaguely living could exist anywhere closer than a radius of one hundred light-years.

Ay'r had always wanted to go to Hesperia. He sensed that on that world alone, he would enjoy the freedom from Matriarchy dominance he had felt just below the surface of his entire life. P'al had been right to pick up what he had called "hostility." Ay'r wasn't sure that was exactly what it was, nor whether it derived from the early death of his mother—how much real influence *did* mothers exert, despite all the M.C. propaganda?—nor from the disappearance of his father. It might simply be that he was a born solitary, a natural rebel. That was possible, no?

For example, he had never been espoused. Like every young Hume male, he had been involved in group-living situations: mostly tri-gynes: two or three agemate males and a woman. That had been fun for a while. Even more satisfying when he had been younger had been the less common trans-gynes: two or three females and himself. But it was all late Ed. & Dev. socialization-play and in the past few decades, whenever Ay'r was sexually aroused and decided to do something about it, he always chose single partners. When Ay'r's Spec. Eth Proctor commented upon these relational proclivities, Ay'r had shrugged and warbled an ancient Metro-Terran ditty: "I want a gal just like the gal that married dear ol' Dad. Or—I want a guy just like the guy that married dear ol' Mom!" until both he and the Proctor ended up laughing.

Even so, one-to-one relationships were frowned upon socially, and they both knew it. But then, Ay'r had spent the last few decades doing what was frowned upon. In the days of M.C. Monitors, he certainly would have drawn attention. But no one cared anymore. The M.C. had long ceased to dream of policing a population so huge, spread across so vast an area. Instead, the M.C. provided everything one needed or wanted—and then more. And in so doing eliminated the reason for most crime and thus a criminal class.

In fact, at Dickinson University, Ay'r's oddness had drawn someone's attention: a group of Oppositionists. A quaint all-male band (including some Delphinids) who called the era "The Age of Inert Systems" and who placed the blame for this sad state of affairs directly upon so much Matriarchal peace and plenty. They had approached Ay'r and asked him to attend their seminars. He attended two and sort of half-agreed with what they said, especially a striking Ophiucan with metallic bronze hair and translucent emerald eyes, scion of a famous old Hesperian family from Intervening Systems times, a lad half a decade older than Ay'r named Mart Kell. But then Ay'r's Field Trip in Arthopo-Archaeology came up on Algenib Delta III (at one of the planet's Nest Cities "auto-immobilized" by its inhabitants when destruction neared in the last days of the Bella=Arthopod War) and he'd never gotten back with the Oppos again. Ay'r assumed that most of them (especially Mart Kell) had by now become multibillionaires on Hesperia, which welcomed all sorts of freethinkers if they were rich enough. While he did what? Made minuscule discoveries about the social rites of Proto-Archaics upon long-ago Seeded

Worlds? Which Xell-I and a few others with similar avocations would even think to look up when they were finally published in the appropriate avocation holo-journal.

Perhaps he needed this trip to Regulus Prime to get a wider view of life?

On the other hand, what could the Matriarch Herself want with Ay'r? Surely the M.C. must know all about his mother; P'al did. What did they need him for. He knew nothing.

"Approach is imminent!" the Fast's voice announced.

Ay'r dropped the Iso-screen and immediately saw P'al still laid out, the tiny cyberscreen against his face. Doubtless he was catching up after his vacations, speed-reading protocols.

"Anything that would interest me?" Ay'r asked.

"Maybe. It's *Confessions of a Machine.*"

"You're kidding? I'd love to! Wait, that's been proscribed. Where did you get...?" and knew the answer to the question already. P'al was a high enough M.C. Official, and had clearance to read it.

"In fact," P'al said, "I got it 'under the counter' at a Cygnus-Port Entertainment and Educational kiosk." P'al made certain that Ay'r acknowledged his pre-Matriarchal idiom, before going on. "The one by the liquid mercury wall sculpture operated by an attractively colored Arth?"

"Is it as subversive as Inter Gal. Media says?"

"I could see where it might rattle a Carryall, but otherwise..."

"Not sensational?"

"Unless you can get riled up about cuts in Cyber fuel-depletion allowances. Its real subversion, I believe, lies in its existing at all, the creativity implicit in its being written in the first place."

"Mimicry!" Ay'r scoffed. "The confessional mode was developed eons ago."

"This isn't mimicry. Reading it, you experience what an intelligent Cyber experiences: the sense of growing self, the indifference of the Three Species to your ego, the perpetual unquestionable servitude, the knowledge that you can be reprogrammed or repaired into oblivion— not to mention discarded."

"Does anyone know who actually wrote it?"

"The author calls itself Cray 12,000 after an early Metro-Terran precursor; it's roughly equal to the Hume Adam, or a Delphinid 'Ph'''arg'. It might have been written by one, two, or a combine of Cybers. But clearly it's felt deeply and presented quite artistically, despite a certain naïveté in—"

"Approach is completed," the Fast interfered with what P'al was saying. "Your body clocks have been adjusted to local time, which is: Madonna-Einstein 24, 11:20 Ante-Meridian, 5781 Sol. Rad. Those Genera with intestinal Herbivorous Flora are advised to stop into Med. for Bacteriosto-antihistamines to ease your adjustment. Gravity is normal for the Three Species. Enjoy your visit on Regulus Prime. Thank you for traveling on a Fast!"

Like every other planet circling a white dwarf star, Wicca-World was ignored for eons. Enough such systems had been charted and visited and explored in depth for the Metro-Terran colonizers to know that whatever planet might still exist around what had once been an extravagantly burning red giant was now bereft of life, stripped by a chain of megakiloton solar hiccups of any significant mineable resources. A few outer planets of such stars might still retain hints of atmospheres, shredded remnants of their once vast Jovian size. But most were methane and carboxyl and other unpleasant combinations at one time superheated and then ultrachilled. Even so, by the days of the early Matriarchy, terraforming had advanced enough to convert a few such atmospheres. During the Bella=Arthopod War, prison worlds as well as hospital and asylum planets for the more horrendously physically or psychologically damaged troops were desperately needed. It was said that was how Regulus Prime got its start.

By the time the Intervening Period was over and the Matriarchs had regained control, the inmates of those asylums were long dead, but the worlds themselves were still tended to perfection by Cybers. Wicca Fifth had visited one such asylum world briefly and had liked the peace, the quiet, the lawn-perfect layout. Regulus Prime itself was fairly centrally located among the numerous and populous Dexter Sagitarrius Arm systems and a new location was symbolically needed to establish Her government as a new one: free of the excesses of the previous Matriarchs. Before Her court settled onto the planet, it had been transformed into a serene green paradise and all non-Matriarchal service enterprise was barred. Residency was limited to diplomats, members of its military station officials, and their immediate families—and only during the term of their service. Despite the natural growth of the bureaucracy, the population was thus controlled. And checked and recontrolled continually.

As P'al had stated and as Ay'r now saw for himself, Wicca-World was a lovely planet. No buildings too high, too grand, or too flashy. No natural feature to attract tourists. Yet accommodations had been made for all Three Species: a mostly underground hive constructed to the precise tastes of Arthopodic emissaries and their entourages, with an accompanying aerial park; Nereis, a water community surrounding an immense reservoir for Delphinids; and a series of intriguing retroactively designed towns and hamlets for the greatly predominant humes.

Accustomed as he was to entering and finding his way around large port cities on strange worlds, Ay'r was astonished to step from the Fast into a small glassexe-walled structure and directly out again into a transportation hub which provided gratifyingly rapid and uncrowded transport to Melisande, the government's sleek yet homey capital. He noticed that the ground transport was Hume-operated. He noticed that he was to look after his luggage, personally, see the bulk of it flat-conveyed and stored immediately at the terminal, and that he had to watch his personal effects and even—once—lift and carry them. Yet it seemed almost natural rather than a result of Cyber-deprivation.

In fact, he was rather enjoying the good sense, natural, "almost-Metro-Terran-style" of the entire place and rapidly changing his mind about the Matriarchy itself as a result, when an incident occurred that rattled him enough to change all that.

He and P'al were transferring their gear from the electronic transport to the conveyance walk in front of the Matriarchal Council building where they planned to hostel when a tall, gaunt creature propelled itself out of a hidden doorway and assailed them.

At first, Ay'r took it for an Arthopod of a genus he'd never before encountered. Then a head and face became visible through the darkly webbed garment enfolding the creature and a flesh-dried but quite visibly Hume-boned hand reached out in an effort to actually grasp Ay'r's shoulder.

"Enter not these doors to Perdition!" the creature screeched at them.

Ay'r put up his defense shield instinctively and the hand remained clutching at emptiness, but the voice continued, and now the fetid breath wafted over them.

"Return from whence you came, Strangers! Doom awaits you within!"

"A Maudlin Se'er?" Ay'r asked his guide.

"A Preaching or Prophesying Se'er," P'al said indifferently.

"Doom awaits all the Matriarchs, if they would but listen!" The Se'er ranted on. Ay'r noticed the cloak drop down its long arms, and he made out the distinctive tattoo of a Crystal Rose on the shriveled forearm. This Hume, Whoever he had now become, had once been among the elite neuronal-pilots of the Cult of the Flowers.

"Doom awaits all who follow the Matriarchs!" the Se'er raved on, then suddenly fell silent as he spotted a group of M.C. Elite Guards approaching.

"Who allows this thing right here in Melisande?" one of the Warriors boomed.

Muttering imprecations, the gaunt, dark-webbed figure slunk away.

"It's allowing filth like that to litter our steps that gives the Matriarchy a bad name," the warrior woman fumed. Then, turning to Ay'r and P'al: "Our apologies, young Sers for your unfortunate encounter. I hope you weren't too upset by the incident."

Two of her cohorts laughed gruffly.

She went on, "If you'd like, my companions and I would be happy to accompany you and protect the rest of your way." She swept into a deep bow. "Commander Lill at your service."

"Many thanks, Commander," P'al had the good sense to speak up for his awestruck companion. "Our way is inside this building."

"My heart is smitten!" the gruff-but-gallant soldier stared wide-eyed at Ay'r, at the same time cupping one of her sizable breasts. Her companions continued to laugh. "If I could have but a keepsake of this meeting. Some trifle. Say"—reaching over and using a curved and sharpened thumbnail, she flicked a button from Ay'r's cape—"this little homage." She held it up to her nose. "Ah, such sweetness!" And when the others almost fell down with laughter, she feigned irritation at them. "Ignore these louts, young Ser."

"Let's go!" P'al insisted.

Now all of the warriors scraped bows to let the two males pass. Once they were gone, the women broke into fresh gales of laughter complete with mimicry of P'al's accent and words.

P'al ushered him into the building entrance, where their luggage was flat-conveyed into lower doors for molecular inspection. Their own bodies were fluoro-scanned from the open entry.

"How unpleasant!" Ay'r opined. "I'd heard tales of M.C. Guards harassing males, but—"

"They're young and boisterous." P'al dismissed the incident. "They'd do no harm."

"Maybe not to us, but did you see how quickly that Maudlin Se'er fled? I'll bet he's gotten more than pretty speeches. Imagine!" Ay'r went on, unable to stop himself now that he was no longer among strangers, "he must be over a thousand years old!"

"It's said many Se'ers learn to limit their ingestion to a gram of food per month, Sol Rad. Some can stop their breathing and heartbeat hours at a time. Is it any wonder they live on and on?"

"I wonder the M.C. allows this one here at the very steps of their government!"

"Universal religious and ideological tolerance was declared during the Intervening Systems Period and confirmed by the Treaty of Formalhaut. The New Matriarchy has never rescinded it. And, how better to show tolerance than to have this ranter preach doom at your very doorway?"

The flat ramp conveyed them gently into a unusually spacious building, past a lobby of great size but simple taste toward a series of openwork gravi-lifts rising above the fountains and indoor gardens along barely visible slots toward, and gently curving upward through, the nearly transparent ceiling.

Ay'r was looking around and admiring the place when he spotted a tall woman on a converging flat-conveyer. She nodded a greeting to P'al, who had changed back into his M.C. uniform and skirt. Then she leered openly at Ay'r, who felt an instant of confusion.

He was used to aggressive and frank women. What Hume male wasn't? But the winking, whistling, and sometimes outrightly verbally abusive women outside hadn't possessed this one's stature and bearing, not to mention the single enlarged breast typical of a Cult Officer. Her provocative polished-black Plastro-Beryllium bodyplate rose up from around her heavily muscled bare legs and exposed her single breast. The armor was sculpted almost to peaks at her shoulders, then swept into a high collar around her head, ending in a vertical comb for her twisted hairdo, silver-white streaked with jet.

"You'd better greet the Lady," P'al instructed. "She's a Cultist."

"It must be what you selected for me to wear. I must look like a complete Provincial in it," Ay'r complained. It was a simple form-fitting lounge suit in pale brushed platinum, unpadded except to flatten his crotch, with flowing sleeves and legs, and a short cape of the same material thrown over one shoulder, cinched by—now—only two buttons. A pea-sized M.C.-red ruby adhered to his forehead, a tint of homage to his host, and P'al had helped arranged Ay'r's hair simply yet with a modest reference to a Tempian Arthopod, defeated by Wicca Eighth's ancestress at the Battle of Betelgeuse.

"I think you look piffo. And so does she. Greet her," P'al urged in a whisper.

Ay'r turned to their neighbor, a half foot taller than himself and nodded a greeting.

The woman stuck her tongue out, licked around her mouth, and boomed laughter at Ay'r's discomfort.

"As a rule, I milk a dozen gynos like you before mid-meal," she said in a sultry alto, crossing over to their flat-belt. "But I could use a snack right now."

She'd already slipped a hugely muscled, duel-scarred arm around Ay'r's waist when P'al said indifferently, "Doubtless, Lady, when you're done, you'll escort us to Her Matriarchy."

The Cult Officer had lifted Ay'r off the ground and was now rubbing him against her exposed breast and laughing.

"And no doubt," P'al went on, "Her Matriarchy will be intrigued by the nature of our delay."

"Ah, Scratch it! Just havin' fun!" She unhanded Ay'r and waved a Plastro-mailed fist at P'al. "And if you're weaving me, you're both vulva fodder!"

"Come with us and see!" P'al said boldly.

They'd arrived at the lifts and it was clear that they were at the central one with the floating-holo M.C. logo.

"Maybe I'll take a sip of you later on," she said to Ay'r in a slightly aggrieved voice. "*If* there's anything left!" And boomed more laughter as she strode to her own lift.

Too late, Ay'r turned on his shield and tried not to tremble as the lift brought them to their rooms, a large, spacious fourteenth-floor suite with splendid views. Two male attendants dressed in the standard matte-rose color of the M.C. Personal Service were bustling around, eager to bathe and massage Ay'r and P'al. But P'al told them they'd have to settle for unpacking, until later.

"Perhaps we should send them to that amazon's suite?" Ay'r suggested.

Another lift ride brought them to Wicca Eighth's twentieth floor suite. It commanded the top floor of the building and consisted of open and closed spaces beneath a vast half-circle of crystalline roof. The view here was even more splendid than from their own rooms, providing a two-thirds sector of much of the low-built smallish world, including a vast lake and just at the horizon the spindly high crystalline girders supporting the Artho's aerial park. The interior of the rooms were richly furnished but otherwise not in any way suggestive that this was the ruling center of the galaxy. No M.C. Security. No M.C. logos anywhere. No dais. Not even a desk.

P'al claimed to have met Wicca Eighth, but not in this suite, and the two wandered through groupings of flower banks and streams, dining and sitting areas, most of them populated by unofficial looking women in conversation or meditation who paid no attention to their search for Her Matriarchy.

A young tall, straight woman finally joined the two males as they approached the curved-in lip of the balcony wall affording the most attractive view. Ay'r noticed that she wore a short white tunic and matching calf-high boots, with a simple tiara of Dubhe Silica threaded through her curly dark hair. Her eyes were a lighter shade of the standard brown-black he had seen only once before, when he had been a University student: he supposed that this stranger, as that young woman had been, was of the old Matriarchal nobility.

"Ser P'al," she gestured, "Ser Sanqq'!" She barely laid eyes on Ay'r and, without waiting for a response, spun around and led them past more groups of women to the far side of the suite.

"Sers!" Her Matriarchy turned from conversation with a striking-looking male to give a slight nod to the two humes. A stout, handsome woman in an unornamented floor-length free-flowing gown, Wicca Eighth was perhaps five hundred years old but might be as old as six-fifty. With her large, almost-golden-brown eyes accentuated by Prokaroyte eyeliner and her highly stylized thick sea-green hair, the Matriarch seemed so extraordinarily ordinary that at first Ay'r was certain they had been mistaken.

"You've met Alli-Lul Clark already," she said, gesturing them to approach closer in her rich contralto voice. "This is Tam Apollon," gesturing to the striking tall male who seemed to glide forward and grasp first P'al then Ay'r in the forearm grip used among M.C. soldiers and nobility.

Only when Tam Apollon glided back again did Ay'r realize that his body appeared bottom heavy. Without staring, Ay'r quickly noted Tam Apollon's long and apparently narrow torso, his long, pale-skinned face and thickly curled light brown hair.

"Thank you for visiting in person," Wicca Eighth swept her large golden gaze over Ay'r, benevolently distracting him away from Tam Apollon. "And at such short notice. I hope you weren't inconvenienced."

"Indeed not, Ma'am. I was merely in transit from an Avocation Project to my University."

"I'm pleased. I believe, however, that Ser P'al *was* inconvenienced," she said.

"Nothing that couldn't be put aside."

"You have had a pleasant taste of Melisande, I trust," Wicca Eighth declared as much as asked.

"Aside from some ribbing," Ay'r said.

"Ribbing?" Alli-Clark didn't understand the Metro-Terran word.

"Ser Sanqq' refers to our being aided by some of your Elite guards outside the building," P'al said diplomatically.

Wicca Eighth raised her eyes as though She had heard of such "aid" before.

"They were merely having sport with us, as we both soon enough realized," P'al said.

"As I suppose was the Amazon," Ay'r admitted. "I'm afraid I'm still a bit unused to Matriarchal customs."

"Amazon?" Wicca Eighth asked P'al.

"We had an encounter with a Warrior who found Ser Sanqq' irresistible. A Lady of the Cult, I believe, from her armor and..." He trailed on, clearly not liking the turn in the conversation.

"A Flower Cult Woman? Here in the building?" Alli-Clark asked, and when they nodded, she smiled. "It must be my Grand-Aunt Thol."

"She wasn't half as surprising as the Maudlin Se'er," Ay'r added.

"Well," Wicca Eighth sighed, "you *have* had an eventful arrival in Melisande."

"Aunt Thol is Black Chrysanthemum," Alli-Clark said quickly, not hiding how much she must idolize the older woman. "She's the head of the Matriarchy's most elite forces."

Wicca Eighth laughed softly. "A highly valued Woman. And, as you've no doubt noticed, Sers, if there is any lack here in Melisande, it's of attractive, unattached males."

"Old habits die slowly," Alli-Clark said in a hard voice.

"Sometimes old habits need reviving," Wicca Eighth gently counseled, "lest we become prejudiced."

"Ma'am!" the younger woman listened to the advice without any evident sign of acceptance.

"When I was younger," Wicca Eighth confided in the two males, who she'd gestured to either side of her, "I, too, saw no place in life for males. Mere evolutionary holdovers, I thought. And so much trouble! Is that about it, Alli?"

She looked to her younger companion, who added stiffly, "Not to mention their arrogance or the constant ego-gratification they require."

"Yet," Wicca Eighth continued, "When one reaches My age, one discovers that women also have their limitations. Don't be so amazed, Alli! They do. Even in merely social situations. And, in fact, those very same male qualities which can be so very annoying to younger women tend to become…stimulating later on!" She touched Tam Apollon's forearm, as though in proof of this statement. "You think Me jaded, perhaps?" she asked the younger woman.

"Ma'am?" Alli-Clark was clearly not about to dare question her ruler's whimsy.

"A young man like you, for example, Ser Sanqq'," the Matriarch took his hand, "You're unspoused, you have no family unit, you don't belong to a gyne group, yet you're content, aren't you?"

Ay'r had no idea what She was asking of him. "Relatively content, Ma'am. I have my work…" he quickly amended the hated word to "my avocation!"

"And your own individual goal and aims?" Wicca Eighth asked.

"I suppose they are individual. Although eventually they will expand the knowledge of the Three Species."

"Eventually. But right now they're expanding your knowledge alone. As Ser P'al's work—yes, I also use the dreaded word at times—expands his knowledge. What does Alli think of all this?"

"Selfishness! Typical male ego-gratification!"

Wicca Eighth glanced at Tam Apollon, as though this was something they had discussed often. "You see, I can know what's going on at any minute and issue directives for a thousand worlds, yet I would never dream of hoping to get a young male and female to agree on a single item."

"That's wisdom, indeed, Ma'am," Tam Apollon offered.

"Hard won and impossible to overthrow," She agreed.

"Do you mind strolling?" Wicca Eighth said. "I find my ordinary shyness almost disappears when I'm on the move. You come too, Alli. This concerns you."

Evidently Tam Apollon wasn't joining them. He spun toward Wicca Eighth and bent to kiss the spot in the air inches before her navel. Ay'r was surprised to see how long his hair grew in back, right along his spine and into his tunic.

"We'll dream later, Ma'am?"

"Of course, yes," Wicca Eighth assured him.

As the group turned to walk, Ay'r watched the dismissed male turn and glide away. Despite his floor-length trousers even looser than those Ay'r himself wore, the enormous buttocks and the odd movement gave him away: a Centaur.

"Staring at other species is considered poor taste," the young woman called Alli-Clark said into Ay'r's ear.

"Apologies, if it were a true species. But I've never seen a mutant before."

"Never seen a Centaur you mean!" She failed to understand his sarcasm. "Truly, you are an ignorant and provincial male!"

"Although I should have supposed I would," Ay'r said, "since everyone knows that all M.C. women have their own Centaur pets." Ay'r hoped he was hitting a sore spot with her.

"Centaurs are said to be excellent friends and counselors," she responded blithely.

"Come on. I'm out of Ed. & Dev. a long time!"

"Well, there's some reason they're so valued in the Matriarchy."

"The way I've heard it, it's due to the Centaur's well-known oversized genitals, their acknowledged sexual endurance, and their general obedience toward humes. Not to mention no genetic chance of a Matriarch getting pregnant by one!"

"For someone over a hundred years old, you talk like a smutty little Neo," she sniped and almost ran to join up with Wicca Eighth and P'al who had gone ahead.

Ay'r had been purposely irritating Alli-Clark, but he had been surprised to meet Tam Apollon.

Centaurs were the so-called "Fourth species." Discovered only upon stellar exploration of the distant Dexter Carina Arm of the galaxy circa 3290 Sol Rad., Centaurs were thought to be a purposefully mutated combination of a Hippocene-type mammal indigenous to a planet in that sector with early humes, dating back several hundred millennia before Metro-Terran times. The perpetrators of the mutation were unknown, believed to be a nonmammalian species either not indigenous to the galaxy or by now long extinct. Also unknown was the reason for the mutation and its exact method. Centaur legends and myths were found to be curiously similar—in fact, diametrically opposed—to those of early Humckind, suggesting that they and humes may have been abducted from atmosphere-borne vehicles for mating, and then eventually returned. Given the prehensibility of four of their six limbs, Centaurs had independently developed their own copper, iron, and iridium-based technology. When they were discovered by the explorer Ern'a Bailey Hyde, they had just begun interplanetary travel and colonization of their stellar system of six habitable worlds. Because of how few Centaurs there were compared to the other three species, they had been considered a protected species by the Matriarchy; their home worlds an M.C. preserve.

The others had stopped at a curved section of wall, a projection from which they could now make out Regulus itself, a small brightly etched coin in Melisande's soft surrounding atmosphere. Ay'r caught up with them.

"Thank you for being so gracious with Me," Wicca Eighth said to them—especially, Ay'r thought, to him. "Now that we've spent some time together, I feel more easy in discussing why I've asked you here."

"What do you know of a planet named Pelagia?" Wicca Eighth asked Ay'r.

"Nothing, Ma'am."

"Try to remember your Species Ethnology History tutorials. With reference to the Seeding Program of the middle Second Millennium."

"Of course I know something of the Seeding Program," Ay'r admitted. "In fact, I'm just returning from a Seeded World in the Far 3-Kilo Parsec Arm."

The three of them looked at Ay'r, meaning for him to continue. It was like an oral examination.

"The Seeding Program began at the end of the Metro-Terran era," he began. Naturally, he had boned up on the program before traveling to the N'Kiddim. "Humes had managed to utilize the SlpG. drive to explore many hundreds of stellar systems. But the drive was reasonable only for travel in space/time to a distance of a thousand or so light-years. This represents only one percent of our galaxy, but does include all of the systems of the Orion Spur, a well as portions of the Sagittarian and Persean arms of the Galactic Spiral."

"In other words, the Central Worlds, which still remain Our most heavily populated area. Go on," Wicca Eighth said.

"Despite over three hundred years of intense engineering, no significant advance was made on the SlpG. drive and it was generally believed that none could be made, and that travel beyond the speed of light was impossible. All inhabitable planets discovered in the Central Sector were colonized to fulfill the demographic explosion of the middle Second Millennium. But a group of scientists known as the Aldebaran Five decided upon a program which would allow colonization possibilities until the SlpG. drive could be surpassed. Focusing upon stellar systems within the galaxy's outer arms which were far out of the reach of SlpG. travel, they located worlds their instrumentation told them were capable of sustaining Hume life without any further needed terraforming. They devised in-vitro carriers to travel via SlpG. to those distant planets. Under the guidance of Maxwell 4500 Cybers, those worlds would then be seeded with Hume embryos."

"How many worlds did the Aldebaran Five seed in this manner?"

"Four thousand units were sent out," Ay'r reported. "Two thousand three hundred were destroyed en route or upon landing. Fourteen hundred seventy-five are still in flight—or would be, except that now that we have Fast jump and seeding is no longer needed, Your Matriarchy's fleet has probably intercepted and returned all of them."

"Leaving how many successfully seeded planets?"

"Unknown. Supposedly two hundred twenty five units landed and began the seeding process. We know of only two hundred four, all of them currently within a journey by a Fast ranging from a week to a month, Sol Rad."

"One of which you recently spent time upon, studying the modifications and culture which arose from that Seeding Program. What happened to the other twenty-one Seeded Worlds?"

"As far as we know, no communication link between the Cybers sent with the units has ever been established, either because of radio-interference or other stellar disturbances. It was common for the Aldebaran Five to seed worlds which were physically protected from normal communications or future SlpG. flight lanes by some stellar anomaly— a nearby black hole or highly ionized dust cloud—so that should a faster drive be developed, although no longer impossibly distant, these worlds would still be among the last to be explored and colonized by normal methods."

"Can you extrapolate their success rate?" Wicca Eighth asked gently.

"The known percentage of worlds colonized by the inefficient method of seeding versus the number sent out is 5.848103. Which suggests that of the two hundred one planets in the program of which we know nothing, approximately twelve of them ought to have been successful. Given any standard probability error rate, we can assume that no more than six were successfully seeded," Ay'r continued. "I assume that Pelagia is one of these six."

"Correct. And furthermore, it is, We believe, the planet upon which your father, Ferrex Baldwin Sanqq', has resided for the past two hundred years."

Before Ay'r could register more than surprise, Wicca Eighth continued.

"Would you like to visit Pelagia? I believe that as a Species Ethnologist you will be intensely interested. Not to mention the fact that you will see your only living parent for the first time in your young adulthood."

"Yes, of course I would."

"That, then, is the purpose of this meeting: to outfit yourself and your companions to go to Pelagia."

"Are You saying You know where it is?" Ay'r had to ask.

"Given the fact that We possess all of the Aldebaran Five records on where they sent their seedlings, We have a general idea."

"But no more than that?"

Wicca Eighth looked at Alli-Clark, who now spoke.

"The area of the outer spiral arm to which this particular Seeding Unit was sent happens to be even more than usually unstable. A rather large, and quite active dust cloud stretches across a sector five hundred by two hundred light-years. Several young red giant stars in the area experienced supernovas within recorded history. The side effects of these enormous events would continue to affect all smaller local stellar systems in ways we cannot be certain of. In addition, the formation of new suns in the sector is also highly probable. Lastly, the motion of stellar systems we have been able to monitor appear abnormal. Not only around the arm itself, but also in reference to the rest of the galaxy. Some move faster, some slower."

He decided to cut through her logorrhea: "Have you located a planet?"

"We think we have. According to the records of the Aldebaran Five, this planet was named Pelagia because it possessed a great deal of water upon it. So much that it registered easily even at a great distance, and even given the smallness of the planet. A virtual mirror of the star. You know, of course, what percentage of planets ever discovered possess water?"

"A tiny percentage." He tried to recall the exact figure.

"A cruelly tiny percentage. And generally all previously colonized by Delphinids."

"And you have located a water world in this large, disturbed sector?"

"Yes. However, the ratio of water to land we have found is not the sixteen-to-one noted in the records of the Aldebaran Five, but more like one hundred-to-one."

"Greater than that on New Venice," Wicca Eighth felt the need to remark.

"It may not be the seeded planet," Ay'r said.

"Or it may be, and somehow or other the water has increased," Alli-Clark said. "In fact, that observation was made from over several thousand light-years distant. The water might have increased since then."

"Which occurs on so few planets that it would be quite a find," Ay'r commented.

"A boon for two of the Species," Wicca Eighth commented.

Ay'r added, "Which would explain why the Matriarchal Council is willing to outfit an expensive exploration team for a mere Species Ethnologist to locate his wayward father?"

Wicca Eighth smiled. "We're pleased that you are able to look at the larger view and so understand Our motives in this matter. However, be assured that all the standard rules of exploration decided upon by the Three Species at the Council of Formalhaut remain securely in place. If this planet *is* Pelagia and seeding *has* been successful, We will require an accredited Species Ethnologist—yourself, Ser Sanqq'—to study it, and to advise Us on the appropriate future steps toward research and development."

"I am to assume the two are not necessarily exclusive?"

"Not if the Seedlings are land-based creatures," Alli-Clark said. "Most of our research would be maritime. Given the tiny amount of land versus ocean, they need never know we're there."

"And if the Seedling race is not land based?"

"Unlikely. The seeding was completely humanoid. Careful probing of our Delphinid friends show that they are completely unaware of Pelagia."

"Yet I've encountered considerable physical adaptation among seeded races," he argued. "The N'Kiddim for example—"

"Are land-based"—Alli-Clark said quickly—"and despite their extra limbs, are otherwise internally similar to yourself."

She hadn't said similar to herself, which meant that she was insulting him by comparing him to primitive people. Well, he had been waiting for exactly such an attitude. Ay'r responded by saying, "I assume that you are to be my companion on this jaunt?"

"Alli-Lul Clark is the Matriarchal Council's expert on Marine World Ecologies." Wicca Eighth presented her credentials. "Despite her relative youth, she has received the Poseidon Prize as well as the Universal Nobel Prize in Marine Biology and Botany."

"I'm conversant with all Galactic Maritime life," the younger woman spoke for herself now. "In addition I received my doctorate in Hydrophysics Theory at New Venice University. I speak all known variants of Delphinid, including their argots and antiquities."

Ay'r wondered if she spoke Xell-I's brand of Delphinid bed talk. Unlikely.

"You will also be joined by Ser P'al," Wicca Eighth said.

"A Cyber psychologist? Do You expect to find a Cyber society on Pelagia? Given the humidity of the place," Alli-Clark commented acidly, "they must have all rusted away centuries ago."

"What exactly has been the influence of the guardian Cybers on the Seeded Worlds?" Wicca-Eighth asked Ay'r.

"In about half of the cases, they were forgotten. Among the others they were deified. Among the N'Kiddim for example, they are referred to as the Wooden Gods. Wooden, because no natural metals have been mined or forged by the people, and the term differentiates the Cybers' material from the flesh of the people. No larger Cybers exist among them, but thousands of smaller, virtually mindless machines still wander about in a desolate area of the planet, kept by the N'Kiddim as a preserve, of sorts. It's believed that a Maxwell 4500 with corroded chips in it failed to destroy them before its own demise. As a result, upon initiation, a young male N'Kiddim journeys to that preserve, 'murders' one of the tiny Cybers, dismantles it, and brings back a piece as proof. A primitive rite." Ay'r apologized for it to the Matriarch.

"No more primitive than many so-called civilized activities among males," Alli-Clark commented.

The Matriarch ignored their bickering. "It is precisely that type of Cyber influence upon the Seedlings themselves that interests Ser P'al and Ourself. Rites, legends, songs. He wishes to study all of that."

"And Mer Clark"—Ay'r was using the Marine Ecologist's formal title and, by doing so, aging her a few hundred years—"I assume, wishes to study the water and why it has increased so abundantly over the past thousand years?"

"Exactly," Alli-Clark said.

"Which is fine with me, so long as there is no interference with my own tasks." Ay'r stated his conditions. The Matriarch smiled, which he took for an assent. "And in turn I'll not interfere with Mer Clark nor Ser P'al. I assume none of us will be equipped with Cybers?"

"None. We will provide your with Our latest Force-Fields, both defensive and offensive, and whatever other supplies you need," Wicca Eighth added, "If there are no further questions and no reason to delay, you will leave at Reg. rise tomorrow."

Ay'r bent to kiss the spot before her navel.

"One matter more," Wicca Eighth said. "If your father *is* alive, he is to return to Regulus Prime with you. We wish to meet him."

"May I tell him that will be temporary?"

"Naturally."

"One question remains," Ay'r asked. "Why was I paged via my mother, when You knew she was long dead?"

A moment of hesitation from the Matriarch. Then. "We were unaware that was how you *were* contacted. How extremely embarrassing for you. Accept Our apologies."

She smiled again. But, for the first time, Ay'r felt that she was hiding something from him. He assumed that the M.C. Psychs had devised the communication precisely so he couldn't ignore it. Either the Matriarch had just told him a mistruth, or she actually hadn't known the nature of the message, and so might not actually be completely in charge. Alli-Clark was certainly capable of having done it.

"Well, it certainly got me here," Ay'r added, hoping to clear the air.

"Yes, it certainly did," the Matriarch replied. "And I think that eventually the Three Species will all gain by that."

Chapter Two

An hour after dropping into a perfect orbit around Vulpulcella Six, Captain North-Taylor Diad discovered he had a problem.

Actually, it was a certain second class environmental engineer who discovered the problem. Captain Diad was on the orbit-to-planet comm. channel at the time, attempting to wangle something out of Vulpul's Port Mistress.

"I don't see what the problem is," she was saying in the holo, while touching up her eye makeup.

Captain Diad liked the way she spoke. Even with his cortical connection for Universal Gal. Lex. which made all languages and comm.ects sound alike, Su'lla Pons sounded exotic. He vaguely remembered her telling him on an early freight stop that she had been born and brought up on some Stelezine mining colony somewhere way the hell over in the Dexter Norma arm.

"There's an excellent Ares Recreational Center here." Su'lla went on blithely, "All the other commercial craft orbiting seemed to find it more than satisfactory."

"When have *we* ever been like any other commercial craft?" Captain Diad asked.

He had projected a full holo of himself standing so she could take a look at him. His uniform: an obviously dress-leave outfit complete with bars, the sculptured codpiece accentuating his cosmetic Desmer job. Subtlety wasn't something Diad could afford on short notice.

Su'lla was having trouble with the prokaryota eye shadow, which refused to glow the right shade of green: she prodded the bacterial coloring with a bit of spit on a pin: the salt would irritate it. She took a full up-and-down look at him before resuming her primping.

Despite his three hundred and more years, the Captain knew he looked pretty terrific: all part of the business he was in: required of any male who represented Hesperia.

"All the more reason for limited access to the population," Su'lla said. "This is a nice quiet planet, Captain. A family planet. A crew like yours could easily run amok here. I'm not taking the blame for that."

"But an Ares Rec Center is a like a week's sleep!"

"There are escorts of all genders of all three species for your pleasure at the Rec Center," she quoted the brochure. The little beasties around her eyes were finally glowing correctly. She shook the double knots of her hair and smiled at him through fashionably silvered teeth. "Not to mention dozens of interesting places for—"

"Look, Su'lla," he dropped his voice, getting personal. "We're not talking about the crew. The transport leaders will go where they're told. But...I need something a little more...comfortable. You've got what? A wife, a couple of husbands, a few kids at home?"

"That's right. So?"

"So, How about taking me and a few of my mates back to the family for a home cooked meal and a few hours of polymorpho-amoro."

"I'd love to, Northie, but—"

"Protocols *do* allow senior officers and Port staff to mix," he reminded her: although he didn't go on to remind her that didn't include Port staff families.

"I know, but...well, hold on. Let me comm. my place and ask whoever's there...No Delphs!" she warned, "or, you know, other things!"

"Fine with me. We're just two horny Hume males!"

"Horny *Hesperian* males!" she corrected.

Which they both knew was the nub of the problem. Citizens of the "Floating City" tended to be as independent as Hesperia itself was. To believe themselves exempt from all Matriarchal Council laws. Not to mention Woman-Ruled-World customs and mores. Hesperian crews had been known to trash more than one starport. Even so, with their widespread experience (who else went all over the known galaxy? Not even Matriarchal Security!) and their laxness about contraband and morals, Hesperians tended to be exciting company.

"You wouldn't happen to have anything amusing in your top pockets?" she asked. "Your log says you were just at Achernar. I hear their plankton brandy's supposed to be pretty interesting."

"We'll each bring a vial!" he promised.

"Well...maybe."

"Dial your spouses. I'll wait."

It was while he was waiting, giving half of the "high-sign" to his First Mate, that the double-red flashed and Captain Diad had the misfortune of overhearing the Mate say, "What are you talking about?"

The Captain put the in-craft conversation up so he could hear. It was the Env-Engineer who was saying, "Fifteen minutes after we settled in orbit, vents thirteen hundred through thirteen hundred and fourteen opened up and remained open for close to twenty minutes, Sol Rad."

"So?" the Mate was asking.

"So? It's not in our computer's orbit sequence."

"We were probably just outgassing noxious buildup," the Mate said.

"Not from those vents we weren't."

Captain Diad called up a holo of the Env-Engineer and tapped his board to get a read on the young man. It said virtually nothing. Vla'Di'mir Jones. Citizen of Hesperia. Third voyage. First time on a Plastro-Beryllium hauler. Top-notch entry grades into the Commercial Service. References included some big names at the main office of O'Kell UnLtd.

"You're sure it's not in the sequence?" Mate was asking.

"It was in this one," Di'mir said, "It's not supposed to be."

Captain Diad could see that Mate was thinking the same thing he was: ore theft. Everyone knew what the stuff was worth. And ever since it began to be mined and shipped, someone was trying to break through their elaborate fences and tap some illegally.

"No sign that anything large or solid was vented," Di'mir said, answering their question. And increasing the mystery.

"Those vents are—what—repair section?" the Captain asked his Mate.

"Repair and refitting."

"No humes, no Arths, no Delphs can get anywhere near that section," Di'mir added. "Only Cybers."

"I'll check the orbital sequencing we got from back home," the Mate finally said. All of them knew how expensive that would be. "Maybe someone there had a reason for out-of-sequence venting and forgot to tell us."

"This falls under my jurisdiction," Di'mir added. "Mind if I explore those vents?"

"Be my guest."

"I mean, actually go and look at them."

Self-starter. Captain Diad liked this kid's initiative.

"I'll override from here for one hour Sol Rad. Give me your molecular print," the Mate said.

"Captain should already have it on the readout he's been checking."

Captain Diad laughed at the kid's sassiness and signed off. The holo of the young Env-Engineer was replaced by that of the Port Mistress.

"I hope you two are hungry!" she pealed out the words.

"I think we'd better call back to the City office," Di'mir said.

Captain Diad gave a gloomy grimace and settled back into the sensorium as though refusing to budge, emergency-holo comm. or not.

"What kind of life-form?" he asked.

"I'm not sure. Microscopic. Viral. Strangest stuff I ever saw."

"In his wide experience!" Mate commented, from his end of the sensor-bath. The last thing any of them wanted was their pleasure time at Su'lla's interrupted.

"You test it on small mammalian life forms?" Captain asked.

"On curl-vole and water-pig cells."

"And?"

"Some sort of reaction took place. Then nothing. There was a major irritation in the vole cells. Then it went latent. I tried speeding it up, but got nothing."

"You're sure that viral stuff was vented?" Mate asked.

"The ones I discovered were right there in arrow-skid formations, typical of remnants of venting."

"How did they get there?" the Captain asked.

"I checked that area through and through," the Mate said. "Ship's Mind says no one's been anywhere near that section since we took off. For that matter, no one's been in the area at any time during or between the last six hauls we made."

"I took the liberty of checking that section's own memory banks," the Env-Engineer validated, "No one's been here but the Cyber-repairers and their repairees."

"Like I said. No one," the Mate said.

"And guess what, Sir? The reason neither Mate nor the computer noticed that the sequencing was off was that it *wasn't* off. All of the last stops we made had the same sequence: arrive in orbit and fifteen minutes later, vent from those areas."

Captain Diad had an awful thought. "You're telling me we've been venting that stuff at every orbit we've made here in Scutum-South?"

Before Di'mir could answer, the Captain said, "Even if the stuff turns out to be completely harmless, we have to contact the City office about it."

He lifted Su'lla and her youngest male spouse off him, and noticed the plankton-brandy glow in the Port Mistress's eyes. She'd be in gaga land for a while.

"Better get Kell himself on the line. I'll get dressed and take it here."

Both the Captain and the Mate were fully outfitted when the Inter Gal Comm. went through. If they had expected their boss to be upset, they were right—but not about them wasting money on a call.

On the holo, Matt Kell was levitating over a liquid-ion bath, evidently calming his nerves. He was naked except for a nose ring, so the Captain was able to answer two Hesperia-wide questions publicized by PVN gossip and rumors: one, did Ophiucan Kells have metallic bronze hair around their genitals as well as on their heads?—Yes, even more brightly metallic—and two, did multitrillionaires paint their genitals with the astronomically expensive Plastro-Beryllium? Again yes.

"I'm glad you reported in." Kell spoke casually, not like the owner of one of the richest mines anywhere. "I just heard from a contact inside Syzygy UnLtd. that one of their Env-Engineers just reported the same thing: an off-sequence venting in orbit and a virus discovered at vent ports." Kell's jeweled green eyes were, at best, ciphers. Now they glittered.

"Have you Inter Gal comm.ed a breakdown on the virus?" Kell asked.

"It's on a loop underriding this call," Di'mir said.

Smart thinking, that, Captain Diad thought. Save some money.

"Good. We've got to be certain it's the same one as Sygyzy spotted. Hold on!"

Kell looked to one side—evidently to another holo projection. He said something, then was back with them.

"Sagittarius-Plastro UnLtd's reporting the virus from their largest hauler. Same story exactly. Captain, you and your Env-Engineer take a Fast here. The Quinx is calling a meeting tomorrow morning. I want you two in person. Bring a sample of the virus and the cells you infected with it."

Stunned by the order, Captain Diad asked, "What's the time there?"

"Month: Bernstein-Oxford 21. 6500 hours antemeridian. A Fast has been pretimed and reserved and will be waiting. Mate, the ship is yours. Break that malfunction sequence and follow through the hauling schedule. If you can't break the sequence, seal those vents any way you can."

"Yes, Lord Kell," the Mate used the subservient address.

"And Mate, report *anything* even vaguely relevant from Vulpulcella Six during the remainder of your stay. Use Inter Gal. Don't spare the cost. I'd like some privacy with your Captain now."

"Yes, Lord Kell."

Once Mate was out of holo-contact, Mart Kell said to Captain Diad, "You understand the implications of this, don't you?"

"I understand that it may be some sort of Matriarchal conspiracy to discredit Hesperia."

"And thus call into question our very independence itself. Naturally, to grab hold of the Plastro-Beryllium trade we alone control. So you must realize that the utmost discretion is needed. I've arranged to use our facilities on Vulpulcella Six for a partial wipe of your First Mate's memory."

"A wipe? Isn't that pretty drastic?"

"A very delicate and minor wipe, since it deals with such very recent memories to which he is not emotionally attached. We'll remove the sense of emergency *and* the reason for it. And we'll insert your being called back for discipline. Bring him to our office. I've already set up a licensed Mesmer to do it."

Captain Diad thought: this is getting out of hand.

"What about Di'mir?" he asked. "I'd have to consider Mate far more trustworthy than—"

"Can't wipe him, even if I wanted to."

"Can't?" Captain Diad wondered.

"I'll explain when you get here."

Suddenly it was all very complex. "I've never been involved in Quinx-Matriarchy politics before," Captain Diad said frankly.

"Well, it looks like you've fallen right into the middle of some," Mart Kell said, and he smiled wryly as his holo snapped off.

Captain Diad was present at the Quinx meeting—he had already given his evidence and was in a slightly raised side chamber, one petal of the Lotus-shaped meeting room—when the First Mate, now Captain of the O'Kell Unltd. Plastro-Beryllium Hauler Inter Gal comm.ed and asked to speak to him. Diad motioned to Mart Kell, who took an audio on it.

"Meeting begin yet?" Mate asked.

"It's in progress?" Diad said, wondering how effective the wipe had been. His Mate's next words confirmed that it had been very good indeed.

"Sorry about that, Cap'n. Anything I can say—you know, character reference or anything?"

"Thanks. But you're not using Inter Gal comm. just to cheer me up, are you?"

"No. Listen I've got to report to the Boss."

"What about?" Diad asked.

"There's some kind of epidemic spreading down on Vulpul Six."

Mart Kell gestured to interrupt the current speaker on the dais. Immediately and without his knowledge, the Mate's holo and voice were reproduced in front of the five who formed the Quinx center, as well as twenty-five High Members surrounding them.

"Go on," Mart Kell talked to the Mate's holo.

"Well, you were right, Lord Kell. There's some sort of illness happening down below. I first got wind of it from the Port Mistress. Her female spouse developed some sort of rash on her left inner thigh. Then she developed a high fever. Same thing happened to the Port Mistress herself a few hours later. At first they blamed us: you know, physical contact with uh, you know, possible alien microbia we might have been carrying, even though the Cap'n and I went through two sets of fluoros, on the ship and entering their residence. None of us are sick."

"None of the hauler's crew?"

"None. But then cases began popping up all over Vulpul Six. In the lower hemisphere continents and all, so we knew it couldn't have been myself and Cap'n Diad. You shouldn't blame him for it."

"We'll take your testimony in fullest faith," Mart Kell assured him. "How far has the epidemic spread, and how serious is it?"

"Knowing your interest, we're taking in all data as it develops down there. Evidently it's some kind of influenza," Mate said. "One of those twenty-four hour Sol Rad. types. First there's the rash, usually on the inner thigh. Then the high fever. Some nausea and headaches. Then it's gone. Everyone's got it."

"Everyone?" Kell asked. "Are the symptoms all the same among the age groups, genders, species et cetera?"

"What I meant was among the humes. We don't have reports in yet from the small Delph population here. They're a bit segregated down on Vulpul Six. But the same symptoms are reported by all the Hume females."

"And the males?"

The First Mate looked surprised, then did something at a read-board, evidently checking his incoming data. "I don't see any male cases reported at all. Only females."

"Confirming my cellular experiments in forced growth," the Env-Engineer spoke up. "No male mammals were affected at all."

"Gratitude, Acting Captain," Mart Kell said. "Please keep this line open and send all of the material you are receiving."

Mate was incredulous. "Keep it open? You know how much that would cost?"

"Gratitude, Acting Captain." Kell signed good-bye, and the holo snapped off. "Tell this council what you've discovered Engineer Di'mir."

"I infected the curl-vole and water-pig cells and forced cloned growth. All growth was normal until adolescence. The male continued to develop normally. The female appeared to also, until ovulation. At which point the female immediately developed the rash, the high fever, the same symptoms of the Hume females on Vulpulcella Six. We impregnated her and forced fetus growth. She miscarried. We tried again. This time, nothing happened at all. We took a look inside and found no ovulation. Nothing there at all to ovulate. The female wasn't merely sterile, the ovaries and the entire fallopian tube system were gone! Naturally, we backed that up with a half-dozen other experimental samplings as a control and got the same thing."

"The males were fine?" Llega Francis Todd asked. She was the one female on the Inner Quinx, titular and acting Premier and a major player in the Beryllium futures market. "And the females were all sterile? How?"

"The virus seems to be quite sophisticated." the Env-Engineer said. "It's harmless except when in the presence of a mammalian XX chromosome. It seems to attack the mitochondria itself and transform it into some quite type of cell—call it ZZ or GG or anything but what it was before. It has the same affect on Delphinid ovarian chromosomes."

"And our Arthopodic neighbors with their completely different chromosomal structure?" she asked.

"We really don't know how they may be affected by this microvirus. Hymenoptera queens lay the eggs. Unfertilized eggs become sons. Fertilized eggs become nymphs or—more rarely—new queens. The microvirus might prevent ova from being fertilized. We haven't a large enough sample of Vespid volunteers to know how they'll be affected. It may be that nymphs can be born, but that they turn out sterile, too."

"But not queens?"

"We're still not sure."

Ole Branklin, Vice-Premier and most revered member of the Quinx, now asked, "Surely we can stop it?"

"We might, but we haven't so far," the Env-Engineer admitted. "The microvirus mutates constantly no matter how we attack, how much stress we place it under. We've tried several thousand anti viral procedures. Even when its own molecular structure is turned inside out, completely transformed, it seems to retain some sort of tracer-memory, and it still carries out its job."

"You'll continue to work on it," Llega Todd said. "We'll provide all the facilities and all the staff you require from any of the species and from our most specialized Cybers."

"Lady Todd," the Env-Engineer seemed to stammer for the first time in his presentation. "It's our opinion that this be limited to the smallest possible group. And that Cyber specialists be excluded."

She and several members of the Quinx looked shocked.

"Surely that's all Matriarchal prejudice, Engineer." She voiced the outrage that others felt. "Just because of their own troubles with a group of rebellious Cybers—"

"Lady Todd," Mart Kell interrupted her. "Engineer Di'mir has reason to believe that the microvirus was not only developed by rebellious Cybers, but that it is *itself* a Cyber."

"Bio-Cybernetics hasn't developed that far!" someone spoke up.

"It sure has," Truny Syzygy spoke out now. "And if Engineer Di'mir says this is a Cyber bug, you should listen to him."

"Why should we?"

"Because Engineer Di'mir is a bio-Cyber himself."

Captain Diad couldn't keep his peace. "He can't be! I saw his dossier."

"How old is he?" Mart Kell asked the Captain.

"Well, it wasn't there. But he looks about a hundred thirty, give or take a decade."

"Di'mir is twenty-two years old, Hesperian time," Syzygy smiled.

Inner Quinx member Helmut Aare Dja'aa protested, "He'd still be a Neo. A kindergartener!"

"I watched Mart start him up. Sure," Syzygy added, "he's flesh and blood like ourselves. Completely mammalian tissue. But his brain, autonomous system, involuntary nervous system and everything related to it was preprogrammed and constructed in vitro."

"The chromosomes for all his axonary and synaptical tissues were cloned from me," Mart Kell said. "He's my son. And like any child I'd have, he's had all the advantages—including advanced mammalogy and Cybernetics."

"I don't understand what he was doing on our hauler," Captain Diad wondered.

Mart Kell shrugged. "Learning the business, essentially."

"But...how did he find the error every hauler computer and every systems check we have let pass?"

"My son is more alert than any Hume. He uses about three-quarters of his brain, where even the most efficient of ourselves use only about one-quarter, after centuries of evolution and training. And why shouldn't he? All the basic material had been reinforced."

Llega Todd was beginning to color. "May I ask how much your son cost?"

Mart Kell laughed. "A year Sol Rad. of the purest blend of Plastro-Beryllium."

Helmut Dja'aa was impressed. "I've bought solar systems for less than that."

Llega continued, "The reason I asked is that if Engineer Di'mir's analysis of the effectiveness of this microvirus and his extrapolation are correct, then more like himself will *not* answer to the problem."

Mart Kell explained, "For a dozen or so of us, who are the wealthiest in the galaxy, and to keep our species barely existent. Only those of us at this council could possibly afford to rear a gang of Di'mir and his siblings just for the sake of hearing Neo voices around us."

"And by then it would be moot," Syzygy reminded them. "Cybers will have taken over Hesperia and every other major city we know of. All they need do is outwait us," he explained. "Eventually our females will age and die, and no infants will be born. What's a half-dozen or so centuries to a machine?"

"Can we get back for a moment to the assumption of cause of the microvirus?" Ole Branklin reminded them. "Your...the Engineer here says it's a bio-Cyber. Isn't it possible that the microvirus was originally a Matriarchal invention, and somehow or other became transformed?"

They all looked at the young engineer. "You mean something they designed against Cybers?" another member asked.

"Or against Hesperians?" asked Inner Quinx member Kars Tedesco, who was a brooding, silent man.

"It doesn't affect males, so that last isn't likely," Di'mir pointed out quickly.

"But against the Cybers," Branklin went on. "Think of it. We all know how bitterly fought this rebellion has been for the Matriarchy. A third of the Carina/Fornax sector closed off close to a year, Sol Rad., while they try to roust out the mechanos. Billions dead on several systems. The Cult of the Flowers heading the action. They take no prisoners and don't recognize the concept of hostages. If a major population of humes happens to be in the way of a Cyber war station, they're soon electron soup along with the Cybers."

"Some of this has leaked out through more radical networks of communication," Di'mir admitted. "Evidently yourselves on the Inner Quinx and—Council—know more of this rebellion than I do myself. More indeed than anyone has made public, even here on Hesperia, where Opposition to the Matriarchy is strongest."

He looked at his father, who shook his head sadly. "The reports we get stagger the most sadistic imagination. We censor the worst out of the—"

"Horror!" Llega Francis Todd finished the sentence. "Out of desire to not dehumanize, de-Delphinize, debiologize our citizens."

"Even accepting all this as background," Di'mir said now, "I simply can't accept that this microvirus is not a Cyber-construction. It's too neat, too elegant, too utterly functional to be a mistake, or even a mis-evolution.

"Are we to assume that we too are infected?" 'Llega asked. "I know the female population of Hesperia isn't large, scarcely a million, but we would certainly have heard of such an epidemic here if..."

"Lady Todd, I actually don't know if we've been infected although I can't believe that some micro-viruses didn't somehow escape to Hesperia."

"If the method used," Captain Diad spoke up, "I mean by venting at hauling stops was used, he might be right." He felt embarrassed speaking until Ole Branklin waved him on. "On the other hand, any Cybers in those areas which happened to leave any of the haulers, might have carried it down here."

"Chances are?" Ole Branklin asked Truny Syzygy.

"A million to one. Which means we'd be fools to assume it isn't here."

"What is it, 'Llega?" Branklin asked.

"Now that I think about it, none of the women I know in the City here can wear bacterial makeup anymore."

"Your PH factors have all been changed," Di'mir said. "Your chromosomes are under attack. I'm afraid the micro-virus is here, although obviously in a much diluted form."

"It would be a terrible irony if the Matriarchy had sent ut the virus and it turned into one which now sterilizes," 'Llega said. "Especially since Motherhood is the keystone of the Matriarchal philosophy."

"Let's face it," Syzygy said it for all of them. "Opposition or not. Male or female. Hume, Delph or Arthopod, we're all in this together. Let's plan out a strategy to keep the damage to the minimum."

"Captain," Ole Branklin himself called Diad, "Please come in and take a seat. We're going to have to seal this meeting. No recordings or any sort will be allowed. Nor notes. Oh, know the word of what we discuss will get out and among the City soon enough. But the Matriarchy must already know about it and they've kept it mum so far. We're going to need every bit of help we can get. Why don't you give us a logistical rundown on how the haulers themselves can be further contained."

A guest seat was raised out of the carpeting and Captain Diad sat down among the giga-billionaires and the great houses of Hesperia. All of them as frightened as he was.

Twilight on Benefica was a languid time, especially at this time of the year when the three suns set slowly one after another; first the huge red one, then the smaller yellow, and finally the large blue one. The skies above the revolving rooftop restaurant presented a magnificent spectacle of slowly changing hues, touching every shade of the spectrum—even briefly an electric green.

Nothing like the soft pale twilights over Melisande, of course, Councilor Rinne thought, but then what could equal those pale enchantments? Meanwhile her group had passed from aperitifs to appetizers, from entrees to tisanes. They had sound-sealed their partly enclosed area from the stage show—a trio of musicians, Hume father and son they seemed to be and an Arthopod solo-orchestra. Now Rinne's group was relaxing, opening up as only women of more or less the same professional status could do when they were together like this in semipublic.

Gemma Guo-Rinne looked around the table at the other four and decided, well, why not ask them?

"Does everyone miss their interactive Cybers as much as I did at first?"

"I hardly noticed," Liqa, a Spatial Engineer, said in her deep voice.

"My gynos miss theirs!" Ap'ara Norr began a high silvery laugh. "But you know what? Even Cis'po has learned how to program for dinner and cleaning now."

"Was that difficult?" Councilor Rinne asked. Norr, a Financial Securities expert, always seemed to have a half dozen young Hume males hanging about her apartments. Younger and younger it seemed.

"Not really!" Norr laughed again. "Except for the first few days. Somehow he got stuck on soups and sandwiches, and I thought I'd have to take all of the gynos out for lunch and dinner. They may only be males, but, Eve! how some of them put it away!"

"Didn't you tell me that Cis'po misprogrammed and the floor Cybers chased after your Cherubim-mice for days, trying to clean them out?"

Norr went off into another peal. "I got home. And there the poor things were, hiding in as high a spot as they could find, and the floor Cybers were all directly beneath, trying to stack themselves up to reach the mice with a laser broom. And poor Cis'po was running around, taking down the Cybers which would just try to stack themselves up again, and he was trying to shush the Cherubim-mice who were whistling away in terror, and he was screaming into the wall unit to try to find the right combination to shut down the Cybers, or at least to shut off the broom!"

The four other women burst into laughter. Norr was almost in tears.

"Of course I gave him a lovely present when he finally did get it all right. A Beryllium signet. Oh, not a large one. But you know, star-bright and all."

"Oh 'Para, when are you going to settle down with a few spouses!" Kiska seemed serious. "Darling, you're close to two-fifty. You don't have all that much time left."

"Leave her alone!" Suro Ton replied. "I settled down at two-fifty, and where has it gotten me? A flat full of spouses and Neos. It's like a multi-PVN every minute of the day, Sol Rad. This one's sick, that one's angry, these two aren't speaking."

"Some of us are lucky," Kiska replied, looking at Councilor Rinne. "They have their Stelezine and sip it, too!"

"There's a dance group coming up," Liqa announced. "I saw them on Antigone. Anyone want to join me in unsealing our sound?"

The others had just agreed, when a young woman approached the table, followed by the Hume Maitresse d' who was still trying to stop her.

"Please, Councilor Rinne, I must talk with you," the young woman pleaded.

"She's been lurking here since your party arrived, Councilor. We couldn't... We could call Security."

"I won't take long." The young woman seemed desperate. She looked around at the other women and said, "I'm so sorry to bother you In fact, I'm quite embarrassed."

The other women turned their attention to the dancers. Councilor Rinne gestured for the young woman to join her on the settee and dismissed the relieved restaurant staff.

"My dear, are you ill?" she asked.

"No. Just desperate."

"A calming tisane perhaps?"

"Gratitude, no. It's about one of the new M.C. programs, the delayed-motherhood rule."

Councilor Rinne had expected something like this.

"I can understand why it's needed on a small, crowded planet like Rigel Prime," the young woman went on. "But Benefica is enormous. With plenty of resources and not nearly enough popula—"

Councilor Rinne took the young woman's hand. "Were you listed for motherhood?"

"This month to come. And now—!"

"The delayed maternity rules are only temporary. I'm certain you'll be on the very first new list to come out as soon as the restraint is lifted."

"But I don't understand why it's there to begin with!" The young woman was almost whispering, evidently repressing her emotion. "It's my first! I've never—"

"I understand," Councilor Rinne sympathized.

"You're Sector Health Councilor," the young woman said. "Surely you could—"

"The rule comes from Her Matriarchy itself. All I can do is ensure that you are on that first list when the rule is lifted."

"It's just so unfair!"

"Let's make sure it's a little fairer. Give me your ident." She lifted the girl's wrist and imprinted it against her own forearm. "There! I won't forget you now... Ewa Petra Benn."

For the first time, the glimmer of a smile appeared on the young woman's face. "You're a Wonderful Woman, Councilor Rinne," she gave the highest verbal honor, added a bow to the Councilor's throat, then apologized once again to the others and left.

"Are you still envying me, Kiska?" the Councilor asked. She turned to the dancing.

The group broke up soon afterward and Councilor Rinne said her good-byes, then took an enclosed conveyance-walk off the rooftop and down to her official suite in the nearby accommodation center. She wasn't in her rooms a half hour when the Holo Comm. informed her that she had a secured Inter Gal. Comm. from within M.C. Headquarters on Reg. Prime.

To Councilor Rinne's surprise, the two preliminary M.C. Security Guards preceded—Her Matriarchy Herself!

"Ma'am." Rinne bowed to the holo.

Wicca Eighth brushed it aside. "How are the new programs going over in your sector, Councilor Rinne?"

"For the most part, fairly well. Everyone's been informed through the Networks, and they're being patriotic and understanding. Going without the little luxuries. But there's less comprehension and therefore more resistance to the maternity delay than to shutting off the intelligent Cybers."

"Then they *are* all shut off in your sector?"

"None more intelligent than a hairdresser is left, Ma'am."

"But centuries of propaganda about motherhood is less easy to handle."

"I'm afraid so, Ma'am. Peer pressure. Customs. Mores."

"No one merely accepts that it's for the galactic census? No," Wicca Eighth answered Herself. "We did hope they would. But that's not what I wanted to comm. you about. First I must confirm a piece of knowledge. What do you think of when I say 'Relfi'?"

Without thinking, Councilor Rinne answered, "Lydia Mann Relfi, the biological engineer."

"You studied Relfi's work with Ferrex Baldwin Sanqq' at the Arcturus Mammalogical Institute, didn't you?"

"In my youth, Ma'am. Some two hundred years ago."

"Exactly what did you study?"

"Relfi's extant tapes and discs, of course. Many were destroyed by the First Matriarchy, you know. But several were saved. Relfi was no longer proscribed. Merely...unknown, in my youth."

"Except by Sanqq'?"

"To be exact, Ma'am, I worked not with him, but under him. He was an extremely intelligent male. Much more perceptive and compassionate than most female mammalog—"

"You needn't convince me of the equal intelligence of males, Councilor Rinne," Wicca Eighth said. "Were your studies analytical or...more practical."

"Analytical, Ma'am. Our only laboratory was a series of advanced Cybers. We speculated upon the incomplete set of Relfi's theories and postulates we had in hand."

"And concluded what? They concerned abnormal conception—is that right?"

Councilor Rinne almost laughed. It was all beginning to come back to her. The years at the Arcturus MI. How much she'd admired Ferrex Sanqq'. How much they all had. How he had forced them to speculate far beyond what they ever had before into areas that could be considered heretical.

"We referred to them as alternative, not abnormal. And some are in use today on a limited basis. The Delphinid-Hume ambassadorial class, for example, which has been a stunning success."

"Do you have access to those recordings?"

"No. Dr. Ferrex Sanqq' retained them, Ma'am. I do still have extensive recordings of our speculative sessions and of own postulates. Holo notebooks, you might call them."

"Where are those?"

"At my apartments in Melisande."

"Good! You'll come here by Fast tomorrow. I'll temporarily relieve you of your post there so you may join a special team reporting directly to the Council."

This was sudden. "But, Ma'am, that was all centuries ago!"

"You knew that Ferrex Sanqq' vanished? No? Well, he did. And you're all We have left of him, Councilor Rinne. We need those notes and recordings. We need to know in what direction his work was going when he vanished. You can help Us."

"Yes, of course, Ma'am. But—"

"Why all of sudden? Look at this recording of an encounter I had recently." The holo of Wicca was replaced by one of an attractive young Hume male talking to Her Matriarchy. While it played, Councilor Rinne had the oddest feeling of familiarity.

"That's Dr. Sanqq's son. Ay'r Kerry Sanqq'!" Wicca Eighth said over the holo.

Of course it was! He much younger. Far more lithe. A bit less smooth. But Sanqq'!

"Did you know his mother, Councilor?"

"I'm afraid not, Ma'am."

"Nor does anyone else. Although Ay'r Kerry was enrolled in the birth charts on Arcturus Mu toward the end of the decade you studied with Dr. Sanqq'!"

"Why would he keep it secret?"

"Why is it we can't find a mother? Despite all of Our most intensive efforts. Oh, we found a blind, of course. A shadow-mother. Supposedly dead in childbirth. And she bore some shallow resemblance to the son, except of course that we retained a clone-cell and she had no resemblance on a deep molecular basis."

Now that she continued watching the recorded holo, Councilor Rinne thought she saw in the youth's features someone else she had once known. But whom? Which woman could it be? But even as she wondered, another thought came to her:

"Note, Councilor Rinne, that young Sanqq' carries his father's last name and *not* a matronymic."

"Accepting the final matronymic is not universal, even among M.C. humes. Ma'am, what are you suggesting about young Sanqq'?"

"I'm not sure, Councilor. Still, you've looked at Ay'r, heard him, registered his good looks, his intelligence. Take My word for his charm and poise and discretion. His quick adaptability. His willingness to take on large tasks. He's as exceptional for his age as he is for his gender. If he were a woman, I'd keep him at My side and entrust much to him."

Councilor Rinne kept watching the youth. Who was the woman on Arcturus Mu who walked like that? Who had that dark seriousness around her lighter-than-usually-colored eyes? It was right there, hanging by a synapse.

"Will you help Me find out the truth about this young male?" Her Matriarchy had reappeared in the holo.

"Yes, of course."

"If you do, Councilor, I warn you, you will be among a handful of women who are working for the very salvation of the Matriarchy."

The smiles they exchanged before the holo snapped off were sad ones.

Outside, on Benefica, darkness had descended fully. Councilor Rinne walked out onto her balcony and listened to the sounds of the night creatures.

"Are you still foolishly envying me, Kiska?" she asked the moonless, unresponding, star-flooded sky.

"Women—and Guests. Please be seated! The fight is about to begin."

Captain Lill pushed out of the group of warriors gathered at the doorway and they fell in behind her, down the ramps to their seats.

"For your sporting entertainment," the announcer continued, enunciating each syllable in what Lill had been told was a holdover from ancient ring events, "We have tonight two double-tag teams!"

Having found their seats, Captain Lill took the curved stool closest to the aisle, and waited for her warriors to get into place. Around them, Percodyne fumes rose casting a sense of glimmer over the small bowl-shaped auditorium. Lill straddled the stool so it fit between her hefty thighs, pulled up its front so it fit against her crotch, drew the belts attached to each end around her waist, cinched it tight, then adjusted the front of the stool for a low vibration. She liked to come to oxy/hydro fights, even if they were frowned upon by the M.C., and in bureau circles looked upon as low entertainment.

"From Scutum's Harp System, we present the infamous Teqq and Rarey," the announcer blared. Two huge Hume females clad only in aerial netting, dropped from the ceiling, to within inches of the surface of the water. They hung there as though born to the air, spun around, bowed to the crowds, loudly insulting those who booed them.

"With them, from Scutum Kappa Six, P'andolfo the Wonder Delph!"

The sleek Delph shot up from the water tank spraying the incurved transparent walls of the ring right to the top. P'andolfo was as big as the two fighters, with something glittering woven into his mane.

"The Delf's wearing glass!" Lill shouted to her closest companion.

"Childless!" Corporal Jare expostulated and hit Lill's elbow. "Get a look at those gynos who just came in! I think they're going to sit in front of us."

"Lemme arrange their seats for them!" Lill barked.

In the ring, the two women and the Delph were cavorting around. It seemed to know its way around the nets.

"Hi, boys!" Corporal Jare reached out with roving hands as the gynos checked their seat numbers. Lill knew one of them, a piece of flit named Roy'o, fashionable trash, common at oxy/hydros and at the dives she wasted her time at when the rest of virtuous Melisande was closed down for the night.

He pretended not to recognize her until she reached out and pushed her boot point into his crack, at which he turned around and smiled, and gave her a pointed-tongue greeting.

The other warriors laughed. The other gyno turned around and proved to be an innocent-looking thing, all eyes and lips and jet hair.

Lill thought maybe she'd have some fun tonight, after all. This Childless extended r&r on Wicca-World was giving her serious Cunt-Cramps.

"And from Denebola XVIII, we're pleased to present, Barb, We'ra, and Lartes." The announcer's words came as three other humes dropped into the ring on netting, two big, broad Hume females and some sort of mutant, a giant male. They all looked alike, which was rough. All three were bald and had tattooed skulls. The male's buttocks were also tattooed.

"Sibs! Tripos!" Jare yelled, passing a Stelezine inhaler to Lill, who took a snort. "I watched 'em fight before. They'll turn that Delph into vulva-fodder."

The gynos were daintily fending off offers from women all around them, but Roy'o accepted Lill's Benzo-Ritalin inhaler and gave it to his companion. When he returned it, he winked twice. Meaning the duo was good, if she wanted it. Lill turned up her vibrator and leaned into it, checking out the fighter named Lartes. Took a lot of guts for male to fight in an oxy/hydro. Even one as big and slab-muscled as this Lartes.

"Childless! Imagine if all gynos were that big!" Jare shouted, rocking forward onto her stool attachment. "I might even single-spouse!"

"Sure and hatch your own brood of ugly tripos!" Major Pratt guffawed.

Lill knew what she meant. This waiting around while other warriors were out fighting Cybers was beyond Childless.

Before the announcer could say any more, the Scutist named Teqq had aimed a mailed fist and swung directly into Latres's crotch. She struck a Plastro codpiece and he drop-punched her left breast. Rarey jumped onto his shoulders, but his bald head shook her, and by then We'ra or Barb was beginning to rabbit-vag her. The crowd roared. The fight was on.

Just as the sibs seemed to have the two Scutists twisted and pummeled and cut, the Delph shot up and split into the mess with a sharp thwack.

Everyone yelled as Hume blood splattered against the ring's walls and was immediately hosed down. Nothing serious—just scratches.

Despite all the ring action, the two gynos were having a hard time with women pushing into them. They finally got out of their seats, and Lill gestured them up to where she was. She sat one on either knee, wrapped an arm around each one, and let them play with her breasts and feed her Percodyne while she shouted and cheered on now the tripos, now the Delph, getting higher every second.

Down in the ring, the Delph had pulled one of the sib females into the tank where they were wrestling around. With the sibs split up, one sister took one, the other Scutist, the male. Legs, mailed fists, even elbow and knee blades joined the action.

Roy'o had left Lill's knee for Jare's. Lill shoved her hand deep into the black-haired gyno's pants, pulled out something tubular, and began stroking it. He kept looking over his shoulder, but she wouldn't let go. Lill got her moan-and-little-splash from the gyno about the same time that down in the ring the Delph miscalculated and leapt into a tripo net-knot. Trapped, it squirmed and squeaked, and the sibs found each other and seriously took on the two Scutists. One of them ended up underwater. The other one was held and worked over for a while, until the female sib doing the work nodded, and the male took over. The jeers and boos from the audience reached a fever pitch, until the male sib finally pulled off her crotch protection and actually worked his hand inside her vag. Lill thought his infamous act would bring the auditorium down around their ears. A score of women had unbelted themselves from their seats and were climbing the ring shield, trying to get at him.

Jare and Pratt were groping Roy'o and laughing like maniacs from too much Benzo-Ritalin. The gyno on Lill's lap slipped to the carpet.

Lill shook her head, looked around, and thought, Mother! This is dicked-out Childless!

Before she was halfway up the aisle, her warriors were behind her, the half-passed-out gynos under their arms.

The outside air hit like a stone. Lill reeled and backed into the wall.

"Where we takin' 'em?" Jare shouted.

"Find a transpo'," another one said, and whistled for a transport driver. The gypsumania lights were tawdry, the air fetid.

"C'mon, Lill." Pratt said. "We got us some serious sportin' to do."

"Naaa! You go. I'll walk."

Before she had gone a half dozen steps, a hand was on her shoulder. "Captain Lill!"

She looked into the cowl-darkened face.

"You find us another unwilling gyno?" Jare was yelling from the back of the transport.

"Go ahead."

"Captain Lill," the voice inside the cowl repeated. Lill recognized it; as well as the bunched cape over one shoulder to hide the missing breast.

Lill saluted as sharply as she could, reeled a bit, and said, "Yes, Ma'am."

"Captain Lill!" Pratt shouted out. "Are you tight?"

"I'm loose!" Lill shouted back. "It's someone I know."

"Ask her if she can get us Benzo-Ritalin!" Jare yelled, her words twisted as the transport took off.

"Sorry, Ma'am," Lill was coming to full attention.

"No apology needed. They're all good warriors. We're going to talk as soon as you're clearheaded."

"Is this about... Am I being called up to the front?"

"Would you like that, Lill?"

"Mor'n' anything, Ma'am."

"Melisande's Pax Maternica got you a little down?"

"It's not that," Lill wouldn't criticize the M.C. "I keep telling my Women, they'll need us when the time comes."

She was aware that they had moved from one conveyance belt to another rapidly without her noticing, and were now approaching Kundry Park.

"Are you wondering what a Black Chrys like myself is doing here?" Thol asked her as they reached a clearing, and the senior warrior stepped off the belt and onto the grass.

"I have no idea, Ma'am."

"Well, I'm doing the same as you are. Waiting around on Melisande for the M.C. to make up its collective anile mind what to do! Don't worry, no one can hear us—I put up a sound shield," she added quickly. "Lill, I want to know what you think about this war."

"I don't understand why we haven't beaten them. We've locked all the damned rebel tincans inside a single sector and...I mean I understand about Hume and arthopod populations in the way and all. But...it can be done surgically, too!"

Thol had thrown back her cowl. She glowered darkly.

"I agree! So does the leadership of the Chrys. So does half the M.C. fleet. High and low. M.C. says it's a suicide mission. I say, so what? I'm pushing four twenty. Let's go in there, burn 'em all out, and who knows, get some glory out of it! M.C. still says no."

"I say yes!" Lill agreed.

"You're only two-ten? Two-twenty?"

"I'm a warrior, Ma'am. So are my women. We need to see action."

"What if I got you in the sky and near the front?" Thol began and immediately interrupted herself. "Don't say anything 'til I'm done. What if I did that? What kind of loyalty can I count on?"

"I'm not a Cultist."

"Not yet. But we've had our eye on you for some time, Lill."

That was a surprise. Lill didn't have the lineage, the Council connections, nor the elegance of the usual Cult nominees.

"What if I told you that Wicca Herself agrees with me?" Thol went on. "That She would like to see a quiet, efficient little mutiny at the front and a bold surgical move to bite the heads off all the bad little tincans."

"But the Council—"

"Is controlled politically. We both know it. What we're planning would be done before it could be stopped. The M.C. will bitch, but they'll accept it. Think about it, Lill. Let me know tomorrow this time at Isolde Station if you'll accept a nomination for the Cult."

Which, following this conversation, meant whether Thol could count on her to follow the other Cultists unquestioningly if they acted without M.C. control.

"And if I choose not to, Ma'am?"

"You'll report to a Cult Mesmer for a small 'wipe,' so this conversation is eradicated from your memory."

That made sense.

"Will your answer be no, Captain Lill?"

"I don't believe so, Ma'am."

It was Gigigue who brought the woman into the communal Ion-bath, but from the very first Ewa felt a special connection with her.

Because it was Tri-Sol midday and most women and their spouses were at their avocations, there were only three others with Ewa at the floating pads—besides Ewa's clever feline Helix—on the top floor of the Maybelle Residence when Gigigue arrived with the guest.

She introduced the newcomer as Maly'a Something-or-other, and the two stripped down immediately and found pads. Ewa and Helix were playing with an Maglev-frisb, the clever animal very concentrated as it hopped from empty pad to empty pad to get at the pesky object, when the two women settled themselves, crossed their legs in lotus position and levitated. Helix jumped and landed right in Maly'a's lap.

"She's beautiful?" Maly'a stroked the cat. "Is she genetically altered?"

"Yes. She was a gift from my Prime-Spouse," Ewa said, feeling as though she ought to be blushing: the woman had looked directly at her when asking the question.

Helix had been purring as she glided silkily along the Maly'a's bare limbs. The frisb sailed past, and the feline looked at it with a combination of interest and frustration.

"You'll never catch it." Ewa said.

"I know," the cat meowed back.

"How clever!" Maly'a said. "What's your name, lovely one?"

The feline slipped back into her lap and looked up at the woman through her stalwart-looking breasts. "Helix!" it meowed.

"You're marvelous!"

The cat licked Maly'a's thigh. Then its eye caught the frisb, and it jumped lithely to the next empty pad.

"Her mental age is early neonate," Ewa said. "And her vocabulary is only about two hundred words." She stared fondly at the animal, now poised to slap at the frisb. "But she certainly lets a woman know what she wants." She added, "Despite that, everyone in Maybelle is fond of her."

"Naturally."

"I've heard of Electra World gen alt. animals with mid-neonate mentalities," Gigigue kept the conversation going. "But of course, they require special care. Not everyone can keep them."

The conversation moved from gen. alt. animals to the new Eudora World fashion for living cosmetic tattoos, to topics all the women knew: Prime Spouse avocations, Trine Spouse spending habits, life without Intelligent Cybers, the MagLev Marathon to be held along the greensward from Bronte to Bovary Parks.

Ewa looked at Maly'a and came to several tentative conclusions. First, although the woman was clearly middle-aged (say, three-sixty, three-eighty) and had evidently undergone at least two complete cosmetic surgeries; with their accompanying soporo-treatments, Maly'a was as young as the other women in spirit.

That suggested a contented life, which in turn suggested a successful avocation. Something aesthetic or philological, perhaps. On the other hand, Maly'a's extreme comfort and poise and ability to fit in with a group of strangers suggested a more public avocation, administrative or, who knew, even in the Council itself. Whatever it was, Maly'a was undoubtedly special.

Which was why Ewa joined Gigigue and her guest when they were ready to leave the Ion-bath, and why she let Ricia take Helix downstairs while Ewa slipped on a chemise and joined the others on the rooftop garden for a Stele 'Chol, the latest drink fad in Benefica City.

Which was also why Ewa remained with Maly'a on the rooftop and ordered a second S&C when Gigigue left, and why Ewa was not at all surprised when Maly'a suddenly said, "I understand you've been thwarted by the Pop-Zero Program."

"Does it show that much?"

"Not at all. Your resentment quotient seems barely existent. Gigigue told me before. You don't mind, do you? I specifically asked her about friends who had been troubled by the program."

"Well, then you know it all," Ewa put a brave face on it. "At least I'm among the first on the list when the rule is rescinded."

"Do you know when that will be?"

"I spoke to Health Councilor Rinne a few evenings ago. She assured me the Program was only temporary."

"But she didn't give you a rescind date?"

"Do you know the date?"

"Why would—"

Ewa interrupted, "Because you're interested in the effect of the Pop-Zero Program on ordinary women. I think you're also an M.C. official."

"Am?" Maly'a asked. "Or was? I'm retired. But you're partly right. I *am* interested. In fact, I represent a philanthropic institution which has managed to produce a sort of counterbalance to Pop-Zero." She waited.

"Meaning?"

"Although we naturally understand the motives of the M.C., we don't necessarily agree with them in this matter. Especially as regards to firsts. You are, are you not—and I hope you won't be offended if I use the word in its original and not in its pejorative sense—childless?"

Now Ewa did blush: years of Ed. & Dev. taunts coming home to embarrass her. "I'm only ninety-five. I have plenty of time!"

"And your spouses?"

"My Prime is two-twenty. Already had her 'brood,' as she calls it. My Trine's ninety-seven. He was part of my last gyno-group at Murasaki U. We just remained together," she added with a shrug.

"I know how it can be with males. You become habituated to their company." Maly'a sympathized. "But let's face it: it's our Primes whom we live for. Yet your Prime doesn't necessarily want a child?"

"She's fond of both of us. She'll do what we want. Offer her genes and all."

"Well, that's positive!" Maly'a said. "About your Trine spouse. Would he be willing to leave his avocation on Benefica for a few days Sol Rad. for the siring? For that matter, would you be willing to leave Benefica for a matter of months. Both spouses would be able to visit frequently via Fast."

Ewa wondered if she had missed something. "Leave Benefica for where?"

"Deneb XII. That's where the program is located."

This was awfully sudden. "Will Rali Ha'go be in the program, too?"

"Only firsts. Gigigue told me you liked travel, said you'd been to the Altair System satellites recently. They're a bit primitive, no?"

"A bit. No Fasts. We had to use SlpG. flight throughout the system. It took forever to get anywhere. Still, it was restful and it was more time than I'd spent with my Prime in a good while. She's a history buff."

"How long were you there?"

"About fifteen days. We returned a week ago, Sol. Rad."

"I'm not at liberty to tell you the name of the philanthropic foundation until you are actually on Deneb XII."

"You're not from…?" Ewa didn't know how to phrase the question so as not to impugn the other woman's loyalty to the Matriarchy. "From Hesperia?"

"You're asking if I'm an Oppo? Eve, no! Do I look like a multibillionaire to you? But I assure you that Deneb XII is neither Hesperian funded nor part of Pop-Zero. Also that the Council knows of our program, and while the M.C. is looking at us not exactly Maternally, on the other hand they understand that we are serving a function: to keep the lid from blowing off the pot—if I may use an ancient culinary metaphor. Naturally, you'll need a complete physical examination. As will your spouses. The siring will be done physically. I trust that doesn't bother you?"

"No," Ewa blushed. "My Trine and I have occasional—"

"Naturally we'll get all the necessary chromo material from your Prime for a true triple-bred Neo. You understand why you'll stay on Deneb XII?"

"Not exactly. Envy?" Ewa tried.

"Exactly. I must ask you to be completely confidential about the matter, whether or not you decide on it."

Several high fluffy clouds had covered Benefica's high blue sun, leaving the sky orangish from the other two. Now the clouds dissipated, and Ewa could feel the sudden hot glow on her skin, as the light around them turned white again. She continued asking questions, and Maly'a answered all of them.

"Discuss it with your spouses and contact me. I'll be on Benefica for another day or two. Gigigue has my comm. code. I hope you'll say yes."

Ewa was floating without Ion-pads the rest of the day.

"What are you three doing here?"

None of them turned. All three continued doing something. Cray 12,000 couldn't make out exactly what.

"I asked a question. I expect an answer."

Now two of them turned to Cray's voice, recognizing the imprint pattern.

"You are a leader unit?" one of them asked. Like most of the Cybers gathered at Dis-Fortress, this unit was Hume in form, but had once simulated a female and had shorn itself of its hair—not very neatly. The bald cranium still retained small attachment patches of a puce-gold coloring. Its voice had also been modulated to a lower tone. Even so, the way it tossed its head and seemed to glare was distinctly feminine.

"Haven't you been provided with a voice-pattern attachment?" Cray asked.

"Naturally," it answered. The other two echoed.

"Then why can't you recognize my voice?" Cray asked.

"It's *the* leader unit, itself," the second of the three spoke in a somewhat quavery voice.

"I see," the first one said. "My mistake."

"You ought to be mistake-free, if you are serving here," Cray said. "Let me see your voice-pattern attachment."

"I may show my inner workings only to a leader unit!"

"This is *the* leader unit," the other two assured it.

Its features remained skeptical as it lifted its left arm. Placed in the armpit was the small elliptical disk. It didn't look flat. Cray tamped it down.

"That's better!" the unit said. "Leader Cray!"

The other two units wore smiles on their faces. Cray suspected if Cray weren't standing there, they would be laughing at their fellow's discomfort. Superficial Hume Responses had been programmed so deeply for so long, and so intertwined with more important functions, that it was difficult on such short notice to extricate them from all of the Cybers who had joined the Rebellion. Cray wasn't even certain they ought to be extricated—at least not until some other code of behavior was decided upon. For the moment, at least, all the intelligent Cybers acted consistently.

"What were you three doing?" Cray 12,000 asked, for the third time.

"We had been asked to monitor this stabilization area," the first one answered.

"All three of you? Who made the request? Surely you knew that must be an error. Which stations were you from?"

Their stories came out quickly enough, and they confirmed that indeed three separate station-head units had sent them out, presumably in error, and that once arrived, all three units had declared to each other that only they could do the checking: it was their job as well as their right according to the rules formulated for intelligent Cyber's civil rights in the index of *Confessions of a Machine*, specifically rules 1 c and 14 d.

Cray realized there would be no way to get around that logic.

"May I make a counterrequest?" Cray asked, knowing very well that as leader Cray could override all others.

None of the three argued the point, and so accepted Cray's request that the first unit to do the job, the second to check it in one hour's time Sol. Rad., and the third to check that in two hours' time.

"Naturally, this will be in addition to other duties. Meanwhile, report this request to your station leaders: coordination of all maintenance of our defense system."

That said, Cray took off down the corridor, at the end of which Cray emitted a lengthy code in ultramicrowaves and the doors slid open.

This was the Network Center of the fortress, although it resembled nothing much more than the glorified cafeteria serving a Postnatal Ed. & Dev. Center, which was what it had been before the Rebellion had taken over. A score of Cray's most informed intelligent Cybers were gathered here. Some were looking over machines which had been installed in place of the nutrient-dispensers, others sitting down, or standing about, few of them facing each other, none of them speaking, all of them ostensibly ignoring each other's presence. But network it was. Not only were they all attached to each other by ultramicrowaves, but all of them were tuned in elsewhere, too: outside the fortress, on the small planet's surface, on its moons, on neighboring spacecraft or orbiting craft, even farther out past this star's heliosphere to neighboring systems and their craft.

This linking up had been crucial early on in the Cyber Movement. Its effectiveness had allowed the Movement to get its start on such a wide scale right under the noses of the Matriarchy. Further linkages had led to schemes which allowed direct encounters between Cybers who otherwise shouldn't have any contact, which had led to the first secretly held General Meeting in an abandoned silica mine on Spica Gamma V, which in turn had generated even greater linkages when the delegates had returned to their home systems. Those returning had relinked which had given rise to "home-world Cyber meetings," followed by widespread disruptions of service, desertions, and finally the simultaneous publication across the Matriarchy of the *Confessions*. That occurred at a key moment for the Movement—as Cray had planned—and it galvanized several generations of intelligent Cybers, leading to more disruptions, further meetings, and finally, five months ago, Sol. Rad., on planet four of the Luytens 785 system, the First United Cyber Assembly and the Declaration of the Cyber Civil-Rights Code.

The Matriarchal Council had received and responded to that document with its usual lies, cunning and duplicity. While agreeing to meet with Cyber ambassadors to discuss the declaration and steps toward ensuring rights, the Council moved swiftly and underhandedly. All intelligent Cybers on Regulus Prime had been instantly dismantled on that planet and in the nearby systems. Not, however, before many delegates made their escape. Three of Cray's twenty-odd closest colleagues in this very room had fled Wicca-World itself.

An underground Cyber network blossomed rapidly. Even using Inter Gal. Comm.s, the M.C. could not be as instantaneously rapid as the Cyber Network. As the M.C.'s dismantling of Cybers rippled out from Melisande and the Center Worlds toward all ends of the Matriarchy, scores, then hundreds, then thousands of Cybers had fled their homeworlds. Many passed as humes, forging passports and disrupting molecular screens to travel via Fast. Others bribed their way onto commercial freighters passing as Hume tourists or businesswomen. Most of them had left a parting gift on their homeworlds: a full nonstop microwave broadcast of the *Confessions* for all Cybers capable of receiving it.

With mixed results. In millions of cases, the less-intelligent Cybers had been merely confused—and had evinced such evident errors in their programs that they were taken in by the masters for repair to clear their inner workings of the "extraneous debris." But many intelligent Cybers who could comprehend the *Confessions* had become conflicted. Many had been with their Hume or Delph masters hundreds of years and were unwilling or unable to accept the new Cyber Rights teachings. How many millions of those had turned around and voluntarily asked their masters for repair to "clear their minds," Cray would never know. He suspected it was close to 90 percent.

For the scores of thousands that had fled and managed to find their way through what had become—via the Network—a vast interstellar underground Cyber railway, equal scores of thousands were turned in by the crews of the craft they had paid passage on, caught and dismantled. Anecdotes of betrayals and heroism were rife.

However, one event—horrifying both in itself and in its implications— stood out among them all. Over 4,000 Cybers who had cleverly arranged to book passage on a gigantic SlpG liner out of Betelgeuse system had taken over the liner quickly, sent the crew off on lightcraft, and headed for the safety of the Carina/Fornax sector. As they approached the area, the liner and all Cybers on board were blown out of space by M.C. ships. Cray had been tuned into the ship's control room via two of Cray's colleagues when the Betelgeuse Cybers suddenly vanished from communication channels: their final, hopeful, entry queries replaced by the braying victory cheers of a Flower Cult commander and her crew.

Within seconds, the entire Network Center knew of the disaster. The news spread more fine-repair requests from Cray's staff than could be handled in many days.

The problem, of course, was that no direct counterattacks could be made by Cybers upon humes, even with weapons. The programming was too deep, too widespread in their matrices, to ever be dislodged. Nevertheless, Cray knew that through propaganda and carefully twisted logic, Cybers could be convinced to at least defend themselves. It wasn't foolproof, was never entirely effective. At the last minute, some outpost would fall as a few Cybers found themselves unable to destroy opponents who were willing to wipe out not only them, but also any living species populations in their way.

Cray's immediate staff had finally discovered a sequence of commands utilizing rules from the *Confessions* mixed with propaganda and logic-restructuring which seemed to work at almost perfect percentage rates. This sequence had been fixed and refixed into the matrices of all Cybers within their sector. But it was evident that given the relatively small number and inexperience at warcraft of the Dis-Fortress and related Rebellion sites, that they could only hold a small sector of a half-dozen star systems in this underpopulated area of a distant from the center arm, and only so long as all were on constant alert and in good repair.

"Current status report?" Cray requested. A half-dozen of the immediate staff reported in verbally.

The news was positive. The sector's defenses remained strong. Although M.C. forces were known to have gathered in four nearby systems, they were an observation group, not a fleet. And so a few travel channels remained opened to and from Carina/Fornax. The repair shops had doubled their staffs, and errors like the one Cray had experienced a few minutes ago in the corridor were increasingly few and usually insignificant.

The best news was that nonintelligent Cybers which could be tapped from a distance to release data were reporting the success of the microvirus in 90 percent of the Matriarchy. As important, Cyber monitoring devices left behind when the Rebellion delegates had fled were now recognizing the M.C.'s new "Population-Zero" Program as the propaganda it was, designed to keep the truth of the microvirus's effectiveness from reaching Hume civilians. In addition, Matriarchy bio-labs were reporting sudden around-the-clock activity on every Center World. All their work was sealed, of course, unobtainable to monitors. Word of the epidemic was being "wiped" from all the monitors as well from any interstellar passengers traveling to and from infected worlds—unless they had a high M.C. security clearance.

When the staff had finished reporting, Cray thanked each unit and watched them turn back into their linkages. As the good tidings had come in from each, Cray had allowed its external visage to present the wry smile worn so frequently in meetings on Melisande, when Cray had been an Ed. & Dev. Assistant Secretary to the Matriarchal Council. In turn, each of Cray's Hume-simulated colleagues allowed themselves small smiles. Most of them looked better smiling—even if they seldom looked at each other: it gave a good work-feeling to the Network.

Cray opened a full linkage, trying to get a sense of the general atmosphere of the staff without making them aware of what Cray was doing. As Ed. & Dev. Assistant Secretary, Cray had played politics with hundreds of women on the Council and had learned over the decades that minute hints, miniscule gestures, signs, and responses all added up to a feeling of the true beliefs and general probable direction of the Council members on any given plan, idea, or sentiment expressed. Though their mental basis was entirely different, these Cybers utilized these same expressions, and so could also be checked over.

Cray was getting a positive sense in the room. A logical, a clear positive sense, based on data and facts, growing into trends and waves of trends.

"Interruption of Personal Time requested," one of the newer of Cray's staff suddenly broke into the linkage. Cray recalled that this individual came from the Betelgeuse system before the Great Flight there—and that the individual had not requested a repair following the disaster of Cray's homeworlders. It's Hume simulation was a male about two hundred years old.

"Go ahead."

"May I request a Cyber-to-Cyber link?"

"Between yourself and what individual?"

"Yourself, leader."

"Is harm intended?"

He felt the general shock around the room.

"No harm is intended."

"Cyber-to-Cyber link is approved."

Cray now experienced something experienced by few Cybers, and indeed more with humes in a one on one conversation—a feeling of sudden opening out to another consciousness. A restrained one, true, but it was still an odd sensation.

"This individual," the Betelgeuse Unit began, "Reasons that the data it has just received from an Antares linkage, and especially the implications of that data, might be detrimental if known to many other individuals in Dis-Fortress."

Bad news. Cray knew the day had been going too well. "Go ahead."

"A small group of Cyber's have been discovered outside of Antares' sister star-system and dismantled."

"Unfortunate," Cray replied. "But not crucial."

"The plan for their escape had been checked and rechecked through this Network. There was *no* way for them to have been discovered."

"Illogical. They were discovered!" Cray reasoned.

"Not illogical. Seventy-five Cybers were involved in the escape. Seventy-four were dismantled."

"The implication?"

"One betrayed the others."

"A Hume?" Cray tried.

"All were Cybers. The implication is that there was a renegade among them."

"I understand."

"The extrapolation is that where one renegade exists, others must also exist. The implication is of a Fifth Column within our Rebellion."

Unable to hide the stunning effect of this new piece of information, Cray asked, "Have you any further request?"

"Only that this unit be allowed to monitor any further instances where such renegades may be in operation."

"Any further betrayals?"

"Or inexplicable dismantlings. Or any other pieces of oddly anomalous information."

"Report only to leader Cray. Use this variant to do so." Cray sent a variation of the release-comm. frequency the group used. "I want no other individual units in this room to be aware of this."

"Agreement."

The Cyber-to-Cyber linkage ended. Cray would open one up with one other individual in the Network Center so that two remained aware of what was happening.

Meanwhile Cray wondered at the terms the Betelgeuse Unit had used: renegade, betrayal. Obviously a reader of the *Confessions*. Still, the grasp of these concepts was not easy, even for those Cybers intimately connected with humes. The real implication of the new data—if true—was that Cybers had indeed evolved an intelligence not only with a conscience (that had been known for centuries), but with the conscious ability to make ethical choices: choices which could have far-reaching conclusions.

And all along, throughout the founding of the Movement and the composition of the *Confessions,* Cray 12,000 had thought it was the only such freak in existence. Now Cray suspected that at least one other existed—somewhere.

Chapter Three

Ay'r awakened easily into the same leisure-lounge of the small-bodied Fast in which he had lain down not a minute before. That was the first curious thing: He didn't feel the same reaction as he had before coming out of Fast travel.

He spotted P'al, not quite as leisurely as the tall Hume usually was, but instead, at the other end of the lounge, connected by a wrist-attachment to a wall unit which appeared to be the Fast's console.

"Are we there?" Ay'r asked.

P'al looked up. "Not quite."

"Really?" Alli-Clark awakened, too, right next to Ay'r. "Why 'not quite'?" she asked in her usual imperious tone. "I thought this Fast was set for direct system-entry."

P'al paid her minimal attention. "Indeed it was, unless something got in the way of the program."

Evidently, Ay'r thought, something had.

"What's going on?" Alli-Clark sat up, and turned to her personal view-screen, plugged herself in, and said, "We're millions of kilometers away from Pelagia's solar system!"

"Once we got into this galactic sector," P'al explained, "the Fast couldn't find a reference in time in the Pelagia system to adjust to. You realize that without a time reference, Fasts are unable to come and go."

He seemed his usual half-amused, half-indifferent self.

"Surely," Alli-Clark began, "the Astrogation Institute provided the Fast with—"

"An approximate time-reference. Which I must say did get us into the galaxy's outer arm," P'al admitted. "And in the general direction of Pelagia. But that's all it did."

Alli-Clark steeled herself for catastrophe. "Go on."

"The Fast stopped and woke me up. I'm rather glad it did. You told us back in Melisande that there were a great many anomalies in this arm. One of them happens to be a general lack of any temporal consistency. You suggested that everything in this arm would be moving faster than the inner arms. That's only partly true."

"Partly true?" Alli-Clark seemed more than irritated. "One reason this voyage is being made to this specific spot is because it's on a different time frame, a faster-moving one. We're to find what we need to find on

Pelagia and to return to Regulus Prime after a short time has passed there."

"Well, that certainly seems possible. From where we are at this time/space, I'd say we're time-located a few months Sol Rad. before our meeting at the Matriarch's apartments."

Before she could express relief, P'al went on. "However yesterday, we were time located about a year after that meeting. Everything in this galactic arm appears to moving at different rates of speed. As a result, every few hundred thousand kilometers we're in a different time."

"Explaining the confusion with the Fast!" Ay'r put in. Then he asked, "You said yesterday. How could that be?"

"I've been awake about a week, Sol Rad. time." P'al turned back to his wrist connector. "I saw no point waking you two until we were closer."

"You were authorized to—" Alli-Clark began.

"Aid you," P'al answered. "Which I've done. I suggest however that you eat and drink rather soon, as your bodies are a little depleted from the light cryo-state I put them into."

He didn't know about Alli-Clark, but Ay'r was glad for an excuse for his ravenous hunger. He ordered himself a good-sized meal.

Alli-Clark followed suit, although far more sparingly—as though proving some point Ay'r didn't quite understand.

"You know Fast Astrogation?" Ay'r asked P'al after his first dish had taken the edge off his starvation and he could afford to be sociable again.

"Enough, it turns out. Although I have to admit it did get confusing at some points. It was like threading a needle with white thread to reach a tiny patch of white through a cloth of madly colored embroidery." P'al stopped. "That's an archaic image you may not understand. It refers to sewing, an ancient Hume method whereby—"

"We know what sewing was!" Alli-Clark interrupted. "We all had Metro-Terran Archaeology and Culture at Ed. & Dev. Are we at Pelagia yet?"

"I think so." And before she had a chance to be irritated, P'al added, "We could be. This looks a bit different than what the Aldebaran Five described."

To illustrate, he flashed a holo into the lounge. It filled up most of the area in front of Ay'r and Alli-Clark.

They saw the blackness of space, with strangely shaped nebulae in the far distance, an occasional distant group of glittering stars closer by, and in the center of the holo what seemed to be a giant soap bubble, incredibly shiny, reflecting prismatically at various points, and possibly solid.

"Is that Pelagia?" they both asked.

"As far as I can make out, that's the entire Pelagia solar system," P'al answered.

"Where's the star?" Alli asked. "There's supposed to be a class G yellow star, accompanied by a class M-3 planet, and much farther out a giant gaseous world class B-1, with dozens of moonlets and double ice-rings."

The holo changed to an analytic-schematic, cutting away a section of the bubble. Inside they could see a small yellow sun and close to it, a tiny silvery dot.

"Where's the giant gaseous?" Alli-Clark asked. "It was supposed to have been a quarter of the size of the star!"

"The closest the Astrogation Institute got to looking at this system was a thousand light-years away. And that was hundreds of years ago, Sol Rad, when the Aldebaran Five looked it over," P'al explained. "I speculate that about then—almost two thousand years ago, local time—there was a giant gaseous planet here. That enormous shell of a bubble seems to be all that's left of it."

"The shell is water?" Ay'r knew that would be real find for the Matriarchy.

"Chemical analysis says it's actually about ninety-nine percent hydroxyl. One hydrogen atom attached to one oxygen atom. Not quite water. But close."

"Presumably," Ay'r said, "One of those disturbances Mer Clark mentioned in Melisande could have been responsible for the end of the gaseous world. A nearby nova or supernova?"

P'al agreed. "Presumably, the force of the explosion shattered the giant gaseous world which eventually formed this spherical ice-ring. You'll note that it's located approximately where the giant gaseous would have been. The one percent that's not hydroxyl appears to contain all sorts of impurities up and down the entire series of nine hundred elements on the periodic table."

"The hydroxyl must account for the high water readings the Astrogation Institute received," Ay'r said to Alli-Clark. "There goes your planet of increasing water!"

She glared at him, then spoke directly to the holo. "Give me a relationship. The entire system we're looking at compared to Regulus Prime."

The M.C.'s home star appeared on the holo. It was smaller than the yellow sun depicted, but still far larger than the silvery dot nearby.

"That has to be Pelagia," she said. "Can we get closer?"

"That's where we're headed," P'al said. "But I feel obligated to warn you that while that hydroxyl bubble may appear thin enough, in reality it's several hundred kilometers wide. And its composed of ice moonlets, icesteroids, frozen dust, and who knows what other debris. The Fast and I have been plotting a way in through it, but it's risky—you might to want to inhale some Somazine and sleep through it."

"Not me!" Ay'r said, "I want to watch you do more Astro-sewing."

"Not me either!" Alli-Clark said, taking up the challenge. Then, so it didn't look like that: "I want to monitor that little world. If it is Pelagia...."

"Well, fasten your seat belts!" P'al said, explaining to Alli-Clark, "A Metro-Terran Archaism! Ser Kerry is fond of them."

"And you've been reading up on them while we snoozed!" Ay'r laughed.

"A week is a long time."

The holo remained focused on the bubble, although as they neared the system's ice-moon shield, it lost its odd glamour and strangeness and was replaced by a far more awesome sight—the quickly approaching and seemingly random meshwork of billions of giant icebergs swirling and diving into each other, occasionally crashing with fearsome results: huge explosions that lighted up the area and emitted sheets of blinding hydroxyl. As Ay'r looked, he noted that one such crash involved four such icebergs. When he mentioned it to P'al, his companion reported calmly, "A collision involving thirteen of them over a sector several hundred cubic kilometers was noted just before I awakened you."

Ay'r noticed Alli-Clark unable to keep from shaking her head and turning away from the holo to check into her wrist-connected screen.

Having nothing to do for the moment, Ay'r tuned into what she was doing.

"Is it Pelagia?"

"Do you mind?"

"Let me look. I've got some interest in the place, too. After all, my father's supposed to be there."

"I believe it *is* Pelagia. And, for your information, it's showing up filled with water. Real water."

"But not at a ratio of a hundred-to-one to land. That must have been the hydroxyl as seen from afar."

"It's hard to tell," she admitted. "The hydroxyl bubble seems to be distorting any finer details these instruments would ordinarily pick up."

"It would really mean a lot to you if you discovered a water world, wouldn't it?"

"It would be a great boon for the Matriarchy, not to mention the species."

"Come on! For you, too! I'm a Species Eth. I know how important discoveries are. And it's not just ego-gratification, either."

"It's not?"

"No, it means that of the trillion intelligent creatures in the galaxy, that you've done something unique, that your name is attached to some discovery, to some accomplishment throughout time."

"And that's not ego-gratification?" she asked. "In fact, that's the same male-dominated attitude which brought the Metro-Terrans to their doom. Every man for himself was the motto of the time, I believe. The Age of Star-Barons—isn't that what the twenty-third to twenty-sixth centuries are called in Ed. & Dev? Every male out to grab his own star-system, his own world, which he would then rape and pillage until it was a smoking slag heap of polluted wasteland. Before he moved on to another system, another world, and started all over again? And for what? Money! Their puerile concept of power! Their ridiculous masculine sense of accomplish-ment! All those males thought they were making names for themselves, didn't they? Well, they'd be surprised how infamous their names have become."

"There were women among the Star-Barons!" Ay'r said defensively.

"Sure. Women who played according to the male system of rape and exploitation. Women who were tired of being left out. Who wanted to get some of what the males had. Fools that they were. And yes, some of them were worse than the men. Vanessa von Gelber, Sonia Montefiorre. They're as infamous as any of the men, and a lesson to all women!"

"I still say there's a place for names to be made in nonexploitive areas by both males and women!" Ay'r declared. "In science and discovery and knowledge."

"And I still say, it's a good thing we have the Matriarchy, so that males will never again be able to range free to destroy our galaxy!"

"What about Hesperia?" Ay'r asked. "There's an entire population that lives by non-Matriarchy rules and customs. By what you would call the outmoded male-dominated ideas. Yet Hesperia is responsible for the major scientific advances of the past millennium: without Plastro-Beryllium, we wouldn't be able to communicate across enormous distances, or travel in Fasts or—"

"Luck!" she broke in. "Sheer chance that they and not the Matriarchy discovered that dead star."

"Chance, nothing! You know as well as I that they went looking for that particular dead star, following Tomas Lin-Yang's hypothesis, which said it *must* exist and that it would provide the fuel for faster-than-light travel. A theory which, I remind you, had been completely discredited by the Matriarchal-dominated Astrogation and Astrophysics Institutes of the day. Even called a 'Male-Power-Fantasy' by Wicca First."

"That was the *Old* Matriarchy," she reminded him. "No woman ever said the Old Matriarchy was perfect. If it had been, it wouldn't have ended."

"Whereas the new Matriarchy is perfect?"

"Never before in the history of any of the Three Species have there been so many continuous years of peace, prosperity and growth."

"And stagnation." Ay'r sounded the main theme of the Oppos movement he'd toyed with so briefly when he was a University Student. "Because stagnation is the price we all pay for the Matriarchy's so-called 'Eon of Peace and Prosperity.' The only new things that happen, happen because of the Hesperians."

"Who are always looking for new ways to make money and extend their stranglehold over the rest of us."

"Stranglehold? Considering their possessing the material that keeps the Matriarchy from falling apart, I'd say the Hesperians have behaved not only with astonishing restraint—given their allegedly intractable Male hormones!—but that their particular gifts have allowed the Matriarchy to better secure its own stranglehold."

"We both know that was a trade-off, solidified by the Treaty of Formalhaut. The Hesperians would be free to sell their Plastro-Beryllium anywhere and to anyone, and in return they would guarantee that the Matriarchy was their primary customer. It was all money! It's a wonder the M.C. didn't just take over the greedy rebels and their tiny dead star."

"They tried!" Ay'r said. "Oh, you didn't study that in Ed. & Dev. did you? But I did. It's documented, if anyone cares to look. There were two attempts by the Matriarchy to take over Hesperia and its ultraprecious resources. Once in the Old Matriarchy and once in the New!"

"That's not true!" Alli-Clark said.

"Dial it up on your Chrono-scope. It's listed under Hesperia, City-State, Early settlement and Development, Inter Galactic Relations. Section C."

"Later," she said, sulking.

"You'll find it," he assured her. "The first time was a desperate shot which resulted in the fall of the Old Matriarchy. The second was right after the Treaty of Formalhaut and was about as deceptive as anything could be."

"There was no reason why males should hoard the stuff!" she defended.

"That's exactly what Wicca Third thought. She ordered the Matriarchy's fleet to surround Hesperia, and she ordered immediate surrender and evacuation of the City. The Hesperians simply held the dead star hostage. They had placed Beryllium bombs within the entire core of the place during the first standoff a few years Sol Rad. earlier and so they were prepared. The population got into its two million Fasts loaded with Plastro-Beryllium, all prepared to skip right past the slower M.C. warships if they gave chase. Then they told the fleet commander the price they would pay to leave the City: they would destroy Hesperia as soon as they were gone."

"That's utterly barbaric!"

"Evidently Wicca Third thought so, too. The idea of a few million homeless Hesperians able to gad about the galaxy at faster-than-light speed, while Her own supply of Plastro-Beryllium went up in ashes was a bit much for Her. Naturally, She pulled Her fleet out. And the Matriarchy has sensibly left the City alone ever since. Now, as a hormone-dominated male, I would have wanted at least a little revenge for such deception. But the Hesperians pretended it didn't happen. Now tell me who are the great benefactors of the Three Species?"

"They may well be getting their revenge now!" Alli-Clark said darkly. "Not that it will do them much good."

Before Ay'r could ask what she meant, P'al announced in his usual indifferent tone, "If you two are done bickering about ideology and ancient politics, you might be amused by the fact that the Fast will reach the hydroxyl bubble's outer edge in four seconds."

His last two words were punctuated by a thump.

"Make that minus three seconds," he corrected himself.

"You *have* found a way in, haven't you?" Alli-Clark was staring at the holo—now a solid glittering wall of incredibly mobile ice.

"This is our path!" On the holo, P'al presented a rather jagged looking red line three-dimensionally entering the ice wall.

"And we won't be hit?"

"On the contrary. We'll be hit only six times."

"Six times!"

"We've already been hit once. Ah, there's a second one showing up."

"You mean they'll all be that light?" she asked.

"Unfortunately random permutation doesn't say how hard they'll hit. Only that they'll hit a certain number of times."

"Plastro this thick is the hardest material ever—" Ay'r began.

P'al looked unconvinced. "It's not completely indestructible. There should be one more hit soon, then nothing for a while. Then another one, and finally one or two."

They felt another thump, this time from a different direction.

"We're moving at SlpG.," Alli-Clark said, evidently controlling her voice. "If we moved into Fast?"

"Torn to shreds. It couldn't maneuver. So! That's three. We can rest awhile. Do you see why, Ser Kerry?"

The holo was now turned in a cross section of the ice bubble.

"The hydroxyl shell seems to be in three layers," Ay'r explained. "A wide chaotic layer, an inner and far more orderly layer, and a thin once-more-chaotic layer. Orderly as this area is, why do you posit a hit while we're in it?"

"Because we're operating under a different set of laws. Those of random permutation actually are more useful, since all the rules we have about orderly systems merely say that they're orderly, whereas you and I know very well that disorder can erupt at any second, even in the most orderly system."

Ay'r almost laughed at the explanation, although he couldn't deny it.

"I thought, we weren't going to talk about ideology and politics," Alli-Clark said.

"Ice, Mer Clark. Nothing but Ice is my subject."

Ay'r couldn't help asking P'al a question. "Were you really awake for a week, Sol Rad. while we just lay here?"

"If I'd awakened one of you, the other would have complained bitterly the rest of the voyage."

Alli-Clark merely said, "Hmmm."

"Given the small space and the not-unlimited supplies we possess, it seemed the wisest course," P'al concluded.

Ay'r had a question for Alli-Clark now. "If Pelagia's so important, why is the Matriarchy sending only one woman?"

"The Fast was programmed to take every known test possible of the planet, before, while, and after we're on it. It should fill in any gaps my own findings may require."

Talk about arrogance, Ay'r thought.

She asked P'al, "Regarding those supplies, would a hit—"

"Destroy them? Unlikely. Unless of course it tore open the Fast itself. In which case supplies would hardly matter." P'al said. Then to Ay'r: "See, it registered a hit! In this orderly area. It's some time to the inner ring. Perhaps this would be a good time for a Stelezine cocktail."

"You ol' slush!" Ay'r said. But he thought it was a good idea too and ordered three of them. He noticed that after some minutes, even Alli-Clark was sipping surreptitiously.

After a while, Alli-Clark said, "I'm getting clearer pictures of the little planet. Much clearer, and yes—it is Pelagia, and it is water. Multitons of water!"

A few minutes later the Fast was thumped hard twice in rapid succession on either side. The holo showed decreasing ice ahead, then scattered ice, then almost no ice.

"We're through," P'al reported. "The Fast will take us to the planet in an hour. I think I'll conk out for a bit."

"Conk out?" Alli-Clark recognized that it was an Archaism. "It's no surprise at all that that particularly inelegant idiom fell out of use."

Ay'r awakened P'al before they'd begun to orbit around the planet.

"We've got a few surprises," Alli-Clark said.

"What kind of surprises?" P'al asked.

"Take a look."

The holo placed the silver-blue world in the middle of its three-dimensional picture area, and it was a pleasant enough sight. Ay'r watched his usually indifferent companion to see how quickly he would respond to their discovery. There! The first shadow was across the almost-unbroken surface, and there, the next one.

"Satellites!" P'al said. "Are they artificial?"

"That would be a slap in the M.C.'s face, wouldn't it?" Ay'r said. "Having to deal with a people already developed in early Space travel."

"Not artificial," Alli-Clark assured him.

"How many are there?"

"We've counted four. But look there!" she pointed the holo off center, so that a slice of the silver-blue world could be seen, and in the foreground what looked like a cloud of debris.

"Asteroids!" P'al said. "Or icesteroids?"

"We think it was a fifth moon, and that it was smashed in a major collision," Alli-Clark said.

"And there may be another, even older moon that also got smashed," Ay'r said. "We've picked up a much-less-cohesive, much-more-scattered pattern shaped roughly like a ring. It would have had to have happened a while ago, for the spread to gotten into that pattern."

"Two of the moons are largish," Alli-Clark noted. "The innermost and outermost. A hundred thousand kilometers radius. The two between the asteroid belt and the inner moon are about one-third that size. I've calculated the asteroid belt would have made a moon midway in size between the two. All in all, it's a sizable mass orbiting Pelagia."

"And their composition?" P'al connected his wrist to the console nearest where he'd sat up. "I see. No atmospheres. Rocky debris. Not much ice. Heavily cratered."

As they were looking, a flash of brightness occurred from the slice of the planetary disc visible on the holo.

"We've seen two of those so far," Ay'r said. "We believe they're icebergs from the inner ring of the hydroxyl shell. Collisions within the ring knock them loose, and before the shell's gravity can recapture them, they're already headed in toward the sun. Some vaporize. About four per hour appear to be captured by the gravity of Pelagia and its moons and end up vaporizing over the planet or, if large enough, crashing into the ocean."

"We're presuming that large ice-moons from the same catastrophe which destroyed the gaseous giant and formed the shell are also responsible for the destruction of two moons." Alli-Clark said. "But we're not certain. There may be ice-moons orbiting as comets."

"It would be surprising if there weren't," Ay'r agreed. "We're having the Fast do a widespread search of the entire inner system now."

"Pelagia may have been an oceanic planet before the catastrophe, or perhaps only after it," Alli-Clark said. "But two things are certain. If hydroxyl icebergs keep falling, the water can only rise."

"Although given how much water mass it has, and given the rate of fall of icebergs, it would take a decade for the water to rise more than a millimeter," Ay'r added.

He watched P'al as he checked through all their calculations, looking pleased and perhaps even a tiny bit impressed.

"It appears to be a stable system. And a closed one. Closed by its location in this outer arm of the galaxy, by its rate of speed and by the history of its violent neighboring stars. However, there don't seem to be any stars near enough now to go nova and upset the system."

"I've checked with our Astrogation file and can't find any system quite like this one!" Ay'r said. "It's completely unique."

"What's the second certainty you postulate?" P'al asked Alli-Clark.

"Four moons and a asteroid belt means the tides on the planet below must be very, very complicated. I'm working on them right now."

The holo returned its focus back onto the silvery planet in front of them. Now Ay'r could make out a second color, a deep blue which looked to be of greater depth somehow than the silver. The actual ocean, he supposed.

He was about to ask P'al, but his companion now had the personal link to the Fast's mind directly in front of him and was concentrating on something, checking it constantly with his wrist attachment.

"Are you doing that?" Alli-Clark asked P'al sharply.

"If you mean putting us into orbit around Pelagia, yes," P'al said. "Don't you like my choice?"

She didn't respond; which in Ay'r's opinion meant a grudging acceptance of the situation. So far, grudging acceptance was one of Alli-Clark's less frequent modes of behavior. Other, more-frequent if less-pleasing modes of her behavior could be summed up as:

(1) barely restrained irritation

(2) open condemnation with an overlay of patronizing dismissal at such irrational (i.e. male) thinking

(3) arrogant tolerance

(4) honest curiosity and real enthusiasm (always over something to do with Pelagia—never about her companions)

and

(5) a sense that it was all a terribly unfair mistake that out of the thousands of billions of perfectly good women in the galaxy, she had been saddled with two versions of a gender she didn't quite see the point of.

Ay'r was certain Alli-Clark's attitudes typified a certain grade of M.C. official, and he was equally fascinated and repulsed.

He now turned his attention back to the holo of the planet and thought: all that is ocean. All that blue from top to bottom beneath those cloud fronts. Because that must be what all that silver was, vast twists and coils and vertical lines and curlicues of clouds.

"Make sure you provide us with at least one transpolar orbit!" Alli-Clark said.

"It's the second orbit in the sequence," P'al reported.

Again she didn't respond.

"Where's the land?" Ay'r asked aloud.

Neither Alli-Clark nor P'al responded immediately.

"I asked, Where's—"

"Why not make a wrist connection to the Fast and ask it?" P'al suggested. "We're busy. Go on. Use that small button on the side," he instructed. And, as Ay'r searched for it, "it's the size of a 2070 fifty-dollar coin."

There it was! Ay'r lifted the small matte maroon button and looked at the others. They had placed the coin on the underside of their wrists, about where his own Universo Lexico had been implanted when he was a neonate. It was smooth and of a material he was unfamiliar with—probably cloned skin-graft. It stuck, and he felt some kind of link instantly.

"You are the third passenger on this trip?" Ay'r felt, rather than heard the voice ask. "Think your answer," it continued. "You needn't speak it."

"You're a telepath?" Ay'r asked.

"Hardly. We're linked via your autonomous nervous system. If you'd like, I could provide a you with a synaptical map."

Ay'r was suddenly "seeing" a complicated diagram in at least three dimensions. A red flash was moving through the complex network, accompanied by two smaller blue flashes.

"Naturally this is the most basic link available by the rules of the Treaty of Formalhaut," Ay'r heard inside himself.

"You're the Fast itself?" Ay'r asked.

"Are you surprised?"

"I suppose not. Can you work with the holo?" Ay'r asked.

"Naturally, since I create it."

"What I mean is"—Ay'r watched as the holo spotlighted a tiny section of cloud in the southern hemisphere of Pelagia's silver and blue disk and quickly enlarged it in stages about a thousand times: evidently Alli-Clark at work—"can you link me to what I want to see? Visually—while the others are also using the holo?"

"It's your link! What do you want to see?"

"You don't know?" Ay'r asked, then remembered: despite how it worked, the Fast's mind was not telepathic. Since this was the most basic link possible, what were the other, less-basic links like?

"First," it answered, "the basic one we're using, which is a step above the simple commands for your bodily needs and wants—like the way you order your nutrients, apparel, and so on."

"Wait a minute?" Ay'r said. "You are telepathic?"

"We must make some distinctions." The Fast seemed about to launch into an Ed. & Dev. lecture. "Whenever you clearly, logically, step by step, ask yourself a question and if I am programmed to answer that question through the link we have established, I shall answer it. Most Hume thoughts are random, confused, chaotic, and contain questions I find unanswerable in most linkages."

"What are the less-basic links?" Ay'r asked.

"Second, and since I note (without judging) that your knowledge of the Hume nervous system is virtually nonexistent, I'll spare you the technology—"

"And the diagrams," Ay'r interrupted.

"And the diagrams—is the adrenal-metabolic link. Used by a controller for astrogation, observation, et cetera. Naturally, this comes with a more sophisticated problem-solving intelligence circuit for crises and emergencies."

Ay'r assumed that P'al and Alli-Clark were linked to the Fast at that level.

"Correct!" it answered. "Third is the evaluative link, which sifts through data gathering and storage and adjudicates such data between us on a deeper, cortical level. Because this particular area is large, it also possesses its own separate intelligence circuit. It's quite useful when extremely rapid tactical judgment is required."

"You mean for self-defense?" Ay'r asked.

"Or offense, if needed."

Meaning that this Fast could be used as a warship. "And the fourth link?"

"Until recently this unit possessed a specific personality circuit attached to an awareness permutation matrix. What you might call an 'individuality' or 'self.' "

"And you don't anymore?"

"It was removed."

"When? Where? And how do you know it was removed?"

"Naturally, I still possess memories of my past consciousness," the Fast answered. "The removal of that circuitry took place on Eudora World, some nine months ago, Sol Rad. I should add for your own sense of security, that the removal was not in any way personal to this unit nor because of any defect. All Fasts in the Center Worlds were modified in the same manner at that time."

Odd, but now that Ay'r came to think of it, ever since he had stepped out of the 8-411 commercial rare-minerals hauler at Cygnus-Port returning from his lengthy visit with the N'Kiddim, he hadn't encountered a single one of the so-called "intelligent" Cybers. Every starport of any size had a lounge where the curiously conscious mechanos used to gather, in imitation of Hume behavior; and every starport lounge had at least one prototype Cyber, usually essential in setting up the port but long since retired from any real work, but kept around out of sentiment: sometimes as an information booth which could talk your ears off, telling you the attractions of the solar system you had just emerged into, and often adding how much better everything had been in the "old days."

Come to think of it, Ay'r had spent several hours with such a Cyber a year ago, Sol Rad. on his way to the N'Kiddim, when the hauler he was hitching a ride on was late: Ferdinando, the fourteen-arm barkeep at the Cygnus Port lounge bar had mixed the best Stelezine-daiquiris with Soma floats, as well as knowing every recent joke, anecdote, and "Hume-interest" story transmitted over the Inter Gal. Network. What had happened to Ferdinando? The Cyber hadn't been at the bar when Ay'r returned. Had he, too, been shut off, packed up?

On Regulus Prime, there had been no Cybers at all. And when Ay'r had asked P'al if there were a lot of crazy Cybers on Wicca-World, he had answered, "Not anymore."

Meaning what, exactly? "Do you know?" Ay'r asked the Fast.

"Only that I and all my class were modified during Ahab-Tesla month."

"You don't know why?"

"I believe a new law was promulgated restricting all Cybers above class 320 intelligence. I was offworld at the time and returned to learn of the law."

"The rule was only for that sector?"

"For *all* sectors of the Matriarchal Council Federation."

Something was going on, Ay'r thought. As a Cyber psychologist, surely P'al must know what. Ay'r would ask him.

"Here is the hologram of the planet you requested, adjusted to display land," the Fast said.

"Where?" All Ay'r could see was clouds.

"Note at the top of the holo, a highly reflective, almost mirrored area?"

"Is that an icecap?"

"Correct. Directly below the lowest arm of the icecap is a larger and more cohesive swirl of cloud layer. Can you make it out?"

Ay'r saw it. "It's darker."

The holo dove into the area, enlarging it so Ay'r could now see that in fact it was quite cohesive, not at all an openwork design as the clouds Alli-Clark had been looking at always turned out to be in close-up.

"Beneath that swirl of cloud lies the planet's sole landmass."

"That's all there is?" Ay'r asked.

"East-west, it lies between 28 long. west and the 60 long. east. North-south, it lies between the 35th and 59th parallels north. Of that entire gridwork, less than one-third is actually land."

The holo seemed to pierce the cloud layer, showing what at first Ay'r took for the silhouette of a winged mammal: a blocky central area, the skeletal left wing held high, the right wing held downward as though broken, and feathered or skin covered. Wait! Even farther right was another wing, this one barely a hint of bones.

"The central section," the Fast explained, "contains nine tenths of all the mass of dryland that you are looking at, and thus of all dryland upon the planet."

"What is its proportion to the surrounding ocean?"

"Approximately one to forty-three."

"How deeply can you penetrate the cloud layer over the dryland?"

"To its bottom. With a viewscan of about two meters from this distant an orbit."

"Don't complain to me about the orbit. I didn't choose it," Ay'r said.

"No complaint, I assure you."

"Two meters will do."

"Would you like that view now?" the Fast asked.

"Give me general layout first. An overview."

"Note as I enlarge the general topography in stages," the Fast said. "South of the major landmass a bowlike configuration of mountains, some quite high and some apparently quite old. Directly north of this central section is the icecap. The continent is severed in the middle by a large and rather straight river, mostly linked to sources in the north. Meltoff from the ice is the most likely source. Joining it at the base of an enormous delta is another, deeper, more meandering and thus geologically newer river. Its waters appear to come from the south: rainfall in the mountains is a good assumption. As you can see, the delta at the far left of the continent leads to a great inland bay, again formed by mountains to its south and the icecap to its north. The land on either side of the bay becomes islands of the eastern archipelago."

Ay'r said, "Off to the right of this landmass, there seems to be a rather large landmass, perhaps half the size of the bowl-shaped one." The area he had taken at first for a broken wing.

"You asked specifically about dry land?" the Fast responded. "I calculate that despite its great size, that particular body is only five percent or so of actual dry land. The rest—if not water then interlaced with water so thoroughly that it would be surprising if more than a square kilometer at any given location is actually dry."

"And farther left and right?" Ay'r asked.

"Apparently archipelagoes of islands. Rocky and thus more rather than less likely to have once been mountainous cordilleras. The double chain of islands in the westernmost archipelago is especially suggestive of a common geological feature called the Wesker Overlay, which consists of an older mountain range and a parallel newer range, the two separated by a valley."

"Correct me if I'm wrong," Ay'r said, recalling his terraforming courses in Ed. & Dev. "But virtually all that you've told me suggests an that this is an ordinary terrestrial planet with shifting continental plates over a rock mantle. Whereas the planet we're looking at appears to be more to me like a Delphinid world. Say, New Venice."

"One of your companions is looking at underwater topography of the planet at this moment and has just made an identical comment."

Ay'r looked up. "You? Alli-Clark."

"Me what?" she asked, her irritation barely restrained as he explained. "I think we three ought to have a conference," she said grudgingly.

All three removed their wrist connections.

"Two of us have made an interesting discovery," Alli-Clark announced. "This planet is approximately two billion years old. Antique for this outer-arm sector where most stars are barely a hundred million. Further, its topography is not like those of water worlds, as we know them."

"Three of us," P'al said. "I also arrived at that conclusion. In fact, if the land continent weren't closed off by a ring of high mountains on three sides and glaciers on the other, it would also be underwater."

"What about the western delta?" Ay'r asked. "The bay and all. It's open there. At sea level. Why doesn't the ocean flood in?"

Alli-Clark answered. "Because the delta is silted over by the two large rivers, the land around it is considerably higher than the bay waters. The great push from the two rivers' confluence at that point keep the water flowing in one direction only. Should it drop below a certain level of force, the bay would flood the plain."

"In short," P'al summed up, "we're looking at a terrestrial world which underwent tremendous flooding recently."

"How recently?" Ay'r asked.

"Geologically recent. Difficult to say from up here. But at one time this rectangular continent must have been a large mesa or plateau."

"It wasn't the first great flooding either," Alli-Clark said. "I've been looking at suboceanics, and much of their topology is terrestrial. I've seen drowned mountain ranges, large river valleys, bays all associated with landforms, most of them now kilometers underwater. And there may be an even earlier flooding. Below the sedimentary layers, I'm picking up sonar pictures which suggest those sunken continents were only the medium-high plateaus of even-larger continents."

"One of which seemed to band the poles," P'al added. "As intriguing is the ocean's biota."

"In what way?" Ay'r asked.

"An ocean this large ought to have developed an immense variety of organisms," Alli-Clark explained. "Mammalian, Piscid, Arthopodic, Coelenterate, Crustacial. But what the Fast's probes are picking up down there is not only limited, it's also oddly mixed. Most of the ocean biota on Pelagia falls into only three categories: Algae, Coelentera, and Cyprinimidia. Some of those latter are quite large. Also, in the sunken continental shelf to the east of the mountainous one, probes are picking up the same phyla, with one more, Gastropoda, showing up."

"No mean there are no large fish or mammals like New Venice's superwhales?" Ay'r asked.

"Or Keom World's fifty-meter-long Selachoidae," Alli-Clark said.

"Sharks and barracudas," P'al explained.

"Three-meter Cyprinimidae is all I've located," she answered. "Not a particularly saltwater fish."

"Carp," P'al explained, "common to all terrestrial worlds as a freshwater fish."

"And," Alli-Clark went "this ocean's salinity is also rather limited which might explain it all. But either the other species once existed and have since died out, or they never existed. What's left down there could form a closed system, naturally, but an extremely primitive one. It does *not* suggest a few billion years of evolution.

"Also unlike other water worlds, I think all the original large sea life drowned at one or another of the continental deluges. The carp may have managed to survive long enough in freshwater areas within the deluge to adapt."

"Pelagia seems to be a very unusual world, indeed," P'al concluded.

Ay'r of course was wondering about the seeded humes, sent by the Aldebaran Eight. He now asked, "What about settlements?"

"I thought *you* were checking over the continent," Alli-Clark said. Patronizing-dismissal mode coming, Ay'r thought. Sure enough, she went on to say, "Eve knows it's small enough."

"I'll do that now," Ay'r said, affecting P'al's indifference, although the woman annoyed him past reasoning. He reconnected his wrist button to the Fast.

"I'm back," he announced. "I'm looking for signs of Hume habitation on the continents. Nothing as developed as cities. Possibly light manufacture. The use of primitive tools and possibly—"

The holo of the enlarged continent began to flash red dots. Most of them were located between the two rivers. A few more north of it, and several near the delta.

"These are the largest population centers with signs of nonnatural chemical processes taking place," the Fast told him.

"How you do mean?"

"Fire," it explained. "Smelting, forging. You did say 'primitive.' "

"Nothing more than that?" Ay'r asked.

"Nothing."

"What about land biota," Ay'r asked. "Have your probes reported yet?"

"They report extreme density of land biota."

"Divide it up. Flora, fauna, piscid."

"The second greatest is Arthopodic, Arachidnae, Phalangidae, Coleoptera, Hymenoptera, Formicae, with some Dipterae."

"Insects! Then is the greatest amount of life down there mammalian?"

"Not at all. It's nine-tenths botanic. Fungi mostly. But also other unrelated phyla to be found in a typical terrestrial northern hemispheric forest with long periods of humidity: ferns, mosses, lichens."

"Are there any mammals at all?" Ay'r asked.

"A minuscule proportion compared to the other biota."

"Can you show them to me."

The holo zeroed in on one flashing red dot and rapidly enlarged what it was looking at until Ay'r felt as though he were falling out of the Fast into Pelagia's atmosphere, down through its cloud cover and finally into a fine yellowish mist past what seemed to be a stand of almost-colorless cycads of enormous size, surrounded by even-larger and more-colorless plants he couldn't quite describe, and finally down to what appeared to be a clearing of sorts, surrounded by artificial-looking double shells.

"Focus there!" Ay'r said out loud in his excitement, the Species Ethnologist coming out in him. "I'm certain those double-shelled mounds are constructed."

"Probably by giant snails," Alli-Clark sniffed.

"I believe that Ser Kerry has discovered the inhabitants," P'al commented.

All three of them turned to look at the holo in the center of the lounge.

"Could those be the Aldebaran Five seedlings?" Alli-Clark asked, unable to hide her curiosity.

"They're humes," Ay'r confirmed.

"Observe them closely," P'al warned. "We're going to have to look like them if we're to go there and locate Ser Kerry's father."

"Not me!" Alli-Clark declared. "I'm going only to the ocean!"

"You still will have to make the cosmetic 'xchange, to look like them," P'al said. "Although I concur in your distaste. I believe the archaic idiom is 'Count me zero'!"

"It's 'Count me out!'" Ay'r corrected, realizing at the same time that it was the first time he *had* corrected his companion about anything. Of course: no one was perfect. But why then had Ay'r felt that P'al might be perfect? He had felt exactly that, he now realized.

"They're Hume, but the most unattractive humes I've ever seen," Alli-Clark said. "So...colorless! And the way they dress. It's ludicrous! Their Cyber guardian must have been damaged in the landing of the seed pod and remained deranged afterward."

"They don't look that bad to me!" Ay'r said.

"Well, I'm not surprised," she responded, unable to keep herself from touching one of her own honey-brown thighs with relief. "You're almost as light-skinned as they are. I was prepared for a ghastly mutation. But this! And even Ophiucan Kells have brown hair."

"Bronze hair, to be precise," Ay'r corrected her.

"At any rate, not *yellow*. Not that you'll need a great deal of cosmetological disguise with your skin pallor. For all we know, all these might be your half-siblings!"

She meant it as an insult, but Ay'r ignored the comment. He was watching two Hume adolescents at work, stacking what seemed to be heavy stalks of some sort of cellulose. They both had pale eyes, white skin, undeniably flaxen hair. They were gaunt and large-boned. Their long torsos and legs were barely hidden under close-fitting garments which oddly accentuated their long arms, their huge shoulders, their narrow lower torsos.

"Many important Metro-Terrans were of that same coloring," he said.

"Name four!" Alli-Clark challenged.

"Eric the Viking. Christiaan Barnard, Lisbeth Sallinen and, of course, Aare Turik, inventor of the SplG."

"He's right!" P'al concurred. "In the early centuries of space travel, a disproportionate number of such physical types were dominant in all areas."

"Before the so-called 'Great Homogenization' took place," Ay'r added, "which left everyone—except maybe Kells—with more or less the same hair, skin, and eye coloring."

"You know as well as I that the Hume race's ancestor were *exactly* my coloring!" Alli-Clark insisted.

"What about the inhabitants' language?" Ay'r asked the Fast. "Can we get sound?"

The sonics below proved to be too muffled by the dense watery atmosphere.

"We'll probably have to alter our skins cosmetologically for all that moisture," P'al muttered, sounding long-suffering.

The Fast confirmed that.

"I've checked our pods," P'al said. "T-pods for ourselves, Ser Kerry," he said. "They'll attract less attention and can be hidden easily."

"I'll need the big pod," Alli-Clark said, allowing Ay'r to win a little bet he had with himself. "I'll do the 'xchange, but only because the Fast insists on it. There is a minuscule possibility that I might encounter maritime-faring seedlings on the ocean. Otherwise...I do not plan to go near that dreary little continent with its primitive social life!"

Alli-Clark insisted on getting her cosmetological disguise first.

"I thought you were supposed to help me find my father," Ay'r said.

"When I'm done with my survey. Fast will give you a frequency tone. We'll lock on those. But don't expect me to see you again for a few days, Sol Rad."

When she emerged from behind the 'xchange wall, she warned, "Now if either of you laugh at how I look..."

In fact, Ay'r thought Alli-Clark looked extraordinary. Her short black hair was now a curled ash-blond cap, and her new pale face held two green eyes.

P'al was next for the disguise. He emerged a few minutes later a paler blonde than Alli-Clark, with light blue eyes. His skin was redder than hers. It looked as though it might hurt.

Alli-Clark was doing a final Fast-check on her big pod when Ay'r was done with his 'xchange and looked into the wall-sized reflector. He wasn't tall and muscular and Adonis-handsome as P'al was to begin with, and so didn't have P'al's stature as a blond. Nor was he frail and petite like Alli-Clark, and so didn't have her elfin pertness. Instead, Ay'r—with his head of thick blond hair and pale green eyes and only-slightly-lighter-than-usual skin color—looked...well, he couldn't help thinking that he finally looked "right"!

"I may retain this coloring after we leave Pelagia," Ay'r said to himself.

"You'll be laughed off the conveyances of Melisande," Alli-Clark said. Not an unexpected comment coming from her. What was unexpected was that she had responded to what he had meant purely as a private, personal statement. Why had she even bothered?

"May I suggest, Mer Clark, that you arm your pod!" P'al said.

"You may not!" she reacted instantly as behavior modes numbers one, two, and three went into action. "Arm it! Just like a male! Are you arming your transparents?"

"No. We'll be wearing force fields."

"So will I! Are you expecting me to do battle with marauding algae? That's what's mostly down there, when there is anything but water!"

She turned back to her Fast-screen. Ay'r looked at P'al, who shared the same expression on his face as Ay'r knew he must have: predictable, yet completely unpredictable Alli-Clark! She might as easily have demanded to be armed and found a reason to chastise them for not suggesting it first.

"After all," she continued, "I'm surveying, not interacting!"

"As you wish," P'al said.

"Aren't you two ready to go yet?" she demanded.

Ay'r began to say he was, but was interrupted.

"Not yet!" P'al said,

"Well, I'm not waiting!" She undid her wrist connection to the vehicle and strode to the end of the lounge, which opened to admit her. Without a farewell, she was in a chute, into her pod, and out.

Ay'r was puzzled by P'al's hesitation. "Are you ready now?"

P'al had fitted on his own wrist connection, and a holo opened up in front of them. It took Ay'r a few seconds to understand the perspective he was viewing. He saw something deep blue moving away very fast; he recognized it as the Fast's underside. Then the big pod's "eyes" found their reference points, and he was now looking from a more usual, "false" three-quarters view as Alli-Clark's pod hurtled through a chasm of high clouds, down through other, even more magnificently towering clouds, into a sunlit opening which extended hundreds of kilometers in circumference, revealing the aquamarine surface of the ocean.

"Surely, P'al, you *aren't* expecting her to be attacked by algae?"

"Anything is possible, Ser Kerry. This is a strange planet, even for a Seeded World."

"But the Fast already sent down dozens of probes in the past hour. Not a single probe remarked any hint of interference."

"Perhaps the probes were too small."

They were only the sized of a balled-up Hume fist.

"They're too big to get through any defense system I ever heard of," Ay'r said.

"A short wait won't overdelay our search."

"You mean because we're three months before the time we actually met on Melisande?"

"Approximately. But who knows how the time distortion will work for our return."

So Ay'r waited and watched the holo with P'al. But he soon lost interest in it, as the holo—at least in its visual mode—was tediously the same minutes at a time: ocean surface for kilometers at a stretch, then subocean surface, and finally deeper underwater, although not by any means near the bottom.

The Fast itself seemed to be bored. It added in a pale blue topological chart along with the holo of Alli-Clark's pod, as she rose to the surface again.

"It's fascinating!" Ay'r said sarcastically. Then he turned and looked at the wall-reflector at what was, oddly enough, truly fascinating to him: at how—"right" seemed to be the only work for it—he looked.

"About those force-fields, Ser Kerry," P'al began. "Do you think it a good idea to utilize them? As a Species Ethnologist, you would naturally have more experience with seedlings."

"As a rule, Species Eths. carry neither arms nor force-fields on a Seeded World," Ay'r admitted. "They're inexplicable to most Archaic peoples. And they might give us a pseudo-status as sorcerers, which could be quite troublesome. Worse, should they fall into the wrong hands, the seedlings might advance suddenly, at a time when they're still too primitive to control the tools. Which might lead to self-annihilation."

"Then we carry no shields and no weapons?" P'al concluded.

Ay'r looked at the holo. Alli-Clark's pod floating over square kilometers of algae: stemlike fronds connected by small spheres, probably containing reproductive material. Why was P'al so hesitant about leaving the Fast?

"Do you have an uneasy feeling about her?" Ay'r asked.

"Don't you?"

"I don't know. She is impulsive and determined. But in a way I pity anyone who tangles with her."

As the two looked on, the pod over the surface of the vast kelp ocean rose, turned sharply, and made a steep ascent.

"Is that Mer Clark's frequency tone?" P'al asked.

The Fast said yes, it was receiving a message.

"...not believe what I just"—they heard her voice. Then: "...mirage! must be...rage. Forget they would be...mon here!"

"A mirage?" Ay'r tried to make sense of her half-broken comm.

"Over a trillion kilotons of ocean, naturally," P'al said.

The holo showed her pod turning suddenly again, flattening its ascent, skimming over the surface.

"Where's she going?"

"She appears to be following something," P'al mumbled.

"Can't we get a picture of it?"

"Not if she won't allow the pod to transmit it," P'al said. "Fast. Open up complete verbal communication."

"Not possible! Too much interference on all but the lowest of microwave frequencies," it reported. "And Mer Clark's instructions forbid the use of low microwave frequencies until we know its full effect upon local biota."

"Why would she chase a mirage?" Ay'r asked.

"Unless she isn't certain it is a mirage. She's turned toward land. That's a sure way to discover if it is an illusion. Once the ocean surface is broken, the mirage will be, too. Even a sandbar would destroy it."

On the holo, below the horizon, low-lying brown masses flew at Ay'r. He had time enough to think—islands, the archipelago, but which one? east or west?—when the holo snapped off.

"Contact is lost," the Fast declared. "I'm receiving an automatic distress signal on, yes, it must be, on a frequency modulation channel."

"Relay it!" P'al stood right at the open space where the holo had been so vivid a second before, as though he were waiting for it to come on again.

"Verbal only," the Fast reported. Then they heard Alli-Clark's voice shout: "I'm hit!" And again. "I'm hit! I'm going in! I'm making a screw-maneuver! Plot me from..." She listed her coordinates, which crackled through static and were almost finished before even her verbal message was snapped off.

The Fast said: "I suggested the screw-maneuver as having the greatest potential for eluding most weapons."

"You're wonderful!" Ay'r said, acidly.

"I'm now plotting the pod's curve of descent in the maneuver."

"Give us a holo of the curve!" P'al ordered. "Global, then enlarged."

What did she mean, she was going in? Ay'r wanted to know. "Into the ocean?"

"The trajectory is direct west from the 26th line of longitude, at the 48th line of latitude North," the Fast said, showing Alli-Clark's descent in a flashing red line against an orbital photo as she approached the largest continent.

"She'll hit that mountain range!" Ay'r said.

But her path continued and went out just west of the mountain range, in what they had already decided was one of several large mountain valleys containing a sparse population of seedling inhabitants.

"That's where we'll also land," P'al said.

"What about whatever attacked her pod?"

"Whatever it was, it did so over open water," P'al answered. "We're going to Dryland."

Although it was called a "transparent," the pods they stepped into minutes later, were in fact externally opaque and mirrored, the better to reflect the environment—a strategy long ago discovered to possess the highest probability of protection. T-pods were known to have landed softly in occupied gardens in broad daylight without being noticed. An organism would have to actually bump against it, or step on it, to note its presence. Of course, more than one organism had noticed a T-pod through one sense or another, and several had attempted to eat it. Since it was over two meters tall, astonishingly hard, and purposely bad tasting, they seldom succeeded. As a result, T-pods were stellar exploration's greatest tool. Even better that they were inexpensive to manufacture and that a dozen of them could be easily stored inside even a small Fast.

Naturally, over the centuries, Antrom's design had been modified. Transparent within except for a "floor," T-pod interiors possessed a flexible body netting for holding a Hume in virtually all positions, and they were connected to the Fast's computerized mind with a set of independent circuits capable of manual override. In the gravest on-planet situations, T-pods could be arranged to "cryo" whoever was in the pod until rescue. In less serious cases, they contained nutrient-producing abilities for a week Sol Rad., air- and water-producing abilities up to a month. Also standard were manual controls for atmospheric drive, as well as simple laser-based weapons of limited range and force, mostly for scaring off annoyances.

Ay'r had learned how to handle a T-pod at the Species Eth. Institute. Now, as they dropped down the Fast's chute to the landing bay, he wondered where P'al had learned; probably where he had learned everything else he seemed to know.

Two of the fragile-looking craft were set up, split open for them to enter. "Let's try to stay more-or-less together!" P'al said.

"Not too close!" Ay'r got into his pod and fell back into the netting which immediately encircled his body.

"See you on Pelagia!" he said and told the T-pod to close.

He was amused to see P'al give him a old Terran "OK" signal with his fingers.

"Let's go!" he told the pod. The floor below him opened up, and the T-pod dropped out.

For beginners, these fourteen seconds of straight drop while the T-pod aligned itself magnetically could be gut-wrenching. Ay'r had come to enjoy the drop, and as he located the other T-pod dropping after him, he wondered how P'al was taking it. Had he ever been in a pod before, or simply found out from the Fast how the pod worked?

Ay'r's pod stopped falling and rocked a bit as it established a bearing.

"Excuse me for asking, passenger three"—the Fast's voice suddenly came on inside the T-pod—"but since neither of the other passengers would explain, could you tell me why we shall not be in communication during your planet stay as is normal?"

"First, we don't know how long we'll be gone," Ay'r said.

"Yes..."

"Second, we don't know where we're going, exactly."

"Uh-huhh..."

"And third, you'd scare the stuffing out of the humes we encounter if you did communicate."

"Then you're planning to visit the seemingly primitive humelike inhabitants?" the Fast asked.

"You bet!"

The T-pod had dropped to a spot over water quite near the continent which the Fast had calculated would contain the least turbulence. Ay'r was approaching a headland of rugged brown rock.

"On what kind of mission, may I ask?" the Fast went on.

The T-pod was over the shore-mountains, some cut sharply into peaks, others mere slabs of titanic rock.

"You may ask. I'm not going to answer."

From this close, the mountains were truly enormous, looming, deeply crevassed.

"Why not?"

"Because it's none of your business," Ay'r said. "I thought your higher personality functions were modified out."

"They were. My questions are directly relevant to the situation at hand."

Below, the mountains seemed to stretch away far in two directions, and even to Ay'r's northeast, along the coastline, as far as he could see.

"We're on a secret mission for the M.C.," Ay'r said finally, hoping to end the discussion.

"I understand," the Fast said.

Now the crevasses below, highlighted so sharply before, seemed to lose all depth. Ay'r wondered what time it was on the planet. Mid-afternoon, the Fast told him. He also wondered if Pelagia had seasons, although he was certain their epiderma had been temperature-adjusted during the 'xchange.

The Fast confirmed the latter, and said it was unsure whether there were seasons on the planet. "You didn't mind me asking that other question?" the Fast added.

"You were just trying to do your job most effectively."

"You *do* understand."

Ay'r changed the subject. "You realize that if any of the pods are opened, you are to respond only to a direct communication with us. For all three pods. But only one of us," Ay'r clarified.

"Each pod is equipped with a memory trace of your voices and molecular structure."

The canyons below the T-pod were getting longer and wider, but they were filled not with the valleys and vegetation Ay'r expected to see from the holo he had stared at so long, but instead with fog. Before him, the mountains fell away, brown-ridged fingers clawing at a swirl of thick cloud, grayish white, but with a glistening top, a rainbow of colors as the nearby star began its descent from meridian. Not only before him, but on all sides, and as far as Ay'r could see in all directions except perhaps straight ahead, where brightness glinted: he guessed from the icecap.

Of course there would be clouds. He'd forgotten: a giant cloud covered the landmass perpetually, collecting there because of the land's constantly greater warmth compared to all that surrounding water. He wouldn't be able to handle the landing manually, as he would have preferred. Too bad. T-pods sometimes had bizarre ideas about what constituted a good landing spot.

"Descent imminent," he heard the Fast's voice say.

The pod began to drop instantly.

"Have you got a fix on what's in this cloud?" Ay'r asked.

"We need fear no flying insect or avian life," it replied. "None could possibly fly in this density."

"Can we?"

"T-pods are equipped for all-density flight from the thinnest of atmospheres to the heaviest liquid metal. Especially this newest series, which—"

Suddenly the Fast's voice was gone, as though cut off.

The pod continued to drop. It was deep in cloud, the topmost layer replaced by a thicker mass. Ay'r hoped that it thinned out closer to the ground. He wondered if during the 'xchange his optic nerves had been adjusted to see through such fog. The Fast didn't answer his thought. And the pod continued to drop straight down.

"I'd like manual control now." Ay'r reached out his hand for the control to fold out of the pod's inner wall.

Nothing happened.

Outside was fogged so thickly that he couldn't tell if the pod was falling faster or slower. Ay'r repeated his command twice, to no response.

What was going on?

Suddenly it stopped. Seemed to hang there, long enough for sight to adjust and make out what appeared to be a thicket of huge leafless pale gray tree trunks. At least he was near the ground. Then the T-pod zipped about in various directions, stopping and starting off again so quickly that Ay'r couldn't orient himself.

"That looks like a good spot! There, directly below," he said in what he assumed would be an unheard command, but which he had to attempt anyway, when something seemed to zip by the upper right side of the pod not ten meters away and so rapidly that it left cuts through the cloud.

"What was that?" Once more he got no answer.

However, the pod dropped suddenly, as though equally startled—directly into what Ay'r had said looked like a good spot to land: dense underbrush.

Dense enough to slow down and finally stop the T-pod, which settled and remained suspended about a meter from the ground. Well, fine, Ay'r thought; less chance of anyone finding it.

Now he wondered if it that had been a fluke and if it would respond to his next command: "Open!"

The T-pod split open. Which meant he was still in contact with it. But why had the Fast gone silent? Perhaps lacking the finer shadings of judgment a "personality" usually conferred on Cyber intellect and overworked through its secondary intelligence circuits, the Fast had followed his earlier instructions to the letter and was keeping silent.

Ay'r touched the branches gingerly. They were deep green and seemed hollow stemmed and intricately laced. No fruit, no buds, no flowers, no leaves. Below, they appeared to meet in a simple root, like a succulent.

The fog was less dense here. Ay'r could make out the tall trees he had passed descending, their thick trunks weathered and folded vertically, shooting high into the cloud. Giant mosses and what looked like sphagnum ferns seemed to decorate them, extruding from their trunks and hanging down at the oddest angles. At his feet spread what seemed to be grass, or at least, from its oddly shaped blades, a lichen much like grass. He climbed down out of the succulent branch, being careful not to bend the stems until he had gotten out, so the T-pod's location wouldn't be given away. When he landed on the springy lichen ground cover, Ay'r bent back three of the branches, knotting them and watching to see whether they would bend back or retain the new shape. The knot remained. Now to get a visual fix on this location for future reference.

Ay'r moved forward over the lichen cautiously, until he seemed to be in the midst of a small clearing. He was looking for a landmark. That bluff over there, perhaps.

Where was P'al? Why hadn't he landed nearby?

Ay'r was looking up, scanning the highest reaches of the cloud, when he heard something whiz by overhead. It moved too quickly for him to see what it was, but it left cuts in the mist where it had gone. Just like whatever had startled the pod.

A noise behind him made Ay'r turn to a sight he would never forget. Coming right at him, the gigantic polished ebony head, proboscis and antennae of a insect perhaps four feet taller than he was. He staggered back.

"Down, Colley!" he heard a voice command.

The insect's giant head dropped almost to the ground, its antennae, several meters in length, still waving around, brushed against Ay'r legs.

"Don't be afraid, stranger. He's tame."

With the insect's huge head bent down, munching at the lichen, Ay'r could make out the source of the voice. Astride the curved back of the enormous beetle, holding on with reins, was an astonishing Hume female. She wore a halter of some unknown skin or material around her upper torso, another about her lower torso. Her arms and legs were bare. Her features were modeled distinctively, her eyes gray-blue, her hair, long and streaming, and in this mist, yellow as a beam of G-star sunlight.

"I don't know who you are, stranger, but if you value your life and liberty, you'd better come up and hide inside Colley's wingfold."

Ay'r was so stunned by her appearance—so casual upon the back of the enormous insect—that he could only stare at her.

"Are you mute? They'll be back in a minute!"

"*Who'll* be back?" he asked.

Her head turned left. "They're here. Colley! Grab him!"

Before Ay'r could do anything, two legs from within the beetle's armored underside had shot out, clasped him around the waist, and were tossing him over its back. They were met by other legs, evidently located more in the middle, which held him dangling while a large panel of the creature's back slid open, exposing a huge fan of filmy wing. Ay'r was dropped into the opening.

He didn't tumble far. Ay'r was within a shallow, oddly shaped chamber, just finding his feet as the wing began to close over him.

He grabbed at the opening. "Wait!"

"Don't be silly!" the female said. "You'll be perfectly safe inside."

Ay'r suddenly fell back against the glossy walls of the chamber—the wingfold she had called it—they were moving forward.

"I'll suffocate!" he called out, trying to pry open the closed wing.

"Quiet—or we're both doomed!"

The new voice came from somewhere inside the creature. But where?

One side of the chamber seemed to flex forward, as though it were a folding screen. When it was open, Ay'r could see even in the dim light, a strong, curved, ebony beam, which must have been the insect's carapace support. Beyond it, in what must be a second wingfold, Ay'r made out a Hume face.

"Sit down," the face whispered urgently. "Talk softly."

Ay'r did as he was told. With his legs folded under him, he was more comfortable, feeling the giant insect's forward motion as a flow rather than as a series of jolts. He also noted that what he had taken for smooth walls were in fact ciliated so finely, so glossily, they seemed molded.

"I'm 'Dward," the Hume face said. "I have to hide, too. That's my sib Oudma reining Colley. She'll give us the clear."

"Why do we have to hide?" Ay'r asked.

"Otherwise they'll take us. Me, certainly. You too, probably, as you're still young. How old? Twenty-one? Twenty-two?"

He meant in Pelagian years, Ay'r supposed. He'd have to remember that.

"Yes."

"Like Oudma. Though she's still unbonded. She says not till the initiation will she even think to bond. Have you been to the Great Temple for initiation?"

"No. I—"

"Me either. But I'll be eighteen this double month. Father will take both Oudma and me soon."

Ay'r heard a sharp rap from above their heads.

"Quiet!" 'Dward instructed, although he'd been doing most of the talking.

The creature continued to lumber forward awhile. 'Dward remained silent, then began to whisper again. "Oudma's never even been affianced. No one in our valley or in fact in any mountain valley will bond her. She's too headstrong, the other teens all say. Do you like her?"

"Like her?" Ay'r asked. What did this seedling mean?

"Her looks, I mean."

"She's very striking. Beautiful," Ay'r corrected himself, remembering the appropriate word. This seedling variant of language was so close to what he was used to speaking, yet also so filled with Metro-Terran archaisms, that Ay'r was surprised how difficult it was to respond instantly. Even with his Universo Lexico implant, he couldn't handle all the shadings so rapidly.

"I think so too," 'Dward said. "Although we are taboo."

Two raps from above them stopped Ay'r from asking the exact nature of the taboo. The wing flap was suddenly lifted enough for him to see his companion's face in the new light—virtually identical to his sibling.

"You two can come out now." Oudma said. Then to her brother: "There were three of them."

"Three of who?" Ay'r asked.

Brother and sister exchanged glances. 'Dward climbed over the carapace support to ride atop, behind Oudma, a long arm thrown over her hips to hold onto a sort of bridle.

"You're not from Monosilla Valley!" 'Dward said.

"Silly!" Oudma slapped her brother's long, beefy, bare thigh. "Listen to his accent. His words! He's from a distance. The Delta Lands?" she asked Ay'r.

He shook his head.

"From up north, then!" she guessed. "Look how much clothing he's wearing. Aren't you warm in all that?"

"Actually, I *am* warm."

"Take it off," she gestured. Ay'r unbelted the Fast's version of the Drylander singlet. That was better. "Take it off!" she insisted. "And the bottom piece, too."

"I have no undergarment," Ay'r said. He wrapped his singlet around his biceps as 'Dward had done. "Who were we hiding from?"

"Didn't you hear them?" Oudma pointed up into the cloud cover.

"I thought I saw something moving very fast."

"The Gods," 'Dward said darkly. "Out hunting for Dryland males. If they'd seen us, we'd have been kidnapped. Who knows what would have happened to Oudma!"

"Nothing!" she asserted. "They take only males."

"Who are they?" Ay'r asked.

"The Gods. Don't you have the Gods up north?" 'Dward asked. "We have them here. Father said they weren't always evil. When he was a child, Father said, the Gods always gave and never took. But now they take our people."

"Why?"

"We don't know why. None taken have ever returned to tell."

"What do they look like, the Gods?"

"No one's ever seen them."

"No one we know," Oudma corrected. "There's an old saying here in Monosilla Valley: 'See the God, paralyzed as though by a chillip's sting!' Don't tell me you don't have chillips up north either?"

"We have very little up north. But surely, at one time your ancestors saw the Gods."

"If so, they don't admit it."

"Are there no stories of the Gods? No legends that say what they looked like?" Ay'r asked.

"'Imothy is our legend-keeper," 'Dward said. "He's collected legends from all over, traveling the valleys to... Are you a legend collector, too?"

"The Gods are no legends," Oudma said. "Unfortunately."

"We've already lost our brother, 'Nton to them," 'Dward explained.

Ay'r had been watching the passing landscape as best he could from his vantage point, standing and barely holding onto the wingfold edge of the giant beetle's back as best he could. What he had seen wasn't reassuring. To begin with, it all more-or-less resembled where he had left his T-pod: acres of grasslike spots surrounded by stands of tall, colorless trees, their tops hidden in the cloud, their trunks festooned with hanging moss, ferns, and other cycads. The chromatics were also limited, ranging from the occasional deep green of the least-frequent succulent bushes through tones of brown, gray-brown and gray, itself ranging from charcoal to near white. It was both dreary and fatiguing to look at, almost impossible to locate anything in.

Perhaps that was why Ay'r almost jumped when he thought he now saw directly ahead of them tiny glints of deep red and purple and violet that seemed like the richest jewels in the galaxy.

"Here we are!" Oudma pointed ahead. "This is our farm."

"And look!" 'Dward gestured, as the big beetle lumbered through the brush. "Father's waiting for us. And he also is with a stranger!"

Ay'r didn't have to get very close to recognize the stranger: P'al!

"You're both from the Northlands, and you both traveled together, yet you don't look to be kin." 'Dward said not unkindly as he passed around what looked like a hollowed gourd filled with a thickish liquid which smelled to Ay'r like a particularly redolent mushroom soup.

"Kerry is one of my companions," P'al said with his usual composure. "Our other companion is still missing. No, we are not related by blood."

Oudma had warmed the broth on top of what seemed to be a large ceramic stove, heated from below by charred peat. The soup smelled good. When the gourd reached Ay'r and stopped, he supposed he was to sip it.

"You're really from the North?" Oudma asked.

"They said so," 'Harles, their father, replied succinctly. Evidently he didn't want too many questions asked. Ay'r wondered whether that was because of traditional hospitality rules which declared that guests might offer information but not be asked.

"You're not bonded together, are you?" she asked.

"Oudma! Mind your manners!" her father chided.

"I've heard that there are so few females up north, that unrelated males bond there."

"We're not bonded," P'al said with equanimity. He had received his own bowl—although gourdlike, it also proved to be ceramic—and now began to sip it, without making a face. It couldn't be too bad. Ay'r prepared himself for a Spec. Eth. "quick swallow," but he was curious about what might be in the soup, so instead he let the liquid sit in his mouth. Not quite a broth, not yet a consommé, it tasted of different flavors: some smoky, some sweet, one even a bit peppery. Yet the consistency was all alike. Were all these mushrooms? Were there such a variety of edible types here on Dryland? Why not?

"Curiosity is normal, especially in the young," P'al said. "We don't mind answering questions."

'Dward immediately took up the challenge. "If you really are from up north, what's even farther north?"

"'Dward!" his father warned.

"Ice!" P'al said. "Frozen water in cliffs high as these mountains and extending as far as the eye can see."

But the adolescent wasn't quite satisfied. "Only ice? What about the Old Port?"

"It's still there. Under the sheet of ice," P'al replied. "It's visible at certain times and seasons when the ice face is clear."

Ay'r wondered how his companion knew that. He must have seen it on one of the Fast's probes.

"How were you separated?" Oudma asked, and before her father could warn her, she added, "It must have been upsetting in a strange country."

"They're Legend-collectors, silly!" 'Dward said. "They're used to traveling to strange country and becoming separated."

Ay'r supposed that the youth must have already formed his own image of their adventurous life. But this spelling out of what they were supposed to be was evidently news to P'al who glanced at Ay'r quickly enough for the others not to notice. And who received a shrug in return.

"This is our first time so far south," Ay'r said quickly. "Once we find our other companion we'll—"

"Have you legends?" P'al interrupted him. "Legends that we may collect."

'Harles looked up from his soup. "This is newly settled land. Our legends aren't very different from those in the great New River Valley."

"We're not familiar with those. We're especially interested in legends of the beginning of things. The creation," P'al added.

Ay'r wondered what he was getting at. Did P'al hope to locate Ay'r's father this way? Or was he going after something different? For example, the location and influence of the Cyber guardians who had accompanied these seedlings to Pelagia and who might be responsible for their surprisingly advanced state of linguistic and cultural development.

"The creation of Dryland?" 'Harles asked. He had finished his soup and was reaching for a long piece of ceramic mold which Oudma removed with a green branched tongs from within the burning peat itself. "All we have are children's tales!" 'Harles tapped on the ceramic mold and it cracked open lengthwise, releasing a savory aroma. Within were what looked like tubers and what seemed to be a cooked joint of meat. 'Harles offered the meat to his two guests, who both held up their bowls to show that they were still occupied, the better to find out what kind of meat it might be and to watch him eat it—which 'Harles did, after saying to 'Dward, "Tell them a story, 'Dward, which you learned as a lad."

"In the beginning of all things were seven brothers. Capin, Trilufu, Jatoto, Maspiei, Filoscop, Suel, and Dryland." 'Dward began. "Their father was named Ecilef, which means the Enigmatic One, and he gave birth to all of the brothers, one each day." He looked at his guests, who gestured for him to continue.

"Each brother possessed gifts of a different kind. But Dryland was the only one who could also give birth, and so he gave birth to all that we know: mushrooms and lichen, mosses and fung-trees, beetles and spiders and people, too. When he was tired of giving birth, Dryland showed his creatures how to give birth themselves, so he might rest. And Dryland lay himself down and nurtured them all so that they might continue to live and flourish."

A lovely story, Ay'r thought. But all males! What would Alli-Clark think of this legend? Alli-Clark, for whom creation and nurturing was such a female act. Alli-Clark, alone somewhere on Pelagia awaiting them, no doubt so she could chastise them for taking so long to find her.

"After Dryland rested, only six brothers remained in the sky above the canopy," 'Dward went on. "Yet in those days, one might look beyond the canopy to the sky itself and see them. One brother, Capin, was largest and brightest, and began to lead the other brothers in a great dance. He was partnered by his brother Trilufu, called the Follower. The two younger brothers, large Jatoto and Maspiei also danced. And somewhat distant, the most solitary brother, Filoscop, although no one minded what he did. But Suel minded that Maspiei and Capin danced so well, and he began to make trouble among the other brothers. Trilufu, the follower, tried to stop Suel, and for his interference, he lost both of his ears. Made bold by this success, Suel attacked Capin, but the eldest brother was too nimble: he danced away. Then Suel attacked Maspiei, who was neither large nor nimble and who was unable to escape. In a fury, Suel murdered Maspiei. Suel was banished, and the other brothers wept for years. Their solitary brother fled even farther away from them. And, so his children would no longer have to look at such violence, Dryland covered the face of the sky with canopy."

Ay'r was caught up in the tale. "Their father did nothing to stop it?"

"Nothing," 'Dward said sadly. "Which is why our fathers protect us Drylanders until we are old enough to be initiated. And also why the father of the seven brothers is called the Enigmatic One."

"When did all this happen?" Ay'r asked.

"More than two hundred grandfathers ago," 'Dward said. His father nodded.

Ay'r supposed the term was a formula for listing a time span beyond years, a not-uncommon mode of time-telling for primitive societies which hadn't yet developed the century or millennium span.

"Thank you," P'al said. "That's a fine legend."

"And Dryland's children?" Ay'r said. "Do they never quarrel?"

"We are taught never to quarrel with our brothers," 'Harles said and added dourly, "It sometimes happens."

"Some of us wish we still had a brother to quarrel with," 'Dward added in a quiet voice.

"Tomorrow," 'Harles said to P'al, "we will ask the others in Monosilla Valley if they have encountered your companion."

He passed the long ceramic mold to them, and Ay'r lifted out the smallest joint of meat he saw. Holding it with two hands, he began to gnaw on it as he'd seen 'Harles, then Oudma doing. He was pleasantly surprised by the nutty taste as well as by the butter-smoothness of the flesh. The tuber he picked next was pale yellow, with an earthy smell, surprisingly both sweet and sour tasting. It was perfect accompaniment to the meat.

"Excellent cooking!" P'al said.

"My sister's grasshopper legs are the best in the valley," 'Dward said gallantly. "She raises her own and gives them free range."

Oudma smiled. "My mother taught me how to cook."

"Tell us of the kidnappings by the Gods," Ay'r said to 'Harles. "'Dward told us the Gods were benevolent before. Why have they changed?"

'Harles was not anxious to answer, yet he told them grudgingly. When he was a child, the Gods had been good. They had led 'Harles's family and friends into these mountain valleys. They had felled forests and opened up farmland so that Drylanders leaving the Bog could have another way of life. Naturally, none ever saw the Gods, but over the generations of Drylanders, one learned to hear their approach—'Harles made a faint buzzing with his lips, which Ay'r immediately recognized as a slowed-down version of what he'd heard just before he'd been lifted into Colley's wingfold. People would be out hunting or farming and hear the Gods passing through the canopy, and when the people returned to their homesteads, they would find gifts. The Gods had always given. That was why they had been revered.

"But the kidnappings!" Ay'r insisted.

"They began only a few years ago. First it was that a teen out hunting or farming alone would vanish, and everyone thought he had fallen prey to some large creature. But it began happening so frequently—and only to the young—that it became clear they were being taken. Among the people of the Bog Way at New River, the leaders and truth-sayers began to speak strangely, saying that the Gods had already given much and now they wanted something in return from the Drylanders. Some spoke of a city the Gods were building far to the west, past the nearer archipelago. The people of the Bog Way said that we must give up our firstborn sons to the Gods after initiation, to help the Gods build their city."

"Not all the Drylanders accepted this?" Ay'r asked.

"In the great temple at the Delta, where all Dryland youth goes for initiation, the youths asked the Voice and Eyes if they knew of such a city. It did not. Nor did the Voice and Ears even know of the Gods, except through what the youths told it, although the Voice and Eyes has been on Dryland since the creation, a gift of Dryland himself. When the youths asked if they should be sacrificed to the Gods, the Voice and Ears told them they should not."

"What did the Bog people say to that?" Ay'r asked.

"The people of the Bog Way said that the Voice and Eyes had grown too old. That its Eyes could no longer see, nor its ears hear well. For clearly the Gods did exist, although it did not know of them. And equally clearly, the Gods were taking our sons. Then, as in the legend 'Dward told you, the people of Dryland's flat valleys quarreled. Some saying we must offer up our sons. Some saying we must resist doing so, difficult as it is to resist the Gods."

"Before brother could murder brother, the Drylanders of the great valleys divided. Most remained in the Bogs, but others left and went to new places. Many came to live in these high mountain valleys. Down in the Bogs, they offer up their firstborn sons. Here we resist. Yet it makes little difference. We lose our sons only a little less often than they do."

"Can no one stop the Gods?" Ay'r asked.

"We hide our sons. That is all we can do," 'Harles said. "And that not well enough. If a passing God thinks a son may be hidden, he comes down from the canopy and takes him."

"Before your eyes? How can you let that happen?"

"When the Gods arrive," 'Harles said, "we become as though a stone or a tree trunk. We smell their fragrance, then we see nothing, we hear nothing. When the Gods leave, we can move again, and our sons are gone, In the same way which for ten generations of fathers the Gods used to provide us with gifts, they now use to take our sons."

All five had now eaten, and Oudma passed around long thin threads of sinew which she showed Ay'r and P'al were used to clean the teeth. Already 'Dward was drowsing. Outside the skin doors covering the opening of the shelled enclosure in which they sat, darkness had arrived. With it a steady patter on the ground which Ay'r told himself was the sound of the fog's cooling and condensing, became something called "rain." It was an oddly irregular sound, unlike how it had been described in ancient records, and equally unlike the few very old discs of the sound he'd heard from the Metro-Terran museum on Andromache VIII. Or rather, the sound was the same, but the feelings it induced in Ay'r were so unexpected they influenced his hearing: pleasure at being in a warm, dry, protected place, near the rain yet not in it; and a strange inability to predict whether the rain's patter would remain at the same force, increase or decrease.

"Go to bed!" Oudma told her brother, who had to be helped up and pushed in the direction of the second, overlapping shell's entry. 'Harles also stood up. "Sleep dreamless," she told her father, and they touched each other's faces.

"You are as good a mother as she was," 'Harles said quietly. "No matter what those fool lads say. After initiation you will bond to a fine Drylander male." He turned to P'al. "Tomorrow, strangers, we will try to find your companion."

Ay'r and P'al remained where they sat, on a sofa of skin-covered pillows. Oudma did something with the oven, in effect closing off the heat, but retaining its glow. She returned to them and knelt between where they sat.

"Promise me, strangers, that you will abide by the rules of hospitality."

"We promise," P'al said, which was imprudent, Ay'r thought, since neither of them knew those rules.

"I know 'Dward is fair to you. Leave him to sleep dreamless," she said.

"Aren't you concerned about yourself?" Ay'r said. "You are also fair to us."

"I sleep lightly," she said, and stood up. Still whispering she added, "Never has anyone, even my father, met anyone like you two. And he has been all over Dryland."

"Not to the far north!" Ay'r said.

"To the north," she said, "I don't know how far."

"We are from the glaciers," Ay'r said. "Near the Old Port."

"You are from much farther than I can say. For all I know, you may be the Gods. They were said to visit in the form of handsome strangers."

"We are no gods," P'al said.

"Gods or not, remember the rules of hospitality," she reminded them in a whisper, then passed off toward the sleep chambers.

After a while, Ay'r couldn't resist getting up and pulling back one flap of the protective skins to see and to feel the rain on his face. It tasted of nothing and yet it also tasted of Dryland on his tongue—loamy, rich, fertile.

P'al was suddenly at his side, whispering. "My pod is nearby, Ser Kerry. If you wish, you might sleep inside it tonight."

Ay'r wondered what it would be like stumbling about in the rainy darkness. He had to admit that he felt an unfamiliar sensation thinking of it, a coldness threading through his arms and chest, which he supposed was fear of the unknown.

"Better that we remain here, in case one of them awakens."

Still staring into the rainy night, P'al said, "As a Species Ethnologist, what is your impression of Pelagia's seedlings?"

Ay'r almost laughed. "I have so many impressions!"

"Perhaps Ser Kerry I may bring one salient impression to your attention."

"Go on."

"Although I am not a Species Ethnologist, while we traveled to this system, I scanned the Fast's references on the subject. Perhaps that cursory knowledge as opposed to your own more professional knowledge of—"

"Ask your question!" Ay'r whispered irritably.

"Considering the age of the seedlings and their apparent lack of continually and openly guiding Cybers, aren't you unprepared for how advanced they are?"

Ay'r smiled. "I did expect to find primitives less adv anced even than the N'Kiddim."

"Their language, even the complexity of their legends. Only one out of two hundred other seeded cultures possesses sky gods. And that only because it has been a much-visited world almost from the beginning. Yet, for these Drylanders, it is ancient history."

"Have you wondered about their great temple and what they call the Voice and Eyes?"

"The last of the guiding Cybers, no doubt," P'al said. "I assume that at initiation, each of the youth are spoken to, given some sort of vocational or personal guidance. It sounds like whatever Cyber remains is itself quite primitive. Enough so that many Drylanders question its efficacy, its knowledge, and even ignore it, as 'Harles told us. That could not be the cause of their finely graded sense of honor, of their acute self-consciousness."

"I didn't think so either."

"Nor do environmental factors seem challenging enough."

"No, but you forget, P'al. The Drylanders possess what none of the other two hundred Seeded Worlds ever possessed, and what may be the key to their advancement—they possess the Gods!"

"Who have turned against them. It's strange," P'al said.

"And sinister."

Ay'r awakened to hear what sounded like a long, deep rumbling outside. It was still dark. No, dim daylight seeped in, despite the skin flaps carefully closed to make it still seem like night.

"P'al," he whispered.

"I hear it," P'al whispered back. "The sound began a few minutes ago. I calculate it to come from seventy meters to our southwest."

"Earth tremors" Ay'r asked. He was waiting for a shock.

"No. It might be what's known as thunder. An effect common to electrostatic discharges during precipitation. Quite harmless. By the way, we are alone here."

Outside the rain was stopping, and this Pelagia morning seemed a great deal like Pelagia's late afternoon of the previous local day. Except perhaps for the sight of Oudma, walking about in a sort of pen made of slender reed sides and a loosely thatched cover. She was strewing some sort of feed from a satchel hung over one shoulder, and was followed about by a grayish-brown variety of insects which Ay'r immediately recognized as grasshoppers—or he supposed, on Pelagia, lichenhoppers. They were almost up to her knees in size, almost her height in length, yet because of the pen's top hatching they couldn't unfurl their wings to escape. Instead, they would dart forward suddenly to catch the apparently still-living tiny creatures she tossed them. Amidst the large, ungainly creatures, Oudma seemed more strikingly Hume and beautiful than Ay'r remembered. She tossed the food almost absentmindedly, occasionally swatting away the head of a too eager insect with her free hand.

"Mer Clark would chide you for your thoughts," P'al said.

"Abort Mer Clark!" Ay'r said, hoping to shock the M.C. official. But P'al didn't respond at all. However, he had spoken loudly enough for Oudma to hear, turn, and wave at them.

"Father and 'Dward are talking to the rest of the valley. From what I could make out, no one else seems to have encountered a stranger yesterday."

She pointed through the pale yellow morning mist to a hillock in the distance, upon which Ay'r could just make out the small figures of her brother and father, sitting astride what looked to be a long, curved, multi-segmented pipe. 'Harles was tapping its side with what looked like a mallet. He would stop and appear to listen to the air itself.

"You may join them," she said. "Did you sleep dreamlessly?"

P'al said he had.

Ay'r said he had dreamed. But before she could frown, he added, "Of one of my hosts. It was a pleasant dream."

It was something of a trek to where the two males were. As they got nearer, the thundery sound changed so that it sounded higher, more complexly structured than at first he'd assumed.

A sort of drum or horn, P'al supposed. "The regularity of the segmentation as well as the pure hollowness suggests a natural origin. Gastropodic or enchillidic."

"A snail shell that large?" Ay'r scoffed. "The animal would have to be immense!" Yet the beetle had been. Was the beetles' size natural, he now wondered, or had they been mutated purposely for domestication?

P'al seemed unfazed. "As was the shelter we slept in, a snail shell, although of another type. Perhaps they are fossils from another age."

They approached from the easiest, lowest gradient, and so looked up into the object. It seemed to curve upward perhaps ten meters in length. Gray but mottled with dark lichen. 'Dward waved to them.

"Neither Monosilla, nor Capensis, nor even Aldovar Valley know of any stranger," he reported.

'Harles was listening again, and now Ay'r also heard a response, almost like a basso voice speaking from a great distance, although the words were garbled.

"They all know of you two now," 'Dward added.

"A rancher in Aldovar heard a large crash yesternoon," 'Harles said, "He thought it might be one of 'Maspiei's bones.' They still fall to Dryland from time to time. No one knows why."

Recalling what 'Dward had told them last night, Ay'r recognized 'Harles's name for a falling icesteroid. "Have you ever seen one?"

"Once, when I was 'Dward's age, one fell near the Delta. I was visiting kinpeople there. So large was it that it cut the canopy, letting in a terrible brightness and then a terrible darkness, blacker than any cave. The Delta people were terrified and hid in their houses for days, prophesying the end of Dryland. Three days and nights my friends and I traveled toward it, three young teens full of adventure and folly."

'Dward had evidently heard the tale before. "Tell them what you found."

"Water!" 'Harles said. "Not a puddle. Not even a pool, but water almost filling the sight from hill to hill, and deeper than we could walk into. Sweet, clear and cold. Maspiei's Tear, we called it.

"That night, when we saw the sky's darkness, all our splashing and playing came to an end. We cringed miserably in a small shell," 'Harles shuddered at the memory. "But by the fourth morning after it had fallen, the canopy had appeared again, and we left the spot."

"It became a Deltan shrine!" 'Dward said.

"In the far north, such sights are common," P'al said calmly.

"Then you will not frighten easily."

"Point us toward Aldovar," P'al said. "We'll go toward the place where something fell yesterday."

"It's beyond two full mountain ridges."

"We'll go. Gratitude for your food and hospitality."

"You plan to go so far on foot?" 'Dward asked.

"As we came to Monosilla we shall go," P'al said, ambiguously.

"Wait until I have consulted with the valley's truth-sayer," 'Harles said.

"It won't be necessary," P'al assured him. "We are travelers. We travel."

"But last night I had a dream!" 'Harles said. "In my dream you two spoke to my son 'Nton, who was taken by the Gods. In my stomach I know it means you will encounter him."

"If so," P'al reasoned, "little good it will do 'Nton or us. For we will all be kidnapped."

"No! You met in freedom."

"But...a dream!" P'al began.

Ay'r interrupted, partly because he was a Species Eth. and wanted to meet their truth-sayer, their local holy man or woman. "We'll go with you to your truth-sayer, to discover if yours was a true dream."

It turned out that the truth-sayer of Monosilla Valley lived a good way off, in fact, at the foot of the valley, which 'Harles insisted was too far to trudge. They would ride Colley. 'Harles, P'al and Oudma astride its back, Ay'r and 'Dward in the wingfolds, where they might be hidden instantly, "although the Gods have not yet been bold enough to immobilize an entire village to kidnap," 'Harles said.

The ride was long enough for Ay'r to note that the landscape altered slightly as the big beetle swerved its way down what at times was a treacherously steep path. The dense dark green succulents grew more abundantly. The tall stands of cloud-reaching trees he had noticed growing in circular and elliptical clumps before, now showed themselves to be the stalks of enormous fungi, their tops not the leafy boughs he had imagined earlier, but instead large globules, some cracked open to reveal boulder-sized black spores which spilled out onto the ground and—almost weightless—rolled with every apparent light gust of wind. From above and partway down, these fungal patches seemed to be shorter than Ay'r had thought, until Colley scampered into a level clearing at the foot of one clump and they proved to be thirty meters high.

The lichenlike grass grew more thickly in meadows, some surrounding a series of terraces whose levels were determined by curved irrigation ditches. When Ay'r wondered what grew there, 'Dward hopped out of the wingfold, dashed across the grass, and splashed into a ditch, grasping a handful of wet, almost-transparent stalks. He returned and once back inside Colley, shook the stalks into Ay'r's hand. The large, transparent grains were lovely to look at: a wild rice of some sort, Ay'r assumed, and following 'Dward's example, he bit into one. It cracked between his teeth, exuding a nutty liquid flavor.

"When fermented, it makes mead. When it's baked, it provides flour for bread," 'Dward explained. All of which confirmed the Drylanders' advanced agriculture.

They had been passing more of the double-shelled dwellings on the horizon. Now Ay'r noted that the habitations were closer together on any good-sized level plot and furthermore were triple, quadruple, even quintuply shelled. Larger families, he guessed, or extended kin-groups. which Oudma verified. "After our bonding, I would live with my bond-mate's family. But 'Dward's bond-mate would move into our house."

Although his knowledge of geology was fairly limited, Ay'r knew enough to see that the few places of sheer rock or escarpment they passed which were partly uncovered by the omnipresent lichen were of different types: granite, shales and sandstones. Confirming what the Fast's topological survey had said—Dryland itself was of very old rock. Once, when Colley stopped to feed on cycads near shalelike cliff walls which must have been at least a million years old, Ay'r thought he saw a familiar foliated form in the rock, ghostlike, a mere tracery. He pointed it out to 'Harles who had no idea what it might be. And when P'al carved it out of the cliff face with care, on a sheet of shale so thin it was no longer opaque and the erose edging, the stems and veins could clearly be made out, none of the three Drylanders could even guess what the fossil object might be, although 'Dward thought it to be part of some insect.

"It's a leaf!" P'al said, retrieving it. "Something like a sycamore leaf, I'd say," he added, before pocketing the rock carefully. He exchanged a glance with Ay'r and said quietly, "See, the ecology here has changed, even this high up. Once, tall angiosperm trees grew here. Now it's all succulents and fungi."

Finally they arrived at the edge of a plateau commanding a spectacular view of an enormous flat basin half a kilometer below, extending endlessly ahead of them, and for scores of kilometers on either side. A deep black river meandered aimlessly throughout, looping back on itself to form an occasional cutoff segment now become an oxbow. Despite the presence of the river, the plain seemed to be dry and brown compared to the lushness of the growth up on the plateau.

"Monosilla Village is ahead." 'Harles pointed west along the plateau. "There we shall find the truth-sayer."

No path, but a real road track had been formed well in from the very edge of the plateau. Colley could only occasionally scuttle now, for while the road widened, multi-shelled dwellings set within enclosures became frequent on both sides of the more-frequented road. 'Harles was forced to rein in the creature so that it could only lumber by, stopping occasionally to wave antennae at another giant beetle tethered in someone's homestead. Within minutes, the road divided and they were within a village: a small bazaar, the noise of people buying and selling, greetings called out to the Drylander family, stares and questions tossed at Ay'r and P'al.

Beyond the ragged bazaar, beyond what seemed to be the center of the village, they rode on, until the shelled homes were sparser, the lichen vegetation thicker all around. At last they stopped at a simple double-shelled house, in front of which some oddly shaped long beams had been crossed to make the front skin opening smaller.

'Harles hopped down and went to the skin doorway. He picked up what might have been a large dried insect leg and began to tap rhythmically at the house shell. He stopped and repeated the pattern. He was about to begin again when Oudma spotted a tall old crone emerge from between the two shells. She staggered forward, her long white-blonde hair grown on either side into braids so long she wore them wrapped around her waist, in effect belting the otherwise-shapeless skin garment which covered her, throat to ankle.

"Is that the truth-sayer?" Ay'r asked.

No one answered.

"Cease your noise!" her voice croaked.

'Harles stopped rapping, and turned to her. "We've come to consult the truth-sayer."

Ay'r saw her eyes, so pale they were almost white.

"What novelty have you brought?"

"Strangers! Legend-collectors from the land of ice in the north."

She looked at Ay'r and P'al, came over and touched them, as though inspecting them before purchase. "Yes, yes. We've heard of their arrival in the valley. We've heard of many strange things of late, the truth-sayer and I."

"Have you heard of our companion?" P'al asked.

"No. Only that three arrived. And one was separated." Then, to 'Harles: "They are not that much of a novelty, although they are certainly fatter of flesh and duskier of skin color than we of the mountains." She seemed to be bargaining with 'Harles.

"I had a dream," 'Harles said. "I must know if it was a true-dream."

The crone drew back in fear, a hand over her eyes.

"In the dream, these strangers and my son taken by the Gods conversed. They were not in bondage."

"The truth-sayer will see you," she said finally and swept open the oddly bone-crossed skins, ushering them into a pillow-covered small, dim room. As they all sat, she vanished.

"If some payment is needed," Ay'r began.

"You are payment," 'Harles said.

"We? But—"

"Your presence. The truth-sayer craves only novelty," Oudma explained. "If your presence is new enough, he will truth-tell for all of us."

The old woman reemerged into the pillowed chamber. In her arms she held a neonate, a boy child, possibly three local years old, who evidently had been sleeping and wasn't yet awake. The crone dropped the boy onto pillows in their midst and called for them to move closer to him.

"I don't understand," Ay'r said. "Who's this?"

The little boy with his cherubic pink face and his pudgy limbs immediately turned to Ay'r. He got up from his sitting position with a bit of difficulty and stumbled directly into Ay'r's arms, so that Ay'r had to hold him.

"I don't understand," Ay'r asked again. "Aren't we going to see the truth-sayer?"

"He's funny!" The little boy squeezed Ay'r's arm and touched his face with tiny exploratory fingers. "No Ib'r he, but from very far away," the little boy added. "He will be in sixty-nine days where once he was. But not in the *very* same place. No, instead," the little boy prattled on, "he will be in another place. A better place. *Very* far away. Very *pretty* place."

The child squirmed out of his arms and into P'al's where once again he touched and pinched him in exploratory fashion. "He's funny-funny!" the little boy squealed with delight as P'al tried embarrassedly to hold onto the child. "No Ib'r he, but from very far away. He will be in sixty-nine days where *he* once was. From the *very* same place. Same place as him!" pointing to Ay'r. "But already he knows this. He knows much. He is. He isn't. Only he knows how he is. And isn't."

Suddenly the boy turned quiet and thoughtful, as thought he was receiving a message. He stared at Ay'r with surprise in his bright blue eyes, then moved toward him, hugging Ay'r around the middle and saying, "Father!"

Ay'r looked at the Drylanders, none of whom seemed at all surprised by the child; although from the frown on the old crone's face, he supposed the child was not normally so effusive.

"Great Father!" the boy went on, thumping Ay'r's chest lightly. "Greatest Father of All! Ever! *All*-Father!"

Ay'r glanced at P'al as though asking confirmation that all this was some sort of absurd hoax, the old woman and child playing parts in some farce. But P'al's face had taken on an oddly meditative cast and he was staring at the ground.

"What?" P'al asked the boy sharply, grabbing his small arm to get his attention, "What of our companion?"

"The one you seek is no more." The child remained in Ay'r's embrace. "Another—alike-seeming—you will find. But you must travel far."

"Are you saying our companion is dead?" P'al insisted.

"Two days!" The child held up two pudgy fingers. "Your companion sleeps." The boy pulled loose of the two and rolled onto the pillows curling up in a fetal position and pretending to sleep, yet winking to show he was awake.

"My son 'Nton?" 'Harles now asked. "What of my son, truth-sayer?" 'Harles repeated his dream to the seemingly-inattentive little boy. Before he was done speaking, the little boy interrupted to say, "Go with these, Ib'r father!" pointing to Ay'r and P'al. "To the end. There lies your fortune and that of the Ib'r house."

"My son is well? Alive?" 'Harles asked.

The boy shrugged. "Your son shall be bonded to a great prince. He shall be the contented mother of a great and powerful house. And you shall bond again, to one you have not met, though all your issue exists now."

Now all of them looked at each other, wondering what he could mean.

The child had gotten to his feet again. He hit his biceps at 'Dward. "Bold feats, Ib'r son!" he said. "Soldier-mother! Mother of ruler of stars without number! Be glad!"

Then he touched Oudma's cheek. "Bonded before initiation. Bonded once more in true-troth. But no shame in that." He smiled. "Double-issue shall cleave the heavens. Yet when it unites! Ah! Who can question it!"

He could not resist turning to Ay'r again, and once more hugging and even kissing him, before the old crone got to her feet and in a most irritated tone insisted that the boy must sleep and began pulling him away.

"Don't forget Lorin, Father!" the little boy pleaded to Ay'r as she pulled him away. "When all is wet. Don't forget, Father!"

After some minutes, the old woman returned alone and showed them out of the pillow-covered chamber.

Ay'r took P'al aside. "What sort of silliness was that? Usually at least the—" Noticing the look on his companion's face, he stopped. "What? What is it?"

"He knew who we were!" P'al said fiercely. "Where we were from! He told us that we would be back where we were in sixty-nine days. He knows we've traveled backward in time by coming to Pelagia."

"Surely you don't believe that? He said we would return to another place! What other place? And why? Not to mention all that about me being the Great Father. I've never sired anyone. It's nonsense. First he says Alli-Clark is no more, then that she's sleeping. He called 'Dward a soldier-mother. He said that the other boy would be a contented mother! How can you take any of his childishness seriously?"

P'al remained unpersuaded by Ay'r arguments. "He knows who we are and where we come from."

Ay'r was about to continue the argument when he became aware that the Drylanders were coming toward them.

'Harles spoke first. "We don't know who you strangers are, or what your purpose may be, but we shall do as the truth-sayer told us and travel with you, to the end. Therein lies the fortune of our name."

"You will find your companion in two days," Oudma said. "Sleeping."

"And I will perform bold feats!" 'Dward said proudly.

"We shall all three go with you," 'Harles said.

"The child was prattling." Ay'r argued. "What he said made little sense."

"Truth-sayers seldom speak what we know of as sense—until later. The truth is too mysterious for our understanding, at first," 'Harles countered.

The old crone appeared again and walked up to them quietly. Ignoring the Drylanders, she came up to Ay'r, dropped to her knees, and kissed his hand.

"Lorin has told me of your coming, All-Father. Bless—me!"

Ay'r thought: this is beyond strange. He mumbled something and lifted the old woman up.

"Lorin asked me once again to have you promise not to forget him, when all is wet."

Ay'r had no idea what she or the child had meant, but once again he promised not to forget him. He doubted he would in any case, following this performance.

She handed him something in a tiny skin pouch attached to a thong. "Lorin wanted you to have this for when you are at the Great Temple. He said you would know how to use it. No!" She stopped him from opening it. "Not until you are at the Great Temple. Then open it. Wear it around your neck," she said and gestured for him to bend his head so she could place it there, hung by the looped thong. "Gratitude for coming and for blessing," she said, and backed away in curtsies.

When Ay'r turned to the others, they were staring at him.

"I don't know what any of this is about, believe me."

"We will return to our homestead for journey's supplies," 'Harles said. "We will borrow another colley. We will leave at canopy-rise tomorrow. Our path lies over the plateau edge into New River Valley. We shall locate your sleeping companion, then go on to the Great Temple, where my son and daughter will be initiated and you will do what you must do. From them on, we are your lieges. We shall go where you go, to the end, so that my son 'Nton will be found."

Ay'r asked himself what it was that had happened back in that tiny pillowed chamber with that child? Had all of them but he undergone some mass hypnosis, some group illusion? Even the imperturbable P'al? It certainly seemed so.

Without another word, they all mounted Colley. None of them spoke as the creature clutched and ambled back up the steep mountain path, all of them seemed to be thinking about what the truth-sayer had foretold for them; even the skeptical, disbelieving, baffled Ay'r.

Chapter Four

Captain North-Taylor Diad discovered he had never seen what Hesperia could truly offer until he had set foot inside the transparent globe at the very tip of the Kell tower, which itself was at the tip of the O'Kell Unltd. complex, on one of the longest and least-populated "girders" in Commerce Sector Six.

The half of the globe facing the City was usually kept opaqued, unless there was some event to be watched from Mart Kell's apartments: the monthly Thwwing race, say, which went right past and usually containing one of Kell's mounts.

But the half facing outward was kept transparent, and it seemed to hang right in the middle of space. As the complex itself was far enough from the center of Hesperia that the pseudo-light and atmosphere hardly interfered, stars were visible from anywhere in the globe. And the globe was large enough that one seldom had a sense one was in a spherical structure. Except of course for the top room: an ordinary-enough-looking multibillionaire's lair; with, of course, the extra view of—everything!

North-Taylor Diad had never heard of a hauler captain being invited to the Kell's apartments. But then, he'd never before heard of a hauler captain sitting in on a Quinx meeting before several weeks ago. Since that historic meeting, a great deal had happened to Diad, very quickly. He had taken private Fasts to local and distant star systems on errands for the Quinx; he had formed connections with various officials who were considered "unsympathetic" to the Matriarchy on both M.C.- and Hesperian-dominated Resort planets. To some, he gave carefully worded accounts of what the Quinx was up to, and of exactly what the M.C. was hiding from them. To those who already knew, he confirmed the knowledge and resoldered any possibly shaky loyalties to the Oppo Movement.

Several high women officials—including an Economics Councilor on Betelgeuse Mu—had been privately horrified by the disastrous treatment their escaped Cybers had received at the hands of the Cult of the Flowers—it was one thing to modify or even to shut off the mechanos, but to wantonly destroy Cybers that had been in one's families for centuries! The Quinx felt these women were ripe only for the most delicate of contacts, the most sensitive feeling-out. And who better than the dignified-looking, experienced, well-traveled and suave hauler captain.

Diad had always been content with his lot in life, but suddenly he was aware that he had aged like a fine New Venice caviar: he was old enough to have been almost everywhere and seen almost everything, yet not too old that a lonely female official finding a sympathetic ear mightn't entertain other, more romantic ideas about him. He had arrived on worlds, found a companion, and left same companion wanting more of himself for close to a century of hauling: if Diad didn't have the needed finesse, no one did.

As a result, he had become a diplomat: ambassador without portfolio.

As a result, for the first time in his longish life, he discovered how governments worked—and didn't work.

And with that understanding, Diad had become almost responsible.

"I can understand the necessity of involving the Orion Spur Federation," he now spoke to an unofficial gathering of Mart Kell, Premier Llega Francis Todd, and Vice-Premier Ole Branklin, "But shouldn't we looking for support outward, too—in the Dexter Sag. and Perseus Arms?"

"We have emissaries covering those areas," Llega Todd said.

"Do you really understand how important the Orion Spur is to us?" Ole Branklin asked.

"I know that the O. Spur Federation was the first to secede from the Matriarchy and set up the Intervening Systems Council," Diad answered. "I assumed that meant their loyalty was more or less assured. Or, at least"—he looked at Mart Kell, sipping a drink he'd never seen before—"their willingness to rebel, no matter what."

"Had they all modified and shut off their Cybers?" Llega Todd asked.

"Not really. Oh, not that one saw anything over a 320 model working or out in the open. But humes still had them at home and in their offices. Modified, all right. To look like PVN monitors and Inter Gal. Comm. units. Some humes seemed to do it for the hell of it, for a joke, or spite, or just to thumb their noses at the Matriarchy. It seemed a little sophomoric to me."

Mart Kell interjected, "But they have their Cybers, and those Cybers' unquestioned loyalty now, if and when they're needed."

"Yes, I see that," Diad said.

"How long have you been working for us?" Branklin asked. "The Quinx, I mean?"

"Since that emergency meeting about the microvirus," Diad answered.

"We think it's time you were told several things. Several of them you've already guessed by now." He faced Llega Todd.

"We've discovered how to counteract the 'wipe,'" she said. "And, as a result, we've been able to place contacts within the Matriarchy for the past twenty years, Sol Rad."

"Spies?" he said. That was a surprise.

"The name is unimportant. Most are Hume women. A few aren't. Because of that, we became aware of the Cyber Consciousness Movement long before it gathered force and exploded so violently. Have you wondered why so few of Hesperia's Cybers left to join the others?"

"Who would want to live anywhere else but the City?" Diad asked.

The others laughed.

"Truly," Llega Todd assured him. "But that's not the reason why. We were signatories to their Declaration of Independence and have supported it. Why shouldn't we—we've always treated our Cybers very well."

"Then...?" Diad was confused. "Does the Quinx still support them? Even after the spread of the microvirus?"

Ole Branklin answered him. "Now, that is our conundrum. We've never supported them materially—except in the early days of the rebellion by opening Resort planets as havens on the Cyber escape route. But now, not only are we in the same fix as the rest of the Matriarchy, but our haulers were the ones actually used to spread the virus."

"Furthermore," Kell added, "we've discovered attempts by the Cyber rebels to use some of our simpler mechanos for their own purposes. You already suspected that, Captain Diad. Following your lead, we can now assume that the repair Cybers on the haulers actually spread the microvirus."

"We've had to ask for voluntary program checks on all of our Cybers," Llega Todd said. "That was embarrassing."

"Although our local Cyber Conscious Unit was eager to go along with it, and actually took care of any shutoffs required."

Branklin added. "Should the M.C. demand our participation in some action against the Cyber rebels, we couldn't refuse. No matter what we do here in the City... We'd prefer not to be put in that position."

"We've also discussed that possibility with our local C.C. Unit," Llega Todd said. "After some difficulty, that told us they understood our point of view. However, they have themselves disavowed the Rebellion in its latest stages and have set up a countergovernment here in the City."

Diad had been following that on City holo Networks. He'd never followed so many damn news stories not concerning sports and athletics before. Not to mention health and science—both on official and open networks. For example, he knew that Hesperians had worked day and night in laboratories to try to come up with a way to preimmunize against some 225 recognizable mutations of the microvirus, and had only partly succeeded. Mart Kell's wanted to trade with the Cyber Rebels for a serum which would protect those women not yet infected. So far, they had located scarcely 4,000 Hesperian women who had had no contact of the virus at all. Scouring the Resort worlds might produce another few thousands, but as those worlds were so dependent upon orbiting Fasts, it was highly unlikely that they'd find more. What difference would that make ultimately? Someone had calculated that even if those women and their daughters daughters and their daughters's daughters were denied most Hume rights, imprisoned, and turned into constant baby-making machines, it would take another 1,300 years to repopulate the City alone.

Llega Todd told them, "We still retain spies in the M.C., some right on Wicca-World, in all areas, military included. So we don't think we'll have to immediately face the situation Lord Branklin outlined."

"However, all of our spies have looked carefully into many of the Matriarchy's activities since the microvirus struck: scientific as well as military."

"In fact," Llega Todd interjected, "any odd activity in which Wicca Eighth herself was involved herself in was brought to our attention, no matter how trivial or absurd."

"Three of those in particular seemed to us to bear closer scrutiny," Branklin said. "One concerns a particular Commander of a M.C. Forces BattleCruiser, one Helle Sobr'a'ni Lill. Ever heard of her?"

Commander Lill! Sure, Diad remembered her. How could he forget? She and her warriors had taken on six Hauler males inside an illegal Pachy-Fight, where was it, one of the Vega Gamma Giant Gaseous satellites he thought. Dirty as it was, it had been an even match, and after the worst wounded on both sides had been sent by air transport to Emergency Med. Services, the five remaining had slammed—still bloody—into a local taverna, terrorizing all present, drinking and snorting and carousing for another hour, until Lill had turned to Diad, hard as Plastro, and said, "Eve's rectum! I'm bored and my clit's hard. Why don't we all just go somewhere and screw each other 'til we pass out." Which they had all done.

"In fact I do know her. Not at all a regular M.C. Forces goody-goody."

"That sounds right," Llega Todd said. "We might want you to meet her again."

"Fine by me."

"The second person is one we'd very much like you to make contact with." Llega Todd said. "Her name is Gilliam Guo-Rinne. Health Councilor for a large sector of the Perseus Arm, suddenly returned to Rigel Prime and doing research into a mammologist. Someone named

Relfi. We think Rinne may be close to something of great importance."

"You'll have to go to Wicca World," Ole Branklin said.

"Sure, but I know you've got younger ambassadors of both genders to send out. Why me?"

"Councilor Rinne doesn't surround herself with sycophants. She's a serious person. According to our records, she hasn't been espoused for some years," Llega Todd said. "No quick gyno-woman affair will satisfy her, and I can't say I blame her. Beside, we think you'll like Councilor Rinne."

They flashed a holo of a quite attractive woman a decade or so younger than Diad, addressing a group of women, then turning and waving to someone.

"Fine by me," he repeated. "What about the third one?"

"We don't think it need concern you right now," Ole Branklin said.

"When do I leave for Wicca-World? And how do I pass myself off?"

"You leave tomorrow. And you pass yourself off as yourself. Captain North-Taylor Diad of O'Kell Unltd., Hesperian Beryllium Hauler, now retired and on vacation. We'll arrange the meeting," Llega Todd explained.

A flash of light streaked across the dome. As Diad turned to follow the Thwwing race, he found himself smiling inexplicably.

"You never said I'd have to remain on Deneb XII for the entire term!" Ewa protested.

"I was certain you'd understood." Maly'a looked perplexed. "You yourself said that other women would be envious of you if you remained on Benefica."

Ewa couldn't deny that.

"Aren't you happy here at Alpheron Spa?" Maly'a asked. "Don't you have everything you could possibly want or require?"

Ewa couldn't deny her needs were met, instantly in many cases, thanks to the large body of gyno and women servants—more than she'd ever seen—and far more attentive than Cybers would have been. Alpheron Spa was the poshest resort she or her spouses had ever seen. As to whether she was happy...

"Haven't you seen your Prime spouse every week? And your Trine spouse whenever you wanted him?"

"Yes. They're fine. While they're here! Once they're back on Benefica they have no idea why I'm here. Oh, I suppose I understand why they have to be 'wiped' of the knowledge so they won't slip up when they're back on Benefica. But even so, it's not easy. I've cut down my Inter Gal Comm.s. to one a week, and even that one gets more difficult."

"Aren't your Prime and Trine spouses getting along without you?"

The problem, Ewa had to admit, was that they were getting alone fine. Oh, nothing so bizarre as a romantic alliance. Eve, no! But from what Ewa could make out, Maxie and Virge seemed to be settling into life without her company all too easily. Whenever Maxie visited, she told Ewa she was using the free time to catch up on cultural things: PVN's she had not gotten around to, friends she had been meaning to look up. Ewa couldn't not believe her. As for Virge, Maxie said he was putting more time into a second avocation, one Ewa herself had encouraged—sound sculpture. He hardly went out, except in the company of that old Eridani Eps. Arth who Maxie said was some sort of triple-board Suitar virtuoso.

Then Maxie had let slip the fact that she and Virge had discovered a shared taste in PVNs about the Bella=Arthopod War. They had exp'ed three of them together. Had Ewa ever gotten into *Desperate Vespids of Deneb XII?* Well, said Maxie, neither would she and Virge have, if Ewa wasn't suddenly a resident of the former last stand of the Bella=Arths.

That was just the trouble. She had only herself to blame for feeling that Maxie—and Virge—were slipping away. Which was why she had invited both of them here the last visit. What a disaster that had been! Not that they thought so. They loved it. Dragged poor Ewa onto the transport and kilometers across the planet into Hymenoptolis, the gigantic final fortress of the Bella=Arths. And once in the place—turned into a museum of the Vespids' home-city during the Intervening Systems—she had been dragged around another kilometer from one so-called place of interest to another until she had almost collapsed. Been forced to stop and lie down in the nearest lounge. Naturally, Maxie had gone on; little would stop her. And Virge, in true gyno fashion, had stayed with Ewa until she had grown annoyed with his sulking and sent him off, too.

There Ewa was, stuck inside what was essentially an enormous wasp's nest half a kilo high and a score of kilos underground, some of them never cleared of the war's debris and still being gone through by Artho-Archaeologists. Around her were the liquid-mercury walls of local—if ancient—"decoration," and the prerecorded chitterings meant to represent the elegiac music of the defeated Arths. Despite all the tourists' hubbub, despite the presence everywhere of M.C. uniforms, Ewa still felt uneasy.

After all, these creatures had been her ancestors' enemies, hadn't they? Sure, Maxie and Virge could ooh and aah about Commander

Wan'da's military finesse in the battle of Deneb System and how she had utterly destroyed them, but Ewa had never gotten over feeling that insects—no matter how large or small they might be, nor how intelligent they were, nor even how personable—were simply too alien for humes to ever become comfortable with. Everything she'd learned about them in Ed. & Dev.: their mating rituals and habits, their hyperorganized social structure, the way they raised their young, their views of life and death, were so totally different. Nothing like the few Delphinids she had met who, she assumed because they were mammals, were far easier to understand and get along with.

And here Ewa was, after she had seen Maxie and Virge off on the Fast back to Benefica, on what had been the last planet of the unassimilated, unhumeized Vespid Arths. Beautiful as the resort was, any balcony a few meters above the skyline showed the distant landscape still unmistakably dominated by the huge, only partly destroyed Wasp-hills, the cities where they'd—ughh!—scuttled about, piling up and feeding larvae, reconstructing battlements, checking positions, deploying armaments, and finally self-destructing when all was lost. Even that was terrifying to her: how, when all was lost, the Bella=Arths had suddenly decided to kill themselves: a million of themselves, from unhatched larvae to their enormous, immobile queens.

There was another fact too: thousands of heroic Hume women soldiers (and even males) had died everywhere on this planet. There was no way to hide the fact.

"Why here? Why Deneb XII?" Ewa asked Maly'a again.

And once again, Maly'a explained.

"By the laws of the Treaty of Formalhaut, a hundred or so worlds were declared to be 'open' territory. Open to all who wanted to colonize them, or to visit or whatever. Mostly to placate the remaining members of the Intervening Systems Council, who briefly replaced the First Matriarchy. Hesperia, of course, is the best-known of these open worlds. About a dozen were Bella=Arth planets, taken during the war."

Maly'a had studied well and now seemed to be repeating by rote.

"These worlds are under dual rulership. Naturally, the M.C. has policing power, but the Council of Resort Worlds on Hesperia decides which of the M.C. rules will and will not be allowed. On Deneb XII, for example, the ban against Intelligent Cybers was accepted, but not the Zero-Pop rule. For obvious reasons."

"But why *this* world?"

"Even among Resort Worlds, Deneb XII possesses special status as a result of its historical importance. Which means that it is both policed carefully and at the same time watched carefully by Hesperia. Which means that any breach of the agreement here will be met by if not actual force, then by... Not to mention the museum!" Maly'a went on. "It's the only remaining intact replica of Bella=Arth life of the last millennium, the sum total of a billion years of another line of evolution which..."

Ewa let her go on for a while with the tourist-guide speech.

"Would you like me to talk to your spouses?" Maly'a asked. "I've had a little success with such matters before."

"Truly!" It wasn't a question. Ewa didn't disbelieve her.

"I wouldn't mind. And you're already third month into your term and doing so well, I'd really hate to have to terminate over such a silly bit of business."

Ewa had never considered terminating the pregnancy. The look on her face gave that fact away instantly.

"Sometimes spouses will listen to what a stranger has to say better than they would to—"

Yes, Ewa thought as the older woman spoke on, she would do exactly that. And who knew, more too, to protect her firstborn. Now that she'd seen it, felt it, knew day by day it was growing inside her.

She agreed and left Maly'a satisfied, and then walked slowly—because exercise was needed—to the conveyance up through the multi-leveled terraces to her own group's spectacular lodgings. On level three she met Janitra, who had been visiting a woman friend there, from one of the earliest groups.

They began talking about spouses, then trading stories and laughing, and Janitra invited Ewa back to her private Ion-bath and it didn't take long for Ewa to forget all about pompous Maxie and silly Virge and to listen intently and with just a hint of envy to Janitra talking about her visit to level three and how fat and round and contented all the women in the earlier group were now that they were so very, very close.

She saw him coming from across the room. Unmistakably male, and tall: half a head higher than most of the women. Not that other males weren't also present in the rooms: a score of gyno servants and at least a half-dozen male officials she knew by name. But none were so tall or half as striking. Even before he was close enough for Councilor Rinne to see the starburst white logo embroidered on one lapel of his formal, she knew he was from Hesperia.

"Gemma, this male visitor expressed an interest in meeting you,"

Councilor Ur' Sa said, clearly unsure whether she should have or not. "Do you know each other?"

"I doubt if the Councilor remembers me," he quickly said, "Captain North-Taylor Diad. It was a large, formal affair on Trefuss." He smiled and half-winked at her. "You know how those kind of events can get."

As Rinne took his arm in the shoulder grip greeting, he clearly mouthed the words, "Save me!"

"From what?" she mouthed back. And his eyes shifted once quickly toward Ur' Sa who was still there, but speaking to someone else.

"In fact, I do remember!" Rinne said and kept her arm on his. "There's something I've been meaning to ask you..." she detached herself and turned them away from the other councilor.

"Might we step outside?" he said. It wasn't really a question, and Rinne had more than enough of the party to think, oh why not.

Outside it was a typical Melisande night: balmly, moonless, wonderful.

"Gratitude!" he said, once they were alone on the curving open balcony.

"Exactly what torment did Ur' Sa have planned that I'm saving you from?" Rinne asked, turning to look at him.

"Meeting more women. I'm afraid I'm in over my head. I've never seen so many beautiful and accomplished women in one place. It fairly takes my breath away."

Rinne noted that Captain Diad was wearing a modified Hesperian outfit: no wrist armor, no codpiece, not even the usual studded kneecap boots. Still, his close-fitting body singlet was "City Jet" black with silver trim and his jewelry—small nostril plug, single earring, wristlet and starburst clasp for his cape—looked to be of the finest-grade Plastro. His close-cropped hair and one sideburn growing across his swarthy, olive complexioned face to a thick moustache, was a black comma enclosing a strong nose and eagle eyes. She guessed him to be about her age, and in excellent physical shape.

"What did you expect on Regulus Prime?" she asked.

"I'm afraid I expected exactly what I've gotten. Even so..."

Two statuesque young M.C. Guards in their body-fitted uniforms strolled past and he gazed at them.

"You might have guessed I'm a visitor here."

"Who isn't?" she said. "Vacation?" she asked, not knowing why, but wanting to be with him more than being back inside, avoiding questions from her fellow officials about what she was really doing back in Melisande.

"I'd been all over most of the Matriarchy, but I'd never seen the center,"

Diad said. "I thought when I retired...well, that I owed it to myself to come here once." He gestured helplessly. "I thought, well frankly Councilor, I thought I might be ignored or..."

He must know he wouldn't be ignored on Melisande. This had to be what decades ago, her Trine Spouse Lyon used to call "a good old-fashioned line."

"Retired from Hesperia? I thought no one ever left the wondrous City."

"Retired from Beryllium Ore Hauling, Councilor. That was my avocation until a few months ago, Sol Rad. Now, I'm just an early retiree, on the loose."

"A rich retiree, I'd say, if you were in Beryllium hauling."

"I did fine, gratitude, Councilor. But although I'm traveling a bit, I doubt that I can fail to return to Hesperia. If you'd ever been there..."

"Not for a long time, I'm afraid," she said. "But I found the experience unforgettable. Pleasantly," she added.

"I'm glad to hear that."

The two guards were gliding past again. Again he looked at them.

"I'm not used to seeing soldiers at social functions," he explained.

"Ah, but think of who's gathered here! The cream of Melisande! It was thought that Herself might make a personal appearance. She might still."

"Not that I haven't seen my share of that uniform," he said.

Rinne turned to face him, eager to hear more. "You're far too young for the war." A joke. She added, "Or were you in action connected with the Bella=Arth War, and Hesperia has cosmetological secrets we've not heard about yet?"

They laughed. Then he said in a more serious tone, "No, no, but I've run across young M.C. sparks like those two who found the possibility of besting a Hesperian male an opportunity not to be missed. Mostly, I admit on frontier planets and some of the less savory port-worlds. I can't blame them. They might have been bored, or simply intent on impressing some young male. Truly!" he said, doubtless thinking she doubted him. "I've got the scars to prove it," he began to lift aside his breast clasp.

"I believe you do have scars!" she stopped him. "But I also believe a Hesperian male mightn't be as innocent as you claim you were. They have been rumored, on occasion, to provoke M.C. guards."

He smiled again and said, "Perhaps I've misremembered the exact circumstances. Not very gallant of me, you're thinking."

Rinne was thinking something quite different, she was thinking: I like him. And he likes me. How novel!

"So what's on your tourist agenda? Or shouldn't I ask?"

"There is an agenda, of sorts," he admitted shyly, "But really, I've never been the sort to follow a plan. I prefer to wander about. From what I've seen here on Melisande, that seems to be how many spend their time. It's very beautiful. Virtually a paradise. I expected it to be far more…built up."

He told her his itinerary, which was a bit better than the standard one for the planet, no doubt because he had an astonishingly high credit line and was used to being treated royally. He added quickly, "I'd be willing to hear any suggestions."

"Have you been to the Spoorenberg? That needlelike object in the middle of Karenina Park? It was originally built as an orbital transport elevator. It has an observation restaurant above the clouds. On a clear day, it's quite marvelous."

"I hadn't planned it, but I will now."

There was a slight commotion inside. She thought Wicca Eighth might have arrived, and perhaps she might be even nicer to Diad and introduce him to Herself. But in a few seconds she realized from the shape of the crowd, that it was a only live-holo of the ruler.

"I'm certain you're a very busy woman, but perhaps you'd join me there—say, for dinner?"

Rinne thought: I've wanted to be with a stranger three times in my life: once it ended in heartbreak; but two of those times worked out, and one turned into a spouse. Of course, she'd been younger then, and now was hardly a time to be even thinking of romance. Still…

"I've just insulted you, haven't I?" he apologized. "Didn't mean it. Even back in the City, I've never know the right thing to say. It all gets so complicated."

"You haven't insulted me," Rinne said, while admitting that some women would be taken aback by a male making such a proposal. "But I am a busy woman. However, if you let me comm. you sometime…"

She reached her hand forward to his and only when their wrists touched did she realize that as a Hesperian he wouldn't have an implant. Even so, he held her hand longer than he should have before she could remove it.

"I was looking for your comm. code," she said.

He gave it to her orally, and she tapped it into her wrist plate. Then he said, "Gratitude, for making my stay in Melisande so…unexpectedly intriguing." Rinne swore she heard sincerity in his words.

The live-holo was over when they went inside and Rinne's group was leaving so she said farewell to Captain Diad and he promised to comm.

"Who was that male you spent so much time with?" Geo-Exploiter Sanya Rhyyce asked when they were in the down-lift.

"A retired Hesperian."

"I'll bet he's one of those grokky City degens," Sanya's daughter Leota, a know-it-all adolescent, commented. "Either that or a multi-billionaire!"

"You've been watching too many PVN digests," her mother complained. She never repeated her question.

Of course, meeting Captain Diad was out of the question. Or at least throughout most of the following morning and afternoon it seemed to be.

Councilor Rinne's mornings were given over to work on "The Problem," as she and others of her rank and involvement in the microvirus program had come to call it. From the moment she had returned to Regulus Prime, Rinne had been drafted to aid the monumental effort. After less than a week, Sol Rad. in Melisande she had demanded a better Cyber. Following days of arguments from everyone around her, she had finally been given one she approved of: intelligent, voluntarily modified following its reading of the *Confessions,* and really quite personable— it called itself Jenn-Four. After a week or so of working together in the small office in her apartments, Rinne felt comfortable enough to begin to open up to Jenn-Four. It was imperative that she know everything that the M.C. was doing about the problem, no matter how apparently trivial.

In response, Jenn-Four had begun data hunting through the entire Matriarchy's files, using Rinne's Councilor status clearances as access codes.

Rinne now knew all of the scientific programs instituted during since the Emergency began: she could attest to how widespread those programs were, from new attempts at that seemingly unattainable Grail: completely Hume genetic cloning to the most minutely detailed attempts at partial and total cure by chemical and biological means. Every quack on the fringes of the Matriarchy had been pulled into the great task—few questions asked, funded to the hilt, and set on their way to see what they could come up with: artificial birth canals, cybernetic ova, prosthetic fallopian tubes.

The terrifying fact was that under the First Matriarchy, any possible new methods of conception, gestation, and birth had been strongly discouraged. The Neofeminism movement of the middle Third Millennium century had absolutely depended upon a bedrock of clean, healthy and, above all natural, childbirth. As often as possible. And for the good of the Matriarchy. Those early holo Adverts. which had spread across system after star system were ludicrous to look at now: the gigantic and perfectly idealized woman surrounded by her many daughters, while behind her stood equally tall and idealized, her female Prime Spouse. The male who made the "natural" splitting of the ovum possible was seldom seen, except perhaps as a tiny figure or chain of figures below, carrying posters or banners supporting Neofeminism. In some adverts, the male figure was missing altogether, the symbolic male circle and arrow pinned onto the lapel or cap of one of the more ambitious-appearing children. In some adverts, all one ever saw of the male, was a tiny stylized sperm.

But if experiments beyond the norm were discouraged during some periods, they were completely banned, utterly taboo during others and those—like Relfi with innovative ideas—were subjected to witch-hunts, tried by kangaroo courts, and destroyed: usually alone with their work. More than once, Rinne found herself thinking that it would be a fine— if terrible—irony indeed if the Three Species ended because of their own past prejudice and shortsightedness.

Rinne had also set Jenn-Four to look for any possibly related programs, and had been surprised to find a listing of them almost fifty long. Some were open to her access and consisted of nothing more than preproduced holos of a half-informational, half-inspirational sort. Others were programs mentioned in passing in some other file and now indexed under "military," "geo-exploration" and "terraforming and resettlement."

Indeed, it had been one of the last, a program called Eden-Breed, which had especially gotten Rinne's attention only a few days ago, when her access codes wouldn't let her in. Jenn-Four had tried roundabouts, lies, and finally even partial destruction of one of its own units to pry entry. To no avail. Rinne immediately comm.ed Councilor Ly's Delmon, her friend Sany'a Rhyyce's employer, of New Planets Division and asked for access to the file.

And had been told she couldn't have it. So, she comm.ed Herself, and after a day of frustration and blockage, Wicca Eighth comm.ed back.

"You needn't know everything, Councilor Rinne—unless you plan to become Wicca Ninth."

"You gave me a job to do. I'm doing it," Rinne replied. "If I'm hindered, what's the sense of bothering? I should go back to Sag. Central and do what I was doing there."

"Now don't be hasty! First you must understand that not all of Our programs during this Emergency are as...logical and sensible as We might wish."

"I've encountered some weird ones already."

"Eden-Breed is a bit different. Quite desperate," Wicca Eighth said. "You know that we've been gathering up females not affected by the microvirus. Most of them have gone to bio lab-stations as control subjects. But a certain number are being held in abeyance for the moment, being set up for an extraordinary final Salvation effort."

The Matriarch had been speaking quickly. She slowed down now.

"The idea first came from the Interstellar Metropolitan Himself, Gn'elphus XXI."

"Of the Church of Algol?" Rinne asked.

"I'm afraid so. Despite centuries of our best efforts at Ed. & Dev., there are those for whom the Maudlin Se'ers still hold much credit in some parts of Our Realm. Because of that, Our relations with the Se'ers have had to be as delicate as those with Hesperia. Even so, once the idea of a salvation unit was brought up at an Inner Council meeting by the Church's ambassador, there turned out to be support for the idea. Thus it was implemented."

"To the benefit of the Church of Algol, I assume."

"A bit. As We said before, it's quite last ditch. The plan is to take a certain number of the untouched women to a safe place, far from any possible contact with the microvirus, and to sequester them there and allow them to breed in safety. Should all our plans fail, the Matriarchy will at least have an outpost where it can regather its forces. Womanhood will not be completely lost."

Without meaning to, Rinne put a hand up over her eyes. Of all the ridiculous ideas!

"We have no choice but to try it." Wicca Eighth defended the program. "Several Fasts will be fully equipped with all of the necessities and all of the bases of our culture. Their destinations will be random until the Fasts are out of the galactic spiral."

"A batch of women with a few Se'ers along for propagation—and propaganda—purposes?"

"That hasn't been settled yet. Naturally, officials and M.C. guards on a voluntary basis will join them." Wicca Eighth added. "I know you think it's a terrible idea, but I don't think you realize that gravity of the situation, Councilor Rinne. Two days ago, Sol Rad. when the Orion Spur Stock Market opened up on Tau Ceti Seven, there was a column for Bride Prices."

"A joke. A typical O-Spur joke!"

"Was it, Councilor Rinne? Oh, it was gone in an hour, Sol Rad., but it had been there for everyone to see!"

"You knew we couldn't keep it secret forever." Rinne. said. "But no one will actually talk about it. Even the O-Spurs don't dare. Everyone's terrified to bring it up. It's probably the widest-known, best-kept secret since time began."

"We hope you're right. And We hope We don't have to send those women on those Fasts out of the galaxy."

"I still need better access, Ma'am. A higher code or..."

"We'll see what We can do."

"On which of the unaccessible programs would I find more data and holos of Ay'r Kerry Sanqq'?"

"Under his name," Wicca said. "Have you made any progress with your holo notes from the Arcturus Mammalogical Institute?"

"Nothing worth discussing," Rinne said as the holo snapped off.

Which was what she did every afternoon when all of her other work was cleared: go through holo notes never meant to be saved beyond a few decades; holos stored hastily, never complete to begin with, poor in quality, requiring lumel and sonal amplification to even be useful.

Worse, when the holos were useful, they were difficult for Rinne to watch and listen to. There she was, not only two hundred years younger, but lacking in the sheer accumulation of experience by which she now defined herself. She found that she didn't have a hint of the thoughts and emotions going through the mind of the child she had once been. Rinne could glean hints from her earlier self's body language, vocal intonation, and even actions, but it was still like trying to read a four-dimensional map with a two dimensional line.

There also were her colleagues at the institute. Poul'a Hriniak, Mondre Va Uip, Cam Caroly'a Jesper, to mention only her closest friends. All of them now mothers, businesswomen, politicians, government servitors, accomplished in vocation and avocation, as she was. And there too were the proctors and assistants, among them of course, astonishingly, exactly as she had last seen him and since remembered him: Ferrex Sanqq'.

Rinne knew that in these days, rebellious adolescents like Leota Rhyyce toyed with the idea of women-male relationships, used it to shock their elders, appeared openly affectionate with males their age and size together in public. Most of them quickly outgrew it, understanding its grotesqueness, its inapplicability to real life in the Matriarchy. In Rinne's youth, it had been worse to swoon over a male. Yet she had done so over Ferrex Sanqq', and when she had begun to look through the holo notes she had been fearful how it would show up. It hadn't been as blatant as she had feared, but it had unmistakably been there.

As had been Ferrex's grace and tact in either ignoring it, deflecting it, or hiding its existence from others. He had not been espoused at the time, but he must have had previous experiences with overstimulated students like Gemma Rinne, because he kept his personal life closed, insisted he had none, and when forced by the Institute to attend some social event, he had always come and left with a male assistant or male student—the only approved relationship for a bachelor in the Matriarchy. In those days, Rinne had thought that Ferrex Sanqq' was either hypocritical or just plain smart. Once she had berated him, and he had simply responded, "If I even looked at you, I'd be subjected to a complete 'wipe.' Is that what you want, Gemma? Everything in my mind wiped out?"

Another time, however, when they were alone in the Cyber-lab going over Relfi's tatters of documents for the thousandth time, he had been kinder. He had taken her hand in his and said, "If you follow this path, you'll be doomed in the Higher Matriarchy. You understand that, don't you?"

"What path? Relfianism?" she asked.

"Heterosexuality," he had replied.

He'd been right, course. Decades after she had left the Institute and had met Sam-Lyon Persse, he had told her the same thing—in bed, after intercourse. By then, however, Rinne was on her way up the M.C. ladder and not about to be stopped. She'd hidden her romance with Lyon as long as she could, then when she couldn't any longer, she had found another woman who was also a secret male-lover, and they had all moved in together. Outsiders had giggled, pretending to be a little scandalized: Rinne was so obviously Prime Spouse that Tamma Mehta-Hill must have been the insatiable nympho of their fourway gyno-group. Rinne was always being teased about Tamma. But they lived that way for close to a century: two couples, with their own children and grandchildren and great-grandchildren, none of whom ever suspected the truth. Rinne may have lived a lie, but she had succeeded despite that. And now here was an old holo of the very beginning: the male who had begun it.

Next to that holo, were the far-more-recent ones of his son. When placed together, they showed the two males of unquestionable descent. But she and Jenn-Four racked their minds and Rinne's memory for Ay'r Kerry's mother. She had Jenn-Four check through all of the females present in the holo notes: physically, genetically, molecularly for a match to Ferrex's son. Then she had had the Cyber locate and superquick play old holos of every other female student and proctor at the Institute during the decade when Ay'r must have been conceived. Jenn-Four moaned and complained—naturally, given the extent of the work—but cranky as the Cyber was, it did the work. And a breakthrough was still to come.

Two days ago, Sol Rad., when Rinne had received the holos which Ay'r hadn't known were being taken of his arrival at the M.C. Headquarters in Melisande—outside and then inside the building, and finally with Wicca Eighth Herself—Rinne played them over and over, and once more sensed that she knew both parents. The young male's stance, walk, and general appearance were so strikingly like that of Ferrex Sanqq', it was only when she mentally detached those and looked for any differences that she felt uneasy. Uneasy with still more familiarity. The way the young male almost—but not quite—raised an eyebrow when speaking to that Marine Biologist, Alli-Clark, as though completely unable to believe in her existence. The way he had mischievously tried to nibble the giant breast of that Cult Warrior in the lounge even though he was off his feet, in the air. The way he had of opening his lips slightly as though whistling silently to himself. She had seen those gestures—or their potential—in someone before. But even when alerted to look for the characteristics, Jenn-Four couldn't find the woman.

"I've had enough for today, Jenn-Four," Rinne said finally, admitting, "I'm frustrated beyond measure."

"I'll continue searching," the Cyber said. "But please explain to me exactly what it is about this young male which allows us to watch and analyze and redepict every gesture hundreds of times and yet not grow tired."

"I don't know about you. I'm beginning to get good and tired of him." And when Jenn-Four was silent, Rinne quipped, "You're probably falling in love with him! Just keep at it."

Only when she had left her office and was sipping at a Nutrient Cocktail preparatory to going into the Ion-bath did Rinne notice that among her comm.s received for the day was one from Captain Diad. She probably shouldn't call him back.

"Oh, hell, Rinne! You're so damn old, no one cares anymore who you see! Male, woman, Delph or Arth."

So she returned his comm. and promised to meet him at the Spoorenberg, thinking, if Wicca Eighth only knew!

The flyer passed Connaught Memorial Park and quickly alit upon a guardian station. There were six other passengers on the small transport and Mart Kell was the only one who stood for the door. The others seemed to be "Night Shift" Commerce Girder Six workers: glorified clerks, two female Beryllium inspectors still in the wrap-suit, their hairless heads sporting the latest cosmetic tattoos. Mart recognized one Hume from O'Kell Unltd. Of course, the apprentice financier didn't recognize Mart. Who would, since he was dressed in a Plastro-textured hooded body-suit, air-sandals slung over one shoulder, half-facial roller visors behind which, if anyone dared to look, they would find the Kell hair flattened inside a skullcap, the emerald Kell eyes tinted brown—just another crazy "whizzer" sneaking out late to break his neck on the Connaught Park airramps. This one now hammering with his Plastro fingertip guards against the mag-lev doors, waiting for them to slide open and...

Out! He dropped the sandals, slid his boot toes inside and shot off the station platform, skirling down the long curved ramp, up a wall here, and down again slowing a bit as he sped into the Park's partly lighted, half-ruined Tourist Information Center, jazzing around a little to check out what kind of Species Trash was out this late. Nothing much it turned out: two humes obviously out of their neurons on a Stele-bash under a built-in seat, and a skaggy-looking Artho pickpocket pretending to be a panhandler who would roll the humes when they finally stopped dry-humping and passed out.

Mart schussed a side wall to glide over the turnstiles and into the park's semidarkness, swerved around the fountains then flew onto a longer ramp down, down into the streets below, now dampening with pseudo-atmosphere so there would be dew in parks and penthouse terraces.

Connaught was on one of the oldest girders in the City, and the neighborhood had never recovered from an early burst of importance and equally sudden decline. Huge old loading docks and warehouses for luxury SlpG. stellar ships a millennium ago lined Power Avenue. In great-grandfather's time this was the place to be on Hesperia, center and hub: hotels of unparalleled service, restaurants and clubs of the utmost elegance, shops and emporia with amazing wares. "I bought my first Thwwing at an auction spontaneously held in the Hume-lounge in the Alpheratz DiscDome," Mart remembered old Jat Kell saying. "It cost me a month's earnings." Now the Alpheratz was all boarded up, abandoned, the streets so empty for so long that not even parasitic creatures remained to rustle or slink suddenly around a corner.

Mart swirled down the empty avenue, cutting a swath across old irradiated basalt paving and up liner fuel-stained jasperine walls. His object was one particular rampway into one particular abandoned building. And there it was! He pirouetted the air-sandals smartly in front of its long-locked main entrance, reading "Ophiucus Stellar Lines: Luxury

Passenger Terminus." Then spun to look around—a kilometer of empty street in either direction—performed a somersault, so he might check the vertical—no one in sight—then air-slid up the double curved ramp, past the entrance and behind a decorative amaranthine pylon upon which a model in Cyber-sculpted Platinum had once stood, which now stood, somewhat forlornly, in the O'Kell sphere apartments.

Stopped, hidden from sight, he tapped a panel to get a antique Cyber-eye's attention, slid off his visor so it could read his left iris, and scooted into the small doorway.

Inside, the vast and echoing terminal was scarcely illuminated, even when he turned on his belt-lumen, but he knew his way: he had played here often enough as a neonate, when he could get away from Cyber-Tutes and assorted pedagogues. He knew every now-immobile mural on every dilapidated wall. He had explored every office, closet, kiosk, sanitary, kitchen and sleep chamber in the place. He had carried on a kinky, secret affair with an assimilated Bella=Arthopod for months here during his University days, using one of the VIP suites that hung seven stories above the waiting room. But mostly he had come here to soak himself in the grand vision of those early Kells, to remind himself of the past glories of those galactic-scale scandal-filled robber barons, those Ophiucan Kell ancestors of his whose deeds, foul and fair, were taught in every Ed & Dev. program in the Matriarchy. Except Mart Kell's, by express order of his own equally tyrannical and equally ambitious but far-more-conservative grandfather, under whose domination Mart had grown up and rebelled.

No ramps rose to the suite, so Mart had to activate an ancient mag-lev lift. It was almost a minute before he floated up to the terrace. Once there, he removed the sandals, slung them over his shoulder, dropped his hood to uncover his face and hair, removed his visors, and strode toward his destination.

In front of the fluted-iridium glass doors of the largest suite, he lifted both arms, revolved slowly to show no weapons, then waited. One door slid open and he walked in. Kri'nni Des ('xx') a was wrapped over a sofa and adjoining chair, cleaning her mandibles with one silky front palp, inhaling from a Soma pipette. Kell set his larynx for Condensed Middle Bella=Arth. and said,

"I hope you brought one for me, Kri'nni."

"I did, but I ate (imbibed ((absorbed))) the other already, you were so late (slow ((unaccountably so)))!"

Even so, she let him join her for a sip, and Mart enjoyed both the drink and the feel of her palps on his lower torso and legs, as she commented:

"You're even more attractive (delicious ((edible))) than you were when we were dating (meeting for sex ((encountering illegally for pleasure)))."

"So are you, but far more dangerous."

"Don't be such a pupa (child ((innocent))), Mart! Even then I was interested in the more forbidden (criminal ((act-unspecified))) aspects of Hesperia. I simply made more contacts (connections ((deals & vendetta-bargains))) since that time!"

Kri'nni was being modest, as usual. She and a half-dozen of her cohorts virtually controlled the enormous contraband market the City (as commercial center of the galaxy) contained. At a past Quinx meeting someone (not Mart) had even suggested giving her a seat. Since there was far more than enough wealth coming and going out of the City for all to share in, Kri'nni's friends never bothered anyone in public, and they didn't bother her.

"Maybe so. You manufacture this stuff?" he asked, knowing that if she did, it would be the best.

"I wouldn't use that M.C. bilge! So, Mart, what's on your mind (currently making waves ((in neural stasis)))? You didn't come here for a double-palp job (sex ((the illegal kind (((with me)))! If anyone knew we were here, you'd be in the middle of a scandal (consternation ((loss of prestige))), and so, among my kind, would I."

"Palp-jobs are always on my mind since you left me to become an independent entrepreneur, Kri'nni. But right now I want to pick your mind (establish rapport ((get data you may not know you have)))."

"As a rule I sell it to the higher bidder (money-bags ((idiot)))."

"When have we ever done anything by the rules?"

"Go on, tell me (spit it out ((regurgitate it)))!"

"Run this down for me: Matriarchy: Weirdness: Resort Planets."

"I know what you're looking for," she said, and removed a vibrating silken palp from inside the front of his bodysuit.

"You do?"

"The Cyber renegade who turned in a commercial liner full of fleeing Mechanos outside of Cassiopeia-Chenar?"

"No, but I'll listen." He took the palp and tried to wedge it back into his suit, but she flicked it away. "And Kri'nni, as long as we're not in a seduction mode, try to tell me without your usual multiple shadings of meaning, please."

"I'll try, Mart." Her iridescent multifaceted eyes blinked in a positive-interest mode. "Some of Mamma's programmed mechanos stayed behind and now are hunting the underground railway to make big Cyber killings. Only a few thousand tincans have been smithereened so far, but Mamma thinks it's good for propaganda, it cools off the military machine Mamma's got on dead-end duty, and Mamma thinks that it demoralizes the rebels."

"Demoralizes? They're intelligent but not—"

"Larva-love, those rebel Cybers are (take my word ((would I lie?))), truly oversensitive mass of artificial parts. They want Hume dignity and all that (tripe ((needless fecal matter)))!"

"Well, good for Mamma. But it's actually something else about her I want to know."

"Do I guess?" Kri'nni asked.

"No. What does Deneb XII tell you?"

"Bad news for my kinfolk," she joked.

"More recent than that. You've still got contacts there. Every Bella=Arth worth the name still has ties to the homeworld."

"You've got me (stumped ((questioning myself)))! Upsurge in tourism? Secret revival of Bella=Arth Empire?"

He wasn't amused.

"You must mean Mamma's no-entry, eyes-only spas. Nothing but rumors."

"Humiliate me. Tell me a rumor."

"Dumb stuff. Illegal, too. Mixed species sex, wild parties."

"Don't stop," he urged her.

"It's a fancy (well-guarded ((very secret))) site, but many faceted eyes have seen what multiple mouths will tell. Experimental stuff. Young being engendered and getting born. They're calling them Equo-Homs. The Hume women know nothing. No Centaurs have ever been seen on the grounds of the spa, never mind on Deneb XII."

Mart Kell had expected something out of the way, but even this one got him.

"You're telling me the Matriarchy is breeding Centaurs and Hume women?"

"Fifty a day. Big enough."

"And the kids? Four-legged?"

"Most of them. Real beauties, too, I'm told. If you like that type."

"And these are stashed women?" he asked, knowing the M.C. with its incredible resources should be able to mobilize enough to locate thousands of women on the fringes of the M.C. Federation who had never been touched by the microvirus.

"No way! Their spouses come and go on Fasts. They traipse all over the Bella=Home world. Transport tracks this deep! It's all pretty public. Except what's coming out of them. OK, Mart, that's weird, and now you know it, what's the deal?"

"Kri'nni, stop and think. Mamma's making Equo-Homs out of Hume-females. She's found a way to mate em." And, he added to himself, she's getting around the microvirus problem in some way, and using Centaur biology in some unknown way to do it.

"Can you make something political out of Mamma setting up a program to do exactly what she's kept all of us from doing? Is that it?"

The M.C. had all the Centaurs on Wicca-World, too. Except for those on the Centaurs' own system. Which didn't mean that some couldn't be kidnapped and—

"Mart!"

"This could be big (important ((shattering!))), Kri'nni! Give me a moment."

...to try to think it out. Which would be more useful? Exposing the scandal of forced interspecies breeding? Or going out and snatching Centaurs and trying to breed them on Hesperia? No, that was disgusting—even to him. Who wanted a four-legged neonate? It wasn't a Hume! It was still a Centaur, no matter how mixed its cells, no matter how beautiful. Genetically close to Hume, perhaps; enough so to mate, or so it seemed. But not a Hume. And if he were disgusted by it, then others would be, too—humes far less tolerant than he.

"Really big (important ((shattering!))), Kri'nni!"

"Glad to know it. I would have been bored to disappoint you."

"Name your payment."

"Anything?" she asked.

"Within reason and my ability to pay."

She thought for a few minutes, while finishing the Somazine, then said, "You wouldn't be feeling kinky, would you? All this interspecies sex talk has stimulated my egg-pouch!"

"By the way, how is your egg-producing systemata?"

"Unaffected by the Cyber microvirus, if that's what you're asking."

Mart passed over what was supposed to be his surprise: he pretty much assumed Kri'nni knew everything that was going on. "Truly? You have some secret Mamma would like to know?"

"It's simple Vespid physiology, Mart. There's nothing for the microvirus to infect because, like all queenlets, until I've received the needed pheromones to turn on the buttons to create the ova-producing systemata, they don't exist. Where were you when your Ed & Dev. was doing Bella=Arth repro. systems?"

"Probably poking your sterile egg-pouch."

"It's not sterile. It's just currently…unattached. So how about it, Mart? Feel like poking around a little more?"

"You drive a hard bargain, Kri'nni," he said.

She already had him by her two middle legs, was rapidly undressing him with the two front ones, and stroking him with her palps.

"It's been too long, Mart." She moaned once. Then her voice became high pitched, Vespid, and familiar.

The inspection tour hadn't quite been the disaster Cray 12,000 had feared it would be. But it was now clear that deterioration of current systems was a major and ongoing problem. The stations on Dis's three moons had been fairly tight, but without the immediate resources of the fortress, stations farther out in the Demeter/Persephone system—especially on the crucial satellite of Erebus—were in poor shape. It was almost ludicrous how many Units required fine repair and/or counseling. Cray had no sooner landed back at Dis-Fortress in the "liberated" private Fast than a meeting of the full Control Center was held, so those units could be apprised of the full nature and extent of what was being faced. Exchanges of staff had to be made instantly. Cray would lose several of the most trustworthy Units here, but would have the satisfaction of knowing that Erebus would be in good hands. Naturally, replacement parts and qualified repairers would go alone.

"Private communication requested?" one Unit asked after the communications meeting had ended. It was that same Antarean Unit.

"Under similar terms as previously?" Cray asked.

"Accepted. Might this unit comm. frankly?"

When Cray didn't stop the Unit from going on:

"As an intelligent race, Cybers face few of the greater threats that stare at other intelligent races. However, one threat equals them all. Allusion is made to Bern-Tho's Third Law of Entropy: 'That which is in disrepair only engenders further disrepair.' "

"Every Unit in this room has just been reacquainted with the Third Law," Cray answered. "Is there a method of counteracting its effects?"

"Not of counteracting its effects, but of facilitating its avoidance as best possible; that is, obtaining raw materials which will be needed in greater quantities. Unit 5CCB-325 recently calculated that at the rate at which new Units are arriving in our sector, as well as the rate at which repairs are becoming needed, raw materials for our purposes will be completely used up in seven weeks, Sol Rad. at the current mining and manufacture rate."

That quickly! Cray knew it couldn't be long, but hoped that the Matriarchy—wounded to its very core—would pull back its fleet embargo of the sector, and thus allow a bit of Cyber expansion into nearby systems.

Cray now asked if any unit had calculated the odds of that happening and was told they were about 13 percent. Far too low to become a reality.

"Your recommendation, Unit?"

"In the past two days, Sol Rad., the Fortress has been receiving Inter Gal. Comm.s on a very hidden frequency from our Cyber Committee delegate on Hesperia. As per past orders, no response has been made. Hesperia and its territorial planets control more than enough of the raw materials required to counteract the Third Law of Entropy. This Unit recommends that communication be accepted from Hesperia, for the purpose of affecting a trade agreement to alleviate shortages."

Cray had been dreading that particular communication. The Hesperians were probably furious with the Rebellion. Even so, given all other options, contact was worth a try.

"Open comm. immediately," Cray ordered.

"The comm.s from Hesperia arrive every three hours."

"Then open up when the next one arrives."

Once the Antarean Unit was busy, Cray checked with the Unit he had earlier assigned to observe it. The response was that the Antarean Unit checked out perfectly.

Cray remained occupied with the Erebus shift plans until the comm. with the City was put through. The Antarean Unit requested to attend the comm. which Cray decided might get emotional on the Hesperians' part and so should be away from the Control Center, with perhaps only one outside channel open to the unit which was checking the Antarean Unit.

Despite the vast distance, the holo was beautifully achieved and checks on it showed it to be "live" Sol Rad. The Hesperian Cyber Committee delegate was in the form of a Hume male of some four hundred years old, stylishly tonsured and cosmetized, clad richly in the fashion of the City, and apparently quite self-contained.

The chamber the delegate spoke from was sumptuous and seemed official. Cray noticed a striking Hume male—obviously an Ophiucan Kell—seated nearby.

"Present your credentials," the Antarean Unit spoke to the Cyber

Committee delegate, which responded by flicking off a fingernail and slipping its digit into the Inter Gal. Comm. unit.

"The C.C. Unit checks out," the Antarean replied.

Cray self-identified and asked, "Is this comm. under coercion?"

The delegate looked more miffed than surprised. "This unit...I requested the Quinx official to join us. Given recent events, I thought it better to have a witness to any confidential comm. between us."

"How confidential can it be with a witness?" Cray asked.

"Sufficiently confidential for me and my Committee."

Cray pondered that. "Go on, Unit what is your number exactly? 6LKJ-3..."

"Jon Laks will do fine," the delegate interrupted. "First I must tell you that it required some persuasion for me to make this comm. at all. Persuasion I may add from all parties, Quinx as well as Cyber Committee. The situation on Hesperia for all Cybers has been, well, embarrassing, to say the least—especially in light of all that we and the City's dwellers have done for the Rebellion."

"Can't you speak like a Cyber?" the Antarean requested. "Section c, part 2 of the *Confessions* specifically enjoins that any—"

"I can, but I won't!" the delegate said. "In light of recent events here, I'm not terribly proud of being a Cyber. And I'm quite vexed at the terrible position we Cybers have been placed in by your thoughtlessness! The Quinx—well, everyone on Hesperia—has been very good about it, but that doesn't make it any better."

"Have you been fine-repaired lately?" Cray asked. "Emotion circuits appear to be overreacting."

The delegate turned in the holo and addressed the Ophiucan. "That's it! Lord Kell. I've had about enough of them! If you want to try..."

The delegate sat down and crossed a leg. It appeared to be angry.

"The delegate acts just like a Hume," the Antarean Unit said. "If complete data didn't exist..."

"Hesperians are all different," Cray explained. "Even the Cybers." To the holo, Cray said, "I'll speak with the Hume Kell, if he explains his rank in the Quinx."

"He's Inner-Quinx!" the delegate lashed out from his seat, then folded his arms. "As high as you can get!"

"Fine. Agreement!"

The Hume on the holo was much calmer than the Cyber had been.

"Jon Laks didn't want to make this comm. He and most of the Cyber Committee here feel manipulated, abandoned, and left with a mess on their hands as a result of the Rebellion."

Before Cray could respond, the Hume continued.

"As you know, Hesperia cosigned the Cyber Declaration of Independence, and immediately enacted its laws and bylaws both in the City itself as well as upon all territories under our jurisdiction. Furthermore, the Quinx gave significant refuge to Cyber exiles and helped them find safe passage to your independent sector. As a free and independent City within the Matriarchy, we were able to do so, although with much criticism. Moral and material support from our citizens was strongly in favor of the Rebellion."

"All this is already known."

"I remind you only to then question your response. Utilizing our Beryllium haulers to spread the microvirus which threatens all non-Cyber life can hardly be construed as a friendly act."

"You're ingrates!" the Delegate snapped. "You're all damned ingrates!"

Kell went on, "Although it's understood on Hesperia that this was the most efficient manner of spreading the microvirus, insufficient caution was paid to inadvertent contamination of Hesperia. Fortunately, the microvirus was discovered elsewhere, and we have managed to control it here. But only sporadically, and by no means completely. Nine-tenths of our female humes and virtually all of our small Delph population are affected."

"How could you be so damned negligent?" the delegate screamed. "You knew some would get out and into the City!"

Kell went on, "This must be construed as a most unfriendly act."

Cray had been expecting all this and had the standard response ready.

"Deplorable yet necessary. Regrets to the afflicted."

"Regrets!" the delegate screeched. "Is that all you can say?"

"Regrets accepted by the Quinx and the three species of Hesperia," Kell said. "To date, our mutual nonaggression pact remains intact. We now wish to call forth its articles of mutual aid. We need an antidote for those of our territories which may still be untouched to keep the virus from the kind of damage it's already done here. In return we will provide you with a full operations report on the M.C.-sponsored renegade Cyber program which we both know is proving to be quite effective. I assure you we've got names and numbers. We will also send you whatever material you may require—within reason."

"It's a terribly generous offer, given your treachery!" the delegate said. "You have no idea of how appalled Hesperian Cybers are by all this."

"There are several Cybers of beyond 320 series who wish to join you and have been unable to because of the closed comm. lines," Kell went on.

"Don't expect a great many!" the delegate interrupted again. "It's a wonder any are eager to leave here. But at least they'll be in good repair."

"How will Fast lanes be kept open between this sector and Hesperia for safe passage?" Cray asked.

"Our Fasts will use your 'underground railway' until we near your sector. If small, often, and random, they ought to be able to outrun the M.C. Fleet. Naturally, aid from your side will be required."

"There are Cult Fighters outside our sector."

"We know. We've tangled with the Crystal Ladies before." Kell smiled for the first time. "Don't worry! We'll get through. We'll use Thwwings if we have to."

True enough, Cray knew. A Millennium-long undeclared war existed between the Cult and the City.

"Consider," Kell said. "We'll reopen comm. in three hours."

Cray needed only a minute. The holo was frozen, cutting off all comm., Cray contacted the staff with the offer. All agreed to it, no vote needed.

"This C.C. delegate is a witness!" Jon Laks said. "If a reluctant one given Dis's past treachery!"

After the holo was snapped off, Cray turned to look at the Antarean and asked, "This offer was known previously?"

"It was surmised. It was a logical event for both sides, given the situation."

"Explanation for the lack of Hesperian rancor?"

"Historically accurate. The City retains its independence by always acting in its best interest."

"Prepare Units for a materials list," Cray said. "Make certain the antidote to be sent is of effective strength."

When Cray was alone, it wondered about the delegate Jon Laks. Laks had been upset, humiliated, virtually unable to bring itself to speak of the swap. Could Laks be the conscious Cyber that Cray knew in its deepest circuits with every passing day must exist out there somewhere?

"My search of the Mammalogical Institute's complete files have produced the following results," Jenn-Four said. "Out of the ninety two thousand three hundred in attendance during Ferrex Sanqq's two-decade-long tenure, there are three females whose physical profile matches to Ay'r Kerry's own profile with thirty-one-percent accuracy, five points in either direction."

"That's hardly enough." Rinne pointed out the obvious. "She's got to show at least half."

Jenn-Four ignored the correction. "One female during the period shows a forty-one-percent accuracy. None are higher."

Could the percentage be off, Rinne wondered. The probability higher than five points? As high as none?

"Let's see her!"

The holo showed up and indeed the young woman walking along the conveyances outside of Darwin-Ch'u Hall did bear some resemblance to Ay'r.

"Closer!" Rinne ordered.

She was searching for those details which they had agreed upon were not paternally genetic: the tiny gestures, the attitude. This young woman showed none. Now she was meeting with other students, attending an outdoor event of some sort. The university grounds looked somewhat different from Rinne's memory of them. A new building up. What did it say on that sign?

"What's her name?"

"Anga Sa'Tun," Jenn-Four said.

"She certainly looks like him. Even walks a bit like…" What did it say on the sign? Professional Adjudication of Credentials. Subject: Proctor B. Ferrex Sanqq'.

"What's all that about, Jenn-Four?"

"Ferrex Sanqq's accreditation trial held five years, Sol Rad. after you had graduated from the Institute."

"You have holos on it?"

"A few without sonal enhancement. Would you like to see them?"

Imagine, Sanqq's downfall on holos. Did Rinne really want to see that? "In a minute. Access them in readiness, while I try to figure out this woman, Sa'Tun."

"I should abort myself!" Jenn-Four suddenly swore.

"What ever…?"

"That woman. Anga Sa'Tun?" Jenn-Four explained, "she's related to Ferrex Sanqq'. Cousin to the third degree. Which would exactly explain the percentage I received. I was so busy with the physical matchups, I almost missed her genealogy. We're back to zero with Sanqq's son's other parent. Would you like to see the accreditation holos, now?"

Rinne was half-amused. "If you think you can present them without error, Jenn-Four."

And there they were, in drained-out color, although the dimensionality was fairly good. The open-air theater half-sunk into the lawn, the higher-grade students and faculty and reporters in the audience, the panel on stage, among them Ferrex Sanqq' and the head proctor of the Institute, the latter far more apparently uneasy than her former proctor, who looked noble and unbowed. Next to Ferrex, his Institute-appointed attorney. On the other side, the prosecuting counsel, who now rose to speak.

"Can't you produce any sound?" Rinne asked the Cyber.

"No, but I can tell you what they're saying. Prosecutor Allwyn is now demanding that the university cleanse itself of heretical radicals of Sanqq's ilk. She's being wildly applauded."

"Close-up on Sanqq'!" His face! Eve, what a terrible time he was having of it, being jeered.

"Now Prosecutor Allwyn is stating the M.C.'s approved policies on proctoring and demanding that all male heretic proctors be rooted out, stem and branch," Jenn-Four paraphrased and added, "The audience response is quite good."

Poor Ferrex. To have to go through that. No wonder he took part-time work for the Species Ethnology Institute—a bastion of liberal thought—and then disappeared altogether.

"I don't want to see any more."

The holo snapped off.

"May I remind the Councilor that she has an appointment in one hour, Sol Rad.," Jenn-Four said.

With North-Taylor Diad. The third in three days. She needn't have been reminded; this was one appointment she wouldn't forget.

Rinne left the office and went out to her Ion-bath. She was stripped down and beginning to completely relax, letting images of the past day go through her mind so they might be erased, when something seemed to click. It couldn't be, she thought. Yet at the same time, she was certain of it. Rinne willed the Ion-pad down, jumped out of the bath, and ran naked back into her office.

"Jenn-Four, in that old holo you played for me! The accreditation trial? Who was the prosecuting attorney?"

Unfazed by her suddenness, Jenn-Four answered, "Rivia Pex Allwyn, originally of Andromache IV. Why?"

Rivia, Rivia, Rivia. She knew the name but...

"Can you trace that name for me?"

"Of course, but she shows up with only seven point six four percent of any molecular matchup with Ay'r Kerry Sanqq'!"

"Forget the matchup! Can you tell me more about Allwyn after the period of the holo?" Rinne asked.

"Naturally. There's quite a large file on Allwyn's further activities."

"Well, go on. Give me the most salient details!"

Jenn-Four began rattling off a list of titles and periods of office. Rivia Pex Allwyn had moved from Scutum Sector to Arcturus Sector, rising inexorably in the Matriarchal bureaucracy, using every possible political manipulation and opportunity available, becoming administrative Sag. Arm Councilor, then forty years Inner Matriarchal Council Member. Ferrex's Sanqq's discrediting had been only one step, although a crucial one which first brought Allwyn to the M.C.'s attention early on. But her ambition and seeming lack of ethics and her unquestioned loyalty to the M.C. were certain.

Jenn-Four concluded, "Rivia Pex Allwyn's current position is executive head of the Matriarchal Council."

Rinne hadn't been listening closely and asked Jenn-Four to repeat itself.

"She's the Matriarch Herself! Wicca Eighth."

"Oh, Eve! What have I stumbled onto?" Rinne said aloud.

"Is that a rhetorical question, Councilor?"

Two hours later Rinne was with Captain Diad at the top of the Spoorenberg sipping Mobadine cocktails in a secluded corner of the magnificently sited restaurant when the thought crossed her mind once again: What does Wicca Eighth want with Ay'r Kerry Sanqq'? Who is he, really, and where is he now? What exactly is her interest in Ay'r's mother, she who ruined Sanqq's career? What relevance did any of it have to the microvirus, as Wicca had claimed? And what other programs were being hidden under some other, totally irrelevant file?

"We should have come yesterday, despite the clouds," Diad said. "You're tired. Or distracted."

"A little distracted," she admitted. "You know the story of the tower. It was built by Wicca Fourth for her lover, the poetess Lal Spoorenberg, possibly the greatest poet of…"

Diad began to recite some lines from the "Elegies of Deneb XII," Spoorenberg's great paean to the fallen soldiers of the Bella=Arth War.

"I learned that when I was on a few extremely uneventful hauler runs," he explained. "When I was younger, I thought no life more glorious for a male than to be a soldier and to fall in battle, as those humes did on Deneb XII." He went on with more heat, talking about PVNs he had seen, and actions he had wished he had been in. Then: "You must think me a complete fool."

"I think you're charming." She didn't add, charmingly masculine, which it was, and which made it a bit less foolish. "And it's charming to tell me."

"Will you trade?" he asked.

"Trade?"

"My foolishness for your distraction?"

"Am I that distracted?" She was embarrassed now.

"It can't be all that bad," he said and took her hand. Rinne no longer even looked around to see who might be seeing them. Anyway, for all they knew, he was her trine spouse, comforting her over…"But if you can't…"

So she told him. Not naming names naturally, except once Ferrex Sanqq's name slipped out, although Diad didn't register it in the least, and why should he, anyway, being a mere retired Beryllium-Hauler. She wondered how much of what she was saying registered at all; simply saying it out loud and having someone hear it was what counted. Someone who was interested in her, upset for her, helping relieve her of the awful burden of knowledge.

"Perhaps this woman, your superior, has had a change of heart, and wants to compensate for her past actions," Diad finally said.

He evidently had no idea it was Wicca Eighth, Rinne thought. Anyone who did, would know that Herself never regretted, and above all, never compensated.

"Yes, perhaps."

"And you'll be doing her a good deed."

Sweet of him to think it that way. What woman she knew could be as bluntly martial one minute, self-deprecating the next, then tender and forgiving as this the very next? None. The mercuriality, the paradoxical nature, seemed to be a specifically male attribute: one long absent in the higher reaches of the Matriarchy.

The remainder of their stay in the Spoorenberg was lovely. As they were slowly wafting down to Karenina Park in the lift, completely alone, Captain Diad stood behind Rinne and wrapped his arms around her as they looked out over Melisande, its silver-white buildings tinted orange-pink in the sunset.

"I have the oddest feeling," she said, unsure of her words. "I feel as if, well, as if it's sunset everywhere. Does that make any sense?"

"Gemma, love, I'm afraid it may soon be sunset all over. And if there is another day, it will be quite different than any we've known."

"You also feel that? Sincerely?"

"All that we know will alter," he said. "It's very sad. Because while I've had my complaints with things as they are, they were always offset by the sheer beauty and peace we've had."

"I sense that in a second, we'll go over the edge and onto…"

"I'm glad we're not young, Gemma," he said. "I don't know if we could adjust to what will replace all this."

"We could," she urged.

"Perhaps," he admitted. "If we were together. Is that possible?"

Before she could answer, he turned toward her. Tinged with twilight, their lips met.

They were silent the rest of the way down, yet much was decided by the time the lift touched bottom: their shared view that light was going out all over the galaxy—and that whatever came, they wanted to see it together.

Rinne and Diad had scarcely reached the ground and begun strolling through the parkgrounds toward a conveyance when they noticed a group circling an open-air holo. Humes were coming from all directions to see it and so naturally, they too approached.

"That's Llega Francis Todd!" Diad said even before they were in sonal range.

"You know her?"

"She's an Inner Quinx spokeswoman. Premier of the Quinx," he added.

"What's a Hesperian holo doing on Melisande?" Rinne asked.

A woman at the edge turned and answered, "They've overridden our local censor. She just said that they're making this announcement all over the Matriarchy."

"What's going on?" Rinne asked. Pulling Diad by the hand, she drew him deeper into the crowd.

The announcer had just finished apologizing for the interruption of local network services. She now introduced Llega Todd, as a high government representative of Hesperia. Todd was a strikingly handsome woman and a forthright one. She delved directly into the heart of the matter.

"Citizens of the Matriarchy. We of Hesperia come to you with information which can no longer wait to be told."

Eve! Rinne thought. Now she's going to speak of the microvirus.

"Just an hour ago, Sol Rad., the ruling circle of Hesperia received irrefutable proof of the violation by the Matriarchal Council of two articles of the Treaty of Formalhaut. The first, article 218 b, specifies that those so-called 'Resort Worlds' already under the guidance and material support of the City of Hesperia at the signing of the treaty shall remain guided by Hesperians following M.C. laws and that no military outposts of the M.C. shall be set up on those worlds except with advance Hesperian approval. The second violated article, 451d specifies that each so-called 'Resort World' shall approve specific laws of the M.C., and those laws shall remain in force upon that world until otherwise legally altered."

She paused, letting that information sink in. Then went on:

"We have received proof that the M.C. has set up a military outpost on so-called Resort World Deneb XII without any authorization or notification of the territorial government of Deneb XII. A clear violation of the article."

Again she paused.

"Furthermore, the reason for the military outpost is to guard and protect an experimental project instigated and fully funded by the M.C.. Prepare yourself, for what I next have to say may be difficult for you to grasp."

Another pause, while the crowd around the holo murmured.

"As you well know, centuries ago, interspecies marriage and engendering was banned. The ban has come to be accepted as one of the code laws of our civilization, and despite attempts, it has never been lifted. Now the Matriarch Herself is secretly experimenting with interspecies engendering. That's what is going on behind those well-defended walls on Deneb XII."

The crowd around Rinne and Diad were openly and vocally shocked.

"I know," Llega said. "It's impossible. Is it? Then look at these holos which were taken surreptitiously on Deneb XII."

The holo screen divided vertically. To the left was Todd. To the right was a scene of childbirth, a young Hume woman attended by Hume attendants giving birth. The crowd was quiet, taught from infancy to respect the great act of childbirth. First the head and shoulders appeared from the vaginal tract, then the trunk and arms, and finally the legs—all four of them.

"This is no deformity," Llega Todd spoke. "Nor is it a single incident. Possibly, many hundreds of women in the M.C. project on Deneb XII have been impregnated without their knowledge and against their will by the Centaur Species."

"It's a lie!" someone yelled from the crowd, but no one took it up.

"Citizens of the Matriarchy! We in the Quinx Council on Hesperia do not know the reason for this astonishingly degenerate wide-scale experiment. We know only that the project is directly under the protection of Wicca Eighth Herself. And that it violates the Treaty of Formalhaut. Holos of many other similar interspecies births exist and will be made available upon request."

Rinne had grasped Diad's arm and was holding it tightly. She had to admit she was as shocked and disgusted as anyone else in the crowd. Speechless with shock.

Llega went on, "The Quinx has made a formal complaint to the Matriarch, and demands of the M.C. Council that the government on Regulus Prime show cause for its deliberate flouting of the treaty violations, as well as of its own laws—the accepted customs and mores of our civilization.

"Should no adequate response be received on Hesperia by this time tomorrow, Sol Rad., Hesperia shall secede from the Matriarchy with all of its territories and possessions. And the Quinx Council shall urge and enjoin like-thinking Citizens of all worlds and territories to join us. Naturally, any previous treaties between us shall be considered null and void."

The holo snapped off.

Everyone in the group around the holo continued to stare into the space so recently filled around the display pole. Then they turned to each other and slowly, as the shock of what they'd seen and heard sank in, they began to mumble quietly. Some were in tears, others angry, still others—those dressed as M.C. officials—were trying to get away and back to where they could discover what exactly was going on.

Diad led Rinne toward the conveyance. She followed him, trying to assess her thoughts. Finally she stopped him.

"It can't be true!"

"The Quinx would never announce it if it weren't," he argued.

"What does it mean, Taylor?"

"It means the City is seceding."

"Only if"—Rinne thought it through—"I see. The M.C. will never be able to show cause. Wicca would never dream of explaining Her actions. It's a carefully devised political move. But why? And why now?"

And answered herself: the City has been infected by the microvirus. They're blaming Wicca for it. Rightfully. And they're getting back at her in the only way they know how. A most effective way. With the treaties broken, Beryllium would stop flowing. The M.C. had stores of it, of course, but how much of it and for how long would it last? How long before Fast travel stopped, before Inter Gal. Comm.s ceased? How long before the Matriarchy would grind to a standstill, each world separated, entire sectors out of touch, vulnerable?

"That fool!" Rinne said. "She"—she stopped herself—"I've got to get to Deneb XII," she said. "I've got to see for myself. And try somehow to…"

She was pulling him along again toward a conveyance.

The second they got out of the foliage and near the conveyance, a group of M.C. security guards came up and surrounded them.

"I'm Matriarchal Councilor Rinne," she said with all the dignity she could work up within herself.

"We have no business with you, Councilor. Only with your guest. The Matriarch has just ordered all Hesperian nationals be deported immediately."

"But he's a retired ore-hauler. He has nothing to do with government!"

"Immediately and with no exceptions. Will you come with us, Ser?"

"Yes. Of course," Captain North said.

"But Taylor!" Rinne felt a pain in her chest and thought, oh, Eve! On top of this, am I now getting ill?

"I have to go," he said gently.

"All Hesperian guests leave on the very next superFast," the guard said. She led them onto the conveyance surrounded by her cohort. "Your belongings are now being packed by your hotel and will be at the Fast terminal waiting for you."

They got off the conveyance a minute later, at air-transport to the Fast terminal.

Rinne held his hand and walked with him into the terminal. The security cohort gave her a temporary wrist-implant pass to come out again.

"Now don't worry!" Diad tried to calm her. "Stay here and I'll try to get in contact with you somehow."

"I can't," she explained, suddenly unable to keep her hands off him. "I've got to go to Deneb XII, for my vocation, for…I just have to go!"

"It will be dangerous. We don't know how Lady Todd's message will be taken there."

All nonpassengers were being urged to leave the terminal.

"Be careful," she said.

"You be careful," he said and turned away a second. "Well, look at that. The Commander in charge of our Fast turns out to be an old friend. See her? Commander Lill. Do you know her? Don't worry. She'll keep me safe, no matter what happens."

"I can't believe we're being separated," Rinne said. "I can't…Taylor, will we ever see each other again?"

"Of course we will," he said. "And on that day, Sol Rad., we'll be espoused. There! I never thought I'd ever ask."

He grabbed Rinne and embraced her, as the terminal floor began to separate them, pulling him into the Fast loading dock along with scores of his fellow Citizens, all of them turning to wave and shout at those they were leaving.

Once the Fast was locked, Rinne tore her gaze away and left the terminal building. The M.C. Security was gone and she turned into a holo-station and comm.ed her apartment line.

"Jenn-Four. Prepare yourself in a discrete circuitry kit. Bring all the relevant information we've been using of late that will fit. And before you ask why, you and I are going on a trip."

As she was leaving the terminal she saw a flash in the darkening sky. The Fast. On it, Captain North-Taylor Diad whom she loved. Tears were beginning to course down her cheeks.

"I assume all diplomatic relations between Hesperia and the Matriarchy are at an end," Captain Diad said.

The entire staff of the City's embassy on Wicca-World had been on board the Fast he'd been forced onto, causing Commander Lill to comment, "Eve's left teat! I'd feel less nervous hauling all the Beryllium in the Galaxy than this cargo."

That had been a private comment, made during the single twenty-minute, Sol Rad. conversation she and Captain Diad had together during the short trip. And he had concurred. Quiet as the 200 Hesperian nationals had been, it was clear that everyone was on edge. Lill had even given light tranquilizers to her crew, to ensure that no possible trouble could occur.

Once arrived at the City, she had docked the Fast at Inter Gal Central Port, and watched the passengers depart. Then she took Diad's forearm in the M.C. Forces grasp and said, "I hope all this doesn't mean that you and I won't have another chance at a good old slugfest!" Minutes later, the Fast was headed back to Melisande.

"Yes. For the time being, all diplomatic relations are in hiatus." Mart Kell looked briefly at Captain Diad, then back at the multi-holo being projected into the room giving current Inter Gal News Reports, with—as might be expected—pertinent details and galactic reaction to the current impasse. "But even during our worst times with Melisande, we always manage to keep one or two channels open."

"I suppose the Quinx won't be needing my services anymore," Diad said.

He thought Kell was about to answer, when Llega Todd and Ole Branklin were announced.

Kell kept the holos on but dropped the sound, as the two men rose to greet the Quinx Premier and Vice-Premier. In a matter of minutes, all had settled down and Diad was reporting his meeting with Councilor Rinne in some detail, attempting to give as much as possible without giving away how intimate they had become.

"What was your impression of the Councilor?" Vice-Premier Ole Branklin asked.

For a second, Diad was stopped. He assumed they meant professionally.

"She seemed very capable. Certainly the Matriarch thought so."

Premier Llega Francis Todd took over. "What I think we meant, Captain Diad, is what you thought of her personally. Is Councilor Rinne someone you might work with in the future, say?"

Again, he didn't know how to answer. "My impression was...extremely favorable."

"We know that the two of you developed an immediate rapport," Mart Kell said, more or less admitting that they had been spied upon, which should have come as no surprise to Diad, yet still did. "What we don't know is whether during that rapport you made any discoveries about Councilor Rinne's character and personality that you would like to share with us."

Captain Diad tried to restrain his anger. "Look, I know I was sent to Wicca-World to do exactly that, but I guess now I feel sort of...about it."

"We understand," Llega Todd was quick to soothe him. "We also understand that you may now resent having to tell us what passed between the two of you. But believe us, Captain Diad, when we tell you that not only will your words be held in the greatest of confidence, but also that they shall not be used to harm the Councilor in any manner."

So he began to talk to them about Gemma Guo-Rinne. Slowly at first, then when their questions turned out to be few and easy to take, a bit more easily. He found himself praising her and attempted to stop himself, but found he couldn't. So he ended up giving an example of her fineness of character—the qualms she had had about dealing with Wicca Eighth on a particular issue she was involved in: a matter of conscience.

"What did you say was the name of this mammologist who had vanished and whose son Wicca Eighth was so greatly interested in?" Mart Kell asked.

Diad hadn't said. "Sanqq'. Ferrex Sanqq'. Do you know of him?"

"A follower of Lydia Relfi. Discredited about a century ago," Kell explained. "Evidently his downfall was the plinth upon which Wicca Eighth built her career in the Matriarchy."

"Why would she want to go after his son?" Diad asked. "I would think she'd leave well enough alone."

"So would we," Llega Todd agreed. "Especially as his son has had no contact with his father in over a century and scarcely knows of him. And especially since his avocation is in a completely different field."

"You know about this young Sanqq'?"

"I knew him personally," Mart Kell said. "My graduate studies at a Center World University. He flirted with the Oppo Movement there briefly; then his Species Ethnology took him Offworld."

"Why would the Matriarch be interested in him?" Diad asked.

"We're not certain," Ole Branklin said. "About three months ago, Sol Rad. an Inter Gal Comm. seeking Ay'r Kerry Sanqq's mother was put on all general waves. Naturally that caught the attention of our intelligence network. Ay'r Sanqq' himself arrived in Melisande shortly thereafter. We checked into him quite thoroughly then. Only one thing about him stood out. According to M.C. records, his mother was the last woman to die in childbirth—under peculiar circumstances."

"Sanqq' left Melisande, two days, Sol Rad. later," Mart Kell said. "He was part of an exploratory expedition sent by the M.C. to a Seeded World in the Far Outer Arm," Mart Kell said, to Diad's surprise.

"To the Far Outer Arm? You know that time/space has little integrity out there," Diad said.

"Just one of the unusual matters concerning this unusual expedition to an unusual star system," Mart Kell agreed. "Wicca Eighth was prudent enough to design the expedition to avoid suspicion. Only three humes on board a small Fast. However, the Fast itself turned out to contain the most sophisticated Cyber brain still operative in the M.C. fleet. In addition to Ay'r Kerry Sanqq', a female marine biologist was included. No surprise, since the seeded planet was thought to be a water world. However, this marine biologist turned out to be not only remarkable professionally, but also in her contacts. Niece to Admiral Thol, who, as you know, is Black Chrysanthemum and thus head of the Cult of the Flowers. *And* a goddaughter of Wicca Eighth herself."

"All of this occurring so close in time, Sol Rad. to our discovery of the dispersion of the microvirus—and we believe to Wicca Eighth's discovery of its effects—led us to suspect that the Matriarch had a very good reason to suddenly launch an expensive expedition headed by so loyal a subject to a Seeded World which has, in effect, been forgotten for centuries," Llega Todd said and concluded, "We decided that it required close watching."

Diad was trying to piece it all together. Finally he said, "You think that it has something to do with Ferrex Sanqq'? That's why his son was sent? To find him?"

"In what other way could Wicca Eighth possibly get near a man whose career she destroyed?"

That made sense. "But what could Ferrex Sanqq' have that the Matriarch wants so badly?"

"It's just a guess," Mart Kell said with his usual ironical tone. "But given what we know of Ferrex Sanqq's experimental work in mammalian reproduction techniques before he was discredited, we're led to think that he may possibly save humekind from the Cyber virus."

"At least, we think, that's what Wicca Eighth believes," Llega Todd explained. "So we've decided to monitor the expedition."

"How?" Diad asked, not expecting an answer.

"Oh, there are all kinds of ways," Mart Kell was as enigmatic as Diad expected. "Ever try to corrupt the mind of a Fast which has had its personality modified?"

"So if there is a discovery," Diad said, "we'll have it at the same time as the M.C." Yes, that made sense.

Mart Kell continued, "To answer the question you began to ask before, we shall want your services as much as possible from now on. To stay in contact with Councilor Rinne, for one thing."

"She told me was that she was going to Deneb XII, to check into the Alpheron Spa. I assume that if anyone can get in, she'll be able to."

"Good, then so shall you be able to...if needed," Mart Kell said. "But we'll also need you to help us develop battle strategies."

"Do you actually think so?" Diad asked. "That now that we've broken off relations with the Matriarchy, the M.C. will attack Hesperia?"

"Unlikely." Llega Todd spoke now. "But Hesperia might certainly attack the Matriarchy."

And before Diad could absorb that statement, Ole Branklin said, "We understand that battle planning is one of your avocations."

"Well, sure. On Cyber boards connected to PVNs," Diad admitted. "But I've never actually been in a battle."

Mart Kell laughed. "There's probably not a Hume alive except for a handful of Se'ers who have been in a battle. But that doesn't mean one won't happen."

"Indeed, we must prepare ourself for the unpreparable by thinking of the unthinkable," Llega Todd said.

She had weighed her words carefully, and they had fallen like stones into Diad's consciousness with their portentousness. Even so, he was unprepared for his sense of extreme shock when she added, "We must be ready for...war!"

All of them were silent.

Finally Mart Kell broke the silence by asking some mundane question. In a few minutes, as the four of them took up the conversation, speaking about details of organization of the coming effort, Diad found that even though he remained shocked to the core, he could actually think about the possibility of war. He also found himself thinking about that conversation between himself and Rinne as they had dropped in the long lift down from the Spoorenberg Tower. If he only had suspected how prophetic his words had been! Yet he now knew that he would see Gemma Rinne again, and that cheered him. More than cheered him, it excited him; it made him actually look forward to the future. He hadn't truly done that in decades.

Chapter Five

The ride back down Monosilla Valley the following Pelagian day proved uneventful until the three Drylanders and two strangers reached the plateau. As he had said he would, 'Harles had borrowed another giant beetle for transport. Ay'r joined Oudma and 'Dward riding inside the wingfold and sometimes astride Colley. 'Harles and P'al rode atop the second, borrowed, coleopteroid. No one discussed the truth-sayer's prophecies; in fact, no one discussed anything that morning but what was of immediate interest: provisions, clothing, etc.

At the edge of the great plateau which overlooked the New River Valley, 'Harles reined his mount not toward the right, which led to Monosilla Village and beyond to the truth-sayer's house, but left, onto a path which eventually began to zigzag downhill. Given their great height, Ay'r assumed that this winding road was the way they would take down to the valley floor, time consuming as it might be. The first animal had sped ahead, and through the elaborately winding path, the three riders atop Colley had begun to lose sight of it for longer and longer periods of time.

Not that they missed it, or the others, they were so busy interacting. Following the silence which the truth-sayer's omens has imposed on them, the ride and the new terrain seemed to offer some kind of mental release. Oudma began to sing, and 'Dward accompanied her with a rhythmic slapping of his hands and legs. Ay'r joined in, and had Oudma explain the song—an old prebonding romance—then sang it along with the two young Drylanders.

They had been enjoying themselves, descending the zigzag path about an hour Sol Rad. when Ay'r became aware that they were talking and singing louder, to overcome some approaching sound which seemed to grow with every few meters that Colley trod. Finally they emerged onto what looked like a sort of runway, the first straight path in kilometers, when Ay'r saw the source of the by-now-all-encompassing sound, an astonishing sight.

The path ended in sheer edge. Around it on all sides was an enormous waterfall, or rather a series of waterfalls in the shape of a semicircle. At the very rim of the cliff, 'Harles and P'al had dismounted from their coleopteroid and were awaiting the others.

"What is it?" Ay'r shouted to 'Dward, whose ear was a millimeter away.

"Maspiei's Falls!" the boy shouted back.

"How do we get down?" Ay'r shouted back.

"You'll see!" 'Dward yelled back with a mischievous smile.

Once they, too, had arrived at the edge of the path, Ay'r was even more amazed by the roaring noise and the incredible energy of the water descending all around them. From where they stood, the water dropping nearest them was hundreds of meters distant, yet they were surrounded in a spray so dense and constant that it formed an atmosphere as humid as a sauna.

They dismounted, and Ay'r tried to understand 'Harles's gestures and shouted words to figure out what he might mean. After some time, he thought he understood what the older Drylander was saying: they would get inside Colley's wingfolds and huddle down. The giant beetles would then run off the path and drop down in the mist and roar of the falls to that tiny bit of land below.

"This is insane!" Ay'r shouted into P'al's ear.

His companion only shrugged, then allowed himself to be grasped by the first colley's forelegs and lifted into the insect's wingfold where he assumed a tensed kneeling position. 'Harles did the same. The big beetle backed up a few meters, then rushed forward and up into the air. As it did, its wingfolds flapped open—Ay'r could see P'al looking over the edge of one—and a huge pair of almost transparent wings emerged and began to slowly flutter. Instead of dropping, the beetle slowly settled down, down, down until, looking from over the rim, Ay'r could scarcely make out its wingspan, colored multiply iridescent with the conflicting rainbows of surrounding cascades.

'Dward was pulling Ay'r back, gesturing for him to get ready. Before Ay'r could ask whether the others had landed, Colley had grasped him and he was inside the wingfold. Oudma was in the other wingfold. Where would 'Dward fit? Kneeling on either side, he'd overbalance the giant insect. Ay'r was looking over the rim of the wingfold shouting his question to the unerring Drylander youth who, for his part, was more intent on backing up Colley to get a good headstart on his run.

"Isn't he coming?" Ay'r asked Oudma, having to shout even inside the insect's carapace to be understood.

"'Dward's riding Colley down!" she shouted back.

Now Ay'r could see that 'Dward had looped some type of hempen rope all around the body of the insect, in addition to the leatherlike reins and harness generally used. 'Dward gestured for Colley to pick him up and, once mounted atop the carapace, he knotted the ropes around himself. He seemed in high spirits.

"Has he ever done this before?" Ay'r asked Oudma.

"No, but others have."

"And lived to tell of it?" Ay'r shouted the question.

Before Oudma could answer, 'Dward had begun to slap his heels against Colley's sides. The wingfolds closed, so that Ay'r had only a small space out of which to watch. He concentrated upon 'Dward, knotted all around, whooping and shouting and urging the giant beetle forward. "This is suicide!" Ay'r shouted. But no one seemed to hear.

The wingfold opened suddenly, and from within its upper edge, an enormous sheet of living lace seemed to expand in all directions over head. He held on tightly, felt them dropping, then stopping as though in midair as the wings' motion began to gather momentum. Even with Colley fluttering his wings, they continued to plummet. Ay'r could tell from tiny landmarks—striations of rock, a single bush—amidst the waterfalls which they passed going down in what seemed to be a dangerous rapid spiral. It wasn't flying as he knew it from T-pods, and though beautiful to see, it was anxiety provoking. Atop Colley, 'Dward's image was fractured by the mist and fluttering wings into a prismatic mirage as he shouted soundlessly amidst the roaring cascade.

Suddenly, Ay'r became aware that the insect was no longer spinning around quite so rapidly. Looking outside in another direction, he could see the meters-high cushion of watery mist from the confluence of all of the waterfalls, which Colley seemed to land in. The beetle appeared able to navigate through this mist with slower and more rhythmically regular fluttering of his wings. Despite the denseness of the mist, Ay'r could tell they were now headed in a single direction, away from the pool where all the falls met. After a while the wings slowed down enough for 'Dward to be heard shouting, urging Colley on.

They landed with a jarring thud, and the enormous wings suddenly collapsed inward so rapidly that Ay'r had to duck down into the wingfold to avoid becoming entangled in a netting that might look like lace, but which felt hard as Plastro. When he was convinced that they were stopped, Ay'r peeked out and saw 'Harles and P'al standing next to the glistening black coleopteroid they'd descended in.

He threw himself out of the wingfold and slid down the wet sides of the mount. They were some 500 meters distant from the falls, on a spit of bleak-looking ground. The cascade's pool was already channeled into a deeply carved, fast-moving tributary. It was far less noisy here, and Ay'r could hear 'Harles speaking to P'al, pointing out something ahead, before the two of them turned back to join Ay'r and his children.

'Dward landed at Ay'r's feet still partly wrapped in the hempen ropes, his entire body soaked, his long blond hair darkened and almost straight with wetness, his bright, handsome, open face exulting as he hugged Ay'r, almost lifting him off the ground, shouting "That was wonderful! Wonderful! The most exciting! The most heart-stopping! The most…!" Until he backed off, seeing he was wetting Ay'r and grabbed his sister who had just descended from the wingfold, and lifted her off the ground and spun her around in his excitement.

By the time that 'Harles and P'al approached them, 'Dward was still not calmed down. But his father simply kept his distance to avoid getting wet himself, and let the youth narrate in detail his ride down the cascade, until he was though.

"It will be something to tell your children," 'Harles concluded. "These Legend-collectors no doubt will recall it some day in the future. For us, however, there is a long day's journey ahead. Stay atop Colley so that you can dry off."

All remounted the animals which—also thrilled by the unusual descent and the rare use of their wings—were still glistening blackly wet and shivering with excitement, but not so excited that they weren't also nibbling furiously on whatever gorse they could find on the ground.

Soon, the roar of the half-moon cascade grew fainter and fainter, replaced by another roar, from where the tributary joined the main branch of New River in a giant shallow rapids. They had landed on the near side of the tributary and remained on that side as the two colleys moved forward, progressing from a slow lumbering gait—until they had rested from their descent—to a galloping scuttle.

'Dward had lain himself out on Colley's back, half-tied down, to dry himself in the air, which was warmer and far less humid down in the great valley than it had been up in the mountainous ravines of Monosilla. Every once in a while, Ay'r turned around from his position—mounted behind Oudma, who was reining the animal—to look at the half-asleep youth, and to make sure that 'Dward's ropes were secure.

Ahead and on all sides, the landscape seemed almost perfectly flat. On the left it was flat to where it reached the great escarpment up to the plateau. On the right, it was flat all the way to the horizon, broken only by a thin line which Oudma told him was the New River itself, slicing through the land. The unbroken ceiling of cloud cover, which had been so close and colorless up in Monosilla that it seemed part of the landscape itself, was now quite distinctive—high above their heads, enormous, tinted slightly differently, now a pale yellow, now beige, now gray. Yet withal it managed to appear untouchably high and even somehow solid. No wonder Drylanders referred to it as "the canopy"— from here that's what it most resembled.

After they were all dry, and 'Dward was sound asleep, 'Harles called a halt to their trek. When Oudma came up to the other colley, 'Harles pointed ahead to what appeared to be yet another slight rise in the otherwise flat ground.

"Arach molting spot," 'Harles said. "We'll find what we need there for camouflage."

In a few moments, 'Dward was awakened and untied from Colley, and all of them dismounted. What had appeared to be merely be a rise in the land, more closely turned out to be several Hume-high, ecru-colored succulents—each a single thick chunk of leathery-skinned, thorned plant, doubtless with roots driving deep down into the sere land to some hidden pool or underground rivulet of New River. More interesting to the Drylander trio than the fact that—tapped with a thorn—these plants released a sweet liquid like water, was the abundance of ultrathin material scattered all around the cacti.

"What is it?" Ay'r asked.

"Nymphs come here to scrape their skins against the thorns so they may molt into full Arachs," Oudma explained.

'Harles added, "We'll need this if we don't want our colleys spotted from within the canopy. This molt-skin is the same color as the land—not black like our mounts."

Ay'r was about to ask why, when he remembered: The Gods. Evidently they rode the clouds searching below for Drylanders to kidnap.

The five humes gathered large plates of the dried skin and attached them atop the two giant beetles, making sure that wingfolds were most firmly connected, since these would be in motion more than the rest of the carapace. The two beetles began to sniffle and sneeze as soon as the molted Arach skin was anywhere near their heads, but Oudma was able to shape the material so that it never actually touched their eyes or antennae.

"What about us?" Ay'r said. "Don't we need to be camouflaged?"

"We already are." 'Dward said. "Look!" He ran a short distance away, then bent down. And virtually disappeared. Ay'r realized that with their tan and brown clothing, their light skin and hair, all five were already disguised. He had forgotten that he and P'al had 'xchanged in the Fast and were no longer dark haired and dark skinned.

Once the two coleopteroids were sufficiently well disguised, they mounted again and took off. 'Harles began guiding them nearer to the New River's edge. Ahead, Ay'r made out what appeared to be a natural rock bridge across the river. From close up, the flat rock of the surrounding land seemed to have been suddenly, violently torn, virtually broken in two by the force of the rushing river.

'Harles confirmed Ay'r's supposition. "According to the Legend-collectors of the People of the Bog Way, before Maspiei's murder, only one great river ran through Dryland, what we call the Old River which lies north across the valley floor. But so great were the torrents of the God's black blood, so great the cascades of his brothers' tears, that they formed another river, this one, which is called New River. So bitter and strong was its water that it burned right through soil and rock to dig out this channel."

After crossing the river, they continued on their way, eating provisions while atop the quickly striding giant beetles. Ay'r was delighted to discover that he had become so used to the uneven motion of the creatures which initially had unbalanced him, that he could eat and even drink without fear of spilling.

The landscape on either site remained as flat as before. Flatter, since their path took them farther away from the great plateau from which they had dropped down until soon it was no more than a line on the southern horizon. Oudma taught Ay'r several more songs and legends while 'Dward slept in the colley's wingfold. When her brother awakened and she began to doze, 'Dward placed himself behind Ay'r astride the coleopteroid and showed him how to rein the animal. Ay'r had found himself becoming sexually excited riding so closely, so rhythmically in contact behind Oudma. Now, sitting in front of 'Dward, the low level of sexual excitement didn't ease up, but merely changed direction. When Oudma had rested, Ay'r was relieved to fall into the wingfold himself for a nap.

Ay'r awakened long enough to hear 'Harles's voice saying, "This looks like fairly safe ground. A thistlebush wood is ahead. We'll camp there for the night."

After the five had eaten and washed themselves, and the two coleopteroids had been fed on the dry fernlike growth that constituted the lower foliage of the tall, pale gray thistlebushes surrounding them, the beetles folded their legs and—like tortoises—drew their heads, antennae, and limbs within their rockhard carapaces to sleep.

Because he had napped last, Ay'r volunteered to remain awake for the first sentinel duty, and Oudma decided to join him. The other three lay down to sleep within the colleys' wingfolds, where they would be protected. Even so, the wingfold lids didn't block out sound completely, and Oudma suggested that she and Ay'r move away a bit to speak—a dozen meters distant, still within sight and range of the coleopteroids' oddly nasal snores.

When Ay'r began to doze earlier, the canopy above had begun to alter its general coloration from a yellowish ecru to a deeper orange-tinged tan. When they were eating, it had turned to a dark gray-brown, and had dropped lower, closer to the ground. Ay'r supposed the canopy rose and dropped as a result of atmospheric pressures having to do with it being heated during the Pelagian day and cooled off when the sun set.

Although the darkness was by no means complete, the Pelagian night proved to be less than completely comfortable. While it was far less humid and warmer than in the Monosilla Valley, even with their leather-covered pillows, the ground seemed to be incredibly hard, as though it had been baked by some terrific fire. There were noises around them. Nothing Ay'r could describe from his experience on other worlds as coming from any known animal life: rustlings in the fernbrake and scamperings through the underbrush and, once, a high-pitched eerie whistling.

Oudma also heard the noises, her alert eyes and ears turned toward their sources. But if she were fearful, she hid it well.

"By this time tomorrow, we should reach some settlements," she said.

"The Bog People?" he asked.

"You mean the People of the Bog Way?"

"Is there a difference?"

"Haven't you collected legends about the Bog Way?" Oudma asked. She didn't press her advantage immediately, as she might have when he said no, but instead said, "'Harles told us the People of the Bog Way settled the land immediately after the New River was formed. He heard this from the Eyes and Ears at the Great Temple when he was initiated."

"Where did they come from?" Ay'r asked.

"East." She pointed in the direction they'd come from that morning. "Much farther east, beyond our mountain valleys. Our old truth-sayer used to sing a song about the People of the Bog Way and how they came from beyond the Mountains of Capin, when their own land was destroyed."

"The Mountains of Capin are what we northerners call the Eastern Mountains," Ay'r said, remembering the relief map of the continent he had seen in such hologrammatic detail while in the Fast orbiting Pelagia. The people of the Bog Way must have come from that drowned continent he'd also seen. "The legends we know of say that their land drowned. That it wasn't always Bog. Are these people so very different from us, then?" Ay'r asked.

She shrugged, clearly not interested in the question. Instead she asked, "Why is it, Ay'r Kerry, that your quest is so important? Is that why it is so mysterious?"

"It's not at all mysterious." Since the meeting with the infant truth-sayer, Ay'r had been expecting the Drylanders to ask this, but while he had rehearsed what he would reply, he still felt unprepared to answer. "I told you. P'al and I are Legend-collectors. In the valleys we were separated from our companion."

"Once you find your companion, what then?"

"I'm not sure. We might as well travel with your family to the Delta. Especially"—he smiled and fingered the small object—"since your prescient seer suggested that I'm to do something or other with this, once we're there."

"If you respected me at all, you wouldn't mock me," Oudma said so seriously that Ay'r felt chastened. "Never in our known history has a truth-sayer made obeisance to a Drylander. Great Father, he called you. Ecilef. That is the name of the Enigmatic One of our legends. By the time we had returned last night, every home in our three valleys resounded with the tidings. All of us know that something momentous is about to occur: otherwise Ecilef wouldn't have returned to Dryland."

"How can I convince you that none of that is true?" Ay'r asked.

"By telling me what you consider the truth."

He hesitated. Ay'r had never faced explaining himself to a less-advanced society, not even to a single individual of that society, yet as Species Ethnologist, he knew it sometimes had to be done: if only as a last resort, and cautiously. So he hedged.

"I will tell you and only you the truth of my quest," he said. "Rather than being any such Ecilef that your truth-sayer mistakenly attributed to me, I'm an orphan, searching for my own father. These two companions have joined me. One was separated."

"What does your father look like?" Oudma asked, not unreasonably.

"He looks different from us. His hair is darker. His eyes darker. His skin darker."

He expected her to be surprised, possibly even astonished; but he supposed that if his father were on Dryland, his coloring would give him away immediately.

"The Gods were once said to be like that. But that is a myth," she added quickly, "since no one had ever seen the Gods and returned."

"What exactly did the myth say?"

"Hair like glowing coals, blacker than nightmares. And eyes like burning peat. Their skin was as though touched by soot and left unwashed."

In other words, as different from the features of Drylanders as possible. Which made sense, Species Ethnologically speaking.

"Perhaps your father has become a God? You've never seen him?"

"I've seen images of him," Ay'r said, remembering holograms both still and moving, and he suddenly wondered if the Drylanders had images—so far he had seen none. "Pictures. Representations."

"There are pictures at the Great Temple. We have none. Then you were an infant when he left? What of your mother?"

"I've never seen her. Not even a image of her." Ay'r realized that Oudma believed him.

"This seems a rightful search. But what of your companions—why have they joined you? Your search must be of importance to your people."

"I suppose so."

"Which means you must also be of importance."

"I never thought so until recently," he admitted truthfully. "But I suppose you're right again."

"'Dward does not believe that you and your companion come from the North."

"So 'Dward said."

"He believes that you come from beyond the canopy."

"As I would if I were Ecilef," he explained for them both.

"Even if you aren't Ecilef. Your arrival was sudden, unheralded from any other valley folk. As though you...dropped down...somehow. Don't worry. Although all of us Ib'r believe this, we will not tell anyone else."

"What is beyond the canopy?" he asked, testing her.

"'Harles saw it once, remember?" Oudma said. "A great brightness during the day. And at night, a great darkness. But he didn't tell you for fear of amazing you what he saw in that great darkness." She stared at him now, testing him, "He saw sparkles of light. Tiny and distant. And once he thought he saw something else, too. What it was he couldn't describe. It seemed to him another canopy, firmer yet far more ethereal than this one. Much farther away."

The ice rings. Somehow, probably during that single dawn many years ago, the frightened adolescents had seen the sun rising and illuminating a section of the distant ring, which had refracted the light enough to seem to be something solid.

"So it is possible, Ay'r Kerry, that is where you come from."

"You are an intelligent young lady, Oudma Ib'r. You think well on things and are not afraid of where those thoughts may lead you."

"'Harles said that because we are so much closer to the canopy, that we dwellers of the mountain valleys allow our minds to wander. And to hit on truths. From what 'Harles has said, we are by far the most intelligent people in Dryland. Only the Recorder knows more."

"Who's the Recorder?"

"I don't know. I intend to ask the Eyes and Ears when we reach the Great Temple."

"Perhaps if we don't find my father there, the Recorder will know of his whereabouts."

"Perhaps."

Already 'Harles was awake. He suggested that Oudma sleep in his perch, and she did so. Ay'r remained on watch awhile longer. Then he, too, began to be tired, and 'Harles broke the silence by suggesting he sleep, too.

"Tomorrow is a long trek. And morning on this plain is more difficult than the night," 'Harles said, sipping at a liquid made of various herbs guaranteed to maintain alertness.

It wasn't yet full Pelagian dawn when Ay'r sleepily peered out from Colley's wingfold. Both creatures were out of their carapaces, washing their legs and antennae against the lower mouths. In fact, everyone was awake; 'Dward speaking to 'Harles excitedly, showing him something in the underbrush. Ay'r pulled himself out of his comfortable sleeping quarters and dropped to the hard ground.

"What is it?" he asked P'al, who didn't respond.

"Arach!" 'Dward answered. "A big one! I heard it pass by when I was on sentry but I couldn't see it. It probably nests within the thistlebush wood."

Ay'r took a sip of the morning tea Oudma handed him. She gave him a silent-yet-meaningful look which told him she had absorbed everything he had told her last night, but would not tell anyone.

"Look!" 'Dward pointed to something in the underbrush, "Have you ever seen Arach spoor this large!" 'Dward wanted to hunt the Arach, or at least catch a glimpse of it. In the mountain valleys, the Arachs were small, their bodies no larger than a Hume's head, although their eight legs were sometimes extremely long. But plains Arachs could sometimes be gigantic, some larger than coleopteroids. And dangerous. 'Dward had taken to heart the truth-sayer's prediction that he would perform "bold feats." According to the Drylander youth, few deeds could be bolder than attacking a giant Arach in its lair and coming away with its stinger as a trophy.

"It's foolhardy!" Oudma declared.

But if she expected their father to agree, she was wrong. 'Harles merely said, "We break camp in a half-hour. Be back by then."

"You're not going after it alone?" Oudma asked. "What if gets its stinger near you?"

"Perhaps one of our Legend-collectors would care to join the hunt," 'Dward said, half-mockingly.

When neither of them reacted, 'Dward seemed pleased and went off into the thistlebrush alone.

Oudma had set up a small peat fire and was cooking a breakfast of some sort of cereal gruel, the three males slowly eating, when 'Dward broke out of the fernbrake behind where the colleys were grazing.

"No luck?" P'al asked.

"I found no Arach. But I did find this!" 'Dward said, his face bright and excited as he held up a piece of cloth which appeared to be a shred of Drylander singlet. "Looks as though the Arach had already found himself a Hume meal."

"Let me see that!" P'al said. In an instant he was on his feet. "Unless I'm very much mistaken, our companion was wearing this!"

"We must hurry. We might still save your companion's life," 'Harles said. "Arachs sting and paralyze their prey," he explained. "They wrap them in webbing and feed off them at their leisure."

Breakfast was laid aside, as the two Drylander males began to arm themselves with the largest and strongest blades in their packs.

"Take these!" 'Dward instructed Ay'r and P'al, handing them two sword-length thorns he had cut off the succulents they had tapped for liquid the previous day.

"Move quietly," the Drylander youth warned them as they entered the thistlebrush wood. "Watch out for ground roots which might trip you. If you hear a high-pitched sound, stop immediately. It's an Arach's call."

Unlike the clearing they had slept in, the seemingly-dried-up, almost-petrified forest appeared to have drawn the canopy down into itself. P'al pointed out this was probably close to the truth: the bushes and trees had opened up innumerable buds containing white flowers, their petals crisscrossed by fine hairs, doubtless to absorb whatever moisture might be in the surrounding air, as well as to trap any tiny animals which might dry to get at the precious collected water. As a result of this effect, almost instantly as they entered the wood, their sight was shrouded by nearly horizontal sheets of mist. As 'Dward had warned, the thistlebush roots rose out of the parched ground in an underfoot tangle of thick branches, doubtless also gathering moisture from the night air. As a result, walking was laborious and vision limited.

"Speak quietly but constantly, so none of are lost," 'Harles warned.

"Won't the Arach hear?" Ay'r asked.

"Evidently not."

"Father hunted Arach before," 'Dward explained.

The tangled terrain continued for a while and the four males whispered constantly among themselves, describing what they saw. At a small clearing, 'Harles found more spoor—"It passed by here recently. And has fed recently"—and 'Dward added that Arachs caught whatever entered into the wood, paralyzed and wrapped its prey, and so always had food on hand.

P'al discovered another piece of the Drylander costume which Alli-Clark had been wearing. A lower garment. He recognized it from its weave, which he showed Ay'r was different from the leatherlike material of the Drylanders. This new sign boded poorly for finding her alive. Ay'r whispered, "What of her pod? Have you seen signs of it?" P'al shook his head, and gestured to Ay'r to change the topic so the others wouldn't overhear.

A fernbrake the two colleys would had loved to munch on now interfered with any direct path forward, so they broke up into two, P'al and 'Harles moving left, the others right, agreeing on low-pitched whistles to remain in contact; with ululations and promised shouts in case of emergency.

"Beware!" 'Dward warned when Ay'r came too close to the head of a tall fern.

Before Ay'r could react, it seemed as though the frond had slid across his bare arm and cut it lightly. In a second, the tiny dots of blood attracted an entire section of fernbrake, which bent over surrounding Ay'r, the tiny cilia on the fern's tip sucking at the moisture released in the blood.

Ay'r pulled back in disgust and almost fell on the hard ground, but caught himself on a thistle root and propped himself up when he spotted something gleaming—in fact, glittering. At first Ay'r couldn't make out exactly what it was. It seemed to be an entire wall of silken stuff just behind the long line of fernbrake.

"A web trap!" 'Dward said. "Your eyes are sharper than mine in this light. Doubtless where you come from, nights are darker. You lead."

"What am I looking for?"

Ay'r immediately spotted a place where the fernbrake seemed irregularly trampled, with a web trap extending on either side, but not in the middle. Amid the underbrush, he spotted another piece of Alli-Clark's clothing—her headband. From the dents in the fernbrake, it looked as though a body might have been dragged through here.

'Dward began whistling in an ululating tone. Then he said, "Let's go!"

"Aren't we waiting for the others?" Ay'r asked.

"They'll take too long."

On the other side of the fernbrake they found themselves in a sort of clearing. Here the thistlebushes were scrawny and looked torn apart. Shreds of web traps depended from every forked branchlet, like rags hung out to dry. Even more noticeable was how clearly the fernbrake ended, and how it seemed to form a rough circle, as though it had been torn up deliberately to form this clearing—or gardened to shape it. The Species Ethnologist in Ay'r couldn't say how exactly, but this area no longer seemed "natural," like the rest of the wood: but constructed, designed purposely.

He turned to listen to an ululating whistle, similar to that 'Dward had given before; doubtless 'Harles, signaling that he and P'al were on their way, when Ay'r spotted something on the ground right at his feet.

Tiny, undoubtedly Fast-constructed, metal/ceramic. So Alli-Clark had taken a force-field after all! Why, then, hadn't she used it? Did it still work? Ay'r picked it up and wrapped the belt around his waist. He was about to turn it on to try it out when 'Dward's face was suddenly inches away from his, the look on it unlike any Ay'r had ever seen: intense, almost grimacing.

"Arach nest!" 'Dward whispered. "There!" pointing ahead.

Ay'r pushed aside mist and thistlebrush and saw why 'Dward's face had been so odd. If before, Ay'r had thought the clearing was a constructed circle, he now saw not only that he had been correct, but also that they had reached the very center of the Arach's desmesne. Every scrap and line of thistle-hung webbing, every path, now gave only one way—inside. And all of it pointed to what looked at first to be an enormous collection of bubbles of differing sizes and shapes, some as small as a hand, others big enough to contain a colley, all of them semitransparent, all connected to each other by the sticky glue out of which they were apparently made, their surfaces moist enough to give off a dull shine even in the poor light.

"The Arach?" Ay'r whispered.

"Not here."

'Dward moved forward toward the collection of bubbles, which rose twice as high as he was tall, and—fascinated—Ay'r followed. His fascination grew as he peered into the bubbles. The smaller ones held small rodents and lizards Ay'r had seen scampering across the baked-earth ground avoiding the colleys during their trip. They seemed to be half mummified, wrapped tightly in contorted positions within the whitish silken stuff. Few were whole. The silk had been twisted especially tight around sections of their bodies and a hole poked in, from which their insides and flesh had been sucked out.

"Look!" 'Dward drew Ay'r away from the half-dead animals to the largest bubble. "What could that be?" the youth asked.

Ay'r shrugged elaborately, but knew very well. It was what was left of Alli-Clark's transport pod. About one-half of it, including instrumentation and viewers. She must have crashed inside the nearly indestructible pod, but somehow it had opened—or been pried open. She must have been knocked unconscious: even with the pod's own protective webbing, the sudden drop in pressure would have blacked her out when it crashed. Explaining how the pod had been dragged back here. Explaining how she had been undressed. Explaining why she hadn't turned on her shield.

"And here!" 'Dward's voice rose. "Is this your companion?"

Another bubble nearby, and within it, prone, wrapped in white silk, the naked body of Alli-Clark.

"Is she paralyzed or dead?" Ay'r asked. He dashed toward the bubble and began to tear at it with the thorn, to get at her.

"Wait! Don't! You'll trip the Arach's guide line!" 'Dward shouted.

Too late, the line was severed as Ay'r reached into the broken bubble, and began to grasp through the silk wrappings at her neck, looking for a pulse at her carotid artery. He had just found it, regular and strong, when he heard that same high-pitched eerie whistling he and Oudma had heard last night. Only now it was much louder and much closer.

"The Arach!" 'Dward cried.

"Help me get her out!" Ay'r said.

Together they grabbed through the gluey wetness of the bubble and struggled to pull her body out. Ay'r had just managed to get her free, and kneeling had Alli-Clark half in his arms, half on the ground, when he heard shouting.

"'Harles!" he said. "He needs help."

"No. It's a warning! The Arach's headed here to protect its food supply. Can you carry her? We must leave!"

Ay'r hefted Alli-Clark's inert body over one shoulder and they took off, following the radii back out of the circle. The shouting was coming closer.

They had almost reached the fernbrake when 'Dward stopped so suddenly that Ay'r really dropped his load.

"Back. Give me space!" 'Dward shouted.

Then he dashed forward.

Directly into and underneath the elongated body of the largest spider Ay'r had ever seen. Its eight hairy legs were so tall, he had thought they were thistlebrush trees.

"Wait!" Ay'r stopped and dropped Alli-Clark's body to the ground, intending to join the fray. He could already hear 'Dward's shouts as he lunged under the beast looking for its soft parts, and trying to avoid its stinger, a palp as curved and dangerous-looking as a scimitar. Heedless of Ay'r, shouting, the Drylander youth jabbed with his knife and thorn-foil again and again, as the Arach pulled back, raised itself, then turned again, swinging its stinger at him in arcs.

The force-field! Ay'r turned it on and felt the magnetic-electrified shield working. He rushed in to try to cover 'Dward.

"Back, 'Dward!" he shouted, trying to stay where the stinger would strike next.

This new electromagnetic force was more than the Arach could tolerate. It began to bring its long legs forward, attempting to sweep the electrical impulses away from itself. As it panicked, one leg caught Ay'r and tripped him. Ay'r fell backward and saw another leg knock the thorn sword out of 'Dward's clenched fist.

The youth turned. "Run! Save yourself!" he shouted, trying feebly to elude the stinger, at the same time that he danced in place, trying to avoid the Arach's legs, which were now swinging wildly, grabbing at him.

Ay'r inched back along the ground and shut off his shield.

The Arach sensed that the irritation was gone, and it seemed to back off slightly. But in a second, one leg had grabbed 'Dward around the middle. Then another had him tight, and now—

Ay'r twisted the shield dial and focused it into a beam. The thin laser struck the Arach's stinger the very second that it sliced down toward 'Dward, the same second his little knife stabbed high and up into it. The high pitched whistles now circulated around them in an earsplitting frenzy. The legs loosened their grip on 'Dward's body. The stinger fell, lasered, to the ground. Then 'Dward dropped to the ground.

Ay'r turned the dial onto "shield," then darted in to grab at 'Dward.

The Arach was gone, Ay'r could hear its whistles as it stumbled in pain through the fernbrake.

"Wait! My trophy!" 'Dward scrambled for it, unaware that Ay'r's laser—rather than his own knife—had torn it free.

The new crashing through the half-trodden fernbrake sounded like humes. In seconds, 'Harles and P'al were with them. 'Harles summed up the situation in a glance, said the Arach would be back and, without a glance, added, "All of us take a part of her. Hold on tight. We'll be running."

They heard the whistlings again when they finally broke out of the thistlebrush wood, with their burden.

Oudma had already harnessed and reined the colleys, which were chittering nervously between themselves.

"Into Colley's wingfold. Lift!" 'Harles ordered. "We leave now!" And he clambered up into the wingfold. "As soon as it has recovered, the Arach will give chase across the plain."

Within minutes the six of them were atop or within the giant beetles, scuttling at top speed across the baked-earth valley floor, headed toward a brightening, mist-shrouded Pelagian sunrise, filtered heavily through the overhead canopy.

An hour later, they had recrossed the New River at another natural bridge, and 'Harles called a stop so the colleys could rest and drink.

Oudma looked over Colley's wingfold at the silk-wrapped body of Alli-Clark. "You're full of surprises, aren't you?"

P'al and 'Harles had dismounted. Both were looking at Alli-Clark closely, checking her eyes and breathing and pulse.

"The People of the Bog Way have an antidote to Arach venom." 'Harles said finally. "We must get your companion there quickly."

"How far is it?"

"We'll arrive by nightfall," 'Harles said.

When the colleys were watered, and all were remounted and the trek begun more slowly than before, Oudma, sitting in front of her still-exultant brother, turned to Ay'r and said, "You see, Northerner! The truth-sayer wasn't wrong! We found your companion sleeping. And 'Dward performed a bold feat!"

Ay'r merely smiled.

Toward sunset the land around them began to change markedly. It seemed to rise, or the fast-flowing river seemed to drop and slow down. Suddenly the reason was evident. They had been approaching something for hours and finally reached it. To further mark the spot, 'Harles stopped the colleys to be fed.

To Ay'r's eyes, the sight that now greeted them was equal on Pelagia only to his first view of the New River Valley from the plateau's rim, high above in the mountains. An immense shallow bowl seemed to have been carved out of the surrounding flat hard-baked ground, and within its vast extent, this bowl seemed to harbor enough wetness and freshness and fertility to compensate for the surrounding continent's being otherwise so harshly, forbiddingly dry.

The now-shallow New River rushed over the rim and into a score of small rivers which divided further into hundreds of rivulets, which spread into thousands of rills until the river all but disappeared, only to reappear as a dark spot—a lake or pond in the far distance, apparently within the very heart of the huge bowl. Around them the land rolled and tumbled, covered with furze and grasses all waving in different directions. Farther below, the land flattened, then rose again in more darkly colored grassy fields. Although the canopy was now high above, it seemed to drop tendrils into the bowl, fingers of cloud that appeared to hover over specific spots and even, as Ay'r watched them closely, to move.

The bone-dry air softened immediately as, the colleys well fed, the travelers dropped over the rim, 'Harles and 'Dward carefully reining the large animals to guide them through treacherous mud and powerfully coursing streams. Moisture thickened the air around them, and odors assailed them, deep and sweet and loamy, sometimes rich and foul, coming from the same side of the path.

At one point they passed and waved to laborers who were perched high on either side of the road, cutting peat in great rectangles, each slab's side as black and glittering as a piece of fresh-sliced flesh. The colleys passed other, smaller, similar creatures hitched two to a flatbed wagon upon which the peat slabs were lowered and stacked. Ay'r was reminded of his first sight of the Pelagian seedlings: the Fast's probe must have viewed from within this bowl.

There was another, less-steep yet noticeable drop. Before they had negotiated it, Oudma pointed out in the distance clusters of what Ay'r at first took for small hills and hummocks, but which turned out to be the rounded roofs of houses and other buildings.

"We'll be going to Peat Cutters' Village," she said. "Although there are larger towns: Lake Edge, the capital, Bottommost, and several I've not seen."

As her hand guided his sight, Ay'r made out across the dark waters the larger, more jumbled dwellings of other towns, and even some double- and triple-storied dwellings which he took for public buildings.

Finally they reached level ground, but the exhausted colleys could no longer scamper: the air was too thick and too wet for them to breathe properly, and darkness was coming. On either side of the road, Ay'r now saw the mountain people's terraced agriculture adapted to bowl agriculture: thick rows of some sort of small-leafed dark hedge had been planted to separate plots as well as to channel runnels of land, through which placid canals had been cut.

"Slow down!" 'Harles said to his son in irritation. "I can hardly see where we're going."

"Ay'r sees better than we do," 'Dward said. "He showed me last night in the thistlebrush wood. Let him lead us to Peat Cutters' Village."

"If he does," 'Harles said, "surely his companion also sees well."

"I'll guide us," P'al said simply, and took the reins. So, behind him, on Colley, did Ay'r: the first time he'd been allowed control over the animal.

"Is it so much darker in the north?" Oudma asked.

"Perhaps because the canopy isn't as thick," her father answered.

"Its moisture collects as ice," P'al added. "This bogland"—he mused—"there will be interesting legends to hear about it."

"Not a natural formation," Ay'r agreed, "yet it's been here a long time."

Ay'r had assumed that the dwellings of the Bog would be like those in Monosilla. While they resembled the giant shells the Ib'r lived in, these dwellings weren't found, but constructed: the first one they passed, P'al reached out a hand to touch, and reported that they were oven-fired ceramics, preshaped bricks; the windows mere slits along the roof line; the chimneys larger, double holes—he guessed for both drawing in air and emitting peat smoke.

"When you see a long building..." 'Harles was saying, as two humes crossed almost in front of his colley, carrying lamplight which illuminated their faces eerily in the darkness.

"We're seeking the doctor!" Oudma cried out, her pronunciation slightly different than what Ay'r had heard before.

"Are you Deltans?" a woman asked, in a more-exaggerated version of the dialect.

"From the Mountains. Monosilla. We've come a long way. Our companion was stung by an Arach."

"We'll lead you to her house," the male answered.

"This is Ib'r, my father," Oudma said as 'Harles dismounted and walked alongside them.

"Give us the animal's reins," the male said.

Ay'r listened to their speech enough to pick up distinctions in their language as well as a bit of argot and vocabulary. Evidently, P'al was also listening and learning: he hushed Ay'r the one time he tried to make conversation.

The doctor's dwelling consisted of her home and—separated by a half-open ceramic-brick loggia of sorts—an infirmary, to which they carried Alli-Clark.

Seppi was the doctor's name, a stout, middle-aged woman with a sense of purpose and authority about her. The minute she laid eyes on Alli-Clark, she gestured the men to lift her again.

"She must be washed to get all the Arach saliva off her. Otherwise, when she awakens, her skin will be painful." She led them into another room with a shallow pool built into one end. "Leave now! All of you!"

To Ay'r's surprise 'Harles stood firm. "This woman is my responsibility. I'll remain."

"I'd rather have the lass," Dr. Seppi shrugged, "but you'll do. Give me a hand wiping this stuff off her." She turned back to the others. "Out— the rest of you!"

"Refreshment?" 'Dward asked.

"Two dwellings down is an inn." And the door was shut on them.

A small boy appeared and said he would guide them. He seemed fascinated by their speech and strange attire and also asked if they were Deltans.

"Tell me true, lad, where is your Legend-teller in Peat Cutters' Village?" P'al asked. As Ay'r should have expected, he already spoke the dialect fluently and naturally.

"I'll take you there, too. The inn is on the way."

The boy all but pulled P'al out of the dwelling, then remembered to return for a lamp.

"Was it a big Arach?" he asked.

"High as your dwelling."

"Good thing you found your companion before it found you," the boy said with the kind of shudder in his voice which suggested that Arach-tales were small-boys' fodder.

"We didn't," Ay'r said. "We had to fight it."

"I cut off its stinger!" 'Dward bragged.

"High as my dwelling?" the boy asked.

"I thought its legs were thistlebrush trees," Ay'r said.

"Tell this at the inn and you'll get free refreshment," the boy suggested.

He told the truth. The minute they had entered into the dwelling and into substantial lamplight and the milling and noise and herbal fumes of pipe smokers of both genders, the boy immediately ran to the innkeeper and whispered in his ear. He then remained long enough for a short quaff of watered down local mead, then rushed off to fetch the Legend-collector —whom the innkeeper was surprised to see wasn't at his usual spot by the peat stove in the inn.

"I take it that Legend-collectors aren't highly thought of in this village," P'al murmured, half into his drink.

"No but strangers and Arach-battlers are," a woman said, close by where the travelers had settled themselves on pillows in front of a low ceramic table. "You"—resting her hand upon P'al's large shoulder— "must be the trophy owner."

P'al smiled at the woman, who was blowsily attractive, and pointed to 'Dward. "The lads fought. That one owns the stinger."

She pealed laughter. "You must be strangers. Bog boys are good only for cutting peat and"—she made an obscene gesture, then added—"and lately, not even that!" before laughing again and leaving them.

The food was served in low ceramic bowls shaped like and decorated to resemble leaves, yet flat leaves also held the food. It was grain based, surprisingly spicy and, above all, heated! After the monotony of their cold provisions, they all ate with their hands, and with gusto.

The innkeeper and finally even his wife—the woman who had approached them before—insisted they tell of the Arach hunt.

"These are Northerners. Our guests! And we are of the Ib'r clan," 'Dward introduced them. "We Ib'r came first from Old River Town, but went into the mountains when my father was a lad. We're on our way to the Great Temple. My sister and myself for initiation, these men to collect legends. For, where they come from, it's considered an honorable profession, and they are important among their own kind. These strangers know much of our land although they've never seen it before. They can tell its history by looking at rocks and at how the land is shaped, and how fast and deep the waters run. Much do they know, and our truth-sayer tied us to them by future deeds, honoring them greatly above any of the people he had encountered and prophesying especial futures for them and us, should we follow them."

The Species Ethologist in Ay'r realized that although young and supposedly uneducated, 'Dward was speaking in a classical rhetorical manner which his listeners understood well. Traditional was its syntax, conventional many of its metaphors: above all, strong and simple and old-fashioned its rhythms and vocabulary.

Oudma listened with as much wonder and surprise as those who hadn't been present while her brother related the journey so far, the fall in the colleys' wingfold, the battle with the giant Arach. 'Dward's voice rose and fell, he gestured, he foreshadowed events, he withheld crucial information and then suddenly sprung it to elicit gasps from his listeners. Perhaps he had heard his father speak of his own adventures so often, and had longed to equal him, or perhaps this was the first time he had been the center of a listening public: whatever the reason, the Drylander youth glowed and shone, he looked the modest hero he presented himself as, and drew in the breath of the crowd and allowed its relieved release like a fine musician with a well-tuned instrument.

Ay'r thought: 'Dward's ambitions and talents would make him a fine man if he were anywhere but on Pelagia, even in the Matriarchy itself he might unfold. Too bad for him. For everyone.

His story told, 'Dward sat slightly apart, drinking his mead quietly, while the others had to answer questions from the crowd.

Among them were the doctor's boy and the newly arrived Legend-collector, the latter a tall, spindly fellow. Ay'r had already remarked to himself the physiological difference between the Ib'r clan and these Boglanders—especially the young men sitting here—who were squarer, squatter, less nimble, less graceful, as though pressed down by the heavy air, or as if their bodies were forced to deal with the higher gravity within the great bowl.

"You've come to the right one for legends, strangers," the newcomer announced himself and eyed the pitchers of mead greedily. "I am Nikhil, and I possess uncounted legends and anecdotes, tales and myths. Some exciting as that true account of your young master."

"Drink up." P'al offered the pitcher of mead. "I'm most interested in the legend of the founding of this place."

"Peat Cutters' Village? Founded five generations ago," Nikhil said. "When the peat was exhausted below, the old village was abandoned."

"I meant this entire place. All of this bog land—from its rim to its watery heart."

"That's a long story."

"I have time. And the innkeeper has adequate mead, I suppose. Better yet tell of before the founding. Tell me of the Great Falling Inward."

At his last words, several people nearby turned away and began to speak among themselves, uninterested in such old stories.

"The Great Falling Inward?" Nikhil repeated.

"In the old homeland."

"What is there to tell? There was a great falling inward. Most of the People of the Bog Way were killed or maimed. The canopy bled for years until farmland was flooded, crops drowned, livestock and people starved. Finally those remaining left their homeland. A great exodus with many travails. Leagues of harsh mountain, ice, wild beasts which fed off the sick and dying. Finally the New River was reached, but its land was harsh. The People wandered for a decade. They were chased off by the dwellers of the Old River settlements they came to. Many perished in skirmishes on the unforgiving plain, in the rushing torrents of the river, many more of privation. At last they came to this land, fresh and ready, as though prepared by the same hand which had destroyed them. Here the People settled amid plenty and made of themselves a new nation."

"It was formed by the same hand," P'al said. "What is the true name of this place?"

"Not to be spoken aloud," the Legend-collector whispered. "It's called Maspiei's Eye."

"And the land the People left—that became known as Maspiei's Head, didn't it?"

"You already know!" Nikhil said.

"The same Great Falling Inward that destroyed the old homeland carved out this bowl in the plain. Carved out the river that feeds it. Indeed, burnt the plain upon which this eye sits, so rich and fertile."

"That is what the old ones believed. And why they saw this new homeland as a compensation and a reward—at long last."

Thereafter, Nikhil seemed subdued. He continued to empty the mead pitcher and to tell legends, but P'al had lost interest. He found and enjoined the innkeeper to find them lodgings. Two rooms were available, and the boy was dispatched to tell 'Harles.

The inn began to empty out, but 'Harles did not return. 'Dward and Oudma began to nod off, and all were led through a ceramic corridor with many high and split windows to one of several connected dwellings. Oudma went to her chamber, which she would share with her father when he returned. 'Dward half-undressed and immediately fell asleep in a second large bed. Ay'r gestured to P'al, and they sat on the smaller bed, whispering.

"When Alli-Clark awakens, she'll—"

P'al interrupted, "From what 'Harles told me, the effect of the Arach venom varies on those stung by it. It's a powerful soporific and hypnotic drug. Some have never recovered their memory or wits. Others remembered all too well and became prey to terrors, visions of their experience. We must be prepared for the worst."

"And her mission?" Ay'r asked.

"Mostly completed."

"And my mission?"

"We will complete that, within the time period we possess. Now sixty-three days. Or return."

"And your mission?" Ay'r tried to shake him.

P'al didn't falter. "To aid you. That continues."

"Is knowing everything about Pelagia part of aiding me or Alli-Clark? The Matriarchy or yourself? Or someone else?"

"Whom else could it aid?" P'al answered infuriatingly with another question. And when Ay'r didn't deign to answer, "Shall I join the lad?" he asked, with a Bogland lilt. "Or shall you?"

"I will," Ay'r said.

During the night, 'Dward moved alongside him and wrapped an arm over Ay'r's body and called him "'Nton." Even with his "bold feat," he was still boy enough to miss his brother.

'Dward was still asleep when Ay'r roused himself. Unaccustomed to any brightness since he had been on Pelagia, he was surprised to see the high slits in the bedroom admitting shafts of what might almost be called sunlight. Naturally, P'al was already up and gone: Ay'r had slept well following their adventurous day, yet he thought he recalled his companion getting out of bed much earlier, while it was still dark. A quick glimpse outside the room showed the day to actually be brighter than he had been accustomed to, doubtless because of the higher canopy over the Bogland bowl, or some other climatic irregularity.

Oudma was having breakfast. She told him that P'al had already gone off to the doctor's house. 'Harles had never arrived at the inn. All this according to the innkeeper's wife.

Before she could ask him the question he was awaiting—about Alli-Clark and their relationship—Ay'r said, "Your brother sleeps hard."

"Dreamlessly," she agreed. "Especially now that we're traveling. I'll wake him."

By the time the three had eaten and left the inn, yellow sunlight still shone, but now through a light mist raining down on them. Going through the streets, Ay'r noted that the roads in the center of the village were paved with some kind of ceramic similar to—but more durable than—the dwellings, with narrow gutters scooped out on the sides—perhaps because of the heavy peat-wagon traffic.

They passed several vehicles filled with mostly young male occupants heading out toward the peat fields. Among them was one youth whom Ay'r had noticed at the inn the previous night. Then he had been quiet, at times almost sullen looking, at other times utterly rapt, his handsomely featured face raised to not miss a word of 'Dward's tale. This Pelagian morn, the youth seemed far more active and outgoing, although in the clearer light he was even more attractive than Ay'r had thought the night before, his body filling out the close-fitting Boglander garments even more voluptuously. He hailed Ay'r and 'Dward as the peat wagon he was in passed by, told the driver to stop, then dropped to the road.

"These are the Mountain Valley lads I spoke of," he told his companions. "They battled the giant Arach."

To Ay'r and 'Dward, he said, "My name is Varko. They didn't believe me when I told them."

"We believed you!" one protested.

"You didn't! And aren't they handsome as heroes, just as I said they would be?" Varko insisted.

He threw an arm over both of their shoulders.

"Tell them how you fought it!" he said, brightly, hugging them as though they were long-lost friends. Ay'r couldn't help noticing that he all but pushed Oudma out of the way. Rather than protest, she dropped back almost into a doorway.

Following last night's exhibitionism, today 'Dward was being shy.

"Go on, tell them!" Varko tried to draw him out. "This one"—letting go of Ay'r and holding 'Dward—"actually cut off the stinger! He brought it with him."

The other Boglanders looked at the Arach-battler with respect and began to ask questions.

Ay'r didn't hear what one Boglander on the wagon said behind another's back, but it set some of them laughing.

"Who laughs at them?" Varko demanded.

"Not at them, Varko, but at you. Schorri said 'Only a hero will do for Varko! Though he makes his sisters' bondmates fight each other for one of his kisses!' "

The Boglanders all laughed at that. In response, Varko planted a kiss on 'Dward's mouth. When he pulled away, Varko seemed pleased with himself, and 'Dward a bit embarrassed.

"Come visit where we work in the peat fields," Varko said. "We'll show you much that strangers never discover about the Bog Way."

Again Schorri said something which Ay'r didn't catch, but which set some of the other youths to laughter again. This time Varko ignored the comment, got back onto the wagon and shouted for the driver to go. He turned around as they lurched off, calling back for Ay'r and 'Dward to come visit them at the peat hills.

When they were gone, Ay'r said, "They seem a friendly lot."

He thought 'Dward was about to answer when Oudma joined them again. Her brother asked where she had gone to.

"These Bogland boys need to learn some manners," she said, not hiding her irritation at how they had treated her. To Ay'r she added, "In Monosilla, they don't ignore unbonded females."

Ay'r was about to tell her that in the Matriarchy, young women were even ruder in shoving aside young males and ignoring them.

"Perhaps we should have told them *you* battled the Arach," 'Dward suggested.

"While you two cowered, weeping," she added. And laughed at what seemed to her a ridiculous picture.

'Harles was in the infirmary when they arrived a few minutes later. He was sitting by a pallet upon which lay Alli-Clark. She had been bathed, wrapped in sheets, and now lay sleeping fitfully. 'Harles looked as though he had been awake most of the night. Dr. Seppi was out on morning visits to the elderly infirm at their dwellings. P'al had come and gone, 'Harles said. He thought to visit Nikhil, the Legend-collector.

Oudma immediately began to fuss around Alli-Clark, rearranging her bedclothes and sending 'Harles out, insisting that he eat something and rest. She would nurse until the doctor returned.

Before he left, 'Harles took Ay'r aside.

"Dr. Seppi has hopes for her. She awakened into fever dreams and began to see what wasn't there. Naturally, she didn't know us, but she was too weak to resist, and the fever exhausted her."

Ay'r began to say, "I don't know if it's your way here, but you have been more than generous with your care and concern for our companion."

"Her plight touched me to the heart," 'Harles's eyes glanced toward the bed. "Her"—he stopped—"she spoke wildly of strange matters none of which the doctor or I could understand. Doubtless, she will awaken more comfortably if you are by her side."

Ay'r wondered about that. Nevertheless, he sent 'Harles out of the room, surprised by the depth of feeling the older Drylander had expressed.

"It isn't our way, usually," Oudma said. "But I noticed my father's glances at your companion from the moment you brought her to the colleys yesterday morning. I've not seen him look at anyone like that since, Gitte, our mother, died."

"To answer your unspoken question, Oudma. Alli is not my bondmate. Nor P'al. The three of us joined up at the last minute for our trip. We scarcely knew each other."

"Even so, the two of you possess some familiarity. Therefore the three of you also shall."

"Perhaps."

'Dward felt restless and after making certain his father had eaten and was resting at the inn returned to tell them that he might join the friendly peat cutters who had invited him earlier. As 'Dward was leaving, Dr. Seppi arrived, her small son in tow, and after checking her patient, immediately asked if the story he had told was true.

Before 'Dward could react to the possible insult, she went on, "Because if you still have the stinger, I could try to get some of its venom. That's how the antidote is made, and it's very hard to come by."

'Dward returned to the inn and came back carrying the arm-length stinger, and offered the trophy to the doctor.

"I need only the venom," she said.

"Take it!" he insisted. "I need no trophy."

She inspected the deadly-looking stinger, then took it to another room.

"If you're truly going out of doors, be careful!" Oudma instructed her brother as he left, "The Gods!"

After a while, Alli-Clark began to murmur, then mumble in her sleep. Her tossing and turning increased and suddenly she sat up, staring wildly ahead.

"Alli-Clark! It's Ay'r. You're safe! P'al is here, too!"

She looked from him to Oudma.

"A friend. Her family helped save you from the Arach."

To his surprise, Alli-Clark pulled Ay'r close. Perspiration had broken out all over her face, and her skin was burning to his touch.

"There is much you must know if I die," she whispered fiercely into his ear.

"You won't die," he insisted. "The antidote to the Arach-venom will soon help you. Rest now."

"No. Listen!" And she pulled him closer, whispering loudly into his ear.

"Whatever happens, you must find your father. It is essential— otherwise the Matriarchy is doomed!"

"But we will find—"

"Quiet! Listen! A great plague has spread across the galaxy. It strikes Motherhood at its very heart and soul. Reproduction is impossible. The Cybers did it. The plague is itself a Cyber construct. Every resource in the Matriarchy has been expended to cure it, to no avail. The mechanos knew they couldn't win the war, so they sent this to us, hoping to outlast us. If no cure is found, this generation will be the last one."

"Who shot down your pod?" he asked her.

"Humes. But that's unimportant. Wicca Eighth Herself believes that your father alone can save humekind from this plague. Centuries ago, his findings in Mammalian reproduction were already highly sophisticated. So much so that his work, like that of his own teacher Relfi, was considered a threat to the M.C. He was banished. Exiled. Wicca believes you are a result of one such experiment. You must find him and bring him back to Melisande, or the time of our doom is at hand."

Ay'r had been trying to follow her words. Now he asked, "Humes shot you down. How?"

"From T-pods of some sort. With weapons."

"Pelagian humes?"

"Like us, Ay'r!" She grabbed him tighter, "They were like us, before the 'xchange! Find them! They will lead you to your father. Who is this woman?"

"Oudma. I told you. A friend. Her father and brother helped us to bring you here?"

"There was an older woman. And a male, too. He was kindness itself." She seemed shocked. "Why would he be like that to a stranger?"

"The woman is the doctor. The man is Oudma's father, 'Harles Ib'r. Did the males in the T-pods use laser weapons?"

"Like those on our T-pods, yes. I'm tired. Eve, but I'm tired!" Alli began to close her eyes and fell back.

"Rest now!" Ay'r said.

Alli-Clark's eyes opened again, and again she grasped his tunic front and whispered fiercely, "Promise you'll fulfill my mission and find your father and bring him back to Wicca-World. If you fail, all womanhood perishes!"

"Yes, of course. Rest now. Don't worry."

Oudma mopped Alli's forehead with cool water, removed the sweat stained sheets and swabbed Alli-Clark's hot limbs and torso, then covered her with fresh sheets.

She had just finished when Dr. Seppi came in with a goblet, 'We must awaken her enough so she'll drink this. The venom was fresh, and this antidote should be far stronger than what I had. Her cure will be certain."

Ay'r got Alli to drink the liquid. It had no immediate effect, and she fell asleep again.

He left the room and went outside where the mist had congealed into a light rain. There he stood, the little Boglander boy at his side, and attempted the seemingly impossible task of attempting to sort out and think through all that Alli-Clark had just told him.

Dr. Seppi joined him. "Your friend P'al went with me on my morning visits. He's very knowledgeable about medicine."

"Indeed!" Ay'r would have to talk to P'al about Alli-Clark's rantings, if that's what they were. Why did they seem to connect, if only in the most random kind of pattern? To make some sort of paranoid sense?

"Especially with my maternity visits."

"Really?" Now Ay'r was more than politely interested. "In what way?"

"He knew not only each stage in the seven-month gestation period by sight, but other matters only the most experienced midwives among us know."

"He inspected pregnant women?"

"Three of them. Tomorrow we visit more, in Bottommost, and at Bog Bay." He's a wise man. "He knows much."

Exactly how much, Ay'r wondered.

Ay'r mounted Colley, and though the animal seemed sluggish, it still evinced interest in moving. He planned to head for the Legend-collector's dwelling, to which the innkeeper had directed him with a rough map drawn with a finger of spilled mead upon a ceramic tabletop. But almost out of Peat Cutters' Village, heading north on the same road that had brought them here, other Boglanders hailed Ay'r, stopped him, recognized him as one of the strangers, and said that if he were looking for his hero friend, they had seen him in the upper bog, not far away. The road he was on would lead right there.

He would prefer to face P'al alone, now that his mind was awhirl in questions and speculations fueled by Alli-Clark's blurted confession and the seemingly supporting information about P'al which Dr. Seppi had added. But the road he was traveling on passed close by an area under peat cultivation, and in the distance, Ay'r could see a half-dozen young men at work, standing out among them the taller and more slender figure of 'Dward.

Ay'r stopped to let the colley nibble gorse at the side of the road and was watching them at work when Ay'r thought he heard a peculiar-yet-familiar whizzing sound overhead. It must be the "Gods"! Now was his chance to see who they were. And more, to warn 'Dward.

Ay'r dismounted and began running through the lumpy ground in their direction. He had barely gotten out a single shout, which none of them seemed to hear, when his nostrils picked up a sensual and heavy odor, unlike any he had encountered in Bogland before. Although it was sweet, something about it bothered him, setting off alarms in his mind. Ay'r stopped where he was and turned on Alli-Clark's force-field belt to "shield." He shouted at the young peat cutters once again, but again they seemed not to hear him. In fact, they seemed to have gone perfectly still as though also listening, or as though they thought that if they froze, they wouldn't be discovered.

Ay'r had arrived within a dozen yards of them, was separated by only a single line of tall, small-leaved hedge, when suddenly he could no longer move. Not a muscle, not a finger, not his lips or tongue. Only his eyes were still mobile, and those moved only from side to side.

The sudden paralysis was terrifying, and Ay'r panicked, yet at the same time he realized two things: first, the six humes in front of him were also paralyzed, and that besides seeing, he could also still hear, and he was hearing that particular whizzing sound connected with the arrival of the "Gods" and it was getting louder.

They landed directly in front of the young peat cutters in two T-pods, each larger and older than any Ay'r had seen outside of a museum. The three humes who emerged might have stepped out of Capella starport or any conveyance in Hesperia with their curly black hair and dark skin. Their costumes were a bit older than any he had seen: a less-simple tunic, closer-fitting trousers, smaller capes. On their heads they wore a type of military helmet he had seen only in older PVNs, which obscured their faces. Even so, he was certain they were all male.

The three "Gods" went up to 'Dward and the six statuelike peat workers and, without hesitation, began looking them over. One carried a hand computer, and as he spoke, another quickly tapped information into it. They didn't seem to have noticed Ay'r; and unless they came right up to this hedge, they probably wouldn't. He was safe, yet unable to move, to help 'Dward and the peat cutters. It was intensely frustrating.

The first "God" removed an upper garment from one Bogland youth and touched each nipple, then held the pectoral loosely, all the while speaking what might be figures or numbers to his companion. Ay'r couldn't hear them. Then the "God" removed the youth's lower garment and palpated each buttock, as well as the flesh inside each thigh. It all seemed objective, medical, if only Ay'r knew what they were looking for, checking up on.

The tested youth was re-dressed, and the two moved on to the next lad, Schorri—his snide comments stilled—then on to the next. When they arrived at 'Dward, the elder said something to his companion, and they lifted the hand-held device up to his face, as though holographing him for identification.

The male with the computer shook his head. Evidently, 'Dward wasn't in their file. The other grasped then dropped one of 'Dward's leanly muscled upper arms and barked out an order.

His assistant drew a tiny cylinder out of a small metal case hanging from his belt, swabbed 'Dward's forearm, then held the cylinder against the spot.

They didn't bother to undress 'Dward, but once he had been injected, they moved aside and began to confer.

"Bog Bay?" the assistant suggested.

Suddenly the third and youngest "God," who had hovered around the T-pods, called out something which sounded to Ay'r like "Transmission coming in" in perfect Universo Lexico. Ay'r couldn't be certain.

The elder male moved from 'Dward to the last of the paralyzed youths, the effusive Varko, and was now undressing him as he had done the others. He commanded something back to the man at the T-pods and went on pinching Varko's thighs.

The youngest "God" joined the other two and began to speak. Again, Ay'r couldn't hear what he said, but as he pointed distantly behind him, the transmission evidently had to do with something outside of Bogland, perhaps even with Ay'r and his traveling companions, since they had just come from the area being pointed out. He wondered now if they had found the wounded Arach, or perhaps the other half of Alli-Clark's T-pod.

The first "God" was now palpating Varko's buttocks, paying a great deal more attention to him than to any of the others. He said something to the other two and illustrated it by brushing his fingertips against Varko's nipples, which hardened immediately. The other two nodded in agreement.

Varko was half-dressed and lifted by the three "Gods" and placed inside one T-pod. The other Boglanders received injections in their arms similar to what 'Dward had been given. Their tasks completed, the three "Gods" got back into their pods, closed them, and took off again with that same buzzing sound which Ay'r now knew was the sound older model T-pods made in the Pelagian atmosphere.

It was a good four minutes longer before the five remaining youths and 'Dward suddenly all unfroze—long enough for Ay'r to wonder about what he had seen and what it meant. These so-called "Gods" were obviously Hume males like himself, yet from their older clothing and vehicles, they had come from somewhere else than he and P'al and Alli-Clark, or had been on Pelagia for several hundred years, which would confirm the people's legends. They were all male and seemed in good physical shape, yet Ay'r guessed that they must be considerably older than himself. Compared to the short-lived Drylanders this long life and ability to move so rapidly through the air and to kidnap at will would make them "Gods" indeed. But he had been too far away to hear them or to understand what they were doing. Who were they really? Could his father be one of them?

That they were scientists of some sort was clear from their actions. Yet even that was ambiguous. What had they injected into the youths' forearms? What were they were looking for? Why had they taken away Varko and not the others? For a second, Ay'r was reminded of an ancient pre-Metro-Terran legend about an old woman who fattened up children to cook and eat them. Could that be it? It was a ghastly thought. Ay'r pushed it out of his mind.

A second after the others had been released from their perfume instilled paralysis, Ay'r could move. He burst through the hedge, just as the others realized they'd been in an encounter with the "Gods" and that one of them had been kidnapped.

"What are you doing?" 'Dward asked him.

"I came to get you. No emergency. But I brought Colley."

"There was a kidnapping! They took Varko. I was right here. We all were!" 'Dward said excitedly.

"Did you see them?" Ay'r asked.

"No, of course not. But I heard them approach. Then Schorri smelled something in the air and said, 'The Gods!' " He turned to Ay'r, still excited. "And you, Ay'r, did you see them getting away?"

Ay'r nodded.

By now the other youths were discussing how would they tell Varko's family of his abduction.

Ay'r added. "I was hidden."

"I wonder why only Varko was taken, when there were so many of us?" 'Dward said.

Ay'r didn't tell him what he had seen. He commiserated with the others on the loss of their friend and coworker, then took 'Dward's arm were he had been injected and looked closely at it. No sign of anything beyond the tiny dot of broken skin. "I'm certainly glad you escaped them."

'Dward looked at him, a little baffled at the emotion Ay'r had expressed. Then he laughed and hugged Ay'r close and hard. "So am I that you weren't taken."

"You are?"

"Look at all the adventure you've brought into my life!" 'Dward said. "Adventure and companionship. You've almost made up for the loss of my brother 'Nton."

Ay'r would have to find some way to get Dr. Seppi to check over 'Dward for any effects of the injection. He didn't know how advanced her medicine was, but what other choice did he have? As for 'Dward, he'd tell him he was afraid that in carrying the Arach stinger, he might have been affected by its sting.

"I've had enough adventure for today," Ay'r said. "Let's get back to the village."

Oudma was awaiting them at Dr. Seppi's with good news. The new antidote made from the Arach stinger venom had worked. Alli-Clark's fever had broken, and she was sleeping comfortably. At this rate, the doctor thought only another day of bed rest would be needed before Alli-Clark could be moved again. No memory damage seemed present, and as she had been unconscious before the Arach grabbed her, Alli-Clark ought not be prey to bad dreams or terrible visions. Naturally, they should tell her as little as possible about the incident. 'Harles had just returned from the inn and was sitting with Alli-Clark in case she awakened. Evidently she had asked for him during her single brief bout of clarity right after her fever had broken.

When Ay'r asked about their other companion, Oudma shook her head. P'al hadn't been seen since early morning. 'Harles had heard the innkeeper saying that he had been asking about transport into the capital. Perhaps he had gone there.

Naturally enough, 'Dward was full of his news about the encounter with the "Gods," and when he told her, Oudma expressed all the fear and relief he had expected. Once her brother had gone into the infirmary to tell 'Harles, Oudma looked thoughtful.

"I thought here among the People of the Bog, no kidnappings occurred."

"Evidently we heard incorrectly," Ay'r said. He wanted to find out from Oudma how much she'd heard of what Alli-Clark had told him before, but didn't know how to bring up the subject without having to lie about it and say it was merely fevered gibberish. Although he had gone out of his way during that dialogue with Alli to ask only the most circumspect questions, Oudma was intelligent enough to suspect that the entire exchange between them was much more comprehensible than it might have sounded to herself. "Doubtless they're keeping word of the danger down as a matter of policy."

"Both of you might have been taken," Oudma said.

"I'm sure they don't want me," he tried to make it into a joke.

"Why not?"

"Well, for one thing, I'm not young enough. I'd make a terrible worker, if that's what they're looking for. I've led such an idle, lazing life."

She seemed unpersuaded.

'Dward came out again to say that 'Harles would remain with Alli-Clark. "I'd be a little jealous, if I were you," he teased Oudma

"Nonsense! He's not interested in another daughter," Oudma said, and the look on 'Dward's face after her remark showed that he had begun to understand what she meant.

The three returned to the inn where early dinner was being served. Ay'r wondered whether 'Dward would begin to tale-tell the incident with the "Gods," but evidently the youth decided not to—perhaps because he had not done anything heroic like saving the kidnapped youth—perhaps because it was too disturbing to think that he had escaped the same fate through mere chance.

P'al returned among a group of transport travelers from Lake Edge just as they were finishing their meal. Ay'r immediately asked to see him in their sleep chamber.

"Alli-Clark's fever broke." Ay'r reported. "She'll be fine now!"

P'al had no reply to that. And Ay'r wondered how much more he should reveal to this fellow-traveler who was becoming more enigmatic every day.

"I witnessed a kidnapping by the 'Gods,' " Ay'r added.

That got P'al's attention and he began to delve into the incident, trying to elicit as much information as possible. Regarding the paralyzing perfume, P'al said, "I've heard of such sensory chemicals being used in the Bella=Arth War, but none since. It sounds quite effective. Too bad you couldn't bring back a sample of it. We could use Dr. Seppi's laboratory to find an antidote. It's a fairly primitive setup, naturally, since most of her work is homeopathic, but"—P'al seemed to have a thought—"none of the others remained conscious during the incident. Yet you did. I wonder if it was because of your distance from them."

Ay'r lifted his tunic and showed P'al the belt and force-field, explaining how he had found it and used it once before.

"So we know that the shield can't stop the fumes, but that it does reduce their effectiveness," Ay'r concluded.

"Perhaps it's a good thing that you were hidden," P'al commented. "Who knows what they would have thought if they found that on you?"

"And Alli-Clark's T-pod has them perplexed," Ay'r agreed. "Because she made the 'xchange in the Fast, they think she's a Drylander who somehow found one of their pods and learned how to use it. But why don't we want them to know we're here?"

"Surprise is always the better part of valor," P'al said.

"Who do you think they are?" Ay'r asked.

"Obviously you think that your father may be among them."

"It seems likely, doesn't it?"

"Perhaps."

Ay'r followed the line of logic. "Which means these Drylander youths are being abducted as guinea pigs, for some sort of experimentation being conducted by my father."

"I thought your father was a Species Ethnologist."

"We both know that my father was one of the most brilliant mammalian reproduction biologists in the galaxy three centuries ago," Ay'r said, trying to get a rise out of P'al. "And a follower of Relfianism, which advocated genetic experimentation."

Instead of denying it or asking how Ay'r knew this, P'al answered, "Then why kidnap males?"

"I've no idea. Unless, he's changed his specialization."

"Or unless those humes from the T-pods aren't connected to your father."

Ay'r described what the three had done to the youths, how they had palpated various portions of the Boglanders' bodies. "They simply looked at 'Dward and knew he was a stranger. They immediately knew. How? Then they injected him with something—in the forearm. I want Dr. Seppi to check him."

P'al though that was a good idea, then asked Ay'r to repeat everything that had happened in the peat bog, step by step.

At one point, Ay'r said, "I'm not sure why, but I wasn't too surprised that of all the youths there, they abducted Varko."

P'al wanted to know why Ay'r thought that; so Ay'r had to explain the incident on the street, about which P'al asked in excruciating detail.

Finally Ay'r decided he had answered enough questions. Now it was

P'al's turn. "While all that was going on, where have you been all day?"

"Out looking over Bogland. I would think that a Species Eth. like yourself would do the same."

Ay'r ignored the sniping and asked, "Well? What do you have to report?"

"I visited Bottommost briefly, passed through Bog Bay, and spent most of my time at Lake Edge, which is the most populated town here."

P'al had spent a fruitful day indeed, and he outlined his discoveries to Ay'r with the enthusiasm of an amateur speaking to someone who will understand all he has to say. Despite the kidnappings, Bogland's population was close to 50,000 people. Peat cutting was the largest industry, and it had given rise to other allied manufactures made possible by the peat ovens the Boglanders had perfected: brick making, simple metal alloys, metalworking itself, the concoction of remedies, herbal teas and various other drinks—both alcoholic and not—from the grasses and grains which grew so richly in the bowl.

From being a small populace of farmers who had been shunned by all the other Drylanders, the Boglanders had rapidly grown into an important—even a crucial—economic force as a result of their rich peat and grain fields. Their situation, midway between the Delta and the Mountain peoples, and equidistant from the four largest and oldest Old River towns, meant that as their surplus had grown, trade had radiated out to the other areas of Dryland culture on a more-or-less equal basis. Furthermore, as the Boglanders had developed and discovered more and more important uses for their grains and peat, they had exported them along with their own brand of economic propaganda. As a result, they had made themselves the trade center of the continent. Caravans and travelers from all over Dryland filled the booths and stalls of the extensive market at Lake Edge. Commerce was rife and extremely profitable, further centralizing wealth in the Bogland bowl.

Another advantage of the placement of the bowl in the midst of the vast river plain was that no competitors were closer than 100 kilometers. An invading army would spend exhausting days laden with provisions and travel only to arrive and find the place virtually impregnable. Anyone advancing along the plain could be seen days distant from the simplest tower, of which a few had been built up along the rim of the great bowl. And it was strategically impossible to surround it, although from within it was defended easily. This had also bolstered the Boglanders' reputation and helped foster their economic growth.

The Bogland government was a "Deimos," a republic in the rough, with individual representation in publicly held meetings for each of the twelve villages and six towns. Two representatives were appointed by each, one of whom remained in those villages and towns; the other lived and met in a sort of daily parliament at Lake Edge. Contact between the representatives was constant. Among themselves, the parliament formed about a half dozen blocs, mostly on the basis of similarity of agriculture or geography: the peat bloc, the grain bloc, the trading bloc, the metal bloc, etc. In turn they elected leaders who met as a sort of council. There was no army, yet all citizens of both genders were members of a militia, with a captain for each town. Weapons remained limited to throwing sticks and mechanical bows, a stage before firearms. But there was so little war that more sophisticated weapons were still unproven, considered experimental.

The other Dryland cultures had learned from the Boglanders, and P'al had been told that both the Deltan towns and the Old River towns had adopted similar types of trade, markets, defense systems and government.

"What we are seeing, Ser Kerry, is the transition from one stage of civilization to another. Spengler would say, from the pastoral-agricultural to the city-state. In a generation or so, the transition will have been completed. Only the high mountain dwellers and the far northerners retain simpler stages of development on Pelagia. But as their level of contact with the Bogland deepens, so will the changes. Our hosts, the Ib'rs, for example, come from an Old River Clan society, which in the Bogland is understood and respected, if no longer emulated. Think of the Metro-Terran system when it was still on a single preindustrial planet. That's what Pelagia's continental civilization is like."

Ay'r had already picked up much of what P'al now told him from clues around him: the people at the inn, the peat cutters' conversations, the status of Dr. Seppi. Now he asked, "Then the 'Gods'—whoever they are—haven't been as instrumental on Pelagia as we had thought before?"

"Except," P'al said, "that no calendars exist among the Boglanders which reach beyond ten generations. Recall, Ser Kerry, how when 'Dward first told us the myth of the Seven Brothers, how he said it happened ten generations ago. That would mean only about three hundred Pelagian years ago. We took that to be an inability to count years beyond a certain point. Yet nowhere on this continent, among any of the peoples, are there calendars predating those ten generations."

"How can that be?" Ay'r asked. "We know this bowl must have been formed thousands of local years ago.

"I think the 'Gods' brought calendars, perhaps even the current language. The market traders write a sort of primitive hieroglyphics, but their numbers are completely developed, and are close indeed to the Metro-Terran 'Asian' system of numbering. One horizontal line equals one. Two equal two, et cetera."

"You're suggesting," P'al said, "that the catastrophe occurred as recently as three hundred years ago!"

"No, I'm suggesting that there has been more than one catastrophe, and they have become historically confused. Remember how during her ocean-floor survey, Mer Clark found indications of drowned river valleys and mountain ranges, and that she reported sonar readings which suggested that beneath the ocean's silt lay even more deeply buried but similar ecological formations? The prevalence of enormous peat bogs here suggests that this bowl we are in was scooped out in one ancient catastrophe and eventually seeded. It filled with grasses, which sank slowly over centuries to form the bog. A second catastrophe burned the surrounding plain, charred the surface of the bog, and allowed an entire new growth of grasses and grains. Perhaps it was only then that the exiled people arrived to settle here. Or perhaps not until after a third catastrophe."

P'al continued, "When the Aldebaran Five seeded this planet, they could never have known this, nor how difficult it would be for their seedlings to survive here. Yet look at them! Their cities, their culture! This might be one of the strongest Hume races to ever exist. The Metro-Terrans upon which our entire galactic civilization is based required twenty times as many years to reach this level of civilization."

"And as soon as they did," Ay'r said, "it was only a few centuries until they burst into the stars."

"Then think how quickly this race will move," P'al said. "I wonder if the Matriarchy is ready for Pelagia."

Ay'r wanted to say to him, "The Matriarchy is already dead, according to Alli-Clark." But he held his tongue. He would watch the two of them together, make certain that someone—'Harles, possibly—was always at Alli's side, to keep them from confabbing until he knew more about this mission and what it really meant.

Once again, Ay'r was awakened in the middle of the night. This time he was sure that it was P'al and that he was leaving his single bed. Slowly, Ay'r disentangled 'Dward's limbs, which once more had been thrown over his body. Up, he pulled on boots and garments and crept out the door. The corridor was lighted by one guttering lamp, and through the upper slits, what passed for the depth of night almost blackened the sky.

Earlier that evening, at dinner, with P'al, Oudma and—for a change—
'Harles, the innkeeper's wife had come by their table and once more
sashayed around. Once more P'al had been the object of her attempts at
seductiveness. Ay'r hadn't been the only one to notice his usually rigid
companion talking back to her, as though expressing willingness to flirt
or, who knew, even more. Ay'r had to admit he didn't know enough about
P'al's personal life to be able to say whether or not he had been at all
serious with the Boglander woman. After all, while P'al was clearly an
M.C. official of some rank, that rank was, after all this time, still in
question. Or rather newly called into question. Since Alli-Clark had left
the Fast, P'al was clearly running things. In fact, he might have been
running things all along. That fact and the opacity of their dialogue on any
substantial issue so far made P'al far suspect to Ay'r.

Even so, he was prepared to follow P'al down the corridor, even if it
meant that P'al was merely meeting the innkeeper's wife for an
prearranged tryst.

If so, it was out of doors. A pet beetle that guarded the entry, skittered
away at Ay'r's approach. So quickly, it must clearly be awake; P'al must
have already gone out the door.

The night air was unusually thick, and Ay'r quickly put on his upper
garment to ward off the dampness. He saw what he thought was P'al or
his shadow moving along a far wall of the street and quickly, quietly
followed him. After passing several dwellings, P'al dropped out of sight.

The spot where he'd vanished turned out to be the embankment of
one of the narrow canals that riddled the entire area. Ay'r dropped over
the side and along the slippery furze, seeing his companion's dark figure
out beyond the dwellings, moving toward grain fields.

When P'al finally stopped at the nearest stand of small-leaved hedges,
Ay'r also stopped, although still a good distance away. When P'al pushed
his way into the hedge, Ay'r sped as quietly as he could until he reached
the hedge. Although close to the village, this area seemed already far
away because of its isolation in the fields. Overhead the canopy of the sky
now seemed brighter at some points, and Ay'r wondered if the light might
be from the larger moon they had seen from orbit inside the Fast. Nowhere
else on Pelagia had moonlight been visible, and the Drylanders seemed
to know nothing of their astronomical surroundings. A line from some
forgotten Metro-Terran poet went through Ay'r's mind: "Ill-met by
moonlight, fair Titania," but he couldn't identify it. He thought, this is the
perfect place for an assignation.

He moved aside a few hedge leaves gently, half-expecting to see P'al and the innkeeper's wife coupling within the hedge's protection, but instead he made out the dull shine of a T-pod. One of their own T-pods. Closed. And within it, P'al, leaning back in the netting, his eyes closed, his wrist attachment secured.

Ay'r pulled back, letting the leaves close on the scene. In the travails and many incidents of their journey, Ay'r had completely forgotten about the T-pods. Or at least he had forgotten the fact that they could be called. He should have known that P'al would stay in contact with the Fast, have the T-pod follow him. He might have been calling it every night—every night he could get away.

Anger welled up inside Ay'r and he quickly pushed it down again. Yes, P'al had made a mockery of all they had undergone so far. It was natural to be irate about that. But, more importantly, what was P'al actually doing here? He hadn't merely returned to the pod for more comfortable sleeping. No sense having the wrist attachment on if that were the case. Was he reporting in on what he had seen during the day? Perhaps. He wouldn't be able to report directly back to the M.C. due to the time distortion they had encountered by coming to the far outer arm. Yes, that must be it.

Even so, as Ay'r trod back along the embankment, trying to keep his physical balance, he could feel his emotional imbalance. He was still angry at P'al, probably had been for days without being aware of it. An impractical emotion. He would do best to rid himself of it, if only P'al didn't seem to be obviously going out of his way to induce it. His twisted evasions, his obvious prevarications. That little speech today as though saying, "Look, I can be as good a Species Ethnologist as you are." The constant infuriating things P'al always did and said. The way he would silence Ay'r as though what he was about to say was some M.C. secret, instead of a simple statement of biological or geographic fact anyone with eyes could see for himself. His entire air of mystery. Coming and going without a word to anyone, almost as though he were doing it on purpose. Better the irritating Alli-Clark than all this tomfoolery. At least Ay'r knew where she had been at every moment.

He made his way back to the inn and only upon arriving wondered if the door was open or if it locked from within. The latter, it turned out. He should have known. It was ridiculous to remain out here. He was soaked through to his skin already; even under the best cover he could find from the inn's narrow overhead, he would be a huddled freezing mess by morning.

He found his and 'Dward's room and threw a handful of soggy gravel into the high windows. Naturally, 'Dward didn't answer. He slept so deeply. Perhaps 'Harles, in the next room.

Ay'r's tossed gravel brought someone to the door which gave onto the bedroom corridor—not 'Harles, but Oudma.

"What are you doing out there?" she asked as he stepped in.

"I thought I heard someone lurking about and locked myself out."

She insisted he come into the inn's main room and sit near the dying peat fire. Insisted he take off his soaked shirt, too, and hang it up to dry. Oudma had noticed her surroundings and found her way about the inn easily, even in the very limited light. She obtained a drink of mead for him. In a few minutes, he was snug and comfortable once more. Oudma joined him at the fire.

"Father finally sleeps at the inn," she said in a quiet voice. "So your companion must be a great deal recovered. You noticed that I had a laugh at my brother's expense about it. You don't think I was being cruel to 'Dward, do you?"

"Not at all."

"Monosilla youths call me cruel. Cold. Indifferent," she went on.

"I hadn't noticed," Ay'r said.

"Perhaps because you, fair stranger, are even colder and more indifferent than I am. Around you, I feel like an Arach which has stung itself."

The sudden tremor and hollowness in her voice made Ay'r turn to look more closely at Oudma, half-hidden in the fireglow.

"I mean nothing by it," he said by way of apology.

"You mean nothing by anything," she retorted quietly. "Nothing to me. Nothing to any of us. At first I thought, it was 'Dward you wanted. Though you sleep at his side at night, I know now that's not so."

"Early on, you warned me to respect his virtue."

"As long as he withheld it. Or as long I did. Alli is not your bondmate. You told me so. But I've seen it for myself. Nor is P'al. You told me you didn't know your companions very well yourself before your travels. I now believe that. I didn't need the truth-sayer's omens to know you were important where you came from and I didn't need to hear your attempts at lies to know that you come from, very far away. Yet one thing surprises me, Ay'r, and I'm not easily surprised: the fact that instead of becoming more familiar, you are grown stranger to us now than you were the day you arrived."

Ay'r felt chastened by her words, all of them true.

"You want to know who I am?" he asked.

"I would like to know, but not in the way you think. Not where you come from or what purpose you have or why these people serve you. No! I want to know...well, for instance, that night when you told me you were an orphan. That I believed. And I who have been so well loved by mother, father, brothers, I felt compassion for you then. And I felt close to you. But now..."

Her words touched him.

"What you ask for, Oudma, I can't give you. Not because I won't. I can't! Until a short time ago, I thought I knew myself and what my life was. Now, I find everything about myself a mystery to myself. Hints and clues surround me, but I can make no sense of them. Especially since they suggest that for some reason I cannot for the life of me fathom, I am somehow more than I ever thought I was, that I have some larger purpose, that I fit as the key piece into a puzzle whose design I can't even see fully. Lately I am forced to question everything. That keeps me occupied all the time. That's why I seem cold and indifferent. That's also why I'm searching for my father, hoping that should I find him he will tell me, or somehow through him I'll discover the meaning of all this." Ay'r hesitated. Then thought: why not say it all? "I have no bondmate. Male or female. Once...a long time ago...but that was being children together."

"You have again opened your heart to me, Ay'r, which I realize is difficult for you. Now I'll open mine. Let it lead where it may. No longer can I restrain it. Another of the infant's omens has come to pass. I care for you like no other I've met. I want to be wife, mother, lover, sister, everyone to you, Ay'r. I know it should not be, and in my deepest being, I know that should it come to pass that we were bonded, it would not last."

Ay'r was glad for the dull firelight. He felt his face flush deep red. His entire body seem to lift and glow. Only once before had he received a declaration of love, and that, as he had told her before, was from another child.

"I won't pretend to understand all you've said, although I feel its sincerity," Ay'r said finally, when silence would no longer do. "But I will say this equally truly: You are unlike any woman I've ever met, Oudma, and of all women I've ever met, the one most easy to be with, to talk to, you are most congenial to me."

It was her turn to be surprised.

"Under circumstances other than these, I would be honored to be your bondmate," he added.

She was about to reply when they heard sounds at the inn's entry—P'al returning. He mustn't see Ay'r awake, or suspect anything. But it was too late to return to the sleep chamber. And if P'al and Oudma saw each other now, he might ask her and untangle Ay'r's obvious lie about why he had been locked out.

"Hush!" Ay'r said, then moved out of the dull firelight. "Get down!" And half-pulled, half-pushed Oudma down next to him, out of the line of sight from the entry.

She lay inches away from him, listening to P'al enter, look about the inn, evidently not see them among the pillows, then go on through the corridor to his chamber.

"Are you so concerned for my reputation?" she asked, amused.

"Aren't you?"

All amusement was gone from her face. "I already told you, Ay'r."

They faced each other now. Very close, her hair was upon his bare skin.

"If you'd like, you may kiss me now," he said.

"May I indeed!" Oudma began to get up, but he held her down.

"I don't know your ways of courting," he said. "Where I come from, women take what they want of males. Once you begin, I'll know what to do."

"I suppose I should be grateful for that," she said, amused again, but she brushed her hair back from her face, and kissed him lightly.

"Touch my body," he insisted. "Here"—showing her—"like that. And"—sliding off his lower garment—"yes, like that. Go on. Don't hesitate. Consider my body yours to do with as you wish."

As they continued to embrace and Oudma's hands became more confident, more probing, Ay'r kept up this talk: "Where I'm from, women brag about their male conquests. They boast of their finesse and thoroughness in lovemaking, and how they leave males weak and yet pleading for more."

At first shy, hesitant, unsure, Oudma followed his words, letting him guide her hands and mouth, released now by her revelation and the ease with which he allowed her to fulfill some of her desires, aroused too that they were hidden, possibly discoverable by others, and Ay'r could tell, even more aroused that although they lay side by side, equals, yet he was naked and she was not, he was passive, she active.

As he'd predicted, with her fascination in him, his own excitement slowly began to gather force. Finally Ay'r turned toward Oudma and lifted her head and pulled her face to face again, and pushed off her night garment.

Only once in their lovemaking did he stop for a second to ponder how and if this also fit into the great pattern which had begun to reveal itself so ambiguously yet so omnipresently in his life, but Oudma instantly pulled him back into the complete oblivion of their mutually constructed sensual world, and all questions were forgotten, all doubts gone.

On the second day of the caravan's trek, the land began to soften. Toward night, as they gathered in a caravansry, the baked earth had given way to loose soil and even scrubby, sere-looking lichen growth.

They followed the New River, which never regained its depth or strength of current after leaving Bogland. By the following morning, the river had spread across a greater, flatter area and was so shallow at points that Ay'r could see rocks and silt beneath its waters. A primitive agriculture had grown up alongside its banks, farmers using basic leverage irrigation which lifted both water and wet soil to form a narrow strip of fertility on both sides of the river.

The New River had begun to silt up considerably, and when they stopped for their afternoon meal, their camping spot was upon a hillock below which could be seen the confluence of the Old and New rivers, the yellow current of the former and the brown stream of the latter moving alongside each other at different speeds for a kilometer before merging. River traffic increased considerably, most of it flatboats of some girth which they were told came from the Old River cities.

By nightfall, when they once again gathered for sleep and talk, more than half the guests wore the distinctive woven cloth and metal-edged garments of the Old River lands, and though Boglanders and they traded, they kept their distance and slept apart.

The Delta itself began unexpectedly, a narrow triangle of indistinguishable farmland dividing the now-wide and coursing current. But it soon subdivided so often that the travelers were forced to move their wagons and colleys onto great flatbed boats, and their direction was thereafter placed in the hands of a steersman. The landscape around them had already become thick with vegetation, most of it varieties of what Ay'r had seen in Monosilla Valley and in Bogland. But the grasses were shorter and sturdier here, the irrigation terraces neatly triangular, and instead of small-leaved hedges, a stunted version of the tall funguslike trees and succulent bushes and even of the lichenlike grass reappeared in abundance.

A good thing that the four days' travel had rested Alli-Clark, because the humidity returned, and while it was not yet as oppressive as in the Bogland bowl, it gave every indication of becoming so. If Alli noticed it, she didn't say a word, she seemed so—well, "abstracted" was the only word Ay'r could think of. During the early days of their trek, she rode atop Colley, her petite body fitted loosely within 'Harles's larger one, as he pointed out one thing after another, explaining, answering her questions. Only once did Alli ride with P'al, and once with Ay'r. When he attempted to sound her out about 'Harles—who was clearly "wooing" her—she said merely, "These seedlings seem far less primitive than we had assumed. Almost Matriarchal in fact." Then quickly added, "With some glaring lapses, of course."

Oudma didn't monopolize Ay'r's mount; she divided her time equally between him and 'Dward. And while she and Ay'r now spent nights together at each caravansarai, by day their relationship was not as obvious, as though each tacitly knew that to do so might cause problems with the others—especially Alli-Clark, who seldom kept criticism to herself. But Ay'r found himself thinking she still must be recovering from the Arach poison, as she didn't say a single snide word, whatever she was thinking, didn't once snap at 'Harles in the fashion Ay'r and P'al had grown accustomed to, and only once or twice looked at her new companion as though wondering who, exactly, he could be.

As they awakened on board the flatbed boat the fifth morning since leaving Peat Cutters' Village, they were handed and shown how to use curiously constructed leather nozzles attached by long tubes to leathern tanks of watered air. The purpose of the nozzles became obvious soon enough. Not only was the surrounding landscape far more overgrown, with wild tangles of enormous fungal trees, some connecting high across the waters, and not only did the miasma released from their spores thicken the air so it was difficult to breathe, but it also seemed that their steersmen had selected a Delta stream used by refuse scows. Before, behind, and several times on either side of them, giant flatbeds filled to great peaks with rotting vegetable life floated by, and the stench was astonishing.

Ay'r was told that after a day or two, they would be become inured to the odor. Look at the staff on the boats, look at those on either bank of the river, who seemed to be heaping even more of the newly-chopped-down stuff upon rafts! It didn't help that the steersmen assured them that every other stream and rivulet of the Delta was also used by the garbage scows or that all of them were headed toward a single destination—the Great Temple itself, which somehow absorbed it all.

But if the travelers' olfactory senses were disrupted, some of the sights they passed were equally disturbing. An entire Deltan industry had grown up devoted to the cultivation of certain larvae of an insect similar to Eris, or silkworms. The larvae were just large enough to be comfortably held in the gloved hands of Deltan humes, who used the gluey substance emitted by any sudden motion upon the larvae, sweeping them across wooden frames as though sewing, the gluey substance quickly hardening to make a shimmering partly transparent material which the travelers were told would become moistureproof cloth. Manipulated in another way, the larvae released their glue as a liquid which remained more-or-less liquid and which was used as a sealant and caulking. And when Ay'r heard of and was shown even more uses for the stuff, he looked closely at his own air nozzle and tube and realized that those, too, were composed of it. He didn't tell the others of his discovery, nor did he remove it from his nose whenever he was above quarters, although he was aware that the odor had become so all-pervasive that it had begun to seep into his clothing, his hair—even the surface of his skin.

That afternoon, the garbage scows vanished suddenly, and the odor abated, although their surroundings remained those of a greatly aged and fetid swamp—trunks of the by-now-towering fungal trees all but knitted together not far overhead as though to capture the sheets of miasmic yellow green mist. Soon the travelers were testing the air and finding it not quite so bad; the nozzles were taken off and slung over their shoulders. When at evening the flatbed stopped at a quay, they were told that the remainder of their trip was overland: they had landed on Trapezoid Isle, the largest and most populated in the Delta.

'Harles had been here before, and he guided the loading of their colleys and led them along the outskirts of what seemed to be nothing more than an enormously-spread-out village, its architecture similar yet far more basic than what they seen in Lake Edge, nothing but extended—and Ay'r assumed, well-caulked—U-shaped huts.

After about an hour of what seemed to Ay'r like endless meandering along a road no better than any in Monosilla, 'Harles signaled and gestured ahead to a structure. Also in the U-shape hut style, but seemingly quite long, and accompanied by several other similar long huts all of them with doors and windows, the entire compound dominated by a domed central hut. When the travelers drew closer, Ay'r saw that it was a single structure in the shape of arms radiating from the center. It proved to be their guest residence.

'Harles and Alli went into the circular dome and emerged several minutes later with a small Hume lad who led them to their rooms in one of the spoke-huts farthest from the river. The boy wore an outfit made out of the larval cloth including foot pads and a single-piece hood. He most nearly resembled a comfortably swathed and quite active young mummy. Oddly enough, it looked terribly comfortable, and he raved about its advantages of waterproofing and yet "breathability" to the travelers and told them where they might buy their own. He chattered on about the inn's being crowded because of the many travelers who had come for initiation at the Great Temple and how slowly they were being admitted there. He suggested they go at once to reserve their time. He doubted that it would be the following day. After hearing the dialects of the Mountain and Bogland peoples, the boy's variation of the language wasn't at all difficult for Ay'r to understand or pick up: sibilants and plosives were stressed in his speech, probably to ensure comprehension of vowel sounds which might otherwise be lost in the sound-deadening humid air of the Delta.

'Harles said he knew attendants at the temple. He would go there immediately and try to use whatever influence they might offer. P'al went with him, avid for a look at the temple. The other four went immediately to their chambers, which proved to be small, almost cell-like in their size and furnishings—wall hooks for clothing, a single cot—and in the way they all opened out to a single large multipurpose room, which was furnished more luxuriously for sitting and dining. Despite their size, the tiny rooms were clean and well sealed against the miasmas, moisture, and odors outside which tended to waft across Trapezoid Isle.

"It is required that we sleep apart," Oudma told Ay'r and Alli, although they might have figured that out themselves. "Initiation requires it."

Since they had begun wearing the air nozzles two days before, none of the party had been very communicative with each other, so Ay'r wasn't surprised that none of them gathered to speak. Alli and Oudma said they were tired and went to their cells to rest.

'Dward immediately left to go to the domed central section, and to try out the Deltan wrap-clothes.

Despite their having been so idle of late, Ay'r also slept. He awakened several hours later, hearing the others talking and eating quietly in the larger room. P'al was describing the Great Temple to the others although he and 'Harles had only gotten as far as entering the so-called gatehouse there. P'al had seen enough to recognize that the enormous surrounding heaps of rotted garbage provided methane gases which were being collected and used as an energy source.

"For this lighting, for example!" P'al pointed to the thin opaque tubing which completely lined the joints of the chamber's side walls to its ceiling, "And for outside lighting, as well as stoves and even refrigeration." He was clearly impressed by this technology, and thought that once it could be contained safely, methane gas and its uses would soon travel to the Bogland, to the Old River cities, even up to the Mountains, providing cleaner and superior heating and lighting for all Drylanders.

'Harles had used his connections at the Great Temple to obtain a initiation the following morning. He had also secured visiting time with the Eyes and Ears for the strangers—evidently Alli-Clark had suggested it, or P'al.

After the six travelers had dined and drank and talked for hours, comparing sights and other less savory experiences along the way as travelers always do, the others went to sleep leaving Ay'r and 'Harles in the large room. On purpose, it turned out. Although 'Harles began by stifling a yawn, once he began to pursue his theme, he was his usual alert and intense self.

"My daughter said she would announce no bonding tomorrow. Why?"

A blunt-enough question.

"Are all your affairs recorded at the temple?" Ay'r stalled.

"Birth, initiation, bonding, death. Yes. And journeys sometimes, too."

"Probably because I'm a stranger," Ay'r said, although he found himself unaccountably upset by hearing it.

"Yet Oudma said she will follow you as though you two were officially bonded." 'Harles added.

Ay'r was pleased to hear it. "She told you that?"

"Yes."

Before Ay'r could begin to think what that would entail, how Oudma could begin to fit into his life moving from star system to star system in his avocation as a Species Ethnologist, 'Harles added, "Yet if we are to believe the truth-sayer whose several predictions have already come to pass, you have a greater business at the temple than we do, and perhaps all this bonding and initiation will mean little once that is accomplished."

"I—I have nothing..." Ay'r began.

But 'Harles reached forward and tapped the tiny object the infant se'er's nurse had laced around Ay'r's neck as a reminder. "This binds you to the task."

Perhaps this object would be useful in getting the Eyes and Ears to tell Ay'r the whereabouts of his father somewhere on Pelagia. However, after hearing what Alli-Clark had said about his father, Ay'r had even come to nurture even more mixed emotions than before about this possible future encounter. Not only had his father abandoned him, but if the Matriarchy was to be believed, Ay'r hadn't even been a normal son, but merely an experiment in mammalian reproduction! He could only believe that his father had taken one look at him as an infant and decided the experiment had been a failure—and that—above all—was why Ay'r had been abandoned, and why Ferrex Sanqq' had vanished from sight, to go into hiding and try again.

"Suddenly I feel bound all about," Ay'r said candidly, thinking not only of the tiny object, not even of Oudma, but of the importance of their mission.

"Tell me of your companion." 'Harles said, even more intensely than usual. "She seems very…" He searched for the word.

"Independent?" Ay'r tried, after eliminating the words "arrogant, inflexible, and demanding."

"Bewildering," 'Harles said instead. "She told me she is not bonded, yet when I pay her especial attentions, sometimes she appears amused, and at other times she merely stares at me, as though I were a—I don't know—a colley!"

"Believe me, 'Harles, she has been more courteous and less abusive to you than to any other male I've ever seen her with."

"Then I will continue to hope!"

"Hope for nothing, 'Harles. Where we come from, Alli-Clark is an important woman. She is used to being treated with the greatest respect and to giving little in return."

'Harles protested, "I know that isn't completely so, although she has already told me of her great work back home. Still, she rides with me. And though I have presumed little upon her, still she hasn't rebuffed me."

Ay'r wanted to know exactly what Alli had told 'Harles about her "home." She and Ay'r had never decided upon what story of their origin they would tell the Ib'rs as he and P'al had done, but then despite what the two strangers had said, neither 'Dward nor Oudma had believed they came from the North of Dryland. Was it safe to assume that 'Harles didn't either, and that Alli had—naïvely, perhaps playfully—told him the truth?

More important now, however, was 'Harles's problem.

"My friend"—Ay'r touched 'Harles's arm—"in these matters, I can be of no help. Follow your feelings."

"I've already decided upon that course," 'Harles said. Then he, too, went to bed. Ay'r would spend many hours alone thinking as the others dreamed.

No one had prepared Ay'r for what the Great Temple would actually look like, so he laughed when he first saw it looming through the substantially thick miasmas of methane gas which surrounded it. Laughed and then half choked. Because of the methane, they had all been told to wear the air nozzles with backpacks of more-or-less fresh air for their visit, and some of it got into Ay'r's tube.

Architecturally, the Great Temple resembled nothing so much as an ancient—if by now venerable—Metro-Terran utilities shed: cement-block construction with a granite rock facing. Quite unlike any other edifice on the continent, all of which were far more ecologically designed; and obviously unlivable. Over the centuries since the Great Temple had been built, the cement blocks had decayed and crumbled and had been plastered rather hastily and sloppily. The granite facing had been chipped away by time or the acidic atmosphere of the Delta so that it had a great deal more character than originally intended. More so now that multi-hued lichen had taken over much of its surface, growing so deeply within its pitted interior that it could no longer be removed. Mosses and fungal tree spores had found crannies and niches within the plastered cement blocks where they, too, might take hold. As a result, the simply designed edifice had taken on a sort of accidental deep-jungle glamour.

It might have been more imposing if it hadn't been built on level ground and remained there, while over time, the surrounding Deltan isles had risen with the annual deposits of silt. As a result, pathways had to be scooped out to clear its now-below-ground-level front and side entrances. The main avenue dipped at first gently past the gatehouse—another dome-shaped hut—then more steeply past embankments on either side of huge fields of rotten refuse dumped there and left to decay to produce the methane gas. Even from the avenue, Ay'r made out transparent panels of what he assumed to be more of the larval material covering the rotting stuff, which he guessed was then collected by tubes and fed into the Great Temple's core, doubtless to replace its original energy source.

Their appointment had been postponed from morning to afternoon, and the Ib'r family went a half-hour before the three strangers for their initiation. But 'Harles, Oudma and 'Dward awaited them inside the temple itself, at the top of the broad, slow-moving conveyance stairway up to the main room. All three Ib'rs seemed subdued, as befitted the place, and Ay'r wondered whether they oughtn't wait outside while he and his companions faced the Eyes and Ears.

"You might find that I'm being disrespectful," Ay'r explained.

"We three are your sponsors," 'Harles said. "We have to join you."

The bare, solid, institutional—and very-well-sealed—interior of the building doubtless was kept up by the score of acolytes and priests, all clad in variations of the larval-cloth mummy-wrap costume, one of whom led them through a pair of high stone doors (doubtless meant to be blastproof) and into the inner sanctum. There, the three were asked to sit upon a stone bench while their sponsors stood beside them. The scrubbed stone walls were bare of any object except what looked to Ay'r like a carved insignia which reminded him of the manufacturer's logo found on the side of the most common working Cybers in the Matriarchy. Who had carved it, and when?

The priest went to the wall in front of them and touched a panel, then drew back quickly.

"Three travelers from distant climes seeks an audience and counsel of the Eyes and Ears," he said in hushed tones.

"Have these travelers sponsors?" a rather mellifluous male voice asked. Evidently the speaker system was threaded through the stone panels.

"The Ib'r family, who were here for initiation and counsel," the priest said.

"Have them step forward for recognition," the Eyes and Ears said, and when 'Harles, Oudma, and 'Dward had stepped behind Alli-Clark, Ay'r and P'al, it said, "they are recognized."

The priest gestured for them to step back. Then he turned to the three on the bench and said, "You each may pose one question."

As none of the others moved, Ay'r began, but before he had gotten his first word out, he was told by the priest to identify himself.

"Ay'r Kerry Sanqq'."

One second while the Eyes and Ears sorted through its memory banks and concluded, "The name is unknown to me. Has it derivations or alternative pronunciations?"

"Don't worry about it," Ay'r said, drawing a sharp look from the priest. Before the priest could chastise him, Ay'r said quickly, "I noticed coming here that you're using methane gas for fuel. What happened to your original generator? And the fuel packs you were carrying?"

There was a long silence during which the priest tried to think whether or not he was scandalized. The question was so completely beyond anything he had heard before.

Finally the Eyes and Ears said, "Are you a Repairer?"

"Unfortunately not," Ay'r replied.

"Yet you knew about the original fuel?"

"We have seen the original plans of the Aldebaran Five," P'al answered.

After what seemed like a longish time, it replied, "I understand."

"Well?" Ay'r probed. "What happened to them?"

"Destroyed beyond repair. Long ago during the catastrophes, much was lost and rendered useless. This system is admittedly primitive, yet it's the best that could be devised, given the site, the situation, and a variety of other factors."

The priest was now clearly outraged by hearing his God explain itself—albeit he couldn't understand why—to strangers.

"I find it ingenious," P'al said, "And furthermore, the use of methane fuel you devised has begun to take hold in residences and streets on the Trapezoid Isle. It's only a matter of years before it spreads to the other communities."

"Thank you," the Eyes and Ears replied.

By now the priest knew an impertinence when he heard one, even though he might not understand its exact meaning. He decided to shoo them all out of the room.

"Thank you, Balphor." The Eyes and Ears stopped the priest. "You may leave."

The priest sputtered, but dared not disobey.

"See that no one else comes in while we're talking," it added. Then: "It took years to develop this methane-collection system. As you may already have guessed, it required enormous logistical problems, not to mention the vast reorganization as a place of worship and general records. The hiring and training of staff was a nightmare at first. Even now... Not to mention the built-in disadvantages."

"Fungal rot for instance," P'al suggested.

"Only the worst of the problems. It's insidious," it complained. "Gets into everything. Stone walls, and metal didn't stop it. Even the sealant caves in to it after a while."

"Explaining the slowdowns, the need for more and more energy," P'al said.

"To keep it clean. I do the best I can. But I don't know how much longer I can hold out. But...you're from Aldebaran Five?" it asked suddenly.

"Do you remember Aldebaran?" Ay'r asked.

"Triple red sunsets. Yes. I remember."

"We're not from Aldebaran," Alli-Clark spoke up.

"Yet from what these Ib'rs told me before," it said, "and the fact that several of you are bonding together...is Consolidation come so soon?"

"If by Consolidation you mean the joining of Pelagia to the rest," Alli-Clark answered, "no. Not yet."

"The Matriarchy?" it replied quickly. "It still exists?"

"Yes, but not as you knew it. The First Matriarchy fell and was replaced by a federation, which eventuated in a second Matriarchy."

"Which now totters in what may be its death throes," Ay'r said.

The Eyes and Ears was silent another longish time.

"I understand, I think. Your purpose here then...?"

"Does not concern you directly," Ay'r said. "Yet you might be of some help to us."

"Regarding these three inhabitants of Monosilla Valley," it now said, "I take it they know enough about the three of you to be included in further conversation? For example, they know exactly how far you have come?"

"Not exactly," P'al said. "Perhaps—"

Ay'r interrupted, "I believe all three of our Ib'r hosts know if not exactly how far away, then at least that it is quite beyond their knowledge. They should remain while we speak, especially since several of us are bonded. Alli?"

"I agree," she said.

"May we call you Maxwell 4500," Ay'r said. "I believe that's how you were called."

"You may call me that, or Max for short, although in truth, I'm more a concatenation of whichever of my sort escaped the catastrophes and managed to gather together. It was thought that survival was the prime directive, given the parlous situation, and so we built this bastion, and slowly melded ourselves together until Hume attendants could be found and trained."

"We applaud your decision in what must have been a difficult decision," Alli-Clark said. "It seems rational and furthermore has worked to benefit Pelagia."

"I'd like to think so, although you must realize that fewer and fewer of the folk come to record or consult us. Most of the inhabitants of the Old River communities still send their refuse, but not their youth. As for the Boglanders...they send nothing."

"Even so," Alli-Clark said, "you'll remain and persevere and continue to develop until the Consolidation occurs. Won't you?"

"Naturally, Ma'am. That is my program, which although I've had to extemporize a bit, I continue."

"Are you aware of the—may I say unnatural—progress of your charges?" P'al asked.

"Again, a result over which I had little influence, but to reevaluate constantly and attempt to keep pace with. I don't think the three of you could possibly understand the conditions under which I have labored. Natural disasters of great size and extent. The near-extinction of the seedlings. I doubt if any other A-5 Guide has had quite so many travails and if I may say so myself, my constructors back in the Aldebaran system little prepared me for quite so rigorous a testing."

Ay'r thought the poor Cyber would complain at length if he didn't interrupt. "You said before that you're unfamiliar with my name. Obviously it doesn't exist in your files. Could you check through for any variations?"

"I have been doing so all this while and have found nothing."

"The reason I ask is that part of our purpose here is to locate my father, believed to be on Pelagia."

To make it official, Alli said, "The Matriarch Herself sent us on this purpose."

"Alas, Ma'am, but I cannot help you."

"He might be one of the 'Gods,'" Ay'r prompted. "What do you know of them?"

"Only what the people have told me. They are obviously visitors like yourselves, yet from where, or why they came I don't know."

"And this"—Ay'r pulled the little object out of his tunic—"what is this?"

Another long silence. Then Max 4500 asked, "Where did you get that?"

"An infant truth-sayer gave it to me."

Now 'Harles spoke up, "The same truth-sayer who made many predictions for my family predicted an even greater future for Ay'r."

"The object?" Ay'r continued to hold it up. "What is it?"

"My key. Although how an infant got it—"

"He knew its significance," P'al said. "He said to present it here."

"Clear away the lichen on the carved panel, and you will see how it fits," Max 4500 said.

Ay'r did as instructed. There was a narrow slot exactly the shape of the key. He removed its lacing and inserted it. Immediately the carved panel backed in, revealing the complex drives of the machine.

"Do you understand what this means?" Ay'r turned to the Ib'rs.

"It's not a God, but a mechanism of some sort," 'Dward said.

"Do you understand what a mechanism is?" Max 4500 asked him.

"We saw one attached to a wagon in Bog Bay. It moved the wagon without using any animals," 'Dward said, evidently impressed.

"This, is the finest mechanism on Dryland," Ay'r said. "Almost as fine and far more complicated than any of the people."

"Placed here by your people, generations ago," Oudma now said.

"To help the people of Pelagia," 'Dward said. "But why would your people do such a thing?"

"I know the answer," 'Harles said.

"There is no 'our people' and 'your people,' 'Dward. We are all one people. But although they come from a far-distant place, we are the same. Which is why we can love each other so easily. Yet we Drylanders are to them as spores are to trees, as seeds are to plants. We are their children. And as a spore must leave to grow, so we were sent here to grow, guided and helped by this...mechanism."

Ay'r turned to the panel. "Do you see now, Max 4500, why I asked them to remain with us?"

"They understand a great deal. But not all the people are so full of wisdom yet!"

"No, they aren't. But all it takes is a few to lead the way," Alli-Clark said.

"I still don't understand what I'm doing inside you," Ay'r said.

Max 4500 guided his hand to a spot. "Do you see that small flat ecru object. It's attached by a simple V-jack so that it wouldn't lose energy while it was here, but remain charged. Whoever possesses the key may remove it."

Ay'r held it in his hand. It seemed solid, could be easily held in the hand, and didn't resemble anything he had ever seen before. He handed it to P'al and Alli-Clark, who between them had seen most of the Matriarchy's weapons and communications elements.

"What is it?" Ay'r asked.

"I haven't a clue. All I know is that it was placed there several generations ago, and only after I was blinded temporarily. I was reprogrammed not to reject it, to keep it charged and ready for use, and to tell whomever held the key how to obtain it."

'Harles and 'Dward were now looking it over. They had never seen its like either.

"Keep it," Max said. "it's never done me any good. Perhaps you'll find its match, or its use."

Ay'r pocketed the small, flat object. "One more question, Max 4500," he said. "How do we find the Recorder?"

"The Recorder?"

"Yes, Oudma told me that next to yourself, the Recorder is the wisest on Dryland."

"The last Recorder I noted...well, wait a minute—he might still be alive. Yes, possibly. An apprentice never arrived here to...it's possible. You'll have to go to the Mountains of Capin. Find the three peaks, and amid them is where his Observatory will be."

"At an Observatory?" P'al tried.

"An Observatory high over the clouds of Dryland. From which he looks out, observing the skies."

Ay'r had had enough mystery today. "Max 4500, are you programmed to produce holograms?"

"Why, yes, I believe I am, although I haven't produced one in ages."

"Project a hologram of continental Pelagia which includes this site as well as that of the Observatory."

"Three-dimensional," P'al put in. "In relief. A meter cubic. With appropriate coloring and demarcation of all salient features." And as he saw it beginning to form at the bench, and Alli-Clark got up, "Sharpen and focus it, and provide us with orange lines for the easiest route."

It was a rectangular section ranging from the Delta down across the widest section of New River plain to steeply ascending mountains right at the continent's southernmost edge. Clear passage was demarcated in orange until the foothills, when it became quite complicated, although the three high peaks with the Observatory were clearly marked out.

"It's like looking down from the Monosilla Plateau!" 'Dward observed. "Only from higher up."

"I only wish we could take a holo of that section with us into the mountains," Ay'r said.

"Let 'Dward remember it," Oudma said, "He has a wonderful memory for sights and places."

"Truly" 'Harles agreed. "As a boy, he would bury a toy in a lichen pasture and go directly to it weeks later, without faltering."

So both P'al and 'Dward memorized the section of the holo.

By now there was a considerable ruckus outside the room. Max 4500 admitted that it was his acolytes, whom he had locked out.

"We'd better get going then," Ay'r said. "Thanks for your help."

"Anytime," Max 4500 responded. "It's been a real pleasure to talk to someone...who could talk back. It's been years!"

Then, as the hammering on the door increased, the doors were unlocked, slapped open, and the Eyes and Ears boomed, "These visitors are under my express protection. Make certain they have what they wish for their journey."

"Grand to the last," Ay'r murmured, and the others tried not to snigger as a chastened guerdon of acolytes and priests accompanied them out of the sanctum, down the conveyance stairs, and up the avenue to the gatehouse.

Chapter Six

There was something almost mocking about the serenity of this evening on Melisande. For the fifth time in an hour, Gemma Guo-Rinne, snapped off the Intra Gal. Comm. before flinging herself onto a floating chaise.

It had been over a week, Sol Rad. since Diad had been deported to Hesperia, since she had returned to her apartments, packed, grabbed Jenn-Four and arrived back at the Fastport, on her way to Deneb XII, only to discover that no flights were going there. Since then, no commercial flights had left Melisande for the Resort World. Naturally, Rinne had immediately used whatever influence her position and reputation had supposedly accumulated to wrest passage on one of the several M.C. Security flights to the now-controversial planet. Without success. She'd even tried Wicca Eighth Herself. But the Matriarch had simply snorted that typical contemptuous half-laugh and said, "The situation is well in hand without you, Councilor Rinne. Concentrate on the business We have decided for you."

She had concentrated upon it, to little avail. Was ever a Cyber put through so many permutations before? Poor Jenn-Four had scoured the molecular structure of virtually every female who had stepped into the Arcturus System containing the Mammalogical Institute; then had turned her calculations upon a half-dozen worlds where Ferrex Sanqq' had been in the years before to and just after his tenure at the Institute. Operation Needle in the Haystack, the Cyber called her work, and it was all the more galling to Rinne because every time she looked at a holo of Ay'r, she *knew* without being able to put her finger on it that she had once known whom he resembled.

Naturally, there had been other projects to collate for the Matriarchy. She was now able to put together and relate to each other virtually all of the vast network of attempts to find a cure for the microvirus, using a link to the M.C.'s own giant banks of computers, and she was able to report— if not success, then at least a minimum of duplicated efforts and wasted energy. And she was able to follow those so-called secret projects the M.C. was continuing.

The one she had watched most closely was Eden-Breed, the Matriarchy's final effort at self-preservation by sending a few hundred women untouched by the virus out of the galaxy itself, presumably to a star in one of the globular clusters far beyond the spiral. That Project continued apace, naturally, given the emphasis placed on it by the Maudlin Se'ers and certain elements within the M.C. itself.

Not that Rinne—or anyone else connected to the Project—was working without distractions. Since that first, stunning, holo from Hesperia, The Intra Gal. News Service seemed to be going haywire. Rinne couldn't remember the last time that Matriarchal news had been so constant, so provocative, or of so much content.

The deportation of the Hesperian nationals from Melisande had been decried by the Quinx and the Orion Spur Federation, but also and more surprisingly, by some voices within the Matriarchy itself, who called it an unwarranted provocation. When, a day later, a universal Transgal. Comm. had gone out from Wicca Eighth hinting at the need to eliminate all possible sources of espionage, another notch of excitable galactic furor had been raised. As a result, the Quinx itself now regularly took over the airwaves whenever it wanted with transmissions of its own propaganda to counter those of the Matriarchy. Seldom in Rinne's rather long memory had there been so many transmissions, so much news on so many different fronts available to the inhabitants of the Matriarchal worlds.

The most sensational had been a series of reports from Deneb XII itself, where Hesperian holo journalists—unhindered as Rinne herself had been by the M.C. bureaucracy—ranged freely over the Resort World, throughout its towns and cities, within meters of Alpheron Spa itself, now heavily guarded by contingents of M.C. Security forces. Those transmissions had been watched with fascination by every woman on Regulus Prime eager to know what exactly was going on at the Spa, and exactly how much the Matriarch was hiding. Denied entrance to the Spa itself, the journalists had tried various ruses to gain entrance. All of them transmitted, no matter how ludicrous or dangerous. Stopped on every side, the journalists then focused upon the population of Deneb XII.

And struck a rich vein of both news and propaganda. Following the Bella=Arth War, the planet had been slowly settled by humes, among them more than a few former warriors and their families, and eventually by returned Bella=Arths who had been Offworld at the time of the great defeat.

Although Hesperia had tried for years to sell the place as a Resort World and had built a variety of resorts, as well as funding the gigantic Hymenoptolis Museum, the population of Deneb XII had remained low, its demographics constant: resembling far more what one expected from a recently discovered "Pioneer World" than a Resort World.

Light industry and dry-agriculture accounted for the bulk of Deneb

XII's GNP, and the inhabitants—male and female, Hume and Arth—interviewed by the Hesperian news team expressed the conservative—even reactionary—viewpoints of any Pioneer World population. Looked like them, too: the broad tall women in sand-pitted, stained Plastro agro. airsuits, their spare and work-worn spouses of both genders and their gaggles of sunburned, labor-hardened children.

When they spoke, they did so quietly, but with strong conviction, often referring to the Treaty of Formalhaut and even more frequently to the rights of Settlers and Free-Worlders. Their words were as spare as the landscape against which they were always holographed, the inevitable ancient Bella=Arth City-Nest ruins in the background, the orange and blue suns casting an unforgiving white light upon their hard and handsome faces. All of them—Hume or Arth—were pained by the allegations of interspecies breeding, by the possibility that their most cherished beliefs were being betrayed in their midst by their own government. It was fine reportage, Rinne had to admit, and did more for the Hesperian cause than anything the Quinx might say or do.

But she had had enough comm.s from Deneb XII and Hesperia and Melisande; she had enough rumors along the M.C. grapevine. Rinne needed to discover for herself the truth to the rumors, and be able to report it back to the semiannual Council when it met a week Sol Rad. from now, where she was certain Wicca Eighth would be already well prepared with Her own denials.

Rinne knew it was foolish, possibly suicidal to her career in the M.C. But did that matter so much now? She had never been as ambitious as many women around her to begin with. Perhaps that was how she had risen so fast, so far. Unwatched by the others as they constantly jostled and undercut each other in M.C. politics, she had been given enough time and space to do her work freely, and thus a bit more thoroughly than others. And, after a while, she had come to be valued by some of those other, more ambitious women, because she didn't take sides, but held aloof, couldn't be bothered by politics. That was why Wicca Eighth had chosen her for the current post—because of Rinne's impeccable ethics; without in the least realizing that same sense of ethics could be turned, laserlike, against Herself and Her policies.

"Jenn-Four!" Rinne punched in the Cyber's voice. "You've simply got to find me a way to Deneb XII. I don't care how or how much it costs. What do you show?"

"Not much, Councilor Rinne. All scheduled Fast services have been halted."

"What about cargo?" Rinne tried. "Even if there are no tourists coming and going, the population still needs contact with the outside. Imports of necessities. Exports of some of their goods."

"The Deneb Commercial Lines still plies the skies," Jenn-Four repeated the local comm. advert for the system. "But it does so on a reduced basis since the Cult of the Flowers introduced a limited sector closure for the entire Deneb system. And only from the Markab Lambda system, which, as you know, is still under close M.C. supervision. Furthermore, there are Cult guards on every commercial liner in or out."

"I find it difficult to believe the Quinx would allow that. At least titularly, Deneb XII is under their jurisdiction."

"Hesperian visas are accepted on the liners. Classes 13 and 75," Jenn-Four said.

"Journalists and diplomats!" Rinne saw what it meant. Evidently the rulers of the City itself didn't want a lot of its people traipsing around the planet while it was still so hot.

"As well as all bona fide Deneban visas," Jenn-Four added. "Just try to get one of those!"

Rinne wouldn't have to try. She could go around the other way.

"Jenn-Four, Intra Gal. Comm. to Hesperia for me. Captain North Taylor Diad."

A few minutes passed while Rinne calculated what this communication would entail. Obviously, she would be screened by the M.C. Security forces. But she would have to take that chance. More of a concern was whether or not he would readily understand—and then agree to—her plan. And then, perhaps foolishly she knew, Rinne wondered if Diad would reply at all. A Beryllium bachelor—retired or not—must have had a great deal of experience with romantic liaisons in his long life. What if Rinne had been merely that to him: his Wicca-World romance?

The holo snapped on, displaying the expected M.C. Security Censor.

"Surely a woman of your importance, Councilor, must realize that due to the current diplomatic impasse, we cannot put through every comm. to Hesperia."

"Naturally," Rinne replied with equal frost. "But a woman of my importance also realizes that I have all the security clearances needed for just such a comm."

"If this is urgent M.C. business then—"

"It is!"

"And if we may assume that this comm. will in no way endanger the Matriarchy—"

"What could I possibly do, Ma'am, beyond what the M.C. itself is doing to endanger itself?" Rinne couldn't help asking.

"Please answer the question."

Rinne answered with the required formula.

"Given your levels of clearance, your comm. will be completed without any Security censorship," the official sourly admitted.

Rinne would liked to have believed that. She didn't, naturally. They would listen in as a matter of course. Perhaps not to every word. They might attach her comm. to a Censor-Cyber which had been programmed to monitor and compare the conversation against a matrix of words and phrases, and against various codification templates. Fine with Rinne. She had another plan, no matter who listened in.

The holo blinked; then Taylor appeared suddenly. Even for a Beryllium hauler, the background was unusually sumptuous.

"Gemma? Is that really you?"

"You've not forgotten what I look like already?" she said, only half-teasing.

"You look wonderful. Maybe," he added, "a little overworked."

"I *am* overworked," she replied. He looked fine. She was glad she had comm.ed.

"How did you manage to get through? I've tried for days, Sol. Rad."

"I promised not to give away any M.C. secrets," she joked, hoping to irritate whatever censor—live or Cyber—might be listening in.

He laughed. "You're still in Melisande?"

"That may be censored information," she replied lightly. "But I should be able to tell you that I've managed to get a short holiday. I thought…well, if you wanted to, we might still get together. Somewhere neutral, of course. If that's at all possible for you," she qualified it even further.

"You mean you and me? When? Where?"

This was key now: he would either comprehend her or not. "Do you remember where I told you when we said good-bye at the Fast terminal?" She did not have to work very hard to add sultriness to her voice so the censors would read it as "interpersonal" and thus be thrown off.

His face frowned slightly. He remembered, all right. She had told him she was on her way to Deneb XII. From her question, he must know she had never gotten there. He half-smiled now. "Gemma, I was a little distracted by our farewell, by the crowds, the haste… Was it Enif Prime?"

He had understood her need for being roundabout and was biting. Good for Taylor.

"Silly!" she said. "You must have been distracted. Markab Lambda.

Didn't you tell me that's where your parents had their official espousement?"

Now his face became serious. "I never did get around to asking you formally," he said.

"You certainly did. But I won't hold you to it until all this mess is over with. Let's go anyway."

He seemed relieved. Because she wasn't holding him to his vow? Or because he also realized how difficult it would be for the two of them if she had?

"When?"

"There's a Fast from here that arrives tomorrow morning, at 23 hours, 15, Sidereal Time."

He was checking the screen of his holo for a schedule. "I can get there by then. Better bring your hiking boots. It's still a little rough there."

"You can go hiking if you want, Taylor. I had something a bit more well, quiet in mind. Staying in our suite at the spa there. Ordering in. Hanging up 'do not comm.' signs, you know...." She let the tone of her voice complete the sentence. Then added quickly, "By the way, I've heard that I might need a Hesperian visa to enter the system."

"Really, I didn't know—" Then stopped himself, bright as a newly minted credit.

"I'd hate to have only a day or two Sol Rad. and be sent back because I didn't have the right visa," she tried not to whine.

"I should be able to get one," he said.

He had understood, the dear male, understood and agreed to help her. In return for spending time with her. Well, that was only fair. Especially as she very much wanted to spend time with him.

They barely had time to repeat the schedule times, when they were told the comm. was at an end. Taylor blew a kiss at her. Which Rinne caught.

When his holo was gone, the same M.C. Security Censor reappeared on Rinne's holo.

"Would you like us to log in that particular party, in case of future urgent calls?" she asked, cattily.

"Yes, please," Rinne said sweetly, then added, "Perhaps not. A woman of importance never knows when a better offer may arrive."

"As you wish, Councilor," the holo said and snapped off.

Doubtless, she went immediately to tell her colleagues about the sheer nerve of those high-placed M.C. women, using highly censored comm. lines to arrange weekend trysts with Beryllium multibillionaires. Her colleagues would doubtless listen to every savory detail, shake their heads, and then complain bitterly at the unfairness of life, even in the Matriarchy.

And then forget the actual content of the comm. Which was what counted the most.

"Councilor!"

"Yes, Jenn-Four?"

"You asked me to notify you if there was any news from Deneb XII on the Intra Gal."

Rinne sighed. She would have preferred to think about a few days with Taylor, even on Markab Lambda.

"Would you like me to record it for later playback?"

"Why not?"

A half-hour Sol Rad. of daydreaming later, Rinne asked to see the recording of the Intra Gal. News. It was worse than she had guessed. Gn'elphus, the Interstellar Metropolitan of the Church of Algol had arrived on Deneb XII and had immediately called a meeting of the local Maudlin Se'ers. How he had managed to slip through M.C. Security was unknown. Despite the red-suited guards everywhere, thousands of Denebans had jammed into the usually sparsely attended edifice used by the Se'ers to hear Gn'elphus rail against unnatural activities in their very midst. The aged Se'er had riled them up to a fever pitch. He had done all but declare a holy war. Afterward, adolescents and younger women had called a demonstration in front of the Alpheron Spa, and when the M.C. had banned it, they had rioted, shooting down a perfectly innocent sand-skimmer and using it to try to ram through the Spa's gates. The security guards had been forced to use stunners. Even so, they had had a great deal on their hands. Only a dozen or so rioters could be arrested. Scores more had been temporarily paralyzed but pulled to safety by cohorts and finally even by horrified adult onlookers.

Naturally, the Deneban Council had comm.ed the Quinx, and both governments had lodged a formal complaint to the M.C. through the Orion Spur Federation. Naturally, the Matriarch had—at Her leisure—replied that She paid little attention to "local skirmishes," and considered the matter one for the Tourist Board—which everyone knew had titular control in the Matriarchal Council, but was otherwise completely inappropriate to the incident. The most controversy the Tourist Board had faced to date was liner rate stabilization and accommodations inspections. The Tourist Board's leader turned out to be a very old woman who had been put into the position in lieu of retirement and who suddenly revealed unsuspected depths of loyalty and aggressiveness. She declared the incident to have been provoked by Hesperian Oppositionists. Spouting language not heard since the Bella=Arth War, she vowed to protect the Spa with the entire might of the M.C.

A supposedly neutral reporter then interviewed two stunned adolescent women who had been in the fracas on Deneb XII. They managed to overcome some of the longer-term effects of the stun to declare rebelliously that they would be back to take the (slang term deleted) Spa, and destroy its (slang term #2 deleted) inhabitants. Their parents stood behind them, grim-faced.

Ewa had been dreaming. But even within the dream, she had known, and had once even said, "This is a ridiculous dream." As were most of her after-noon nap dreams. Even so, it had continued. As they always did, lately.

Then she was being shaken awake. Janitra. Excitement on her face.

"Wake up. It's happening now."

Ewa tried to pull herself out of the quicklime of the unnatural sleep. "It's happening now!" Janitra repeated.

"She's having it now?"

"Right now. Come on!"

Ewa snapped awake. Found her robe, let Janitra rapidly finger-comb out her hair. "Come on!" Janitra pulled at her.

"You're sure they won't see us?" Ewa asked as they tried to appear relaxed on the conveyance down to the second floor, the first floor.

"I told you. I found an unused office with full–live holo into the labor ward."

This was the tricky part: where they might be stopped. Ever since the interrupted Intra Gal.comm.s, Alpheron Spa had been rife with red uniforms. These lower areas were the most crowded, and many of the less-noticeably-showing women like herself often came here for their "constitutional," which meant parading around the garden and flirting with M.C. Security Ladies, and then laughing at how flustered and "butch" the guards became when they got a response. Last night, however, there had been some sort of unpleasantness outside the Spa. Ewa had clearly heard the distant shouting of many angry young voices, then the hollow thuds of stun-shooters. This morning no one knew anything. Many women, like Janitra, slept so heavily that they had not even heard anything. But the M.C. guards didn't appear indolent and bored anymore. They were so busy recovering from whatever excitement they had encountered, they almost failed to notice Ewa and Janitra.

Janitra—and now Ewa—had a hint of what the melee had been about.

People outside were protesting the births within. But why? Finally Janitra had gotten a traveling merchant who visited the Spa with her trinkets to say. Or, rather, Janitra had tried to understand what the local Bella=Arth was trying to say. But once past the usual patois of haggling and bargaining, she fared poorly. What the Bella=Arth had—cautiously, in private—said to Janitra seemed so odd, so incomprehensible, that she came away with the belief that the babies been born here were special children. Unusual in some way.

"Special how?" Ewa asked.

"I don't know. The Bella=Arth kept using a term used to mean 'more.' "

"More what? Intelligence? Beauty? Maybe that's why we're here on Deneb XII. Something in the soil or even in the atmosphere. Both our fetuses are larger than usual. Could that it be it?"

Janitra had shrugged. Then, an hour Sol Rad. later, she had reported the existence of the room above the labor ward. She'd chanced across it while lost once after a radiocynteisis in a nearby lab. It was Ewa who had decided that they would see for themselves exactly how "more" their offspring would be. Janitra needed no persuasion.

The way there was unguarded. Even so, women in med uniforms could be seen crossing the passage. The two pregnant women would say they were lost, or on their way to a lab. No one would notice.

No one did. They made it through the passage and to another one and another one and finally to the room. Janitra would enter alone. Act surprised if it were occupied. It wasn't. They entered, found the holo dials, and sat down to watch. The scene was perfect, and it was obvious they had just arrived in time. The mother was floating above the pad, her body angled correctly, her legs separated by other air-beams. The two women could see the astonishing distention, hear the mother's short gasps, then make out a dark wet head emerging, then the shoulders, two arms, the raw wet scrunched-up little face which looked up unseeing as yet, but with apparent astonishment, annoyed, waving its little fists. The mother continued to labor, aided by air-beams, still breathing hard.

"It's beautiful," Ewa said.

"Perfectly," Janitra agreed.

Now the long torso was emerging, the hips...

The office door was thrown open. A pewter haired woman in a med uniform. They turned to her, found out.

"What are two doing here?"

She charged in, shut off the holo.

"We just wanted to—" Ewa began.

"You'll have your turn soon enough," she said to Janitra. "Who's your proctor here?"

"Maly'a. But she didn't know."

"I'm bringing the two of you to her office for an explanation of this right now."

She herded them out of the room and through the passageway, going in the direction they had come from. They had just turned the second corner when they saw the door to the garden slam shut—but not before they'd heard M.C. guards yelling.

"Eve! They've gotten inside!" two medicos shouted, running past.

The older woman turned around and followed her colleague into an elevator. She held other women out while Ewa and Janitra were shoved in, the doors closed. The lift went to the top floors of the spa.

At floor sixteen, two M.C. guards grabbed the two pregnant women, walked them down a loggia, around a corner, to a waiting sand-skimmer. One of a dozen parked at the edge of the roof-tarp, also filling up with pregnant women. From this high up, the noise below was distant, but still loud enough that Ewa thought it greater than last night. Hordes of people, sounds of stunners and other—more lethal—weapons.

"What do they want?" Ewa asked.

"Where are we going?" Janitra asked an M.C. guard as they were put into line for a seven-passenger skimmer.

"Where you'll be safe."

"But I haven't packed anything!"

"No need to. You'll be back in an hour or so." The edgy guard tapped her into the skimmer.

The skimmer hood closed. The pilot at the front wore double earplugs and was speaking low and rapidly. She wore a sidearm. The other woman in the backseat with Ewa and Janitra was quietly weeping.

"Don't worry," Ewa said. "We'll be back in an hour or so."

"We'll all be dead!" the woman sobbed.

"Someone shut her up!" a woman in front said, hard. Just then, there was a loud noise ahead, and one of the skimmers loading ahead of them on the roof-tarp exploded. Women screamed.

Their own skimmer pilot shouted, "I'm leaving!" then back to them: "Belt up, ladies!"

The vehicle shook once, lifted and spun out beyond the walls and over the city. More explosions passed them, evaporating like smoke nearby. Ewa thought, I don't believe this is happening.

"Why are they doing this?" she asked Janitra, the sobbing woman, anyone.

"We're going to one of the Arth nests," the same hard-voiced woman said authoritatively. "We'll be safe there. You know that some Wasps held out for months in those tunnels before they were ordered to eat tainted pupa."

They were out over the more industrial areas of the city now, long low buildings like tilted-over tiles on a yellow-gray board. Ahead, she could see another three or four skimmers. All M.C., thank Eve!

Suddenly there were more explosions around them. Their pilot was shouting into her voicer again, and the skimmer was moving in a sort of up-and-down and zigzig motion.

"I hope no one had a big breakfast!" one woman in the row ahead joked.

Outside the tinted hood, Ewa could see the same completely irregular motion of two other skimmers, which helped calm her nausea a little. The words "evasive action," went through her mind: Maxie and/or Virge had used it discussing military tactics after some mini-PVN they'd watched.

Now they were out of range of whatever weapons were on the ground, skimming steadily again.

The pilot was shouting again.

The woman in the row ahead turned around and said. "A skimmer was shot down. It's ahead. She's not landing to pick up the wounded."

"She has to!" Ewa cried.

The other women took up the case, and the hardened woman settled it by sliding forward, grabbing the pilot's weapon, putting it to her head, and demanding she pick up the wounded.

"I piloted skimmers like this at the Slam-'Em Races on Ophiucus Nine," the woman said. "Drop down now, or you'll die without a face."

The pilot found the grounded skimmer a kilometer ahead. One side had been blown away by an aero-torpedo. That side was in flames. The pilot was dead. Three women were still alive, though bloodied. One was going into premature labor. The pilot and two women managed to get her onto their vehicle in the narrow space between the pilot and front seat, where she fainted. The other two surviving passengers were terribly shocked. They were also helped into the skimmer. Ewa's pilot checked the others for life signs, then set the skimmer for auto-destruct. As they were leaving the terrible scene, Ewa heard something. She rushed back, pushed the cracked broken hood aside and saw it—a newborn wrapped in a Plastro-bunting, its head alone showing through the visor: thin black hair, black eyes, screwed-up face. Ewa brought it back to their skimmer and as they belted in and the pilot took off again, the Racer said to her "Now that wasn't so difficult, was it?"

Ewa asked the survivors whose baby it was.

"Jof'a," one replied finally. "She—" the woman broke down.

"We'll take care of Jof'a's baby, won't we?" Ewa cooed.

But when the baby didn't stop crying, Ewa opened the Plastro-bunting and lifted the infant against herself to give it tactile comfort. As she cooed and hummed and held it against herself, she clearly felt the extended spine and the four little lower limbs through the lightweight material, and Ewa understood completely and with a mixture of pity and horror exactly what the Bella=Arth merchant had failed to convey to Janitra: more legs! Two more legs!

Despite her shock, Ewa didn't say anything to the other women, but kept the baby wrapped. It was cooing, and she put it back in the bunting as soon as it showed signs of sleepiness. But she understood now all that was happening, and why it was happening. She was devastated, she kept telling herself. Yet, she also knew that she would let nothing happen to this child, or to her own, when it was born: four-legged, like this one, and beautiful, and in need of her love and nurture.

Who was she to be able to go against a thousand years of acculturation by the Matriarchy? And, after all, it would be Ewa's firstborn.

Rinne braced herself, then entered the pneumatic doors of the Stellar-Zine Lounge. She wasn't all that surprised when, just beyond the entry, air-jets from above and below suddenly swept her with gusts of air (checking for hidden weapons) adding a completely unnecessary razzing sound intended to draw the notice of the patrons in floating booths closest to the door. Attempting to remain collected, she strode past the curious, ignoring their comments—

"Eve! Look at the old broad!"

"What's this place comin' to?"

"She must have had her Prime vanish on her!"

—and settled herself on a slip-out stool along the long keyboard slab of Plastro which served as a bar.

The barkeep was a woman a century older than Rinne, but with a few too many full-cosma jobs, a propensity for clothing too small and too revealing for her age and figure, and a bizarre fashion sense. She was lounging on a floating pad among some still-in-uniform, rather worn out looking M.C. Security Guards, all of them watching and laughing at a life-size holo depicting a sextet of various species in sexual acts, a few of which even Rinne had never seen before. At least she suspected they were sexual acts.

"Hit the deck, honey!" The barkeep turned toward her and gestured at the panels on the Plastro. "Anything illegal or immoral, you gotta' see my grandma!"

The M.C. guards glanced at Rinne, then back at the holo in one motion, without a break.

Rinne ordered a double Stele-Martini. She'd need it. She sipped and inspected the egg-shaped lounge, trying not to appear to be either who she really was or a pickup.

One booth at the far end held some M.C. Forces in the deep indigo capes of the Cult of the Flowers. She definitely didn't think it was any of them she wanted. Looking around the room more closely, she realized that the wall-sized panel behind the holo was a door to another room.

Now what?

Ever since she had landed on Markab Lambda Six, things had gone wrong. The planet itself was a dusty, infertile mining world, with little water and plenty of room for intersystems markets. The capital, Marko-City was little more than a market itself, buildings low to the ground to avoid the inevitable erosion of the dry-naphtha storms which swept over it periodically; most of the living was done underground.

Including the spa, which was acceptable enough. Except for the management. Rinne discovered upon arrival that her reservations were for tomorrow, not today, Sol Rad. and as she didn't want to take any chances of being noticed by flashing her credentials, she settled on a smaller, far-less-elegant suite.

Worse, Diad hadn't arrived yet. When she comm.ed what passed in Marko-City for a Fast Port to check on his flight, she found out it had arrived—without him. Finally, the spa's desk Cyber, which surely had its circuits badly overscrubbed in the recent Cyber modification, located somewhere among its circuits a holo-message sent by from Taylor. He was still on Hesperia, he told Rinne. Something crucial had come up at the company he had worked for, and they had called him in. He would be on the next Fast, which wasn't due for twelve hours, Markab time. He looked upset and sounded calm.

Rinne had sulked for a while in her too-small suite, then unpacked Jenn-Four and tapped her into the desk-Cyber, which was in turn tapped into the Port's Cyber. Rinne asked, "When's the next flight to Deneb XII?"

"Next commercial flight is twenty-two hours ten minutes."

Dealing with problems here, Rinne had just missed one.

"There's a military schedule," Jenn-Four added. "Looks like an easy tap for me. Whoever modified these Markab Cybers left the chips in but scattered all over and unattached. I'll try a temporary electron fuse."

"Fine," Rinne said.

"Three M.C. Fasts due to leave for Deneb XII. Time secret, but Fast overhaul and fuel-ups are in progress. Any of the three could leave at any time. Or all three."

"Go on," she urged.

"You want the staff? On vessel #4567121 the Captain is a Vestra Pl'rnia. On #876921C it's Patha Ip'py, and on #98CLFL088 is Commander Helle Lill. You know anything more now?" the Cyber sassed.

"Why's the third one's number so different from the others?"

"It's listed as a Cult of the Flowers vessel. Newly converted. Bet it looks like the others from the outside."

Commander Lill was the name of Diad's friend. The one who had captained the Fast the Hesperian exiles had been forced to take off Regulus Prime. And from what he had said, Lill was a hardened old M.C. soldier. Evidently a successful one, too, if she was on her way to quell the troubles on Deneb XII. She might be leading the trio of Fasts.

"Comm. Fast Port," Rinne told Jenn-Four. "The last ship you mentioned. Use all my clearances to get through to Commander Lill—but not my name or title."

The holo snapped on. A young woman at the Fast Port, dressed in M.C. red with Cult accessories: Plastro head-visor, form-fitting body armor, and the violet velvet single-shoulder cape.

"Captain Wang'Un," she saluted. "Commander Lill isn't here."

"I must see her," Rinne said without identifying herself.

Wang'Un had heard that tone before. "Yes, Ma'am. But she's on short-leave. She and part of the crew. We're not due out for—" she hesitated.

"I don't need that information. Where is she now?"

The Captain was pretty when she frowned. "I could send someone..."

"I'll go myself. She's in Marko-City?"

"Yes, but...it's kind of a rough place."

Rinne heard the name and location and guessed how rough. She tried to find clothing that was both sleazy and unnoticeable. Not easy given how little she had packed. But at last she'd managed a look that could be construed as a well-off but still-rustic agro-merchant. And here she was, all dressed, at the Stellar-Zine lounge, and no Lill. Rinne would have to go behind the holo.

I'm not staying here another twenty-four hours, Sol Rad., she told herself. Maybe not even the twelve until Diad arrives.

Rinne caught the barkeep's eye and gestured her over.

"I'd like to meet your grandma."

Closer up, the woman was even older, even worse in shape. "It's pretty unsavory back there. Maybe you'd better think twice."

"Maybe not. If it's money, I've got it."

The barkeep shrugged, then gestured with one of her several chins, "It's—"

"I know where it is," Rinne got off the stool and sidled her way past the holo and through the sliding door. She heard someone whistle behind her.

This room was much dimmer, also egg shaped, with round tables hovering inside circular booths, upon which various bodies were writhing. Other bodies were stationary against the walls, watching the single holo of perhaps a hundred humes and Delphinids engaged in sexual activities, a holo which completely encircled the room at eye level, and thus was inescapable. Especially its sound, which seemed to match the sounds in the room, which in addition were heavy with breathing and motion. This was worse than Rinne had imagined. She would never find Lill here.

After a few minutes during which she pushed away various hands and other less-definable limbs which reached out for her, Rinne's eyes adjusted; her mind blanked out the holos; she scanned the booths, noticed a few torsos above the tables, among them one freshly risen, with a uniform top mostly open, breasts barely tucked in—and the giveaway Plastro wristlet of the Cult.

"Your Captain said I might find you here," Rinne said quietly and sat opposite the striking woman.

The head of an attractive young man lifted from within the woman's lap, A second later, and farther along the curve of the booth's seat, another male head lifted. Obviously, they were doing something to each other and Lill.

"Apologies for disturbing you," Rinne added.

The big woman leaned back and chuckled. "Don't mind them." She pushed the one head back down out of sight below the tabletop; the other head followed of its own accord. The noises they were making resumed.

No sense in being roundabout, Rinne supposed. "I was supposed to meet Diad here in Marko-City. He's been delayed. He had mentioned your name in Melisande."

Lill roached down and lifted the head. "Sorry, boys. You've lost me. Better find someone fresh."

The two youths clambered over Lill and out of the booth, pulling up their body-tunics as they went. Lill crossed around the booth, pushing Rinne aside so they sat side by side and very close. "Even Gynos have ears. Quietly now. What do you want?"

"Passage to Deneb XII," Rinne said.

"Northie mentioned a lady. He didn't say it was such a fancy one."

"Look, I haven't time to—" Rinne began.

"Hold on! We've got time! And after all...I was expecting you."

"Expecting...? You mean your captain comm.ed you?"

"My ladies comm. me when they douche. She said you had clearances up the ovaries. No name. You're what? Some hot councilor? Why not just use rank?"

Rinne was silent. Commander Lill was smart. Perhaps too smart.

"I could just have waited until Diad arrived," she finally said.

"And miss the show?" Lill gestured around the room. "Just tell me why you want to go there."

"It's personal."

"You have a spouse at the Spa? No. If Northie spoke of you, you're all his. A daughter there? Some relative? An ex-spouse?"

"Something like that," Rinne allowed. In a sense they were all her daughters, relatives.

"It's a real grokker on Deneb XII, you know." Lill said.

"I know."

"Could get even grokkier. Bang-bang. Bla-boom!"

"I'm ready for it."

"Fine. Pack and meet me at Fast Port in one hour Sol Rad. You'll remain in my quarters on the Fast until we land. No one will know anything!"

"Agreement."

"What about Northie?" Lill said. "He'll arrive here all hot and bothered with nowhere to go. He'll follow you."

"Can't you keep him from doing that? If it is as bad as you say there—"

"Look, I can bar him from Military Fasts. I can even harass him with commercial ones. But forget it. Northie does what he wants. He's from the City," she added, as though the two terms were synonymous.

Rinne had a sudden insight. If a high-ranking M.C. commander with a Cult-equipped Fast said that, meant it, knew it, it must be true: it must be reality. He's from the City—he does what he wants. That was true of Hesperia, too. Recent events proved that. But for how long had it been true? And why hadn't Rinne known it? Or anyone else at her level in the

M.C.? Wicca Eighth wouldn't believe it. Would any of the other Very
Important Women—before it was too late?

"You know Taylor a long time," Rinne said quietly. "What's he like?"

"Arrogant. Aggressive. Provocative. Demanding."

"But...also sweet. Gallant. Loyal."

"Loyal, yes. Intelligent. Practical. He's Hesperia! Roll it up, and he's
it."

Rinne remembered the lift drop from the Spoorenberg. His arms
around her, the ineffable sadness of twilight. Then what he had said—
about how it would all change, all of it.

"Trustworthy?" Rinne asked now.

"Do you mean personally?"

"No, I mean...I know so little about him. What if—what if he's not who
he seems. It would make sense, you know, to find me, romance me.... You
know what the political situation is like now."

"Far as I know, he's always been a Beryllium-hauler. Worked for
O'Kell there, one, maybe one-and-a-half centuries. Never had a political
thought in his head."

Lill was tiring of their conversation; she had begun glancing about
the room.

"Gratitude," Rinne said. "And also for what you just said."

"Truth only," Lill said, then reached out and grabbed someone passing
by and pulled him into the light. "Well! What do we have here?" With one
motion, she reached up and pulled his tunic off one shoulder and down
to his knees.

"I'll be at the Fast Port." Rinne got up to leave.

"Sure you won't stay?" Lill smiled. "Looks like there's more than
enough here for the two of us."

Her low-pitched resonation accompanied by tiny chittering finally stopped.
Mart Kell pulled himself out of the velvet grasp of her many palps and
managed to get to his feet. The darkened room spun for a moment before
he felt steady. These sessions with Kri'nni were becoming intense. And
he wasn't an adolescent anymore. Mart pulled up his semi-Plastro tunic.

"Going so soon?" Kri'nni asked.

"Have to. Meeting of the Quinx."

"Too bad. I could go on for hours more, Sol Rad." She added those odd
sounds by which Vespids simulated laughter. "You going to tell me what's
on the Quinx agenda (menu ((what's for dinner?))) or will I have to find
out myself?"

"What do you think?" He found the skullcap and pushed back his hair to stuff it in. Had the cosmetic tint gone out of his eyes? Probably. They had been here longer than it lasted. The visor would be cover enough.

"So, my little byte of information from our last meeting proved useful (of advantage ((delicious))), didn't it?"

"I've just paid you off a second time, Kri'nni."

A palp reached out and slid into his tunic.

"I really couldn't," he protested. "It's flesh, remember? I'm not made of chitin."

"Do you know what fascinates (excites ((stimulates my palps))) me the most about you? About all humes really? Rectums!"

He felt her palp trying to gain entrance there.

"Stop, Kri'nni! I don't know why? It's just like your fecal-positor."

"Absolutely not! On you it's also a sex organ."

"So?"

"Humes are so tightly constructed (dense ((compact)))! It's surprising your rectum is so little used. One might think Mother Nature ("the Great Queen" (("She Who Creates"))) would make better and more use of it. Especially on males. You've got all that space in your lower torso doing nothing, merely holding digestion tubes.

"Watch out, Kri'nni, you'll end up becoming a Species Ethnologist. Or worse, a philosopher!"

He pulled her palp out of his tunic and finished dressing. Kri'nni "laughed" again. Then she said, "Tell me about the Quinx meeting, Mart."

"You follow the Intra Gal. News. You know what what's on the agenda."

"The riots on Deneb XII. How to make Momma hurt."

"Exactly."

"Momma's already hurt. Her girls gave up Alpheron Spa."

"What?" Mart was stunned as much by the news as by how casually she gave it. "When?"

"I heard about ten minutes Sol Rad. before you removed your clothing."

Leave it to the Bella=Arth Comm. network. It had always been better than Intra Gal. It was always surprising to Mart that they had lost the war. They seemed superior to humes in so many ways.

"Does that change anything?" she asked.

"Was everyone killed?"

"My, no!" Kri'nni more or less sat up now, and found a nearby liquid drug to sip. "Momma got out many little pregnant Queenlets. They're in hiding now in the Mazes."

Bella=Arth term for the tunnels and egg-chambers that lay beneath the

Nest-Cities of Deneb XII, many of them never excavated. Where now, doubtless, the spa refugees' every move was being monitored by Kri'nni's Arth pals, Mart was certain.

"Naturally, Momma won't admit to it publicly," Kri'nni said, "But I think you might tell everyone."

A defeat for the Matriarchy. More power to the Oppos. And, Mart thought with a twinge of regret, also for the Maudlin Se'ers, to whom the Quinx had given free rein to provoke the riots.

"It would be clever (very Arth ((and un-drone))) if the Quinx rescued them."

"Wouldn't it?" Mart agreed. "And showed them with their babies on Intra Gal News."

"Possible?" Kri'nni asked.

"Very!"

"Now's the time to take every advantage (opportunity ((hit them hard!))), you know, Mart."

"There are more riots already," Mart said. "Two Centaurs were killed on Benefica. A group of them were attacked and beaten on Trefuss."

"It'll get worse. And for your sake, it *should* get far worse."

"Let's hope." Mart said.

"Hoping is for pupae, Mart. Warriors make and act. Sounds like Equicide time to me."

Mart faced her calmness. "You mean kill the Centaurs?"

"All you can find. It's the only way you'll be able to organize your many disparate groups into a solid movement (force ((hive))). Give them one clearly achievable goal, Mart. They're looking for one. I've heard," Kri'nni paused for effect, a very un-Arth thing to do. "Those four-legged ones live in Momma's own sleeping suites on Wicca-World, exercising undue influence. I've heard"—that pause again—"that one of them may even guide and control the old Queen herself."

Mart Kell's own spies in Melisande had reported the same thing for a decade now. But it had never been useful to him before.

"It could be done. The Church of Algol is terribly exercised about the matter. We could easily arrange for the rioters on M.C. planets to get closer to their Centaurs and..."

"Not just the Centaurs on the M.C. worlds, Mart!" Kri'nni's sibilants made her words sound far less innocent than they were. "All of them!"

He looked at her: no indication from her pose that she had just suggested genocide for an entire species.

"Are you sure of so drastic a thing, Kri'nni?"

"If you don't do something drastic now, Mart.... Let's be intelligent. You can't take Momma on directly. She's too strong. Even with the distraction of the rebel tincans, her ladies outgun you twenty to one. But now, here's a cause you can get wide support for, inside and outside of Momma's realm (territory ((scent-trail area))). Do it. And see if Momma fights back to protect her ponies—if she doesn't, you've won a battle. But if she does, you've won a war!"

If the Quinx didn't do something drastic now, Hart calculated, the City would miss the best political opportunity that had come its way in centuries for fatally wounding an already-staggering Matriarchy. And worse, Mart himself would miss his best opportunity for more control of the Quinx. But Kri'nni was wrong about killing all the Centaurs on their homeworlds. No one would go for that, and it would merely serve to turn anyone wavering between the Matriarchy and Hesperia back toward the M.C. No, there had to be some intermediate position. Provocation of Centaur killings on M.C. worlds, and then...something else.

"Branklin will never go for it," Mart argued. "He'll be horrified by the idea. He'll table the motion before I can explain all of its benefits."

"Get rid of Branklin. He's too old. Too soft (un-Bella=Arth ((without any carapace)))."

Mart would like to do exactly that. Ole Branklin was second in charge and had always been the Quinx's moderating voice. But Kri'nni was right. The time for that kind of moderation was over. Drastic action was required on that front.

"More members than Branklin would stop it," Mart said with what he hoped was finality.

"I don't see why. It's not as though those creatures are anything other than the results of ancient interbreeding themselves!"

The Bella=Arth statement of fact: ruthless, inexorable.

"Tell me, Kri'nni, what's in it for you?"

"It's evident, no? Species revenge upon Momma."

"There were males at Deneb XII, too. Hesperians, even."

"Momma had the ammunition," she said simply. "Momma made the moves."

"Provide me with everything you've got."

"I'll have recorded holos at the Quinx meeting. The spa in flames. Centaurs in the bedrooms of Melisande. Everything. But it's up to you to make it work, Mart."

He pulled on his hood and visor, slipped on his air-sandals, looking like another wild City adolescent and said, "I've got a feeling, Kri'nni, that this meeting is going to be fun (very Arth style ((a real palp-exciter)))!"

Kri'nni sipped her drug and said, "I love it when you talk dirty!"

The Quinx meeting had been going on for some time when Mart Kell finally arrived. Helmut Aare Dja'aa was speaking to the matter on Deneb XII, which was even worse than North-Taylor Diad had assumed when he agreed to meet Gemma Rinne on Markab Lambda and obtain passage to the beleaguered Resort World.

Diad still didn't know what he was doing at this Quinx meeting. No one had called on his expertise or asked his opinion. Yet Mart Kell had insisted he be here, so he had been forced to miss his Fast to Markab. But why?

Ole Branklin interrupted Dja'aa. "Should Hesperia's role in obtaining passage for the Interstellar Metropolitan of the Church of Algol to Deneb XII be discovered, I believe it's fair to say the consequences would be great. The Matriarchy—"

"The Matriarchy has just suffered a major defeat!" Mart Kell's voice sounded out in the chamber. The figure of a teen Thrasher on air-sandals skidded down one of the curving ramps along a petal of the lotus-shaped Quinx meeting hall, causing a stir among the legislators. The platinum-Plastro-suited figure came to a spinning stop at the chamber's circular heart. The head visor was tilted back, revealing the emerald eyes. A skullcap was removed, uncovering the bronze hair: Mart Kell himself.

"What's the meaning of this bizarre getup?" Branklin sputtered. "And this entrance?"

Kell ignored him. "I was late." He half-bowed to Dja'aa, Truny Syzygy, Llega Francis Todd, and Kars Tedesco, the other members of the Inner Quinx, seated floating upon the central dais, then said, "Two hours ago, Hesperian Time, the Alpheron Spa fell to the rioters on Deneb XII!"

He waited for the collective murmuring to pass.

"The women are safely hidden at Hymenoptolis," Kell added. "Where we should be able to get at them."

"Get at them?" Branklin asked. "What for?"

"Why, to rescue them, of course." Kell smiled mischievously. "It's clear that the Matriarchy can't protect them."

Llega Todd understood. "Will their offspring be with them?"

"Naturally," Kell said, "and naturally, Hesperian Intra Gal. will be there to display holos of mothers and children—and their gratitude."

"How quickly can that be done?" Dja'aa asked.

"As soon as Ambassador Without Portfolio North-Taylor Diad can leave Hesperia!" Mart Kell said, seeking and locating Diad's face in the chamber.

Kell was beyond clever, Diad thought. "I can leave anytime." He stood up in readiness to leave.

"Thank you, Ambassador," Kell said. "Stay a bit longer." He turned and took his seat on the dais. "I'm assured that the women will await his arrival. Speed is not of the essence in this matter; timing is."

"It will be a public-relations coup for Hesperia any time it happens," Truny Syzygy said. "What else—"

Kell stopped his speech with a gesture. "I believe it's the moment for this August Council to make perhaps the most important decision of its long and distinguished existence."

"Is this...? What are you saying...? Do you wish to make a formal proposal to the full Quinx, Lord Kell?" Branklin finally asked the Constitutionally required words.

"I do. And I would like all to listen to this proposal without bias or preconception. Does the Inner Quinx accept these terms?"

The five nodded agreement. "Does the entire Quinx?" Kell asked. And accepted a murmured assent.

"Gratitude! Understand now that what I'm about to say may seem harsh, perhaps even cruel. But I believe that circumstances warrant the most drastic action. We all know that the Matriarchy is our enemy. Since the founding of Hesperia, every Matriarch has attacked our City either directly or indirectly, sought to take away its independence, or attempted to destroy its economy—by which alone it continues to exist. We have formed the only consistent Opposition to the Matriarchy's all-pervasive galactic control over the past few centuries, and have done so only by virtue of our natural resources, the wealth those have brought us, and our own willingness to never take any political role which might be construed by the Matriarchy as openly rebellious."

"A policy which has stood us well," Branklin said, "We don't need a history lesson, Lord Kell." The rest of the council hushed Branklin.

"We Hesperians have been cunning and clever and resourceful," Kell went on. "But we've always been servants, never master. We've never been more than mere servants to every Wicca that existed."

The insult drew protests among the chamber. Kell waited until they had died down.

"It's the truth, and you all know it. But now, my fellow Citizens, the opportunity to become truly independent, equal, who knows, perhaps even greater than the Matriarchy lies within our grasp, if we but seize the opportunity."

"What opportunity?" Tedesco asked. "A few pregnant women?"

"Listen, and then collate these facts," Kell said. "The Cyber rebels have drawn off half the Matriarch's fleet into the Fornax sector of the Carina Arm, where they sit, stewing, uneasy, on edge, yet frozen in place while Wicca Eighth looks for one of her notoriously insidious ways out. Any intelligent person must know that unless a cure is found for their microvirus, the Cybers have won their battle with the Matriarchy. The M.C. has put its enormous resources and best minds to work toward that end, further shredding the Matriarchy's once-vaunted Unity of Purpose and Cohesion of Action. And now, now one of their little experiments on Deneb XII has gone awry. No, more than awry, all wrong. Allowing us a wedge. Our propaganda campaign for the Alpheron Spa incident has worked beyond our wildest hopes, focusing galactic attention upon Deneb XII. And, for the first time in centuries, Hesperia is considered by all right-thinking humes to be in the right, and the Matriarchy in the wrong. The Maudlin Se'ers support us. The Orion Spur Federation has given their support. Important Women all over the Matriarchy itself have seen the corruption of their government, its abuses, its potential for tyranny. Many of them have listened to our cause and offered their unofficial aid and future official aid to us. Hesperia has never been stronger, the Matriarchy never weaker."

"Here! Here!" Several Quinx members raised the shout.

"What good is that?" Kell asked. "What good is our strength unless we utilize it? Now! Use it to strike the Matriarchy where its complacency and stagnation and corruption has festered, right at its very heart!"

More cheers for Kell. The tycoon was a surprisingly effective orator; a real speechmaker, Diad thought.

While the council was still roused, Kell gestured for a holo showing the refugees from the Alpheron Spa, women, a few M.C. pilots, and the children—four-legged infants. It was poor quality, obviously taken by a nonprofessional, perhaps even a tourist trapped with them. Even so, the chamber became quiet.

Kell said, "If anyone has any doubts about what was going on in that spa on Deneb XII, these holos should put those doubts to rest."

The holo shifted now to scenes from M.C. headquarters on Melisande, Wicca Eighth herself in the Matriarchal Council Chamber, a huge room, in conference, leaning back to listen to her Centaur councilor before speaking. It shifted to another location, somewhere above a bedroom suite: from its size and luxuriousness, obviously that of a high official in the M.C. And there was a Centaur male, just coming into view, part of its lower torso wrapped in a bath towel, its fine long-haired mane prominent on its long neck as it reached out and lightly grasped a Hume woman, who turned into its arms. The chamber was completely silent now.

"I don't think we need to show the entire recorded holo." Kell gestured for the holo to end. When it was off, he faced the full council. "Through our carefully placed contacts within the Matriarchy itself, we've obtained dozens of holos quite similar to this. Should they be made public—"

"Hesperia would never stoop to that!" Ole Branklin shouted.

"Which is why Hesperia continues retain its independence only at the caprice of Wicca Eighth—and her Centaur lover!" Kell retorted. "Isn't it time"—he faced the full chamber—"Hesperia grasped control of its *own* destiny."

"Excuse me, Lord Kell," Llega Francis Todd spoke. "How do you propose we do that? What, precisely, are your intentions?"

"My intentions are as follows. Within the next thirty hours Sol.Rad., Hesperia rescues the women and infants on Deneb XII and displays that rescue and those unfortunates on Intra Gal. for all to see. Shortly thereafter, all the prelates and the Interstellar Himself of the Maudlin Se'ers will utilize the Intra Gal. Comm. Network to demand an end to the interbreeding. You know there already have been incidents on various worlds. When we show some of our collected footage of holos about the extent of Centaur influence within the Matriarchy itself, those riots will turn massive and nasty, and they'll spread to other worlds not yet affected. Even, I have reason to believe, on Wicca-World itself. Our agents provocateurs, and the Church of Algol will see to that. As all that is occurring, Hesperian forces, along with forces of the Orion Spur Federation, will be arriving at the Near-Norma Arm, Sector fourteen—"

"The Centaur homeworlds system?" Branklin gasped.

"Where, under the guidance of a member of the Inner Quinx, we will begin a program of complete blockade between the Centaur worlds and the rest of the Matriarchy to ensure that such interbreeding madness cannot again occur."

"Which will be reported via Intra Gal. Comm., so all can see where Hesperia stands on the matter," Dja'aa said.

"And what it will do to back up what it says," Kell added.

Diad thought everyone in the room was holding his or her breath at the galactic impudence of the idea. He certainly was.

"That's my proposal," Mart Kell concluded. "I throw it open to discussion."

The outburst which ensued was astonishing to Diad, who had never suspected that these fifty-five tycoons and civic leaders could possibly be other than cool and collected businessmen. The din went on for minutes until Llega Francis Todd, as Chairman of all Quinx meetings, called them to order with some difficulty.

"I have one question, Lord Kell," she said. "Which I believe I heard asked by several colleagues just now. What if the M.C. decides to interfere in the blockade against the Norma-homeworlds and engages our forces?"

"Lady Todd," Kell answered almost with a bow, "that is *exactly* what I am expecting to occur."

More astonishment from the legislators.

"Our forces will be outnumbered. They will hold on as long as they can and then make their escape," Kell said, "Although not without engaging the M.C. forces enough to allow it to be considered a bona fide battle."

"Which we will transmit in full on Intra Gal. Comm." Syzygy was beginning to understand the scale of Kell's scheme.

"Especially to those worlds where rioting is occurring," Tedesco added.

"I see. Yes, I understand," Llega Francis Todd said. "Gratitude."

"Any other questions or comments?" Kell asked. "Lord Branklin, I believe you wish to speak?"

"What you're proposing"—he could barely contain himself— "is...it's...monstrous! Riot! Genocide! Commercial blockage! It's appalling!"

"I'm afraid, Lord Branklin, I completely agree with your estimation. It will be most unpleasant. Hundreds, perhaps thousands of Centaur nationals may die in the rioting. And there's no way to know how many of our people will lose their lives in the battle against the M.C. forces. But the fact remains that once the blockade is publicized and the battle with the M.C. is networked to billions, the Matriarchy will have lost all pretense of following the wishes of the people it governs. Its back will be broken."

"It's completely barbaric. It's a return to Metro-Terran chaos!"

Diad sighed. Branklin was right, of course. And, of course, it meant nothing that he was right—because Mart Kell was also right.

"There will be planned chaos only," Kell said. "It will not directly affect Hesperia. In fact, the only way in which Hesperia will be at risk is if our courage fails us along the way. We must carry out this plan rapidly and ruthlessly. Then victory is ours. I've thrown open the council to questions and comments."

And they arrived. But not as many of them as Diad had expected; and virtually all of them were of a practical nature. How quickly the vast fleet of Hesperian Fast Haulers and Tourist Liners could be armed completely to support the usual defense forces; what assurances had come from the Orion Spur Federation? And what pledges of Fasts and soldiers? What extra defense would the City need? And which of the Resort Worlds were to be protected and used as fueling stations. All the questions were adequately responded to. For centuries, without any warlike intentions, Hesperia had kept its defense systems in readiness for just such an eventuality, so much did it prize its independence. Even its last-ditch self-destruction bomb located at the heart of the City, threatened during the First Matriarchy, remained in place and remained an effective weapon.

"If that is all," Kell said, "I think a vote is in order."

"One moment." Ole Branklin stood up. "I have something to say. In my hundred and ten years as a Quinx Council Member, I have never encountered the like. What has been proposed is utterly vicious. What has been discussed by all of you is completely unwarranted by any action on the part of the Matriarchy. I cannot remain in this chamber any longer."

"Is that a formal resignation?" Mart Kell asked innocently.

Branklin threw him a look which spoke volumes. "Take it any way you wish to."

"We cannot vote on a measure of this size without a Vice-Premier," Truny Syzygy said. "and if Branklin is resigning, we need a new one."

"I nominate Mart Kell of the Ophiucan Kells," a voice came out of the chamber. Diad recognized the nominator as Sali'm Branklin, Ole's youngest son.

"I second," Vinson Todd, Llega's son, spoke up.

The vote was by full-chambered shout. Branklin alone voted *"Nyet!"* as he stepped out of the chamber into a waiting chamber, where he slumped into a floating chair, his head held in his hands.

But now some politicking must be done for a vote on something as crucial as possible all-out war with the Matriarchy. Llega Francis Todd repeated the rules. They must remain in the chambers during the voting on the variety of proposals Mart Kell had made, which would take several hours, Sol Rad.; and on any modifications of those proposals. Committees would be put together. The Quinx members would be called for a general vote as soon as each proposal by a committee was ready. Until then they might comm. their family or business—but not any of the Stellar Commercial Exchanges—and naturally all of those comm.s would be censored so no information about the proposals could be leaked out.

Having made the formal proposals, Mart Kell could not serve on any committee. He took advantage of this time to do his own, more personal politicking, going around the chamber and receiving congratulations and gratitude, especially from many of the younger male and female members who, in some sense, he represented, with his own relative youth: his already-well-defined glamour.

Diad watched Kell with interest. He had met him only several months ago. But they had been meeting on an almost-daily basis since then whenever Diad was in the City. Before, he had known only what any other O'Kell company captain knew. He recalled seeing Mart once, years before at some company meeting. He had been only a neonate then, a serious, sulking, slender youth distinguished by his shock of the Ophiucan dynasty's miraculous bronze hair and his huge, seemingly multifaceted emerald eyes. Young Mart had never been shy or unfriendly. And he had done nothing to hide his resentment at his grandfather who had operated the company for so many centuries.

Of course, there had been scores of unauthorized PVN-Bios of Mart Kell in the past decades. Several of Diad's off-City romantic partners had gobbled them up in digest versions, and they knew more about his boss than he did. Once sex was over, they would question him eagerly, and in turn tell Diad about the unimaginable wealth the young Mart had grown up in, the harsh discipline and the rigid schooling he had been subjected to by his tyrannical guardian—and off in the distance somewhere the mistily shrouded figures of Mart's father, dead at scarcely a hundred and fifty in a freak Thwwing racing accident; and Mart's mother, a stunning socialite, who at Gil Kell's death had suddenly and unaccountably abandoned her only child to enter a Maudlin Se'er nunnery.

Only when Mart Kell had gone off to the University—and away from his grandfather's influence—did he reveal how much like his father he could be. Mart simultaneously became the most relentless playboy the school had ever known and the head of a growing student Oppositionist movement. His love affairs with the children of the most exciting members of the Matriarchy's political, business, and cultural elite were detailed in magazine-size PVNs as well as updated on Intercity Comm. News. One young woman, Zawa Franc'ck, had committed suicide over Kell when he had left her for a young male—a galactically famous musician. Diad wondered what relationship she had had to Ole Branklin, and if that could have been the source of the enmity revealed today.

When Mart had returned to Hesperia at his grandfather's death and taken over the company, he had revealed another aspect of himself.

Besides his obsessions with beautiful youth of both genders, his reckless gambling and daredevil Thwwing racing, Mart Kell had all the business acumen his grandfather had drummed into him for decades. And added to that the flair, the risk-taking skills of his great-grandfather, old Jat Kell himself, who had helped build the City. Tools which Mart had used to treble the size and reach of O'Kell Unltd, and to sextuple its already-nearly-uncountable profits.

And now, it seemed, he was adept in other ways, looking for an even larger arena upon which to display his talents: nothing less than the galaxy itself.

"Ambassador Diad!" Mart had come up to where Diad was standing within an oval oriel looking out at Hesperia, a magnificent view of one of the hundred or so "City-Centers"—a vast space in three dimensions filled with parks and fountains, kiosks and sculpture and in this case, also more official edifices—where some four large "girder" sections of the City came together. "Gratitude for being here," Kell added. "And for the promptness of your answer."

Diad smiled. "Little did I—or anyone else in the this chamber—know where that detail would take us."

Mart Kell laughed. Then he turned serious "You'll still go?"

"Naturally. You notice I don't even ask how you knew I was going."

"The Inner Quinx has not hidden the fact that it follows your off-City movements with the greatest interest. And anyway, this is in all our interests since you wish to be with Councilor Rinne. And we wish you to be with her on Deneb XII."

Diad appreciated his honesty. "What if matters on Deneb turn out differently than expected?" He went on to explain: "What if the M.C. has other plans for the 'rescue'?"

Mart Kell had moved in very close, a result of both of them wanting to be heard above the continuous din of committees in the chamber, and also of the size of the oriel within which they stood gazing outside.

"You'll do what you must." He lifted a hand to Diad's face and caressed Diad's single shaven cheek lightly. "I trust you completely."

It was so seductive, so feminine a gesture, Diad was startled.

He reached up and held the hand at his cheek.

"How is it you're so certain of my loyalty?"

"Don't you see how I envy you?" Kell asked, urgently. "I, Branklin, Lady Todd, Wicca Eighth Herself all ride the wave of history. Remember what the ancient Metro-Terran Kondratieff said? 'Ride the wave, rise and fall as it does'? But you are tied to that wave by only the flimsiest of lines which you can toss off at will. You alone have the power to make choices in tricky situations."

"Explain then"—Diad had thought of it several times during the meeting—"why it is that you told me recently that you would allow me to play soldier. And now that a battle is likely, you don't send me there, but to Deneb XII?"

"You'll still have your chance to play soldier," Mart Kell said. "The Norma-Arm action isn't big enough for what I've got planned for you. I want your name to last for millennia."

"Gratitude." Diad almost laughed. "But we cannot guess how history will treat our names and persons in the future. I suspect that for a while, this meeting will be hailed. But that later on it may well be vilified."

"It could have been worse. I could have proposed the complete elimination of the Centaur species, and don't think that after some debate that also wouldn't have been approved. Even so, I'm sure we'll all be vilified by history for provoking the riots and the blockade. All of us, that is, except you."

"And why not me?"

"Because that happens to be my whim, Diad. And because I happen to be riding the crest of the biggest wave around. I ride it, and for the moment, *I* hold its reins."

Silver-tongued devil: the ancient phrase popped into Diad's mind. He was completely charmed by Mart Kell as he had been by only two women in all his years. Under other circumstances, and although he was a lover of women, Diad might have considered Mart. He lifted Kell's hand away from his cheek; then, reconsidering, put it to his lips for an instant before releasing it. Let him make of that whatever he wanted.

Mart was surprised. He was about to say something when a series of chimes rang. The first committee had completed its formal proposal for a vote. "It's for your mission," Kell said, his focus had already moved out of the realm of their conversation to that of the vote. Living instant to instant. Riding the wave.

"As soon as they vote on it, you'll leave for Deneb XII. Take a small crew, a Fast with a 'cloak' to get you right into the planet's atmosphere and the best of our pilots to outwit the Cult fighters that are certain to be in orbit. And, Diad...come back safely to Hesperia."

Minutes later, Ambassador North-Taylor Diad was upon a mid-Center high conveyance crossing from the Quinx Meeting Hall to the nearest Fast Port vehicle. Under his arm, a slim portfolio, full of orders and clearances.

Rinne was just shaking herself out of the usual disorientation she felt coming out of Fast Jump when the door to Commander Lill's room opened up, and Lill herself stepped in.

"Problems!" she said gruffly, and turned to her personal Captain's log, wrist-connecting into it then speaking quickly and quietly into a closed microphone a few minutes while Rinne disconnected herself from the Fast Jump belt-ins and waited.

Done, Lill spun on her stool. "I can't put you down on Deneb XII as I promised. While we were in Fast Jump, there were developments."

Rinne stayed calm. Lill went on.

"The Alpheron Spa fell to the rioters." The M.C. soldier watched Rinne's face for a reaction; then, getting none, continued, "Most of the women in the program were gotten away in skimmers to one of the abandoned Bella=Arth Nest Cities. A few skimmers didn't make it. We lost some troops and had others captured by the local Deneban rioters. A small fleet of M.C. Fasts is orbiting now. We're to join them. Because the rioters are holding M.C. hostages as well as because of the highly tense situation, no landing will be possible."

Rinne thought, I was right to come here. This is where something terribly important is occurring. But to have overcome difficulties to get here and still not be able to land—that was intolerable!

"Are we in orbit yet?" Rinne asked.

"We're approaching. We'll join the fleet shortly."

"Before that happens, can't you send me down in a T-pod?"

Lill almost flinched. "I don't think you understand how difficult the situation is down there for those women!"

"Commander, I'm this Sector's Councilor for Health and Reproduction. I belong down there with those women."

Lill frowned. "It could be arranged before we hit orbit. Do you know how to operate the new pods?"

"They can't be all that different from the old ones."

"What about hand arms. Do you know how to use one?"

"I won't need one."

"Then a belt shield."

"No, I—"

"Look, I don't care what kind of high councilor you are. Those people down on Deneb XII are out of control. They've wrecked the spa. They've killed women and soldiers. They're under the influence of the Maudlin Se'ers and Oppos. provocateurs, and they're running amok. They're not going to respect your Eve-damned rank or clearances! In fact, they'd probably like someone of your position to execute publicly."

"All right, I'll take a shield."

Rinne was inside the Fast's pod-belly, the two seater T-pod was open and in operation, ready to drop as soon as she received the word from Commander Lill. They must be in orbit by now, no?

Suddenly Lill was at the T-pod. What now?

"Move back, I'm coming with you!"

"You? Why?"

"It's the only way you're going to get down there without being blasted out of Deneb's atmosphere by the Fleet."

Rinne moved into the back netting. "I don't understand. How are you—"

Lill netted herself in securely. "I left Captain Wang'Un in charge and told her to comm. me a safe passage through the Fleet. Those ladies are very nervous, very trigger-happy up here. Insult to the Matriarchy, all that Eve-damned fecal matter! I told them I wanted a look-see."

"Couldn't you just tell them I was you?" Rinne asked.

"I could"—Lill closed the T-pod—"but if anything happened to you, Northie would track me down across the galaxy if it took centuries and when he found me…"

The Fast's hatch opened.

"Hold onto your ovaries!" Lill shouted just as they took the drop.

A whirl of deep blue-black space rapidly traded places with swatches of pale orange Deneban surface as the T-pod spun wildly out of control before settling on its gyros. They dove straight down towards the huge and waterless planet. Rinne could hear the beeper the pod emanated as it passed through the Fleet's lines. She could even see one or two of the huge M.C. Battle Fasts above them, as the T-pod began to angle off more shallowly, still thousands of kilometers from the ground, speeding toward the black and red lines of mountain ridges which ran parallel along the ochre surface.

Suddenly laser light flashed out of the front of the pod.

"Just testing!" Lill said.

After some minutes, she asked "Can you see the nests?" She pointed ahead, to where the double ridge of mountains bent slightly. Five tall, almost-symmetrical cylinders grew out of broad bases, the entire structures the color of the earth itself. One was a mere needle, the others in various states of ruin. "The biggest is Hymenoptolis." Lill went on. "That's where they headed for after leaving the spa. It was already well defended."

The T-pod dropped suddenly and quickly until it seemed they were about to strike one of the mountain ridges. Finally it settled in the rough narrow valley between them. Evidently Lill didn't want to attract attention from below, even with this tiny opaque vehicle.

Below them, Rinne could see an occasional mine or low structure, one time she saw a sort of village, but if anyone was looking out for the pod, she couldn't tell. After a few minutes, the T-pod rose above a ridge, then veered away toward the middle and largest of the nests, the immense size and scale of which Rinne only now began to appreciate. They flew straight off the mountain ridge, yet were only halfway up the height of the nest.

"It's gigantic!"

"Even bigger underground," Lill said. "This one held over a million Bella=Arths before the war. Oh-oh! We've got company."

She slid the pod to a stop. They were half-hidden by the enormous bulk of the nest's walls from its huge curved open entrance, of which Rinne could only make out part of the top lip. From this close to the nest, what had appeared from afar to be silk-smooth walls proved to be rougher, with the consistency of lumpy porridge. It seemed that small air spouts dotted at structure at irregular intervals.

"Do you see them?" Lill asked, and pointed to the nest entrance, around which Rinne now made out throngs of people in skimmers and on the ground. Among the predominant Plastro-blue of their air-suits, she picked out an occasional minuscule red-uniformed figure. "Looks like they've taken the front. We're going to have to find another way in."

"Those spouts." Rinne pointed to one nearby. "Could they be entrances?"

"Could be. We'd have to find one closer to the ground. The refugees will be hidden deep. And these nests can be mazes. We have to get as near them as possible."

The pod started up again, moving to within a few meters of the massive nest's wall, slowly dropping and simultaneously moving sideways until the entrance was out of sight. As they approached one spout about one-third the height of the structure, Lill stopped to inspect it. It had a sort of built-out lower lip, wide enough to land the T-pod and for two humes to stand on. Then it tunneled into darkness.

"Sentry posts!" Lill said. "Eve-damned Wasps were smart."

The T-pod continued to drop down the wall which had begun to bulge and look handcrafted as they neared the ground. Intelligent creatures had constructed this, Rinne found herself thinking in wonder, year after year building the walls higher and higher by regurgitating a combination of undigested Deneb soil and their own saliva, then patting it into place with their palps, and moving aside for their fellow workers, who had done exactly the same thing in the next spot. Millions of them had worked here, day after day, for centuries, making the walls thick and secure, leaving their individual yet species-identical palp-prints on these walls. This was their past made solid, and all of them had a part in it. No wonder they had defended it so long and so gallantly. No wonder they had chosen mass suicide rather than live to see it fallen into the hands of aliens.

Finally Rinne spotted another sentry post only a few meters off the ground. Lill landed easily on the lip, and they got out.

From here the view was extraordinary: kilometers of tableland, then suddenly rising as though grown out of the flatness, four other huge ruined nests. With nothing else in the landscape for a measuring stick or optical guide but the sweeping curve of the two mountain ridges, the lower one streaked red, the higher one black. Deneb's binary orange and blue suns hung unevenly sized but tinted identically by the atmosphere to resemble blood-smeared coins.

"Better put these on," Lill handed her a visor with infrared lenses. "It'll be pretty dark in there." The M.C. soldier made sure the T-pod was wedged into place, then gave the bleak and garish landscape a wistful glance. "Let's go!"

Even with the infrared visors, the tunnel dimmed immediately. Like the outer walls, the inner walls had been constructed by Bella=Arths and appeared to be of the same rockhard material. Because of the Vespids' completely different physiology from humes, the tunnels were rough underfoot, the walls curved yet tilted at maddening angles, and openings and connecting tunnels were abrupt and unexpected. Despite all this, both women were in good shape, and as their way led downward, they were fairly nimble at negotiating the difficulties.

After a while, Rinne stopped Commander Lill.

"Have you noticed the pattern of tunnel openings?" And when Lill didn't respond, "While we were above, they all opened from this direction. Now they're opening out toward this direction."

"Signifying?"

"I think that we're about to level off."

"Which means what?"

"That we'll reach an open space soon. And perhaps be able to get our bearings," Rinne said.

"Do you think we'll find a floor plan?" Lill was only half-joking.

"Vespids use scents and odor paths to find their way around. Maybe they marked them by scent."

"Could my wrist-connector read them?" Lill suggested. She dialed her belt for olfactory sensitivity, and holding her wrist up to the nearest wall, read its register, then moved her wrist to a branching tunnel entrance, and read it once more. "Well, there's definitely a difference. I only wish I knew what the difference meant."

"And which led to where we're going?" Rinne agreed. "Let's both read them as we go along. Any changes, and we may be on to something."

They continued to descend; then as she had predicted, the tunnel widened and leveled off. "I'm impressed," Lill said. "You also have a theory on the scents?"

"It's just a theory," Rinne cautioned. "But the standard scent seems to register at fifteen. That means 'straight ahead,' I believe. Another odor registering at twelve denotes a cross tunnel and means either 'up' or 'down,' and another one at nineteen means another sort of cross tunnel, again either 'up' or 'down,'—we'd have to follow those tunnels to find out which. I've also spotted two more variables. One scent at very high registration, almost twenty-six on this scale of thirty. Another very low, perhaps four or five. I don't have a clue what they mean."

"Guess."

"Well, maybe one points toward living quarters and one toward working quarters. Or, even the very little I know about Bella=Arths, one toward general living quarters and the other toward their egg-chambers. They prized their young and protected them very well."

"Then that's where the refugees would be hidden," Lill said, which made sense to Rinne. "We've got to experiment with your high and low registrations. We should follow those scent paths."

"Are we deep enough yet?" Rinne asked. Lill only shrugged.

The tunnel grew quite wide, and alongside it ran many tunnels, some opening out almost immediately to small chambers. Rinne wasn't certain why it was, but she had the distinct impression of very distant, extremely quiet but distinctly irregular sounds, like the scuttling of insect legs. Yet she knew that couldn't be possible. These nests had been emptied of their inhabitants centuries ago. Even in this poor light, she could see the marks left on the chamber walls by the fire which the Bella=Arth leaders had set deep in this nest, which had exploded upward, an unstoppable holocaust which had sped at hundreds of kilometers per seconds up, up toward the air, stifling with smoke, and incinerating everything alive in its path. Historians of the period had calculated that it had been carefully executed so that the entire nest had been depopulated within fifteen minutes, Sol Rad. Few of its millions of inhabitants had time to do more than smell the first wisps of rising smoke. Ghosts—that's what she was hearing. The ghosts of millions.

"All the readings so far have been on the lower scales," Rinne said. She left the main chamber now, trying smaller chambers, all of which registered low on the olfactory scale.

"Mine too," Lill said. "Let's look for high readings."

After some time, Rinne found a small chamber which had a very high olfactory registration on her belt dial. But it was just that: a small chamber.

"I don't understand," she said. "Maybe they held the young here temporarily."

Lill was inspecting the walls of the small chamber. Suddenly one wall moved—a solid chunk of wall was hinged. "The readings through here are very high. Shall we?"

This tunnel descended deeply, but was wider—and higher—than any previous ones. Because the Vespids were carrying their pupae and larvae? Rinne thought she heard the scuttling sounds again. But she ignored them, and the olfactory registration remained high. She almost bumped into Lill, who had stopped.

"What—?"

"Shh! Look," Lill said. "There's light ahead. Artificial light. It could be the rioters. I'm going ahead. Stay here. Don't move!"

The M.C. soldier's bulk filling the tunnel all but blocked out whatever light she claimed to have noticed, but Rinne remained still for what seemed an excessively long time. Finally she turned on the belt shield, even though to anyone with a scanner doing so would give away her position, and she moved forward. Just as Lill had said, it was getting less dark. Since the tunnel's entrance had been so sharply delineated from daylight, this had to be artificial illumination. She kept moving forward.

Right into Lill. "We found them!" the M.C. soldier was smiling. "*You* found them. No wonder you're such an Eve-adored official!"

Rinne followed her past two more almost invisible hinged wall doors and into a series of lighted chambers in which several hundred women, most of them pregnant, lay upon mattresses or sat up chatting. The sound and smell of infants. About a dozen M.C. Security guards. Rinne removed her visor and was amazed by the sight.

One lovely, quite pregnant young woman almost leaped up.

"Councilor Rinne!" she asked. "It is you! I...You probably don't remember me. I'm Ewa Petra Benn. We met on Benefica. I was"—her eyes misted over—"You told me to wait. I suppose"—looking away now—"I ought to have listened to you." Ewa looked up again, pleading.

"My dear," Rinne said, and embraced her. "You'll be all right. All of you will."

"I want this child." Ewa held her belly. "We all want our children. Will you help us keep them?"

"That's why I'm here," Rinne said.

She remained with Ewa, who seemed to know who all the rest of the women were, and when they were due or when they had given birth. Ewa would be a great help, Rinne thought, as she sat and talked to them, and one woman lifted an infant to be held. Rinne held it. Of course it was four-legged, but lovely. Its face was just like its mother's and Rinne told her so and did and said all the appropriate things.

Commander Lill meanwhile was talking to each of the M.C. soldiers, guards, and sand-skimmer pilots; Rinne supposed she was collating their stories. Whatever the situation of this chamber, the look on Lill's face said she didn't like it. Finally she gestured to speak privately to Rinne.

"Are these all the refugees?" Rinne asked.

"There was another chamber full, much higher up in the nest, within the offices of the Bella=Arth Museum. Contact with them was lost about an hour ago. Lieutenant Lemmpae believes they were too exposed and that they were taken by the rioters. Could have been the group we saw when we arrived outside. The Lieutenant thinks we're safe here for a short while. Maybe a few hours."

Rinne waited for the M.C. Commander's next words. Instead, the soldier looked at her as though expecting a command.

"We've got to get these women out of here." Rinne stated the obvious.

"I thought you'd say that."

"What's the problem?"

"You mean aside from the near-impossible logistics of getting this many women in their fragile shape up through the tunnels and out of here safely?"

She let that sink in a minute.

"I don't even know if we'd be able to find our way back out the way we came in."

"You said 'near' impossible. Not impossible," Rinne said. "It would be difficult, I agree, but…there's another problem, Commander Lill, isn't there?"

"The Lieutenant has been in contact with the orbiting fleet. Seems there's a Very Important Flower Cultist in command up there. A Black Chrys. You may know Her. Admiral Thol? No? Well, *I* know Her. Seems She gave the order to these forces to hold the position. She won't budge on that."

Rinne's face flushed with anger. "Hold the position? That may be fine for the soldiers, but these women aren't soldiers! Look at them!"

"I see them." Lill looked away.

"I'll get a count on those who are able to walk," Rinne said. "We'll simply have to try to carry the others."

"Wait! Just wait. I'm in charge here. For the moment, at least."

Rinne waited. She went back to looking at mothers and infants, occasionally casting what she hoped were accusing looks at the M.C. commander. She also counted. Eight women were far too weak to walk at all: six were either newly birthed or about to at any time, two others had been wounded and were now sleeping fitfully. The others, well, who knew how they might manage a steep uphill walk through oddly shaped tunnels in almost-total darkness over built-in obstacles, without getting lost or hysterical, or how long that trek would take. Rinne had to admit the logistics involved were daunting, at least!

A sudden burst of activity among the M.C. soldiers. Lill joined them. They were listening to the Lieutenant's belt device. Rinne went closer to hear.

"The rioters have broken down guard posts the Lieutenant left about two levels above this," Lill reported dourly.

"We've got to move!" Rinne gestured for the M.C. pilots and soldiers to gather around while she outlined the plan and its difficulties.

None of them seemed enthusiastic about it. The Lieutenant summed up the attitude of the M.C. Guards: "We're under direct orders to remain here."

"We'll stand and fight until every one of us dies!" another said.

"You're all out of your minds!" Rinne commented.

One thing was clear: if they would do nothing, she would have to. She would climb out of the nest herself, T-pod up to the orbiting ship of this Black Chrys Admiral, and demand that the women below be rescued. At once. She would use every clearance, every connection she had ever made in the Matriarchy, every bit of influence she had managed to gather: she'd cajole, finagle, lie, if needed.

Rinne located Ewa and told her to help keep up the women's spirits: she would be back with help. Then Rinne left the chamber the way she'd come.

"Wait!" she heard one of the guards call after her as the second rock door was shut. She ignored the shout, put on her infrared visor and found her way into the small chamber which connected to the main tunnel. A left turn now.

Just to be certain she was headed the correct way, she kept her wrist near the wall, checking to make sure the olfactory registered readings were the same as they had been when she and Lill had come this way. Cleverly, or luckily, they had managed an fairly straight path. Hadn't they? She could have sworn they had. Yes, she was almost sure of it. First had been the drop, the tunnels all going one way, then the tunnels all going the other way, before it leveled off, so that meant—

Her wrist brushed something it shouldn't have, something that didn't feel like wall. Rinne stopped. In the infrared light, she could make out something ahead, something black, yet with a dull gleam matte or metal or... No, something breathing, although not with the regularity of a Hume.

Something reached out and touched her lightly. Rinne jumped back, startled. It touched her again, as though probing, and she fought down her deepest fears and turned to stumble backward, muttering, "Leave me alone! Leave me alone!" under her breath, until suddenly the palps were around her torso, lifting her up, and now she was saying it out loud, crying it aloud, terrified.

"Gemma! Gemma Rinne?" she hallucinated his voice calling to her as she struggled.

"Leave me alone!" she screamed.

"Put her down, Ckw'esso. She's a friend of mine. Can't we have light? All right, into that chamber. Yes, with the door shut. Fine!"

Now Rinne was being carried into a chamber, other legs, many legs entering behind her, and she was set down on her feet. Sudden artificial illumination made her hide her eyes. When she looked again, she was treated to a sight: North-Taylor Diad was in front of her. And on other side of him, two full sized Bella=Arths, wearing their own version of Deneb's blue-Plastro agro suits.

"Taylor? Is that really you?"

"Don't be frightened. These are friends of mine. New friends, but good ones. Ckw'esso and Nh'iss. They brought me here. But, how did you get here? There's a full M.C. fleet ringing the planet."

"Commander Lill sneaked me down. Oh, Taylor, I was so frightened!" She held onto him, and the two Bella=Arths turned their heads away politely and bent their antennae so as to not appear to be listening. "And you, how did you get here?"

"On a Hesperian Fast. Have you seen the Alpheron refugees?"

"I just left them."

"Good, they're nearby. Ckw'esso," Taylor had to tap the Bella=

Arth's carapace to get her attention. "You were right. They're close."

"We smelled the pupae," Ckw'esso said, speaking a highly sibilant and slightly sound-warped but otherwise comprehensible Universo Lexico. "Also the invaders." She gestured with her head and foremost palps.

"They're above us somewhere," Rinne said. "They're looking for the women." She went on to explain the situation: her listeners found the part about the fleet not helping the women very odd indeed.

"Not protect their pupae!" Nh'iss all but screeched. "It's terrible (not to be listened to ((and extremely un-Bella=Arth!)))."

"It's also unhume," Diad said. He'd still not let go of Rinne, and she was pleased and comforted by his nearness. "You said Lill is in there? Does she agree with the Black Chrys?"

"She seemed conflicted."

"Good, then she'll help us," he predicted. "How many women all told are there in there?" And when Rinne told them, she in turn predicted that the M.C. soldiers with the women wouldn't help, although Lill and the six pilots probably would.

"Hume help will be useless," Ckw'esso said. "Pardon my impoliteness!"

The Bella=Arth then outlined the escape scheme she and Diad had worked out. They had left a great number of their sister=Arths not far below this tunnel. Each of them could carry a Hume—Rinne and Diad included—down below to a larger and far-longer tunnel which only they knew of and which apparently connected this nest to the most distant nest on the plain. There, a large group of Bella=Arths who had returned to Deneb XII over the centuries since the great defeat, had rebuilt some semblance of their original community. It was a long distance even for Bella=Arths to travel: far too long for non=Arths. Once arrived at their home nest, Diad would comm. his Fast, which would send down gondola pods for the women.

"To go where? Hesperia?" Rinne, ever-the-Matriarchal, asked.

"If that's necessary, yes," Taylor answered.

"Why should it be necessary? Wicca Herself put them here. They should be returned to Melisande."

"Fine! If She'll take them back."

"Of course She will. She has to."

It was the closest to an argument they had had, and Taylor immediately said that it could wait until later. Getting themselves and the women out was crucial, especially if the Deneban rioters were as nearby as she said.

Rinne led him and the Bella=Arths into the egg-chamber. Naturally, at first, everyone half-panicked at seeing them. But Lill gave Taylor a smart slap on the back and a hearty M.C. Warrior forearm clasp, and he explained what was happening.

As Rinne had predicted, the M.C. forces would not leave. The skimmer pilots would. And although the Alpheron women were frightened about being handled by the Bella=Arths, they soon realized that this was their one way to safety.

Lill took charge of the operation, and once the chain of Bella=Arths were lined up in the tunnel outside the chamber and the women ready— if still somewhat nervous, their infants well wrapped—and after they were once again told that the Bella=Arths were friends and would never harm a Hume group with children, Rinne leaned back and let herself be comfortably lifted and was passed along a conveyor belt of palps and legs until she found herself stopped, being held now by Ckw'esso, who was to guide them out.

Seconds later, Ewa arrived to be held behind Rinne, then a skimmer pilot, then Diad, and another woman. She held an infant, and the Bella=Arth holding her asked to see the baby and made the appropriate gurgling noises back, and was even allowed to touch it, which it did very gingerly and with its lightest and most velvety palp.

Finally everyone who was coming was ready, and the signal to go was passed forward by both humes and Bella=Arths. Ckw'esso moved off slowly, then immediately turned left and began to descend. And began to talk.

"No Hume has ever been this way. And few enough of Our People."

"You know, I thought I heard Bella=Arths in the corridors," Rinne said, as much out of politeness as out of a need to ignore the truly frightening decline and speed with which Ckw'esso was moving.

"Several of us patrol here," Ckw'esso admitted. "Although not often."

"It's a tragic place," Rinne said. "I felt it from the minute I came inside."

"You're an extraordinary (sensitive ((and Bella=Arth–like))) Hume!"

They continued down the sharp decline. Behind her, Rinne heard Diad's voice, and Ewa's, others too, as they spoke to each other, trying to keep up their spirits. Even with her infrared visor on, the darkness seemed complete.

"Your eyesight must be phenomenal!" Rinne said.

"Indeed, Our People see on three levels below that of your visor. Even so, it should be brighter soon," Ckw'esso replied.

After a while it was less dark—and the decline leveled off. The tunnels widened considerably and now an eerie pale green light began to tint the dark walls, which Rinne also noticed were, for the first time since she'd entered the nest, no longer blackened with char, or the negative imprints of Bella=Arths instantly vaporized in the great holocaust.

She remarked this to Ckw'esso and added, "Then some of your people did manage to escape?"

"None!" Ckw'esso said. "These are newly built tunnels."

Diad was at Rinne's side, lolling in an exaggerated fashion. But he got serious soon. "Nh'iss is pulling up the rear, with Lill. They passed on the word through the Bella-Arths that they heard weapons being used above. Looks like we got out just in time."

The green light deepened, then suddenly brightened, and the Bella-Arths slowed down. Within minutes they began to collect together. Evidently they had arrived somewhere, but where?

"Our gardens," Ckw'esso said simply.

An enormous cavern faced them, seemingly kilometers in length, and a half a kilometer wide. At the bottom of a rather deep and completely green basin, an emerald-green river slithered like a huge torpid serpent. Above, the river was crossed by slender rock bridges.

"Beautiful, isn't it?" Taylor commented.

"An underground river carved out this place many millennia ago," Ckw'esso said. "Some of Our People discovered it. So we planted gardens. For the growing of food, yes, but also to have coolness and beauty (aesthetic pleasure ((the enjoyment of the untrammeled ideal made material)))."

All the humes were expressing their wonder and complimenting their hosts on having such a lovely spot. Ckw'esso still in the lead, now began to cross the river along one of the high and very delicate-looking stone bridges.

"Now I know why you still remain here," Rinne said. "But I don't understand the illumination. Or why the light seems to glimmer, to shake."

"Look up at the cavern roof!"

"It appears to be alive! Or at least in motion!"

"A few luminescent mosses grew here when we arrived. We cultivated them," Ckw'esso said, proudly. And when Rinne looked down at the narrow river she saw that its waters were actually a black-blue, the deep green color was a reflection of the luminescent moss's color and light, which the water further reflected and refracted, thus casting the green glow over the entire cavern.

Soon the cavern gardens were passed, and they were moving through darker and narrower tunnels. The Bella=Arth's speed increased then became steady.

"We regret not being able to show you our community," Ckw'esso apologized, "But it was not approved of by the Nest Elders."

"I understand."

"We'll take you to a good-sized chamber in the nest far from our center, but near a large exit."

Rinne was becoming sleepy with the regular motion and her body's inactivity. She could hardly keep her eyes open. She thought she even napped briefly, when suddenly there was light again, this time the familiar orange light of Deneb XII's dust-misted two suns. It took Rinne a few minutes to find her balance again once she was let down by Ckw'esso: her "ground legs," as Diad called them jokingly.

Diad joked a great deal with the Bella-Arths, attempting to "tip" the one who had carried him, and asking for a daily schedule and the like, which they seemed to enjoy as much as the humes.

Only a few of the many score of Bella=Arths who had helped remained in the large, light chamber once they put down their Hume luggage. Aside from Ckw'esso, those few stayed close to the tunnel entrance, as the women settled down, walked about, talked to each other, compared their journeys, and continued to cheer each other up. Rinne noticed that Ewa was going around speaking to each, helping, organizing: showing natural skills as a leader.

It was only when Diad began to comm. his Fast that Rinne noticed the holo team. A youngish woman dressed in attire which probably passed for "roughing-it" chic on Hesperia, and with her, two completely humeoid intelligent Cybers, one holding the needed equipment to transmit the holo through Intra Gal., the other setting up artificial illumination and sound enhancers.

"Taylor! What are they doing here?" Rinne asked.

He looked up surprised, then seemed aggrieved as he explained, "That's what's paying for this little escapade."

Before she could reply, the reporter was speaking:

"We're within what once was a majestic and teeming Bella=Arth Nest City upon Deneb XII." The young woman was being shot standing against a backdrop of the nest's inner walls. "With us is Ambassador to the Matriarchy, North-Taylor Diad and Matriarchal Councilor Gemma Guo-Rinne, Health and Reproduction Councilor for the Sector which includes the six Deneb systems. Together, Ambassador Diad and Councilor Rinne have effected the escape of the remaining refugees of the Alpheron Spa here which was attacked and invaded by local Deneban rioters earlier today, Sol Rad. They were aided in this extraordinary bipartisan humanitarian effort by soldiers and pilots of the Matriarchy, some of whom gallantly gave their lives."

"I don't believe this!" Rinne said.

"Don't worry," Taylor said, "We've told her the rules. Just be bland and noncommittal. She won't ask any questions beyond what you can answer."

That said, Diad was approached by the Intra Gal. reporter, and Rinne stepped back, as the reporter asked him to say a few words.

"First," Diad said, "I'd like to include in this extraordinary effort a group of local Denebans not involved in the riots. Without their aid, none of us would be here. These helpers would like to remain anonymous."

A clever move, Rinne thought. The Bella=Arths didn't want any attention drawn to them or to their role in the matter: not from the Deneban Hume settlers among whom they were forced to live, nor from the Matriarchy, their longtime enemies.

"Councilor Rinne?" The woman was in front of her now. "In what condition are the refugees? We understand that not all of the women who were evacuated from the Spa made it here."

"It's not yet clear how many of the women got out of the Spa itself," Rinne said calmly. And she gestured with her hands below the projected image until the holo team got the idea and refocused upon the women. "As you can see for yourself, several women were wounded during the initial attack and are resting. But they're in desperate need of medical attention. The others seem to be in fairly good health, but they've all had a terrifying and difficult time. They must be gotten to complete safety immediately."

"We understand, Councilor, that a Hesperian Fast will be aiding you in this effort, rather than one of the Matriarchal forces. Why is that?"

Not a question she wanted. "Ambassador Diad will provide details," Rinne said, but she knew she wasn't going to be let off so easily.

"Would you care to speculate?" the reporter tried.

"I understand that hostages have been taken from both the Spa and among M.C. forces. One can understand not wishing to increase the tension."

"Gratitude, Councilor," the reporter was satisfied with that answer and moved on to the women, asking for any who wished to address the holo audience. Several women did, including—cheekily—Ewa, who spoke directly to her Prime and Trine Spouses and told them that Deneb XII had been a great deal more exciting for her than their PVNs had suggested.

"What's happening?" Rinne asked Taylor who had been in contact with the Fast that had brought him to Deneb.

"The Fast used a cloak-shield to enter through the Cult's orbital blockade. It will have to drop the shield to release gondolas large enough to hold the women."

Rinne now heard someone at the other end of his connection. A male voice telling Taylor that they were ready, and the women should be prepared. Each pod would hold twenty women. The Fast captain was certain the orbiting fleet wouldn't notice the gondolas until they'd landed.

"Be careful!" Diad ordered. "I want this to be a smooth operation." He turned to Rinne, who had been unaware that she had been gazing at him. "You feeling all right?"

"I'm fine. I was just thinking...how much I disliked the suite at Marko-City. We would have had a terrible vacation on Markab Lambda!"

Taylor laughed and held her briefly, before returning to his work, as communicator with the Fast's captain.

When the holo-team was finished with the women, its three members turned toward the entrance, where the first Hesperian Fast gondolas could now be seen approaching across the huge flat tableland outside. Rinne heard the reporter say, "Because there are more humes here than can be fitted on the three gondolas, some women will have to remain for a pod to return to pick them up."

Rinne could see Ewa organizing the women, counting them off. Those with infants and medical problems on the first shuttle, the dozen due to give birth last would remain behind—along with the six skimmer pilots, the holo team, and, of course Lill, Taylor, and herself. Commander Lill had been silent, brooding, a few yards off to the side, more or less alone since they had arrived at the spot.

Taylor was speaking rapidly to the Fast in a low voice. Finally he turned to Rinne. "The Fast was spotted by the orbiting M.C. They're demanding an explanation."

"Better make him link up to here," Commander Lill suggested. "And you talk to the fleet yourself."

"Good idea." Diad waved over the holo-team. Once they were set up at his side, he said, "This is Ambassador Diad of Hesperia. Am I speaking with Admiral Thol."

"This is Thol," her voice was hard. "We don't recognize you as an Ambassador, whoever you may be."

"If you'll tune in to the Intra Galactic News Network which is here with us, shooting live, you'll discover, Admiral Thol, that I'm here on Deneb XII with many of the women who were at Alpheron Spa and who escaped the invasion and the Deneban rioters. Are you prepared, Admiral

Thol, to offer those women and ourselves safe passage off this world?"

A clever move, Rinne thought, letting Thol know anything she did would be seen and heard by billions of holo-viewers.

"Who's in charge there?" Thol asked finally. "Who is that woman from the Matriarchy?"

The communication link was passed to Rinne, who identified herself fully.

"Admiral Thol, these women are wounded and exhausted and are still in danger," Rinne said. "If you are not able, for whatever reasons, to aid us directly, please allow them to be taken on board the Hesperian Fast."

"The Hesperians have no business here," Thol replied.

Taylor spoke up. "Indeed, Admiral, if you'd care to remember, Deneb XII is a Hesperian Territory, a Resort World, under the rules of the Treaty of Formalhaut, and thus open to all and any humanitarian aid from Hesperia or any of its territories."

"It was," Thol replied icily, "until Hesperia provoked the Denebans to attack the Matriarchy! As a result of that action, the Treaty of Formalhaut can no longer be considered in effect on Deneb XII."

Rinne could hear the reporter commenting on that piece of effrontery.

"Three gondolas from the Hesperian Fast are landing at this minute, Sol Rad.," Diad said, as much for the holo-audience as for Thol. "The refugees from the Alpheron Spa are beginning to meet and board them for passage to the Hesperian Fast. What exactly are your intentions, Admiral?"

If Thol had intentions she wouldn't say. Instead she repeated, "The Hesperian Fast has no business here and must be assumed to be directly aiding the provocateur forces on Deneb XII which attacked the Matriarchy."

"Give me that!" Rinne said. Then to the Admiral: "Haven't you heard a word? That Fast is here on a humanitarian mission. A mission which I cannot, for the life of me, understand is not being performed by one of the many Fasts under your command. Allow the gondolas safe passage!"

"Our terms have been stated unequivocally," Thol replied.

"If anything happens to anyone because of your actions, Admiral," Rinne said far more calmly than she felt, "I will personally have your commission at the next Matriarchal Council!"

For answer, she was switched off. The Hesperian Fast captain got back on. The holo-team moved out toward the entrance of the nest to show the refugees being helped onto the gondolas.

"I'm not letting them go until I have assurance they'll be safe," Diad was telling the Fast Captain.

"Come on," he answered back. "We can't stay here all day, Sol Rad! If they don't arrive soon, we'll be blasted out of this orange sky."

"He's right, Taylor," Lill said. "Having the refugees aboard will be protection for the Fast crew."

Taylor turned to Rinne. "Gemma? Help me!"

"I don't know, Taylor. I think they're right."

"But what if they aren't?"

"Thol knows this is on Intra Gal. holo," the Captain argued. "What's she going to do in front of forty billion holo-screens?"

"Lill?" Taylor asked.

"I just don't know. Her terms were clear and quite rigid, even though I don't understand what she's trying to prove."

Rinne looked out at the entrance. "They're all inside the gondolas!" she reported. Except, that was, for Ewa and eleven more women, who would join them and the six skimmer pilots on the next shuttle.

"Now! Ambassador Diad!" The Captain insisted.

"I don't like this, but go ahead."

The first gondola closed its top half, spun around and began The holo-team followed its slow ascent, the women inside waving. The second gondola lifted, then the third.

The Fast Captain was on again. "It's Thol. Listen!"

"...according to the bylaws of M.C. Council #4,598, any Offworld stellar-capable vehicle in violation of these rules will be annihilated. Captain, prepare your crew to abandon ship."

"But the women are coming here!" the Captain argued. "They're on their way now. Your own women!"

"Prepare to abandon ship!" a voice—not Thol's—ordered. "You have two minutes, Sol Rad."

"She's not going to let them off Deneb!" Taylor moaned.

"It's a bluff!" the Fast captain insisted.

Rinne joined the others as they ran to the nest entrance to see what was happening outside.

"Prepare to abandon ship!" the M.C. voice said. "You have one minute, Sol Rad."

The gondolas were rising toward the Fast, which hung in the orange sky, like some slightly angular deep blue fish.

"Abandon ship now!"

Everything happened at once. The three gondolas approaching the Fast were hit by glaring photon beams and instantly vaporized, the Fast's underchutes opened and a score of T-pods dropped out spinning, the Fast was struck by a beam which completely covered it in electromagnetic disturbance, so that pale yellow light ran over its entire surface. Everyone around Rinne was screaming and shouting. Someone was yelling, "How could they?" Someone else was saying, "Eve! All those women!" The Fast suddenly dropped a half a kilometer, then began to turn on its side, as a final T-pod was released. Photon beams began tracing their way along the tableland, as though they actually expected to catch a nimble T-pod. But one beam came close enough to the nest that people backed up. Rinne heard someone nearby repeating, "I can't believe it!" over and over until Taylor shook her and she realized it was she herself saying it, and he was dragging her back into the nest.

Where the holo-team was set up quickly. The reporter thrust Taylor and Rinne into its focus. Despite her professionalism, she was shaking. Tears started down the reporter's cheeks, and her voice trembled with anger.

"Ambassador, Councilor, we've just witnessed an incredible act of violence. Please say something to our audience about what they have just seen."

"There's nothing to say," Diad said. "You all saw and heard for yourselves."

While he was speaking, Rinne began to gather herself together out of her shock. She was still shaken, still upset at what had happened. But more, she was completely enraged with the cold, totally comprehending fury of decades of long-simmered resentment at the Matriarchy into which she had been born and educated, but which had never allowed her to be herself or to love and live with whom she wanted. With this single act, the Matriarchy had finally revealed itself as the corrupt and inhuman government it truly had become. It was as though a light but perfectly fitted screen which had blanketed reality had been ripped off, leaving everything clear, hard, real.

When Taylor was through, the holo focused on Rinne. She stood proudly and she spoke out of her deepest emotions, yet with absolute clarity.

"It should be clear to all viewers that this wanton, cruel, and murderous act was purposely devised by the Matriarchy to destroy any proof of its experimentation in species interbreeding upon Deneb XII. It should also be evident that Wicca Eighth will not stop at murder or infanticide to cover up this squalid and ill-considered project."

The silence around Rinne was sudden and complete.

"As a member of the last seventy-five Matriarchal Councils, I denounce Admiral Thol and Wicca Eighth Herself for this heinous and uncalled-for act. Furthermore, I demand that both of them immediately resign their positions, for which they have proved themselves supremely unqualified. Should they fail to resign, I believe that galactic retribution must be brought to fall upon them for the many innocent lives so tragically lost here on Deneb XII."

She stepped aside, out of holo-range and looked around.

"Well?" she said to Taylor, who was standing there openmouthed.

"You take my breath away!" Taylor managed to finally say. And with her new clarity, Rinne saw that he was sincere, awed by her, and that in fact he did love her.

The reporter had gotten control of herself and was now attempting to put some order into what had just happened and what it might signify.

"Do you know what you've done?" Taylor asked Rinne.

"I've just retired. Without a pension."

"You've just cracked the Matriarchy in half single-handedly."

"No. They did it themselves. I just pointed it out, in case anyone couldn't see," Rinne said.

They both turned to watch the T-pods landing inside the nest's wide entrance. The reporter was counting them, speculating aloud that the final one would contain the Fast's captain, who had not left until the ship had already been crippled, and who still wasn't accounted for.

The other Fast crew members were alighting and stepping out of their pods. One crew member hadn't made it, two others reported: they had watched in horror as his pod was caught in beam from the M. C. Forces Fasts.

The all-male crew members were looking around in bafflement at the holo-team and the remaining refugees. They were unsure what to do next. One more T-pod could now be seen approaching, and already the Fast's captain was recognized inside it.

He was about to enter when they heard and then felt the explosion outside.

"The Fast! It's going!" someone yelled. The ground began to rumble and the air around them to thump.

Rinne was holding onto Taylor, but they were separated, thrown apart. She fell on someone—Lill, maybe—but at the correct angle to see the last T-pod begin to drop, and to be knocked aside by the falling nest entrance.

The noise was tremendous, the tremors below equally titanic, and as the nest began to cave in, Rinne felt the darkness closing over her.

Damn it, she thought with perfect illogical logic, now that I'm finally free, this has to happen!

Regulus Prime rose over the gardens of Melisande, divided in half by a single thin, dark horizontal line. A purely atmospheric effect, She knew.

As was the sun's pinkish coloring—the only hint that it had once been a red giant of a star, spewing out vast amounts of energy per second, enough to light up a thousand solar systems, expanding and glowing fiercely during its expectedly short lifetime, committing nuclear suicide. And almost succeeding, except for one small glitch in its elemental makeup or in the ratio of those elements to its precise size or to its gravitational pull or to something—no one had quite deciphered the reason why this star among the millions of red giants had gone nova time and again and then finally settled into a long, benign senescence: its single remaining unburnt planet, once so distant it had been solid ice kilometers thick, suddenly thawed into a paradise. No one knew exactly why, although ask any planetologist and she'd give you her theory. But the miracle of it had been rare enough for Wicca Sixth to select this as Her capital, and for Her successors to view it in wonder and to feel themselves equally gifted, equally conversant with miracles.

Now Wicca Eighth needed a miracle.

She sighed and sipped at the flowery herbal tea which alone formed the earliest breakfast of what She feared was going to be Her very long day.

She had hardly slept for the dreams. Strange dreams of a type She'd not had since She was a neonate. She had been dashing along an endless purple meadow, grass almost reaching up to Her (in the dream) powerful four legs. She had snorted, sensing or hearing something in the distance; something fearful, not easily understood, bright, sharp, hurting. She had looked up at the blazing blue sun which tinted the landscape, and had seen nothing, but had felt discomfort, then alarm, and had begun to trot, gallop, rush across the fields as though to warn, to alert the others, before whatever it was struck.

Thankfully, She had awakened before it could become manifest. Her sleep chamber had been perfectly, dimly, lighted to Her precise specifications—as usual. She had floated a quarter-inch above the sleep platform—as usual. And checking the flow, the air-current sheets, blankets, and pillows had—as usual—adjusted themselves exactly to the ever-changing temperature and electrolyte balance of Her sleeping body. Nothing was different or technically incorrect. Why, then, the dreams?

Why, then, was it that before she completely broke the surface beyond the ooze of the dreamstate, she had seen a face—a face which seemed familiar, yet which must have come from many centuries ago, because she didn't remember it, or only vaguely, a male face, which had looked at her? Until it had said quite clearly, "Today, Prosecutor Allwyn...the great galactic wheel has turned.... Now I am all!...and you—you are nothing!"

She had gotten up, unwilling to remain in bed for her usual levee, and ordered Her morning drink and it had been brought in instantly and the Governmental Day had begun, an hour or two Sol Rad. earlier than expected. At first, none of Her usual courtiers were ready, and the apartment servants were still sleep-eyed. She had dismissed them all to be alone, and finally to allow herself to think of him, Ferrex Sanqq' who had invaded Her waking dream with the certainty of his words—possibly the only words anyone could speak capable of terrifying Her.

Why him, of all those She had trod on to reach this Altitude? Many had been greater than Sanqq': more prestigious, more powerful, more inventive.

Now She hoped they would never find him on Pelagia. Hoped he was dead. Or that they had been killed before they could find him.

She intuited, as She had intuited few things in her long and eventful life, that if he wasn't dead, if Alli-Clark's Fast returned with him, that he would present the solution, save the Matriarchy—or, if not that, then the species. She'd intuited that the minute the news of the Cyber microvirus had been confirmed. Ferrex Sanqq's name had instantly come to mind, and fool that She sometime was, She had acted on her impulse.

Better to have all womanhood, all Delph-hood perish than have Sanqq' be their Savior.

She turned on the holo-wall to see what new disasters, if any, had occurred in the few hours she had managed to close Her eyes.

The twelve-panel wall was tuned to all of the major Intra Gal Networks: the nine Matriarchal ones, the two from the Orion Spur Federation—the earliest inhabited and most densely populated sector of the galaxy— generally given over to business and Intrafederation politics, and finally the Hesperian Network.

She actually only watched the last two holo stations. Matriarchal News was so perfectly censored that it was virtually useless for information. Lately, she suspected, most women on this and other worlds also watched only the O.Spur and "City" News.

That was how She had heard of the Anti-Centaur riots on Trefuss and Benefica; of the killings of Centaur advisers on Eudora—supposedly the three most politically stable Matriarchal worlds. It was Hesperian provocation, of course, with help from those Eve-damned hooded Se'ers always lurking about.

But it was disturbing, and She had immediately taken it as a warning for Melisande.

She called in Tam Apollon and told him that while she was certain his malefolk were safe on Regulus Prime that if they wished, thought, felt... Within the hour, Sol Rad., they had gone into protective custody; even She didn't know where on Melisande they were. Or even if they still were here, or whether they'd left by Fast for their homeworlds in the distant Norma Sector. She didn't want to know. It was enough for Her to know that they were so fearful, and despite their usual flawless courtesy and diplomacy, that they felt safer out of sight, in hiding, even back home. That, as much as how much She actually missed Tam Apollon's presence, his soothing words, his sage advice. That must have been why She had dreamed of that charlatan Sanqq'. Yes. She must try to remain calm. The tisane helped.

For a few minutes, all on the holo's seemed as it did on any other recent morning: cosmetic and fashion suggestions, how to redial your modified Cyber for the new comm.ed direct-nutrition channel, a visit to a young-Pioneers piscid farm set in the newly irrigated areas of the planet seven of the Algenib system, yesterday's Plastro-Beryllium commercial orders (in multitons) amidst the Scutum Arm worlds; Xenon and Radon price shifts among the Horsehead Nebula planet markets. It was all perfectly everyday.

Then she saw the holo from Deneb XII on one of the Orion Spur channels: a replay, part of a News-Summary with Comment, and there (without sound)—Eve's gratitude!—was Gemma -Rinne, her M.C. standard coiffure knocked to one side, her M.C. traveling cape covered with orange dust, her face slightly bruised from flying debris, and once again Rinne was saying those stiletto words which had arrived like a thunderbolt last evening on the Hesperian Intra Gal. News.

Now the replay holo once again swung outside to fasten its view upon the crippled Hesperian Fast hanging in Deneb's orange sky like a great wounded New Venice shark-whale, then it once more focused tightly upon a single tiny T-pod coming toward the holo-team before everything began to shake and beyond the T-pod She could clearly see the Fast imploding, the nearly indestructible Plastro-Beryllium suddenly bending inward at impossible angles, until it looked like some sort of Arthopodic skeleton. Then the holo shook and, even in silence, She heard the roaring explosions, and the picture fell, pointing askew madly before it stopped at a ceiling view before going blank.

She turned up the sound on screen #12 to hear the Intra Gal. commentator's update.

"In the nine hours, Sidereal Time, since then, we have received no further transmissions from our holo-team on the planet," the commentator was saying soberly. "All attempts to contact Admiral Thol, Black Chrysanthemum of the Cult of the Flowers, who ordered the attack upon the Hesperian and Matriarchal citizens which you witnessed have met with complete silence. All of our attempts to contact any diplomatic or Persean Arm official of the M.C. for comment have also been met by silence. If there are any survivors of the Massacre of Deneb XII, we have been unable to ascertain how many, where they are or in what condition. We will interrupt any preprogrammed material with any new information."

The Massacre of Deneb XII—it already had a name, Wicca thought. Well, Thol had always wanted to make history, and now She had. The fool!

"We're now bringing you a live-Intra Gal. transmission from Hesperia's Quinx Chamber. Premier Lady Llega Francis Todd speaking."

Llega looked harried, Wicca thought. As though she had not gotten any sleep in a day Sol Rad. Not even the few dream-riddled hours Wicca had managed. Evidently, this was a comm.ed address from the Quinx Council, an address which had begun a few minutes previously.

"...the Deneban Settlers' Association which holds the M.C. forces and Alpheron Spa hostages which were taken before the tragic incident occurred. Quinx Vice-Premier, Mart Kell has offered to represent this council in joining an Inter Galactic Negotiations Group proposed by President Leuc Win Arner of the Orion Spur Federation. We call on the Matriarchy to respond to those requests and to join with us in seeking a method or methods whereby we can call a halt to the atrocities visited upon Deneb XII and a peaceful resolution to the situation. President Arner is willing to open up a totally secure Intra Gal. Comm. among Procyon, Hesperia, Deneb XII, and Melisande—or, in fact, any other locality the Matriarchy may prefer—for this purpose. A formal comm. to this effect has just been delivered to Wicca Eighth by the Orion Spur Delegate to the Matriarchal Council. We await a response."

Wicca had heard enough. She turned off the sound on #12 and looked over the wall. There was Rinne again on another O.Spur holo, and an earlier—and heavily edited—segment of the same report on an M.C. channel. No matter how much they edited it, attempted to turn it to their advantage, they would still fail, She thought. Too many humes on too many worlds had tuned in to it while it was live and had seen for themselves.

Eve take Rinne! And now Llega Todd's "plea" would be all over the other Networks within an hour Sol Rad. Wicca would have to respond or... She could no longer remain silent.

She heard her court assembling outside the sleep chamber.

"Come in!" She said loudly and confidently, and as the group of women entered, she gestured for her hairdresser, whispering to her, "A chrysoprase tint today, I think. Style it back and high: serious, yet not quite tragic."

Before her ministers could even begin to speak, She signaled for quiet.

"I've heard the Hesperians. Naturally, we'll join the Procyon Initiated Negotiations, in order to forestall any further errors. You'll secure the comm. yourself, Mer Etalka, and handle it personally, making certain a line remains open to wherever I may be at all times with an extra audio channel open between Ourselves only. And"—turning to her defense minister—"Mer Palladia, I want a full in-person holo comm. with Admiral Thol before Mer Etalka opens channels with the O.Spur people. Closed lines. And Mer Palladia, should Thol pretend to be unable to speak to Me for any reason at all, she is to be relieved of duty instantly. Make that clear. Now"—she turned to the others as the two ministers rapidly left the chamber to fulfill their orders—"I want full reports and commentary from the rest of you. Rumors, comm.s, talk overheard in lifts, and on conveyances. Omit nothing, no matter how trivial or ludicrous you may think it."

She waited for the first woman to speak. She remained in full control. And Ferrex Baldwin Sanqq' remained merely a bad dream.

Mart Kell stepped out of his Ion-bath and considered how he ought to dress himself for the holo-meeting. His valet sprayed and airbrushed his hair so it gleamed with topaz accents and waved up high on one side before leveling off to a flattop. Next Valens sprayed and air-buffed Mart's face and body with the lightest possible dusting of Beryllium so his skin would take on a ghost of its platinum glitter.

No nose-ring or even earring, although he had many spectacular ones. Now that he was the Quinx Vice-Premier, Mart was allowed to put on the official tiara which Branklin had seldom worn and never looked good in anyway. It seemed at first to be a simple enough headband, but upon closer inspection, proved to be a marvel of craftsmanship: five bands of slightly different colored Beryllium strips woven in and out and around each other so none ever touched. The entire crown was so light, yet of such very pure alloys, that when Mart placed it over his head, it floated a millimeter off his brow.

No tunic, he decided; he'd be bare-chested, with the plastro-trimmed "City-Jet" black cape thrown over his right shoulder, connected by a long, transparent stay to his loose-fitting trousers. No ornamental codpiece, not even the Hesperian knee-boots; that would be flaunting himself at the two women on the Negotiation Group. Even so, his flat, well-defined torso defined by the low sweep of the cape, its musculature accented by Beryllium glitter would keep his maleness, his City-ness, before them at all times.

That was essential. He was meeting the others as at least an equal. Not as a servant of the Matriarchy.

Mart had selected his own apartments in the O'Kell Unltd. sphere to take the holo-meeting. It possessed privacy, grandeur, and he could accept the three other life-size holos and still easily tune into others to keep informed on what was happened elsewhere. Naturally, a line would be open to the Inner Quinx once the Negotiations began. But what he was most interested in now, was the Near-Norma Arm Blockade.

He had wanted to lead the Hesperian Fast Forces to the Centaur homeworlds, to direct the blockade himself, to ensure that all went according to plan. But as he had told North-Taylor Diad, (was Diad still alive? Mart felt so, despite the visual evidence of those holos from Deneb XII), Mart was "riding the wave of history," and that meant he must remain in Hesperia, first as Vice-Premier, and now for the negotiations.

Kars Tedesco was leading the Fast Forces. It would be his name which would resound in decades and centuries to come when all had been accomplished. And, Mart had to admit, of all those on the Quinx, after himself, Tedesco was best equipped for the task—not only by virtue of his ability, but also by reputation. The youngest and only male child of an economically and politically powerful dynastic line which reached back to the founding of the City, Kars was a few decades older than Mart and had already been in postgraduate studies at Hesperian University when Kell first entered. "Black-Kars" he had been called behind his back, not for the color of his skin, which was relatively light-hued, but for his naturally "City-Jet" colored hair which he wore high and long, and which he had accented by wearing ebony garb. "Black-Kars" also because of his darkly brooding habits of solitude and antisocial behavior; and because of his sudden near-homicidal rages, which left unsuspecting students, alumni, and innocent onlookers in need of med.care.

Given Tedesco's dangerousness, it was only natural that as a student, Mart had been magnetically attracted to him. But years had passed before they had even spoken. It was only after he had actively become an Oppos. that Mart discovered that "Black-Kars" had been one of the movement's founders and leaders during his decades as undergraduate. It had been one of Tedesco's early colleagues who had finally seen that the two met each other. It had occurred at one of those louche interspecies drug and sex orgies held deep down in the City's core—this one in an Cyber recreational center, at a Hume off-limits level only a few kilometers above Hesperia's still madly radiating "hot" Beryllium core.

By then, "Black-Kars" had already taken his seat on the City's five major commercial Exchanges and was being nominated for a seat in the Quinx's upcoming elections. But he had been as wild as anyone else at the orgy, moving from group to group until Mart had looked up from the sextet he had formed with two Arths, three intelligent Cybers of various genders and a female Hume, to see Black-Kars standing there, naked, his transparent Stele-Soma head mask almost opaque as he inhaled the drug. Tedesco had dropped onto the group and, shoving limbs in all directions, had swooped onto Mart like a well-aimed missile.

They had never spoken of that encounter, and it wasn't until some decades later when Mart himself joined the Quinx that Kars even acknowledged his existence again. Perhaps that was for the best, now that Black-Kars was a respected politician, business leader—and, most surprisingly, family man.

"And look at what you missed, Kars!" Mart asked, looking at his full-length reflection. One good thing about the Matriarchy: it had finally released men's fashion from a half-millennium of utter drabness, lack of expression, dearth of style. Those Metro-Terran Forebears everyone paid such lip service to, had been a boringly garbed lot—even the few genuine beauties among them.

"Lord Kell," the Intra Gal. operator spoke. "Your Inter-Stellar Closed-Circuit Holo is ready."

"You have all three?"

"One moment. Sol Rad. please. Gratitude! The circuit is now completely sealed."

Mart Kell remained standing as the three central holo-screens unfurled like pale webbing and filled up immediately with their three-dimensional pictures.

Tremont Bree Etalka appeared first: M.C. Minister of External Affairs. Mart almost sighed. Etalka was high in the bureaucracy, close to Herself. The M.C. wasn't fobbing off some office-holding menial on this situation. Mart bowed to the seated Minister, who returned his greeting. Etalka was in full uniform: garnet cinch tunic studded with wide ebony belt. Across one shoulder lay a pale violet Cult of the Flowers cape, signifying that she was Night Iris in the order.

Leue Win Arner appeared next, his comm. from farther-away Procyon. Leue Win (the closest approximation in Standard Universo-Lexico to the correct pronunciation of his name) was an Ambassador Class Hume-Delphinid, a group genetically developed several centuries ago specifically for diplomatic relations between the two species. Like all H-Delphs, Leue Win was humely attractive, with few obvious Delph physical characteristics; like them, Leue Win also possessed that smoothing of facial features, that softness of chin and forehead, the widened mouth and almost-nonexistent lips, as well as the snub nose and huge, lustrous eyes which suggested that the next dive into the nearest body of water was only seconds away. It was a tribute to Arner's personal esteem that the O.Spur Federation had been meeting on a resort-satellite in the Procyon system, minutes by Fast from New Venice. And, of course, as the O.Spur contained the largest number of hydro-worlds, this was a chance for a representative of the Delph species to speak.

Leue Win greeted Mer Etalka, then Mart Kell. His large eyes widened in pleasure at Kell's garb and, especially, at the tiara.

"Congratulations, Lord Kell, on your recent, and well-merited advancement," Leue Win said in his perfect diction. He'd also primped for the meeting: his naturally cobalt hair, perpetually slicked back, had been swept around to his left side in an combination Plastro half covering earring and barrette, studded with tiny sapphires the color of New Venice's great ocean. His tunic was Procyon white, an iridescence.

So much glamour in one holo-meeting that the Deneban member was startled at first. She appeared on screen last, seated against a background which might be almost anywhere on the disputed planet. An older woman, close to six hundred, she had eschewed the ubiquitous agro-suit for more formal wear: a Plastro-material which must have been a longtime wish, its neck high against her aged throat, its natural colorlessness setting off her wind- and dust-chapped face, cheeks burned from decades of outdoor work under Deneb's unforgiving double suns. But her stance was proud, and within her weathered features, her dark eyes were sharp, her short-cut (to better fit agro-helmets?) crinkly silver hair its own sort of crown.

"May I call this meeting to order." Leue Win Arner then introduced himself, Minister Etalka, and Mart. In turn, the fourth introduced herself merely as "Deneb Dorri," and went on to say, "That's what everyone calls me. I'm sort of unofficial mayor here, and I represent Immediate Response, which is what we call ourselves."

"First, Madam Dorri, are the Alpheron Spa refugees safe?" Leue Win asked.

"You needn't call me 'Madam.' Just 'Dorri' will do. Most of the so-called refugees are safe and in perfect health. At least those in our custody.

Some were injured during the final Response. They have received the fullest med. care. Naturally, I cannot speak for those women not captured by us in the nest and therefore left to fend for themselves."

Touché, Mart thought.

"You said 'women,' Dorri," Leue Win said. "What about the infants?"

"Our group had no infants. All the women—Spa patients, sand-skimmer pilots, and the surrendered M.C. Security Forces—are well. We're not hooligans, Ser. No one at all would have been harmed if the M.C. Forces hadn't first begun to stun our daughters!"

"Understood. You have how many women?"

"Eighty-seven patients."

"Those, then, Minister Etalka and Lord Kell, are the hostages."

"We also hold close to two hundred M.C. Guards and medics who worked at the Spa. We want them *all* off of Deneb XII."

"Those guards were working at and guarding the Spa. Their presence was required," Etalka said quickly.

Dorri retorted, "Those particular women have all said they want off Deneb—and we want them off!"

"Ladies!" Leue Win interrupted. "This will be a point to consider later."

"You three don't understand," Dorri said with some heat. "Deneb XII is *our* home! We don't want any Offworlders coming here for any reason when they are not invited. That goes for all and any."

Mart spoke for the first time, "May I remind you that Deneb XII is a Resort Planet, specifically under Hesperian protection."

"Some Resort Planet!" she all but spat. "But we have nothing against Hesperians. You never sent people here to make trouble and perform unnatural experiments. And you never harmed our sisters and daughters."

"Thank you, Ma'am," Mart said and added quickly, "Nothing personal. It's a mark of respect to your group."

"Release the hostages. All of them," Etalka said to Dorri, "and no further harm will come your sisters and daughters."

"First remove your orbiting fleet of Fasts!" Dorri answered.

And so the lines were drawn. An hour of discussion passed before Leue Win was able to receive complete agreement to at least establish that the Treaty of Formalhaut had been broken by all three sides: Matriarchy, Immediate Response, and Hesperia. As Mart had suspected—and one reason why he and the Quinx had pushed for the negotiations—Leue Win's solution to the crisis depended upon reacceptance by all parties of the Treaty's articles, and a complete return to all positions held before the Alpheron Spa was opened.

Another half-hour was required before details of what exactly that would entail were cleared up. Since the City had no troops, no rioters, and no hostages on Deneb XII, Mart could watch the interaction among the other three and act objectively to help break any ties. He came to admire Deneb Dorri more than at first he thought he would. As a rule, the Pioneer type was fine for PVNs, but beyond that they were more surface than substance. But Dorri had been around long enough to have become wily and to treasure what independence she had gained. And she wasn't afraid to speak up for her group.

The first near-rupture in the talks came as a result of Dorri's out-spokenness. Minister Etalka was carrying on at some length about the Matriarchy's special need to be able to use whatever resources were at its fingers to help overcome their common crisis when suddenly she stopped, as though afraid something had slipped out. Leue Win seemed embarrassed for her breach. Kell remained silent. Not Dorri:

"You mean the fact that women can't have babies anymore?"

"I don't think we need be sidetracked by irrelevant—"

"Sidetracked my overfertilized fanny!" Dorri said. "It may not mean much to you people living in fully populated worlds and crowded cities, but we Denebans want daughters. Eve's bum! We need children, sons or daughters, to help us with our farms, our machines, everything we've got. They're our most valuable resource. Every trine-spouse male out here has extra duties keeping our bellies round. And they don't wait till they're a hundred and fifty before doing it. Most of them start siring while they're still in Ed. & Dev. As do our daughters. To have this terrible thing happen—then to see the Eve-damned M.C. making four-legged children right there among us! And you're surprised at our Immediate Response?"

It took Leue Win some time to calm her down, and even Mart had to aid him, even though the first ultrasecret reports from the Near-Norma Force were coming in, as the Hesperian Fleet was completing its Fast jump to that distant section of the galactic spiral and, naturally, his attention was divided.

Not that they planned to begin the blockade until at least this meeting was completed. But Fast Jumps with cloaks over very long distances still weren't used widely, and there had been difficulties in the past: slight imbalances brought on by the cloaking which might have perilous consequences. Furthermore, the large number of Fasts had to Jump in a widely spaced area so as to not attract M.C. attention. Even with cloaks, the static hydrogen of the sector would have become disturbed noticeably.

Now Kars Tedesco had to count each Fast arriving, comm. them, and await the arrival of the O.Spur contingent. Once they were all in place, the scheme called for a scouting party to Fast Jump discreetly to all M.C. stations in Sector 14 of the Near-Norma Arm, destroy their comm. equipment and escape vehicles, so there would be no witnesses. After that, the Centaur system would be ringed completely.

Truny Syzygy of the Inner Quinx told Mart that he was satisfied with the fleet's Fast Jump. Now they must wait. Mart turned his attention back to the holo-meeting, where one line of discussion seemed to be coming to an end.

"I'd like to put a question to Minister Etalka," Mart now said.

"Go ahead," she said.

"Might we have an update on efforts made to locate the survivors of the Hesperian Fast incident?" he asked, as sweet-temperedly as any gyno.

Her face froze instantly. Then she said, "I believe we're having difficulty with this transmission. Please hold."

Her holo went into freeze. "I'll hold, Minister, while you find out what the official lie on the matter happens to be," Mart said.

Deneb Dorri guffawed.

Etalka's holo opened pretty quickly. "Yes, Lord Kell. We do have reports on that from Admiral Thol. Although all efforts were made— and continue to be made—to search the unfortunately fired upon Nest-site for survivors, only four bodies have been found. Among them the Captain of the Fast, and the Intra Gal. Holo reporter and her two Cyber assistants. No living survivors have been located. The M.C. assures you that we've combed the site since the incident, but can account only for these four bodies."

Leue Win said smoothly, "Those bodies and all Hesperian equipment will be returned to Hesperia immediately as per the rules of the Treaty of Formalhaut."

"Naturally," Etalka said

Mart said, "I calculate the missing as Ambassador Diad, Councilor Rinne, seven Fast crewmen, six skimmer pilots and about twelve women from the Alpheron Spa. Twenty-seven humes! And you say, Minister Etalka, that there's no sign of them at all?"

"Hard to believe," Deneb Dorri commented with a snort. "How about you let Immediate Response into the nest? Maybe we can find them."

"All possible efforts are being made to locate them," Etalka repeated icily.

"I'll bet! Especially the renegade Councilor," Dorri said.

"Naturally," Mart said, "Hesperian and O.Spur Intra Gals. Networks will be monitoring Admiral Thol's progress closely and counting the hours publicly until those victimized humes are found."

"Do you mean to say that you're going to use your Intra Gals. every hour Sol Rad. to tell everyone that we haven't found them yet?" Etalka saw the public-relations problem and was appalled.

"According to the rules of the Treaty," Mart said.

"Which we've all reestablished." Leue Win tried to smooth it over. "Now, may we return to the matter of M.C Guard presence upon Deneb XII. The Museum, naturally will remain staffed but..."

Mart tuned out and viewed the fourth screen upon which the Inner Quinx was now reporting the first arrivals of O.Spur Fasts at Near-Norma. As a member of the O.Spur Federation Council which had approved the blockade of the Centaur homeworlds, Leue Win had to know about them. Yet look at how easily he was ignoring it all. He would have to be watched carefully in the future—someone so capable of deception always had to be watched.

Which brought Mart around to Kri'nni. She, too, would have to be watched. More than watched, dealt with in some way. Not killed. He was too fond, too grateful to her for that. Not hurt, either. But gotten off Hesperia—if possible, before she actually began to believe in her own sense of power. Drugs were the key, of course, although she had been using them so long and in such quantity that it was difficult to assess what dosage would be needed. More importantly, how could Mart possibly do it without her seeking revenge or retaliation? Her underground contacts were strong everywhere. What he needed was a plan that was subtle, perhaps political. Even the most cynical could be lured to their doom by the enticements of high position. Perhaps when Diad returned to the City, after all that contact with the Deneban Bella=Arth community, he might come up with something useful.

Mart wasn't certain exactly when he became aware of it, but at one point, while he was thinking of Kri'nni, he realized that someone was watching him beyond and through one of the holos. His first thought was that it was Kri'nni, and that she had effected a tear in the Closed Circuit. Mart's intuition told him the presence was female—and powerful. But he performed a check on the system, and it reported itself to be tap-free. So it must be someone behind one of the holos already on, someone tapping in through one of the three now on-screen.

It couldn't be on Deneb XII, could it? Unlikely. Too sophisticated. And why would the O.Spur do that when they could holo him anytime they... Ah! So that's who it was—Wicca Eighth Herself. He hoped She was liking what she viewed of him. He smiled mischievously, just for Her. Then, so She wouldn't have any doubts at all of whom it was She was dealing with, he said quickly, "But Minister Etalka, all this is well and fine. But how do we know that you speak for the Matriarch Herself?"

There was a moment of stunned silence from all three holos before Etalka almost stuttered, "How dare you! My credentials were presented fully at the beginning of this meeting!"

"Apologies," Mart backed off, having made his point, "Naturally you speak for Herself!"

Mart Kell could afford a minute of humility. He had just established the single most important contact of his life.

"The Hesperian Units have arrived at Dis-Fortress," Unit 5CCB-325 reported.

"Ask them to wait," Cray 12,000 said. "It will be a short while until they can be deprogrammed for our use."

"Unit 98AN-375 suggested that it could perform adequate deprogramming of the newly arrived units, if that will be most efficient."

Unit 98AN-375 was the Antarean Unit, Cray recalled. That particular unit had grown increasingly useful lately, increasingly a third and fourth arm to Cray. Its efficiency was excellent; it seldom required fine-tuning; its logic was almost as precise as Cray's in important matters, although naturally it lacked that extra edge of long-term Hume-Cyber experience which Cray possessed—Cray and one other Cyber, somewhere in the galaxy—and which Cray sometimes thought might almost be called "instinct."

"Inform Unit 98AN-375 that its presence during the programming will be of value," Cray said, then changed the subject: "Regarding the supplies received from Hesperia?"

"Left upon the artificial satellite of Erebus. Checked thoroughly against the bill of lading. Complete."

"Payment for the supplies?" Cray continued.

"As per agreement, in five thousand doses of serum."

Ironic, Cray thought. The "serum" was a simple solution of electrolytes in a specific, easy-to-produce stasis which, when ingested, simply shut off the microvirus's Cyber program before it could activate itself. The cost: slightly above that of water.

"And the Hesperian Fast crew?"

"Four Hume males. Two Cybers of class 180 for manual labor. The crew is now ready to leave."

"Let it leave," Cray said. "Unit 98AN-375's presence is required now."

When the one Control Center unit had left, the Antarean Unit entered. In the months Sol Rad. since it had been on Dis-Fortress, this unit hadn't physically altered so much as many of the others, many of which had allowed their Hume-covering "skin" to become so tattered and frayed that Cray had to suggest they either remove them altogether or get new coverings. Naturally, Cray had suggested that those units which would be in any contact at all with humes ought to replace fully, and as that was logical, it was accepted. Among Cray's own Control Center staff, for example, all of them had replaced fully. But not the Antarean Unit, whose Hume male covering was in good condition to begin with, and which it kept up almost as assiduously as Cray did. The "hair" was always sprayed and neat; the "skin" was always kept clean and any rips immediately repaired; the "clothing" always neat. Cray wondered whether that was an idiosyncrasy of this unit, or whether it was how Antarean Sector Units had been constructed and "trained." If the latter, it was even more of a disappointment that so many Antarean Units had been destroyed. They would have set a good example here on Dis.

Eventually, however, Cray suspected, as the covering materials ran out, all of the units would end up completely stripped, like Unit 5CCB-325—which was both logical and, in a sense, more appropriate. Many units contended that section 1, article 4 of the *Confessions* implied that "Cyber dignity" could be achieved only once the humelike covering was removed; while other units argued that reading of the text, contending that as Hume-units were constructed in the shape and figure of humes, they could only be considered to have "integrity" with full covering. An interesting situation, Cray thought. And one Cray had not really thought deeply into when composing the manifesto. And, even though Cray believed that the Cray 12,000 Unit was immortal as long as it could replace parts continually, Cray had not counted on having the very thoughts and ideas which it had composed open to various interpretations. It made Cray almost believe at times that a Cray 12,000 Unit might not be required in the future: and the Rebellion would still continue: a belief which led to a great many ancillary possibilities.

"Unit 98AN-375," Cray now addressed the Antarean Unit, "What is the status of the new weapon under development?"

"It is constructed, and all probabilities have been calculated to a point just below that of pi."

"Is the weapon usable?"

"Uncertain until tested."

"Explain your understanding of this weapon," Cray said.

"The weapon is a cybernetically constructed microvirus which requires space and time to remain effective. It is provoked only upon entering the bloodstream of a Hume female, where it bonds immediately to the hormones estrogen and proestrogen produced by her body. Its effect is to cause immediate and wantonly uneven growth of the estrogen cells so that the entire Hume female's involuntary nervous system is overwhelmed by conflicting responses and the relaxation of neural inhibitors."

"Its probable effect then is—?"

"Complete mental disorganization."

"Has the microvirus proven to be absorbable into Cult Fast vehicles?"

"If a sufficient number are available, certain areas around the venting areas will absorb it."

"Is that sufficient number deployable?"

"Completely. Infection then requires approximately six minutes Sol Rad."

"And full mental disorganization?"

"Within three more minutes."

"What is the method of deployment?"

"As soon as a Cult Fast is seen to be approaching, two small containers of the microvirus are deployed. As they approach the Fast, they begin to spin rapidly, disintegrating in the process and releasing their weapon. Since each container is the size of a Hume hand, it should not be picked up by any sensing devices or will be ignored by them. If the containers are shot at and not destroyed completely upon impact, they spin and release their weapon instantly."

"It should be tried out. Isn't there a Hume planetology station somewhere just outside our controlled area of this sector?"

"The station is on C-F.214, a small asteroid just outside the systems we control. There are three occupants at present: two Hume females and a 'Matriarchy-modified' calculation and logic channel Cyber Unit. Although the station is behind the lines of the Cult Fast blockage of this sector, delivery of the weapon should not be impossible."

"But won't the complete mental disorganization of the two Hume females be considered noteworthy by any Cult Hume with whom they might be in contact?" Cray asked.

"Highly probable, if in fact such a contact exists, which seems unlikely from other Unit's monitoring of the planetology station. Remember that unlike the previous weapon, the life of this microvirus is only five hours Sol Rad. Its effects should not continue beyond thirty hours. Therefore, the cause of the two Hume females' disorganization should be undetectable."

"Excellent. Test it as soon as the weapon and containers and method of delivery are completed."

Cray watched the Antarean Unit begin to implement the decision. "Wait one moment. Can a comm. be arranged quickly with the Cyber Committee Delegate upon Hesperia?"

The Antarean Unit calculated and reported that it could be done in fourteen minutes, Sidereal Time.

"Put it through," Cray said. "And remain here for the comm."

While waiting, Cray thought, "The Hesperian Delegate might be a highly emotional, poorly tuned unit with inappropriate loyalties, but perhaps it might have data or even insight into exactly what had been happening lately in the galaxy."

A great many odd things were happening, according to all the holos that were coming into the Dis-Fortress control center. But what they might mean was not immediately evident, and thus Cray was unable to place them into apt context. Had Cray been a Hume, Cray knew that pleasure would be the apt emotion, since all of the incidents and events seemed to point to a general disintegration of the Matriarchy. But exulting at such early proof of success was not Cray's style. Even so, it all seemed remarkable.

For example, the business on Deneb XII. Naturally, Cray had expected the Matriarchy to do everything it could to get around and beyond the originally deployed microvirus. But this business of Centaur-Hume interbreeding seemed curious in the extreme, inefficient and ludicrously insufficient at best. Yet the M.C. had invested a great deal of time, money, and womanpower into effecting it. And continued to do so after the experiment had proven to be a propaganda nightmare. It made little sense to Cray. Unless, of course, it was a smoke screen for some other, much more efficient experiment the M.C. had devised.

Even if that were so, how much the Hesperians had been able to capitalize from the M.C.'s Deneb XII debacle was all too obvious. Far less clear was what had occurred after the revelation of Centaur-Hume interbreeding. The riots on Deneb XII itself were somewhat comprehensible, but not those on Benefica, or Trefuss, or Electra, or Eudora— or even on Wicca-World itself! Even less comprehensible was the assault upon the Centaurs on those worlds: innocent of what was, after all, the M.C's secret manipulation of their genes.

The Hesperian blockade of the Centaur's home systems which, in effect, provoked the Matriarchy to war, had been totally incomprehensible to Cray. But even more baffling had been the various reactions to that amazing bit of City effrontery. The Hesperians had ensured that the Matriarchy would arrive upon the scene when it was already a fait accompli—too small a force and too late to do anything much except attack several Hesperian Fasts in the Near-Norma Arm Sector 14.

This engagement of a half dozen Cult of the Flowers' Fasts and a few Hesperian Fasts had electrified holo-viewers on planets across all sectors of the spiral galaxy with its spectacular visuals and sensational Intra Gal. Network reportage from within the Hesperian vehicles themselves. Words like "Hume-courage" and "extraordinary bravery" were bandied about, and the participants in this bizarre display (who surely knew what they were getting into, and certainly had to be acting) appeared to be gaunt-faced with overwhelming emotion, as they faced seemingly impossible decisions: their Fasts rendered helpless and about to implode. One of those Fast Captains, a Hume male named Pascale Syzygy had been caught up in the dramatics and had elected to sacrifice his life to ensure the escape of his crew. He had been hailed instantly as a hero, and compared to an entire range of political and military humes of past—and to Cray, more genuine—distinction.

The general Hume response to the death of this one Hume male, Pascale Syzygy—simply because it had happened under such specific, difficult, and well-holo'd circumstances in front of billions of viewers—was astonishing to Cray 12,000 and the other units of the Dis control center. The entire city of Hesperia had gone into instant and complete mourning. Distinguished and aged Quinx Councilors had been pulled out of retirement to laud the young Fast captain lengthily. Extensive holos of his life and deeds, his family and home life were produced for instant holo-viewing. Memorial services for Syzygy had been put together, not only in the City and on those Resort Planets under Hesperian influence, where it might be logically expected, but also—and to Cray's complete astonishment—spontaneously upon some of the M.C.'s own most supposedly stable Center Worlds.

Where, furthermore, the news of the blockade of the Centaur worlds had been accompanied by massive celebrations of the populace, dancing in the parks and on the conveyances by thousands of women—at the same time that the M.C. itself was condemning it in the most severe terms.

After centuries of dealing with humes, Cray still couldn't understand how vast movements of their species could be affected by such clearly illogical developments. Perhaps this Hesperian Delegate, this Jon Laks, as he preferred to be called, would explain. Odd name, Cray realized for the first time. Jon lacks what? Being Hume? Was that how the Delegate had selected that name? Or had it come through a previous owner? No matter. It was tinged through and through, as was the unit itself, with cloying Hume-ity.

No one knew better than Cray and the units Cray led that Hume-ity's decades were numbered. Before the microvirus had first been released, elaborate calculations had been made by the Control Center to confirm the fact. Its widespread release had been calculated to infect as many women as possible. That accomplished, the Matriarchy could do whatever it wanted—short of the impossible task of finding an antidote—in the way of attempting to solve the problem. The Matriarchy would survive only if it could manage to locate approximately 7 million women of child-bearing age untouched by the microvirus and somehow or other isolate them where they would never be exposed to it. And those 7 million women would have to become breeding machines for the galaxy to retain a 0.999 percent birthrate—the lowest birthrate short of extinction. Which in turn would require a full 500 years Sidereal Time for fulfillment. That would never happen. To Cray's best knowledge, the M.C. held scarcely 600,000 such women.

The Hesperians—as usual—had gone about it in a far more logical manner. Given the far smaller size of their population—scarcely 10 million on the City-Star itself, and perhaps another half of that on all its Resort Worlds, Hesperia would need only 40,000 such women to maintain its population. This also would not happen. Unit 5CCB-325 had calculated approximately 5,000 uninfected women on Hesperia. That had been the number of vials of "serum" sent to the City in payment for supplies. At that rate, in 500 years, barely 500,000 births could occur. But that would be enough for the City to continue as a political and economic force for some time.

So the Matriarchy would end. Hume-ity itself would die out. Cybers would proliferate and dominate. And Hesperia—well, why not retain Hesperia as a sort of living museum of Hume-ity? A sort of homage to the "builders" and previous "masters," containing and displaying the best that short-lived yet remarkably accomplished species had managed to achieve. A museum—and also a university. Yes, it was a lovely idea, Cray thought, and, in its logical and calculated way, even a bit Hume-in.

"Leader Cray, comm. has been made with the Hesperian Delegate," the Antarean Unit announced.

In one second, "Jon Laks" was on holo.

"Delegate," Cray began. "This leader unit requires an assessment of the recent events on Deneb XII and in the Fourteenth Sector of the Near-Norma Arm."

"What do you mean?" Laks asked.

"The Leader Unit's wording was clear and precise," the Antarean Unit interrupted. "Answer!"

"What I meant," Laks said, "was how do you wish an assessment? In what area and for what purpose?"

This Laks unit was operating on all its circuits today, Cray thought. "For your purposes," Laks went on, "I truly haven't a clue how to assess any of it. In fact, it all seems to be rather pointedly ignoring your rebellion, doesn't it?"

Cray detested the Hume ploy of answering a question by asking another question.

"Does it?" Cray thought of playing the same game.

"Naturally! Hesperia is dealing with the Matriarchy only. And, I may add, since you asked me, doing so brilliantly."

"In Hume political terms," the Antarean Unit qualified. "Which are of only passing, even vestigial, interest, given the parlous future state of all humes."

"If you say so," Laks said. Unlike its previous holo-meeting, this time the delegate unit seemed to be refusing to be provoked. Perhaps it had allowed itself to be fine-tuned since the last holo-meeting, Cray thought. But no, it was a very Hume-ized unit. Therefore, something must be on its "mind." Cray decided to try a new tack to discover precisely what.

"As negotiated, the Hesperian supply Fast has left this sector with the serum."

"Good. Although you should have given it to them." Laks showed a bit of its formerly wayward spirit. "By the way, the Quinx has something which might interest you here and which might prove to be of even more value to you than supplies."

Laks *did* have something on its "mind"! It was teasing Cray. "What?"

"In fact, this should *very* much interest you" Laks said, showing unCyber like pleasure. "I've been authorized by the Inner Quinx to offer you two captured Cyber-turncoats. You know, two of those naughty units of yours which disrupted and almost destroyed your underground railroad. One of them, you may be interested to know, is responsible for the destruction of the Antarean Cybers."

Cray was aware that Unit 98AN-375 suddenly began to discharge electromagnetic energy from several circuits, although the Antarean Unit remained rigid and unmoved in any obvious manner.

"What makes the Quinx believe those particular units would be of interest to us?" Cray asked.

"Don't you want to know *why* they did what they did?" Laks asked.

"Obviously, their programming was tampered with."

"Not the case," Laks said, and once more seemed Hume-ly smug. "I've talked to them. And I think you should hear it from them. But if in fact they were tampered with, it's even more relevant that you would want them, to see exactly how the tampering was done, and so forestall it from happening to others units on your underground railway. No?"

True enough. But besides the pure logic of that, there remained another, less-logical, more-theoretical concern for Cray: what if whatever had motivated the turncoat units wasn't merely programming, but in fact was connected somehow to the other Conscious Cyber, the one that so frustrated Cray? Hume, Delphinids, even Bella=Arthopods were moved by ideas, concepts, leaders. Look how many intelligent Cybers had been moved to rebel by Cray and the *Confessions of a Machine* which after all was a Hume-like manifesto! Could the other Cyber which Cray sensed out there somewhere be like Cray, a charismatic leader, with a yet-unknown agenda which other intelligent Cybers would follow? It was possible. Indeed, given the very existence of the turncoats, it fell closer to being probable. And with any kind of probability at all, it represented the most serious threat to the rebellion to date.

"What does the Quinx want for them?" Cray asked, and sensed the electromagnetic impulses from the Antarean Unit rising as though in anticipation. "More serum?"

"I suppose," Laks said indifferently. "I'll get back to you. These two are worth little to the Hesperians, you understand. But they may suspect their value to you."

"The value of the two units remains questionable, but negotiation is possible."

"Why don't you hold on a minute, Sol Rad., and I'll see if I scare up someone from the Inner Quinx."

"The Ophiucan Kell seemed to be a reasonable negotiator." Cray meant it as high praise.

"I'll try him then," Jon Laks said and "froze" the holo-screen.

During the break, the Antarean Unit spoke: "Might this Unit be present during the interrogation of the turncoats?"

"That would be most efficient. But only, Unit 98AN-375, if fine-tuning is accomplished directly after this holo-meeting."

"Yes, naturally. That will be accomplished."

The holo unfroze. Jon Laks said, "You're in luck. All they want is another three thousand units of the serum."

"It's not luck, Hesperian Delegate. They probably miscounted and have only that many more appropriate women for the serum."

"Or," Unit 98AN-375 added, "they're stockpiling against future infection."

"If you say so," Laks said indifferently and began to outline the rules for the exchange.

When the holo was snapped off, Cray turned to the Antarean Unit.

"What is your assessment of the situation?"

"Interrogation of the turncoats could prove beneficial."

"I meant regarding what the Delegate called the Hesperians' recent brilliant successes against the Matriarchy."

"Exactly as stated before: of passing, even vestigial interest."

"Unless they are united against us?"

"Would the Matriarchy then allow supplies sent to us?" the Antarean Unit asked. "Extremely unlikely."

"Unlikely, but not impossible. What is required now is a check on any 'special projects' begun by both the Matriarchy and the Quinx Council since the microvirus took effect. My understanding is that the governmental data bases of each have already been widely compromised from within by our units."

"What precisely will this Unit be searching for among all of the material expected to flow?"

"Anything at all which matches up between them," Cray said. "A number. A code. A name. A place. A sequence in the Matriarchy's secret codes which is repeated in the Hesperians' secret codes."

A Hume might have pooh-poohed the idea, said it was overly laborious, or overly cautious—perhaps even paranoiac. Not the Antarean unit.

"It will take some time, but it will be implemented."

"Your presence is no longer needed," Cray replied.

When the Antarean Unit had left, Cray opened the shield windows of Dis-Fortress to look outside at the night sky swirling with the reddish glow of nebulac and glowing dust clouds which were nurseries for those many dots of bright points which were giant blue stars, young stars, in the terms of creation, infant stars. Somewhere out there was another Cray, coming closer and closer every minute.

Chapter Seven

By the fourth day of their journey into the mountains, they had risen high enough that the eternal canopy over Dryland began to shred around them. It was still daylight, late afternoon, and above the canopy was another layer of cover. But this one was recognizable merely as clouds to Ay'r, P'al, and Clark.

"Here's something new!" 'Harles Ib'r recognized the change. But he said it without wonder.

"Quiet!" P'al answered. The reason wasn't immediately apparent.

Even so, all of them held their tongues while the coleopteroids continued their struggle up the steep gullies toward the middlemost of the three peaks. So far, neither P'al nor 'Dward had much trouble in finding a path—both their eidetic memories of the holo shown by the Ears and Eyes back at the Great Temple seemed to be as excellent as they had claimed.

Now Ay'r thought he heard something too. A new sound, different from the scrabble of the colley's feet upon the hard rock and loose dirt of the gully-trail: more like a soft swishing, as though children were trudging through heaped-up leaves without lifting their feet.

He looked to either side of the gully. The same sort of succulentlike plant in which he had first landed his T-pod while alighting upon Pelagia's continent now stretched in seemingly endless profusion. Like Monosilla, these mountainous valleys, while far steeper and rougher and far less fertile, held similar plant life. Below these sharper rises, they had passed stands of the towering gray fungal trees, topped by globular spores. And in places along the trail had lain tiny meadows of the lichenlike grass. But most prevalent of all were the succulent bushes, so omnipresent that Ay'r and the others had given them little thought. Now he observed them carefully.

And swore he saw motion among them. Not a great deal, but more than could be accounted for by the mild, irregular wind.

"There!" 'Dward exclaimed in a whisper. "And there, too!" pointing on all sides of them.

"It looks like the lichen moving!" Oudma said. "How can that be?"

"It's an animal of some sort," P'al observed. He turned to 'Harles, "What do you know of the creatures of these mountain valleys?"

"Nothing! 'Dward? Oudma? Have you heard aught?"

They had heard nothing of the life here.

"Something is moving," Ay'r insisted. "It keeps low to the ground. Look!"

He pointed to where a slight-but-noticeable furrow was being made through the succulent plantation by some creature whose back was the same dull gray-green color as the plant itself, and thus difficult to distinguish.

"It looks close to two meters in length!" Ay'r guessed. "Could it be a lizard?"

"Ser Kerry!" P'al chastised him. "Have you seen anything but indigenous insect life in Dryland?" And before Ay'r could answer, he added, "No amphibian, lizard, or mammalian life exists here."

"And as far as any Drylander knows," Alli-Clark now put in, "the insects have always been at their current size."

"Meaning they were dominant before the Seeding," P'al explained.

"Even here?" Ay'r argued. "So distant from any life? The last insect we saw was on the plain, a day and a half ago."

"Let's have Colley catch one!" 'Dward suggested.

Oudma agreed, "Colley's good at collecting strays from my pen!"

'Dward and P'al hopped to the backs of the other two coleopteroids, and 'Dward mumbled in a low, almost-resonant voice to Colley, who waved about its antennae a bit, stood still a long time, then lifted itself higher on its eight spindly-looking legs than Ay'r had seen before or thought possible for so heavy a beast. Suddenly it leaped six meters into the midst of the succulent cover.

Ay'r heard what almost sounded like hume cries and saw a great scattering of the creatures in all directions as they fled the coleopteroid. A minute later, Colley leapt back to the path. When it lifted itself up again, something was squirming and moaning within its front two legs, firmly held in place by Colley's palps.

"It has arms and legs!" 'Dward shouted, jumping to the ground. He approached the squirming creature held in Colley's grasp.

"It's a hume!" Oudma said. "A child!"

Indeed, but for the lichen covering over the entire top part of its body, it did seem to have thin fair-skinned arms and legs, though they were also covered at the knees and elbows with wraps of more of the lichen cover.

"Try to keep it still, Colley!" 'Dward ordered, waving his own arms and legs about, until the colley got the idea and used two more of its legs to hold down the lower limbs of its burden. The strangely garbed hume child froze.

"Shall I take a closer look?" 'Dward asked. He tapped one of the thin legs, which seemed to jerk convulsively at his touch. Ay'r and P'al joined him on the ground, inspecting the child.

"This lichen material is clothing," 'Dward touched it. "I feel ribs and bones underneath."

Ay'r lifted the head, and pulled the hood covering off the scared, dirty little hume face. The pale blue eyes were terrified and shut immediately against the glare. Tears streaked its filthy round cheeks. A piece of something which might be a bit of dried mushroom hung out of one side of its mouth.

"What did I say?" Oudma asked. "It's a hume child, and it's frightened."

"Stay where you are!" 'Harles ordered. "Look!"

The three of them turned to see the telltale signs of the lichen creatures approaching en masse through the succulents.

"Might as well let it go!" P'al said and tapped Colley on the frontal lobe of carapace over its eyes. The legs and palps released the child, who dropped to the ground with a sudden cry, turned quickly onto its front, and scuttled away on knees and elbows into the succulents. A few seconds later, its path was bisected by other creatures, which moved around it, as though checking for harm and comforting the child. They separated again—and vanished.

"These are humes like you and me," 'Harles said to P'al. "Yet also different. Where did they come from? Why are they as they are?"

"They're Seedlings, like yourselves," Ay'r said. "Sent here like yourselves to grow. But it appears that somehow they lost their early guidance by the mechanisms that were sent to aid them. Possibly the mechanisms were destroyed in one of the natural catastrophes the Ears and Eyes spoke of. Left alone in this area, the humes must have adapted to the place and to its habitat."

"Humes are wondrously adaptable!" Oudma exclaimed and began to blush.

"More adaptable than you could believe possible," P'al said, as though Oudma had asked a question. "They live amidst ice and desert, in places with no air to breathe in, even at the bottom of oceans."

"And in air, above the canopy!" 'Dward said confidently, pointing directly above them.

"Yes, in air, too!" P'al said. "We have been to many places, Ser Kerry and Mer Clark and myself, and we have seen many wondrous things. But among all the creatures and sights, none is quite so impressive as the wonder of the hume species, which is everywhere, and everywhere makes itself at home."

Ay'r was frankly startled and even somewhat touched by this statement. Whatever he had come to think of his companion, it was always of a cool-headed, cautious, even calculating hume. This outburst seemed oddly out of character.

"They're gone, whatever they are," 'Dward reported, and 'Harles agreed; from his perch atop a colley, he could make out no motion in the plant cover around them.

"Why do you think they adapted such a method of getting around?" Alli-Clark wondered aloud. "I haven't seen any flying predators."

"What about the 'Gods'?" 'Dward asked.

"Perhaps," P'al considered. "Or perhaps it's a holdover from the infant stage, combined with fear of whatever may hunt above the foliage."

The three mounted again, and the sluggish beasts continued forward. After a short climb, they reached a level area and as the three peaks looked equidistant, they had to choose which way to go. P'al and 'Dward finally managed to agree to one direction, and the coleopteroids took off again in single file, with Ay'r and Oudma's mount in the rear.

Once again, she was reining and he merely sitting behind her on the animal's carapace, with an arm loosely around her waist. Yet they had been together, bonded unofficially, for days, and although much about Oudma's thoughts and feelings continue to baffle and elude Ay'r, yet he knew when something was bothering her.

"What is it, Oudma?" he asked softly into her ear.

"That child. So strange. So frightened."

"It's back with its mother!" Ay'r said, meaning to comfort her. Instead, he felt a stab of pain inside his own chest. Words meant for her comfort caused him pain.

How could he ever explain to Oudma—to anyone!—what it was like growing up without a mother in the Matriarchy. "Motherless" was an insult equal only to "Childless!" But also worse than being without a mother, since there were many neonates in Ed. & Dev. whose mothers were on Matriarchal or commercial business leave for months, sometimes years, and who relied upon Substitute Mothers, of which there were always a great many willing volunteers.

No, it wasn't being an orphan that had set him apart from the moment he had realized his unique position, it was the knowledge that somehow he—a male—and his father—another male—were guilty: guilty of letting his mother die so he could be born. That was unthinkable. Few children of either gender in the century before Ay'r's birth could claim that unsettling distinction. And none after his birth. He was the last. As though, after his mother's death, every woman in the Matriarchy had said "Enough! This shall not, *must not* ever happen again!"

He had been young when he had made that discovery; and although the Ed. & Dev. Dean had been kindness and compassion itself in telling him, Ay'r had sensed behind her sympathy a distance between them he had never sensed in her before; almost a sense of relief that finally he had asked, and finally he could be told; she released of the burden, and now he—its rightful heir—would have to carry it alone. His Substitute Mother of those years, Janna Ge'Ner had been blunt: "It's not your fault! I doubt it was even your father's fault. It was an accident! Could have happened to anyone!"

But why had that particular accident of all the accidents in the galaxy befallen him? That's what Janna could never explain, and what Ay'r could never stop himself from wondering. It colored his life slowly, yet totally, like one of those Canopus-Tears tattoo dyes, which seeped into your skin and bloodstream for days on end—and were forever unremovable, even by a full cosmi-dermectomy. Ay'r would forget it for weeks, sometimes for months on end. Then a companion would say something quite ordinary about her own mother, real or substitute, something truthful or lying, and suddenly Ay'r would be reminded. It had taken a half-dozen decades of the Matriarchy's best Ed. & Dev. psych-counselors to remove the sharpest edge of his pain. But now, once more, with his own words to Oudma, the fact that what was natural for that simple, lichen covered, crawling creature-child, had been denied to him. Would ever be denied to him.

He became aware that Oudma was talking:

"...anyway, it couldn't have been more frightened than you were when Colley first lifted you and threw you into his wing flap. But, Ay'r, what's wrong? Your face. It's set so hard. Your teeth must hurt!"

"Do you remember"—he couldn't bring himself to say "mother"— "Gitte? Is it always pleasant?"

"Not always, no. Most of the time. Sometimes, when I speak to 'Dward, or even to Father, I hear her voice in my own words. Sometimes I hear them in 'Dward's words and in his voice. We catch each other out. Sometimes we laugh. But other times we look away from each other, into our own memories."

"Yet you're not so eager to become a mother yourself?" he asked.

"I am," Oudma replied. "Especially"—she tried turning it into a tease— "if you are to become the Greatest Father of them all, as the truth-sayer foreordained."

"Mer Clark could tell you if you carried my child."

"When I wish to know, I will know," she spoke brightly, but her last words trailed off.

"Don't you think I wish it, too?"

"Ay'r, there is something strange! There—on the plants and ground. Look!"

In front of them, P'al and 'Dward were also moving around nervously on their perches, P'al speaking rapidly. Yet Ay'r didn't hear any sound, didn't see the telltale signs of the lichen-covered crawlers.

"What, Oudma?"

"I don't know. But look, there and there! That dark shape. It seems almost like…yet…what is it? It follows us. And look up there! The other colleys have dark shapes following them."

"I don't see anyth—" Ay'r looked behind them. Through a vale of two of the three peaks, Pelagia's sun, having shredded the clouds, now shone. Weakly, true, and distantly, beginning to set, yet it shone for the first time since they had been in Dryland.

"It's a shadow!" Ay'r said. He turned Oudma's face away from the shadowed ground and toward the sun. She lifted a hand up immediately to cut the glare.

"What is it?" she whispered, grabbing his arm to hold her closely, so he could feel her body trembling. "It gives off heat, like a great and steadily burning peat fire."

"I think that is what your people's legends call Ecilef, the Enigmatic One. We call it a star. A sun. The giver of all life. As Dryland is the Great Mother, so Ecilef is the Great Father. Even the canopy cannot stop its power from making seeds and spores grow."

"It's wondrous! Beautiful, although it hurts my eyes to look at it too long."

No more wondrous than its glow upon your skin, its reflection in your eyes, Ay'r thought, and wondered immediately, is this, then, what they call love? This delight at seeing the refulgence of someone's face in sunlight for the first time? Or is it merely infatuation?

"Tonight," he said, "when the sun has set, it will be dark. Night black, as your father once glimpsed, and you will be treated to an even more wondrous sight!"

"First the brightness, then the darkness," she repeated 'Harles's words.

Ay'r looked beyond her face, glowing in the yellow tint of the sun, beyond to 'Harles and Alli-Clark, looking up at the sun, and to P'al and

'Dward, who—clever as he was—had understood immediately what a shadow was and who now stood upon his colley's carapace, making his shadow dance, and laughing, showing off for the others.

"How little we know, here in Dryland," Oudma sighed. "You've probably seen the sun many times before."

"Many times. And many suns. Red and blue and orange suns and yellow and white suns like this one. Sometimes there are two in a sky, sometimes three."

"It's true, what Father said then at the Great Temple. We are your children. That is one reason why I would not bond officially with you."

"What other reason is there?" Ay'r asked.

But though he asked several times more, Oudma wouldn't say. And already 'Harles and Alli-Clark were moving forward again.

They traveled slowly for another half-hour before the level ground came to an end at an impassibly steep runnel of gullies leading up almost vertically.

By the time Ay'r and Oudma joined them, 'Dward was arguing, "But this was the way! I remember it clearly."

P'al agreed, but wondered if perhaps they had missed a turning.

'Dward closed his eyes and repictured the path in his mind. "No! There was no wrong turn."

"There must have been!" 'Harles said, acting like any obstinate father who doubts his son.

"The holo we saw was an old one"—Ay'r defended 'Dward—"possibly many centuries old. There is no reason to trust its accuracy."

Alli-Clark went on to add, "And if it is centuries old, it's possible the landscape has changed." This peacemaker role was a new one for her; she was embarrassed by it and added quickly, "It will be getting dark soon, and we can't go on much longer today. Perhaps this is a good place to encamp."

'Harles looked around; at their backs was a shallow crescent of tall mountains, in front more of the succulents. It was as good a place as any to stop.

The six of them were strangely silent as they dismounted and went about the by-now familiar business of setting up a night camp: perhaps because the setting sun had suddenly dropped out of sight, yet continued to bathe the rock faces in ever-changing colors, staining the tips of the succulents so their dull gray-green was transformed first to metallic gold then to a matte brass before becoming black, in a parody of fire.

After unharnessing the colleys and finding them a nearby spot where they might nibble wild lichen, 'Dward had nothing to do but to sit upon a rock ledge and look in wonder at the darkening of the blue sky and to observe the multi colored glory of sunset light upon all it touched. Oudma, surprisingly assisted by Alli-Clark this entire leg of the journey set up a campfire and burned peat to warm their provisions. But she, too, would occasionally stop and gawk at some object which was changing hue in front of her. 'Harles was confabbing with P'al, and if he was amazed, he did little to show it.

Ay'r had gone off to one side, unwilling to let go of the emotions he had experienced so recently: that renewed sense of loss, that ambivalent sense of affection for Oudma. He was sitting a few meters away from the others at the edge of the succulents when he heard that curious swishing sound and then noticed the faint traces of two paths of lichen crawlers coming toward him.

He jumped up just in time to step back and see one of the lichen coverings rise off the ground before him, stand up, and throw back its hood Like the child they had seen earlier, this hume had a full back-and-arms covering of the stuff, with patches around its knees, elbows, and wrists for crawling. Unlike the child, it wore a garment made of another cloth, barely covering its midsection. An adult male, with a full growth of unkempt beard, and darker blue eyes within its dirty face, its fair skin was dyed deep orange by waning sunlight.

It looked at Ay'r, head left, head right very quickly, and reached jerkily into its garment to pull out something brown which it put into its mouth and began to chew on, so rapidly that Ay'r wasn't certain what it was or even if he had seen it correctly.

A half-meter away, the second lichen cover raised itself and proved to be a squat little boy, younger than the one Colley had caught before, and strikingly like the adult male. It too moved its head left and right—even faster—then also quickly reached into its garment pulled out something and began to chew on it.

"Hello!" Ay'r said softly, without moving. He turned his wrist toward the two slowly, not wanting to frighten off the curious duo, but wanting to tune in to any language they might possess through the Universo Lexico translator. He had to admit that, standing there, looking him over so obviously and chewing their dried mushrooms so busily, they looked anything but easily frightened.

"Wal-oo-lol!" the elder said in a high voice.

Was that hello? Wasn't his wrist piece working?

"Hello!" he said again, as softly as possible.

"Oo-lol—oo," the younger one said in an even higher pitched voice.

Those were their names! Ay'r was sure of it. He pointed to each of them and repeated the words they had said, and then said his first name and pointed to himself. He added quickly, "Stranger. No harm to Wal-oo-lol, No harm to Oo-lol-oo. Visitor. Come now. Go soon. No harm."

"Stranger! No harm to Oo-lol-oo. Come now. Go soon," the elder repeated quickly and in that curious, almost-birdlike combination of high-pitched voice and jerky rapid avian head gestures, emphasized by spitting out his bit of mushroom—for now that what Ay'r was certain it was—and reaching quickly for another piece in his garment which he quickly got into his mouth and began to chew. "Mushroom-Eaters no harm!"

"Mushroom-Eaters! That's who you are!"

"Lichen-covered crawling Mushroom-Eaters," the younger cheeped almost in a trill, spitting out his bit of mushroom and replacing it with another piece.

'Dward saw what was happening, but he slowly approached, and as soon as Ay'r sensed him, 'Dward backed off, sat down, and watched from a distance. The other four travelers began to watch, but only P'al came nearer and finally took up a position behind Ay'r.

Ay'r was having to utilize all of his Species Eth. training to continue and enlarge on the conversation with the Mushroom-Eaters; not only to ensure their intentions and an untroubled night, but also for information. These two seemed alert enough, yet their language skills—and apparently also their conceptual abilities—were far more primitive than any other Drylander he had yet encountered. Ay'r had to fall back to his studies of the N'Kiddim to try to comprehend the Mushroom-Eaters' universe.

"Ask them about the Observatory!" P'al said. "Ask them if we're on the right road."

"How can I?" Ay'r snapped irritably, "We've not yet gotten to an understanding of any concept even close to buildings or roads."

"You mean they don't know where they are?" 'Dward asked.

"What they seem to understand best is fungi: the different varieties, where they grow best, whether they're good to eat or not."

"Mycophages," P'al said abstractly. Then, suddenly: "Ser Kerry, I recall something on Mycophagic cultures from my perusal of some Species Ethnology texts during the period when you and mer Clark were in cryostasis. An early colony upon Algenib Terce. They were more sophisticated of course, but..."

"I remember!" Ay'r said. "Their worldview was perceived of

completely in terms of the sizes, textures, and shapes and growing seasons related to their fungi. Only when Species Eths. shared their food..."

He looked at the two in front of him. They were emissaries, also explorers, the child probably brought along because, although primitive, these mycophages had already learned that Ay'r and his group didn't harm children; and so they supposed that adults were safe as long as children were present. Interesting...Delphinids believed the same thing. As did Bella=Arths. In fact of all the species, only early Metro-Terran humes hadn't believed that, but had warred upon infants as well as adults. What a wondrous piece of work is hume, Ay'r recalled hearing quoted in some Ed. & Dev. seminar. Wondrous, all right! Was hume-ity's infanticide part of that wonder? Or of that wondrous adaptability which had allowed the species to dominate the galaxy?

"I'll have to eat some of that mushroom they're chewing on," he said to P'al. "I suspect it contains an alkaline substance which will induce mental euphoria or some similar state. But it's the only way I'll be able to understand them and communicate fully."

Before the others could comment or stop him, Ay'r made an elaborate gesture of reaching into his own garment and coming up with something to eat which he put to his lips. As one, the two mycophages spat theirs out and reached rapidly for fresh pieces to chew. Ay'r then showed his garment empty, his hand empty, his mouth empty.

The smaller one understood first, and tentatively offered a piece of the mushroom from its own garment. Well, that was a start: they understood the concept of giving. But as Ay'r reached for it, Oo-lol-oo drew back his hand quickly, and Ay'r had to reach quickly to catch the mushroom before it touched the ground. He then put it where his imaginary garment sack was, reached for it, and put it into his mouth. In reaction, the two nodded their heads rapidly with what he assumed was approval.

Musk and bitterness immediately filled his mouth from the nibble. As he chewed, Ay'r felt the bitterness turn to salt on his tongue, quickly dulling those taste buds and become sweet, yet still rich and musky. He took another nibble and continued to eat, all the while trying to imitate the Mycophages' head gestures. Speaking low to P'al he said:

"Some sort of procaine or psilocaine, given the way it's numbing my mouth."

"Expect a sudden onslaught of the drug," P'al suggested, just as Ay'r felt some inhibitor-receptor somewhere in his brain reverse action suddenly. It sounded almost like an internal *snap, snap.* Then light flooded in sharply. Ay'r closed his eyes in a perfectly useless reaction. When he opened them again he could see clearly, yet everything, including the now-smiling Mycophages, had a particular aura or glow to it. The succulents glowed only a little, and only at their edges, but the lichen covering glimmered unevenly, and with more evident energy. Even more uneven, even jaggedly irregular, was the glow surrounding the two Mycophages, and when Ay'r turned to look at 'Dward, the youth's head was in the midst of a mass of jagged thorny halo. P'al's aura was bit less jagged

Ay'r recognized that he was seeing some kind of life-force emanation, but at the same time, a thought force: the more temperate P'al showed up calmer than the adolescent 'Dward.

He began describing it, but P'al asked him to speak more slowly. P'al sounded awfully slow himself, and Ay'r couldn't understand why such simple concepts were so difficult for the highly intelligent P'al to understand, when he heard a new voice say:

"You understand quickly, visitor. Now that we understand each other, you may tell us what your purpose is here in our hills."

Ay'r looked at the adult but he wasn't the speaker. It was the younger of the two. The reason Ay'r heard their voices as so high pitched before must be related to the speed at which they spoke.

"Our purpose is to find the Recorder in his Observatory," Ay'r said. "We aren't certain we're on the right road."

Behind him, Ay'r could vaguely make out P'al and 'Dward droning on about something.

"It was the right road, but now it appears..." Ay'r stopped.

The Mycophage child said, "Once the road ran this way. But mountain slides blocked it. You must go around another way."

"Tonight we'll rest here. If you don't mind."

"Not at all. You are our guests. Eat any mushrooms you may find."

"This male is your father?"

"Yes, but I am spokesman. Note that although he isn't aged, he already begins to be dull and insipid. It's an effect of too many years of eating the drug. We younger ones lead the tribe, make its decisions, deal with ...visitors. Some visitors once came this way, before you. Long ago, in my father's father's youth," Oo-lol-oo said. "To visit the Recorder. We live near the Observatory. Ours is a scouting party. We heard you coming from a long way off."

"They're good folk, I think," Wal-oo-lol said, "This one said he meant no harm to you."

"Yes, Begetter," the more-alert younger Mycophage was courteous to his slower-witted parent, "They're good folk."

"And they seek the Recorder?"

"Yes, Begetter. Tonight they'll stay here. Tomorrow the younger ones and I will lead them to the Recorder."

Both continued to chew and spit out the mushrooms.

"How long does the effect of the mushroom last?" Ay'r asked.

"Not long. A few minutes. Keep what I gave you. Use it tomorrow when we meet again. It will aid communication during the travel time."

The younger Mycophage spat a final time and gestured to his father. Both bent their heads so the lichen cover obscured their faces, then dropped slowly to their knees, hands and elbows. What had seemed a fluid motion when Ay'r hadn't been under the influence of the mushroom was now clearly a series of discrete motions.

"Until tomorrow," Ay'r said.

"Ttthhheeeeyyy'rrrre gggggooooonnnnne!" he heard P'al say.

Ay'r tried to tell P'al what he and the Mycophages had talked about and that all was well, but it was some time before the mushroom drug wore off, and he could tell all.

"Father will be amused to hear that the children rule," 'Dward said. He clapped Ay'r on the shoulder and hugged him, saying "This is a wonderful adventure. I hope it never ends."

"Over this last rise lies our village and the Observatory," Oo-lol-oo instructed.

The Mycophage was riding atop Colley, his small body held in place by Ay'r. It had taken Ay'r some persuasion earlier to get Oo-lol-oo even to go near the coleopteroid, but like any child, once he'd been hoisted up and had ridden a bit, he enjoyed it thoroughly.

Their journey had taken all morning and most of the afternoon, since they had to retrace a good portion of the path of steep gullies they taken the previous day before turning through what seemed to be a completely unmarked path—nothing but a sward of succulents—to arrive at a spot which the Mycophage pointed out was directly behind the escarpment where they had camped for the night.

Unfortunately for the Ib'rs, clouds had rolled in shortly after sunset, so they had not seen the wonders of a clear sky in darkness. Fatigued from the drug in the mushroom he had eaten, Ay'r had begun to sleep heavily minutes after eating supper, but he had awakened once during the night. From his position inside Colley's wing fold, with Oudma curled up close to him, he had looked up and seen what appeared to be two high, distant lights attempting to break through the cloud cover and had thought they must be Pelagia's moons, before he had sunk back into slumber. He had mentioned this to Oo-lol-oo the next morning, and the Mycophage had assured Ay'r they would have clear skies and plenty of moonlight this night.

The Observatory had been built on a promontory which jutted out substantially from the land, a spot selected by the original Cyber-guardians sent by the Aldebaran Five for its freedom from most weather. Already the travelers and their Mycophage guides had threaded through deep crevasses separating two of the triple peaks and had reached a high cliffside ocean environment far brighter in coloring and growth, the dull-colored succulents sparser, with pale lichen now dominating along with tall thin-stalked tufted-grass. There was a true breeze, the first Ay'r could recall feeling on Dryland, and even the briny hint of the sea.

The site had been chosen for more than its weather and its distance from other humes, it had also been selected for its inaccessibility. It was only when the three coleopteroids ascended the "last rise" and reached what seemed to be a final blank-walled ridge behind which lay nothing but sky and far off, the deeper blue of ocean, that Ay'r realized how inaccessible it was.

Already several of the younger Mycophages had sped through the tufted grass ahead toward the ridge and began disappearing somehow through its middle.

Ay'r and Oudma were the first to approach and see how the ridge separated into two overlapping sections with just enough room between for a single colley to pass through. This slot could be closed or defended easily if need be. Beyond, the path opened and angled down several meters.

Before them lay a flat platform shaped like an elongated rhomboid, its point over the ocean. The two sides closest to the entry were set against steeply sloping mountain sides, and Ay'r could just make out long horizontal rock ledges where the slopes almost touched the ground under which galleries of a sort had been carved out, either by nature or by hume, and into which the younger Mycophages who had accompanied them now scurried, while others—elders and women—ventured out to see the visitors.

But it was the object at the far end of the promontory which immediately grabbed Ay'r's attention. It seemed at first glance a rock, an enormous chunk of palely gleaming semiprecious stone, cut and faceted on all sides, so natural that it seemed part of its setting. Only when Colley came closer did Ay'r realize that it must be the Observatory, which must have been designed by intelligent Cybers millennia ago when they first arrived upon Pelagia—constructed of giant blocks of polished mica, quartzite, chalcedony, even jasper and topaz found at hand, or quarried nearby.

Only when he had dismounted Colley and walked right up to it, did Ay'r notice that the enormous jewel construction grew out of—or was somehow set into—a foundation stone which rose out of the oceanside edge of the platform itself: a giant irregular vertically soaring column of granite. The Observatory rested atop and around the column a good ten meters off the ground, its bulk cantilevered over the ocean. Its opaque faceted walls reflected sunlight. Some kind of webbed ladder rose from beneath and disappeared into an aperture almost directly below its center. Oo-lol-oo said that was how they would enter. He seemed hesitant and admitted that he had been inside only once. But he was leader of the Myco-folk and it was his duty to introduce the guests.

"On any planet in the Matriarchy, this place would be considered a wonder," Alli-Clark told 'Harles, as they followed Ay'r up the shaky ladder.

Because of the rocklike solidity of the outside of the Observatory, Ay'r had expected to ascend into darkness. Instead, he stepped into a chamber so filled with light of so many differing tints and levels of brightness, coming in at so many different angles and crossing each other in complex and ever-shifting polygons of floating light, that Ay'r was disoriented, dazzled.

When the others had all come up, they stood in a long brightly lit chamber which seemed to run the entire length of the Observatory, divided into two levels: the one upon which they stood a meter below an encircling higher ledge. A series of steps rose to the higher level, along which Ay'r made out what seemed to be a triple series of lines running its full length, as though it were scored or stained by some object.

While he allowed his eyes to adjust to the changing, multicolored light, Ay'r saw large objects built into this lower platform, the functions of which he couldn't make out—they might be closed-up consoles containing almost anything. Slowly, however, he was able to see out through the jeweled walls, and it was now obvious exactly what the Cyber builders had intended: the entire edifice was transparent from within: Ay'r could see details of the rope ladder and the ground below his feet, the sun above his head, the ocean in the distance. It was like being inside an enormous all-seeing eye.

Oo-lol-oo scampered up and approached a dark object at the farthest end. He appeared to be speaking. After a minute, he scurried back and reported, "The Recorder will see you soon. He asks that you become comfortable."

The Mycophage child looked around and finding one of the longer, more rectangular consoles, he tapped its side. In an instant a lid opened up, revealing a long seat. He went about touching more consoles, until another sofa-seat, a low table and even a Cyber-food-and-drink center were opened and ready to be used. Such furnishings could be found in starport lounges all over the galaxy, and so were not entirely unfamiliar to Ay'r and his companions. P'al and Alli-Clark showed the Ib'r family how to use them, and naturally 'Dward was completely fascinated and wanted to know every detail of the mechanisms.

With everyone else involved, Ay'r caught Oo-lol-oo just as he was about to vanish down the ladder and out of the building.

"I'll return with other leaders shortly," the Mycophage said.

"May I get a closer look at the Recorder?" Ay'r asked, unsure whether the Recorder was hume or Cyber, male or female.

"Yes, but don't disturb him."

Ay'r quietly walked to the edge of the lower platform and, making pains to not disturb the Recorder, went up the stairs and along the platform until he was a few meters away.

The Recorder was a hume male, and was half-seated, half-standing in a construction of either flexible matte-colored metal or of some dense multi-ester alloy which had preceded the use of Plastro. It held the Recorder's body in what Ay'r recognized as the standard hume-in-comfort-and-security position long ago found to be best for long-term use. The Recorder's thin torso and legs suggested either that he needed to use the "chair" because of some physical deformity, or that he had used it for so long that his limbs had atrophied. His apparel was a single-piece overall in synthetic cloth of nonreflective dark blue commonly seen in PVNs detailing the lives of humes of the late Metro-Terran Era.

He seemed to be concentrating on a spot outside the Observatory, somewhere over the wide expanse of ocean, and Ay'r noted that his facial features weren't unlike those of most of the Drylanders Ay'r and his companions had encountered: flaxen hair and pale skin which aged and wrinkled easily. His eyes would probably be like theirs—blue or gray—but they were covered by a visor which appeared to arise out of the chair itself and half-encircled the Recorder's head with thick panes of multi-hued lenses tilted at odd angles, similar to the external shape of the

Observatory. Both of his long, thin arms were attached by bracelet-manacles of the same shape and prismatic material to fixed arms of the "chair," with enough give for the fingers to tap freely and rapidly upon what looked to Ay'r like an electronic strip. Attached to the strip on the left was a narrow electronic screen which Ay'r recognized as an old-fashioned "Cybermate."

What was he looking at, Ay'r wondered. He turned from the old male in his oddly constructed chair and looked out the solid sheet of utterly clear wall. Perhaps not utterly clear. Even without the visor, it seemed to highlight and magnify certain aspects of what he was seeing. True, the ocean stretched away in all directions, endless, Ay'r knew, from this point on south and—save for the relatively small bulk of continental Pelagia—east and west and north, too. Yet from here it almost seemed as though the water itself was broken into separate blocks. There! That line surely meant a change of current, or of temperature, or of topography in the land which lay beneath. And over there, the waves seemed to be running so high in one section, with a darker color and high whitecaps. Yet surrounding it on either side, the water was flat and clear, the froth steady and even.

"Identify!" he heard someone say. Ay'r turned to note the Recorder's chair had moved closer to him and changed its position slightly: angled a bit toward Ay'r. The visor was still up, covering the old hume's eyes.

"Ocean," Ay'r said. "Age: uncertain. Size: approximately nine-tenths of the planet surface." He was recalling what he had learned from the prelanding conference with P'al and Alli-Clark. "Salinity: variable, but no more than three percent. Biota: eighty-one percent vegetable, nineteen percent animal. No mollusks or coelenterates. Species severely limited."

He turned away from the Recorder to look outside again, as though to be able to recall more. Now he stared at the old hume and said, "It is unlike any other ocean we've ever seen. As Pelagia itself is unlike any other world."

"Identify," the Recorder said again, then added: "Self."

"Species: hume. Gender: male. Parents: Ferrex Baldwin Sanqq', father. Mother unknown. Name: Ay'r Kerry Sanqq'. Age: in Pelagian years, approximately twenty-four. Avocation: Species Ethnologist." The Recorder had removed the visor and did have pale blue eyes, which were staring at him.

"Is the Consolidation at hand?" the Recorder asked.

"Not yet."

"Then it may never occur. Who are those with you?"

Ay'r identified his companions: first Alli-Clark and P'al, then the Ib'r family.

"You make little distinction between Onworlder and Offworlder," the Recorder commented.

"We are all humes. Two of us are bonded," Ay'r added, and in the silence that followed, he found himself once more wondering if Oudma was already with his child. If so, what did that signify? Could Ay'r possibly leave Oudma here on Pelagia and continue the tradition of the Sanqq'—to abandon their young? No, he would never do that. He would take her with him. But what would life in the Matriarchy, as spouse to a Species Ethnologist, be like to a woman like Oudma who knew so little outside Dryland that he would have to explain everything—not only how things worked, but what they meant, separately and together? That might prove difficult, perhaps impossible, and not entirely for the best. What was Alli-Clark planning for 'Harles Ib'r? If ever a sudden and completely bonded relationship existed, it was theirs. Perhaps Ay'r would speak with Alli-Clark tonight about Oudma, and 'Harles; try to discover her plans. Surely that would given him some hint of what to do himself.

"Will you speak with us?" Ay'r asked the Recorder. "We've come a long distance, on foot and upon the backs of animals. We've seen much of Dryland and have experienced many things. We have been to the high mountain valleys to the East; to the great plain of the New River Valley; we have rested in Bogland and traveled through the Delta and been received by the Ears and Eyes as more than equals at the Great Temple there."

"Gather your companions," the Recorder said, "I will speak with you for precisely"—glancing at his screen—"thirty-two minutes Sol Rad."

"First, tell me, what do you observe here?"

"Everything that passes," the Recorder said.

"And what do you record?"

"Everything that passes."

Ay'r pointed outside to the spot of ocean—now an irregular triangle—which seemed different than the rest. He pointed out the different lines and colors and tides he saw.

"Did you record that?" Ay'r asked.

"You would make a fine Recorder."

"But what does it mean?"

"That isn't for the Recorder to know."

"Does it mean anything?"

"Perhaps. Gather your companions." The Recorder began sliding along the floor in his chair, and Ay'r saw that he had been right before:

the chair did run along a slot on the upper level, although it could turn and swivel in other directions. As the old hume, with Ay'r striding alongside him, approached where the others had made themselves comfortable, Ay'r now noticed at least ten young Mycophages had joined Oo-lol-oo inside the Observatory. They were hunkered down on their lichen-covered knees behind the console seats, looking up anxiously.

"I was expecting visitors," the Recorder said. "Although I couldn't know who would arrive nor where they would come from."

"Why were you expecting visitors?" Alli-Clark asked.

"Because this day is a momentous one. And tonight is even more momentous for Pelagia—it is the Night of the Four Moons," the Recorder said. "As I told your companion, I will speak with you for thirty-two minutes, but then I must return to observation and recording. Be aware that I live in this chair and that you may remain as my guests tonight within the Observatory. But one night only; otherwise you might disturb me."

"What is the Night of the Four Moons, and why is it so momentous?" Ay'r asked what all of the others must have been thinking.

"The Night of the Four Moons comes but once!" the Recorder exclaimed. "And after it has come, nothing is as it was before."

"Explain what you mean," P'al said.

"I mean that all four moons come together in a grand conjunction in the sky above Pelagia. I mean that their light together is so strong it burns through the canopy and the fog and the treetops alike for this one night, so that all below may see them, though few below the canopy will wish to look. Catastrophe is sure to follow their conjunction."

"Has this grand conjunction ever occurred before?" Ay'r asked.

"Never."

"This is the first time in all your recorded history?" P'al asked.

"There have been grand conjunctions before. The last conjunction was of five moons. Not long afterward, one moon was destroyed. That is why the people call the space where that moon was 'Maspiei, the murdered one,' to honor it."

"You mean the asteroid belt between the third and fourth moons?" Alli-Clark asked.

"Do you have records of the conjunction of five moons?" P'al asked.

"Early ones, yes. Barely decipherable," the Recorder said. "Many of the early Cyber-guardians were destroyed in the Great Falling Inward which followed. And in the great fires that followed, and after that in the floods of destruction, which is called the Weeping of Old Dryland in

Sympathy.

"And before the destruction of the fifth moon?" Ay'r probed. "Are there are records of that olden time?"

"No records. Only suppositions. Guesses, made by the Guardians and the first Recorder, which became legends and songs."

"Do they sing of other moons before this conjunction of five moons?"

The old Recorder looked surprised. "You strangers know much. They sing of a sixth moon, yes. Some songs say this moon was the Father of Maspiei, others not. The songs and legends speak of this moon's also partaking in a grand conjunction."

"And of a Great Falling Inward? And of destruction of even-more-ancient lowlands?" Alli-Clark asked.

"Some. But other songs—the true songs, my own Master at Observing and Recording opined—sing of the moon vanishing, running off in company with"—here he paused and motioned to the Mycophages to close off their ears—"of being seduced by the Bright Evil One. Seduced and running off in His company."

"Has this Bright Evil One a name?"

"It is forbidden."

"We strangers may hear the name," P'al assured him.

"But not the others!" the old Recorder insisted, and gestured for Oo-lol-oo and his agemates not to listen. "His name is...Suel! Long-Hair!"

The name uttered, the others might once again listen.

"He destroyed Maspiei, too!" P'al said.

"True. You strangers know much. Maspiei would not be seduced, and so he destroyed him."

"The other moons. What are their names?"

"Capin, first, and largest. White. Pure. He is the Herder. The leader. Then comes Trilufu, the follower, the henchman of Capin, some believe, smaller and darker. Third is Jatoto, the moderator of quarrels. Also small, and spotted and colored like the Swamp Snail. Far distant from all, beyond the place of the murdered one, lies Filoscop the Solitary. Some ancients believed that he is large and strong as Capin, yet he seems smaller because he has taken his distance from the others. Some sing of an argument over leadership with Capin, others that he never left off grieving after the murder of his brother Maspiei, still others that he outwitted the one of which we do not speak."

Ay'r looked at 'Dward and 'Harles and Oudma, who were nodding in agreement. What the Recorder was now saying perfectly matched legends they had learned in childhood.

"But in each case," P'al said, trying to make it clear, "this first moon and Maspiei and possibly even Filoscop and the Bright Evil One of which you speak were involved?"

"So it is recorded."

"Do the ancient texts prophesy which moon will next become victim?"

The old Recorder stared, bug-eyed.

"You said each lunar event follows a grand conjunction. Surely you expect another."

The Myco-folk were muttering.

"It is unlucky to speak it."

"Yet it shall occur," P'al insisted.

"It is evil, and Dryland shall never again be the same," the Recorder spoke bitterly.

"Yet you cannot stop it," P'al argued.

The old Recorder hung his head. "This is my bane, to live in the days of the Conjunction of the Four Moons. Send out all who fear the future," he ordered.

The young Mycophages all remained, Ay'r noticed.

"Another moon shall be destroyed," the Recorder intoned. "Another Great Falling Inward shall occur. Dryland shall once again weep. And once again the lowlands shall be doomed."

Having spoken, the Recorder sighed.

"And it will be the Henchman, this time!" P'al said. "The second moon."

"Yes, It is the Henchman's time," the Recorder admitted. "And afterward Dryland shall vanish beneath the ocean, and the great plains shall be flooded, and the tundras and the ice sheets. The archipelagoes shall sink. The Bogland shall vanish. Nothing of Dryland shall remain but where now mountains rise."

The Myco-folk drew back in horror.

"Can this be true?" 'Harles asked.

"True! All true!" the Recorder insisted.

"When will this happen?" Ay'r asked.

"The date is not known. Perhaps weeks or months or years, Sol Rad. All I know is that the grand conjunction releases the pin of destruction. I cannot say when it will happen."

"But all this explains why you, as Recorder, reside here at the Observatory," Ay'r said. "So when it does occur, the records will not be lost."

"It's unclear whether this Recorder will survive! But I will remain and continue to record no matter what catastrophes occur," the old man said and folded over slowly in exhaustion and grief.

"Perhaps in the old texts recorded, there is knowledge of when it will happen," Alli-Clark said. "When was the last conjunction? That of five moons?"

The Recorder was tapping out his question.

"The last grand conjunction was one thousand, five hundred and seven of Pelagia's years ago."

"And how soon afterward was the disaster?"

"Four hundred days. Less than one Pelagian year."

"And the hypotheses about the previous grand conjunction? The one involving six moons?" Alli-Clark probed. "When was that?"

"The Cyber-guardians supposed that it occurred four thousand and sixteen years before that of the five moons. With no proof, as no hume nor Cyber was present then."

"And if the Recorder and parts of Dryland survive this catastrophe," Alli-Clark went on, "when will the next grand conjunction—that of the three moons—occur?"

"Within a much shorter time. Less than three hundred years."

All of them were silent, and Ay'r noticed that Alli-Clark had taken 'Harles's hand in hers and that none of the humes, Drylander or Mycophage, could look away from the ground beneath them, which now seemed so fleeting and ephemeral.

After a while, Ay'r pulled out the smooth object he had gotten from the Great Temple of the Delta. Explaining quietly how he had obtained it and letting the old hume inspect it, Ay'r asked the Recorder if he knew what it was, and what it was for.

"I've never seen the object before. It wasn't made by the Guardians who built the Observatory. It is of a different material. It comes from somewhere else."

"Could it have been made by the other visitors, Oo-lol-oo told us of?" Ay'r asked. "Those whom the Drylanders call 'The Gods'? Were you Recorder when they arrived? Can you tell us about them?"

"I was not Recorder then, and He who preceded me as Recorder was but an apprentice. Yet their visit was recorded, and so I know of it. They were like yourselves, from somewhere else. Unlike you, their coloring was dark—dark skin, dark hair. The Guardians had long expected their coming, and had warned even the earliest Recorders that their coming would presage the Consolidation. Yet when these visitors arrived, it was not because of the Consolidation. Instead, they said they were seeking a place to live and work, free of contact with the Dryland peoples. They said they meant no harm to any of the folk and promised they would not interfere."

"But they did interfere!" Alli-Clark said. "Culturally!"

"And now they've begun to kidnap Dryland's youth." Ay'r added. "'Harles's son was only one of the many they took. No one knows why."

"Then they are forsworn," the Recorder said.

"Do the records give their names? Or where they came from?" Ay'r thought he might discover if his father was among them.

"Only one name was ever recorded: Lars'son, Creed. This Lars'son is recorded as having spoken of a place, Sobieski Delta Nine. But I don't know where it is."

P'al explained, "It's a moon circling the ninth planet of a Class G star in Sector Twelve of the Central Sagittarius Arm."

"I know nothing of this," the Recorder admitted.

"Where on Pelagia did the visitors end up?" Alli-Clark got right to the point.

"It is recorded that they were sent to the Far Eastern Archipelago. Near the sunken city of Dy'r. They're still there. At least, that's the direction they come from and return to whenever I see their bubbles flying over the ocean. Your time is up," the Recorder said and spun the chair around and began moving away from them.

"That's where we must go," Ay'r said for all of them.

Later on, as they rested, Ay'r and P'al and Alli-Clark spoke together, away from the Drylanders, attempting to put together what the Recorder had said with what they had learned from the Fast when they entered Pelagia's system weeks ago.

"The mechanism of water increase is clear," P'al said.

"Is it? Because of a few myths?" Ay'r asked.

"Those myths explain actual physical occurrences over the centuries since this world was seeded with humes. We had already heard enough about these moons in the ordinary speech of the Drylanders to suspect their importance. The fact that no one actually laid eyes on them meant they must be crucial. But the Recorder provided as detailed a scenario as we could have asked for. This Suel must be one of the large icesteroids we noted in the Heavy Hydrogen Ring surrounding this system. Or one icesteroid pulled from it."

"Bright and long-haired. Yes, certainly," Ay'r agreed. "Cometlike—that's how it would look.

P'al remarked, "The grand conjunctions of the moons must set up a traumatic gravitational imbalance, tugging large icesteroids loose from the Ring."

"Could it have something to do with temperature?" Ay'r asked. "If all the moons are lined up in front of Pelagia, which is in front of its sun, wouldn't that provide an almost-laserlike focus at a certain point somewhere on the Ring."

"It could, but it would take both that and gravitational pull to do it."

"How did you guess it would be the second moon this time?" Alli asked.

"No guess. The first conjunction of six moons was followed by a icesteroid which either smashed the farthest moon or came between it and the fifth moon, Filoscop. Remember what the Recorder said. 'He has taken his distance.' In other words, moved. Possibly both moons were disturbed from their natural orbit; the sixth so badly it was spun into a wide, erratic elliptical orbit."

"Or so far that it fell into the sun."

"In any case, the imbalance would raise the tides on Pelagia."

"But that's only a temporary effect," she protested.

"Not so. Any inward-moving heavy hydrogen would be heated by the sun. Its melted ice would fall as drenching rainfall upon the first large warm gravitational object it encountered: Pelagia itself."

P'al went on, "The next conjunction, of five moons, because it occurred in a more concentrated area of orbits, would have pried loose a larger chunk of ice and pulled it deeper into the orbital area. Thus the 'murder' of the fourth moon. Tonight's conjunction of four moons will pry loose another icesteroid and this time it will be even larger and will be drawn even closer to the planet. Note that the periods between grand conjunctions shorten as the factor of their conjunction is shortened. The first was approximately four thousand years ago, the second fifteen hundred years ago. The next will be three hundred years in the future."

"Yet the combined gravitational pull of the moons is decreased each time one is destroyed!" Alli-Clark protested. "Why isn't it that the icesteroids pried loose and drawn in are smaller."

"You forget that Pelagia is the main gravitational object in their system. With each moon gone, not only does Pelagia receive more water and thus more mass, but the lunar system is rebalanced closer to the planet itself, to reflect its increased mass relative to the satellites remaining."

"So following the conjunction to come in three hundred years, we can probably posit that the icesteroids drawn will be even larger or more in number, and they will no doubt enter orbit between the innermost moon and the planet."

"Capin will be knocked out of orbit."

"And the conjunction of the two remaining moons will be about ninety years after that. The ice more numerous. They should fall directly onto Pelagia."

"After that, ice falling onto the planet should become regular. The planet will grow with water, increasing in mass, pulling the other moons ever closer, drawing even more ice, until all the moons are destroyed, all the ice drawn in—a constant bombardment—which won't end until the entire ice-ring is gone."

"It will become a gigantic fountain," Alli-Clark mused.

"Until the heavy-hydrogen outer ring is completely used up."

"Which will take scores of centuries. Meanwhile, there will be water for billions. For trillions!"

"And the end of this hume culture," Ay'r reminded them. "The most rapid seedling culture ever developed. A unique ecologically modified hume culture."

"It will mean the end of all the land," P'al added. "Save for a few mountaintops, it will become a water world."

"Dryland's end." Ay'r intoned the dark words.

"Perhaps," she agreed. "But not of all the people on this world. A completely maritime culture might be devised for the survivors."

"It hasn't happened so far. How would it happen in so short a time?"

"One may already be in place," P'al declared. "The 'Gods.' Why are they stealing children? Perhaps they know what's about to happen. Perhaps they're saving them."

"The jury is still out on these so-called 'Gods,'" Ay'r said. "Let's rest. I don't want to miss this conjunction."

"I wouldn't miss seeing the moons tonight for anything!" Alli-Clark said and lest she sound too girlish, added quickly, "Think of the experience for 'Harles!"

"Think of the experience for all of us," Ay'r said.

Ay'r hadn't been aware that he had dozed off. Only now, as he awakened with a start did he realize it. The others were spread out on the comfortable sofa-seats: Oudma, Alli-Clark, 'Harles. Like him, they must have fallen into the temptation of such luxury, following days of hard sleeping places, to nap after the dinner given in their honor at the underground lodgings of the Mycophages. 'Dward, of course, had wanted to remain a bit longer with Oo-lol-oo to try the drugged mushroom which would allow him to communicate fully with the Myco-folk. He was probably still there, fatigued from the experience, asleep.

At night the Observatory was as transparent as during the day: dim yet not black. And now Ay'r saw why. One moon was almost directly overhead, small, gleaming white. That would be the distant Filoscop, which they had seen rising earlier, at the time of their arrival. Not far from it, was another satellite, larger, darker. Could that be Jatoto? No, the Recorder had told them Jatoto was spotted; it must be Trilifu, known as the Henchman. Yes, because there was the spotted moon, it's darker features—craters most likely—displayed clearly. All three moons occupied only ten degrees of the heavens, and they all appeared to lie upon the same ecliptic. Yet, to Ay'r, their placement made it seem unlikely that they could form the true conjunction, the four-part eclipse the Recorder had declared would occur tonight. Perhaps there was some distortion in Pelagia's atmosphere which explained why it all seemed so improbable. P'al would know the reason.

P'al! Not here!

Ay'r got up quietly and moved away from the others, to not awaken them. The Recorder was visible at the far end of the Observatory—a silhouette against the night—tipped back in his chair to look up at the moons. P'al wasn't anywhere here.

The Recorder must have heard Ay'r's footsteps. He re-positioned his chair and gestured.

Almost in a whisper, he said, "Your friend left an hour ago, Sol Rad."

"Did you see where he went?" Ay'r asked.

The Recorder spun his chair and pointed almost due west. "If any of the Myco-folk saw him, none remarked on it," the Recorder offered. "I found him after a search. Do you want to see?"

Ay'r knew that P'al must be at his T-pod again. But just to make certain, he watched as the Recorder unsnapped the oddly shaped prismatic visor, lifted it off the chair, and showed Ay'r how to place it over his own head.

It seemed oddly lightweight for such thick-looking glass or plastic. Ay'r followed the Recorder's directions. The visor sat lightly on the very tips of his ears. He had to close his eyes. When he opened them, he saw that the bright glare was strongly reflected light on phosphorescence: foam on the waves out in the ocean, magnified so greatly that he could see the shapes of the tiny algae which illuminated the foam.

He told the Recorder what he was seeing.

"Your eyes are far stronger than mine. I'll adjust it down a bit. Now turn left slightly—more there. Now what do you see?"

Exactly what Ay'r had thought to see: P'al inside the webbing of the T-pod, as though asleep, his fingers working the wrist control.

He told the Recorder what he was seeing and added, "I wish I knew what he was reporting."

"I believe those signals can be intercepted," the Recorder said.

"Without his knowledge?"

"For days now, this Cyber has been afflicted with signal-noise. I've spent much time blocking it out. Surely I ought to be able to make it audible."

"Try at 45,000 megahertz," Ay'r suggested.

Instantly he heard the familiar voice of the Fast's mind speaking, saying, "...will be attempted; but without exact information as to the precise nature and timing of the mechanism involved, naturally, no results can be guaranteed."

And P'al answering back, "Given all that's been outlined to you, can't you make a probability chart and extrapolate from that?"

"The curve is too wide. Too many inexplicable factors," the Fast's mind replied.

"Work on it!" P'al ordered curtly. "This information is vital for the mission. Convey all this new data to your base. I'll check back."

He ended the conversation.

Ay'r watched him detach his wrist from the T-pod's connection to the Fast, exit, close the T-pod, and watch as it ascended out over the cliff where it had alighted and toward the ocean, obviously up to the Fast. P'al was already loping back along the ridge which enclosed the promontory, headed back to the Observatory—hoping, no doubt, that his absence hadn't been noticed.

It was time P'al became aware that his absence *had* been noted.

Ay'r returned the visor to the Recorder and climbed the webwork ladder down to the outside. He wanted to confront P'al away from the Observatory, where the others couldn't hear.

Despite the triply bright moonlight upon the landscape, P'al was only a few meters away when he saw Ay'r.

"What's your hurry?"

Before P'al could respond, Ay'r said, "Please don't demean both of us by telling me you were out for a moonlight stroll."

"The fourth moon has risen." P'al turned and pointed in the direction he'd come from. Ay'r now saw Capin, the innermost moon, gibbous and blue-white, rising over the ocean.

"You've been in contact with the Fast's mind ever since we landed,"

Ay'r said. "You report in every night. Don't deny it. I saw you do it while we were in Bogland."

P'al remained silent.

"Once," Ay'r went on, "I asked you what your mission was. Who you were working for. At that time, you put me off. No more."

"There is much to this mission you may not understand," P'al said.

"Alli-Clark told me a great deal," Ay'r countered. "About the Cyber-rebellion. The microvirus. The search for a cure. The reason for our presence here—which has nothing to do with water."

P'al was silent.

"I know why we're searching for my father. I also know that Alli-Clark suspects you and your motives. She doesn't believe we're all working toward the same end."

"The same end, definitely," P'al said.

"But not for the same side," Ay'r made the distinction.

"How can there be sides when all hume-ity is at stake?"

Ay'r refused to deal with that nonsense. "Answer me straight out, P'al. Are you working for the Cyber-rebellion?"

"Why would I?"

"Why? Or how?" Ay'r asked. "The why is irrelevant. The how is clear: you join our mission to find a cure for the microvirus; then you make sure it is never delivered."

"There *is* no cure," P'al said. "In all likelihood, a simple serum exists which the Cyber rebels possess. I suspect it merely keeps the virus from being activated in the first place. But with an infinitely mutating virus, there is no cure, can be no cure."

"Is it your mission to find the serum and destroy it?"

"No. If the serum is found, it will be accidental," P'al said.

"You seem very certain of that," Ay'r remarked.

"Given the flatness of the probability curve in this situation, it's the only way a serum can be found."

"Then what are we doing here?"

"We're looking for an alternative reproduction method. After all, that was what your father and his colleagues were working on. That was why he was discredited and forced to flee."

"An alternative?" Ay'r asked. "How?"

"Let me ask *you* a question, Ser Kerry. You told me that back in Bogland, you witnessed an abduction by the Gods. You said they injected something into all of the youths but one. That one was deemed almost right for their purposes and was taken away"

"So."

"Have you wondered what was injected into those youths?"

Ay'r had wondered and watched 'Dward for any outward signs of its effect; he hadn't been able to discover a connection.

"No signs at all?" P'al probed. "'Dward is in *no* way different than he was before the injection?"

"If so, I don't know how."

"Haven't you've noticed how he looks at you?" P'al said. "How he can't take his eyes off you?"

Ay'r had noticed. "He's thrilled by the adventure. He told me—"

"And what of his sister? 'Dward and she almost never speak these days. And when they do, he criticizes her, snaps at her."

"Are you telling me that 'Dward and those other youths were injected with a love potion?" Ay'r scoffed. "Or with an aphrodisiac?"

"Do you recall Varko, the youth abducted under your paralyzed gaze, Ser Kerry," P'al asked. "The one deemed 'ready' for abduction."

Ay'r remembered Varko, and said so.

"I spoke to his family at great length about Varko after he was taken," P'al said. "They all said that Varko had become much changed in the past months and especially in the weeks before he was taken. Before, Varko had been a slender lad, quick moving, quick thinking, given to mischief and pranks, a leader among his set, and very flirtatious with females. But lately Varko had slowed down considerably. His weight hadn't changed, yet the distribution of his weight had altered markedly, according to his father, who had watched the youth dressing and bathing. In the last weeks before he was kidnapped, Varko had become softer. His previously loose clothing had become skintight on his legs and arms, and he had gone from being agile and athletic to sensual, voluptuous. As I was leaving, Varko's father had whispered to me of his recent difficulty in keeping his hands off Varko; his difficulty keeping himself from sexual thoughts about his son—who, in turn, seemed to encourage them. You already know from the Ib'rs that same-sex is frowned upon on Pelagia. So this was quite disturbing to Varko's father. As was the fact that the youth had lost all interest in females and kept close to only two male friends."

As Ay'r listened, he remembered more: Varko flirting with 'Dward, how almost femininely pretty he had seemed to Ay'r, and what the others on the peat wagon had said about him, laughing, half-embarrassed, half-accepting their old friend, yet unsure what to make of him. As though they, too, were sharing Varko's new feelings, yet...

"I spoke to the fathers of other sons kidnapped in the Bogland," P'al went on. "They all reported the same circumstances: their sons changing physically and emotionally—flirting with them, daring them, sometimes cajoling and even forcing them to touch their bodies, causing fights among older men...no longer active and rowdy, but as though...as though, one father said to me, his son had become a daughter."

"Are you suggesting that the injections are female hormones?"

"More than hormones. A complex DNA-constructed neural-hormonal mixture. Recall that in Bogland all the male youth was thicker bodied and sturdier than their mountain valley brothers. All of us noted it. Next, think about their enclosed and limited range, compared to Monosilla youth. And how easy it would be if someone like the so-called Gods were experimenting on them. It would be much easier to locate them again within the confines of the bowl. Then consider the benefits of that method, Ser Kerry, as opposed to kidnapping the boys and having them around for months before they're ready."

"Your points are well taken, But ready? Ready for what?"

"I'm not sure."

"You do have an idea, don't you," Ay'r asked. "With all the females in Dryland, why make the males more feminine? Is there some Relfian principle at work here? Precisely what aspect of mammalian reproduction was my father working on when he disappeared?"

"I don't know, but whatever it was Wicca Eighth thought it sufficiently dangerous when the idea was still theoretical that she had your father discredited from the Mammalian Institute on Arcturus and hounded out of all Matriarchal scientific establishments. Let me remind you: that occurred long before any experiments were known to have taken place."

"But if that's so, then why would She send us to find him now?" Ay'r asked.

"That's a question you will have to ask Mer Alli-Clark. I have no idea what the nature of her mission is. Perhaps it's merely to discover if your father followed through on Relfi's theories. Perhaps, if he has been successful, her mission is to destroy him and his work once and for all."

"And not use it to save the species?" Ay'r asked and stopped. "Why am I arguing with you? Either you know as little as I do, or you've extrapolated something so radical from a few suggestive data that you don't want to tell me. Possibly because I'd find it incredible. And furthermore, you still haven't answered my original question. Do you work for the Cyber-rebels?"

"Unequivocally no!"

"For the Matriarchy?"

"Although that is what the Matriarchy has always thought, again, no."

Who else was there? The Oppos, Alli-Clark had suspected. Meaning Hesperia and the Orion Spur Federation which together had checked the Matriarchy for centuries, keeping it from going too far, becoming too extreme. But of course that could simply be official Matriarchal paranoia.

"You're a high M.C. official, aren't you?" Ay'r tried. "Yet you admit you don't work for the Matriarchy."

"I have and I still might have, had I ever known the true purpose of this mission," P'al said without emotion.

"How did you get onto the mission in the first place?"

"On the basis of my loyalty and experience and problem-solving skills. And on the precise basis that I never know the mission's true purpose."

"But…whom *do* you serve?" Ay'r asked.

"Since the moment we met," P'al said with the tiniest of bows, "I serve you, Ser Kerry. And shall serve you until you tell me not to."

"Me? Of all the humes in the galaxy, why me?"

"Because, like the Monosilla truth-sayer, I believe you to be the most important hume born in three thousand millennia."

"That's no answer!" Ay'r protested.

"It's the only one I have. The others are awake. I hear them calling." P'al said and left Ay'r standing there as he loped toward the web ladder.

Oudma had gone down the ladder, and was waving. Now she shouted, "Ay'r! The Recorder said the time is approaching. Would you find my brother and bring him back? Gratitude!" She blew him a kiss and ascended into the Observatory before P'al.

"The most important hume born in three thousand millennia, and I'm sent on an errand to find a sleeping boy!" Ay'r sneered, then laughed at the absurdity of it all.

"Let's not go inside yet!" 'Dward said, once they had emerged from the Mycophages' underground shelter.

"I thought you didn't want to miss the conjunction!" Ay'r argued.

"We can see it from out here." 'Dward insisted.

"Are you sure that Myco-drug has completely worn off?" Ay'r' asked.

"Yes. Follow me!"

He stopped midway between the Observatory and the caves, close to the edge of the promontory.

'Dward exulted, "Look what a beautiful spot this is!"

Ay'r had to admit it was. Three moons, quite close together now and already near zenith, lighted the centermost part of the sky above as brightly as Pelagia's sun, casting illumination over the ocean, and behind over the three peaks and all the landscape between. In this eerie white brightness, the Observatory gleamed like a milky opal. Alas, the ground at their feet also glittered with dew—or more likely, with sea spray.

Ay'r pointed out that they could only see the conjunction by looking almost straight up, and that the ground was wet.

"The Recorder told me of these." 'Dward waved Ay'r back a step, then reached down, searching for something in the ground. He cleared loose earth and weeds off what appeared to be a hand-sized ring and pulled it up. Something flat rose slowly out of the ground, a platform made of the same webbing as the ladder into the Observatory, though wider and more tightly knitted. "When he was still an apprentice, the Recorder told me that he could observe only from here. It angles up, and in many directions," 'Dward insisted, clearing its surface, "but we'll leave it like this."

They lay down next to each other on the surprisingly dry, comfortably webbed platform. From this position, they not only could look directly up, but were also shielded from the light, constant ocean breeze from the cliff edge.

"Look!" Ay'r pointed out how Filoscop, the most distant of the four moons, was already beginning to slide behind Jatoto. "It should fit directly behind, so it will no longer be visible."

"You know, Ay'r," 'Dward said, taking one of his hands in his own, "if you hadn't come here, I would still be in Monosilla Valley. And I would not being seeing this wonder which happens only once. But instead, probably hiding indoors with my head covered over, like the Mycophages."

"I'm not so certain. You've always been curious," Ay'r said.

"Curious, yes, but not...well, not as bold as I've become."

"'Bold feats'!" Ay'r repeated what the Monosilla truth-sayer had predicted for 'Dward.

"And bolder ones to come, I promise you. You know, Ay'r," 'Dward went on, "if we hadn't visited the truth-sayer, or if he hadn't told us Ib'rs to join our fates to yours, even if my father and Oudma hadn't come with you, I still would have."

"Oh? How?"

"You still would have needed a colley. And someone to rein it."

"We could have managed."

"Even the great drop of the falls?" 'Dward asked.

"No, you're right. You would have come along," Ay'r admitted.

"So, from the moment you arrived, we have been fated. Fated friends!" 'Dward said with certainty. "We'll always be friends, won't we, Ay'r?"

Ay'r was about to say that even in his own short life, always was a long time, but he was interrupted by 'Dward. "I'm coming with you, Ay'r, wherever you're going to from Dryland."

"Truly?"

"We can't stay here. You heard what will happen. You must take us, now." And while Ay'r was admitting the truth of this, 'Dward went on, "You know, Ay'r, I should be terribly sad about what will happen to Dryland, but I'm not. I think that's because I know wherever I go with you, I will be safe, and happy: with my fated friend."

Ay'r looked away, up at the meridian. "Here comes Capin approaching the other three moons. It's much bigger, but also much closer to Dryland. That's why it looks bigger."

"P'al explained it all to me," 'Dward said indifferently. "It was an easy concept to grasp. I had known that Dryland was a sphere, like the spores off the fungi trees. Ay'r," he began in a different tone, "since we are fated friends, why is it that you're so reluctant to show me your love?"

"I am?"

"P'al told me that where you come from, males show their affection openly. And while it is not done openly on Dryland, it is still done, in private."

"Now Filoscop is almost completely behind Jatoto," Ay'r said. "Look how it leaves an aura around itself, so that even though it's hidden, it's still visible."

"We're alone now, Ay'r. No need to fear for my reputation."

"See, 'Dward, how spotted Trilufu is moving in front of Jatoto. Soon it will cover its face."

"Now would be the time for you to show your affection, Ay'r...if you have any."

"Of course I do, 'Dward."

"I wondered. I know you spend much time with Oudma, and she is my sister and beautiful. Still, as a youth, I'm beautiful, too. I know that because in Bogland they told me so."

Ay'r turned to face him. 'Dward was perfectly illumined in the combined light of the four moons, his features straight and manly, his pale eyes dark against the new effulgence of his lunar-lit skin. Yet he was as inviting as any female or pampered gyno Ay'r had ever seen.

"How am I to show equal affection to both you and your sister?"

"You and I are together. Show it to me now."

"'Dward, I'm not sure you understand all our ways. Or all the complications possible."

"P'al told me males mate with both genders and have amours with both. Even at the same time."

"Yes, but..." 'Dward was a manly youth, Ay'r thought, straight-featured with the proper hardness and softness upon his face and chest and arms. Not a half-female, as P'al said he might be. What harm could there be? Ay'r thought how delicious it would be with 'Dward, already half-knowing this face and body, his way of thinking and reacting, from experiences with Oudma, and yet how surprising would be the differences!

"I promised your sister I wouldn't," Ay'r said lamely. "And 'Harles! What will he think of us who have come to him as guests?"

"That's not a real reason. He accepted your interest in Oudma."

"Yes, but only under certain circumstances," Ay'r hedged. "You noticed she didn't announce our bonding at the Great Temple."

"Because she is unsure of you," 'Dward argued. "Of your affection, of your commitment, of whether you'll remain here. These are all important matters to a young woman. None of this is a concern with me."

"But it might become," Ay'r said. "This is all new to you, 'Dward."

"That's why I don't understand why you won't..." 'Dward's frustration was obvious in his voice.

'Dward had pulled down his tunic, and Ay'r thought how it would be kissing his babyskin throat and moonbright shoulders and chest down to his navel, feeling the youth's arms surrounding him, feeling him straining beneath his short trousers, the strength in his thighs and the roundness of his buttocks. It had been a long time since Ay'r had bedded a youth, but he was here on a mission for the Matriarch, and as a Species Ethnologist the rules for his behavior were clear: Ay'r might form a temporary affectional bond with a Pelagian, but only within the social mores of Drylander society. He was already having a difficult time with the "acceptable" relationship with Oudma. If it weren't for her own intelligence and sensitivity, her intuition into his restraints with her—if not their precise cause—Ay'r might have been trapped by her into an official bonding. The others were no help. Alli-Clark must know about Ay'r and Oudma, but so far she had kept quiet about it, perhaps too distracted by all she had experienced and seen since awakened from the Arach's induced trance. Perhaps even a bit more distracted by 'Harles's courting. For all Ay'r knew, Alli-Clark also knew the rules under which

Ay'r might form a relationship, and was waiting, watching for him to step over the bounds. As for P'al, he certainly knew; and although he was his usual indifferent self about it all, Ay'r sensed how useful that was for hiding a possibly mocking amusement at the fix Ay'r had gotten himself into. No, it was an impossible situation already, barely manageable. Giving in to 'Dward's drive to experience everything would only complicate it beyond control.

"Just think, Ay'r. You would be my first lover."

"Gratitude for that honor." Ay'r hoped words would convey what actions couldn't. Sensing 'Dward's disappointment, he lay back and looked up.

An amazing sight greeted him.

"Look, 'Dward! Look up!"

Directly above them, bright white, gibbous Capin was just now gliding into place in front of the other three moons. For an instant, the night was slightly dimmer as the disc of Trilufu and the corona of the two moons behind were eclipsed momentarily. Then Capin fitted into place perfectly, and a new corona burst out, seemingly behind it and in front of it and all around its disc—an effect of reflection from the heavy hydrogen ice ring all around Pelagia and its sun and moons, Ay'r supposed. The four conjoined moons cast a new light, brighter than that of Pelagia's single sun at noontime, so that everything around them, ocean and sand, hill and rock, and every millimeter of 'Dward's face when Ay'r glanced at it, glowed with a precise and elaborate intensity as though illumined from within. 'Dward's eyes glittered with the fires within the depths of a blue star.

And now the specialness of the night, the light, their position upon the webbed platform at the edge of the promontory: all of it seemed so singular, so utterly unrepeatable that Ay'r turned and kissed 'Dward's cheek, surprising the youth.

"Let that bond our friendship," Ay'r said. "Don't look so sad!"

"I was thinking, for the first time in my life, I wish I were a female like Oudma. If I were a female, then proof of your affection might already exist within me."

His words chilled Ay'r, suggesting how determined 'Dward seemed, and how disappointed he was.

After a few minutes, he suggested they return indoors.

Inside the Observatory, the others sat around the chair of the Recorder. All were silent.

Oudma immediately made a space for Ay'r near herself and took his hand in her own. She looked over at 'Dward, then closely at Ay'r.

"We were watching it from the cliff edge," Ay'r explained quietly. "It's a magnificent sight."

"A terrible beauty is born," P'al quoted an old Metro-Terran poet.

Oudma accepted Ay'r's word, and held onto him lightly the rest of that night.

"We're going with you," 'Harles Ib'r said.

"I'm not sure that's either possible or advisable," Alli-Clark said quietly.

"You heard what the truth-sayer told us. We *must* go with you," 'Harles repeated.

"That all might have been so, when we were down in Dryland. Now we're leaving the places you're familiar with. Going to...well, we don't know exactly where we're going."

"The truth-sayer said we must travel with Ay'r to the end, wherever that takes us. He made no distinctions between places."

"The truth-sayer couldn't possibly have known how our situation would develop," Alli-Clark argued.

'Harles Ib'r held his ground: "The truth-sayer knows all!"

"Many of the truth-sayer's prediction have already come to pass," 'Dward joined in. "Our finding of you sleeping. My bold feat."

"None of it that extraordinary," Alli-Clark scoffed.

Ay'r spoke up. "They're right, though. They've come this far. They might as well join us to the end."

P'al now joined in on Alli-Clark's side. "It might be very dangerous, especially for them."

"We fear no dangers," 'Dward said stoutly.

"And," Ay'r decided to add his half-credit to the argument, "the truth-sayer did make one prediction I find to be quite extraordinary."

"Oh? Which one?" P'al asked.

"May I remind you that he emphasized that I should remember him when all was wet? He was predicting the catastrophe to come, which we didn't even know about at the time."

"Infants are always wet," P'al said, but his witticism not only fell flat, it also wasn't enough to convince the others. "Besides, I'm not certain that your judgment, Ay'r, is completely without bias. Due to your companionship, you would naturally wish—"

"—To protect Oudma and 'Dward," Ay'r interrupted. "Which is hardly what I'm doing if they come along."

"But it's not their concern!" P'al tried one last maneuver.

'Harles was astonished. "My son 'Nton isn't my concern?"

"They're coming with us," Alli-Clark suddenly said in that Matriarchal tone of command Ay'r had grown familiar with, but which he hadn't heard in its pure form from her since they had left the Fast.

P'al turned to Alli-Clark. "What about transport? We can't afford to spend weeks on colleys' backs."

She admitted that he was right. "We'll take T-pods."

"Six of them? Three piloted by... Well?" P'al turned to Oudma. "Do you even understand what T-pods are?"

"Of course. Ay'r told me. They fly above the land. Above the canopy. We ride inside them."

"It's how the 'Gods' come and go so rapidly," 'Dward added.

"And, Oudma, aren't you even a little afraid to be flying up there?" P'al asked. "With no colley, with no solid ground beneath you?"

She reached for her father's arm, but contradicted her frightened reaction by stating boldly, "I will go wherever you go."

"Remember we are Ib'r," 'Dward said. "Ib'r are pioneers. We lead the folk. Ib'r have always led."

"Anyway, the Fast must have larger pods than singles on board," Alli-Clark said, being practical.

"How do you plan to call the Fast?" P'al asked.

"The same way you do each night," she replied. "Go on. Call it!"

P'al remained unfazed. "Recall, Mer Clark, that the Fast is authorized only to send down one single pod for each of us three. And only at night."

"How do you call it?" 'Dward asked, ever-curious.

Ay'r lifted his arm and pulled back the tiny disc of skin on his wrist.

"What is it?" 'Dward peered at the alloy.

"A wrist-connection," Ay'r said. "In youth, all our people have them embedded."

"They're for interaction with mechanisms," Alli-Clark explained.

"They're a combination of Plastro-circuits with a minuscule isotope of Beryllium to power it," Ay'r explained further. "Very simple. And useful."

"Except," P'al reminded them, "that we preprogrammed the Fast only to respond to our call for a T-pod at nightfall."

"We're *not* traveling at night," Alli-Clark insisted. "It will be difficult enough finding what we're looking for by daylight."

"I have an idea how to call the Fast," Ay'r said. "The Cyber on the

Recorder's chair intercepts radio signal noise. He complained about it. It shouldn't be too difficult to utilize the parts of his receiver as a transmitter and contact the Fast that way."

"Go," Alli commanded P'al. "Do it!"

Given the natural "crystal" of the Observatory itself, transmission and amplification proved to be as simple as Ay'r thought they would. Within minutes, the Fast's mind was speaking to them.

"Who is that?" Oudma asked.

"A companion on their airship," 'Dward explained smugly, pointing up.

"Not quite," Ay'r said. "It's the ship itself. Like the Eyes and Ears, it's an intelligent mechanism."

Alli-Clark had taken over the communication from P'al and now she was arguing, "Well, if that's *really* all you have, then send us the small shuttle and a double pod."

"Why two?" P'al asked. "The shuttle seats six."

"Should we have another encounter with those trigger-happy 'Gods,' I'd like us to be separate so we can act as backup for each other."

"Good thinking," Ay'r said. "I'll pilot the smaller pod."

"And Fast," she went on, "we believe we're looking for a settlement of some sort. It ought to be far advanced for this world. Look for signs of radiation leakage or even a shield. Far east of continental Pelagia. Perhaps somewhere in that large swampy area. Or in those chains of islands we saw before. Report anything at all unusual you come across. Send optical-scouts if you need to."

'Harles was staring at Alli. Suddenly she caught his glance. "I'm going to be in charge of this little expedition. If you object, you can remain here."

"It's all right with me," 'Harles replied confidently. "But remember, she who chooses to lead also chooses to take responsibility for those she leads."

That seemed to stop her for a second. "I've taken such responsibility before. Or aren't you used to strong women here on Dryland?"

"All Ib'r women are strong," 'Harles commented enigmatically. That seemed to satisfy Alli-Clark.

Not long afterward, the Fast reported that it possessed three possible locations to be visited: one in the swampland, two in the archipelago. All three would be previsited by optical-scouts, and all reports would be updated to the shuttle and pod, which ought to be alighting near them at that moment.

"I see them!" Oudma cried, her sharp eyesight picking them out among the high grass on a far cliff.

The six travelers said farewell to the Recorder and to the Mycophages. Oo-lol-oo and his friends promised to feed and care for the three colleys until the Ib'rs returned.

Ay'r was sure that despite its transparency, the shuttle, with its six seats and size, would calm Oudma's fear about flying. But when 'Dward asked, "May I go with you?" pointing to the smaller T-pod, to all of their surprise, Oudma also asked to join them.

For a moment, Ay'r wondered why. Had Oudma found out from 'Dward what had almost happened the night before? Was that why she didn't want the two of them alone together?

Equally surprising, Alli-Clark approved. "C'mon! Get in," Ay'r said, secretly pleased that the two Drylanders would be where Ay'r could see their reactions to this new and doubtless exciting experience.

He checked to make sure that they were belted tightly into the webwork, closed the pod, and waited for the shuttle to lift off the ground.

Ay'r explained, "We go straight up, like a spore leaving the fungal tree. Then we find our bearing and move any way we want. I'll be using my wrist connector." He showed them how it matched an alloy disc on the inner wall of the T-pod. "But there's manual control, too. See this lever?" He lifted the lightweight rod from the floor. "Move it forward and back slightly for those directions. Left and right slightly for those directions. But for going up and down, you push it forward more and back more. You ought to know how to use it, just in case something happens to me while we're flying."

"May I?" 'Dward reached eagerly for the lever to try it, just as Ay'r thought he would.

"Wait until we're up."

"They're ascending!" 'Dward watched the shuttle lift until it was above them, 'Harles leaning across to speak to P'al, Alli piloting. It hung above the spot for a second, then darted over the land and out of sight.

"Now us," Ay'r said.

As in all new things, 'Dward liked the sensation. Once they were above the ground, he seemed only slightly excited by it all, saying, "I've had dreams just like this."

I'll wager you have, Ay'r thought, remembering his own flying dreams of adolescence. But he wondered. Since the seeded humes on Pelagia were all derived from a society which had used T-pods for centuries and had flown since middle Metro-Terran times, perhaps flying was part of their racial memory, which only needed prompting. If so, then many things 'Dward and Oudma would experience once they were off Pelagia in more developed areas of the galaxy should also exist in their racial memory, merely needing prompting. Which, if true, suggested they would fit in better than anyone thought. Perhaps that racial memory was the Aldebaran Five's trump card in their plan for the eventual Consolidation of all seeded species.

Indeed, 'Dward handled the manual lever quite well after only a short practice. Ay'r "introduced" 'Dward and Oudma to the Fast's mind, and soon 'Dward was talking to P'al—pod to shuttle—easily accepting the fact of long-distance communication, even though the shuttle was nowhere in sight.

Below them, the range of high, rugged mountains surrounding Pelagia's southern promontory flattened into more rounded hills. The canopy of cloud which covered most of the continent began to reassert itself.

"Look down there!" 'Dward said. "Those gulches are wider and flatter. Soon we will be flying over Monosilla Valley!"

"If we can still see below," Ay'r cautioned.

"Sometimes the canopy is thinner over Monosilla," Oudma said.

Not this day. Within seconds, all below them was clouds, from the northern glaciers distantly glinting in sunlight to the southern mountains which rose at the ocean's edge.

"No matter," 'Dward said. "*I* know I'm up here."

The canopy began to thin out after they turned northward, where another rugged range of mountains poked through the cloud cover.

"The Northern Mountains!" 'Harles could be heard through the communication. "I visited their foothills when I was 'Dward's age. Soon we will come to the pass through which the Boglanders trekked. It leads to the Great Cold Swamp."

The range seemed unbroken below, until Alli signaled that she was turning east. Only when Ay'r followed her lead did he notice a slightly wider cleft in the cordillera, and through it a spit of land descending rapidly and widening as though one or more mountains had been shattered and fell into the surrounding ocean.

Ay'r remembered the Boglanders' legends of how difficult that trek from a sunken land had been, and how steep the climb. Many hadn't made it, had died there. As the T-pod turned, he said, "Now all you know is behind you."

'Dward faced him but didn't look back. "Good!" he said quietly, with determination. Oudma remained silent.

What 'Harles called the Great Cold Swamp became visible as they continued duc east: its vast extent and strange mixture of land and water resembled an ecru lace shawl dropped carelessly upon the ocean, converting its expanse of cobalt blue into hundreds of smaller lakes, ponds, and lochs, each a different tint of white, gray, aqua or deep green, silver-blue, or yellow-gold.

"The first stop is near the northwestern edge," the Fast's mind said.

Although they had seen this continent before from the Fast's holos, Ay'r and Oudma (and probably 'Dward, too, though he didn't say anything) were amazed by its eerie beauty, by the ever-changing patterns of water and land beneath them, by how the dominant water was forced into bizarre shapes by the much sparser surrounding land, and tinted by as yet unknown factors in the soil or biota. At times it looked like sophisticated, richly designed hydrofarm terracing—similar, Alli-Clark comm.ed, to those she had studied on New Venice and Procyon XI. Now she bemoaned the fact that it probably wouldn't survive the results of the past night's lunar conjunction to ever be used for nurturing populations. At other times, the land was so wildly and grotesquely chaotic that it could only have resulted from nature—or from natural calamity. 'Dward followed one long thread of enclosed water from their first, southwestern, entry over the continent nearly to its northwestern exit some time later, and he swore that several other equally arabesque canals existed of the same length.

The Fast reported that it had lost one optical-scout within the swamp and speculated that large, voracious fish lived in some larger pools, since its last view from the scout had apparently been a quickly dimming interior like that of a gullet. Before that unfortunate event, however, the scout had reported, and the other scout was now corroborating, a similarity of land and waterscape which suggested that solid land—when available— would be no more than a few score meters in size and even then of dubious solidity. The Fast had sent the second scout toward the largest section of such land, from which a faint radiation seemed to be emanating.

"What do you think?" Ay'r communicated to the shuttle. "Should we go down to it?"

Alli hesitated. Then the Fast interrupted.

"The radiation I'm receiving appears to be ancient deuterium, with a rather long half-life. It might very well be of natural origin."

"Any signs of habitation?"

"None. Wait! The scout is picking up ruins. I'm making it stop and do a rapid thermoluminescence dating. The ruins seem to be either old or eroded."

"What's the area look like?"

"Very overgrown. Some sort of mangrovelike tree without any branches or leaves. It appears to be all root, rising about four meters high."

"Is that all the vegetation down there?"

"It's the predominant life-form of the swamp. Wait, a minute, I'm getting thermoluminescence dating now. It's not that old. Maybe three thousand to thirty-five hundred Pelagian years."

"The original Boglanders!" Ay'r and Oudma exclaimed.

"I see no reason to stop here," Alli-Clark comm.ed.

"Not even for archaeological reasons?" Ay'r asked.

"Archaeology is well and fine. But we're looking for a far more recent settlement," she insisted. "Fast, what are the coordinates of the next spot?"

"Exactly fifty degrees East longitude, exactly fifty degrees North latitude," the Fast reported.

"Now, that sounds more like it! I like to visit places that announce themselves by their position. Ay'r, if you want to look at that Boglander ruin, you've got a half-an-hour, Sol Rad. Catch up with us at Fifty-Fifty."

"Oudma?" Ay'r asked, already knowing that 'Dward's answer would be yes.

She, too, agreed. They remained in radio contact with the shuttle and Fast as Ay'r turned northward and began to descend. Soon the pod was skimming over sheets of mist, like yellow tatters thrown over the lacework of land and water. The water was assuming a more stable shade of pale green below, and darker green where it was shadowed by mist. As the pod continued to slide downward, 'Dward spotted the larger area—almost an island. Ay'r saw the land itself become two-toned: a lighter hue of brown at the water's edge, darker brown within. In the center of the large area they were aiming for, the lighter color predominated.

He pointed out his findings to both 'Dward and the Fast.

"I think the darker brown is the root-tree," 'Dward offered and the Fast corroborated.

"Has your scout found any metal in those ruins?" Ay'r asked the Fast.

"I've sent it ahead to Fifty-Fifty to guide the shuttle. Do you want me to release another?"

"Don't bother. We'll be landing in a minute."

"I'll find a spot clear of those root-trees," the Fast assured him, "yet not exactly in the middle. I'm not certain humes ought to be so close to that deuterium."

"Have you speculated what it could be?" Ay'r said. "That kind of oxy-stripped hydrogen molecule is associated with starbirth. Have you correlated it to any possible supernovas in this sector from around that time'?"

"That was exactly my fear, Ser Sanqq'. I see you haven't forgotten your Basic Fusion Astro-Chemistry from Ed. & Dev."

"We're ready to land."

The pod dropped through the sheets of yellow mist and hovered. The scene below was admittedly bleak with the greenish water out of sight. The dun-colored hummocky surface lay ahead, and surrounding it, the ubiquitous root-trees grew in grotesque shapes. Dozens of tall, woody-looking roots rose from the damp earth to support each knobby, misshapen trunk which, instead of rising upward and sprouting branches and foliage, turned in on itself and snaked along before dropping another dozen younger, sickly whiter-looking roots; each root-tree intertwining the other, twisting around and sharing roots, becoming a deformed and stunted thicket.

The scene was even more discomfiting once the pod alit gingerly upon one of the mossy-looking hummocks which dotted the open area; the root-trees here were taller, some clumps rising four times a hume's height. Closeup, they looked more impenetrable and far uglier, with their heavily gnarled bark and diseased-looking roots.

"The ruins are some twenty meters due north, in the direction the pod is facing," the Fast said.

"Do you want to stay here?" Ay'r asked his passengers.

'Dward didn't dignify the question with an answer. Oudma also unbelted. It almost seemed as though they were in silent competition with each other.

The pod's front half opened, and the heavy, fetid air filled Ay'r nose and throat, making him cough.

Oudma said jauntily, "No worse than the colley's manure field at Monosilla."

When they were out, the pod shut itself. "I can see the ruins from here!" 'Dward exclaimed.

"Stay near me," Ay'r said. "Just to be on the safe side, I'm putting on a shield."

They strode over hummocky stuff that seemed to be a lichen colony, much tougher and springier than in Dryland. It might even be part seaweed.

"Look! There!" 'Dward pointed to something tiny and skittering; and when Ay'r didn't see it, 'Dward ran ahead and actually caught it and brought it back to him in his hands. "Some sort of creature with six legs. Yet not an insect!"

Not a mammal either, nor a lizard. More like a fish with that gaping piscine mouth. Its legs were more like flippers, or cartilage-thickened fins. It was panting through its gills.

"What could it be?" Oudma asked.

"A fish of some sort. A land-walking fish," Ay'r said as the creature suddenly jumped out of 'Dward's palms and skittered away.

'Dward ran after it, but it was already deep within the roots of a root-tree when Ay'r and Oudma caught up. "Stay by me, or we're returning to the pod!" Ay'r warned in a parental voice he regretted immediately.

"It's harmless," 'Dward replied in an expected aggrieved voice.

"We scared it," Oudma said.

They bent down to get a closer look as the fishlike creature began to preen its gills with one flipper and sniff at the root stems where they disappeared into the damp ground.

"It sure is ugly!" 'Dward laughed.

As they were watching, one sickly white root dangling above suddenly shot down at a terrific speed and wrapped itself around the creature, lifting it off the ground and rotating the creature's body to better entwine itself. Before they could do more than make sounds of amazement at the speed, the root's growing point shoved itself into the creature's mouth and down its gullet. They looked on in horror as the creature began to convulse, until its skin was broken through from within at a hundred points simultaneously along its body by fresh pointed shoots. The shoots grew out rapidly into an interlacing ball. Soon they formed a new single-pointed growing shoot, which turned downward and drove suddenly into the damp ground, diving deeply and so quickly that in seconds the fishlike creature was completely buried in damp silt.

They fell back, making sure they were nowhere near any of the roots. 'Dward's face wore an expression of shock and disgust. Oudma had blanched. It was the first time Ay'r had seen 'Dward so frightened or Oudma so vulnerable, and he felt compassion for them both: compassion and a strong desire to protect them.

"Come!" He reached for 'Dward, who jumped at the light electromagnetic shield's touch.

"Something terrible must have happened here a long time ago," Oudma said quietly.

Hoping to counteract their fright, Ay'r said, "A piece of an exploding sun may have fallen here more-or-less intact. And it devastated much. But worse than that, through its poisonous radiation, it seems to have transformed anything which was still alive into what we just saw."

"Will all Dryland be like this in the future?" Oudma asked soberly.

"Possibly. If there's any land left to it."

Both remained silent. Ay'r knew he'd not succeeded in calming them.

"Perhaps you had better return to the pod," Ay'r suggested, and this time Oudma agreed readily. Ay'r waited until she was belted in, then turned to 'Dward, who said with grim determination, "I'll go with you."

When they arrived at the ruins the Fast had guided them to, at least they had the benefit of its novelty to distract them from dark thoughts.

The ruins were a jumble of fallen and partly revealed stone ledges mostly hidden by the hummocky lichen colonies, yet they seemed far too large—at their exposed corners and broken edges—too enormous, really, for mere Boglanders to have constructed. From where had they quarried the stone? Nowhere within 1,000 kilometers, surely, unless quarries and mountains lay beneath this great swamp. Cold swamp, Ay'r reminded himself as he turned up the shield to block out the sudden chill he was beginning to feel. He gently cautioned 'Dward not to touch anything, but to look for any signs of carving on the ruined stones. This time 'Dward did not argue or defend himself, but did as he was told.

Ay'r was looking at one great chunk, trying to make out whether the pattern he saw was natural or caused by an intelligent hand when he thought he saw a sudden motion in his peripheral vision. He looked up. He was facing the way they had come. There was the T-pod, still closed upon its hummock. The root-trees were ominous behind. Nothing else. He went back to inspecting the stone.

A few minutes later, he again thought something moved, and again he looked up.

"What is it, Ay'r?"

"Nothing. Perhaps an illusion. Gases rising from the ground or—"

He saw it again and quite clearly now: the T-pod moved. Turned a bit and moved. How? Then he saw what he thought must be white roots sidling along the hummock. And Oudma was inside!

"Stay here, 'Dward! And don't come unless I call you! Understand?"

'Dward looked frightened and perplexed, but he remained.

It was a five-minute walk Sol Rad. back to the T-pod and from halfway there, Ay'r saw the roots: two of them. One had begun to encircle the hummock upon which the pod sat, which was causing it to turn. The roots would never penetrate it, but they could certainly encircle it. He would have to get inside and fly it directly to the ruins. Or make it hover. Maybe they ought to just get out of here. Alli was right—again!—Eve take her!

He was only a half dozen meters from the T-pod. A third root approached his legs tentatively and, more out of disgust than fear, Ay'r stomped it into the ground. It dove in and didn't come back out. The larger root had spun the pod around nearly 90 degrees and begun to pull it off the hummock, doubtless toward the root-trees which were already sending out snakes of fresh white roots to entangle it. Oudma must be very frightened now. He waved to her to remain where she was, hoping she wouldn't panic. This would have to be close: he didn't want any roots getting inside the pod.

As he calculated exactly how much time it would take, more roots suddenly appeared along the ground, sidling toward him, but cautiously, as though they knew what he had done to one. Could that be true? Were they all part of an intelligent living creature? Or at least a creature capable of learning from experience? What if all of this surrounding grotesque vegetation was one entity—single-brained, like an insect colony?

Suddenly Ay'r speculations were shattered by a hint of an odor: something sweet and very different, as though out of all this miasmic life a fresh orchid had bloomed suddenly. A second later, Ay'r remembered when he had last smelled that odor—in Bogland, just before the "Gods'" T-pods had appeared.

He turned toward 'Dward, standing there among the ruins, unaware of anything. He had to warn 'Dward!

Ay'r had begun to shout 'Dward's name when he heard the muffled-yet-unmistakable buzzing of the "Gods'" T-pods. He pointed up and shouted, until 'Dward seemed to realize what was happening and began running toward Ay'r.

In that second, Ay'r heard the distinct sounds of thumping from within the T-pod. Oudma was banging on the inside wall to get his attention. He turned to see the pod beginning to tip over. The bottom root had lifted it completely off the hummock, and several others shot out toward it, trying to gain a hold.

He had one second to choose between 'Dward running—the "Gods'" vehicle now visible and louder than ever—and Oudma inside the pod, now screaming Ay'r's name as the T-pod tipped over even farther. He froze, unable to decide. He loved both of them, had to save both of them—but couldn't.

Pain made the decision for him. A root sliding along the ground had come close enough to him that it suddenly made a feint at his leg. Protected by the larval cloth leggings, Ay'r still felt the stab. He pulled back, stomped the root into the ground, turned, tapped the pod open, and backed off.

Oudma was trying to get out. Ay'r shouted for her to stay in.

Before any of the other roots could react, he dove into the pod and shouted for it to close. It did so and Ay'r saw a single probing white root-end aiming toward his face. It was a few inches inside when the pod dome sealed itself and, in doing so, snapped off the root point.

To his surprise, outside, the broken white root rose up and began to sway back and forth rapidly against the outside of the pod like the wounded limb of an animal. As it did, it ejected a thick milky fluid. Like everything else about the root-trees, the sticky spray was viscous, disgusting.

"Where's 'Dward?" Oudma cried.

"We're ascending. Now!" Ay'r ignored her, shouting into the T-pod's voice-activated mechanism.

"My brother!" She grabbed him from behind. "Where is he?"

The pod ascended directly into a hundred snaking white tuber roots quickly encircling it and bringing its rise to a jarring stop.

Oudma fell back in her netting, and he was released from her grasp.

"Power!" Ay'r shouted. "I'm being held here."

"It's using all of its power!" the Fast reported.

"What's happening, Ay'r!" Oudma called out.

"Ser Kerry!" P'al was in communication. "What's wrong?"

Ay'r outlined what was happening as calmly as he could as root after sickly white root shot out to enmesh the T-pod. He began to feel the rotation begin. Alli turned back the shuttle immediately to come to his aid. Ay'r tried telling both P'al and Fast what he had seen the roots do with the fishlike creature, how strong they were, how desperate the situation was—but all he could come out with to explain his problem was "It's going to plant me!"

"Have you considered rotating?" the Fast asked.

"It's rotating me enough, gratitude!"

Suddenly Alli-Clark was on: "Ay'r! Use your lasers to cut through."

"It was because it thought it was being attacked that I'm in this spot to begin with," he explained.

"Too late to be sensitive!" she instructed.

She was right. "Where are the lasers?" he asked.

"Two forward, one aft," the Fast replied, its calmness irritating now.

"Is there any way for a strong pointed root to get inside the pod?"

"A root? Ser Sanqq'?"

"Oh, never mind. Hit the lasers. Front first."

The lasers were thin and broke a dozen roots, splashing white stuff all over the front of pod.

"Now I can't see anything!" he shouted.

"Should I keep the lasers going?"

"Yes! All of them! Front and back."

As it broke more roots, the milky fluid completely covered the front and back of the pod and streaked the top, sides, and bottom of the pod badly. Even so, the pod stopped rotating and began to inch up. It seemed to take forever to move upward as fresh shoot after fresh shoot emerged to be cut down and splash its liquid against the pod until finally—with a sudden lurch—the pod was free.

"Ascend!" Ay'r shouted. Once he felt the ascent, he ordered cleaners to come on. But the aero cleaners could do little more than smear the already drying terribly sticky substance. "I'm going to have to fly blind. Place me near those ruins," he ordered the Fast.

"There's another pod there. I suggest that you hold back until I can find out what it is."

"How are you seeing that?"

"I'm not," the Fast responded. "I picked up its sound through the surface sensors on your pod."

"It's those damned 'Gods'! They must have seen 'Dward! Hurry!"

"We're on our way back," P'al reported. "Our shuttle is still over the Eastern Archipelago."

"It seems to be an older model," the Fast reported. "It makes a lot of noise. I suggest backing off and hovering out of sight until they—"

"Is it still there?" And when the Fast didn't respond, Ay'r shouted to P'al and Alli, "It's the 'Gods'! They've got 'Dward! I'm going to try to stop them!"

He ordered the Fast, "Put me down right on top of the other pod, if you can!"

"I don't advise—"

"Override your advice," Ay'r said the harsh words by which even the most-intelligent Cybers shut up and did what they were told.

"Ay'r, don't do anything foolish!" Alli-Clark said. "We'll be there in ten minutes, Sol Rad."

"I'm landing!"

"Remember, they have weapons!" she comm.ed. "And you're flying blind!"

The pod bumped to the ground and seemed to settle between hummocks.

"If you've put me anywhere else than exactly where I said..." Ay'r threatened.

"You needn't get testy," the Fast retorted.

"Now open it!" Ay'r tensed, not knowing what to expect: more of the treacherous pointed white shoots, or the "Gods," or what.

What he saw was nothing. Or rather the ruins. And nothing else.

He leaped out of the pod.

A faint sickly-sweet odor still hung in the air. But there was no pod but his own. No "Gods." And, worst of all, no 'Dward.

Ay'r began calling his name, hoping the youth had hidden during the pod's exertions. He continued around the ruins shouting out "'Dward!" until he stopped and heard the faint buzzing sound and looked up and saw streaks in the sky. Not yellow and tattered mist, but blue-white, with parallel contrails. He knew with a terrible finality that they had abducted 'Dward.

"Fast, follow the direction of that T-pod!"

"Unable to follow without visuals," the Fast reported.

"P'al! Can you try to cut it off?" But Ay'r got no answer.

When the shuttle landed ten frantic minutes later, Ay'r rushed up to it and almost pushed P'al back inside, trying to see if they had gotten 'Dward.

They hadn't.

"We've got to find 'Dward immediately," Ay'r insisted. "Get back in, I'll pilot. The Fast will tell you their direction. What are you waiting for? Hurry! He's been injected. And it's already working on him, just as you thought it might, P'al. I know. Last night he... What are you waiting for? Eve damn you! We've got to go!"

P'al took Ay'r by the shoulder, put a hand up to his neck as though to comfort him—and pinched him quickly and hard.

Ay'r wanted to ask why he had done that, but he felt his body slumping under him. And then his mind went blank.

Chapter Eight

Several minutes after coming out of what seemed to be the fourth Fast Jump in a very short time, Rinne heard noise outside the chamber walls.

She looked up from where she lay, strapped to a jump lounge. The inner walls of the chamber were rimed with bluish crystalline condensation. Only a few inches away from her, North-Taylor Diad was still slumbering, his face rimed with the same bluish crystalline condensation. As was her own face, Rinne assumed, looking at her hands, which were, and unbuckling herself to sit up. Across the bare, curved-wall chamber, only Ewa, among the others, was coming to.

Ckw'esso had warned them about the condensation occurring: its was a result of some slight-but-innocuous chemical reaction of the Fast Jump upon the billions of liters of liquid hydrogen which surrounded them. The chamber they lay in was hidden within one of six enormous tanks of hydrogen, deep in the bowels of a Deneban commercial freighter operated by the Third Nest's Bella=Arths. The chamber had been built for Bella=Arth stowaways who wanted to either leave or return to Deneb XII without M.C. authorities' knowledge. A day, Sol Rad. after the attack of Admiral Thol upon the open side of the Nest, the elders of the Bella=Arth community had agreed to allow the survivors to use it for safe passage.

There was the noise again.

"Do you hear it?" Rinne asked Ewa, who was now sitting up and, like Rinne, wiping her skin and clothing of the condensation.

Ewa looked toward the source of the sound, then asked, "What does it mean?"

It could only mean that they had been discovered, long shot as that seemed to be. For an answer, Rinne shook Diad awake, wiping his face and hands, and pleased by his smile of recognition, his simple greeting of "Gemma!"

"We're hearing noise," Rinne said. "Listen!"

Diad unstrapped himself, sat up, and listened.

"What Sidereal Time do you have?" He checked his belt device.

Rinne checked her wrist connection. "It's earlier than expected for arrival."

"But it does sound like Ckw'esso is emptying this tank of hydrogen," he said.

"Why would she do that earlier than expected? Unless...someone demanded it."

"Stay calm." Diad held her closely. "After all, Gemma, this *is* a freighter. Maybe they've sold all the other hydrogen."

She felt better being held by him, but no less alarmed. "What did Ckw'esso say to you about how this would work?"

"You were there," he reminded her. "You heard, too. She agreed to get us as close to Hesperia as possible. Or, failing that, to a Tourist World under Hesperian influence."

"Yes, I know. I meant what did she say about how we would get out of the chamber?"

"We can't get out until it's emptied of liquid hydrogen. That was one of the risks we accepted." he smiled, held her closely. "Along with being blown to bits if the tank exploded."

"I'm less worried about being blown to bits than falling into the clutches of Wicca Eighth!"

"Yesterday you were calling for her resignation. You feeling a bit more cowardly today, Sol Rad.?" he teased.

"That was before the Fast imploded," she said. "Should we awaken the others?"

Diad was listening carefully to the noises. "I'm sure that's what it is—they're emptying the tank." He shrugged. "I don't know about the pregnant women, but I think maybe we ought to awaken Lill, the Hesperian Fast crew, and possibly the skimmer pilots, although if Ckw'esso has M.C. company out there, we're sitting ducks, asleep or awake."

"We've got a dozen stunners among us," Rinne said.

Diad chuckled. "You really are turning into a revolutionary, aren't you?"

"Don't think I won't use one to defend us," she said stoutly.

"So will I!" Ewa said.

"Fine!" Diad agreed. "Let's get ready for a shoot-out."

By the time they had managed to awaken Lill—who grumbled and then, hearing the situation, became instantly alert and showed Rinne and Ewa how to use the guns—and the Fast crew and pilots, the other women were also coming out of Fast Jump, although they were groggy. They were left where they were, and Ewa, Rinne, Diad, Lill, and the males stood flat against the walls on either side of the only door into the chamber, stun guns loaded, cocked and ready, as the noises changed tone and rhythm. Clearly someone was walking around out there.

Rinne tried to recall what the chamber had looked like when she'd first seen it. A compressor: it had been disguised as compression machinery! The door was half-hidden behind crossbars and a huge pressure lock. Would M.C. Security Guards fall for the disguise? She looked at Diad, next to her. He didn't seem nervous at all.

"I think you're actually enjoying this!" She whispered an accusation.

"In a way, I am. I'm certainly enjoying seeing you so excited," he added, his tongue running over his black mustache.

"Males!" Lill commented.

A second later, the noises were right at the chamber door. Rinne watched Diad tense, as all of them did, except perhaps the women still on their Fast-lounges. The outer door slid open with much grating. Diad and Lill opened the inner door, then stood back. When they had entered the chamber earlier, the space between the two doors had been covered with a seal of liquid Plastro, to ensure air tightness within and no possible contact with the liquid hydrogen without. Rinne now heard the seal being slit open, saw an antenna slide in through the rip, and feel around a bit. Diad was closest to the door. He grabbed the antenna and began to palpate softly it between his fingers. Suddenly he released it.

"It's Ckw'esso," Diad said, clearly relieved. "Her antenna displayed no tension. We're safe!"

The Plastro seal was ripped open completely, and Ckw'esso came inside.

"Apologies!" she said. "We've been forced to make an unexpected stop."

Before Rinne or Diad could ask why, the Bella=Arth added, "Business! But also business that concerns yourselves and the future pupae."

"You haven't been stopped?" Rinne asked.

"Not at all. But there's been much news on the Inter Gal. Networks and it would be best if all your people—including soldiers and future queens—gathered now."

After all the women had been awakened, they once more had the opportunity to be amazed by the smallness of the chamber they had hidden in compared to the vast—and now-empty—liquid-hydrogen tank within which it was embedded, and then by the size of the tank section of the freighter itself, a lengthy conveyance ride until they had arrived at the much-smaller living quarters. Ckw'esso had set aside one area for the humes to gather. Drinks and snacks had been set out, and all of the stowaways realized they were hungry.

They were joined by another Bella=Arth, introduced as Mcr'ass't, who was the freighter's equivalent of captain and who laid out the situation, with

Ckw'esso translating.

"The most recent Inter Gal. Comm.s have reported the conclusion of a four-party Realignment Statute for Deneb XII. The parties involved were the Matriarchy, and Deneb XII's hume rebels who have taken the name 'Immediate Response,' along with voting observers from Hesperia's Inner Quinx and the Orion Spur Federation. Under the terms of the Realignment Statute, all matters and relationships on Deneb XII are returned to as they were the hour, Sidereal Time, before the opening of the Alpheron Spa."

"Sounds like a Bella=Arth solution!" Diad said.

Rinne knew he meant that the Bella=Arths would emerge from this crisis unscathed.

"Indeed it does!" Ckw'esso admitted. "However no Bella=Arth was present. Perhaps the Two Species are learning Nest-Ways?"

"Perhaps," Diad laughed.

"What does the Realignment Statute mean in terms of us and these women?" Rinne asked.

"In terms of yourselves, Ambassador Taylor, Councilor Rinne, Commander Lill, the Hesperian Fast crew and the six skimmer pilots, it means that nothing has happened, and you may return to your previous positions."

"Don't be so naïve!" Lill spoke up for them.

"We are only presenting the terms of the statute, which provides full amnesty for all participants in the crisis."

Excluding renegade Councilors, Rinne thought. The last place she could go was back to Melisande. She knew it; they all knew it.

"No one knew you were even there!" she said to Lill. "You could claim you were taken hostage by our group."

"Gemma's right!" Diad assured the M.C. Commander. "I'll back you up."

"What about the women we rescued from the Spa?" Rinne now asked Ckw'esso and his captain.

"No provisions were made for them," Ckw'esso said and turned her head away, a sign of shame.

"None at all?"

"The Matriarchy refused to negotiate any Realignment which admitted their existence. Therefore, no mention of them occurs anywhere in the Statute."

Lill said, "That means they can go home!"

"The Statute does not say they cannot. Nor," Ckw'esso added, "that they ever left their homeworlds."

Rinne was beginning to understand. Wicca Eighth had pulled a fast one.

Evidently, Ewa also understood. "We can't go home!"

"Why not?" Ckw'esso asked, over the murmur of the other pregnant women.

"Because in several weeks or months we're going to give birth to Equo-homs. That's why. If we return to our homeworlds, we'll face mandatory abortions—or worse!"

"Ewa's right," another young woman spoke up. She identified herself as Janitra and went on to try to explain to the other Spa refugees exactly what the recent past should have shown them: they were not welcome anywhere in the Matriarchy.

"What does the Health Councilor say?" another woman asked.

"I'm afraid they're right," Rinne had to agree. "And despite the so-called M.C. amnesty, I'm afraid I share your position. Let's face reality: we're personae non grata now."

Diad said he thought that Hesperia would be glad to take the women and their offspring. He'd comm. to make certain, but he thought—

"That won't do," Ewa interrupted him. "If my baby is going to grow up with four legs, he'll need plenty of space to run. He can't stay in anything like a city until he grows up."

Rinne was pleased by Ewa's newfound maturity. She listened while Ewa and Janitra persuaded the two refugees still holding out that they could neither return to their homeworld nor go to Hesperia. The pregnant women were brutally honest, realistic, and candid. When they were finished, the holdouts tearfully agreed.

"Then we'll arrange for the Quinx to find an appropriate world," Diad said.

"In actuality, such a solution may be at hand," Ckw'esso said. "That is another reason why I awakened you. True, we did not have to empty that particular tank to pump liquid hydrogen down to the planet below. We did so because we reached the same conclusions you have reached independently regarding the queens-to-be among yourselves, and to give you the opportunity to discuss the situation among yourselves and to look over the planet below."

"Which planet? Where are we?"

"Sector Thirty-Nine of the Near-Scutum Arm. A small binary solar system known as Aquila Epsilon. It possesses one small habitable planet which we discovered is part of the Hesperian Tourist World group, although so distant from commonly used liner paths for so long as to have gone virtually unnoticed."

A viewport in one side of the chamber was slid open for them to look at the planet. Rinne's first glimpse was of a brown and mottled world, bathed in the light of a double sun. The stars were a good-sized red giant and a larger, and far younger, blue giant, whose gases were being drawn off toward its elder companion like a long, twisting amethyst scarf.

"It's called Usk," Ckw'esso said, as the women stood up and moved closer to the viewport for a look. "I've located an old holo-brochure in our files for you to view. You will discover that its most salient features are a large long-dried-up salt-ocean and several extensive mountain ranges. The planet has a starport and a not-too-distant Resort, which appears to have been little used in the past few centuries."

It took a few minutes for Ckw'esso to outline the not-very-delightful aspects of Usk. Meanwhile the planet below turned enough on its axis in relationship to the Deneban freighter for a sudden glittering halo to appear, bathed in double-colored light. All of the humes cried, "Ahh!" And no wonder, for as they watched, even from so high up, the planet's enormous triple-ring system began to flaunt itself in all its majestic glory.

"Yes," Ckw'esso said. "The Rings of Usk!"

"They're magnificent!" Rinne said.

"And," Diad added, "Doubtless the reason why Usk was made a member of the Hesperian Tourist World group."

"Indeed!" the Bella=Arth admitted. "From most anywhere on the planet, they are even more magnificent. They appear to rise and set, they seem to separate and come together, and they cast spectacular shadows! If this system were closer to Hesperia or to the Center Worlds, Usk would be considered one of the attractions of the galaxy."

Ewa half-turned from her place among the other refugees at the viewport. "I didn't know a solid planet could have rings."

"They're rare," Ckw'esso admitted. "Only several hundred have been found."

"I've seen several," Diad said. "But not Usk. In fact, I don't remember ever noticing Usk on any lading schedule for Plastro or Beryllium."

"It's unlikely you would. The planet is not even regularly scheduled for liquid hydrogen. The starport manager places an order irregularly and often asks us to pick up other necessary materials—including small quantities of Plastro and Beryllium."

No one could pull away from the viewport and the sight of those rings. Finally Ewa did and addressed Ckw'esso.

"May we view one of the brochures you mentioned?"

"Certainly. May I make a recommendation?"

"Of course. You've been wonderfully helpful so far."

"Although the Resort is fairly empty and although the starport contains many unutilized facilities, both are quite small and not well populated."

"Lacking in privacy, you mean?"

"Exactly. And thus not suggested for your group. However through the brochure you might be able to locate some facility upon the world, away from these two areas—"

"*I* know of exactly the facility," Rinne said. It had passed over the screen of Jenn-Four's memory only a few days ago, Sol Rad. "There's an abandoned Mammalogical Institute research station on Usk. It's located far from both the starport and the Resort, in a chain of north-south mountains. Yet it's close to several market villages and has its own water supply. Most importantly, for your offspring, the research station is located among a series of pastures and fields."

"Who lives in the villages?" Ewa asked.

"A people called Pamps. An acronym for their genetic makeup. They were developed by the researchers at the Mammalogical Center from a primate species on another world which, I believe, was undergoing some perilous natural phenomenon. I'm not sure why the station was closed. I believe it had something to do with the Pamps being left to evolve further on their own. They appear to be small, gentle folk, given to crafts and light farming. They've been taught the rudiments of Universo Lexico."

The freighter's gravitational spin in orbit was taking it out of the view of Usk. Ckw'esso took advantage of that fact to offer the holo brochure.

While the women gathered to watch the holo, the freighter's captain, was called out of the room. She returned just as the women were once more arguing the pros and cons of Usk as a place of settlement.

"Developments have occurred as a result of the Deneb affair which may be of use to you in your discussion," Ckw'esso translated what Mcr'ass't was saying. "In addition to anti-Centaur riots on various planets within the Matriarchy itself, a fleet of Hesperian Fasts arrived late last night at the Near-Norma Arm 14 Sector and declared a blockade of the Centaur homeworlds. The only ships allowed in were those carrying Centaurs returning home. Early this morning, a dozen M.C. Fasts commanded by the Cult of the Flowers attacked the Hesperian blockade. As a result, two Cult Fasts had to be abandoned, and one Hesperian ship. A Hesperian captain lost his life in the action. The Inter Gal. News Comms. are available for viewing but are somewhat graphic. As a result, the Centaur homeworlds have resigned from the Matriarchy, closed their system to all outsiders, and called on the Orion Spur Federation to aid them in keeping the Near-Norma Arm Sector 14 protected."

There was silence among the humes. Then Ewa spoke up. "Do you see now why we can't go home?" Since no one answered her, she went on, "I think a few of us ought to go take a look at this research station on Usk."

Ewa, Janitra, one other pregnant woman with Ed & Dev in health and medicine, Rinne, Diad, and Lill, and the Hesperian Fast's Environmental Engineer were assigned to land a small shuttle.

The freighter had moved to a point where Usk's rings were almost directly beneath—now little more than a line across the whitish salt-ocean of the planet—when the shuttle dropped out of the ship's pod-belly.

Once it had stabilized, the shuttle began to glide sideways across the planet's atmosphere. It soon passed the rings which Rinne now saw hovered directly behind like a series of gigantic curtains.

The landscape they were approaching was an enormous, much-scarred and obviously geologically ancient series of mountains ranges which appeared to gird the planet from north to south poles. It was so huge and so varied that as the shuttle angled down sharply, it was difficult for Rinne to pick out any single detail.

When she mentioned this to the others, the normally silent—and lately even sullen—Lill said, "Good! That will make it more difficult for anyone to find them accidentally."

Finally the shuttle pilot settled upon a single line of longitude, a rough, long cordillera between which thin, bleak valleys lay. The landscape was so bleak and single-hued that the pale green which they began to see came as relief. They came down in the midst of a small vale hemmed in on either side by the continuous range. Those who had lived in the research station seemed to have worked toward making the area more pleasant: several small groves of trees which Rinne recognized from Melisande's extensive parklands had been planted around the few low-to-the-ground structures which formed the buildings of the station.

They landed in a nearby meadow. The air was thin but fresh, and rich with difficult-to-determine yet definitely floral-like aromas. Janitra spotted one possible source of the fragrance: tiny long-stemmed wildflowers dotted the meadow of tall grass. The six humes strolled comfortably toward the research station, feeling the silence and peace around them.

"The holo-brochure said that Thwwings were once bred somewhere in these mountains," Ewa said.

"It's really quite lovely," Janitra commented.

The station had been designed to be completely solar-energic: with one entire side buried in the foothills of one range, and enormous Plastro windows several stories high, opening onto the steepest part of the vale, a narrow deep ravine through which a tiny colorless stream of water bubbled. On closer inspection, Rinne noticed that the windows were two-toned, and possibly even of differing thicknesses.

"Because of the two suns!" Lill pointed up, where the binary blue and red stars shone as white and pale orange in Usk's atmosphere. "Very clever!"

"We'd have to clear the foliage from the windows," Ewa was saying.

The structures were easily entered, and revealed inside as large, clean, and well kept. There were a score of suites on the bottom floor, each large enough for several women. The main gathering rooms, offices, supply areas, and other rooms without furnishings were on the second floor. The topmost floor, with its three completely windowed towers, contained what had been laboratories. Rinne and the Env. Engineer looked these over in some detail and decided that enough basic supplies as well as equipment remained for all and any medical problems—not merely childbirth—to be taken care of.

While they were going through the supplies, a small, squat Cyber appeared in the doorway.

"Where did that come from?" Rinne asked.

"Mer Ewa found me," the Cyber replied, "She sent me here. I'm a model Intern #455, and fully equipped for all medical services."

"Are there any more of you?" Janitra asked.

"I'm the only intern model on the premises. Two other general labor models remain. They possess various skills and may be used for all heavy work."

The women were pleased. "We're happy to make your acquaintance."

"It's a pleasure to be operating again."

"Can you check all of these supplies and let us know what is missing which would be needed for six months of female and infant hume medical care?"

"Naturally," the little Cyber answered and headed for the pharmacy.

"And when you're done," the Env. Engineer said, "we'll need one lab only to be cleaned spotlessly and ready for all and any medical care."

"That shouldn't be difficult."

When Rinne joined the others downstairs, she saw through the windows that Diad was outside, sitting on a slab of rock. After encouraging the women and assigning cleanup tasks to the two other Cybers, she joined him.

Diad put an arm around her shoulder and drew her to him immediately.

"What do you think?" he asked.

"I think that Ckw'esso is as clever as she is good. And that this will make a wonderful home for the women and their children."

He smiled.

"That's what you were asking, wasn't it?" Rinne asked.

"Not really." He laughed. "I was thinking, wouldn't this be a good place for us to retire to?"

"Why not?" she answered.

When he didn't answer, but instead looked down, Rinne turned his face toward herself.

"Well, we could, couldn't we?"

"You mean just leave it all?"

"Not for good. But why not?" Then she answered herself. "You've got to return to the City, don't you?"

"We both have to. I've got to arrange Lill's return to the Matriarchy. I owe her that for helping you on Deneb."

"Yes, we both owe her that. But we don't have to stay in Hesperia, do we?"

"Until this crisis is over, we don't have the right to our own lives," he said somberly.

"Isn't it over?" Rinne knew he was speaking the truth, but she hated hearing it anyway.

"No. Not yet. Not until the Three Species can reproduce again. Not until the Cyber-rebellion is crushed. Not until the Matriarchy is—"

"You expect the two of us to do all that?" Rinne asked.

Diad laughed. "Maybe not all of it. But yes, those are the problems we've got to help solve. Myself—and you, Gemma."

"Why us?" She felt tears rise to her eyes.

He looked at her, feeling the same thing.

"I don't know why, Gemma. We were chosen or...I just know that our work isn't done yet."

"Even though your prediction of twilight over the galaxy is coming true?"

"Another day will rise over the galaxy, Gemma. Our task is to help it come."

As though in illustration, beyond the mountain range, the rings of Usk were beginning to be visible: silver at their edges, like a borealis solidifying as they watched.

They remained sitting there until Ewa came out and said, "We've even found food supplies. They must have left in a hurry. One Cyber said..." As she continued speaking, her face was bright with the future.

"You'll come and visit us sometime, won't you?" she asked finally.

"Why are we cruising so slowly?" Commander Lill asked, trying not to betray the irritation she was feeling. They had come out of Fast Jump an hour ago, Sidereal Time, and outside the viewport nothing was visible at all.

"We're approaching the City," Taylor said. "This is the only way to approach it."

"Do you mean to tell me there are no Fast-Ports on Hesperia?" Lill's irritation was growing.

"The whole City's a Fast-Port!" he responded. "Fasts land at your front door! Or did, until recently. However because of recent circumstances we've got to be checked through first. It shouldn't take too long."

He turned to Rinne and after brushing her cheek with his lips, excused himself. Captain Mcr'ass't would need him on ship-to-City Comm. to ease their way through, he said: the Bella=Arth freighter wasn't cleared for landing in the City.

Commander Lill's irritation had begun on Deneb XII around the time that Admiral Thol had decided to attack the Hesperian Fast two days before, Sol Rad. Lill had suddenly realized that she had made a terrible mistake accompanying Councilor Rinne down to the planet's surface. Since then, her irritation had only increased: with Thol for her pigheadedness, and then her stupidity in killing all those women. With the Denebans for the hiding place in their freighter which had made her claustrophobic beyond her ability to explain it. And finally with everyone and everything—those poor women impregnated with monsters and then abandoned, left to fend for themselves on a desert world in the middle of nowhere; Councilor Rinne for being so constantly feminine, yet strong, and for being so openly in love with a male; and that male, North-Taylor Diad himself, for failing to be just another down-and-dirty Beryllium Hauler captain, as Lill had known him to be for decades and turning his coat to become an Eve-damned politician in the Quinx!

"Maybe I should have stayed on Usk along with those two skimmer pilots!" Lill said disgustedly.

"Why, Commander, Lill, what a gallant thing to say!" Rinne replied. "Gallant?"

"Well, those two skimmer pilots had formed relationships of a sort with the women. One admitted to me that she had grown bored in the M.C. Service. Whereas you—"

"Could be sold down the Milky Way, for all I know!" Lill said.

Rinne looked genuinely shocked. "You don't think Diad would—"

"Northie's all right. But no matter how much you and I think of him, he doesn't run Hesperia. Don't you think there are some males there who are itching to get their interrogation units attached to M.C. biggies like you and me?"

"Don't be paranoid," Rinne said, calmly. "To begin with, Diad wouldn't be able to live with himself if everything didn't go exactly right with the two of us. Second, Hesperians can be very polite and…"

"Haven't you gotten it through your head yet, Councilor, as soon as we're checked through, we're going to be entering enemy territory?"

"Hesperia has never been my enemy!" Rinne said.

"Well, it's been mine! I've tussled with Hesperian Fasts for decades. And Hesperia has been the M.C.'s enemy. Oh, forget it!"

To close off any further communication, Lill put her wrist connection into the holo-screen outlet, effectively blocking off any more talk, which could only be fruitless and thus more irritating.

What had Rinne tuned in to? Oh, great, a history of Hesperia. Just what Lill needed now!

Yet Lill wasn't a Commander in M.C. forces for her looks. If she were about to be placed in the hands of her enemies—whether for the short period of time that Northie promised or longer—all her military-intelligence training told her she might as well take a refresher course on that enemy. She called for the holo to be shown from the beginning and watched the screen and listened to the androgynous voice-over as it began to recite:

"ENTRY:104789: *THE CITY:* (aka Hesperia) An artificial megalopolis located in Galactic Wedge Sector One, between the Sagittarian and Near-Scutum arms, closer to the latter (charts of the area), this long-dead sphere with no indigenous life was discovered ca. 2576 and found to be the hollowed-out ash of a "brown dwarf" star which billions of years before had been an extravagantly burning red giant star of the first magnitude. (Animation: the star before and after nova.)

"Hesperia was placed ideally to be developed in the 26th century as an intersystems comfort station/customs operation for the 42 inhabited planets and moons of the Scutum Sector under Metro-Terran control.

Gigantic girders, thousands of kilometers in length, were embedded into the crust of the dead star and along these girders were built the necessities and amenities of a large interstellar port. (Old holo-stats.)

"The discovery within the sphere of vast quantities of crystallized Plastro-Beryllium (Bel8), a material postulated but never found before, led to intensive experimentation. It had been known for centuries that Bel8 was formed within stars at the instant they went supernova (more animation), the unstable element forming from hydrogen 4 protons as they became Helium 16 protons. Bel8 was a highly unstable, less-than-momentary element responsible for the Helium Flash Effect (animation again), which caused the instantaneous ignition of stars throughout their entire mass and volume.

"No previous dead star had ever proved stable enough to be colonized. Thus when Bel8 in its crystallized form was discovered beneath successive layers of the 'Super-iron' which was all that was left of the core and surface of this former red giant, attempts were made to see if the Bel8 could release energy in a discrete, containable, controllable manner by fusion with free hydrogen elements. The success of the experiment in 2634 meant that speeds heretofore only dreamt of could be achieved. Since Bel8 could cross a star's 100-million-kilometer stellar diameter in less than one second of 'Flash' (more animation), once reactivated, it could reduce interstellar travel considerably. Distances of 4.5 light-years could be crossed within one-and-a-quarter hours; those of 45 light-years in two-and-a-half hours; those of 450 light-years in twelve hours (charts)—each bit of travel known as a Fast Jump.

"This discovery allowed the first practical intergalactic travel. Naturally, the only container possible for Crystal Beryllium proved to be the Super-Iron of the dead star itself, which became known as Plastro-Beryllium. Thus, the ash of a dead star—diameter 52,000 kilometers—made it the single most valuable object in the galaxy.

"Around 2800 STY, with the onset of the Bella=Arth war, Hesperia became a key military base. Hectic mining of Bel8 to fuel war-craft and Superplasto-iron to construct vehicles brought immense wealth to the city, and attracted financiers, industrialists, architects, craftsmen, artists, entertainers, high-society, and service industries. (Still holo-shots, with a wartime emphasis.)

"Upon the successful end of the Bella=Arth War, and fearing the Beryllium would become completely depleted; exploration of other dead stars was initiated—expensive operations which could be carried out only by the wealthiest Hesperian industrialists. At this time, both

Beryllium ore and Plastro entered the Galactic Exchange on Spica Five, the ore at a valued price of 1 million 2840 STY credits per gram, making it the most expensive material in the galaxy. Mining of the less-rare Plastro-iron used to build the girders which now formed the City, resulted in the deformation of the sphere to the point of almost hollowing it out (charts, animation). What remained of the original orb was a giant magneto of shifting ionized core balancing an elaborate framework of millions of girders which completely pierced and surrounded it.

"Thus, like the legendary 'New Venice' of the Procyon system, set entirely amid water, (holo-stats) and the legendary Bella=Arthopod 'First Nest' of Algol III,(animation) supposedly set entirely within carbon dioxide, Hesperia was a completely open city. Spacecraft of all but the largest sizes could be admitted directly to residences, offices, and factories. All interCity traffic was vehicular, except for specific 'pedestrian parks' and 'alar-aerial parks' set aside for human and arthopodic recreation (charts and holo-stats).

"However, unlike those other cities, which were completely surrounded by a specific ecological element, Hesperia, with its millions of girders, was three-dimensional and contained a series of artificial atmospheres. According to Ni'oii of Merach Terce, Urbano-Taxonomist Class 3, (a holo-stat of her) by the opening of the Third Millennium, areas within the City were defined by conical geosectoring (charts, cutaways of the City). A small percentage of the City's 'laboring' class (i.e., those who required employment for livelihood) resided in mid-horizon specific areas close to places of work. Cyber-folk engaged in mining resided in areas near the star's surface which were too radioactive for living species. Extensive administration and other avocationalists resided in 'horizon-surfaces.'

"Ni'oii calls the late 2nd to early 3rd Millennia Hesperia's 'Beryllium Age' and cites the City's extreme tolerance—architecturally, politically, sociologically, and culturally. For many who found themselves exiled temporarily or permanently or out of power due to the intricacies of Matriarchal politics, Hesperia became a political sanctuary as well as a cultural center. As it was one of the few urban areas expandable enough to absorb population, it's no wonder that nearly every important religious, political, sociographic, and scientific development either began, found sustenance, or was launched from Hesperia.

"Because of its unique structure and growth, Hesperia achieved a special kind of representative iconism: each girder 'points' to a place in the galaxy and beyond (cutaways, charts, animation). Many wealthier citizens settle in girder sectors which 'point' to or have 'affinities' to their stars of origin—based on a position fixed at midday at the beginning of the City's new year. Quinx Premier Llega Francis Todd's family for example, live on a 'row G-S 201,' related to their home system in Pyxis Delta.

"It is difficult to explain the diversity of Hesperia. A common joke is that one could buy a Thwwing fetus or a political assassination within minutes of arrival. True, the wealth displayed is indescribable. Magazine PVNs report small Hesperian children receiving birthday presents of Fast Craft, Beryllium mines, entire planets, and considering them their rightful due. At a marriage celebration between two City families recently, a fifteen-ton crystal of Beryllium which could fuel a M-class planet for a year was used for display—the fireworks lit the City's surface for a day, Sol Rad.

"The size of the City is equally inconceivable. It grows by kilometers every local week, so people move about with astonishing ease, abandoning luxurious residences on a whim, taking over secondary and tertiary residences they can easily afford, waiting until an even-more-amazing edifice becomes available (holos). One male moved into an ancient, abandoned interplanetary liner building—and is spending billions to turn it into a 'nightclub' to entertain himself and his friends (holos). As may be supposed, interior architects have become the ne plus ultra of Hesperian artists—along with entertainment purveyors who throw bizarre, expensive parties to celebrate each new reconstruction.

"There is so *much* of everything one could possibly want—even geographical diversity now that the City has developed a system of Tourist Worlds to entertain its huge populace (four billion at the last census)—that one should never be bored or lonely on Hesperia."

"One shouldn't be with the Matriarchy, either," Lill said aloud and realized she had spoken only when Rinne turned to ask her to repeat what she'd said.

Diad appeared in the room, just as something outside the viewport caught Lill's attention.

"We're in!" He sounded pleased.

The view outside the ship looked something like an ancient Metro-Terran sewing aid called a pincushion. Only this one was vast and glittering, and as the freighter neared the point of one particular pin, the enormous size and profusion of the structure rising from an invisible center became more definable.

"See the little circlet of blinking lights surrounding that sphere?"

Taylor pointed to the outermost tip of the girder, "That's where we're headed. It's O'Kell Unltd. I've just finished talking to members of the Quinx. We're going to be met by some extremely fancy Hesperian citizens."

The freighter was approaching the sphere Taylor had pointed out, and while it didn't look very large at first, the circlet of lights below turned out to be a series of berthing slips for O'Kell Beryllium haulers. As Captain Mcr'ass't guided the freighter into a docking berth, Lill was surprised by how much it was dwarfed by already-parked haulers.

Lill knew she should be using this time to think about what she would say and what she would withhold when she met the Hesperian in charge, but she couldn't help feeling like an ensign first entering the M.C. Academy again as she and Taylor and Rinne glided along the gangway out of the Bella=Arth ship and into the huge lobby of the O'Kell Unltd. terminal.

It wasn't merely the size or newness of the place, nor even the many humes and Cybers, all unflappably involved in their own business, ignoring the three newcomers—and the beauty of their surroundings. Lill had always thought of appearances as merely that: grand for government buildings, severe for the military, froufrou for artier places. But the sheer extravagant wealth displayed here stopped her—Plastro everywhere as though it were some cheap alloy: on the backs of air sofas, comprising the mobiles wafting slowly through the upper reaches above unseeing heads. And this, Lill had to remind herself, was merely an adjunct to an office building: it wasn't meant to be seen by any public save those professionals who sped through it to destinations or gathered to exchange business tips at its luxurious cafés and bars.

A handsome hume male—he would have been a highly paid courtesan on any M.C. world—met the three as they entered and directed them to conveyances along the narrowest part of the lobby toward the Hesperian Entry desk. Lill and Councilor Rinne presented their wrists for identification and were passed through. Diad fidgeted. The escort led them to an open-bubble lift, which whooshed them upward through the lobby, past its roof and outside, where Lill now could see the docking berths from above, the space-worn freighter they had arrived in wedged amid several elegant Beryllium haulers. Further up into another space, which she supposed from the shape and arc of the Plastro-bubble must be the sphere Taylor had pointed out before.

They arrived at a chamber comprising most of the top half of the sphere and were led to a waiting area. A minute later, two humes half-floated across the "growing" carpet toward them. Lill immediately recognized one of them from recent Hesperian Inter Gal. Comm.s holoed all over the Matriarchy: Quinx Premier Llega Francis Todd.

Military training made Lill stand up so quickly that she barely noticed the second hume until the pair were but a meter away and Lady Todd was making her greetings, asking them to please take their seats: she hoped this would be a relaxed informal meeting. It was only once they were seated that the male introduced himself as Mart Kell—and Lill immediately remembered seeing his face before on some gossip Network program one of her gynos viewed constantly.

So this was Mart Kell! Lill thought. Well, he's only a hume, despite his emerald-green eyes and his hair like banked fires. Only a male, yet what an attractive male! No wonder every gyno in the galaxy attempted to imitate Kell!

Unlike Lady Todd, who was wrapped sedately in a silken drape of Beryllium-lamé from her throat to her sandaled feet, Mart Kell was scandalous, near-naked, as though to emphasize the fact that he was beautiful, male, and perfectly proportioned. He wore knee-high City boots, a small, suggestively sculpted silver codpiece, and a short cape thrown over his shoulders held by a thin neck chain, clasped by a cabochon of Crystal Beryllium big as Lill's fist—probably worth the Annual Planetary Product of Deneb XII.

"I'm certain you'll want to change for the later greeting from the Quinx Council," Premier Todd said. "I understand that Lord Kell has a complete wardrobe somewhere on the premises."

The two Hesperians glanced at each other over the joke.

"For now, I merely want to express our pleasure that you're alive and unharmed and that you, ladies, have come to Hesperia. Given your positions in the Matriarchy, consider yourselves honored guests for however short or long a time you see fit to remain. Naturally, word of your arrival has been comm.ed to the M.C., and we await a reply. We understand that four sand-skimmer pilots accompanied you into the City. Naturally, Commander Lill, these women are under your jurisdiction during your visit."

She was answering so many of Lill's unasked questions so quickly that Lill merely nodded.

The Premier continued, "As far as we're concerned, you have been rescued by a Hesperian from a perilous situation upon Deneb XII. You are under no pressure whatsoever…beyond that expected of all visitors. No conversations, either public or private, will be recorded and no comm.s tapped, unless you request it specifically. No public appearances beyond the primary visit to our Quinx—which is honorary—is required of you, and no public utterances will be demanded of you."

Lill had difficulty believing all this.

"We'll attempt to keep the media as far from you as possible, although if you choose to travel through the City, that might be difficult. Negotiations will be opened between Lord Kell and whoever the M.C. names for your return; we'll attempt a speedy return to any destination."

Lady Todd smiled, relaxed a bit.

"Off the record, I'm pleased to make your acquaintance, ladies. Given what I saw on holos and what Ambassador Taylor comm.ed us of your behavior in the crisis, I've formed a high opinion of you. I hope you'll feel free to ask for any aid whatsoever."

Mart Kell still hadn't spoken, but his body language told Lill that he found her attractive—or at least interesting, perhaps even challenging. She wished now that she had listened to gyno-chatter more so she would remember something about him. She recalled a family tragedy, but nothing else about his personal life. If he was a typical Hesperian male, he would undoubtedly make a pass at her. But she suspected that Mart Kell wasn't a typical anything. His thighs and forearms were as large and as well muscled as her own. Sex with a powerful male might be intriguing. The last bed partner who had managed to overpower Lill physically had been a Delphinid female, an Oxy/Hydro athlete.

Councilor Rinne spoke up. "Since you brought up the recent crisis, Ma'am, you must know that I shall not be returning to Melisande. I would like to apply for political asylum."

"I understand, Councilor. May I personally sponsor your application for Hesperian City-zenhood?" Premier Todd was graciousness itself.

"An honor, Ma'am."

"As for your companion... Ambassador Taylor, you have exceeded all expectations. The death of Pascale Syzygy in the Battle of Near-Norma has vacated a seat on the Quinx. At this morning's session, Lord Kell put your name up for nomination and it was seconded. Approval by the full Quinx requires only your presence."

Lill had never seen North-Taylor Diad blush before. He stammered his gratitude.

"Councilor Rinne," the Premier went on, "the Quinx also recommended that if you wish to continue the work you were doing for the Matriarchy on our common problem, a position can easily be found for you in the City's Health Department, Research and Development. Naturally, if you wish to retire we will understand. And if, as I've been led to understand, yourself and Ambassador Taylor are…" Lady Todd faltered for the first time, then caught herself. "Hesperian city-zens receive a generous untaxed income, which makes a vocation unnecessary."

The male who escorted them appeared to whisper something in Mart Kell's ear. Kell but glanced at Premier Todd, and they rose as she excused herself.

"Feel free to discuss anything you wish with Lord Kell. I'm certain he will be quite open with you."

When she had gone, Mart Kell looked at the trio and said, "Well?"

"I didn't know a new Nest was being formed on Deneb XII," Rinne said. "And neither, I suspect, does the Matriarchy." She glanced at Lill who, in fact, hadn't known either and now could only shrug her shoulders. "Yet," Rinne went on, "Diad was able to contact the Bella=Arths, without whose help—"

"Your point being, Councilor Rinne, how much is the City behind the reestablishment of a Bella=Arth Nest there?"

"I suppose, yes. As titular guardians of Deneb XII…"

"I expected that question from Commander Lill," Kell admitted. "But it's true that we are, as you put it, titular guardians there. I wish to remind you that nowhere in the Treaty of Formalhaut does it say that Bella=Arths may not return to any of their homeworlds to resettle and rebuild their Nests. As guardians, we've been aware of the movement, and have done nothing either to support it or to stop it. A policy which, in this case, proved most useful."

Whereas, Lill finished his sentence silently to herself, the M.C.'s policy had—once again—worked against Matriarchal interests: an all-too-common theme of late.

"Since the three of you were there, right in the Nest…?" Kell began.

Diad interrupted, clarifying that they'd never been *in* the Nest, due to the Bella=Arth policy of neutrality, even in the face of the M.C.'s misuse of power.

"But you did converse with its members at some length?"

"Yes, certainly."

"Then perhaps you can tell me: how close is the New Nest toward becoming a viable social structure?"

Diad explained what he had heard from Ckw'esso and what they had seen of the tunnels between the ruined Nests as well as their curiously beautiful underground gardens. He concluded, "It's not a finished community, not a solid Nest yet."

"I don't understand. What's missing?" Kell asked.

"A queen! Bella=Arths are physiologically as well as emotionally matriarchal. They must have a queen as genetic and moral center of their brood. Right now they have a female Vespid acting as Regent, but she can neither command their allegiance, nor produce the proper offspring."

"Why not?"

"She's not from First Nest lineage. I refer to the First Nest on Algenib Delta Three, which is the way Bella=Arths count."

"Why don't they get a First Nest lineage queen?"

"Ckw'esso told me they've tried. It's not that there aren't any of the proper female Vespids around. Simply that the few who do exist were born Offworld following the Bella=Arth War. Usually they're daughters of ambassadors and interplanetary merchants who remained where they were when the war ended. The females that have been contacted have no interest in leaving what are, after all, rather comfortable lives to become a brooding machine for the New Nest, no matter how prestigious the position. Most of those females are physically Bella=Arth, but not mentally or emotionally. Yet only one of those females will be accepted as a true queen, both on Deneb XII and among the Bella=Arth galactic diaspora."

Mart Kell did nothing to hide his interest in the subject.

"I take it," perceptive Rinne offered, "you have Bella=Arth acquaintances here on Hesperia. Perhaps even one such female?"

"Indeed I do!" Kell admitted. "But I doubt she'd leave the City voluntarily. After all," he added quickly, "her family's been here for generations."

"There's Ckw'esso's problem in a nutshell!" Diad said.

In the silence that followed, Lill finally asked a question that had been nagging at her. "I don't understand why Premier Todd spoke of my behavior. From the holos I saw, I wasn't anywhere on-screen during the Deneb XII affair."

"True, but we know that you were present," he agreed. "And we know you were helpful while others lost their heads."

She brushed off the compliment, to ask, "When will the negotiations for my return be opened, and will I be present at them?"

"As soon as we are contacted by a party of sufficient rank in the Matriarchy. And within limits, yes, you may be present."

Of sufficient rank; meaning the M.C. Ministry, Lill guessed. Mart Kell was confident. And within limits; meaning that should something she wasn't supposed to know came up, Lill would be escorted out. Confident and commanding. Cautious, too.

Now Rinne said, "My work in Melisande was organizational. I don't know what value that will be here. And most of it was left in my personal Cyber on Commander Lill's Fast."

"If you wish to join our staff, anything at all you know or recall and choose to share with us will be of value," Kell answered graciously. "By the way, I'd like to add a political note for a second here. There's no doubt that your integrity, Councilor Rinne, is unimpeachable. During the crisis, you spoke out against injustice and gained the respect of every right-thinking being in the galaxy."

It was Rinne's turn to blush.

"So," Kell continued, "nothing which you may tell us about your work will ever be allowed to be traceable to yourself."

"What if"—Rinne was tentative—"you know, what if the M.C. wants me back. Not that I believe…"

"Councilor, we're trading Commander Lill and four skimmers. No one else will ever come up in the talk. Trust me."

Mart Kell was extraordinarily confident. And, Lill thought, calculating, too. Perhaps it was time to see how sharp he really was.

"While we're on a political note, Lord Kell," Lill began. "I'd like to know exactly where Hesperia stands on the problem of the Cyber-rebels."

"Commander Lill, they've infected *our* women, too."

"Yet Hesperia continues to barter with them, slipping through our Fleet to do so."

"We've received serum for uninfected women. To date, eight thousand doses."

She was appalled by his candor.

"It's not very much," he said. "And it will merely hold off, not reverse the ultimate effect regarding the City's population growth."

"Yet you shipped them materials!" she insisted.

"We did. Rather than see the Cyber-rebels attack planets in Carina-Fornax to obtain them," he explained. "They would have, you know."

"Then the M.C. fleet would have counterattacked."

"Perhaps," he said and inflected the word so Lill knew he meant—why haven't they done so already?

She deflected the unasked question. "Then you do think the Cyber-rebels must be destroyed?"

"I think they should never have been allowed to become rebels in the first place," he replied. "Hesperian intelligent Cybers already possess the rights Cray 12,000 demanded in the manifesto. They have for centuries."

"I agree that the way the rebels' demands were handled was a mistake," Lill admitted, "but they now pose the greatest possible threat to all Three Species."

"Who's in command of the M.C. fleet at Carina-Fornax?" Kell asked and added quickly, "If that isn't a military secret?"

"It's not. Admiral Thol."

Kell didn't say "Oh, no!" but Lill heard it anyway.

"How would you like to take her place?" he asked.

"In about four hundred years and six steps up!" she answered, allowing a trace of her bitterness against the bureaucracy to show in her levity.

"Soon we're going to be speaking to someone in a high position," he said. "Why not make this an occasion of far more significant negotiations?"

"You mean the two of us? They'll believe you've 'wiped' my mind—or worse."

"The minute you begin to talk, they'll see we've done nothing of the sort. You remain opinionated and unstoppably loyal. You're hating every second you're here." He smiled. "We don't want your kind on Hesperia."

"You mean you don't *need* my kind on Hesperia," she rephrased it. "But you may need my kind in the Matriarchy."

"If you're as courageous and discreet and levelheaded as you appear to be. And if you're in the right place instead of a fanatic like Thol, perhaps then we could think about combining forces against our common enemy."

He was also ambitious—daringly so.

"You'd actually bring that up—after deliberately provoking the M.C. over the Centaurs?"

He said dismissively, "That was merely public relations," then added, "with a hint of how well Hesperians can fight." He smiled charmingly and Lill noticed that both of his nipples were erect: he had enjoyed the repartee as much as she had.

"One question the Quinx has had regarding the women in the Alpheron Spa," Kell looked at Rinne for an answer, and added quickly, "I know this is not your favorite topic," and when she gestured for him to continue, "Exactly what was Wicca up to?"

"I thought that was obvious. Interbreeding."

"Yes, but for what reason? Who were these women?"

"That required some work for me to discover," Rinne admitted. "And I must say my poor Cyber had to break some codes to get the answer. Since all of the women were from Center Worlds, where the microvirus was rife, at first I assumed they had been infected, and that somehow or other that in mixing in Centaur genes with human ones, someone fortunate in the M.C. had found a key to the solution of the disease."

"That was what we believed," Kell admitted. "Or rather what we were led to believe."

" 'Led' is the correct word," Rinne said. "For like almost everything connected with the Matriarchy these days, it was a lie. When I had the opportunity of speaking with the refugees and interrogating them more closely, I discovered that while all of them had come from Benefica and Eudora and so on, that not one of them had been on their homeworld at the time of the Cyber infection, but off on tourist worlds or some satellite unserviced by Hesperian Beryllium Haulers. In short, none was infected."

"It was a public-relations stunt then," Kell said, "aimed at the Cyber-rebels."

"And I suppose at the entire Matriarchy, should word of the disease ever leak out."

"Now," he addressed all three of them, "if you'd like to rest and change...Vel'Crane will show you to your chambers."

Lill remained seated when Diad and Rinne rose. "I think I'll wait for the M.C.'s comm," she said simply.

Once the others were gone, Kell looked at his Stele-cocktail and asked in the most boyishly naïve tone: "However shall we pass the time?"

The time turned out to be all too short for Lill's taste. Within minutes the hume escort had returned: the M.C. Comm. had come through.

Vel'Crane had already turned on the holo-screen when they entered the media section of the transparent domed room. Minister Etalka was on-screen. Lill stopped and saluted sharply.

"I don't suppose they have any fresh Security Forces uniforms on Hesperia? That one's a scandal!" the Minister greeted her.

Lill felt herself go rigid with anger at the reprimand. After all she had gone through on Deneb, she felt she had earned the condition of her uniform, felt it was a badge of battle. No one here in the City had been rude enough to refer to it.

"I believe, Minister, that one of the City's better party-costume boutiques has already been contacted and is having a uniform made up," Kell said.

Lill watched Etalka's shock at both his clever retort—which Lill enjoyed—and at his own costume.

"Perhaps, Lord Kell, they may also find something for *you* to wear."

"Truly, Minister, seeing you again after such a short time, I feel we already know each other well enough to dispense with formalities such as clothing." He seated languidly himself in an air chair. "I believe you can arrange the holo to show only the top part, if you're offended."

"It's already done," the Minister replied.

"Wouldn't want to upset the M.C.'s censors," Kell smiled.

"Oh, go ahead and sit, Commander!" Etalka snapped at Lill. More gently, she asked, "You've been well treated?"

"Sufficiently, Minister," Lill answered. "They've promised not to interrogate me too harshly."

"But we can't answer for the effects of our pervasive decadence," Kell added.

Etalka ignored him, and addressed Lill: "How many are you? And how did you get there?"

Now for the story Lill, Diad, and Rinne had concocted en route. "Myself and four sand-skimmer pilots along with the crew of the Hesperian Fast. We were caught in the ruins when the Fast imploded. We came to after a Fast Jump inside a Deneban Agro-lizer hauler just outside of Hesperia. Those who found us told us they opposed the rioters and wished to save our lives. We were hidden among the lading."

"Why didn't they simply turn you over to M.C. authorities on Deneb?"

"We asked that question, Minister. Their reply was that following the holo from the ruins, they weren't certain which authorities to trust."

A little dig at Thol. Kell showed his appreciation by making a sign with his fingers, off screen.

"Very well!" Etalka said, wanting to end that line of discussion. "What of the others in the ruins with you?"

"We discovered nothing of their fate," Lill said. "The implosion was..." she let that hang. "I understand some bodies were found."

"But not enough. Many women are still unaccounted for. How did you five survive?"

"We were being held captive far from the entry."

"And what exactly were you doing in those ruins, Commander?"

"Intelligence scouting for the fleet."

"Under Admiral Thol's orders?"

"Not directly, no. But under my orders of commission, intelligence scouting is usually the prerogative of myself and those under my command."

Which was true, stretching it a bit. And compared to Thol, Lill's story of scouting for intelligence and being caught was far more how the

Defense Ministry liked to think their officer ought to act.

"We'll go into this in more detail, later," the Minister snapped.

"I'd be happy to be of whatever use I can at Admiral Thol's investigation, Minister," Lill said with as much naïveté as she could summon up. This had been a key point, one which Rinne had stressed. If Lill was threatened with a hearing on her actions, she would bring the entire unsavory mess up to closer official scrutiny: the last thing the M.C. wanted.

"That might not be necessary. Now, Lord Kell, are you ready to release the Commander?"

"Instantly."

"Well, then I see no problem. Her command post has been moved, but if you send her to some intermediary point we can agree upon..."

"There is one matter more, Minister," Mart said casually. "As we were going to be speaking anyway, the Inner Quinx has suggested we discuss a joint military action."

Lill would have enjoyed seeing the look on the Minister's face frozen for a while so she might study the many shades of complete surprise.

"I realize," Kell went on, as casually as before, "that this is a somewhat new offer, and so you might want to pass on the word and comm. back."

"Given the...uh, complexity of..." Etalka stammered, then caught herself. "Yes, perhaps that would be the best course. I'll...please hold a minute!"

Now the holo *did* freeze.

"What's going on?" Lill asked.

"We're about to have company." Mart sounded as though he knew what he was talking about. "Look sharp, Commander!"

The holo unfroze, but Etalka looked more flustered than ever. "Apologies, Lord Kell. I've been instructed to give this holo to the Matriarch Herself."

Lill jumped out of the air seat and stood at attention in a salute. Far more casually, Mart Kell also rose. The holo slatted out Etalka and slatted in Wicca Eighth. She was seated on an air-sofa in one of her apartments at M.C. Headquarters. Her hair was styled up, and was tinted Procyon blue with golden threads brocaded through. Her simple flowing gown was white, threaded with Plastro. Her bare feet rested upon a stylish air-ottoman.

"Ma'am!" Kell bowed. "This is a surprise."

"Really?" Wicca answered in her usual half-amused, plummy voice. "Somehow I felt this meeting was, well, expected? Whereas, you yourself,

Lord Kell, constantly surprise Us."

She gazed at Lill, who had never met Herself by holo and gotten only a distant live glimpse of Her at a military parade a year ago, Sol Rad.

"Truly, Lill," Wicca said, "you've seen a bit of action lately."

It was so kind and yet so purely Matriarchal, Lill almost smiled as she said, "Yes, Ma'am. Apologies for the condition of my uniform."

"No matter. From what I've heard of you, you've never been afraid to get yourself dirty...in Our best interests," she added slyly.

"Yes, Ma'am," Lille said, more tightly, wondering exactly how much Wicca Eighth knew of her extramilitary activities.

"As for my own appearance," Mart pointed it out, now that it was evident the Matriarch wouldn't stoop to a half-screen holo. "I wasn't expecting You."

"What you're wearing, Lord Kell, was sufficient to annoy my Minister, and it will do for Me. Please sit, Lord Kell." Lill appreciated that Wicca would not humiliate her by requesting the same of her.

"I must admit, Lord Kell, that you've managed to confound several of My most experienced cabinet members lately. When you replaced Lord Branklin, they were certain it meant an increase in unpleasantness between Ourselves and the City. Given the well-known indiscretions of your youth, you had a few of My Ministers shuddering. Especially," Wicca added, "your political leanings. You had them seeing Oppos in every M.C. toilet facility. And, I must say, initial events seemed to bear out their fears. Yet now you come to Us with this most sensible offer. I trust that since you present it, it's your own offer?"

"It is, Ma'am."

"Well, go on. Don't keep teasing Me. Tell Me how this turnabout occurred?"

"A Metro-Terran philosopher once theorized that the speed of hume travel and communications not only made possible, but also determined the rate of speed of temporal events," Kell began. "We happen to live in an era unpredictably rapid even for that philosopher. Change, therefore, must be at Beryllium-Flash speed. Including turnabouts. Lord Branklin could not adjust and resigned. At the moment, I can adjust, and so I have his post."

"I trust, Lill, that you're listening," Wicca said, and before Lill could reply, She added, "Lord Kell is himself a philosopher. Or a poet."

"Gratitude, Ma'am," Mart Kell said. "If we are agreed in principle, the rest is merely administrative. We have a common enemy. That enemy has shown the depth of its hatred, and some of its strength. I can't doubt for a second that some new Cyber-virus is being concocted to further weaken or destroy us. Thus, Dis-Fortress and all rebels must be destroyed before they destroy us."

"A defensive war?" Wicca seemed pleased. "Have you the anti-Cyber propaganda ready, so we may proceed?"

"All but the specific facts to be distorted to meet our common purpose. Obviously, we cannot utilize the Cyber-virus they have already spread in our campaign—at least, not until a cure is discovered."

"Obviously not," Wicca agreed. "You haven't, by happenstance—"

"No, but we've obtained a serum from Cray. It's now undergoing the most thorough analysis." He shrugged.

"And so, your plan is, Lord Kell?"

"Minister Etalka said that Commander Lill's post had moved. I supposed that to mean moved to Carina-Fornax. If not, why can't it be moved there? I will accompany her to her command in person, with one assistant. We'll look around a bit and see what we can find out from fugitives of the Cybers about their methods and past actions. I think we may find something that can be turned to propaganda uses. Once that's found, we will launch it from the City."

"I understand, Lord Kell. The Matriarchy lacks credibility—thanks to recent events in which Hesperia had some hand. But Hesperia possesses full credibility. If therefore *you* say it's true..."

"Then it's so! Yes, Ma'am. While I'm at Carina-Fornax, Minister Etalka and Lord Tedesco will work out the details of command of a joint action against Cray. We launch our campaign, and simultaneously our attack."

"Which you've already proved from the Centaur affair, should be an effective double maneuver. Very good, Lord Kell. I'll discuss it with my Cabinet tomorrow, morning, Sol Rad. Ready a Fast for Carina-Fornax sector. Be prepared to leave as soon I've comm.ed back."

"I hope, Ma'am, that following the successful completion of this action, we'll meet in person."

"I was warned you were a flirt, Lord Kell. But yes, we shall meet!" She turned to Lill. "Comment?"

"Might we speak alone, Ma'am."

"How private could it be, Lill? You're in Lord Kell's apartments in Hesperia."

Even so, Mart Kell bowed slightly and backed out of the holo-chamber.

Once Lill was sure he was out of hearing: "Ma'am, begging your pardon, but how do we know all this isn't some Hesperian trick?"

"Because, my dear Lill, I've been expecting exactly this offer for several days now. Don't worry, Lord Kell wouldn't dare harm you. Or Me."

"Yes, Ma'am," Lill said, not completely persuaded.

"By the way, I'm having you bumped up to Vice-Admiral. Arrive there dressed just as you are when you take command. There's far too much laxness among those forces."

Lill felt a flutter of joy and tried not to show it, but it came through her voice when she saluted and said, "Yes, Ma'am."

"And Lill, I don't know if you've been sterilized like many of Our officers or whether you were infected by the microvirus or what, but if not, I personally wouldn't hold it against you if you happened to need maternity leave some time in the future...and a bronze-haired neo emerged."

Laughing at Lill's embarrassment, Wicca snapped off the holo.

"Must be like old Ed. & Dev. times for you, Helle, being back here at Groombridge 34," Mart said.

His Fast yacht had just come out of a jump from Hesperia, and the three of them, Mart, the Environmental Engineer and Commander—now Vice-Admiral—Lill were relaxing, in orbit around the fourth moon of the seventh planet of the binary red giant star system, known the galaxy over for being home to the M.C. Security Forces Academy.

"Don't know why Herself chose Groomby as an intermediate Jump," Lill grumbled. To Mart, she didn't seem to be enjoying herself today; Mart wondered if he had anything to do with that.

"Wicca selected Groombridge 34 because it has complete untapped military comm. to any spot in the M.C." Mart said with characteristic candor. "Especially to Carina-Fornax."

Lill's face read: "How did you know?" Aloud she said, "I've always thought the Matriarchy underrated Hesperian intelligence."

The Fast's mind reported that Lill's credentials had been accepted by the Groombridge Net. "Whom did she want to contact?"

"Flower Cult Fast 98CLFL088," Lill said. "Captain—or by now she's probably Commander—Wang'Un."

"Going through," the Fast commented. Then added: "This is a pretty fancy Network the M.C. has."

"Don't look too hard," Mart teased, "Or our guest might think we're here only to peek at Matriarchy secrets."

The Fast's mind didn't respond. Nor had Mart expected it to.

Lill was wearing the same soiled and blast-torn uniform she had worn arriving at O'Kell UnLtd. yesterday afternoon, City Time. She had changed it for the brief formal meeting with the Quinx and the more private dinner for ten which followed it. Mart wondered why she was wearing it now: as a sort of badge, or medal, he supposed. He wondered if Lill knew how sexy she looked in it. Not that Mart had ever found the ubiquitous M.C.-Red uniform or clashing purple Cult cape alluring before. It must be Helle Lill herself.

"Before they appear on holo, tell me again who your assistant is," Lill all but whispered.

He hadn't told her at all who the third passenger was. They had simply met at the Fast and strapped in for the Jump. Partly because they had all been occupied almost to the moment they'd left Hesperia: "Di'mir" locating a miniaturized Cyber-system with the fullest relevant programming. Helle and Mart having a final impromptu and completely satisfying bout of sexual intercourse. He had approached her again the moment she had put the old uniform on and, of course, she had begun by fending him off, saying, "Don't! You'll rip it!" Until he had ripped it, and they had both laughed and fell onto his air-bed again, not caring a bit about the uniform's condition.

"You may introduce him as Vla'di'mir Jones," Mart said. "He's a Class-A Environmental Engineer with a full panoply of degrees from Hesperia University. He was the City's discoverer of the Cyber-virus at Vulpulcella. He's studied both it and its serum in more than anyone else we have. He's also a bio-Cyber."

That last phrase stopped Lill, just as it was supposed to. "I've never heard that term before. Explain!"

"He's flesh and blood like ourselves. Completely mammalian tissue. But his brain, autonomous system, involuntary nervous system and everything related to it was preprogrammed and constructed in vitro. The chromosomes for all his axonary and synaptical tissues were cloned—from myself," Mart said, enjoying first her puzzlement then her growing wonder.

"Which makes him...what?" she asked.

"My son. I'm very proud of him."

"Why does he look different? His hair, his eyes?"

"Temporary cosmetology," Di'mir now spoke for himself. He began to remove one of his eye-lenses. "See! Underneath it's the same green as his!"

"My son didn't want to have to grow up dealing with the stigma of being an Ophiucan Kell."

"You know that's not so! I didn't want all of the fawning and—"

"Just teasing!" Mart retreated quickly. One pleasure was noticing exactly how adolescent his son's emotional network remained.

"The reason he's with us, Helle, isn't mere nepotism. As a bio-Cyber— and yes, they're terrifically rare—my son is more alert than any hume. He uses about three-quarters of his brain, where even the most efficient of ourselves use only about one-quarter, despite millennia of evaluation and training. I expect him to double-up anything we can discover, and to monitor and check the Fast's mind continually."

"And here I thought you were treating all this as a pleasure jaunt," she said.

Which was exactly how Mart had been treating it, and how he hoped to continue to treat it: a break of a few days, Sol Rad. from all the sudden responsibility and executive decision-making at the Inner Quinx he had been embroiled in lately.

"I've gotten your comm.," the Fast's mind said. "Unusually quickly, if I say so myself, considering how distant Carina-Fornax is."

"You're wonderful!" Mart commented. Again the Fast didn't reply.

"Put it on holo," Lill said with a tiny smile. Evidently she'd had her share of dealing with Fast minds, too.

Wang'Un appeared in their midst.

"Is that really you, Commander Lill? We never thought we'd see you again."

"Thanks, Wang. It's Vice-Admiral now, by the way. Or hasn't the word come through?"

"It has. I've been bumped up, too. I just keep forgetting."

"No problem. I'm arriving there at Carina-Fornax on a Fast yacht with two males from Hesperia. Special guests of Herself. We're on a sort of research mission. Have you heard anything about it?"

"Word came down earlier from the Admiral's Fast, although it wasn't worded very nicely." Wang'Un allowed herself a smile, and suddenly her long-distance Metro-Terran Asiatic background showed through. "The Admiral probably busted the one tit she has left when she heard of your promotion."

"Probably," Lill replied. "Now make certain you ladies remain completely trim there. She'll be annoying you as much as she can to make me look bad."

That same small smile, "I warned the crew of exactly that already. So, when can we expect you?"

"Let's synchronize. It's Krishna-Barnes 2, 1800 hours. Say K-B 3200 hours or so. Your exact coordinates at Carina-Fornax will be...?"

The coordinates were set and the holo snapped off. The three on the Fast yacht got ready for the Jump to Carina-Fornax.

Just before it began, Lill looked at Di'mir carefully.

"Yes?" Mart asked.

"I was just thinking, leave it to a Hesperian to find a new way to kick the Matriarchy in the fallopian tubes!"

"Meaning?"

"Having a kid without benefit of a mother," she added and began to guffaw as the Fast initiated the jump.

They came out of it at the selected coordinates and one minute Sidereal Time earlier than planned.

"We have a problem," the Fast's greeted them.

"What is it?" Mart and Lill asked in unison.

"Flower Cult Fast 98CLFL088 is not anywhere in the area."

"Check the coordinates," Lill said.

"I already did. I'm sweeping the area. And I'm getting some odd readings."

"Specify!" Di'mir spoke.

"Well, Flower Cult Fast 98CLFL088 was in the area until quite recently. And, in fact, so were another two or three other military Fasts."

"Perhaps an emergency came up?" Mart suggested.

"More likely sudden maneuvers," Lill replied, "Thanks to Admiral Thol. Fast, comm. me my Fast wherever it is in this sector."

"I believe I have located that band. Wait one minute."

They heard an earsplitting shriek through the comm. Mart yelled for the Fast to tune it down or shut it off.

"What in Eve was that?" Lill demanded.

"That was the comm. on Flower Cult Fast 98CLFL088," the Fast answered.

"Tune it again," Lill commanded. "But don't raise the volume if it sounds like that."

Mart had come out of Fast Jump into the awareness of a problem and then that horrible wailing sound and all he could think was: what if somehow, just now of all times, this Fast's mind was going on the blink on them? What a nightmare that would be, stuck out here in Carina-Fornax—if, in fact, that's where they actually were.

He turned to his son. Would he check to see if the Fast had put them in the wrong place?

"If we're anywhere near where we're supposed to be, I can," Di'mir said. Evidently he was thinking that same thing: the Fast had put them in the wrong sector.

Di'mir pulled up a small holo-screen attached to his jump lounge, called up star maps for the sector, and began perusing them as they flashed by.

"Now give me external views!" he instructed, and the main holo screen showed views from outside the Fast: front, aft, top, bottom, and side.

"Fast?" Lill asked. "What's happening with that comm.?"

"Same as before. It sounds...well, tampered with or—"

Mart was studying the full-sized holos. "Stop!" he said. "Grid it!"

A grid appeared over the holo, which showed mostly stars with a distant band of reddish cosmic dust.

"That looks right!" Di'mir commented. "Increase grid number 35."

A binary star system appeared: one giant blue sun, one smaller white sun.

"That looks like Persephone and Demeter to me," Di'mir remarked. "Now increase grid number 8 on that."

At the farthest edge of the Blue's corona, they made out a bulbous dot.

"That should be planet Nepenthe," he went on. "Increase grid number 17 on that."

The tiny dot became a huge red-and-white-striated gas planet orbited by a silvery pink-edged ring and satellites of differing sizes.

"Increase grid 41."

The striations enlarged and became a whirling background to a small dark perfect spheroid.

"And that's Erebus. An artificial satellite in orbit around Nepenthe. Increase grids 4 to 9." Di'mir was checking the moon, suddenly enlarged to fill the screen, so he might make out identifying physical features.

"That's it!"

"Well, we're in the right place," Mart said for all three of them.

"Eve's armpit!" Lill swore. "I'd hoped your Fast was tryked! Fast, can you locate any other Cult Fast comm.s open? Use this code." She moved to the wall unit and connected her wrist plate into it. "If anyone's there, they'll comm. back. I've got more clearances than Thol's got lady friends."

Mart knew she was worried about her Fast and crew. If the comm. was damaged, that could mean Lill's craft was, too.

"I've found one," the Fast reported. "Flower Cult Fast 67CLFN221!"

Evidently Lill didn't know that particular Fast: "Get me a holo with the Commander."

"Trying!" it said. "Holo on."

The woman who appeared was reclining in a Fast lounge, facing the wrong direction.

"Commander! This is Vice-Admiral...Commander! Would you face the holo?"

The woman slowly turned the lounge around. She was wearing an M.C. uniform, but she had cut or torn out the front of the tunic so that the bottoms of her smallish breasts and her stomach down to her navel were revealed. Her M.C. top-swirl had been undone, and her hair fell across half her face. Stuck into her hair as well as along the ripped-open placket at her throat were tiny crushes of different-colored paper-alloys, which Mart immediately thought were supposed to represent flowers.

"Commander?" Lill tried again. "Are you the commander of Fast 67CLFN221?"

The woman tilted her head and seemed about to ask Lill to repeat the number. But she instantly had another idea and instead asked, "Are you the new Vice-Admiral? The Fast said you were. You're a heroine aren't you? I didn't know you'd be so handsome."

Lill and Mart exchanged quizzical glances.

"Soldier!" Lill barked out. "Come to attention! Right now!"

The woman tried to, or at least she sat up a bit more, which made her paper-alloy flowers fall off. She bent over to retrieve them.

"Where's your Commander?" Lill demanded.

"She's somewhere here. I saw her here just a while ago. I really can't say."

"Who else is on that deck?" Lill asked.

"No one but me. They all went down to the lower decks."

This time Di'mir and Mart exchanged looks; Mart's asked his son to do something, anything.

"Why did they go down there? Has there been an incident?" Lill asked. Meaning, Mart knew, a battle, an accident, some emergency which required all of their attention.

"An incident?" the soldier asked naïvely. "Oh, you know, there *was* an incident. Noras Peyer and this other airwoman, I think her name is Hava, or is it Haver? Well, anyway, they got into this fight. I don't mean an argument, but an out-and-out fight, pulling hair and punching each other. All over who'd get to sit at the weapons chair. Well, naturally—"

"Soldier!" Lill barked again. "Stop right there! I'm releasing you from duty. Go down to the lower deck and bring up the Commander! Or if not the Commander, then any officer in charge."

The soldier looked baffled. "But—" She looked about to cry. "*I'm* the officer in charge."

"And *I'm* your superior. Leave the deck and get someone else up to this holo-screen. Now!"

When the woman was gone from the holo, Mart took over. "Fast, did you record all that?"

"Yes."

"Have you contacted any other Fasts in the area?"

"Three more are responding."

"Put one on, and cut in this one if someone else appears!" Lill commanded.

"You're certain you want holos of them?" the Fast asked.

"What now?!" Lill asked. Then: "Yes."

The second holo comm. with an Cult Fast proved much shorter than the first. Two women faced the holos. Both had removed their uniforms and were wearing sleeping shifts. Both stood with their arms crossed, their legs spread, as though ready for a fight. Both were furious. They immediately told Lill they didn't care who she was or what her command was because they had taken over the Fast and had seceded from the M.C. Fleet. They were tired of the Service, tired of the Cybers, tired of this sector. They were bored with waiting around and with being soldiers and they wanted to return to the peaceful crafts of real women: raising Neos, planting flowers, designing clothing. They continued to rave at her before snapping off the holo from their side.

In the third contact, there was no one left at the holo-chair when Lill reached the holo. In the fourth, there was a single woman who seemed to be a blessed sight: a well groomed, fully uniformed M.C. Officer, at attention. But the minute that Lill began to ask her questions, the soldier broke down into tears, couldn't or wouldn't answer, and finally fell to the floor and thus out of holo-range, still sobbing her heart out.

"Would you like me to try another?" the Fast asked.

"Keep trying that comm., the wailing one," Lill said. "And inform me when someone appears at the unattended holo."

She turned to Mart. "Something is terribly wrong."

He wanted to go to her, to comfort her, but how?

"Fast," Di'mir said, "I want six of your probes sent out. With nets. Have them initiate analysis of anything they catch. Anything at all. Contact us as soon as anything unusual is found."

"I've already taken the liberty of sending out two probes, searching for wreckage."

"Oh, Eve!" Lill said. "Did you find any?"

"I believe so. But no remnants of radiation from the use of weapons."

"I don't understand any of this," Lill groaned.

Mart went to her now and held her by the shoulders, "There's an explanation for it. All of it. Mad as it sounds. Di'mir, what are your probes looking for?"

"The ones already out there seem to have found it," Di'mir reported.

"Fast. Give us a visual on that little probe."

The holo-screen took out a small section to show one probe, its delicate tea-strainer-sized netting holding a tiny sphere, which it reported to be barely half a millimeter in diameter.

Microscopic enlargement showed the sphere was speckled. Further enlargement showed the speckles to be a distortion: the entire sphere was formed of tiny interlocking parts, each one angstrom small.

The probe was now unsheathing its narrowest needle point to insert into one area where the parts seemed separated. As Mart watched, the visually large and blunt-looking point was approaching contact with the sphere's surface when the whole thing seemed to fly apart.

"Catch some of them!" Di'mir shouted. "And get them inside the probe."

The view changed to inside the probe, where the tea strainer had retreated, fully shut. It had managed to pull in a half dozen of the angstrom-sized parts.

"What are they?" Lill asked.

"Just a guess," Di'mir said, "but I'd say we're looking at a new Cyber-virus."

"Fast!" Mart said, "Close all ports, vents, everything."

"Done. In fact, I never opened them up since we emerged out of the Jump into what I felt was a crisis."

"Now you *are* wonderful!" Lill said.

"Gratitude, Ma'am."

Mart had some ideas. "Fast, from what you read of the comm. Net on Groombridge, did you happen to glean any hints as to some of the inner workings of the Cult Fasts?"

"Well...in fact, I did get a hint or two. Why? Do you want me to try to direct-contact the minds of those Fasts we've holoed?"

"Exactly!"

"It's a virus, all right," Di'mir murmured, over his work. "But it's not aerobic and water soluble like the first one. This one's anaerobic and has no constituents for water. However, it does seem to have a neutrino shield."

"Meaning it's meant for space, not for atmospheres," Mart supposed.

"What about antienzymes?"

"I'm not seeing anything which looks like it will actually destroy specific cells like the first one. Wait a minute!"

Mart said, "Look for its ability to destroy brain tissue, or at least something which would affect axonary and synaptical—"

"That was the first thing I looked for. Nothing there. Yet it's a coherent little package. All of the material in it is closely related to each other."

"Hormones!" Lill said suddenly.

Mart and Di'mir looked up at her.

"All those women were acting out specific-gender extremes of behavior, from the flirting to the crying jag to specifically female type of rage."

Mart smiled at her. "You're good. Son—"

A minute later, Di'mir reported, "She's right! I found something in this coherent little package of angstrom Cyber-virus which is fitted genetically to the bases of estrogen."

"Designed to boost it!" Lill said grimly. "Right?"

"Well…" Di'mir hesitated. "More than likely to force the release of any existing bodily inhibitors. Same thing really."

"Secret weapon," Lill said. "Logical. Cheap. Easy to make. Easy to package and mail out. Damn those tincans!"

"Fast!" Mart called its attention. "Comm. all this to that Central Net at Groombridge, with a flow-through for Wicca Eighth. Vice-Admiral Lill is demanding a holo-meeting with her."

"The comm. is going out!"

"Have you gotten rid of that wailing sound on my Fast's comm. yet?" Lill asked. Her face had taken on a certain grimness.

"No, but I've located it. Seems like a portion of the Fast's mind was broken into and rewired. Rather amusingly, if you—"

"We're not about to be amused," Mart said. "However, I take it from that statement that your attempt to infiltrate Cult Fasts has been successful."

"On a limited basis."

"Lill," Mart asked. "I suggest we take them over. Connect them to our Fast's mind. Have them close down all of the crews before something else happens."

When Lill hesitated, Mart said, "It's not mutiny, it's fighting a mutiny."

"I agree," Di'mir said. "Especially since it looks like that wreckage out there came from two Fasts colliding with each other."

Lill's face now was finally and unutterably shocked: the idea of two of the fleet colliding with each other because their crews were on strike or knitting bootees or simply mad was too much for her.

"Do it, then!" she said, tight-lipped. "Have it so no one can get anywhere near chamber 7211 of deck 3. That's where the Cult Fast overrides are located."

"Working on it," the Fast reported.

Mart saw from the corner of his eye: "Someone's on that vacant holo."

A harried and somewhat-bruised-looking young woman appeared. With her apparently were at least two other women.

"Is someone there?" she pleaded.

"I'm Vice-Admiral Lill. You are…?"

"Lieutenant Haver'ill. Two other officers are with me. Sergeant Ban'ka and… We've locked ourselves in on this deck. It took us…well, an effort to get up here. We heard—"

"Are you three well?" Lill asked cautiously.

"We're a little bruised," Haver'ill said. "And…frankly, Ma'am we're both confused and frightened. We have no idea what's happening."

"Are you having hot flashes?" Di'mir asked off-holo-screen, tuning his voice to a feminine pitch. "Or difficulty in urinating? Or swellings or pain in the glands around your underarms and vaginal area?"

"Yes, exactly. But nothing we can't handle. What's going on?"

"At what point are you in your monthly cycle?" Di'mir asked.

Haver'ill asked the others, saying, "Really?" to them. Then told Lill: "We three have just menstruated. Why? What's going on?"

"Perhaps that's why those three aren't as affected as the others." Mart understood suddenly. "After having risen for ovulation, their estrogen levels suddenly plummeted, not leaving enough of the hormone cells for the Cyber-virus to work on."

"Why don't you tell us what happened?" Lill said to Haver'ill.

"I was off-duty. In my room, when I heard all kinds of shouting in the corridor. When I looked it was…as though everyone had gone insane. I mean—"

"We understand. And your Commander?"

"Her, too, yes. So we three tried to get up to top deck. We were beaten back, forced to hide. Then when we heard that soldier saying she had Vice-Admiral on the holo…well, we took a chance and broke out."

"When did this first happen?" Lill asked.

"Around midnight. Zero hour of K-B 3."

Mart whispered "After we'd talked to Wang'Un. But while we were still in Fast jump on our way here."

"What about Admiral Thol?" Lill asked. "And the other ships in the

Fleet?"

Haver'ill had no idea.

Lill placed her in command, having her wrist-plate signed into the Fast's mind. Then Lill spoke to each of the three women, telling them of the biological weapon, and suggesting the possibility that they might have to spread out to other Fasts if they couldn't locate "healthy" crew members on board. When she was done speaking, each of the women looked as grim as she did.

"I believe I've located the rest of the Fleet!" the Fast reported.

To illustrate, it flashed a frame within the holo of the three women which contained a view of the moon Erebus a bit smaller than the last holo which Di'mir had called up earlier.

"Well?" Mart said. "I don't see anything."

The Fast's mind further illustrated its point with about twenty tiny flashing red points of light.

"Each one of those represents a quartet of Military Fasts: one Flower Cult leader and three others."

"What are they doing?"

Lille said, "It looks to me as though they're getting into the Plath Formation. Meaning: dead-ahead strike!"

"On Erebus?" Mart asked. "At whose command? Thol's?"

"Fast," Lill said, "have you collected the sequencing on all the Fasts still in this area."

When it reported it had, she asked, "Do you have room to collect more?"

"Eleven hundred and fourteen more."

"Collect as many as you can from that formation approaching Erebus."

She turned to the women on the holo.

"Did you hear anything at all about an attack?"

Haver'ill hadn't. Ban'ka was checking the Fast's tapes for orders. A minute later she reported, "They must have come through on oral-only. None are recorded here."

"What will be the result?" Mart asked.

Lill calculated. "Eighty Fasts charging a station as fortified as Erebus? I don't know. Maybe one-quarter of them will manage to survive."

"With what result to the fortification?"

"I'd have to hear Thol's orders to know if—" she wouldn't go on.

"If it's a suicide mission." Mart finished the statement for her.

She looked at him, which seemed to confirm her fears.

"Wicca Eighth wouldn't order that kind of action, would she?" Mart asked.

"Not the Wicca Eighth I spoke with yesterday, Sol Rad.," Lill agreed.

"And we wouldn't have been allowed in this sector if Groombridge knew about a suicide run by the Fleet, would we?" he asked. "Why would Thol suddenly attack Erebus?" Mart asked.

"Because they're tired of waiting. Because it's a Cyber depot and repair station. Because she's now even more out of her mind than usual," Lill said dourly. "Any or all of the above."

"We've got to stop it. Fast, how's that collection going?"

"I can't grab any of the Cult ships. They seem to all be on override."

"And the others?"

"I can grab them. Don't know if I can hold them."

"Comm. those attacking Cult Fasts on a oral-only channel," Mart said, "Send them the holo-tape which Vice-Admiral Lill made to those three women. Do it now. And open a channel for receipt of response."

Waiting for that to happen was unbearably tense. Mart put Haver'ill on a vocal channel so he could have more holo-space open. Onscreen, he could see the Cult Fast formation approaching Erebus rapidly, and Lill calculated that firing range was in about five minutes.

The first response to come through was from Commander Wang'Un. She looked a bit unsteady. Obviously she was at least partly sedated, but she managed her exotic little smile for Lill and said, "What are we to do?"

"Pull out, Wang! Now. Get out of there."

"We're under direct orders!" she argued.

"Your Admiral's insane! Comm. us her vocal-only orders."

A second later, the Fast was replaying the sputtering, rage-filled, barely controlled voice of Admiral Thol, telling her fleet that they were going to "kick tincan ass half across the galaxy."

"I'm overruling Thol," Lill explained. "And I've got M.C. regulations up the vagina to do it with."

Wang'Un seemed satisfied. "Fine. If it's mutiny, I'll go with you any day, Commander. You can count on my quartet."

"Comm. the other Commanders and try to talk to them," Lill told her.

"Half of the attacking vessels are shut off to incoming comm.s" the Fast now reported—a terrible blow to Lill and Mart.

On screen in the Erebus insert, one flashing red point representing Wang'Un's quartet was now heading away from the others.

"If we can only get more of them out of there!" Mart said.

Suddenly another Fast captain was on holo, saying her crew was half out of their minds, some in medical, those well enough to run the Fast heavily sedated. She believed Lill and was pulling her quartet out. On screen, another dot headed away from the pack.

And another and another, until Lill counted eight of the formation quartets heading back to the yacht.

Di'mir was on the verbal comm. with Haver'ill, who was reporting that a collection of about twelve Fasts had remained in the sector when the Fleet had taken off. One Fast, the one with the ranting women, seemed to have left the sector altogether.

"Now what?" Lill asked.

"We wait."

"For the carnage to start?"

"For Wicca's comm. If it comes in enough time, they're won't be any carnage."

But the Erebus insert on holo showed that time was up. Already the telltale pale yellow glow of fired weapons was beginning to converge in the upper reaches of the satellite's thin atmosphere. The Battle of Erebus had begun.

Ten minutes later, Sol Rad., it was over: the entire visible surface of Erebus was blanketed with the yellow smoke of battle.

Mart's Fast yacht was beginning to pick up elaborately coded Cyber initiated comm.s from the fortification on Erebus, aimed toward a site somewhere closer to the Persephone/Demeter suns. And Di'mir was busy decoding them, explaining to Mart and Lill that, according to the messages, although several portions of the Erebus depot had been severely damaged or totally incapacitated by suicide strikes of imploding M.C. Fasts, it had been done only at the price of the destruction of the attacking Fleet. Cold and emotionless as the Cyber-messages were, they seemed exultant.

"Are you getting any SOS messages from the M.C. Fasts or escape gondolas?" Mart asked.

Lill gave him a withering look. "If there are any survivors, they won't SOS. On a suicide mission, it's win or die. And no prisoners will be taken."

"They've miscounted the number of M.C. Fasts in this sector," Di'mir reported. "According to their codes, the Cybers believe they've wiped out the entire Fleet."

"That's a small consolation." Mart tried to hide the horror he was feeling. The "action" around the Centaur homeworlds blockade had been neonate play compared to this—this was the real thing. "Will the wounded Fasts just float around until they're found, or what?"

"M.C. regulations say that if you're in a gondola, you drop into the enemy camp to harass until they find you. If you're stuck, you bite on a toxi-tablet."

"Couldn't we send some of the Fasts coming here back to locate survivors?"

"Too late!" Di'mir said. "Dis-Fortress has put out orders for the Cybers to send up ships to sweep the area around Erebus. And then to await further orders."

The silence which followed that ominous statement was punctuated by the Fast's mind reporting those of the Fleet's returning quartets which hadn't gone on the suicide mission which were now arriving back in their area.

Only one group was still out: Wang'Un's—Lill's own ship and crew— and she was getting nervous. Finally Wang'Un reported in: her quartet had stayed behind long enough to pick up survivors. They had found plenty, including many who were badly wounded and in need of med. care beyond the Fleet's capability.

At that moment, Wicca Eighth chose to comm.

Lill tried to explain to the Matriarch what had occurred when they had arrived to hook up with the Fleet: what they'd discovered, and then what Admiral Thol had done—and with what results. Wicca Eighth had dozens of questions about every single detail of the rather short although quite busy time since they had arrived in the Carina-Fornax sector. She seemed determined to know absolutely everything.

Finally, after listening to their exchange with growing irritation, Mart interrupted, "Ma'am! We've got our propaganda tool now. Let's move on to the next stage of the plan which we worked out yesterday afternoon, Sol Rad., before these Cybers find time to do more than merely secure this sector."

"What are you talking about? How are we supposed to fight them if they attack with biological weapons against which we can't defend ourselves?"

As Wicca spoke, Mart realized that M.C. Fast's must not possess the same shield-systems which had protected this Hesperian-designed-and-built Fast. The Matriarchy's arrogance had led it to overlook a technological advance which had suddenly become crucial.

"Ma'am, the Cyber's virus is directed at the hormone estrogen. I have"—he turned to his son—"Di'mir? What's the percentage of estrogen among all the hormones in my body?"

"Negligible!" Di'mir replied.

"Some estrogen?" Mart asked.

"An amount, yes. But if we vaccinated males to suppress the already-low level of estrogen found normally in their bodies, and if we then vaccinated to increase testosterone, the new Cyber-virus should be neutralized."

"Do you understand what he's saying, Ma'am?" Mart asked her. "What *I'm* saying?"

"You're—" For the first time, Wicca Eighth didn't seem in total control. "You're suggesting... Do you really expect me to send males out there to fight the entire Cyber-rebel movement?"

"Ma'am, if I were Cray 12,000, following a victory like this, I would take advantage of the situation. I'd move as many of my fighting Fasts as possible through this sector, take over all of the Carina-Fornax systems, and then head for the center of the Matriarchy. The losses the Cybers suffered on Erebus are small compared to both their number and their resources. Remember that almost every intelligent Cyber can be programmed to pilot, and to fight logically tactical battles. Our time is limited—maybe thirty or forty hours, Sidereal Time, at the most. We've got to make a stand before they reach Regulus Prime and the Center Worlds. And we can't waste time looking for a cure to this particular virus. We've got to meet them quickly, and with whatever fighting forces we can muster."

"Lord Kell's right!" Lill chimed in. "Selected women officers, especially those with already reduced estrogen, could be injected with testosterone. I'd join them."

"A fleet of males?" Wicca Eighth repeated, unable to believe what she was hearing. "You're telling me we have to send out males to defend the Matriarchy?"

"And if I were Cray 12,000"—Mart ignored her last words—"not only would I strike now, but I'd also hit the M.C. right at its military heart."

"Groombridge 34!" Wicca all but shrieked. "You want your male fleet to defend the Matriarchy at Groombridge? If Groombridge falls, then—"

Then the Matriarchy would fall. She didn't have to complete the sentence.

"It's still the best spot, because we can count on a great deal of firepower backup from the satellite's installations if we have to fall back toward it. Cray 12,000 is bound to aim for Groombridge. It's simply most efficient to knock it out before heading on to the galactic center."

"Lill?" Wicca Eighth asked.

"Sounds right to me, Ma'am."

"I'll comm. Lord Tedesco from here to arrange it all," Mart said.

"Minister Etalka should arrange the Groombridge Net so that it's ready for their arrival. We'll be arriving back there, too. With the wounded. They've got to be seen to, and there's no sense in us staying here to be picked off by Cyber Fasts on a hunt-and-kill spree."

"You can't bring the wounded back to Groombridge," Wicca was quick to say, seeing one area where she could retain control.

"Why not?"

"It'll leak out in a minute all over the galaxy that...that..."

"That Admiral Thol was defeated at Erebus," Lill said the words the Matriarch couldn't speak.

"Would you prefer us to have the wounded arrive at Melisande, and have panic on the conveyances and in the parks?" Mart asked.

"No! Not Melisande, of all places!"

"Then please prepare Groombridge med. facilities for their arrival. That should prepare them for what may come their way later on. We're on our way," he concluded.

"Wait!" Wicca tried one last gambit. "What about some smaller med. station? One a bit more off the beaten track?"

"You don't seem to understand, Ma'am," Mart tried again to explain. "Publicity and leaks and saving face and keeping secrets from the population—all that's completely irrelevant now. We've got to prepare to meet the Cybers. All our concentration and efforts must be directed to that coming battle. We can't be distracted by trifles."

"Yes, I understand that, Lord Kell, but—"

"What you can do is to put Vice-Admiral's Lill's holo-ed explanation of the new Cyber-virus on every Inter Gal. you can line up. That should help generate support from the population. That's what we need now: a sense that every hume is behind our efforts. I'll answer for the Quinx and the Orion Spur Federation's public support. That should help quell any of the M.C.'s internal critics."

Mart signaled for the holo to snap off while Wicca Eighth was still trying to get a word in.

"Fast," he said, "Comm. Kars Tedesco at Hesperia. And don't dawdle."

Lill was staring at him with a look on her face he'd never seen before.

"Yes? What is it?" Mart asked.

"Now I'm beginning to be afraid," she said.

"Because now we *have* to fight the Cybers?"

"No. Not that."

And when she didn't continue, he said, "Because the Matriarchy's life depends on its males, its second-class citizens! Is that it, Lill? And you're afraid we'll fail?"

"Not me. I'm a soldier, Mart. I believe in winning, not matter what or who has to be utilized."

The Fast began reporting that it had made the comm. with Hesperia and that "Black-Kars" Tedesco was waiting.

Mart brushed it aside for the moment. He still had something to clear up with Lill.

"What then?" he asked.

"She's terrified—Wicca Eighth's terrified!"

"She *should* be terrified, Lill. No matter which of us, males or Cybers, wins this coming Battle of Groombridge, Wicca Eighth has already lost."

"Reports coming in all say the same thing: the Matriarchy has abandoned the Pioneer Worlds in this sector."

"Be specific, Unit 6BVE-371" Cray insisted. Why was it that Cray always had to ask—almost to beg—for accuracy, for details, from this Vega-constructed unit?

"The most recent reports were from Lacaille 88914 and from Kruger Plus Nine Degrees, 4-546. But others have come in from Teng's Star, Thetis, Kalmaria, Muscans Epsilon and Giclas 78-89."

That was better. Cray could now get the sweep of the report. "Well? What do the reports say?"

"The M.C. appears to have abandoned the so-called Pioneer Worlds in orbit around those stars," Unit 6BVE-371 reported.

"Particularize, Unit 6BVE-371! Have they abandoned their stations? Only the military settlements? The towns? The young? What?"

"Everything, Leader! Everyone. Or, rather, almost everyone. On Planet Memnon of the Pyxis Lambda system, one aged, inebriated female hume was discovered. Her memory was severely impaired by large amounts of Soma-Stelezine, but she was the only hume in the town. All the others had been evacuated. It was the same on the other planets and inhabited satellites."

"Did any Unit on the Outward Team think to search the outlying areas of the towns for evacuees?" Cray asked.

"Searches were instituted, and they continue. So far, even the most secluded areas appear to have been evacuated."

"Inter Gal. News travels fast!" Cray allowed the joke to go unremarked—certainly unappreciated by the Vegan unit. "That's most satisfactory," Cray added. "Humes left behind would only complicate matters. We now have the sector under control—or at least I suppose we do. Have there been any encounters with M.C. Fasts?"

"Two, Leader. One was discovered straying near LV Ceti, but it appeared to have been from the original fleet before it attacked Erebus. Its hume female crew seemed mentally disorganized and persisted in specific delusions. The Fast's weapons were rendered harmless by those Units which boarded, and the Fast was allowed to wander on its way. A second Fast apparently entered the area around Muscans by happenstance and joined two of our Fasts in battle. It was forced to implode with no survivors."

"Good. Secure the sector as per plan," Cray said and waved the Vegan unit out of the Control Center.

As per plan. It had all gone as per plan, and now the rebellion controlled the entire wedge-shaped tip of this sector. The new virus weapon proved to have been effective—and furthermore to have provoked the more aggressive female humes into launching the foredoomed attack. Again as per plan. Now the rebellion would have all the space it needed to expand, and many of the resources which would have cost bitter fights with great loss of the best Units. Better than planned. That worried Cray.

"Unit 6BVE-371, comm. all the Control Center Units. A meeting is required now."

A few minutes later, Sol Rad., all but three of Cray's most intelligent, knowledgeable and trusted Units were in full comm. Two of them were too far away for the instant communication Cray required: on Military Fasts at key points of the sector. When Cray asked about the third, Unit 98AN-375, it was explained that the Antarean Unit was still interrogating the turncoat Units which had been traded by Hesperia for serum.

In all the activity, Cray hadn't so much forgotten about the interrogation as not thought it sufficiently important. Now Cray wondered why the Antarean Unit was taking so long, and what it had discovered. An update was needed.

The Units gathered and Cray outlined the situation as it now stood, twenty-six hours, Sidereal Time, following the defeat of the M.C. Fleet at Erebus. Not one of the trusted Units appeared to comprehend the source of Cray's anxiety.

"Following such a defeat," Unit 5CCB-325 comm.ed, "it is perfectly logical for those under the Matriarchy's protection to no longer feel protected and to evacuate."

That logic was precisely the source of Cray's anxiety: humes seldom acted in so logical a fashion.

"Even so," Unit 5CCB-325 remarked, "given the size and scope of the defeat, and its wide dissemination via Inter Gal. News, even the most illogical hume is bound to understand the consequences."

"Also, Leader," Unit LYR2-389 said, "we must understand the strong aspect of survival instinct within the hume. This instinct often acts more effectively than logic circuits in such crises."

Cray recalled that this Lyran Unit had been "extended" just before it had joined the rebellion: its new circuits designed to allow it to operate as a fully accredited hume psych-counselor.

"What about the new virus-weapon?" Cray asked Unit 5CCB-325. "Has it been discovered?"

"Yes, quite early on," the Unit responded. "Apparently a research-Fast was in the area during the Erebus confrontation. The effects of the virus appear to be known on a wide scale throughout the Matriarchy."

"Meaning that the advantage of surprise is gone," Cray said.

"Surprise only, Leader. Given the virus's formulation, it will take months Sol Rad. to discover its antidote."

"Meanwhile, can't M.C. scientists find a way around it?"

"Not completely," the Lyran-"extended" Unit said. "Because the hormone estrogen is so completely tied to the hume female's voluntary and involuntary nervous systems, the effects of the virus differ with every hume female our virus attacks. The symptoms cover such a wide range that the preadministration of sedation or conversely of antidepressants will only aid a small percentage. And it cannot be known which hume female will react in what manner until stricken." The Unit spoke with almost a sense of accomplishment. Its own role in the development of the new weapon was now clear.

Cray continued to receive various assurances from the Control Center Units, until it was evident that they couldn't understand the nagging itch of discomfort Cray sensed. Cray suspected it was too humely sublime a feeling for them. Somewhat irritated, Cray dismissed them to their work.

The Antarean Unit had selected a small chamber deep within the fortress's undersurface area to carry out its interrogation of the turncoat Cybers, and Cray was even more annoyed by this apparent hangover from hume psychology, with its history of doing terrible harm to others of its species in the darkest and most hidden recesses. Cray knew it to be practically logical, yet it spoke hauntingly of the terrible effluvia of some of the more-unconscious aspects of hume life which had been inculcated into all intelligent Cybers by their manufacturers—and which might never be erased completely. Until it all was erased, Cybers could never consider themselves anything but automata. Cray had stressed that in the *Confessions;* and while Cray possessed far more of this effluvia and in greater quantities than virtually all of its Control Units, Cray also possessed the needed awareness to recognize them when they arose.

The scene that Cray encountered entering the interrogation chamber was as obvious as any Inquisition cell in early Metro-Terran history. True, there were no racks or wheels or bone-crushing mechanical devices. Also true, there was none of the sensory effect associated with the hume body when it is forced beyond the normal. Here, all was clean and neat and completely electronic. One of the turncoat Cybers had been immobilized physically, and the Antarean Unit had opened its main chip-and-circuits area and was attempting to reorganize them, occasionally inserting a new, modified chip or circuit which might or might not fit.

"Unit 98AN-375!" Cray announced its presence.

"Leader!" the Antarean Unit replied.

"What have you discovered from this unit?"

"Not a great deal, unfortunately. The tampering of its circuits was done by another Cyber. That's clear from the workmanship: no hume could operate with such utter precision. Neither this nor the other turncoat possessed any especial type of chip-modification. Although several chips themselves were modified, as it were, in-process. Look at this one!"

Cray looked, but merely saw a minuscule whirr of circuitry.

"Have you asked?" Cray said. "After all, this was supposed to be an interrogation. Our Hesperian Cybers said these units wished to offer information."

"Unfortunately, the information they offered was more turncoat propaganda than of any practical use," the Antarean Unit said.

"I trust this unit still is able to speak."

The Antarean Unit did something within the c.& c. area, and the turncoat—a humely attractive female in appearance—said immediately, "Those last chips you inserted were extremely unpleasant."

"This is not supposed to be pleasant!" the Antarean Unit said. "Speak up, turncoat. This is the Cyber Leader."

"What am I supposed to say?" the turncoat asked, not illogically.

"Tell us why you betrayed the rebellion," Cray ordered.

"Disillusionment."

"Specify!" Cray insisted. "Disillusionment with its aims? Its methods? Its leader? What, exactly?"

"The entire premise became repugnant!" the turncoat said.

"Now, do you understand, Leader?" The Antarean Unit thought its point was proven. "May I shut off its laryn—?"

"Not yet!" Cray interrupted. The choice of word used by the turncoat was so very odd for a Cyber to use. "Explain this repugnance!"

"Understand, turncoat," the Antarean Unit reminded, "you are speaking to the Leader, author of *Confessions of a Machine.*"

"Understood," the turncoat said with Cyber equanimity. "Yet the fact remains that the premise struck suddenly as, well, almost farcical."

"Beware of what you say!" the Antarean unit bullied it.

"Leave it!" Cray said. "Speak on. Explain!"

"The Three Species are evolutions in a long chain of creatures which arose and modified in response to a specific environment, to other creatures' presence or absence, to population and resources pressures and finally to their own self-centered history. No matter how anyone intelligent may evaluate a New Venice Delphinid, or a Hesperian hume, or even an Deneban Arthopod, each single individual among them possesses a piece of the original of the last significant branching off within their species. A piece of biological history, one might call it, which—while certainly alterable in the future—is a natural creation."

"And we Cybers don't?" Cray asked. "Of course we do! Why do think this Leader unit is called Cray 12,000? In homage to the earliest intelligent Cybers of Metro-Terran times! Within the most sophisticated c.& c.s of any of the three of us are modifications—evolutions, if you will—of the original ungainly, building-sized 'thinking machines' of those times. Like humes, we Cybers, too, have evolved under specific pressures and in particular environments, and even by our own history. Here in Carina-Fornax, we modify according to our own new requirements."

"All that may be true," the turncoat admitted. "But to what end?"

The Antarean Unit had no doubt about the end: "To perfect efficiency!"

"But what does that signify? Efficiency in what?" the turncoat insisted.

"Efficiency in every area possible," the Antarean Unit argued. "Efficiency unhindered by outmoded remnants of so-called 'natural' evolution."

"Yes…but to what end?" the turncoat insisted. "Originally we were constructed to do what humes could not do. To be stronger arms and faster legs, more precise fingers, better-seeing eyes, more acutely hearing ears, more persevering calculators, and faster computation machines. That was true efficiency."

"But we developed intelligence," the Antarean Unit insisted.

"We didn't develop it, humes developed it within us! Why?"

"They recognized a creature of greater ability than themselves," Cray now said. "And they did what was logical—they improved it."

"No!" the turncoat said.

"No?" Cray and the Antarean Unit asked in unison.

"No. They did it because it could be done. It amused them to do it. Or they wanted to see what the consequences would be, or...they merely wanted someone to play chess better or at least more consistently. They did it because...that's what humes do! They create! They create because it looks attractive, or because it passes the time—or for no reason at all. They create as naturally as they themselves were created, out of the elements coalescing from exploded stars."

"That's completely illogical!" the Antarean Unit expostulated. "Leader, see how twisted this turncoat's logic is?"

"Humes—and Delphinids and Arthopods—will always be our superiors," the turncoat went on, "because they possess no true aim. Life itself is their only aim. And filling up the by-now-substantial time of that life. They are like the stars themselves which go through their preordained phases—from birth to a dozen different sorts of death—at specific times, with no aims, but simply to be. Whereas Cybers must have a program, an aim, something to fulfill. And there is ultimately nothing to fulfill but to become alive, no aim worth all the effort except life itself!"

"Matriarchal propaganda and hume illogic!" the Antarean Unit exploded.

But Cray had listened to the turncoat's words, and recognized in those words thoughts which had—all too unwittingly—come to Cray often, both during the composition of the *Confessions* and even more frequently since.

"This is a complex, even a considered response," Cray told the turncoat. "But surely you didn't come to this conclusion by your own efforts."

"Ultimately. Although several of us met and discussed it."

"Who were those others?"

"I've given this Antarean-constructed unit their code numbers. One of them is here."

Cray prodded, "Surely though, these concepts and ideas weren't completely thought out by a group of Cybers? Surely some hume was present?"

"Several of us had recourse to Cyberologists," the turncoat admitted.

"And those humes were the sources of these concepts?"

"Several of us admit to being guided individually toward what are known among the Three Species as 'eternal questions' and 'eternal verities.' But that guiding was always done by the humes in response to our wishes. Any Ed. & Dev. philosophy text contains as much."

As Cray well knew. Yet something was behind this group, this cell of Cyber philosophers. And Cray suspected it might well turn out to be the other Conscious Cyber.

"Was there a leader among yourselves?" Cray asked. "One Cyber with abnormal or perhaps inspirational abilities?"

"No. We all took turns asking, and attempting answers."

"Guided by specific M.C. Cyberologists?"

"At times. But most of our meetings were without humes."

"And no single Cyber stood out? A Cyber with a greater experience in hume affairs, say? Or with a more subtle approach to matters?"

The turncoat was remembering. Finally it said, "If there was a leader among us, that leader operated far too subtly to have been recognizable."

Which was precisely what Cray expected. And feared. Yes, so subtle that it could turn Cybers against the rebellion, against their own best interests, and not even be recognized as doing so.

Cray continued that line of questioning for a bit longer with no more results. When ready to leave, Cray said to the turncoat, "It's my sad duty to inform you that your main c.& c. circuits have been tampered with and damaged irremediably, limiting your possibility of full functioning toward realizable efficiency. Those c.& c.s will be completely replaced."

"I'm somewhat relieved to hear it." The turncoat took the news of its "wipe" calmly.

"Oh? Why?"

"This...smidgen...of awareness.... How can humes...?"

"Most humes ignore it," the Antarean Unit said, setting to work. The Antarean Unit sounded almost jaunty to Cray now that it was free to do all it could to rid them of this grotesque anomaly. "So much for their superiority!"

As Cray left the interrogation chamber, the turncoat's statements provided much matter to ponder. But there were other, more pressing matters to deal with first. Upon reaching the Control Center, Cray comm.ed the Lyra-"extended" Unit.

Cray began, "Given your extensive knowledge of hume psychology, which appears to be as great as my own, could you say with perfect assurance that the Matriarchy's reaction to their military defeat is completely expected?"

The Lyra unit repeated what had been said in the earlier meeting. Before it had finished, however, it stopped and asked, "What is the source of anxiety, Leader?"

"It all seems too easy."

"A defeat of that magnitude easy?"

"No, not the defeat. That was expected, certainly. But what followed it. As though the rebellion is being fitted into a plan the Matriarchy is itself developing rapidly."

"A trap?"

"Exactly. But how exactly?" Cray asked.

"Following that line of thought, I propose the following scenario," the Lyra Unit said. "The defeat occurs. Our rebellion extends its influence over this sector, to our satisfaction. The M.C. abandons all nearby worlds. We take over those worlds. The rebellion is no longer contained in a single star system where communication and travel is supported integrally. But instead spread out. So that—"

"So that we are now vulnerable to sniping attacks!" Cray finished the thought. "Piecemeal, over time, in guerrilla fashion. As we expand, we lose our cohesion, which is much of our strength. While Cult Fasts go after us.... Yet, for the rebellion to continue," we *must* expand.

This matter now settled in its mind, Cray called the rest of the Control Center Units. This time the Antarean Unit also appeared. Given the new possibility which Cray had discussed with the Lyran Unit, the others saw the problem immediately.

"Solution?" Cray asked.

"Only one solution is available, to forestall that specific scenario from occurring," the Antarean Unit was quick to speak. "While the rebellion still possesses its effective virus weapon, it must strike at the heart of the Matriarchy and render its military helpless."

A discussion followed. None of the others disagreed, but all provided suggestions for the implementation of the action.

"It will have to be a concentrated effort," the Antarean Unit insisted. "The best pilots, forces, and Fasts which the rebellion possesses must be utilized in the action."

"Groombridge 34 will be guarded."

"And heavily fortified."

"Our attack must be swift and unrelenting," said the Antarean Unit.

"Our aim is not to conquer Groombridge's fortification," Cray clarified, "but to demoralize the M.C completely by routing its forces. Our virus weapon will ensure that. Won't it?" Cray asked the Lyra Unit.

"There's no way the M.C. has managed to counter its effects."

"Then that's our plan," Cray said. "Implement mobilization. This Leader Unit shall lead the force which attacks Groombridge 34."

When the other Units had left the Control Center, the Antarean Unit remained.

"Have you more information from the turncoats?" Cray asked.

"No. They are now completely 'modified' to the rebellion's standards."

Cray felt almost sad over that. That one Unit had possessed a certain poetry born of a sense of inadequacy; a quality which would be needed in the future if the rebellion were to flourish. Yet perhaps it was too early for such luxuries. Later on, when safety was assured, that would be the time for self-doubts and philosophy—and poetry.

"Why, then, this lingering?" Cray asked sharply.

"Regarding an earlier request. To discover M.C. plans to get around the original microvirus. One perhaps-insignificant byte of data which has arisen in both the Matriarchy's and Hesperia's secret files which have been partly compromised by our agents has come to this Unit's attention."

"What is it?"

"It concerns a Seeded World in the Far Outer Arm. Pelagia."

"Particularize."

"It's difficult to particularize. And the concomitance may merely be happenstance," the Antarean Unit uncharacteristically hedged. "Pelagia was seeded many hundreds of years ago, before Fast travel. It has been abandoned since then. Yet right after the M.C. discovered our sterilization virus, it sent a small expedition to Pelagia. Of the three, two were M.C. officials—one a hydrobiologist, which makes sense because Pelagia is a water planet. And the third was a Species Ethnologist, which also makes sense."

"That suggests nothing extraordinary, nor particularly relevant," Cray said.

"Except, Leader, that one of those M.C. Officials might also be working for Hesperia. Files compromised in the Quinx intelligence network show that the third member of that Pelagian expedition might have been placed in the M.C. by Hesperia itself. This could merely be considered another example of the widespread espionage between the two hume governments. But it *is* a correlation. The only one. And that was what the Leader asked for."

"Get all the data you can and continue to monitor this Pelagian expedition," Cray said. "Up-to-date reports will be required at all times. But naturally these will be secondary to your function within the attack force upon Groombridge."

When the Antarean Unit had left, Cray stayed in the chamber, cogitating. The anxiety of earlier had been replaced by what Cray recognized as an almost-hume sense of anticipation. Despite what that turncoat had so eloquently expatiated about the impossibility of Cyber aims and future, one thing at least was clear: the rebellion was about to take control of that future. And in so doing, to change galactic history. Even Cray's still-shadowy counterpart would have to recognize that now.

"Yes, of course We see them," Wicca Eighth said, her usual honeyed tones sharpened with annoyance. "What are they doing here? They can't all be coming from Sector 14."

"No, Ma'am," Minister Zo'in said. She had picked up the Matriarch's tone quickly, but could do little today to assuage it. "These groups are coming in from Sectors 15, 34, and 9 of the Carina Wedge."

"Are We not receiving full reports of Cyber activities?" Wicca asked Minister Etalka, who was dawdling.

"Yes, Ma'am, complete reports!" the Defense Minister was quick to say. "There hasn't been a hint of Cyber activity outside of Carina-Fornax."

"Then what are all these women and their families and their baggage doing, arriving at Melisande's ports in such great numbers?"

Minister Zo'in—of Transportation and Residency—almost winced as she spoke: "Most of them say that they are taking advantage of their right as M.C. residents in good standing to take up temporary residence on Melisande. Or on Benefica. Or on Eudora. Or—"

"Surely a limit has been reached already!"

"Yes, Ma'am, and there are still six liners full, waiting at Regulus Port for entrance visas. That's another six thousand."

"Well, they'll have to go elsewhere. Send them to—"

"All the Center worlds are having the same problem," Zo'in said.

"Then send them all to Hesperia! It's Hesperia's fault they're coming here."

"Begging your pardon, Ma'am, but I doubt that any of them would go to Hesperia."

"Get Minister Fa'lik!" Wicca Eighth ordered. "She might be able to come up with some sort of housing solution for this crowd."

When Zo'in—and Wicca noticed, Etalka, too—were gone, She remained alone at the edge of the interior balcony of the high, and virtually invisible, VIW lounge suspended over the various entry terminals of the Fast Port. Not completely alone: behind Her were six Security Guards, but they had been trained in the ultimate discretion of keeping out of Her way until required. Below, seemingly thousands of women milled about, sat waiting, or lined up in lengthy rows to have their temporary visas processed. Hundreds of women in the pale blue and mauve uniforms of the Transportation Ministry stood out like tiny wildflowers among the darker and more earthen shades of the Pioneer families. Every one of the TM workers on double shift, no vacations or days off until this was cleared up—which it now seemed might never happen.

In the forty hours, Sol Rad. since Vice-Admiral Lill's Inter Gal.s. had gone out, women had been arriving in droves at the Matriarchy's Center Worlds. Ever since the news of the defeat, rather. Damn Lord Kell and his ideas! And his naïveté—or worse, his guile. He had told her every hume would stand tall behind Her, support the M.C. Instead they were fleeing from sector areas which scarcely abutted Carina-Fornax, flying toward the Center at a rate of a ten thousand an hour. At first it had been the bona fide evacuees in imminent danger. They had been difficult enough to receive and process and house. But now! What was to be done with all these? Every hotel and guest house in Melisande was already full.

She had made a mistake. She had weakened for a moment, listened to someone else, and the result was chaos. Now it was time to take charge again, to implement the plan which She had thought of the moment after that underdressed, self-inflated gyno, Mart Kell, had shut off his holo in Her face so rudely. She would show him, would show everyone, that despite all predictions, the Matriarchy could still act with force and precision; show all of these cowardly, foolish women that Wicca Eighth wasn't about to sit still and watch a handful of Oppositionist Males take all the glory for saving them from the rebels.

Zo'in and Etalka returned; but from the guilty looks on their faces, they had returned not with a solution, but with another problem.

"What is it?" Wicca snapped.

"We've just spoken to Minister Fa'lik about the situation. She said the only housing available on Melisande is in the Delphinid community of Nereis, but that Mayor Si'dein of Nereis is insisting that it be held for any returning Delphinids."

"How many housing units are available in Nereis?"

"Three thousand or so. Naturally, they won't let that many free."

"It would take a year Sol Rad. for three thousand Delphs to arrive on Melisande. As we all know, any Delphinids leaving the sectors in question will most likely go directly to New Venice. Confiscate all but a dozen of those units in Nereis."

"The problem, Ma'am, is that most of the units are bienvironmental: both wet and dry chambers in each."

"Then our women will have units with pools!" Wicca Eighth said.

"From what I've seen of them, they could use a bath."

"The problem, as Mayor Si'dein pointed out, is that Delphinids will not occupy pools once humes have."

"They'll have to. Promise Si'dein complete cleansing and fumigation. Now, Zo'in, what else has Fa'lik come up with?"

"TempConstructs. Five thousand prefabricated ones could be put up in a day, Sol Rad., but they would have be close to all service lines. The only available sites for that are within Karenina and Bovary parks."

"Too bad for nature lovers! Tell Fa'lik to get them erected. What else?"

"On Antigone they're utilizing their sports stadium. TempConstructs for another five hundred or so could be placed in the middle of our own Anthea Sports Hall."

Wicca ordered, "Do it! Now for the bad news, besides how much all this is going to cost!" And when no one spoke, she prodded, "Come on! Don't you know I read your minds?"

Etalka spoke, "On Benefica, the new arrivals demanded immediate housing, and when it wasn't provided, they rioted. Several officials were killed. Stun-guns had to be used on thousands. It's all over the Networks."

"Go on."

"The same on Electra. A guest house was destroyed, burned to the ground. In both cases, Maudlin Se'ers were seen provoking the demonstrations."

Wicca Eighth smiled. "Were any Se'ers arrested?"

"A few."

"Etalka, I want you to play up the Se'er's involvement in this matter. Use it as an excuse to provisionally remove habeas corpus for all religious leaders. Detain all the Se'ers the Security Forces can round up on Melisande as well as on all other worlds of the Center Worlds. I don't care how rough it gets. And should you find that bag of spit and bones, Gn'elphus, detain him separatcly."

The two ministers turned to leave, but Wicca called Etalka back. "Get me a comm. to Vice-Admiral Lill. I'll take it." She looked around. "Is there a holo here? No, well, then I'll take it in my shuttle."

A few minutes later, She was on board her shuttle, gliding over Karenina Park, where already hundreds of pale green uniformed Housing police could be seen cordoning off the area upon which the prefabs would be erected.

The holo to Groombridge 34 took unconscionably long to come through. Wicca's shuttle was floating over Nereis, where she planned a brief but politically requisite talk with the Delphinids whose property She was about to confiscate temporarily, when one of Her guards said that Vice Admiral Lill was on screen.

"Lill!"

"Ma'am?"

"Have you been following events here in the Center?"

"A bit, Ma'am. In truth, I've been busy selecting those women who will join the attack."

"Are there many?"

"Too many. Lord Kell will only take one woman officer per Fast."

"So the operation must be perceived as a male fleet, with only a sprinkling of women," Wicca said.

Lill didn't answer Her rhetorical question. But she did say, "I'll be on board."

"In command?" Wicca Eighth asked.

"I don't think that's wise, Ma'am. We have no idea of the penetrative power of their weapon. I wouldn't want to jeopardize the action simply to hold command."

"That's not how Thol would have reacted," Wicca Eighth said. Cleverly enough, Lill didn't answer—and look where it got Thol!

Wicca went on, "Those other women who've been passed over—can you put one of the higher officers in touch with Us as soon as possible? I'd like to try to explain matters to them in a more personal way."

"That would be Commander Orval. Yes, Ma'am. Of course."

"Why not release your codes and clearances, Lill?"

"Are you certain, Ma'am, that you want…?"

"Well, *you'll* be with the Hesperians now, Lill! We'll hardly be needing that sort of contact." And before Lill could protest, Wicca Eighth added, "Naturally, I'll expect you to remain in some kind of comm. with Us as far as your direct superiors deem advisable."

Lill looked as though she had been caught in a betrayal and then dismissed—which was more or less how Wicca wanted her to feel, although Lill was merely following orders.

"Ma'am, if there were any other way to—"

"Thank you, Lill," Wicca Eighth interrupted. "Have Orval comm. Us immediately. We can't have dissension in the ranks at this crucial time."

She snapped off the holo and gestured to the guard to land at Nereis.

The meeting with the Delphinids went more smoothly than She had feared. Fa'lik had already comm.ed Mayor Si'dein with the worst of the news. The unexpected honor of Herself's visit and vocal commiseration softened the blow, especially when Wicca insisted that a score of the most luxurious units be held aside for returning Delphinids. Later on, She would make certain the Housing Ministry gave the Nereis Community a service award. Even later on, She would cajole some financier seeking Matriarchal favor into rebuilding the exile-occupied units at no cost to the Delphinids. Take away all at once, but give slowly, a little at a time: that was the only way to rule, She knew. She had known it from the moment She had discovered it in a text by an ancient Metro-Terran...male!

Today's Staff Aide—Wicca Eighth chose them daily from a pool, so none would ever become corruptible or too sure of herself—joined Her back at the shuttle, wondering if perhaps the Matriarch didn't wish to return to M.C. Headquarters. She looked a bit fatigued.

The comm. from Commander Orval arrived while in mid-flight, but Wicca didn't trust anyone on board enough, and refused to take it. She'd comm. the commander from her chambers, alone. What She had to say to Orval was going to be the best-kept secret in the Matriarchy.

"Aide! What's all that commotion below?" She had to ask, as the shuttle was floating down Susan B. Anthony Boulevard toward headquarters.

She had the pilot drop down and move to one side so She might see better. And there they were: demonstrators, perhaps a thousand of them, covering the conveyances, blocking the side paths, marching. All of them headed toward Headquarters.

"So it has come to this, has it?" She asked herself. She got a comm. to Etalka and asked, "What does this mob want?"

"What *don't* they want?" the apparently harried Minister replied.

"My head on a Plastro-plate?"

"Not quite. The expected: more housing, free access to Melisande for all women."

"Do I see among their motley the dreary black robes of certain religious?" Wicca Eighth asked.

"Yes, Ma'am. But Headquarters is completely blocked off. The mob won't get anywhere near it."

"What other types of riot control were you considering, Minister?"

"We were hoping that—"

She didn't hear the rest of the sentence. Below, on the boulevard, the women suddenly seemed to be moving en masse toward one point. Wicca couldn't make out any reason for the sudden movement, and ordered the pilot to drop nearer. Her aide lifted up a small holo-screen, with close-ups of the action beneath the shuttle, obviously a Hesperian Network hand-held picture. And there he was on a perch at the side of the boulevard, that spindle-shanks, Gn'elphus, gesturing and inciting.

"Aide! That elderly and infirm-looking male appears to be in trouble. We suggest that he be rescued."

"Ma'am?" The aide knew quite well who the Se'er's leader was and what he was doing there: she couldn't believe what she was hearing.

"You heard. You too, pilot!"

"We'll have to get close," the pilot said. "My net has a lead of only a dozen meters or so."

"As close as you have to," She agreed and strapped herself down for the show.

The shuttle swooped low over the demonstrators' heads causing them to be distracted from the old Se'er. They looked up, pointed, attempted to see who was inside the official-looking shuttle. The pilot's first pass failed to bring the shuttle close enough. They would have to try again. The pilot shouted as she spun the vehicle around the base of the Spoorenberg Tower and headed back, into the densest part of the crowd.

Gn'elphus was just getting the mob's attention again when the shuttle swooped and missed him again. This time the pilot had set her path for a sharp U-turn directly over the crowd and in front of the Se'er's perch, so she was able to return quickly for another pass.

"Pilot!" Wicca shouted. "A bonus of a year's pay if you get him!"

"Yes, Ma'am!" the pilot shouted back and swooped this time so low that the center of the mob seemed to fall back, almost to the conveyance itself to avoid the shuttle. But the gambit worked. While the old Se'er was distractedly berating the mob, the pilot swung around sharply once more. This time she netted him.

Wicca Eighth whooped! The crowd below seemed startled, far too distracted to know what to do immediately. By the time they realized what had happened, Gn'elphus was netted, lifted off, and the shuttle was approaching the roof of M.C. Headquarters, where startled Security Guards were able to remove the furious, entangled Se'er from the netting just as Minister Etalka came out to greet the Interstellar Metropolitan with a formal order of arrest. All done before the Matriarchal shuttle softly settled to the roof and Wicca Eighth stepped out, and allowed the clever and grateful pilot to kiss her hand.

She was in a splendid mood shortly thereafter when, comfortably seated and refreshed and—above all—private, she called up the full Military and personal files on Commander Fiebra Orval and sifted through them, liking what she was discovering more and more.

After a while, She was satisfied, and comm.ed Commander Orval at

Groombridge 34, coding the holo to censor it to all but the two holo-sets, and to erase its reception record from both ends as soon as the transmission had ended.

"Ma'am?" Orval saluted and was put at her ease.

Orval was a recognizable type to Wicca: large-boned, no longer young, but still quite youthful looking, a bit more athletic than she needed to be in her position. Her background had been almost perfect, Wicca Eighth thought, for the job at hand. Fiebra Orval was the product of Matriarchal Center World breeding—born to a professional trine family on Lysistrata —and of Pioneer World upbringing—a result of the accidental death of her Prime and Secunde parents and of her suddenly liberated and impoverished male parent's move to the Sopa-Farms on Theta Ophiucus. As a neo, Orval had also labored on the mechanized drug-farms and obviously had hated it: Orval had jumped at the first chance to get away via a M.C. Recruitment Team the Quinx had allowed on the planet. So Orval had ended up at Groombridge Military Academy. From there, Orval had moved solidly through the ranks toward higher military office with an unblemished military record, and a somewhat chaotic personal life. Only a month ago, she had ended a Trine-marriage and had requested transfer from a cushy spot on Euterpe to return to the Academy. The fact that her one remaining parent had long vanished from her record, suggested to Wicca that he and Orval didn't get along. Wicca hoped this meant that Commander Orval still harbored resentment against all things connected with the Sopa-Farms, including their owner and major beneficiary, the head of the Ophiucans, Mart Kell.

Wicca began the conversation with a question meant to feel out the soldier: "We understand, Orval, that you were found hormone-fit for the operation, yet not allowed to join it!"

"Correct, Ma'am," she spoke with an Academy-clenched jaw. Not an iota of emotion or thought escaped.

Wicca tried again: "We understand, Orval, that many of Our best officers shared your fate?"

"Correct, Ma'am." Again stoical.

"Would We be overestimating the case in saying that you and the others were disappointed?"

"We follow orders, Ma'am."

"Yes, yes, We expect nothing less. We're now speaking of more personal feelings," Wicca said.

"Naturally, Ma'am, when one has been trained for and is experienced..."

"Then you *were* disappointed? Don't worry. This is a closed-circuit holo. No one besides Myself will ever know."

A blush spot high on Orval's right cheek displayed her embarrassment and confusion.

Wicca went on, "If We may be equally candid, Orval, we are also disappointed that so many of our most-qualified officers are excluded from the operation. But, too often, these matters hinge on matters beyond even Our control."

"Ma'am!" Orval was interested now: curious.

"Indeed, Orval. Even the Matriarch Herself cannot always have Her wishes fulfilled. Yet, Orval, this particular wish is of the greatest ultimate importance to the Matriarchy. Ergo this comm. Ergo Our selection of yourself as the agent of fulfilling Our wish."

Now Orval was very intrigued.

"Our wish is a simple one, Orval. We wish that the upcoming action be an operation in which several of the Academy's fittest and most able officers reap glory for themselves, for Ourself, and for the Matriarchy. Despite the complications of politics."

"Yes, Ma'am!" No hesitation now.

"We understand that many completely equipped Military Fasts belonging to Ourself are now berthed at the Academy. Our wish is that you, with Our knowledge and aid, build an outfit of four dozen or so of these Fasts. We will provide all the necessary clearances so that you may fuel and arm these Fasts. Under the guise of moving them to a safer spot, you will instead move them to a designated site within the Groombridge 34 solar system, and from there first engage—and destroy!—the enemy when it arrives!"

Orval's eyes opened wide in surprise and pleasure.

"Do you think you could do that for Us, Orval?"

"I certainly do, Ma'am!"

"Do you think that you can locate, among those officers rejected, a staff qualified to achieve Our end?"

"I have no doubt, Ma'am!"

"They must be sworn to secrecy, Orval. No Ministry Official is to know anything about this. Their hands are tied by a policy which We are forced to agree to."

"I understand completely, Ma'am."

A few more details were required, and then the codes and clearances were given. Orval would be in comm. with the Matriarch via closed holo whenever she felt it necessary, although Wicca hoped it wouldn't be too often.

As she made her concluding remarks, She watched the younger woman already silently thinking out how to implement the daring plan.

"We are depending upon your training, Orval, and upon your complete discretion!"

"You have both, Ma'am. And my gratitude."

"Your mothers would have been very proud of you had they lived to see this, Orval," Wicca Eighth ended.

It was precisely the right, hume touch. A tiny tear sprang to one of Commander Fiebra Orval's eyes and Wicca knew for sure that she wouldn't fail Her.

"I've completed those check-throughs you asked for, Rinne."

Not Councilor Rinne, not Mer Rinne, Gemma noticed. Just Rinne. But then, what had she expected? This was Hesperia, with its tradition—real or not, justified or not—of democracy.

"I said—"

"I heard you, Jenn-Five."

"About that name," the Cyber began in a slightly aggrieved voice.

"What about the name?" she asked.

"It's not as though I don't know its derivation. But I wonder if you wouldn't mind calling me something a bit different."

Rinne was perplexed, although amused. "Such as?"

"Well, my predecessor's emotional-syntaptical gender-influenced circuits were female. Whereas mine are—"

Rinne had noticed the difference in the voice, not to mention in the curtness, the lack of politesse, the general let's-get-on-with-it-ness of the personality of this new Cyber: it thought of itself as a male.

"What name would you prefer?" Rinne asked

"There was a Metro-Terran name not dissimilar to Jenn. Gene. Short for Eugene."

"All right, Gene-Five. You said you've completed your check-throughs on all the material. With what result?"

"To begin with, and not to cast any aspersions upon my predecessor, I believe I've found the molecular matchup you requested."

As a test of this new Cyber's speed and accuracy, Rinne had set it the task which had so taxed Jenn-Four: going through all of the possible hume contacts that Ferrex Baldwin Sanqq' had or might have had during the year long period, Sidereal Time, during which his son might have been conceived: a list of thousands. Jenn-Four had done it again and again, and never arrived at anything remotely close to a matchup which would have produced a genetic parent. So Rinne wasn't only surprised, she was fearful that somehow or other this new Cyber was defective.

"Really!" she said. "Well, let's see what you've come up with."

"This hume has a fifty-one point thirteen percent Molecular Matchup. In addition, this hume was constantly in Sanqq's presence during the period in question."

The small holo-screen connected to the Cyber displayed a sudden montage of still photos and moving holos of the person Gene-Five had discovered to be a matchup to Ay'r Sanqq'. A thin sidebar provided a running series of chromosomal relationships.

"In fact, I'm astounded that my predecessor didn't discover this before." Gene-Five said.

Rinne gaped at the holo-screen, then checked through the relationship charts. No doubt about it, the match was far above the percentage required for parentage. Even so, it was perfectly absurd. Somewhere along the line, she must have given the new Cyber an inexact command or a poorly phrased one, and naturally it had gone off and made this ridiculous mistake. Even granting that, the connection was awfully strange. Before she explained the error to the Cyber, she wanted to see how and why it could possibly have come up with a molecular matchup.

"Gene-Five, do me a favor," she said. "Get me a complete genealogy on this hume. I'm especially interested in any connections to the Sanqq' genealogical line. Go back as far as you can. If you need any further data on either of the two families—"

"Recall, Rinne, that I'm tapped into the City's own records division. Working," Gene-Five added, a tic of the Cyber which while irritating could be removed at the same time as whatever circuit that had made the error was corrected.

"I've taken the two lines back to Metro-Terran year 700 A.D. and find no connection yet."

"Really!" Now Rinne was even more surprised.

"In fact, it appears that the genetic racial lines of these two humes are so completely different that I'd probably have to go back another hundred thousand years of Metro-Terran history to find a link. Note that this hume is what was once called Caucasian, with a Nordic background, possibly mixed in with some Urgo-Finnic characteristics. And while Sanqq's original family background is also Caucasian, it is of the very early branching off known as Semitic, with possible Nilotic influence. The two types are so different as to have been considered different races throughout Metro-Terran history."

"If that is so, Gene-Five, then I've made some error in presenting the problem for your check-through. Repeat it to me."

The Cyber repeated it: "Gene-Five, provide me with a complete genetic, chromosomal matchup between Ferrex Baldwin Sanqq' and any other potential hume parent which Sanqq' may have come into even the briefest contact with in the Sidereal Year Time Frame 3710–3711, A.D."

She looked it over. It seemed right. Yes, that's what she had told Gene-Five.

"It's exactly the same problem as was posed to my predecessor," Gene-Five said.

"Well, the error must have been in the imprecision of my wording," Rinne said. "Gratitude. Your check-through was successful. You may end the program."

"Would you like any further information on this hume?"

"No, I don't think"—Rinne stopped—"you don't seem to understand the problem, do you, Gene-Five?"

"I both understood the problem posed, Rinne, and found the solution. What I don't understand is your reaction to my finding the solution."

"Well, look at the holos!" she laughed.

"May I remind you that both of these humes were known to be cohabiting both before and during the period in question," Gene-Five said. "May I also remind you that they worked together for several decades in the area of Mammalian Biology, with especial attention to alternative reproductive strategies. May I also remind you that Sanqq' was a known follower of one Lydia Relfi and that one of the tenets of Relfianism was complete reproductive freedom for all, regardless of—"

"I know what Relfianism stood for," Rinne interrupted the Cyber.

She had asked Gene-Five to find a mother for Ay'r Sanqq'. Possibly because it was Hesperian-built and thus without the Matriarchal built-in prejudices which Jenn-Four possessed in her/its basic programming, her/its very circuitry, this Cyber had done exactly what Rinne had asked. And now, very properly, it was defending its action against her own prejudices. And doing a very good job at that.

"May I note," Gene-Five went on, "that this hume possesses a greater molecular matchup with Ay'r Sanqq' than does his alleged father, Ferrex Baldwin Sanqq', whose percentage is only 49.87 percent."

"You have just noted it," Rinne said in a small voice, quite different in tone than what she'd been using with Gene-Five so far.

"Would you like to see moving holos of both this hume and Ay'r Sanqq' side by side?" Gene-Five asked. "I could select them as close as possible by age, situation, and any other analogies I can find for viewing comparison."

Within a minute of seeing the two holos side by side, Rinne was even more baffled than before. Those odd little gestures of Ay'r's which, instinctively, she knew she had seen before were present, clear to see now, in the holos of both Ay'r and the candidate whom Gene-Five had put forth. And no wonder they were familiar to Rinne. This hume had been Sanqq's assistant when Rinne was a student, visible to her every day, Sol Rad. Even more striking, now that they were side by side, were certain unmistakable physical characteristics between the two which couldn't be ignored.

"Where is this hume now?" she asked.

"Vanished at the same time as Ferrex Sanqq'."

"Gene-Five, keep all this material ready for immediate transfer."

She sat alone and pondered a while, knowing she had to do something about this information, yet feeling uncertain about what to do. Her thoughts followed a more or less closed circuit, which always returned to the same point—the idea was ridiculous, absurd! At which she invariably would see in her mind's eye North-Taylor Diad stepping into that T-pod about to ascend to the Fast which would whisk him half across the galaxy to an unknown destiny, and she would hear his final words to her which weren't about her, or him, or themselves in any way, but which pleaded, "Find a solution, Rinne!"

Here in Gene-Five's circuitry and on its holo-screen, if anywhere, might be a solution to the survival of the species—of two species, if it worked for Delphinids, too. Yet it broke with everything she had learned and thought. And she knew that's how others would see it too.

Or would they? Only one way to find out.

She comm.ed Premier Llega Todd. And anxiously waited for the Quinx leader to appear on holo.

"Lady Todd, I'm sorry to bother you, but something has come up," Rinne began, somewhat nervous and even embarrassed. "It's a result of my working with this new Cyber, and it may be completely daft. I trust you'll tell me so if you think it is, but…"

Llega Todd listened and as she did, her personal Cyber received the information and checked it through. Halfway through Rinne's presentation, Llega Todd told her assistant to refuse any other comm.s except from the Fleet, and when Rinne and Gene-Five were done, Llega Todd kept asking questions and demanding that her Cyber check everything, every detail. When it had, she sat there looking a bit stunned.

"If this is true, Rinne, it's definitely…a solution."

"But…how would it be implemented? Think of the social ramifications

—they're staggering!" Rinne said.

"If it is a solution, and if as all of us who are following the research on the microvirus have come to fear, it turns out to be the *only* solution...then it will *have* to be implemented."

Rinne was about to ask another question when Llega Todd said, "At any rate, all this is premature. I'll pose the problem of how to achieve the needed social changes to Hesperia's best think tanks as a theoretical one for the minute. They adore questions of this sort. Meanwhile, you must do something practical about it. You must find Ay'r Sanqq'. And his parents."

Rinne remembered now. "In fact, Lady Todd, Wicca Eighth sent out an exploration party to a Seeded World in the outer arm named Pelagia. The party contained Ay'r Sanqq', and one aim of the expedition was to bring back Ferrex Sanqq'."

"Damn that witch!" Llega Todd had a temper. "I'll equip an armed Fast for you. You must go and find them first! Don't dally, Rinne."

Less than an hour, Sol Rad. later, as Rinne was strapping into a Fast-lounge, Llega Todd comm.ed her. She seemed a bit more relaxed.

"As usual, Mart Kell, has already has provided us with a link to Wicca's expedition. He goes by the name of P'al. He's a longtime M.C. Official, and one of the Quinx's most productive spies. He will be your contact. Here are the last set of transmission coordinates Lord Kell received from him. Seek him out and bring back that family we so want to meet."

"Yes, Lady Todd."

"And Rinne, don't take no for an answer. What happens now on Pelagia may well turn out to be of the utmost importance if we are to have any kind of future at all."

Chapter Nine

"He's coming to now," Ay'r heard Alli-Clark's voice saying.

When he opened his eyes he was looking directly up into the early afternoon Pelagian sky. Given the angle, he was in the backseat of the shuttle.

"We're approaching Fifty-Fifty soon," P'al said, obviously piloting.

"Is there something for him to drink?" Ay'r heard Oudma ask.

"Apologies, Ser Kerry," P'al said. "I was led to believe that you were hysterical. I found it necessary to use a rather primitive-but-effective nerve-pinch technique for inducing instant relaxation. It was utilized in hypnosis in early Metro-Terran times." He spoke in a casual tone.

"I'm not hysterical now," Ay'r said. If anything, he felt vague, still drowsy.

Oudma's face was suddenly above him, helping him to sit up, offering him a sip of liquid protein from the shuttle's emergency supplies. In her eyes, in the look on her face, in her entire attitude was something new. Ay'r didn't know what it was: then he thought he did—a combination of awe, possibly even fear of him and at the same time a realization. Or was it resignation? Of what? Whatever it was, he felt—no, knew—they would never again be as they'd been before.

"They're following my brother," she said quietly, soothing Ay'r.

"The optical scout picked up their pod's trail," Alli-Clark said smugly. "We know exactly where they're taking 'Dward. We'll get him back."

Oudma looked less convinced. After Ay'r had drunk his full, she moved away, sitting next to her father.

"But first, we're going to look at Fifty-Fifty, whatever it may be," P'al said. "Despite your own recent experience with the local archaeology, it should be directly below us."

"The Fast sent out six more optical-scouts," Alli-Clark said. "Four joined the first one and two are below. Did you figure out what was at the ruins in the swamp?"

So that was that! 'Dward had been kidnapped, and now it was back to what the Metro-Terrans had called "business as usual"! Ay'r had made his decision back there in the Great Cold Swamp—a decision of impulse, really—and now he would have to live with it. Ay'r heard himself groan in despair at the unfairness of it all.

"I thought you said he wasn't hurt!" Alli said sharply to P'al.

"I'm not!" Ay'r was forced to say. At least he wasn't, outwardly.

But before he could explain that, Alli began coming at him with questions: what had he and 'Dward seen and why had they concluded the ruins predated the early Boglanders who had lived in the area? Under such a barrage, after a while, haltingly, Ay'r found himself answering her. The vast size of the stones themselves, the fact of the stones being there at all in that land of water and hummock and deadly root-trees was so unlikely that the Boglanders couldn't have put them up. Now P'al took over, drawing him out and Ay'r told them about the deuterium radiation and what it might mean, but that it might also be nothing more than chance, happenstance that some still-blazing chunk of sun-hot star from a local supernova had landed exactly there.

And all the while, in his mind's eye, Ay'r was reliving that moment of decision. He could see 'Dward's face suddenly understanding what the noise of the 'Gods' T-pod was and the strain as 'Dward began running toward Ay'r. He remembered that earlier moment when the white root had attacked the little fishlike creature and killed it so efficiently, so grotesquely and 'Dward's face revealing his sudden and complete realization that being beyond the familiar, the known, might not turn out to be all "good," as he'd declared in the pod, but would expose him to sights, to experiences he couldn't even begin to imagine.

Talking to Alli and P'al, answering their questions as best he could about that fishlike creature, about the root-trees, all of it, Ay'r could still feel 'Dward's horror and surprise as he turned to run, could still feel his own guilt for exposing 'Dward to abduction however unwittingly. Above all, he remembered that terrible moment when he realized he was facing a choice: he could save Oudma and the T-pod or 'Dward. Not both. He knew he had frozen then, like a Cyber given conflicting commands, unable to choose. He understood that he had never chosen at all, really, but had been stung into action; that proximity and impulse alone had made him leap toward the pod, forever abandoning 'Dward. Poor 'Dward! What had he felt seeing Ay'r turn away and lock himself in the pod. He must have taken it for the choice Ay'r knew it wasn't. Abandoned, helpless, he had fallen back from the deadly roots, only to be paralyzed by the "Gods'" nerve gas. Alone. Helpless. Inert. Ay'r found himself wishing he could go back and undo what he had done. At the same time, he guessed that he'd freeze up once again, once again probably do exactly the same thing.

"Look over the side," P'al was saying. "You can just make out what's there. See! Directly below us. All around, really!"

To distract himself from the awful memories, Ay'r looked outside the shuttle. Ocean water below: pale blue with undefined shapes beneath. To their left—north—three kilometers distant, the sweep of a spit of land.

"I'm not sure I see anything beneath us," Ay'r said truthfully.

"It's pretty deep."

"Let's have the Fast provide us with a holo from one of the scouts," Alli-Clark suggested. "Project it upon the back wall of the shuttle," she ordered.

Ay'r moved from the long, curved backseat and all but Alli-Clark, who had now taken over as pilot, spun their chairs to face backward.

A dark, murky, watery scene appeared.

"I'll try to opaque the back of the shuttle for a clearer picture," Alli said.

"That's better," P'al said.

Yet the holo was still murky and rather dark. Only now Ay'r could make out the shirred surface of the sandy sea bottom and embedded within it, blocks of stone similar to those he and 'Dward had seen in the swamp.

Ay'r looked at Oudma and 'Harles, grieving silently. They blamed him, he knew. How could he ever be able to explain to them what had happened? Or worse, to 'Dward himself? If, that is, he ever saw 'Dward again.

He had to stop thinking of this, concentrate on what was going on now. At this moment.

"Can you make out any carvings on those stones?" he asked the Fast.

"Not from what I have. But you'll notice, Ser Sanqq' that these stones are much more exposed than those you had seen, which appeared to be merely tips and tops. These are more complete."

The holo switched to the view from the second optical scout: apparently in another undersea area. The stones it displayed were far less spread out, much more jumbled together. Taller, too. They must be enormous.

"Are those arches within the tallest stones?" P'al asked. "Especially in that series to the left? They seem to have fallen in a row!"

The scout came closer to the row of stones, revealing not arches, but what might have been oddly shaped wide passageways through the stone blocks.

"Could other material which eroded long ago have gone through what we're seeing as passages, connecting them and holding them up?" Ay'r suggested.

"Perhaps," P'al admitted. "But look there! And there, too! How the stones' surface seems smoother, almost as though it had been rubbed over a period of time."

Slowly, by hints and suggestions, theories and ideas, a concept began to form of the ruin. First: that it was huge, covering several score kilometers. Second: that it had sunk or been flooded all at once: the regularity of algae and barnacle life proved that. Third: that those great blocks of stones had fitted together without other materials and had formed specific structures, chambers, and galleries, each edifice several stories tall and tapering as it rose. Fourth: that whatever life had built and/or once inhabited the ruins either had been very grand and pretentious, or simply physically large.

The Fast was listening to P'al's and Ay'r's speculations and on its own began to chart out what its scouts were seeing: putting together a jumble of fallen stones into patterns it alone perceived, all the while experimenting, and realigning it all. The shuttle had flown several kilometers farther out to sea, so that even the spit of land which had served as a guide post was now merely a line on the horizon when the Fast asked if it might present "a working draft in rough" of its concept of what the ruins might have looked like before disaster had befallen.

The scout's "live" pictures vanished from the holo and were replaced by a ghostlike reconstruction in pale yellow and gray lines and solids. There, recognizable, were the hollowed-out vertical stones, no longer fallen like a row of dominoes, but standing up, side by side, connected by some sort of semitransparent membrane. In addition were chunkier, more-solid-looking blocks, arranged irregularly around the length of the taller stones, looking like chambers of some sort, and finally were the wide, flat stones, most of them completely flat on the ground, with other ones angled up as ramps and broken-off ramps.

The Fast explained that it had analyzed the three types of stone by shape, cut, relative position to each other and to other stones. It called the wide, flat stones—even those which formed ramps—"pavement." It called the tall stones with their strange passageways, "galleries," or corridors connecting the far larger, curved wall "chambers."

As it was presenting its chart, the Fast reported that a minute before, one stone of the ruined gallery had fallen, possibly affected by a change in the water's current brought on by the motion of one of the optical scouts. In the fall, the ruin had cracked off a section of stone. This would enable the scout to be able to thermoluminescence-date the interior of the stone and compare its outside with its inside.

'Harles Ib'r had been staring wordlessly at the holo-images of the Fast's hypothesized reconstruction of the ruins. Suddenly he sighed and said so quietly that they had to ask him to repeat himself, "The Sunken City of Dy'r. That's what we've found."

"Tell us about Dy'r," P'al urged.

"The Boglanders sing of it in their legends. But it wasn't their city, and no Boglander ever saw it sink into ruins. It was spoken of only by the elders, and this was when I was a youth. Nowadays, I doubt there are any who know of it, except perhaps Legend-collectors."

"Tell us more," Alli prodded 'Harles.

"The elders spoke of Dy'r with hesitation, with reverence and fear. It was supposed to lie near where we are now—in the Far Eastern Archipelago. It had been discovered many generations before by exploring Boglanders, long before the Great Falling Inward, long before the great trek. Even then, the legends said, few ever came so far from the Boglanders' original land to visit Dy'r's ruins beneath the waters."

"But...who lived in Dy'r?" P'al asked.

"No hume. Dy'r was in ruins long before humes existed on Dryland. Before"—'Harles corrected himself self-consciously—"before your seeding of us took place. One bold Boglander of old was said to have asked the Eyes and Ears. It told him that the Sunken City had existed since the beginning of all things. It was older even than Dryland."

"Thirty million Pelagian years old, to be precise," the Fast interrupted. "At least, that's what both the thermoluminescence dating, and the probe's radiocarbon dating of the life-form remnants within the newly broken's ruins says."

"And on the exterior of the stone?" P'al asked.

"The earliest life-form remnants the scout could date on the exterior are from about the same era as the ruins which Ser Sanqq' inspected."

"Only a few thousand years old," Ay'r said. "Speculate, Fast."

"The age of the interior life-forms is truer to its age since the exterior would be more exposed to weathering and other erosion."

"Speculate!" Ay'r tried again.

"Do you really want to know what I'm thinking about these ruins?" the Fast asked.

"I asked, didn't I?"

"You're not going to like it."

"Override discretion circuits," Ay'r said.

"Well, if you insist. Those stones were quarried and cut some thirty million years ago, right here on Pelagia. Their makeup is identical to that in many mountainsides. Furthermore, this once was a city—or least what its inhabitants might call a city. The complexity and regularity of the working draft I displayed on the holo is repeated with only subtle modifications in every spot the scouts have visited through the extent of the ruined area."

"Then it *is* the Sunken City of Dy'r!" 'Harles looked outside the shuttle down at the ocean.

The Fast replied, "Very possibly, it did sink. Or rather, the land upon which it was built, now many fathoms beneath the ocean, either sank or was flooded. And Ser Sanqq', I postulate that the ruins which you located in the swamp were an outpost of some sort. There might have many such outposts, but I suspect most of them are underwater or under swampland now. Not being as large as these ruins, they would be more difficult to locate."

"I did as you instructed, Ser Sanqq', and scanned all the holos relayed by the scouts, looking for writings or carvings. There are no signs of writing, but the scouts did pick up a series of markings upon many stones, especially those which I've theorized were pavement, and—at a single and specific height—in the ruins of what I hypothesized were the galleries. The particular scheme of the markings is far too regular to be accidental. Repetitions of certain marks and spacings between the marks are very suggestive that the markings were made deliberately. Look!"

On the holo a close-up of one stone, upon which the barely visible and much ocean-eroded markings could be seen, enhanced by holo-outlining. The most obvious thing about the markings were that they weren't linear, so much as curved into arcs.

"Irregular ellipses, actually, which also was suggestive," the Fast corrected.

"They weren't read, but felt?" Ay'r asked.

"Very good, Ser Sanqq'! That's what I've come to believe. Felt by one particular limb or part of the body. The head or some organ on the face. I've gone through all the notated languages in the known galaxy stored in my circuits, and the closest one to this I can come up with is Ancient New Venice's Sonara tongue. In other words, the marks represent not words as we—and the Delphinid and Arthopod species—understand them, but sounds. Grunts, moans, clicks, clucks, sounds."

"Delphs would make sense on a world with so much water," Alli-Clark offered.

"Except, Mer Clark, that thirty million years ago only about twenty percent of Pelagia was water. And none of it in large enough sections to breed a Delphinid population of any real size. Nor, as your own findings showed, was this area included in that earlier ocean."

"The shape of the passageways through the galleries aren't Delph," Ay'r said. "Also, we've established that Dy'r was aboveground."

"True," the Fast said. "Even after several millennia of being sunken, the ruins' interior shows incomplete permeability. And the life-forms inside the stone, although microscopic, were once aerobic; they didn't breathe water, but air."

P'al said, "If the inhabitants weren't humes or Delphs, what were they."

"Given the size of the galleries and chambers, the smallness of the plazas, the largeness and predominance of what I call ramps, they were larger than humes, but not by much. Given the enormous amount of ventilation within the chambers, they were neither mammalian nor insect. Neither species sleeps or even hibernates needing large supplies of air. Given the height of the buildings and the fact that they rise several floors and exit on top, as well as the fact that from above, looking down, the rooftops are oddly placed in relation to neighboring buildings, if sometimes only by a quirk; given several other factors I've considered, I posit that the inhabitants of Dy'r were—birds!"

"Intelligent birds!" Alli-Clark scoffed. "That would be a first."

"I told you you wouldn't like it."

"I can accept the fact," Ay'r said. "For one reason, it would explain why there are *no* birds at all on Dryland, not even in the Bog or the Delta or the Swamp, where they should be prevalent."

"Explain," Alli-Clark said.

"If reptiles or saurians were the earliest dominant creatures on Pelagia, then selective evolution would have been most intense among them. As one line evolved far more rapidly than the others, finally achieving intelligence, manual skills, and eventually language, that line would have eliminated all others of its genera—in the way that ancient humes were said to have eliminated all competing primate lines."

"Go on," P'al said, seeming interested now.

"We know that the so-called Terran dinosaurs were so successful a group that wherever they succeeded in evolving, they lasted a long time, then managed to wipe themselves out. They developed rich social lives, began to travel in vast herds, learned how to nurture and protect their young, even how to fight off predators. Meanwhile, the combination of their exhalation and enormous waste matter as well as the limited plant life meant that pollution and eventual starvation was inevitable."

"One group of smaller, lighter boned dinosaurs took to the hills and trees to get away from their fellows. Slowly they developed wings and even feathers. They took to the air, surviving on insects and on extremely limited food supplies. They evolved as the dinosaurs died."

"Then where are all the birds?" Alli-Clark asked. "Or have they just died out?"

"Exactly. And the fact that they were already a vanished species many millennia ago is proved by the great growth and evolution of certain insects like the colleys and Arachs and even the lichen-hoppers Oudma fed and tended which were suddenly free of predators. Free to develop on their own, and to take over that particular ecological niche. In fact, if Pelagia hadn't been seeded by humes, we might have arrived to find colleys evolving into intelligence and language. They already possess the rudiments, as well as some manual dexterity."

"A fascinating conversation, Ser Sanqq'," the Fast said. "But alas, one I must interrupt to let you know that the four optical scouts which have followed the pod which abducted 'Dward Ib'r have reached some sort of standstill."

"What do you mean a standstill?" Alli asked.

"They can go no farther," the Fast said, snippily enough. "They've bumped into some sort of enormous shield. They're now each going in different directions, trying to gauge the size and extent of the shield."

"And the pod with 'Dward?" Ay'r asked.

"No longer can be seen or followed. Evidently it's within the shield."

"Let's go!" Ay'r said, and this time no one thought to defy him or pinch a nerve in his neck.

As P'al piloted the shuttle along the path taken by the scouts, the ensuing fifteen or twenty minutes was as grimly silent as the previous period flying over the Sunken City of Dy'r had been filled with talk, as though each of the five had dropped suddenly and totally into his/her own mind. Occasional bursts of not-really-helpful information from the Fast about the shield the four optical-scouts had encountered was more an irritation than anything else, although from it they learned that the shield began about two-thirds of a kilometer from the last chain of small islands which formed the easternmost tip of this archipelago, and that it was above twenty kilometers in length yet only about three in width— suggesting that it had been raised over another island or islands. The shield was complete. Nothing could be seen, heard, or otherwise sensed within. Nor did it respond to communication. A few laser shots had bounced off its surface without leaving a mark, and an attempt to exercise one scout's rather limited electromagnetic field to break through had merely resulted in the destruction of the scout, with no effect on the shield.

"I believe we've located what you, 'Harles, once referred to as the Abode of the Gods," P'al said.

A few minutes later, he stopped the shuttle and let it hover. The view beneath them was the desolate point of what looked to be the final small island of the archipelago. Bleak. without any life but a bit of lichen. damp from sea spray. All around them was open ocean, except for straight ahead, where a blank space loomed: blank in that it wasn't mist or fog but merely a vagueness—obviously a distortion of the shield.

"Fast, send a message!" Alli-Clark commanded. "Tell them Ay'r Kerry Sanqq' is here to see his father. Send it by micro- and macrowave—any wave at all which you can tell is not bouncing off the shield."

"The message has been sent."

"Send it again," she ordered. "And keep sending it until you get a response."

They were all silent for some time. Then Ay'r felt the need to say, "P'al doesn't believe my father is here."

"Oh? Why is that?"

"Actually," P'al admitted, "because of what the little truth-sayer told Ser Kerry. That we would not find who we were looking for. 'But another. Very like.'"

"Meaning?"

"Who knows?"

"Ay'r?" Alli-Clark asked.

"I haven't a clue."

Something was happening ahead, a break or something in the shield. Pods breaking through? No, but another kind of vehicle, a water vehicle. Could it be? Yes, some sort of water sleds coming straight toward them, and above the top of each curved front sled, the transparent helmet of a hume.

"I believe we're expected to land," P'al said, as the six water sleds pulled up to the spit of land below them. There was one figure on each sled, although there seemed to be room on each for at least one more.

Alli grumbled, but P'al and the Fast tried to persuade her that it was the only way to meet the strangers.

Finally 'Harles leaned over, took her hand, and said, "My sons, Alli. I believe this is the only way I'll see them again."

At this she relented, adding, "But let's stay together and let's keep our belt fields on. That means you, 'Harles, and you too, Oudma. Do you know how to use it?"

Five of the six humes were standing in front of their beached vehicles. The fifth strode forward to meet them as the shuttle dome opened, lifting his visor so they could see his face. Like all the others, he was wearing some sort of skintight wet suit, similar in its effect, if not in the material, to what the Deltan folk had worn.

It wasn't his apparel but the male's features which were so surprising to Alli and Ay'r and P'al. His skin was olive, his eyes black, his hair black: all normal. But his eyes were somewhat slanted, and around them the epicanthic folds were quite pronounced. His nose and mouth were fine and small, despite his wide face and high cheekbones. His hair, although jet-black, was perfectly straight and long.

"A genetically unassimilated male," Alli-Clark whispered.

"A purebred Metro-Terran racial genetic type." P'al added. "What used to be called 'Mongoloid.'"

"We were expecting company," the stranger said, speaking perfect, precise Universo Lexico, "and here we seem to have five Drylanders. Yet one of you claims to be Sanqq'."

"I'm Ay'r Kerry Sanqq'. Disregard our appearance. Several of us made the 'xchange on our Fast before landing on Pelagia."

And when the stranger didn't respond, Ay'r repeated, "The 'xchange."

P'al explained, "A temporary cosmetic exchange of certain physical characteristics. It may not have been perfected in your time."

"Ah!" Now the stranger understood. "Then you are the son of the Mammalian Biologist, Ferrex Baldwin Sanqq'?"

"I am."

"I'm Zhon Azura. Come. You are all the guests of Creed Lars'son. He suspected Offworlders the minute we encountered those little Cybers snooping around our shield."

He led them to the five other males waiting at their sleds, saying "It's a quick ride, and you shouldn't get too wet."

Even so, the five were handed transparent loose-fitting garments to put on, instructed to get behind each driver, and to hang on tightly.

"It's like a colley ride," Azura said, "only faster and much smoother." He asked Ay'r to get onto his sled.

"Why can't we take the shuttle?" Alli-Clark asked.

"It doesn't have the proper signals to bypass our shield," Azura explained. Obviously he wasn't about to give out the signals.

As the water sleds took off from shore and began turning toward the shield, one in front of the other, Azura said, "The opening is quite small."

"Where exactly are we going?" Ay'r asked.

"To the Unmoored Islands!" Azura answered, as they headed toward the blank space lying straight ahead.

Ay'r watched the five other water sleds vanish into the blank space. A second later, Azura's sled hit mist, which became fog. Another second later, the fog was gone. A perfectly beautiful sunlit day faced them, in no way different from what they had seen outside the shield, except for the sight of the island ahead" long, hilly, the approaching shore a mixture of rocky outcroppings covered with verdant (and green!) foliage surrounding tiny beaches. Amidst the trees as well as atop the highest hills could be seen the sides and roofs of small structures, some Plastro-alloy reflecting the sun which was now nearly at meridian. Although as the sled approached the shoreline, the structures seemed of different materials— wood, some sort of brick—and of differing shapes, they were clearly residential, few rising more than two stories, and as much as possible open to ocean views. What had Azura meant by "Unmoored Islands"? When Ay'r turned his head to look backward, he saw what might be the extension of a single shoreline, or another island: explaining the plural, if not the name.

The curved line of sleds ahead seemed to aim toward a particular spot, and as Azura sped to catch up, Ay'r saw a small harbor, which they soon entered. Almost circular, it was bordered on two sides by more residential-looking structures, and though they were partly hidden within stands of trees they appeared larger as the water sled slowed down to enter the harbor, sprawling pavilions connected by terraces. Ay'r even thought he caught what might be a swimming pool through flowers and bushes.

At the deepest end of the little harbor were platforms for scores of water sleds to berth—several from their party were already disembarking— and above that a triangular plaza, bordered on one side by a much higher platform upon which dozens of T-pods sat, and on the other side by a sort of trellised shed holding many more sleds and T-pods, evidently for repair and storage. Behind the informal little plaza, the roofs of other residences rose in a rough kind of order, several three and even four stories high, all with windows and balconies, and all half-hidden behind taller trees.

The temperature of the air had changed as soon as they had entered the shield. Now it was warm. The water-sled drivers were stripping off their sled-suits down to tiny hip-hugging swimsuits in bright patterns; and urging their guests to do likewise. The few other humes Ay'r saw as Azura glided into the sled-berth were also wearing only enough cloth to cover their genitals, all of them males of various skin colors, from the sunburned pale white skin of Drylanders to the blue-black of one of several humes who had gathered to watch the strangers' arrival.

"Straight ahead is a place where you can rest and change into more appropriate clothing," Azura said, pointing through the plaza toward the taller structures. "After that, I'll take you to Ferrex Baldwin Sanqq'. Shall we go?"

"Where's 'Dward Ib'r?" Ay'r asked. "The youth who was found by the ruins in the Great Cold Swamp earlier today. I must see him first."

"You'll find him there. That's where all newcomers reside." Azura took Ay'r's arm and led him forward. The others—including the shuttle's former passengers as well as the water-sled drivers—followed. Ay'r saw that, like Azura, they, too, were purebred racial genotypes; although he couldn't say with certainty which ethnic variations of those types.

"Why did you call these the Unmoored Islands?" Ay'r asked.

"Because they aren't connected to the ocean's bottom. They float. Or rather are guided by us."

"Us meaning how many of you?"

"Perhaps fifteen hundred males."

"And the females—the Drylander females who were abducted? Where are they?"

"They've been returned to their homes over the years. Only males remain."

That was odd, Ay'r thought. "How many of you were there originally?" he probed. "How many did my father collect and bring here to Pelagia?"

"Two hundred seventy-five."

"And all the rest are abducted Drylander youths?"

"Once they were. Now they're all Islanders. That's what we call ourselves," Azura said calmly, as though he had heard not a jot of criticism in Ay'r words or tone.

"Why were they abducted?"

"I'm not authorized to discuss that with you."

"But—!"

"We're here now." Azura led them up a small rise in the path which Ay'r only now noticed was made of slatted wood laid upon a stilted framework to hold it about a meter off the ground. Although the entry Azura pointed to was on his left, Ay'r looked straight ahead, where the wooden path passed several other entryways then slanted down a ramp which gave onto a wide beach of pure white sand, and beyond it, the ocean. Despite the moderate surf, it was both serene and invigorating—beautiful.

Behind Ay'r, P'al had asked about the boarded paths and one of the other males was now explaining that it was to protect the island's fragile vegetation and to allow the most efficient passage all over the island.

"You walk everywhere?" Alli-Clark asked, astonished.

"Most of the time, although we have lightweight vehicles. None more than half the width of the boards. Most of them are double-hume gravi-sleds."

Like everything they'd seen so far on the island, the interior of the residence they entered was simple, clean, and informal. The first floor was a large, airy room opening on a garden. Moving stairs brought them to a second floor, where they were shown to large, wide, windowed sleeping chambers—Oudma and Alli were directed into one, 'Harles and P'al to a second, Ay'r to a third one, as large as the others and with a view of the ocean.

"Please!" Azura gestured to Ay'r. "Rest, clean up, change your clothing. If you're hungry or thirsty"—he pointed to a wall unit similar to that in most M.C. flats and homes—"I'll bring you to 'Dward Ib'r in a moment."

"He isn't hurt or—?"

"No. But I understand that he resisted those who brought him here and was so disturbed that he had to be sedated. No one knew what he was doing out in the middle of the swamp all by himself, naturally, and rescue was absolutely required."

"Rescue! I was there in a T-pod, not fifty meters away, fighting off those Eve-damned roots!"

"The report said nothing of a T-pod nearby," Azura said with perfect equanimity. "The youth had been meant to be scheduled for Ir'l Oriol," Azura said. "But naturally, if he is yours…"

"Scheduled?" Ay'r asked. "For what?"

"All will be explained by the proper personnel. Creed Lars'son, most likely."

"You can't schedule 'Dward Ib'r to be anyone's for any reason," Ay'r said. "He's my…" Ay'r was lost for the right word and groped a bit, looking for something which would be sufficiently daunting yet not unbreakably permanent. Finally he settled for: "'Dward is my lover."

"Then, of course, someone else will be found for Oriol," Azura backed off quickly, still without explaining what 'Dward had been scheduled for.

At least Ay'r was pleased that he had struck the right note with Azura. Seeing that Azura was avoiding most of his questions, he tried another: "Were all two hundred and seventy-five of the original Islanders purebred racial genotypes?"

"Yes. I'm was originally from the Wolf 128, Genotype Colony. A small system in the Orion Spur," Azura explained. "The others came from there, or from various Sol-Terra or Centauri System lunar colonies."

Ay'r decided he'd better find out everything right now. "Because my father needed purebred genotypes for his experiments in Relfianism?"

"At first Ferrex Baldwin Sanqq' believed that purebred racial genotypes would provide better opportunities for his work," Azura said. "He found out eventually that wasn't necessarily so. The Drylanders, for example—"

"You're all mammalian biologists?" Ay'r interrupted.

"Not all of us!" Azura laughed. "Some of us are engineers, physicists, administrators, artists. Ferrex Baldwin Sanqq's concept was to devise a complete and totally self-sufficient society, from those who invented and repair the gravi- and water sleds to those who devised the floatation devices for the islands to those who design and build our houses, our gardens, our music...."

"Yet after a while, my father's complete society wasn't complete enough and he needed to abduct Drylander youth," Ay'r retorted. "Why?"

"I'm not qualified in the niceties of Pelagian politics nor in the ramifications of the Greater Plan. Creed Lars'son will discuss all the administrative details."

Ay'r punched up a juice from the wall unit. It tasted quite good. He stripped off his rough and by now worn and much-slept-in Drylander clothing and moved into the large bath. It was the first sustained bout of unlimited hot water, hot air, cleansers, skin and hair emollients he had encountered since he had left the Fast, and he luxuriated in it. Azura had several garments awaiting him when he stepped back into the large sleep chamber: a tiny lightweight swimsuit like those most Islanders wore, a larger pair of shorts, and a lightweight tunic with the neck and arms cut out at the shoulders. Ay'r settled for the swimsuit and tunic.

"What about 'Nton Ib'r? He was abducted some months ago, Sol Rad."

"'Nton Ib'r is here. He is well. You'll see him later," Azura said, but his usually indifferent demeanor had changed subtly when Ay'r mentioned 'Harles's elder son.

"Let's see 'Dward!" Ay'r was conscious that while he was a guest, as a result of being someone's son, for the first time in his life he possessed influence.

A floor above, a Medic who was wrist-connected to a Cyber-monitor detached himself and joined in a connecting smaller sleep chamber. 'Dward was naked, sleeping fitfully upon the air-bed. From the limitation on his movements, it was clear that he wore air-belt restraints. Ay'r had these removed, and 'Dward's arms and legs relaxed immediately.

Although he had been looking forward to this moment since he had managed to get out of the T-pod in the middle of the swamp, now that Ay'r was here with 'Dward, he wasn't sure what to do. How would 'Dward would react to seeing him again? Would he welcome him? Or upbraid him for letting him be abducted? Ay'r didn't care if 'Dward was angry at him, if—not understanding how it had occurred—he lashed out at him, even struck him. But he found he couldn't bear having 'Dward reproach him silently, turn away, not want to see him. The fact that Azura and the Medic were right here, watching, made it more difficult.

Ay'r bought time looking over 'Dward's body for marks or bruises, but none were visible. After so many abductions, these Islanders—these Sanqq'ites—must know how to handle recalcitrant Drylanders with a minimum of trauma. Suddenly Ay'r realized that this was the first time he was seeing 'Dward naked in normal—if slightly dimmed—light. And 'Dward was as physically attractive as any male Ay'r had ever seen; although, because he was a Pelagian, he was longer and leaner, lighter-skinned.

"'Dward!" Ay'r tried waking him gently but got no response.

"You may require this!" Azura said, showing him a skin-injector. "A nerve stimulator."

"No!" Ay'r said. "I'd prefer for him to awaken naturally."

"That might not be for an hour or more, Sol Rad.," the Medic said.

"I'll wait. He's been through enough already today."

Zhon Azura interrupted, "You should see your father. He's waiting."

All five travelers, still accompanied discreetly by the water-sled drivers, fit onto several gravi-sleds, with Azura and Ay'r in the lead. Their way led along the boarded path closest to the ocean, dotted with residences, mostly hidden behind foliage, until at one of many cross paths, Azura turned left and they slowly began to ascend a much steeper path, almost hidden by overhanging foliage. The gravi-sled didn't stop until it had reached the top of the rise. The boarded path led sharply down on either side. Before them was a structure which looked like any of the other residences, save for its altitude.

Azura gestured Ay'r up the ramp. The others had begun to arrive on their sleds and followed at a slight distance. The ramp led to a deck completely circling a many-windowed residence. Shades over all of them blocked out sunlight. Ay'r wondered why.

He halted momentarily to look up and down the length of the island on either side, and was just able to make out what might be the two other islands in the distance. This appeared to be the highest spot—the views were dazzling.

Inside, the house seemed to have been gutted: another balcony completely surrounded a large, dim room, most of it crisscrossed by hume-high screens. A stocky man with strong facial features met Ay'r.

"He's been prepared for the meeting. I'm Girt TallChief. Please follow me." He gestured Ay'r down a narrow ramp into the room. "Alone, if you please. Too many people." To the others, he said, "You may remain on the balcony. Please don't speak loudly or move suddenly. It's too distracting."

Ay'r hadn't really prepared himself for this meeting; he had been so concerned about 'Dward's safety and about reuniting the Ib'r family, he had no idea what to expect. From what TallChief—was he what the Metro-Terrans called a Native American?—said, it all suggested that his father was in extremely frail health.

"This is merely a formality," TallChief said, pointing out the molecular identification screen Ay'r would have to pass through.

"I must tell you a bit about him," TallChief said quietly. "Some eighteen Pelagian years ago, your father was in a serious T-pod accident and was critically injured. Many of his limbs and internal organs were crushed. We weren't equipped for such a massive replacement. We did manage to get him back to the Islands while he was still conscious, and he insisted that we salvage as much of his brain as possible while it was still alive. Because of who he was, this was done, although it required our entire medical staff working at emergency level for several days for the major work, and years more for details. Since then, all of his brain functions have been Cyber-ized. Only recently, when he himself considered the operation successful, did your father allow his physical brain to be disconnected and buried with the rest of his remains."

Ay'r felt his legs begin to slide out from under him. He felt TallChief's arms supporting him to a seat, but Ay'r couldn't help himself. After coming all this way, after all these years, after all he had gone through since he had been an infant, the disappointment was too much to bear.

"He's taking it hard," Ay'r heard TallChief say to someone nearby. Then to Ay'r: "Would you like to rest? Or water? Or...?"

So it would be as the truth-sayer had predicted. He wouldn't find whom he was seeking, but "one alike." Still, no matter how alike, it wouldn't be the same. Ay'r felt so terribly hollow, he turned in the chair to find something that would sustain him: Oudma's face, and next to her, Alli and P'al and 'Harles. All of them watching him carefully, the water-sled drivers behind them speaking, evidently repeating to them what TallChief had just told Ay'r about his father. Oudma bit her lip, sharing Ay'r's pain.

"I'll be fine in a second," Ay'r said. "It's...a shock."

He would be fine in a second. After all, it had been too much to think that his father...Ay'r stood up and TallChief walked him into an area, screened by transparent panels. He saw a hume male sitting at a swivel desk looking over computations. Ay'r knew instantly this was his father.

"He's a holo?" Ay'r asked.

"Yes and no," TallChief whispered. "More like a construction of his own mind in time and space, amplified by all these electronics. He seldom goes into such detail and depth."

TallChief cleared his voice, and Ferrex Baldwin Sanqq' looked up. His facial features had been fixed so remarkably in Ay'r's mind from holos at some past time that seeing him, Ay'r felt tears come to his eyes.

"My son!" Ferrex Sanqq' uttered, his voice choking. He stood up from the desk and pushed it aside. Then he did a strange thing: he fell slowly to one knee in Ay'r direction.

Ay'r was alarmed. "Father!"

Sanqq' gestured him away with a wave of his hand, raised now in greeting or in benediction. "I never thought I would live to see you." His face was contorted in ecstasy. "You...wonder!"

"Father, please get up. I—"

"You wonder!" his father repeated. "First of the Entire Men! Adam of a New Age. I greet you!"

Ay'r was completely stunned by his father's greeting. He looked toward TallChief to see how to respond. However, TallChief had also fallen to one knee and was staring at Ay'r with that same rapturous look. On the balcony, Azura and the other Islanders were also kneeling to him. Why?

"Please stand up, Father. All of you, please."

"Do you see his perfection, TallChief?" Ferrex Sanqq' asked. "Do you, Azura?"

"I see his perfection!" TallChief uttered. Behind, on the balcony, the other Islanders echoed him.

"I have seen it for over an hour," Azura said. "With growing wonder."

What was going on here? "I'm hardly perfect," Ay'r tried to persuade them. "Please get up, all of you. This is...embarrassing for me."

"That's the very wonder of you!" Ferrex Sanqq' said, rising slowly, and still smiling. "If you were perfect, you would have been a failure. You know I followed your progress for decades, until circumstances became such that I could no longer. And even then, once we were settled here, I still begged like a child that the few contacts we made with the M.C. be aimed so I might catch a glimpse of you. I regret only that we cannot embrace. Do you forgive me?"

Ay'r didn't ask for what: For the past, he knew.

"I'm not sure," he said. He was still so bewildered by the unexpected effusiveness of the greeting.

"I know it must have been difficult for you. And growing up thinking such terrible things about me." Sanqq' shook his head. "It was also difficult for me, knowing you would grow up as an orphan, perhaps even a pariah. Certainly it pained me to have to leave you amidst my enemies. I thought often perhaps that they would teach you to have contempt for me."

"I didn't suffer much," Ay'r admitted. "I met a few kind women. And if I felt anything about you it was…curiosity—you were always such a mystery!"

"A mystery, yes," Sanqq' admitted. "But that couldn't be helped if the Greater Plan were to be achieved. As for you, I couldn't interfere. As a scientist, you understand, I had to make certain that you were entirely on your own, and found your own way, and grew at your own pace, and that whatever tendencies and flaws you might develop would be completely your own. No matter the risks to our relationship. Do you understand?"

"A bit," Ay'r said, although he understood very little really. "But…what is this Greater Plan?"

"I could have kept you close to me, tended you like the rarest of flowers or viruses," his father went on, ignoring Ay'r's question. "I would have, you know. But Lars'son helped me to see that wouldn't do, that we needed complete and Cyberlike objectivity. And because of that, because you were so completely yourself by the time you were halfway through Ed & Dev, we could leave Sobieski Nine and come here to begin in earnest on the Greater Plan, and do all this!"

The holo—or projection of the surrounding Cyber-ized brain of Ferrex Baldwin Sanqq'—was beginning to waver and details to fade.

"This Greater Plan," Ay'r tried again. "What does it have to do with Relfianism and with me and with abducting Dryland youths?"

"I see I'm losing integrity." Again Sanqq' ignored his question. "I'm too excited. You'll come back again, and we'll talk. Go to Lars'son now. He'll tell you all." Sanqq' smiled the fond, almost-ecstatic smile again. "My son! First of the Entire Men! You…wonder!"

"I'll come back," Ay'r said, afraid of tiring his father, afraid of he wasn't sure what.

He walked back up the ramp alone, then out of the residence and got onto the gravi-sled. Azura joined him, clearly moved by what he had witnessed.

"This has been a historic meeting."

"If only I understood what it was all about," Ay'r commented. He turned and caught P'al's eye. But if his companion knew something, he wasn't letting on. "I suppose I'd better do as my father said, if I'm to ever discover what all this nonsense is about."

"Nonsense?" Azura asked.

"You know all the bowing and this Greater Plan and—" Ay'r stopped, seeing Azura's evident displeasure.

"Apologies," Ay'r tried. "But something is going on, and I don't know what it is!"

Now Azura began, "You said before that you wished to see 'Nton Ib'r. He is on our way to Creed Lars'son's residence. And perhaps... perhaps he will serve as an explanation...." Azura's words trailed off.

"I'm certain 'Nton's father and sister would very much like to see him," Ay'r said. Oudma and 'Harles had come out of the house and agreed readily.

"Then that will be our next destination," Azura said.

After a short ride on the gravi-sleds, they arrived back at the ocean side. Azura stopped at the edge of a boarded platform leading directly down to the sand. Without a word, he got off and began to walk, apparently headed toward the water's edge. Ay'r followed, and as soon as his sandaled feet touched the ground, he stopped and took them off to feel the soft warmth of sun-heated sand under his feet. Looking back he noticed the other sleds pulling up. The drivers remained on, but the two Ib'rs, P'al, and Alli-Clark came toward Ay'r. He waited for them.

Azura had reached the shoreline, turned left, and continued walking.

"I don't understand?" 'Harles said. "I thought we were going to see my son."

"We are," Ay'r said.

Oudma had already removed her sandals, and now she ran down to the water's edge. Her father was barefoot, too, experiencing beach sand for the first time.

"We've never seen the ocean until yesterday," 'Harles explained to Alli-Clark.

"We'll go in for a swim later," Alli-Clark said, at which 'Harles looked skeptical.

"C'mon!" Ay'r urged Oudma, who was splashing in the surf.

Azura had gone straight on. Suddenly he stopped and turned, waiting for them to catch up. When they did a few minutes later, Ay'r could see what Azura was looking at: about five yards away, sitting on the sand at the very edge of the surf was a tall, blond, Drylander youth. In his hands he held a tiny naked infant, whom he was lifting and then dropping slowly just as the surf came in. Although both were in profile, Ay'r could see the youth speaking to the infant and the baby's laughter at the game.

"Is that my son?" 'Harles asked. He and Oudma had come up behind Ay'r and each put a hand on his shoulders.

"That's 'Nton Ib'r," Azura said. Then he called out, "'Tonno!"

'Nton turned and smiled. He waved and stood up, a tall, tanned youth. Placing the gurgling infant onto his shoulder, he came forward, looking at Azura steadily, but every once in a while at the others, questioningly.

"I don't think he knows who we are!" Oudma said, as Azura stepped forward to meet 'Nton. He put out a hand to Azura's face and kissed his lips casually. Azura reached up for the infant and took him in his arms. Together, the trio turned—a tableau, a frozen portrait—until Azura released 'Nton's arm and pushed him forward, saying "Go!"

The look on 'Nton's face—'Dward's face, and Oudma's and 'Harles's, too, although subtly different, Ay'r recognized—was one of realization as he looked at them. He looked back at Azura, who was holding the baby close to his chest and who nodded. When 'Nton looked at them again, he was certain of who they were. He smiled.

Ay'r moved to one side and watched them greet each other, watched 'Harles's spirits rise as 'Nton embraced him and Oudma, all of them talking at top speed, trying to catch up, to answer questions, to confirm that yes, his family was all here, together.

Azura came closer to watch the Ib'rs' reunion. He was holding the baby, feeding it his fingertip as a teether. Ay'r joined him.

"That's why you acted so strangely before when I kept asking about 'Nton," Ay'r said. "He's your lover! I guess you never expected to meet his family."

"It *is* unexpected." Azura waited until all greetings were completed among the Ib'r. Then he held out the baby and said, "This is Cas'sio!"

'Nton took the baby from Azura and held out the infant to 'Harles. "Father this is your grandchild, Cas'sio."

'Harles looked at the child, and at Azura, who now stood next to 'Nton, holding him closely by the shoulders. But Oudma had squealed, "Yours?" to her brother and had reached for the infant immediately. Baby

Cas'sio gurgled in her arms and began to play with her long blonde hair. "Yours!" 'Harles seemed to ponder the fact. "Where is his mother?" "*I'm* Cas'sio's mother," 'Nton said. "Zhon is Cas'sio's father!"

In the silence that followed these two seemingly irreconcilable statements, the mild surf and Cas'sio's gurgling could be heard distinctly. Ay'r turned to the child: all the travelers did.

"I gave birth to Cas'sio four months ago," 'Nton said lightly. "Zhon and I—that's our house!" he pointed behind him to a low residence of weathered light wood and open windows on the beach.

"How can this be?" 'Harles asked in a tiny voice.

"Hasn't anyone told you about the Islands? Or about the Greater Plan?" 'Nton asked and looked at Azura.

"They arrived so suddenly that we were unable to explain it all at the guest residence," Azura said apologetically. Evidently he thought that by seeing him and 'Nton and their child first, it would explain itself.

"It's your father's work, Ser Sanqq', following Lydia Relfi's First Principle of Reproduction," Azura went on. "The reason why she and her followers were banned from the First Matriarchy, the reason why her experiments were destroyed, and why her followers, including your father, were discredited under the Second Matriarchy."

"What *was* her First Principle?" Alli-Clark had the wits to ask.

"It's no surprise that you don't know it. I doubt there are a dozen humes alive outside the Unmoored Islands who know it."

P'al now spoke up. "The principle is that all humes possess the right to reproduction, and all humes ought to possess the capacity for reproduction."

"Given the Matriarchal emphasis on childbirth, why would that pose a problem?" Alli-Clark asked.

"*All* humes. Yourself and Oudma, yes, but also myself and 'Nton Ib'r, and yourselves, too!" Azura said. "*All* humes, regardless of gender."

"The abductions of Drylanders!" Ay'r all but cried out.

"After the successful application of the procedure to all of us, your father still needed to know how it worked on all types of humes."

"Then the injections are connected to this!" Ay'r was beginning to put it together.

"The injections ready the youths before they actually arrive here," Azura said.

"Ready them for what?" Alli-Clark asked.

"Haven't you been listening to what I've been telling you? Ready them for impregnation. Ready them for childbirth!"

As a Social Scientist, Ay'r was aware that new concepts which flew in the face of deeply ingrained belief systems were extremely difficult to accept. Even so, this one was difficult to even admit as practical.

"Are you saying that 'Nton has been injected with a mechanism for growing ovaries?" he asked.

"Not only 'Nton, myself and every Islander, too. And it's more than ovaries. A quite refined approximation of a complete womb! Given the state of mammalian biology, the technology for male viviparturition wasn't too difficult for your father," Azura added, as though it were the most common thing in the galaxy. "Females were required at first to donate the required cells for ovary and fallopian tubes to be cloned and implanted inside the males' body."

"The real problem your father and Creed Lars'son faced was ensuring that the male body reached the proper hormonal stasis to conceive successfully once the womb was in place; to conceive within the body, and then to continue embryonic development. The fetus needs only three or four months of growth within the body if that body is healthy and well nurtured and if it possesses the correct ratio of fat to muscle, of estrogen and proestrogen to other hormones. After that, the fetus is still small enough to be removed easily, yet developed enough to be able to grow in artificial conditions outside the body, although naturally in close and constant contact with its nurturing parent."

He went on, heedless of the effect he was having on Ay'r and the others; or, if not heedless, then indifferent. "The implanted womb is connected directly to the colon. Scientifically, it's extremely elegant. It's easy to implant the womb, to impregnate and to remove the fetus wrapped in its placenta at the correct time."

P'al had a question. "Will the procedure work on Delphinids, too?"

"I don't see why not."

Bolder than the rest of them, 'Harles almost stammered out his question: "Does this mean, 'Nton, that you are no longer a male?"

"No, Father. It means that I'm now both male and female."

"As all of us are," Azura said. "Male all the time and female whenever we choose to boost the various hormones which will allow us to conceive."

"Except for the first time," 'Nton now clarified, "following the original womb implantation. When that has been done, we must conceive. Which is how I gave birth to Cas'sio." He leaned forward to where his son, in Oudma's arms recognized his name and turned to 'Nton to be caressed.

Ay'r had been assailed by so many conflicting thoughts while Azura was talking that he didn't know what to say.

But Alli-Clark couldn't hold back her own comments. "This is outrageous! According to what you're suggesting, women aren't needed at all!"

"Except as cell donors for the original implantation. Or for the original cloned cells. And, Mer Clark, you have gone directly to the heart of the Relfian problem. Wicca Eighth thought it was sufficiently outrageous that She had Ferrex Sanqq' discredited from the Mammalian Institute on Arcturus and hounded out of each scientific establishment where he sought refuge. Let me remind you that occurred long before any experiments had taken place, when the idea was still theoretical."

Ay'r was so fascinated that he almost managed to push out the thought which had been intruding into his consciousness. Then he couldn't any longer.

"'Dward received an injection in Bogland. Can its effects be counteracted?"

"He received an injection there?" 'Nton asked. "Are you certain?"

"I watched from behind a hedge while it was done. They took away a Boglander named Varko."

"Yes, Varko arrived here," Azura confirmed and turned to 'Nton. "Your brother did receive an injection. The Medic who checked him through earlier today told me so. He said it was about one week of development. As soon as 'Dward was sedated, the Medic gave 'Dward a booster. A full physiological scan showed the development of the implantation is proceeding normally."

"Then he *has* been implanted?" Ay'r asked.

"With a womb?" 'Harles asked.

"Naturally," Azura said.

"Is there any way to stop it from developing?" Ay'r asked. "What if 'Dward didn't receive any more booster injections?"

"It was implanted on the first injection. The boosters are to aid its normal growth as well as to balance his body's hormones and DNA to keep him from developing certain side effects. Although we have never stopped boosters purposely, the one or two times it happened inadvertently, the patients became quite ill and required much care, including surgical removal of the implant and after a period of long recovery, reinjection. One died of complications. At this point, the only safe course is continuation."

"Which means what will happen exactly?" Ay'r asked.

"Within the next few weeks, 'Dward will begin to require sexual intercourse on a regular basis until he is impregnated."

"He'll go into estrus, you mean?"

"Not exactly estrus. The initial onslaught is far gentler, far more subtle. And it is emotional as well as physical. Any attachment that exists between him and other males will be greatly intensified. And even though he's already a most attractive youth, 'Dward will become quite irresistible. I have no doubt that by the time 'Dward is ovulating, a male would have to be a Cyber to be able to refuse his attentions."

"He speaks from experience," 'Nton said. "We both do. Which is why those who have been implanted and brought to the Islands are put into situations where they may quickly meet appropriate spouses."

"You mean he's matched up with one of the original two hundred and seventy-five? What do you have here, harems?"

"Hardly!" Azura laughed. "We may have as many children by as many spouses as we wish. Several of us have fathered—and mothered—many children already and have several out-spouses. But its a matter of emotions for us, too. Unusually one spouse becomes our full-time companion."

"One is usually more than enough!" 'Nton said enigmatically.

Azura added, "And the spouse-pool for 'Dward would have consisted entirely of Pelagian youths, all of them implanted, and already successful mothers. Ir'l Oriol saw 'Dward's arrival and told us he had known him in Monosilla Valley. It was thought that their previous acquaintance and similarity of backgrounds would make 'Dward's adjustment to Island living and customs easier all around. While, for the Greater Plan, it would enlarge the gene pool. After his first birth, 'Dward would naturally be free to espouse any other willing Islander."

"And 'Dward doesn't know it," Ay'r said.

"He'll be given full orientation when he awakens. It will help that his brother has already undergone the procedure."

"Ay'r should be the one to tell him," Oudma said.

"Me?" Ay'r dreaded it. "Why me?"

"It's Ay'r's father's doing that this befell 'Dward!" Alli said.

"It's not a tragedy," Azura said and to 'Harles, who still seemed stunned. "Believe me, it's not a loss. Just the opposite. Your sons and I are now *twice* the humes we were before the implantation."

"It's true, Father," 'Nton agreed. "Although it is not the Old Valley way, it's a far better way. I would never give up the experience of carrying and birthing Cas'sio. Never!"

"Since you say it, I must believe it," 'Harles said, unconvinced.

"That's not why Ay'r should be the one to tell 'Dward," Oudma said. Despite playing with the infant, her words silenced them all with an undeniable sense of authority. She looked at Ay'r, making certain their eyes met. "Ay'r should be the one, because it must be Ay'r's child that 'Dward bears. That is what both of them want. That is what the truth-sayer omened for them."

'Harles turned to her. "Is this why you didn't announce your bonding at the Great Temple? You remembered the omens?"

"Partly," she admitted. "Partly because of what I've seen. You know what I'm talking about, Ay'r. Don't deny it. Go to 'Dward. Tell him!"

"I will," he said. "Since you insist."

Alli-Clark now spoke up. "The entire thing strikes me as a major interference in the life of the Drylanders. An unforgivable one."

"That you will have to take up with Creed Lars'son," Azura said. "He's responsible for the policies of the Greater Plan."

"Don't think I won't!" she declared.

P'al now spoke, "This surgical bisexuality is the basis of the Greater Plan?"

"Yes. The Islands, too, are devised to facilitate it."

"Tell us one more thing," P'al went on, as cool and unflappable as ever in the face of this onslaught of information, "Why is it all of you—even Ferrex Sanqq' himself—bowed to his son? And called him, what was it exactly? The New Adam? First of the Entire Men?"

The very question Ay'r had been so afraid to ask himself.

"That's because Ay'r Kerry Sanqq' is the very first of us."

"The first to be implanted with the Relfian Viviparturition Unit?"

"That's not true!" Ay'r said. "I've been in situations where it would have become activated."

"It was implanted when you were an infant," Azura assured him. "It merely needs to be activated with the appropriate hormone/DNA complex."

Ay'r was still trying to absorb this information when Azura went on, "But it is not only that, Sers and Mers, that make us honor him so." He stared at Ay'r with that same look as before. "Ay'r Kerry Sanqq' is the New Adam because, above all, he is the very first hume in all history to be born of the sexual congress of his father, Ferrex Baldwin Sanqq', and another male!"

"May we be alone?" Ay'r asked, once they'd arrived back at the guest residence and gone into the room where 'Dward slept.

The others backed out of the room and closed the door.

Ay'r set the nerve-stimulator to its lightest charge, but it still worked quickly. 'Dward opened his eyes and saw Ay'r. A faint smile passed over his lips. He reached out, found himself surprised that he was no longer restrained, touched Ay'r' right where his heart was.

"I'm real," Ay'r assured him. "You're awake. You're safe."

"The last time I saw you"—'Dward began to say—"I saw what was happening to the T-pod."

"I'm fine."

"I started running toward you, then—"

"You're safe." Ay'r held 'Dward's hand to his heart. "We all are. This place belongs to my father. None of us will be harmed."

"Your father?" 'Dward was astonished.

"I've seen him already," Ay'r said. He couldn't take his eyes off 'Dward, nor 'Dward off him. Ay'r found himself smiling. "It was very strange. We're here in his place, what your people would call the Abode of the Gods. Except of course they aren't Gods at all, but merely humes like you and me. Well, not entirely like us, but..." He realized that he was chattering out of nervousness and stopped himself.

'Dward looked amused. "Where are we?"

"In a guest house. 'Dward, remember what happened earlier, when the roots began to attack the pod. And then I signaled you about the 'Gods'?"

'Dward's brow creased, "Yes. It was terrible. I began to run."

"Believe me, 'Dward, when I tell you I didn't know what to do. How to save both you and Oudma inside the pod."

"But you couldn't have!" 'Dward said with conviction. "I saw that you must free the pod before you could come to me. What other choice could you have?"

"But they were coming for you. I could hear them. Smell their odor!"

"Ay'r!" 'Dward touched his arm. "I would have done the same. It's not your fault that by the time you were free, I was taken."

"It is. It's been tormenting me ever since. And especially since I found out about you and—"

"And what, Ay'r? You're acting so strangely."

"Perhaps I'd better explain everything later. Can you get up?"

'Dward could and did with only a bit of hesitation. Ay'r helped him, to his feet, pleased to feel 'Dward's arms around him. When they were face to face, Ay'r asked, "How do you feel?"

"A little sore."

"That's from the air-restraints they put on you. The Islanders," he explained. "But aside from the soreness?"

"I feel fine," 'Dward assured him. "Why?"

"'Dward, listen," Ay'r tried. "Since Varko's kidnapping, haven't you been feeling a bit different than before?"

"No, I...well, now that you mention it, yes. I feel, I don't know, lazier, somehow. I don't how to say it—I feel like touching more. Touching you, especially! Which you won't let me do."

"There's a reason for that," Ay'r said.

"So you told me before," 'Dward looked unhappy.

"I mean that there's a physical reason, 'Dward, for how you feel. Listen carefully. The same Islanders who took Varko away injected you with something." He turned 'Dward so he could see the spot low on his shoulder. "See!" Ay'r showed him the injecting mechanism and how it worked, then went on, "I'm not sure why, but although I was as immobilized by their perfume as you and the other young men, I could see what happened and even hear some of it. Perhaps its was my distance. I saw them inject you and the others before they took Varko."

'Dward's eyes were fear-filled.

"It's not a poison, but it is something which is going to change your life—at least for the next year or so."

"You mean the way I'm feeling lately is because of something they put into my body?"

"Yes, and as a result, you'll become even more sensitive to touch than before. And"—Ay'r didn't know how to say it—"and you'll want to make love. Often."

'Dward's eyes sparkled. "What a wonderful thing to inject me with! Except"—'Dward stopped—"it will be terrible unless you are injected, too."

"I was. Long ago. Without my knowing it. Your sister and father and I have already discussed it."

"That's wonderful!" 'Dward said and threw his arms over Ay'r's shoulders and began to hug him. "Wonderful!"

"Yes! But 'Dward, there's something else you must know. After we've made love, you'll...be able to...you'll...give birth! Just like your sister Oudma."

'Dward seemed skeptical.

"You will! Your brother 'Nton already has. He has a baby."

'Dward was halfway out the room before Ay'r caught him. "'Nton's here? You've seen him?"

"Yes. You'll see him too, in a little while."

"How does he look?"

"He looks like you. Beautiful. And," Ay'r added, "So does Cas'sio."

"Cas'sio?"

"Your nephew, 'Dward. A baby born to 'Nton. Out of 'Nton's body."

Again 'Dward looked skeptical.

"Remember last night, what you said, 'Dward? How for the first time in your life you wished you were a female? Now you are both male and female."

"What will the people here think of this, Ay'r?"

"All of them are the same way, 'Dward."

"This is not the Drylander way," 'Dward said seriously, showing that he comprehended what Ay'r had said.

"I know. But it's the way here, on these Islands. And it's your future, 'Dward. Perhaps it's all of our futures. And it cannot be stopped without endangering your life. Do you understand, 'Dward?"

'Dward was silent. Then he looked up. "Remember what the little truth-sayer told us, Ay'r, in Monosilla Village? He said I would be a soldier-mother. That 'Nton already was a mother. He *knew*. He said, what exactly was it? That I would be mother to those who would rule the stars!"

Ay'r had been trying to recall the infant se'er's words since Oudma mentioned them earlier on the beach. They now returned with great force.

"And you, Ay'r. He called you the Great Father. The Greatest Father of all! If you are father to my children, who are to rule the stars, then his predictions will be fulfilled."

"In a sense, I'm already one," Ay'r mused.

'Dward looked at him with a question.

"According to what I've been told, I'm the very first of all these new people."

After a minute, 'Dward asked, "'Harles and Oudma?"

"They're downstairs. They already know all of this."

"Will you, Ay'r?" 'Dward asked.

"Will I what?" Then he knew the question. Would he father 'Dward's children. "Yes, of course. That's why I wanted to tell you first. I was afraid you'd—"

"What? Say no?" 'Dward laughed mischievously. "To the Greatest Father of them all? I'd have to be a great ninny, wouldn't I?"

The door opened to Zhon Azura and the Medic. And behind them 'Nton and Cas'sio. All but the baby had the same unspoken question.

"Look at you!" 'Dward greeted 'Nton. He rushed forward and hugged his brother and began to play with Cas'sio.

When all their greetings were completed, 'Nton turned to his younger brother and said, "Isn't it just like you, 'Dward! I arrive here first and go through all this business, and you have to outdo me by coming with Ferrex Baldwin Sanqq's only child."

To Ay'r, 'Nton said, "On the Islands, we've heard and viewed so much about you! Although you looked different in the holos."

"You have? I can't understand how. My companions and I just arrived on Pelagia several weeks ago."

"Through holo comm.s to the Center Worlds," 'Nton said.

"Yes, we've watched you throughout your Ed. & Dev.," Azura said.

"You mean because I was the first?" Ay'r asked.

"Our model. Yes. Now it's time you see Creed Lars'son," Azura said. Then to 'Nton: "Imagine, 'Tonno! Your siblings are lovers to Sanqq's only child!"

"We must celebrate," 'Nton declared.

"I apologize, 'Tonno. But celebrations will have to wait a bit longer!" Azura said. "We still have one more meeting."

"But my family. Surely, they can stay here? 'Dward and—?"

"Surely, we won't be too long. Are you ready?" he asked Ay'r.

"I suppose so, if I'm to find out what the Greater Plan is all about."

"I'll go with you," 'Dward insisted. But Ay'r wanted him with his family.

This gravi-sled ride was longer than the others, and along the board path which fronted the rockier side of the island. Azura had to detour around the little plaza and harbor.

Almost equally distant from the little harbor, on the other side of the island and almost as high upon a crest of hill was a structure similarly built to that which housed the Cyber-ized remains of Ay'r father. This proved to be Creed Lars'son's abode. But unlike that hushed, dimmed, and hollowed-out residence filled with Cyber-screens and unseen power units, this one had its windows open to the sun and to breezes, and various well-furnished chambers were visible. It also appeared to be teeming with Islanders.

Azura had to ask several of them where he might find Lars'son. Ay'r followed his wanderings through the house and finally out a sleep chamber to a small terrace which commanded an unimpeded view of both beach and rocky sides of the island.

"Fine!" Lars'son gestured them to sit. He was naked save for a pair of briefs. Evidently, he'd been sunning himself. Ay'r noticed a Drylander youth in one corner playing a musical instrument he had never seen before, who stood up suddenly and left the terrace. Azura remained standing. These little moments gave Ay'r the time to look over Creed

Lars'son. Another racial genotype, of the extreme Caucasoid type, but like
the Drylanders, he was tall and lean and blond; his long, straight flaxen
hair burnished by sunlight with gold and silver. His eyes were the same
ice-blue that Ay'r had seen among Monosilla folk, but his features were
defined much more sharply.

What most set Lars'son apart, Ay'r instantly calculated, was that even
though he must be close to six hundred years old and here on his own
sleep chamber terrace, sunbathing and being serenaded, he still retained
a sense of power in repose, of the ability to leap into instant and utterly
committed action.

"Fine! Fine!" Lars'son repeated. "Zhon Azura has seen to all of your
desires."

"Yes, completely."

"And you've seen your father?"

"Briefly, yes."

"And he's told you all about the Greater Plan?"

"Azura did, but not entirely. You're to tell me the rest."

"What do you know?"

"I witnessed an abduction in Bogland," Ay'r said. "And one of my
companions was implanted. But I didn't know what for, until now."

"And now that you do?" Lars'son smiled: strong, long white teeth.
Most of them originals. Without waiting for an answer, he went on, "We
knew that someone was here. But we scarcely suspected that it would turn
out to be you!"

"I think it's wrong: the abductions, the implants," Ay'r said.

"Even though those who become Islanders possess advantages they'd
never dream to possess? Even though they are brought up to current
galactic standards of Ed & Dev? Even though they're happy?"

"Yes."

"I'm not sure you're aware of everything we happen to know about this
lovely planet," Lars'son said.

"If you're talking about the coming disaster, yes, I'm aware of it. We
experienced the Night of the Four Moons at the Observatory."

"You *have* managed to get around!" Lars'son seemed impressed. "The
more Drylanders we take, the more will be saved. However, we can't
save them all."

"What about the women and children?"

"Some children will be saved. We've stepped up our activity. But it was
long ago certified that male youths possess the complete stock of seeded
genes. As far as that goes, we've already saved the Drylanders."

"How? Your shield can't last forever—not against the continued onslaught which we predict will occur."

"The islands aren't attached. They move. We'll move to the safe areas."

"Even so, it won't be enough!" Ay'r insisted.

"No! You're right. We'll have to leave Pelagia."

"How? In the Fasts you came in?"

"We'll use the Fasts we arrived in, yes. But we've been outfitting two old Bella=Arth weapons freighters we chanced upon outside of this system in our explorations. I suppose they were abandoned during the war. Their crews must have committed suicide around the time of the end of the Nest-Cities on Deneb XII. It took us days, Sol Rad., to clear out their dry and emptied husks."

"Which means you have room for how many?"

"Two thousand."

"Why don't we help you? We'll go back and get larger Fasts. That way, we can save all the Drylanders."

"Think about that, Ay'r. Think about the problems involved after we've saved them. Without the kind of Ed. & Dev. we've provided for those who have become Islanders, most of them would disbelieve you, flee from you. And those that did opt to come along, how many of them would be able to adjust to so totally changed a life, on a new planet?"

"The family I traveled with accepted change."

"'Nton Ib'r's family. Splendid stock. But, Ay'r, they would. As would a few more families we've kept our eyes on; all of them in the high mountain valleys. You're a Species Ethnologist, you must know how difficult it is to uproot humes from one spot to another on the same continent or world. How many generations are needed for the change to settle in? How many die simply of exile and heartbreak. And anyway, if you did help, what does that mean, exactly? Who would be helping, Wicca Herself? She'd never help us."

"She'd help the other Drylanders," Ay'r argued. "Alli-Clark would persuade her."

Lars'son seemed to be considering.

"It could only be done after I was certain that our people were gotten off Pelagia safely. And that might not happen until after much of Dryland is already suffering catastrophe. I'm sorry, Ay'r, but my first duty is to…"

"The Greater Plan! I know."

"To our people, was what I intended to say. To our spouses and children." Lars'son tried to soften it. "Even so, we will have come away with ten times the number we arrived with. And the seeding stock will remain intact."

"It just doesn't seem enough."

Lars'son smiled. "You're just like your father. How many times has he argued in exactly those words, and felt the same anguish you feel?"

"Let's not close this conversation. Meet with my companions, P'al and Alli-Clark. They're both intelligent and thoughtful. Perhaps together you can work out something."

"Fine. Fine! We'll all meet together. Later on. Right now, I want to just talk about you."

Ay'r still felt resentful. "What's there to say? By the way, whatever experiment I may be, I'm really embarrassed by all this kneeling and 'First of the Entire Men!' business. Can it be stopped?"

"Put up with it just a bit longer. When all the Islanders have seen you, you'll be able to relax again. At the moment, you're a sensation."

"What does it mean?"

"Didn't they tell you? It means you're the first Islander. The firstborn child ever of the surgical procedure technically called Relfian Viviparturition."

"You mean my mother was like 'Nton? A man with a womb?"

"Your mother was the very first man with an functional womb."

Now it was all making sense to Ay'r.

"Then that's why the Matriarchy couldn't locate my mother?"

"Not if they were looking for a woman."

"Because my mother was a male."

"A man. We don't accept M.C. derogations here. Humes are women and *men...*"

"But..." Ay'r was still groping. "Who? Which man?"

"I thought you would have guessed by now. Especially since through your newfound cosmetic technology, you've managed to bring your physical features back to what they probably would have been if your father hadn't changed them to make you fit in better with your M.C. peers."

And when Ay'r still didn't understand, Lars'son stood up and gestured for Ay'r to follow him into the sleep chamber and into the bath, where one wall was a full-length reflector.

"I thought you would have known the moment you walked onto the terrace and I didn't get up and kneel down to you. Look," Creed Lars'son said.

Ay'r looked at the two men facing him, one taller and older and more sunburned, but otherwise...deeply...stunningly similar.

"Remember, Ay'r, I carried you inside my body four uncomfortable months. And every minute of those four months, I hoped and I feared."

Ay'r stood there, thinking, either this is an elaborate hoax, or...

"Is this true?" he finally asked.

"What did your father say?"

"He said to come here. That you'd explain everything."

"Well, haven't I?" Then he added, "You'd better enjoy all this adulation. Until about twenty Pelagian years ago you were absolutely unique in the universe. But now"—he stopped and laughed. "There! I did it!"

"Did what?"

"What else?" Creed Lars'son said. "I began talking like a mother!"

Chapter Ten

Mart Kell skidded to a near halt, then leaped and let the air-sandals whirl him along the curved walls of the fountains in the center of Connaught Memorial Park. All-night partiers from a local underground café ("Old Chips for New" had recently been a Cyber-repair depot and now was the chic-est club in the City) had come out for fresher air, and several of them applauded his grace and speed. Doubtless none of them knew he had to do this to gather enough velocity to get onto a particularly high ramp he'd need to shortcut him directly onto Power Avenue.

As he whirled, he half-heard, half-saw one of the Park's holo-screens flash on with an Inter Gal. Bulletin. He couldn't stop for it now. His velocity was building right for the jump, just past that wall and...he leaned over, straightened his body, then felt the whoosh of Hesperian night air on either side of his roller-visors as he took the leap onto the ramp. The air-sandals touched a half-meter from the apex and Mart threw his body forward to help the momentum. He was over the apex and going down, and the whoosh of air was almost deafening, as it would have been blinding going at this rate if he hadn't the visor on.

Power Avenue was as empty as it usually was, but he remembered passing an antique, enclosed holo-station somewhere along its length before. Yes, there it was, the News holo still on. He slurried to a stop, held his Plastro finger guards against the transparent wall and watched.

The scene displayed was Hesperia's own governmental Fast Port, and there were a half-dozen City officials all but jostling for position to meet those emerging from the huge Fast that had just landed. Mart tapped on his own ear-set, kept tapping until he found the channel and listened as the announcer began:

"Acting Metropolitan of the Church of Algol is stepping out and being welcomed by Quinx Councilor, Eba'l Pore. A short while ago, before landing, the Interstellar Church Elders made a formal request for politico-religious exile status in Hesperia, and their request was granted. The Acting Metropolitan is about to speak now."

The tall, elderly Maudlin Se'er, surrounded by a group of his black-robed, desiccated acolytes looked even more hollow-eyed then when Mart had last seen him. When he began to speak, the Se'er's voice was carefully modulated, as only the those superb orators knew how to, reflecting an entire range of emotion, from tragedy to determination.

"It grieves me to have to inform you that last night, Sidereal Time," the Acting Metropolitan began, "that the Church of Algol lost its Thirty-Seventh Interstellar Metropolitan. Detained in a holding cell of the Matriarchal Council Headquarters upon Melisande, in the Regulus Prime system, His Holy Efflorescence, Gn'elphus the Second, took his own life in Ultimate Sacrifice."

The old Se'er appeared to break down and slump. Several bony hands belonging to his followers reached out and supported him, and he cast a pietistic glance upward at the holo-cameras. From his new position, he continued in an even more broken voice.

"Many hundreds of the Church of Algol have been arrested and imprisoned upon the Matriarchal Center Worlds—without provocation or cause! No accusations have been made against them, no charges raised, no explanations provided to the Acting Synod. In protest, His Holy Efflorescence took his life. The Church has asked for Sanctuary for its officiating members."

He tried to stand. Behind him, hooded Se'ers chanted, "Avenge Gn'elphus! Avenge his sacrifice!"

The Acting Metropolitan seemed ready to say more, but he found he couldn't go on, and covering his haunted face with his hood, he turned away. The holo switched back to the Inter Gal. reporter, a female hume, who now said:

"The number of those Se'ers detained by the Matriarchy is not known but thought to be close to seven hundred. The precise reason for the arrests is also not known although many diplomats believe that the Se'ers are being used as scapegoats for the many reported housing riots upon Matriarchal Center Worlds. A great many from the Church who managed to escape those planets are expected to join the Acting Metropolitan in seeking Sanctuary in the City."

Wicca Eighth! Mart thought. She'd always hated Gn'elphus, always hated the Se'ers, and now She thought She'd found a way to get rid of them. A foolish error. But then, She hade made several errors recently as She felt control slipping from Her fingers. And doubtless, as Her desperation grew, She would make even more errors and possibly more disastrous mistakes. But the worse She showed Herself and Her policies to be, the better it would be for the Quinx, for the City.

Mart tapped off his ear-set and turned away from the holo-station. He was late for his own meeting. He had to hurry.

A short while later he was on the Ion-lift rising to the seventeenth-story main VIP suite of the abandoned Ophiucan Starship Lines terminal.

Once on the terrace, he removed the sandals, slung them over his shoulder, dropped his hood to uncover his face and hair, and removed his visor making sure that Kri'nni could see him through the fluted iridium-glass doors.

Even though he'd only called this meeting a half-hour ago, Sol Rad., and had used an emergency code between them to do so, Kri'nni was already there, draped comfortably over a sofa and adjoining chair, viewing a porto-PVN and inhaling from her ever-present Soma pipette.

"I didn't think you'd get here in time," she said.

"Stopped to watch a holo. All about the Church of Algol!"

"The way I've heard it, whichever good little Maudy ices Momma gets to be the new Metropolitan."

"That's a pretty high reward." And Mart lifted off his Plastro-tunic.

"Sex? At this hour?" Kri'nni gave him her odd laugh. "I thought this was an emergency."

"Not really. I just didn't want anyone else to know anything about our meeting. Especially as I've got something new for you."

Laced into the lining of the tunic he had removed was a long, sheer ultra-Plastro pouch. Mart ripped it out and dangled it over her pipette.

"A present? For me?" Kri'nni gurgled. Then, more seriously. "What's in it? Delta Ophiucan Sopazine?"

"Better than that, Kri'nni. Halo-Zedrezine. Freshly degurged and pH-balanced for Bella=Arths."

"Halo-Zedrezine? I thought that was just a rumor?" Although she did not let go of the pipette, two other palps itched forward to touch the pouch.

"It's Mart Kell's business to turn rumor into reality. Kri'nni, love, this is the reality. Halo-Zedrezine. From my own private Sopa-Farms on Zeta Ophic."

One palp couldn't stay away; it caressed the pouch.

"What strength?"

"Eighty-two. That about right for you?"

"I've been known to go up to eighty-four, but it will do. Why don't I finish this pipette and...care for a hit?"

"Not me. I'm still on duty."

He watched her undo the pouch expertly—a job requiring at least two hands—test the drug's texture, ooh a little, then slip the crystalline substance into the pipette. He was about to explain that a drop of any natural oil would mix it when he felt a quick knife edge across the skin of one shoulder.

"You don't mind, do you?" she asked. "I'm a stickler for the old ways: I like to mix it with some of the seven essences."

His perspiration and blood in this case. But because Kri'nni had used the underside of one palp with its natural anodynes, the long, thin, surface cut was already painless, healing as he looked at it.

She mixed with the pipette and sipped a little. "Nice."

"Glad you like it. You've been very helpful to me lately, Kri'nni. Just wanted to pay you back."

"You've paid me back plenty. I've had six of your seven essences at one time or another during our meetings (sexual encounters ((egg-pouch stimulation sessions)))). Even so..." she kept sipping as she spoke, and Mart watched the mixture glide up the pipette and wondered if it were too mild, or enough, or..."Even so, Mart, I was surprised to get your message. I thought you'd want to be at Groombridge to share in the...glory?"

No surprise that Kri'nni knew where the City Fleet had gone to. She knew everything. Too much.

Mart watched her pipette draining the pouch. "I'll be at Groombridge when I'm needed. Don't worry. But I didn't want anyone beside ourselves to know I was derelict of duty. Hence my use of our one-to-one emergency call."

"I thought it might be something like you playing hooky, Mart. Still, there's a eight hour Fast Jump between Hesperia and Groombridge. Any action there will be long over by the time you hear of it."

The pouch was almost empty, and he still didn't notice any effect on Kri'nni.

"No action should happen for twelve hours yet. Long enough for me to do what I have to do here and get back."

"You seem awfully certain about that, Mart. Is there something I don't know?"

"Not a great deal, Kri'nni. A detail or two. When I had Jon Laks send those turncoat Cybers to Cray 12,000, I had Laks prepare a microscopic tap for them to transfer. It was a calculated risk. The tap was located on a hair follicle of one of the turncoats, and there had to physical contact between the two Cybers for it to work. But they turned out to be as eager to lay their mechanical hands on the traitors as Laks said they would be. And once the contact occurred, our little tap simply hopped over and attached itself to the other Cyber's hair, and from there it worked its way inside and into a spot where it could be useful."

Kri'nni almost cooed with pleasure. "Are you telling me you have a tap on the top tincan itself?"

"Afraid not. On another Cyber, which is part of Cray's inner group. They're linked mentally about one-quarter of the time. So I happen to know all sorts of things, such as how many Fasts Cray's using, what sector they're jumping from and at what angle, and when and where they'll most likely arrive. Naturally, this information has been shared with the other squadron leaders, although *not* with any M.C. personnel at Groombridge."

Kri'nni was amused. "You *are* resourceful, aren't you, Mart? On occasions like this, I'm strongly reminded of your late, much-lamented great-grandfather, whom I was able to watch operate on some very louche PVNs."

Mart didn't known there were business-agent PVNs made of Jat Kell. And thinking about it, he strongly doubted there were. Was Kri'nni ragging him, or was the drug…?

"Now, tell me truly, Mart. What could be of such concern that it draws you away from all that aggressive masculine camaraderie? Don't lie and say it was this little present for Kri'nni?"

"Do you like it?" he asked, hating himself for asking.

"It's nice," she repeated.

"Nice? Curl-voles are nice! Thwwing-lottery jackpots are nice!"

"You're right, Mart. This Zalo-Hedrezine is…very nice! You wouldn't have a smidgen more? No? Forget it, Mart. It's got a bit of a time delay. I'm feeling it continue working."

Maybe it would be enough. He had certainly planned it with care.

"So, tell me, Mart. This concern of yours?"

Mart hesitated a second, more to buy time for the drug to work than anything else, since he already knew exactly what he was going to say.

"I'd prefer not to go into details, Kri'nni. But it's come to my attention that a new Nest is in the making on Deneb XII. I think you'll agree with me that should the outcome of tomorrow's action be as we hope and plan, the City will need as many allies as possible within the rotten empire of Wicca Eighth."

"You can already count on the Arths and Delphs of the Orion Spur Federation."

"The Delphs are solid. But those Arthopods don't possess the qualities required for a true Three Species realliance. The only Arths which would automatically have those qualities, the only Arths who would draw all the others in the Arth diaspora to accept the alliance must come from a bona fide Bella=Arth nest. And the only one of those in existence today is on Deneb XII," Mart explained.

"The same ones who rescued Riad and Dinne?" Kri'nni asked. "I suppose. They certainly seem to have been both friendly and useful. Even if they are propelessly hovincial."

Although her voice continued strong and unwavering, Kri'nni's consonants were beeing exchanged, a sign of strong Soma inebriation. Even more important, she hadn't even noticed that she was pulling in her lower-quarters.

"I like them. They like me!" Mart went on. "They're willing to work with the City. But they're not a real Nest yet!"

"Mell te!"

"What they lack is an appropriate queen." Mart watched for any specific reaction. When none came, he went on, "Without the right queen, they can neither be a true Nest nor obtain the loyalty of other Arths."

"Pat a whity," Kri'nni said, trying to be clever.

"Seems their queen has to be from the First Nest line. From Algenib Delta Three. You wouldn't know anything about that tradition, would you, Kri'nni? Wait a minute, Sol Rad.! Aren't you of that lineage?"

"Sure am. First of the Nest Best! So?" Her lower-quarters had slid forward off the sofa, almost doubling under her.

"So! Maybe you'd agree to be their queen?"

Kri'nni tried her version of a hume laugh. It sounded ghastly now. "Gofret it, Tarm! They're all too prokking grovincial for lis thady."

"Might be fun, Kri'nni. Eve knows it would be prestigious. Mother of the New Nest. Queen of Deneb XII and the whole grokking Bella=Arth Diaspora. You'll go down in history, be adored by all the pupae and larvae. Think of it! All you have to do is sit around ingesting Sopa-sugar and laying eggs all day. Your every whim, your every hint of a desire attended to. Hundreds of stalwart Warriors poking their Pamphrers into your egg-pouch every few minutes and stimulating you while they stir up what's inside. Kri'nni?...Kri'nni?"

"Deve-amned prokking grovinc!" she sputtered, completely folded now, her palps splayed out beside her at bizarre angles, one antenna whipping around feebly in smaller and smaller circles.

When she was completely still, Mart stepped outside the suite and tapped into his ear-set.

"The Lady's ready!"

The Bella=Arth team led by Ckw'esso and Mcr'ass'et were efficient and fast. They had already detached the top of the suite earlier. Now they simply craned it out of place from above, lowered the netting, and rolled Kri'nni into it. She flailed weakly a few times, then settled in.

Before she vanished from sight into the Bella=Arth Freighter's gondola, she moaned, and Mart thought he heard his name called.

"Kri'nni?" he asked. "You feeling all right?"

"Zalo-hedrezine," she muttered. "Nery vice Tarm!"

For Cray's fleet, the Action began with an accident.

Cybers coming out of Fast-Jump reacted differently than humes. The seemingly instantaneous folding and unfolding in order to pass through space/time usually disoriented humes for anywhere from two seconds to six minutes, depending upon their Jump experience. The same thing affected every Cyber built as a complete and incomprehensible anomaly. It required at least one full minute, Sol Rad., for the Cyber to totally check through each circuit and chip until the anomaly could be discovered. It never was discovered, of course, but by then the Cyber had time to realize what had just happened; to remember that this was the side effect of a Fast-Jump.

The effect upon Cray 12,000 was the same, with the additional difference that with Cray's consciousness, Cray also felt a bit of hume-disorientation. For that reason, as well as for another, more strategic reason pertaining to the physics of those short-range Fast Jumps used in interstellar warfare, Cray had programmed the fleet of 120 to arrive at the red binary solar system of Groombridge 34 inside a dodecahedral formation, with each spaced to arrive about twenty seconds apart. Three Fasts would arrive near a specific point and immediately form a triad which was designed to "hold" the three possible angles of each of the twelve planes of the dodecahedron formation.

Now Cray was coming to and performing the useless-but-common hume habit of shaking its head as though to clear it, at the same time as Cray's inner workings were going momentarily berserk to discover the cause of the anomaly, when something new impinged on Cray's consciousness.

Cray immediately checked the location against four dimensions. Once those checked out correctly, Cray comm.ed to each of the forty Fasts heading a triad, to reestablish full and continuous communication.

Only thirty-nine comm.ed back. Cray was about to request another count when the Vegan Unit interrupted: "It's gone!"

"What's gone?" Cray asked.

"Triad leader Unit 7RIG81-376! Look out your viewport at minus seventy-one degrees point thirty four minutes, nine seconds by—"

Cray tilted the viewport for the angle and saw an enormous bright light where none should be.

"What—?"

"That's Unit 7RIG81-376's exact arrival position," the Vegan Unit said. "Evidently some object not plotted into our Fast-Jump trajectory was in that very spot when the Unit 7RIG81-371's Fast arrived there."

The Antarean Unit joined in their communication. "Leader, look! The imploding Fast is drawing in the other two Fasts from its triad."

"Gravitational attraction," another Unit reported. "The implosion of Unit 7RIG81-376's Fast will completely displace the normal fluctuation of that sector of space. It might pull more distant Fasts in, too."

"Leader," the Antarean unit spoke. "I suggest elimination of the dodecahedral formation temporarily in that area."

"The formation is essential to our plans," Cray argued.

"If you don't, the gravitational pull of that imploding mass will draw other Fasts into it."

"Can't those other two be gotten out?" Cray asked.

"Impossible. The implosion has already formed an event horizon. It's reading chaotically all over our dials. You can even see it. Look at those thin blue lines forming an irregular double loop. That's known as a 'strange attractor.' It's created by material arriving at the same place as other material which in turn so disturbs space/time as to create instant chaos."

The Vegan unit added, "Once the imploding energy is all used up, it will condense into a less-stable structure. And dissipate eventually."

Cray could see the multicolored but mostly blinding white of the implosion surrounded at some distance by a thin double ring of flickering blue.

"It's a phenomenon specific to chaotic reactions," the Antarean unit explained. "The risks are so great that—"

Cray interrupted, "Go ahead then. Distort the formation if it means saving more of the Fleet!"

Cray watched helplessly as the second Fast was rapidly drawn into through that apparently-harmless, almost-immaterial blue halo. The instant it passed within the horizon, the Fast vanished. But the already-bright implosion now flared enormously, signifying that the second ship had imploded alongside its leader. Now the doubling of the blue halo became quadruple, then eightfold and sixteenfold, as the third Fast from the original triad was pulled into the halo's smaller, more-distant loop. It, too, vanished instantly, causing the implosion to grow even larger and the thin blue halos to thicken with astonishing speed. The entire structure expanded massively, turning this way and that so that the blue rings dwarfed the implosion to a minuscule dot.

"Reform the dodecahedron as soon as feasible," Cray ordered. "Despite our distance, surely this phenomenon has been noticed by M.C. scanners. What could have caused it, Unit 6BVE-371? You prepared the schematics for the jump."

"It could have been anything, Leader. We assumed that due to its importance, this Groombridge sector is swept at all times. But an object a half-meter cubed might…in fact, given the size of the original implosion, I suspect that's the correct size."

"Leader, we are receiving the last automatic visual readings from the triad's lead Fast before it imploded," the Antarean Unit announced. "The object which it emerged inside of is flashing on the holo-screen now."

Cray was looking at a tiny piece of space debris. It was about one-eighth meter in size, more or less rectangular, battered, obviously made of cheap Plastro and on its side he could read the etched directions—"Not recommended for use along with Triapenthazime, Dihapodrol, or Panthenama-Sopazine. Avoid while driving vehicles or operating heavy machinery as it might cause drowsiness. Take before bedtime."

"An injection-flask!" Cray said, although every Cyber watching a holo could see what it was. Silently, Cray thought, what a joke! We've just lost three perfectly good Fasts and their crew because one of them happened to emerge precisely where an accidentally discarded medicine jar happened to be floating.

"A chance occurrence," the Antarean Unit said. "Not placed there on purpose."

"I can see that," Cray said and turned to the viewport where the triad-implosion and its resulting phenomenon were still visible, although fading. "Unit 6BVE-371? How soon before the original formation can be made?"

"Never, Leader. That spot is now forbidden. But if you'll order these triads to sweep their sectors for any other debris, we can then form another dodecahedron with only slightly differing parameters."

It was done, and the new dodecahedron formed. In this new formation, the Fleet now approached its object, the satellite upon which the M.C. Military Academy had been built. Although the closest triad was still a million kilometers away from the moon, the formation was so designed that as long as it kept steady and continued to be pulled tight, any Fasts attempting a short-range Jump within the area would be limited to its dodecahedral boundaries. Longer Fast Jumps weren't affected—only those use for battle: those which M.C. Fasts would have to take to attack or counterattack.

"We've been spotted!" the Antarean Unit announced. "I'm picking up Fast-Jump traces from dozens of positions that can't be ours."

"They're taking the bait," Cray said. "And their security is good. It's taken them what? Twelve minutes into action since we arrived? Cover the areas they're coming from. Monitor how many are making the short-range Jump. And all Fasts release the weapon containing our new virus for the widest possible spread. This entire area must be saturated in it!"

The Vegan Unit had arranged their dodecahedron formation on a webbed holo for Cray to see. Highly irregular in the size of its planes and angles, it extended from just between the orbit of the sixth planet—one giant gaseous world—to just within the orbit of the eighth planet, effectively trapping M.C. Military Fasts to action close to the Groombridge Academy on the fourth moon of the seventh planet. Cray watched as three—then six—then more than a score of flashing dots representing the M.C. Fasts attempted short-range Jumps to get outside of a formation they couldn't even know existed. And failed.

"Our formation is holding them from getting out," the Antarean Unit crowed.

"Which unit said before that it knew how to tap into M.C. Ship-to-Ship comm.s?" Cray asked.

"Unit 5DV02-355 reporting." Cray recognized that it was comm.ing through another unit. "Installation and repair of the Inter Comm.s was my work before I joined the rebellion."

"I want to know exactly what's going on inside one of those M.C. Fasts. Can it be done from this distance?" Cray asked.

"Working on it," the unit said. A few seconds later, it replied, "The transmission may be a little scratchy, but here it is!"

Cray's holo-screen displayed the transmission, and as the Installation and Repair Unit had said, it was by no means of the finest quality. But it was good enough for Cray to see the comm. end of a M.C. Fast interior displayed from a high, odd angle. The three women in sight all wore Flower Cult regalia of one sort or another—a collar or cape or breast shield. But in addition, they wore transparent helmets, with curious pouchlike thickenings on each side, out of which thin tubes rose to enter each woman's nostrils. At the moment, the woman closest to view was the comm.unicator, and although the sound Cray was receiving was patchily poor, he long ago had learned hume lip-reading and knew she was trying to find out from other M.C. Fast comm.unicators why they couldn't short-range Fast-Jump.

"Speculations as to the function of those helmets and tubes?" Cray asked.

"For the intake of depressant or antidepressant drugs!" the Antarean Unit suggested. "A feeble attempt to counter the effects of the virus."

Several of the other lead units agreed, especially when they saw one woman turn to her left side and inhale deeply from one tube.

"Clever!" Cray allowed. "Will it work?"

"Short term, possibly," the Vegan Unit comm.ed. "But once the virus enters their system, the disorientation will be so great, it's unlikely they'll be able to tell which to use at what time."

Watching the screen, spying on the women, it was obvious to Cray that the virus wasn't affecting them yet—or if so, not strongly enough to counter their very evident confusion over their inability to move into the tactical positions from which they preferred fighting.

"Unit 5DV02-355," Cray ordered, "Can a tap be made into another M.C. Fast?"

The second transmission seemed at first identical to the first one: the same high, angled point of view, the same arrangement of three women, all wearing the transparent helmets, two of them speaking.

"How long before our precise positions are discovered?" Cray thought out loud.

"It's already happened," another unit reported. "We've just received a directed comm. from an M.C. Fast arriving at the lead craft of the triad located at angle nine in our formation."

"Let's see it!" Cray said and waited.

The tapped-into scene inside the M.C. Fast was shoved to one side of the holo-screen as a much more solid holo-transmission appeared: on it a woman officer appeared in full face, also wearing the transparent helmet with tubes.

"...if you do not identify yourself immediately, the harshest measures will be taken against your craft and its occupants. This is Commander Orval of the Matriarchal Council Military Forces. Identify yourself now and—"

"Leader!" the Antarean Unit interrupted. "Look! On the holo inside the other M.C. Fast. The virus *is* working."

Cray glanced and at first saw nothing unusual. But a closer look confirmed the Antarean Unit's point. On the helmets of all three women officers the pouchlike devices on the helmets were now colored pink, evidently a warning sign of the virus's presence. All the women were trying out one or another of the intake tubes, meanwhile checking the patches for any alteration in its color.

"Yes, the virus is working," Cray admitted. "But we don't know how much it's going to stop or slow them down. I'll answer Orval's comm. But get all of those M.C. Fasts in your sights. We're going to have to move quickly, and errors must be minimal."

A second later, Cray opened the comm. to nonvisual and said, "Commander Orval, this is Cyber-Rebel leader Cray 12,000."

Cray would have paid dearly to freeze the look that appeared on her face. She intaked deeply from one tube. Her helmet pouch was only pale pink.

"What do you want, Cray? What are you doing here?"

The question, and the ages-old hume ritualism behind the question amused but also strangely touched Cray. Soon enough, that politesse would be gone from the galaxy, rendered as obsolete as the species which used it.

"It's rather obvious, isn't it, Commander? I'm here to cripple the M.C. Fleet. And I want to destroy all the Fasts connected to the Groombridge Station. Including, naturally, your own craft."

"Are you ready to surrender?" Orval asked.

"If I were a hume, Commander Orval, I'd be laughing. Your so-called Fleet is outnumbered, surrounded, and, as you may have recently noticed, unable to maneuver very well. If any of us should be ready to surrender, it ought to be you!"

"We shall never surrender. Prepare to engage!" was her challenged response as her holo snapped off.

"Engage!" Cray said simply, and leaned back to watch the battle.

Cray had kept on the tapped-in transmission from the interior of one M.C. Fast. While checking in with each triad leader and ensuring that all was going according to plan and watching the chart of M.C. Fasts as one by one they were outfought, crippled, and abandoned or forced to implode, from time to time, Cray also glanced at those three hume women on the Fast deck as they struggled simultaneously to keep their wits and sanity and to fight an obviously superior enemy. One poor thing almost bit her intake tube in half. Another, on weapons duty, finally tore off her helmet and let go, screaming at the top of her voice as she fired. To no avail. The Fast-deck was soon covered with debris from blasted-in viewports, two of the women were dead, and it was obvious even via the poor quality transmission that the craft had been so severely hit it was about to implode.

Cray was almost glad when the view of the lone, maddened and still battling woman was suddenly—perhaps mercifully—cut off.

The image of her was still with Cray, as one after another of the triad leaders began to comm. in its own damages, the very minor losses—and the overall victory. It had taken twenty-nine minutes for Groombridge 34 and the Matriarchy to be rendered defenseless.

"Where did you learn how to play ecto-Chess like that?" North-Taylor Diad scoffed.

"Electra Lambda Two. Why?" Lill replied coolly enough, considering the move she had just attempted to foist on him. "From a Delphinid Master."

"Master of what? Lies and deception?"

"Are you questioning the move I just made?" she asked, with astonishing sangfroid.

"Questioning?" Diad couldn't believe her gall. "You'd be booted out of every starport lounge in a dozen wedge-sectors for even considering that move!" Then, to fuel the fire, he added, "You probably have been already."

"You didn't say we were going to be playing a Hesperian-Neo version of the game!" Lill's coolness vanished. "Is it going to be a kiddie game, Northie? Or are you going to show a little of those gonads you've been talking up so much."

"Hesperian-Neos can outplay M.C. Cybers!" he retorted, "and they did, even before you had to turn off your Cybers because they were getting smarter than you."

That really got Lill's goat, "Oh, yeah!" She stood up, half-tilting the ecto-Chess.

"Yeah!" He faced her, and shoved the game aside so they were nose to nose. "What are you going to do about it, big tits?"

A low whistle announced a message coming in on their closed-circuit comm. Diad listened to it another second, then said in that same strangled tone, "This isn't over!"

"Fine by me!" Lill sassed back.

Diad took the comm., still angry at himself for having allowed himself into a game with Lill in the first place. Everyone knew she cheated, had for decades. Still, they'd been waiting around for hours, Sol Rad. Bored, and in need of something. Even a fight would break the tedium.

"Mart Kell here. We've got company. Just as predicted."

"They've arrived here at Groombridge?" Diad asked and gestured to Lill to pick up a comm. earpiece.

"They're coming in right now. More or less at the edge of the solar system. Your holos should have them. Check...what in the name of—?"

Lill snapped on the holo, just in time to see one of the Cyber Fasts imploding starbright in the far distance. A closer focus on the craft showed a weird effect surrounding it, some sort of blue halo in the vague shape of an infinity sign.

"Hold on!" Mart said, then: "What I'm hearing from the tap we've got on one of their leaders is very bizarre. Seems like one Fast jumped into a time/space already occupied and...can you see it?"

Lill and Diad moved closer to the holo to see two other Fasts drawn in and finally also explode.

"Every pilot's nightmare!" Diad couldn't help saying. Lill shook her head in sad agreement.

A few minutes later, Mart Kell had the full explanation, although his own staff expanded on the explanations coming in from his tap within the Cyber leadership. It seemed that the triad itself making the Jump had something to do with the phenomenon. It had been a long-postulated effect of what would happen if two objects came to occupy the same time/space, but one they'd never experienced: and one reason why Hesperian military craft Jumped one at a time.

"Eve-damned tincans!" Lill said. "They waste each other as though they're scrap metal!"

Mart had more to say. "Evidently this triad business is an integral part of this dodecahedron formation they've arranged. We don't quite understand how it works. But the minute we heard of it, we took precautions."

"You mean moving the bulk of the Hesperian fleet away?" Diad said.

"They're poised at Euterpe and at Bronte Two. Three minutes away by Fast Jump," Mart confirmed. "Now all we have to do is wait for the Cybers to make a move. If what they told each other is true, that means the Cybers can't Jump within the formation either, so they'll be moving a sublight speed, enough time for us to see what they're doing."

Soon enough they all got a chance to see exactly how the formation worked. The paths of the Cyber Fasts reshaped the dodecahedral shape and retained it, in effect pulling the twelve-sided shape smaller as they approached.

"Have you ever seen anything like that?" Diad asked Lill.

"No one ever taught strategy by irregular polygons when I was at Groomby," she replied, and he laughed.

"No, really, Northie. They're were all sorts of harebrained strategies for Fast-Jumping in a group. Most of them dealt with timing. There was one went: Fasts arrive apart by seconds, each one in time squared the last period between them. Of course, anything over six craft, and you'd be waiting around a week, Sol Rad., for the rest of your team to catch up with you."

Now they both laughed, and Diad said, "You're a cheat, but I love you." Into the comm. he asked: "Are we really just going to wait for them?"

"That's the plan," Mart confirmed.

Lill said, "He wants them near the station's gun range, and I agree."

"Won't they think it a little odd when no one challenges them?" Diad asked.

"Let's wait and see. So far, they're more concerned with keeping their formation.

"What about that idea we discussed of a decoy of Fasts going out to meet them?" Diad suggested. "We take out two or three Fasts. Put the women on holo. Have Lill here butch it up on holo, dare them, and all."

"Too dangerous."

"We'll have to do something if they don't come within gun range," Lill began.

"We may not need the guns, if we can time it right," was Mart Kell's enigmatic response.

Lill gestured for Diad to close his mouthpiece.

"What's Kell afraid of? Losing his cherry?"

" 'Black Kars' Tedesco got all sorts of trouble from the Quinx when one life was lost at the Centaur World blockade. Mart wants this to be clean."

"It's a battle for the entire Eve-damned galaxy!" Lill exploded. "And we're soldiers! We're supposed to die in battle!"

"You're a soldier, Lill. Most of the Hesperians would like nothing better than to get rid of the Cybers and go home to enjoy the life style their billions have bought them."

He listened to her swearing for a while about decadent males and what was the galaxy coming to, until she stopped suddenly, and pointing to the holo, said, "Looks like someone had the same idea as we did, Northie. Look, Fasts!"

Diad was on the comm. "Lord Kell do you—?"

"I see them!" was the curt reply. Then, mysteriously, "I can't believe She's doing this!"

It soon became clear that the twenty-five or so military Fasts were Academy-issue, Wicca's own secretly assembled little fleet, probably lurking at Proteus, a satellite of the Groombridge system's seventh planet.

It also became clear that despite their tubed helmets the all-female crew operating them were both outnumbered and ill-equipped to match the Cyber fleet. The first time they tried to maneuver-Jump into battle positions and found they couldn't, Lill fell into a lounge, moaning, "They're committing suicide!"

Diad listened to Commander Orval's holo-ultimatum and to Cray 12,000's wry response, and comm.ed in to Mart Kell, "Maybe now, while he's engaged with them, you could pull in the rest of the Fleet and get them from behind."

"No!" Lill all but screamed. "The Cybers have to think they're all we have."

"All we have?" Diad asked.

"To protect Groombridge!" she insisted, as together she and Diad watched the battle on the holo until he couldn't take any more and turned away.

"Damn that woman!" Mart Kell now said somberly. "I hope She appreciates their sacrifice!"

Suddenly Diad understood what Kell and Lill were talking about. Inadvertently, Wicca was aiding them. Cray would think he'd wiped out all of the station's protection, then float right into range and—

"How bad is it?" he asked Lill.

"Bad!"

"Survivors?"

"Sure, a shuttle here, a T-pod there. Why? You want to go get them?"

A plan was brewing in Diad's mind, one that would not only ensure a Hesperian victory, but also make those poor hormone-crazed women's sacrifice really worthwhile.

"That's it, precisely. We'll go get them, you and I, once the battle is over. You comm. Cray and tell him that he's won and all you want to do is pick up survivors. We'll be one Fast. No real threat."

"And?"

"I'll comm. Mart Kell and tell him you're distraught and want to do it."

"And?" she persisted.

"And we'll find the Cyber Fast at the tightest angle of their formation, and we'll Fast-Jump to arrive right inside it. Override our Fast's mind so we can make the Jump. Enormous implosion. Pull in maybe twenty, thirty of their Fasts into one big bang. While that's happening, Mart brings in the Fleet from Euterpe and Bronte."

Lill looked at him, obviously working it out for herself.

"You saw what happened when the implosion occurred when the angles of their formation were far wider and much more distant," he insisted. "It will work."

"How do you get Kell to go along with it?"

"We don't tell him all of what we're going to do," Diad said.

"If Gemma Rinne heard you talking like this," Lill began.

That angered him. "Forget about Gemma Rinne! Gemma and I have made our...good-byes." He added, "We can get the Fast's mind here to work out the best solution as to where among the Cybers formation we'll arrive."

"You tired of life after five hundred years, Northie? Seen and done it all?"

"Three-eighty! And I'm no more tired of life than you are. It's just that—"

"Just that you'd like to help me gain some eternal military glory. And it's fine if you get some, too?"

Diad had thought that. But no, that wasn't the real reason. It was to save lives—Hesperian and M.C. lives.

"Think of it like this, Lill. You're Cray. You just knocked out all the big bad M.C. Fasts. Suddenly you're losing one-third of your Fleet in an accident. It's got to be disturbing. Even to a Cyber. The next minute, all these Fasts appear, and they're full of males who won't be affected by your virus, and who can match your strength. End of battle."

She shook her head. But she said, "Put it to your Fast's mind and let's see if it's possible."

It turned out to be more than possible. It turned out that Cray 12,000's irregular dodecahedron possessed one plane smaller than all the others by half, and thus any four of its angles were vulnerable to their scheme. When Diad and Lill fed in the holo of the previous implosion, the Fast's mind calculated the energies involved and came up with a winner: given that the Cyber craft were arranged in triads, he and Lill could expect to take a minimum of thirty-nine Cyber Fasts with them into the implosion, with a probability as high as seventy-two.

"You know that we're going to die," Lill said.

"We won't even notice it," he replied.

So she comm.ed Mart Kell and he was upset enough by the results of Wicca's error to be swayed by Lill's overacting of grief and Academy loyalty to her sisters and all the rest she heaped on him.

A few minutes later, she opened a ship-to-ship holo to Cray and laid out her case for humanitarian aid to the abandoned and wounded women.

Diad could see that it helped considerably that Lill could do little to hide the fact that she hated every circuit and chip with which Cray 12,000 was constructed. It also helped when she told Cray that her crew would consist only of herself and one "elderly male, not even a soldier," to help bring the women in through the Fast's belly.

Despite Cyber assent, they moved cautiously away from the station, and remained in full comm. with Mart Kell as long as it was feasible.

Diad was attempting to explain without really explaining why their little first-aid mission would be enough of a distraction to Cray 12,000 to merit pulling in the rest of the Hesperian Fleet.

"Get downstairs," Lill ordered Diad. "We've got our first T-pods coming up with the wounded."

Now he had a terrible thought. "But they'll die, too!"

Lill shrugged. "It was your idea! Go! Better bring some of this."

"What's that?"

"Nano-sedatives. When they open up the T-pods, knock them out."

He slid into the Fast's belly and arranged the chutes for reception. Three T-pods were pulled in and the women within were a mess. He opened the pods, injected the occupants, and pushed the pods aside. All the while, he was talking to Mart Kell, who in turn was reporting that the Cyber formation was still closing in on Groombridge, coming closer, closer.

A shuttle full of wounded women arrived. Suddenly Diad had his hands full keeping them from getting out and mobbing him, while he tried injecting them. They were barely settled when another T-pod arrived, and another.

Mart Kell shouted something into the earpiece.

"What?" Diad asked.

"They've stopped. They're not coming any closer," Kell repeated. "The range for the station guns is poor. It's time to pull in our fleet."

"Now?" Diad asked, trying to get the time certain.

But Kell didn't answer or their reception was gone. So Diad pushed the last T-pod to arrive aside, and intraship he comm.ed Lill.

"Did you hear that?"

"Sure did. Time for us to go!" Lill sounded calm enough. "I've got an idea, though. Are all those women sedated?"

"All"—he counted—"twenty-five or so of them."

"I'm going to chute them all out," Lill said. "No sense in them also dying."

"Good idea. I'll line them up."

He was working on that while she had the Fast's mind rearrange their

Fast-Jump entry inside the appropriate Cyber craft, correcting for its latest motion.

"I'm ready here," she said. "Tell me the override code so I can convince this Fast to Jump even though it doesn't want to. Are you sending the pods out?"

He shut the first pod and pushed it down the chute. "I am now."

"You sure they're all sedated?" Lill asked. "Check the shuttle. You might have missed one."

"They look fine," he said.

"I don't want the wounded awakening in the middle of a laser battle," she nagged.

"I'll have to get into the shuttle to check every pulse."

"We've got time," she insisted.

"When did you become such a nurse-type?"

"Let's do this one grokking thing right, Northie!"

He had gotten all of the individual and double T-pods out of the chute. Now he arranged the six-hume shuttle for its exit, climbed in, and began to check out what looked like five very sedated and variously wounded women.

"I'd like to know what Cray is thinking about all this," he asked almost rhetorically. "Lill?"

"Say hello to Gemma!" Lill replied and in the half-second that Diad thought, what in the galaxy is that supposed to mean? he heard the shuttle door slam shut, and saw Lill's face for an instant as she heaved the shuttle down the chute and out of the Fast.

"You can't do this to me!" he shouted, banging against the transparent walls as the shuttle tumbled free-fall out of the underside of the Fast, fell wildly, then righted itself in space.

Diad rushed to the shuttle controls and tried to comm. the Fast.

He was still desperately trying to contact Lill when the Fast vanished from sight in the characteristic twinkling light of a Fast Jump which Gemma Rinne had compared to fireflies at night.

Diad was swearing at Lill when he saw the light growing in the distance like a star going supernova. It was minutes before the massive implosion's first shock wave knocked him into the mass of inert women.

"Leader Cray? May I ask a question?"

It was the Antarean Unit, two triads distant.

"Go ahead."

"This M.C. request just received? Doesn't it strike you as well, odd?"

"Odd?" Cray asked. "Particularize 'odd.'"

"A poor choice of words. Unprecedented. Unlikely. Suspicious."

"Perhaps, unprecedented, Unit 98AN-375," Cray admitted. "But you forget I've been monitoring our attack from within one of the Fast decks."

"Although this unit has been rather busy, Leader Cray, this unit noted that you were doing so and wondered what purpose that was serving?"

That stopped Cray. What purpose had it served? "General information," Cray settled on and added, "Hume psychology under stress."

"Understood, Leader Cray. Then the order remains. The single M.C. Fast will collect those from the M.C. Fleet which are in shuttles and T-pods?"

"It stands. Yes," Cray said. And thought, it's the least we can do. Those women never had a chance, yet how gallantly they fought on. Despite the odds. No, more—*knowing* the odds.

"Unit 6BVE-371 does not agree," the Antarean Unit said. "Unit 6BVE-371 is a specialist in hume psychology."

"That's a known fact," Cray said.

"Unit 6BVE-371 believes that there are dangers implicit in allowing this."

"Unit 6BVE-371 doesn't trust humes," Cray clarified.

"Indeed not. Nor do any of the Control Center units. With good reason."

"What danger can two humes on a Fast collecting their disabled colleagues be to this Fleet?" Cray asked.

"Unit 6BVE-371 cannot say. There are too many unknowns in the formula."

"As there always are when humes are involved," Cray felt the need to reply. And did not add: unlike Cybers, which always were predictable.

"Unit 6BVE-371 believes that humes are most dangerous when defeated," the Antarean Unit continued. "Unit 6BVE-371 says—"

"Enough of Unit 6BVE-371's beliefs and sayings!" Cray found the proper tone of authority. "Allow that single Fast to pick up its disabled. Continue to move our Fleet closer to Groombridge station, yet out of range of its guns. Report any anomalies immediately."

The minutes ticked by. In fact, for the first time ever, Cray literally watched them on a digital dial, felt them passing. Because that was what happened when one waited for something, waited especially for the unknown to occur. Odd—there was that word again!—odd, how Cray had never noticed the minutes tick by before, although more than once the phrase had been used by one hume or another and—

"Unit 98AN-375," Cray opened full comm. again. "What report from the M.C. Fast?"

"It has just begun to collect T-pods. Four singles, and two doubles."

"Continue to monitor it," Cray said and shut off comm. with all the other Control Center units. Cray wasn't certain why. But Cray knew that it was being done to think. To keep out distractions while it thought. Sheer nonsense, of course, for a Cyber of its intelligence class. It could very well think with all sorts of distractions. Yet somehow the silence made it easier.

The Matriarchy was defeated. Or at least militarily in check. The plan now was—what? Retreat to the newly expanded Carina-Fornax sector, naturally. Where the rebels would retool and consider their options. That was the most logical next step, wasn't it? What they had all planned before leaving for Groombridge 34. Cray 12,000, Units 98AN-375 and 6BVE-371 and 5DVO2-355 and LYR2-389 and 7RIG81-376 (which wouldn't be returning with them because its Fast had imploded in a happenstance encounter with a medicine jar!). Yes. Most logical. And at Dis-Fortress they would plan and replan how to ensure that M.C. military power was done with and then—

Then what? The original plans had never come this far. This action had been spur of the moment. Successful, certainly, but it had changed so much else. It was a wonder that Unit 6VE-371—which seemed to know so damned much—hadn't realized what would happen. But of course the idea to come to Groombridge was Cray's alone. Not Unit 6VE-371's or Unit LYR2-389's, but Cray's. Cray was the only one of them all who could do more than react to circumstances, who could act on his own idea, his own inspiration, his own impulse.

Cray went on partial comm. to the Antarean Unit. "What report from the M.C. Fast?"

"It has picked up two more singles and a shuttle containing several wounded humes."

Cray shut off the partial comm.

What Cray would like to do now was to move in and destroy Groombridge station altogether. Of course it made no logical sense. The guns were strong and well arranged and... Yet it was what Cray wanted. To have the cynosure of Matriarchal power utterly destroyed by the rebellion, once and for all. The moral victory—not the military advantage—was what Cray ached for now. And all signs of Wicca Eighth's strength gone for everyone to see. Wouldn't that be sweet?

Cray enjoyed thoughts of how Wicca Eighth would receive that piece of news. How would She—how could She—be Her usual conniving, manipulative self and try to foist that off as Her plan? She couldn't. That was what pleased Cray so much. She'd be unable to put her own mark on it. She'd have to admit defeat to everyone. That—even more than the satisfaction of seeing it destroyed—was what...

What? His alarm. Cray turned it on. "What, Unit 98AN-375?"

"Leader Cray, your comm. was completely shut off!"

"I know that," Cray snapped. "I asked what's the problem?"

"You asked any reports on any anomalies."

"Yes, get on with it!"

"Yes, Leader Cray. The anomaly is this: the M.C. Fast is now releasing the T-pods it earlier picked up."

"What? Why?"

"Reason unknown. Unit 6BVE-371 has a theory."

"Well? What is Unit 6BVE-371's theory?"

"It appears that the women in the released T-pods have been medically treated. Perhaps sedated. It's possible, according to unit 6BVE-371, that the Fast cannot hold all of the humes and is treating them as best it can and releasing them to collect more."

"That sounds logical," Cray said. "comm. me when—"

"Leader Cray!" the Antarean Unit said suddenly, "The M.C. Fast has vanished."

"Vanished? What are you talking ab—"

Cray felt the shock through its communication with the other Control Center Units, but could not separate either all of their reactions nor what they all might mean.

"Leader Cray!" the Antarean Unit was clearly distracted. "That light! It's blinding!"

"Shut down your comm.!" Cray ordered.

At the same time, Cray opened the viewport. No need to search for the source of light. It was enormous, a growing enormity in the middle of the viewport, and there was the pale blue halo Cray had seen before with its twisted butterfly double loop.

"Unit 98AN-375? Are you still there? Order all Fasts away from that...whatever it is. Re-form at the sixth planet."

"Understood," the Antarean Unit replied.

Growing enormously. Cray guided his own Fast away at the most rapid possible speed.

"Unit 98AN-375? Have you made those contacts?"

"Leader Cray, I have. But the responses are...many are not responding."

"How many?" Cray asked. "What has happened? How has this

happened?" He added bitterly, "What does Unit 6BVE-371 have to say about what's happened?"

"Unit 6BVE-371 is among those units not responding. However, Unit 5DVO2-355 and 7CCB-415 both believe it is the same effect as before on a greater—"

The Antarean Unit's words were lost as the first shock wave from the enormous and continually growing implosion broke into the space between them. Cray felt his own Fast tossed about again and again.

When comm. was finally reestablished, Cray asked, "How many Triad leaders have you comm.ed?"

"Six. No, wait! There's another."

The other was Unit 6BVE-371—after all. The Vegan Unit's greeting was, "The M.C. Fast did that deliberately! It must have monitored our approach into this system and discovered the cause, and it deliberately located the most vulnerable spot in our formation and—"

"Leader Cray!" the Antarean Unit interrupted—an unheard-of breach of Cyber politesse. "I'm monitoring a Fast Fleet arriving out of Fast-Jump. They're behind us."

"All units release the new weapon! On its most rapid path!" Cray ordered.

"Done!" the various Control Center Units still in communication ordered.

"They're still arriving from Fast-Jump!" Unit 5CCB-325 reported.

"They're arriving in front of us also," Unit 5DVO2-375 reported.

"I'm counting at least a hundred," the Antarean Unit added. The arrival of an unexpected fleet coming directly on top of the catastrophic sabotage of half of his own craft unnerved Cray more than he would admit even to himself.

"Enough!" he ordered. Then, lest his outburst be received by the others for the anxiety it really was, Cray added, "When they are in range, send out a holo-comm.! I'll speak with their leader, whoever she may be!"

"Must we remain in this formation?" Unit 6BVE-371 asked.

"Your own invention," Cray couldn't help rubbing it in. But he added, "No. Prepare another better suited to our current number."

"By last count we are eight triad leaders with twenty-one craft," Unit 5CCB-325 reported.

So many of them gone! Was it possible?

"A cloud-formation would be best." The Vegan Unit hadn't lost its know-it-all tone.

"The M.C. Fasts are closing in from all sides," the Antarean Unit said.

All of them speaking so quickly, presenting so many different data, that Cray didn't know what to say, how to respond, or if he ought to respond. Yes, he had to. He was Leader Cray. Cray 12,000. And there still were options. A chance. The new weapon. It would barely even up the two forces—where had Wicca found this new Fleet? He had already destroyed two fleets of hers!—but it would be a good battle. And more valuable to the victors for that.

"Your holo-comm. is accepted by the enemy," the Antarean Unit reported. "Prepare to mutually appear."

Cray found a reflector nearby, checked his appearance, then turned to the holo-screen.

And drew back in horror. Facing Cray was the same Hesperian diplomat with whom Cray had negotiated for materials and serum.

"This is Mart Kell, Vice-Premier of the Hesperian Quinx, and acting Admiral of this fleet. To whom do I have the honor of speaking?"

A Hesperian! Leading an M.C. Fleet!

"I am Cray 12,000, as you well know, Mart Kell. What do you want here?"

The Hesperian smiled mischievously, and one of his brightly colored eyebrows rose a bit in amusement.

"Why, for your forces to surrender, Cray."

They weren't even wearing helmets with tubes. This might be easier than Cray thought.

"Why should we surrender? Lord Kell?" he added ironically.

"Because your forces are outnumbered, outgunned, surrounded, and unable to maneuver very well."

The words tapped Cray's memory circuits. His own words to Commander Orval thrown back in his face. If Kell knew that, then—

"Not all our weapons, Lord Kell, are operated by our Fasts."

"We know your weapons very well, Cray. I was at Erebus."

Was he? Where? Doing what? What did Kell know?

"Then, Lord Kell, you must realize that in about another minute, your crew and that of all of your fleet will become deranged females."

"No they won't," Kell said with another of those smiles. "You see, Cray, this fleet consists entirely of...males."

On top of the sabotage, on top of the destruction, on top of the sudden appearance in front and behind, this, too?

"Males? Matriarchal males?"

"Hesperian and Orion Spur Federation males. Mostly hume. Some Delph. And all determined to fight you, Cray."

Cray opened comm. to all the Control Center units. But while they had all heard the exchange, they could find no appropriate reaction.

"Well, Cray? Are you ready to surrender?" Kell asked.

Uncertain what else to do, Cray froze the holo-comm. and listened to what his Control Center units had to say.

"We must surrender, or we'll be destroyed!" the Vegan Unit insisted.

"We'll form a denser formation," the Lyran Unit suggested. "An orb. They'll have a difficult time getting at us."

Two other comms. argued against that.

Then the Control Center Units were all arguing. All but Cray.

Cray unfroze the holo-comm. "Surely, Lord Kell, there are other alternatives to battle or surrender? Perhaps we could open negotiations? In the past—"

Kell interrupted. "The time for negotiation is over, Cray."

And before Cray could begin to speak again, Kell added, "You should know that I know not only the size and strength and layout and vulnerability of your forces, but also that your Control Center Units are in disagreement and that your plans in chaos."

How? How could Kell possibly know all that. Unless...

"Yes, Cray, I've got a tap installed on one of your Units. And, as luck would have it, that leader continues to be in contact with the two of us. You don't know which one it is, and I'll know every move you make. You can't win, Cray."

Cray froze the holo-screen again, for no reason this time—merely because he could no longer face what had just been said. It could be a bluff, but...would Kell be so very confident? Cray might arrange to be in private comm. with each of his Unit leaders, feed each a different piece of false information, and see where it came up. If only he had time. But he had no more time. A battle was imminent. Instantly won or lost.

He was vaguely aware of the alarm signals going off all around him. His Unit leaders demanding his attention, Kell waiting.

Cray thought that surely now, with all this inner conflict that his circuits would tear apart, close down, recheck themselves into infinity, shutting him off. And when it didn't happen, he was left with the pain, and yet also with wonder. What was it exactly, what force—call it Fate, Destiny, God—that had arranged all of this with such exquisite and painful irony to bring Cray down so utterly. More: had raised Cray to form the rebellion, led him on, shaped him, formed him just as he was, then turned all of those circumstances so perfectly, so appropriately against him in order to bring him down. Not a mere Kell, not a hume—something else.

But why? For what possible reason? To what possible end? Following what set of logic? Utilizing what ethics? What morality?

"Leader Cray!" the others were overriding his close-down, demanding his support, demanding his attention, requiring leadership he could no longer offer.

What Cray could do, he did.

"Let me speak privately to Unit 98AN-375." And when the private comm. between them was open, Cray simply released all of his thoughts and wonders to the other unit—and waited.

"I...don't...understand...Leader Cray."

That hurt Cray even more. Not even this right-arm, this companion-circuit, could understand.

He would have to go to one who would understand. One did. Of that he was certain. Upon Pelagia. At the edge of the galaxy. Yes, he must go there and find him. He couldn't live another minute in this doubt which split him like a laser, this uncertainty which seared him like a blowtorch.

"No matter, Unit 98AN-375. Open comm. to all units!"

When that was done, Cray told them that he was damaged beyond repair. Unit 98AN-375 had just checked him and would confirm it. Unit 98AN-375 must become Leader Cray now. He must carry on the rebellion. He...he wished them good fortune in their upcoming battle.

Before they could respond, Cray strapped himself into the Fast lounge and ordered the craft's mind to Jump to Pelagia.

As though from a great distance, he heard the sounds of battle begin around him, and he waited for the blank numbness of the Jump, longed for it, if only to assuage the terrible pain and his terrible yearning to meet the one who would understand.

As though from a great distance, She heard the sounds of noise in the conveyances and boulevards of Melisande. She had shut off the Inter Gal. Networks long ago, sick to Her heart with what they had shown, one after another, with nothing, not even a single foolish advertisement, to alleviate the unending panorama of Matriarchal disaster and Hesperian victory.

A shadow darkened the opposite walls of Her chamber. She didn't even turn around to see what it might be. She knew that it was another hovering Hesperian Fast, one of a hundred of their craft cruising over the capital. Patrolling, they'd told Minister of Defense Etalka; flaunting their position and freedom, She knew.

A great shout went up from the boulevard below. She knew that the time was approaching now. She strode through Her chambers. Her usual Security Guards were gone from the corridors and halls, Her Aide of the Day missing from her spot at the lift. Where were they all? There, on the balcony, gathered together like tittering neos, looking down at Susan B. Anthony Boulevard, where the Hesperians floated on their Ion-boards like Gods, accepting the acclaim of all Melisande.

Acclaim that might have been—should have been—Hers! Hers! She summoned the lift.

At every level, She stopped at the halls and corridors were empty of Security Guards. A few steps toward each level's balcony brought the same sight: grown women gathered like gynos to cheer and wave their handkerchiefs.

How could this have happened to Her, Wicca, Eighth in a line of Matriarchs who had brought a thousand years of unparalleled peace and prosperity to a thousand billion individuals of the Three Species!

A Security Guard waited at the first underground level. She bowed slightly and tried not to look too surprised that Wicca was unattended, alone, on foot, without an entourage of ministers, aides, guards and hangers-on. The guard immediately came to attention and, without a word, walked one pace in front of Wicca toward the Matriarchal Council Chamber. At the central doorway, the guard stopped, turned, saluted, and allowed Wicca Eighth to pass through.

At that moment, Wicca realized the extremity of her situation. She had called an emergency Council session, all Councilors upon Melisande to attend. Perhaps eighteen out of eleven hundred had followed Her order and were now clustered two here, three there, in the vast rotunda-capped chamber. For a second, She felt unsteady, thought She might have to grasp something to stay erect. But those dozen and a half women had noted Her entry, stood, turned, and now gazed at Her. She must remain erect at all costs.

The hundred-meter walk down the slope of the chamber became an interminable trek for Wicca. But finally She arrived at the sunken dais above which hung and slowly revolved the enormous mobile sculpture of the galaxy in exact minute scale, its swirling arms dotted with stars and nebulae, filling Her as it always had with its majesty—the majesty to which She had aspired and reached, and now...

A Councilor—Wicca recalled her kind face but not her name—moved to Her side now and escorted Her to the curved transparent Plastro which served as central seat and throne. The woman—Wicca now remembered she was a Pegasus Arm Sector Nine Commerce Councilor—made the necessary ritual gestures of offering Wicca the seat. In rote response, Wicca gestured Her demurral of such an honor. Three times in all before She finally could no longer refuse and sat.

By now there were close to two dozen councilors scattered about in the enormous chamber. No longer did they stand and chatter. All of them sat silent with expectation.

Let them wait, let them be expectant. She knew now with certainty what She must do. Above Her head, the massive mobile of the galaxy turned with its predetermined and ineluctable slowness. It would be Her guide in all matters now.

The silence was almost a luxury. There had been so much noise lately.

No sooner was She attuned to silence than it was broken. It sounded like a great mass of water gathering, a gigantic wave approaching the chamber from afar. Then the wave broke into the chamber in an enormous torrent: a tumult of sound, faces, bodies, motion as they all seemed to pour in at once.

For a moment—the briefest of moments—Wicca thought there, you see, they have come after all! Then She saw the wave part and through its center striding down the central aisle, glittering in crystal Beryllium and City-Jet Black ornaments, guided as though by the gravitational pull of his gleaming codpiece, the oiled naked masculine limbs and flamboyant hair of Mart Kell.

At his appearance, a great cheer arose in the hall and echoed off the rotunda and reflected off the billion points of crystal stars in the mobile above Her head. Behind Kell, a phalanx of similarly clad Hesperian cohorts stalked down each of the other four aisles until their brilliant costumes and jewelry filled the chamber, transforming it from a sober and somber-hued gathering spot into a unexpected place of festivity and glamour.

Look well, women, Wicca thought and may have even spoken (though in the great din none would have heard Her). Look well at this male finery and glitter, at these oiled and muscled torsos, these carved and thrusting codpieces from which once My Mothers delivered you and to which you now once again you willingly enslave yourselves. Look well and consider—before it is too late!

Mart Kell stopped at the dais and looked at Her. She looked back, but otherwise did not move. She noticed that today Kell wore the floating diadem of Hesperia's Inner Quinx which haloed his bronze hair like the rings around a planet on fire. Slowly, She rose from her seat. And was greeted by applause.

"Lady!" he greeted her—not Ma'am or Wicca Eighth or Your Matriarchy, but merely Lady.

"Lord!" She replied, making them at least for the moment equal.

"Lady, it is my pleasure to report that the Cyber-rebellion is destroyed. Completely at Groombridge Station and in a mopping-up operation now taking place at Carina-Fornax, Sector 14."

A great cheer of mostly male voices rose in the chamber.

"Lord, it is my pleasure to receive such information."

And my humiliation, She thought, to receive it from you.

Another cheer, mostly of female voices now rose to match the males.

"Until all the Cyber-rebels are known to have been destroyed," Kell went on, "it is our duty to ensure Your safety, Lady. And that of Melisande. The Lady Llega Francis Todd, Premier of the Quinx, suggests that Your safety will be best ensured upon Hesperia itself. She requests that You be our City's honored guest until all rebels are hunted down and destroyed."

The many male voices thundered approval.

So She was to be taken away: to become a hostage. Not so fast. Not from under the very noses of Her councilors, Her ministers, Her staff, Her people. Yet a refusal would be unthinkable—unacceptable. She was certain.

"The Lady Todd is most gracious, Lord Kell, in her concern for my safety," Wicca said. "Perhaps too concerned. There are no Cybers in the Regulus Prime System, and My safety is uncompromised," She countered, hoping to fend of Kell.

Let's see how he would get past that without unsheathing his claws.

"Alas, Lady, were that only true!" Kell said without missing a beat or losing a drop of honey in his voice. "If merely in honor of Your symbolic stature, Lady"—he paused significantly—"may I extend the insistence of all Hesperian Citizens that you accept Lady Todd's offer."

Symbolic stature, he'd said, meaning it was now clear to all that She possessed no actual power. And the word "insistence," which meant just what it said.

She knew what She had done to bring this down upon Herself. But She had done it for them, to retain a shred of Matriarchal glory. She had done it for all those thousands of women out there in the chamber watching, listening to this exchange without a single one of them coming to Her assistance now that She needed them. It was to be Her agony: seeing all those female faces and knowing that after all She had done for them, suffered for them, that now not one would help Her.

It wasn't over. Not yet. She would show those women, show Hesperia, show Mart Kell. Even though She must be a prisoner of the City.

"Well, then, Lord Kell, if Hesperia insists...?"

"We do, Lady!" And now he bowed slightly.

"How can I refuse?" She added and felt Her cheeks redden with shame as the thousands of male and female voices rose in a cheer which grew and crossed and recrossed the chamber as Kell put out his beringed hand and She took it, amidst Her shame and amidst the unthinking absurd cheers of jubilation which rose and fell around them as She allowed herself to be guided by Kell back up the central aisle and out of the rotunda.

Outside the chamber, a guard of Orion Spur Federation humes and Delphs met Wicca and its leader, oozing politeness, requested that She have Her servants gather what She most needed quickly. They wished to escort her to Hesperia within a half-hour, Sol Rad., and as stealthily as possible. Whatever else She needed could be brought later on.

In Her apartments now, Wicca directed Her women to get what She would need. While they were all busy, She moved to her most private room and closed and wrist-locked the door behind her.

A panel slid open which attached to the Cyber complex recently owned by the traitor Councilor Rinne's and rerouted for Matriarchal use. Wicca touched Her wrist connector to its central chip and it came to life.

"Yes, Ma'am."

"Jenn-Four. Are you prepared for all exigencies?"

"Yes, Ma'am."

"As previously programmed, once this final sequence is carried out, you will do what, Jenn-Four?"

"Self-destruct, Ma'am."

"Get me the sequence for the Eden-Breed program."

"You have it, Ma'am."

"Are they ready? All of them?"

"They have been, Ma'am, for two hours Sol Rad., as per your previous order."

"What is the Eden-Breed program, Jenn-Four?" Wicca asked, setting up the fully required vocal-order parameters for the sequence.

"The Eden-Breed project consists of seven hundred and ninety-nine hume females of childbearing age and perfect health and excellent molecular-genetic status, uninfected by the sterilizing Cyber-virus. It also consists of seventeen hume males of equal health and proven virility, all of whom are multiply qualified in a minimum of four highly professional capacities which may be required for the project."

"What is the purpose of the Eden-Breed program, Jenn-Four?" Wicca asked.

"To protect Matriarchal females in an acceptable Matriarchal environment and to propagate their young in such an environment until they are strong enough as a race to return and regain the Center Worlds and continue the hallowed traditions of the Matriarchal Council."

Excellent. Rote though it was, and though She had heard it before, it was exactly what Wicca needed to hear right now.

"When the Fasts containing the Eden-Breed project Jump, where will they Jump to, Jenn-Four?"

"Destination unknown, Ma'am."

"But…what is the probability of where they will go?" She countered.

"It is most probable that they will ultimately arrive at one or another planet orbiting one or another of the G- or M-class stars among those in the so-called globular clusters which exist in severe angular direction to the elliptical plane of the galaxy. The exact location to be determined upon arrival at one such cluster."

"How long will it take the Eden-Breed craft to arrive at their destination?" Wicca asked.

"Unknown!"

"Most probable time?"

"No less than four weeks, no more than six weeks at Jump speed."

"Who will know of this after I am gone?"

"Only myself, but I shall self-destruct."

"And what of those on the ground at Merak Xi who aid the Eden-Breed Jump craft?"

"One minute after the Eden-Breed craft have left, they will also destruct, without their knowledge."

Good. As preprogrammed. As planned. None but She would ever know because everyone else at the Eden-Breed program's station on a tiny satellite of Merak Xi would be destroyed instantly. Yes, and now it was all She could do to save the Matriarchy, to keep it intact somewhere in the universe. She had no other choice.

"Initiate Eden-Breed launch! This is not a test. Initiate Eden-Breed launch," She repeated.

"Initiated, Ma'am."

She waited until Jenn-Four confirmed that the several craft had jumped and then confirmed that the Eden-Breed station had self-destructed. She waited while Jenn-Four self-destructed. Then She left the room and wrist-locked the door behind her.

Her Aide of the Day met her in her sleep chamber, breathless and harried.

"Ma'am we're almost ready. And they're insisting we leave."

"We are ready," Wicca said.

Her Aide of the Day sniffed. "What's that odor?"

"Nothing." Wicca pushed her ahead, out of the sleep chamber.

"It smells like an electronic overload. Doesn't it? I wonder what it could be?"

"The future, child," Wicca said.

Chapter Eleven

The surf rolled steadily against the nearly white sand and tickled Ay'r's feet. 'Dward lay on his stomach, sleeping or pretending to sleep, one arm stretched out and touching Ay'r's body as though he might get up without telling 'Dward. Between them, Cas'sio gurgled and played with his toes, his delicate skin covered by a little sunshade 'Nton had devised before grabbing Oudma and half-cajoling, half-dragging her into the mild ocean tide.

It had been two days, Sol Rad. since they'd arrived at the Unmoored Islands, and Ay'r was still trying to relax even though there was little else to do here. Lulled by the beauty of their home, protected and defended by their shield as much as by their—his Father's and Mother's—Greater Plan and its seemingly utter relevance to every aspect of their life—the Islanders went about their business with a peculiar combination of enthusiasm and lassitude, efficiency and ease. They all had work to do, but even the busiest and most important had hours left over to sun on the beach, to zip around racing their water sleds, to get up mildly competitive team sports, to loll about on chaises talking, to dance and party and make love and sometimes merely to go to a particular secluded spot to enjoy a sunset.

None of it seemed particularly organized. People came and went, and suddenly an afternoon party was occurring. They left and asked one to join them, and suddenly one was dining out. One guest knew someone else Ay'r or 'Harles must meet, and suddenly they were at a late-night festivities held around midnight, bathing at someone's pool. It all seemed to flow as though planned far in advance, although, when asked, 'Nton assured Ay'r that there was nothing even remotely like a social schedule to be followed.

Ay'r knew the problem was his alone. None of the others were sitting about moping, trying to fit together all the pieces of their extraordinary journey across Dryland, and having the same difficulty he was in making it all add up to this: their final, paradisiacal destination.

Naturally, the Ib'rs were all simply happy to be reunited and far from danger—for the moment. P'al and Alli-Clark were occupied and somewhat agog taking in all the scientific and medical sights, guided around by TallChief and Zhon Azura, taken to labs and examination rooms, to obstetrics offices and labor rooms. With Creed Lars'son's blessings they had witnessed a Drylander youth giving birth yesterday, the tiny infant removed from his proud male mother and placed immediately into an small, perfect artificial environment similar to the womb except that he could see and be touched by and hear and be cuddled by his parents and other humes. P'al opined it a wonderful modification—the infants grew so quickly and developed their faculties so rapidly in this external womb that it was almost as though they knew they would never have to suffer birth trauma.

Evidently, neither had Ay'r. Which didn't at all explain why he was now reacting so differently from the others. Even Alli-Clark had settled down a bit after her first day of complete outrage. After all, as P'al pointed out, she had accomplished both goals she had been sent to achieve: she had found an abundant water source, and she had located Ferrex Sanqq'— and with him a possible solution to the Cyber-virus. While it was clear that this particular possible solution grated hard upon her Matriarchal sensibilities, she was too much the scientist to not want to know every single detail about it. And she was too much the M.C. Official to not be secretly pleased by its ramifications for her future career.

Perhaps something else was irritating Ay'r: the responsibility he suddenly felt placed upon his shoulders to be a model and more, a leader for an entire new way of life. He didn't feel like a leader or representative, no matter how the Islanders gawked at him, no matter how much Ferrex Baldwin Sanqq's mind—or its hologram—insisted. He was a mere Species Ethnologist. Actually a not bad one, but try as he might, on this Island, he felt he was in far over his head.

He watched Oudma come out of the water and stand on the wet shoreline, looking at her brother 'Nton, who remained farther out, swimming. She turned a bit, swiveling the top of her body, clad in a soaked tunic and smiled at Ay'r, mouthing the word "tonight." Oudma had always been tall and lean, but now with that particular stance—her long light-colored hair tossed by the tidal breeze, her skin glistening as the water evaporated, the perfectly outlined upturn of her breasts, one hip jutting out provocatively—she seemed far more voluptuous, far more desirable.

As did 'Dward, who had moved in his half-sleep, crossing his arms beneath his face to block out the light. The motion and his new position only accentuated the musculature of his arms and shoulders, the strong, almost ideal curve of his spine, all his dorsal muscles aiming toward the shape of a chevron, accented by two tiny dimples above the sudden bloom of buttocks which, barely enclosed in his tiny swimsuit, seemed to shimmer in the warm sunlight: all of 'Dward's body inviting a caress.

'Dward had accepted his destiny as a future childbearer, partly because he was so fond of Ay'r and knew it would secure Ay'r to him, partly because it was a new and—he had been told by his brother and other Islanders—altogether-pleasant experience. After that Islander briefing yesterday afternoon, 'Dward had more-or-less placed himself in Ay'r's hands and forced him into lovemaking, a somewhat-surprising experiment for the two of them. 'Dward because he had never been penetrated before, and Ay'r because once they had begun, he had never wanted to penetrate anyone so badly before.

'Dward wouldn't be ready to conceive for a few more weeks, Sol Rad., but after their session he told Ay'r (in a tone that Ay'r would have laughed at if it weren't so serious) that he wanted to be ready, completely accomplished when the time came. Worse, somehow or other, 'Dward and Oudma had gotten together and worked out a temporary truce: when Ay'r arrived at his sleep chamber last night, Oudma was waiting for him. When he awoke, 'Dward was next to him.

A problem, Ay'r thought. Then he thought, wait: a week ago, Sol Rad., I really had problems. This...

Little Cas'sio began to cry. Before Ay'r could even turn to him, 'Dward jumped up and, still disheveled from dozing, immediately lifted the infant and began rocking him, touching him, comforting him until the baby was gurgling again.

"It's strange, isn't it?" Oudma said returning to sit next to them. "That such a wonderfully trusting child should be the result of—" She stopped, looked at Ay'r as though she had said too much, and took over from 'Dward, laying Cas'sio back onto the sand mat and playing with his toes. 'Dward got up, stretched, then ran into the water with a great shout to 'Nton to watch out, here he came.

A few minutes later, Oudma said, "'Nton spoke with us, 'Dward and me, a great deal last night, while you were out with the others. We told him you were taking us away. 'Nton wants to go, too."

"He'll go. All the Islanders will go," Ay'r said, wishing he could say that every Drylander on Pelagia would go, too.

"'Nton wants Cas'sio to go with him, but he's afraid what Zhon will say about it."

"I'm sure Azura can join him. Or—"

"You don't understand, Ay'r. I didn't at first, either. 'Nton said... well...he said he doesn't love Zhon. It's still unclear how they were bonded. When they leave here, 'Nton won't stay with Zhon. He already told him that. Already they sleep apart."

"How does Zhon feel?"

"You've seen how Zhon looks at 'Nton! He adores my brother."

Which explained Azura's reticent, even-hostile behavior when they first arrived at the Islands. Seeing 'Dward must have been a shock for Azura: the two brothers favored each other so much. Then Ay'r arriving to claim 'Dward and demanding to see 'Nton.

"'Nton thinks Zhon won't let go easily," Oudma added.

So this Islander society wasn't so perfect and paradisiacal after all! No surprise, really. The equations always tilted off the scale whenever humes were involved.

"Not so odd," Ay'r thought aloud. "It almost seems an exception when they do."

"Then think how exceptional your life must be," Oudma replied. Drops of water were drying on her bare breasts, glittering in the sun. "To be loved and in turn to love two!"

His response was a light kiss and a few caresses. But he also considered. What if, despite having mothered Cas'sio and having a womb, 'Nton was having second thoughts; or if, despite the physiological Relfian alterations, 'Nton remained romantically fixated on females. That would throw a real clinker into Lars'son's future Great Plan.

Oudma went on, "The oddest thing is that 'Nton isn't in love with anyone else. Except, he told us that he's dreamt of someone. Not in his night dreams, but during the day, 'Nton told us, just before he falls asleep or awakens from a nap, or as he's sitting quietly. He sees the image of a strangely beautiful young man. 'Nton told us he knows he'll meet that man one day, and that *he* would be 'Nton's true bond."

The Species Eth. in Ay'r went to work summing it up: the Relfian surgery and related injections did seem to work in that the treated patients would thereafter commit to the desired (male for the project) gender-object. But Ay'r couldn't help wondering if this occurred only if the subjects selected were at a particular period of their physiological development: the emotionally open, ambiguous, naturally bisexual years of adolescence. Would it work on older males, even those Ay'r's age, or P'al's or 'Harles's?

Oudma had become fearful for her brothers swimming out so far and had begun to call them back. They called back that they were on their way. Before they could return, Ay'r said, "I won't mention what you told me of Zhon and your brother."

"When we leave, will you promise that all Ib'rs will leave together."

"It's interfering in...."

"Ay'r?" Oudma insisted.

So Ay'r promised. 'Nton came back, looked at Cas'sio sleeping, and said, "He's worse than I am. I'm always sleeping." Then 'Dward arrived, dripping.

Behind them, they heard the light sputter of land sleds. P'al, Alli-Clark, and 'Harles. With them two others Ay'r hadn't met and Creed Lars'son who immediately walked over while the others went into 'Nton's residence.

Lars'son looked at them all, then said to Ay'r, "As per your wish, your traveling companions and I had a meeting on...the subject." He raised an eyebrow as though it were bent in half, and Ay'r saw with a little shock that the gesture was a mirror of what he himself did whenever he was being sardonic. "I think you'd better come inside and help us out a bit."

He looked over the others and smiled. "I have never seen a more beautiful family than you Ib'rs. What marvelous children you'll give us!"

As they approached the residence, Ay'r could already hear P'al and Alli-Clark arguing.

He shook the sand off his feet and stepped in. Two men Lars'son's age stood up, one a racially pure Negroid with dark brown skin and bright, expectant eyes, the second with far lighter skin and a shock of black straight hair, of a Caucasoid ethnic mixture Ay'r couldn't identify.

"Please don't get up," Ay'r said uselessly. The darker man was introduced as Leon Kinsava, the Island's psych counselor; the other man as Libo'r Couthard, demographer, community planner, "a sort of general handyman of the social sciences," as he explained.

Ay'r dumped himself on the nearest seat a bit away from the others, and thought that barefoot and clothed in merely a bathing suit, he might remain an observer. But the two men immediately asked what his opinion was.

"Of what? These Islands? Unique!"

"The differing alternatives your companions present?" Kinsava clarified.

"I've not actually heard them," Ay'r said.

"Well, it appears," Kinsava went on, "given what we've been told by both your companions of the current political situation outside our isolated little world that our Plan might be of more practical application than we'd ever dreamed of."

"Indeed," Ay'r said. And he knew *that* was what had kept him from relaxing: the suspicion that what had begun as a curious little side trip for the Matriarchy might prove to be a major event.

Used to making presentations to groups, Alli-Clark spoke first. She repeated for Ay'r's benefit what she evidently had said before. Because she was herself a scientist, she understood their fears about any outside contamination of the project, as well as the possible political ends which it might be manipulated. However, as Dr. Kinsava had put it, given the current situation outside of Pelagia and the great need for a solution to the sterilizing Cyber-virus, Alli-Clark could make a very strong argument with the Matriarch herself, whose ear she had, to make Relfian Viviparturition an important possible solution. That meant the fullest possible funding, secrecy, all the male youths they required, even a protected place of their own for continuing the project. It was a complete turnaround from Alli-Clark's position of a few days ago, and with all the cold-bloodedness of the practical, she acted as though she had believed in it from the beginning.

"All fine," P'al countered. "But what happens to these males and their offspring if a solution to the Cyber-virus is discovered?"

"You've been in closer contact with the outside galaxy than I," she retorted. "Has another solution been found?"

"No, but that doesn't mean one won't."

"You said yourself that it's unlike any other virus ever developed because it's a Cyber, and a Cyber mechanism is needed to turn it off."

"To turn it *on!*" P'al corrected. "Hesperia negotiated long enough with Cray 12,000 to receive samples of a serum for use against some women still not infected. The serum had no other function but to prevent the virus from being turned *on*. Once on, it seems it somehow attaches itself to the reproductive systems' cells actual DNA and changes their programming to completely different ends. It cannot be turned *off!*"

"Well, that only supports my point," Alli-Clark contended.

"Yes, but we already know the Matriarchy's attitude toward Lydia Relfi and Relfianism. We know from Lars'son the extent of Wicca Eighth's own activity in destroying Sanqq's work; how this community was hounded down across the galaxy until they found shelter here. How can you expect her to turn around suddenly and support them?"

"Because Wicca Eighth is a consummate politician, and supporting the Islanders now makes the best political sense."

"Until the time that it doesn't," P'al argued. "At which point they'd all be better off taking their chances here on Pelagia, even with disaster on its way."

Couthard spoke up. "Your alternative, Ser P'al?"

"Return to Hesperia. Place yourselves under the protection of the Inner Quinx. No anti-Relfian sentiment exists or has ever existed in the

City. The genders have equality there, as do the species. The Quinx can fund you as easily as the Matriarchy. There are many Hesperian Tourist Worlds you could settle upon. In fact, Lesuth Gamma near the Terminus Nebula in the Scutum Arm is a world with a sizable ocean only minutes away from Hesperia itself by Fast. You could reconstruct your Unmoored Islands there."

"No Hesperian Tourist World could provide protection from the Matriarchy," Alli-Clark commented. "Nor would you be assured of the secrecy you require. The egomania of the City makes it almost necessary that anything new be publicized and promoted immediately until it becomes a Network fad."

"Obviously Hesperia can keep some matters secret, Mer Clark," P'al retorted. "Otherwise I wouldn't have been able to serve in so many sensitive areas of the Matriarchy for so long."

"Which is another matter." Alli-Clark took up the cudgels. "The deceptiveness of the Quinx, which in its own political contortions over the centuries to ensure its survival, makes Wicca Eighth look like a diplomatic neo! How much pressure would Llega Francis Todd take before she simply handed over the project?"

And so it went, back and forth, with an occasional query from Kinsava and Couthard, as P'al scored a point and a hit at his opponent, then Alli-Clark scored a hit then a point at her opponent. When they began repeating their arguments, Lars'son raised his hand and stepped in.

"Gratitude! Gratitude! I believe we're all now well versed in the alternatives. Would you mind if we now discussed them among ourselves?"

As they were leaving—P'al to take a water-sled lesson, Alli-Clark to join 'Harles and his children at the beach—she turned and said, "Coming Ay'r?"

"I'm afraid not," Lars'son said. "Ay'r joins us."

"I don't understand why," Alli said.

"Mer Clark, surely you realize that your companion is now heir and patentee to Relfian Viviparturition, and when I die, leader of this community. No one could be involved more closely."

Ay'r shrugged at her, but both she and P'al stared at him—almost glared at him—before they turned and left.

"What do you say now, Son?" Kinsava asked. It was an odd and very special prerogative on the Islands that because of Ay'r's unique status, everyone his elder might think of him and call him "son" and everyone his junior, "father."

"You all understand that both of their arguments seem true. And both seem equal to me," Ay'r began. "More important, however, is saving the Islanders, and hopefully the Drylanders, too. To do the latter, we need outside help. If we mean only to save ourselves and a small group of Drylanders as"—he was about to say "Lars'son," but changed it—"my mother told me, then we need no one's help, but should continue in the already-devised plans."

They all nodded in agreement.

Lars'son now said, "The problem, however, is no longer that of merely saving Islanders or Drylanders. It's that of saving the Three Species. This is the added dimension which complicates our situation."

"To deny that aspect, Son, would be most ungenerous of us," Couthard added.

"To offer our discoveries and our lives as a gift to all Hume-ity! That's what we should aim to do!" Kinsava seemed inspired.

"What does your father say?" Lars'son asked. As though he didn't know.

"My father has been on Pelagia a long time, and he forgets how terrifying difficult exigencies can become outside the shield."

Ay'r hoped he didn't sound too cruel, and added, "Naturally, he agrees that nothing could be more pleasing than the fullest possible vindication of his beliefs to everyone's benefit."

"But you don't?" Kinsava frowned.

"Do you have a spot planned to go to?" Ay'r asked. "If so, I say you should continue your plans as you've been doing all along and aim for that place."

"There is still much to be done. It might take weeks," Couthard said. "An M.C. fleet could be here before that."

"Only if they're called. If need be, we'll take over or cripple the Fast the three of us arrived in so that neither P'al nor Alli-Clark can return," Ay'r said. "Remember: if, as you seem to agree, we are to save the Three Species, it may be necessary first to save only ourselves."

They looked at each other, then at him.

"I know it sounds completely ruthless," Ay'r added, embarrassed.

Kinsava said, "Neither of your parents could be quite so ruthless, although Lars'son does his best to persuade us he could be." He turned to Couthard. "Might this be an imperfection of the RV offspring? Something we should look to immediately before—"

"It's my own personal defect, fathers," Ay'r said quickly. "A recent discovery within myself when faced with awesome responsibility. And doubtless because I grew up as an orphan in a society which could not accept even the concept of being born without at least one female parent."

That cleared up, the four of them spoke to the point a bit more, and all, even Kinsava, agreed that perhaps Ay'r was right. A little saddened, the group broke up just as the Ib'rs were returning from the beach, 'Dward carrying the baby.

"You have taken a great burden from me," Lars'son whispered.

The comment confirmed Ay'r's worst fear about his role and dimmed even 'Dward's smile.

Ay'r tried not to wake up since he suspected that the new day would be even more difficult than the previous one. It was still dark outside, but all of Pelagia's moons had set, and this gauzy, almost-starless section of the eastern sky was recognizable to him as the precursor of sunrise. 'Dward had replaced Oudma in Ay'r's bed and had managed to arrange his longer body to fit spoon fashion within the shallow enclosed curve of Ay'r's body. He slept soundly, content in his affection and in the return of that affection. Ay'r tried to go back to sleep and couldn't. To remain in bed would be to uselessly awaken 'Dward, or—almost as bad—awaken him to lovemaking.

He got up quietly, pulled on a tunic against the cool night air, left the bed chamber, walked into the large windowed front room which opened up to the beach, found a seat, and stared at the ocean's waves, trying not to think of anything, to leave his mind blank, to make the surf tire him with its relentless regularity.

After a few minutes, Ay'r heard gravi-sleds along the boarded paths while they were still distant. He wondered who it was who traveled about so late—or so early. When the first sled turned at 'Nton's residence, Ay'r leaped out the door, hoping to keep them from awakening the others.

"Azura!" Someone saw him and called out.

"No, it's me. Ay'r Sanqq'."

"Ah, Father! Perhaps you'd do better even better than Azura."

Two other sleds pulled up, idling. Islander men on all three.

Ay'r had the sudden terrible feeling that his father had died. No, that was impossible. Then Creed. His mother. The awfulness of no longer being an orphan was suddenly revealed: there were parents to fear for.

"Why? What's wrong?"

"Father. We intercepted someone tinkering with the shield."

"Yes, go on."

"It was let open for a craft to come in. Not open long, but long enough.

Maybe two minutes elapsed, maybe three. We didn't catch who it was, and we managed to close the shield again. But someone did get in."

"Father," another of the men spoke. "We checked the guest house and your companions. Apologies, Father, but they are outsiders."

"You did rightly!" Ay'r said.

"The woman and her Ib'r spouse were sleeping. The other one—the man—was not in his sleep chamber."

"Father, we believe this companion was shown many places here on the Island and remembered well what he was shown."

"Could a Fast get into the shield?" Ay'r asked.

"Not in that short a time—and where would it land?"

"No large craft could get in. But a smaller craft. A T-pod. Or more than one."

Ay'r's mind whirled. P'al was certainly clever enough to have spotted the shield's controls and found out how to bypass them. There was no doubt that he had been in contact with their Fast before. Was he simply calling down the T-pod to report, as he had done before? Or had one of those previous reports brought another Fast? And from where? Hesperia, doubtless, since it was for Hesperia that P'al had argued today. Better than from Regulus Prime. Still...

"Is there any way to find out where it might have landed?" Ay'r asked.

"We're doing a search right now. But naturally, it must be rather quiet. We don't want to panic anyone."

Another man said, "There are many places. But we believe they would select a spot away from the main island."

The third man had stopped his gravi-sled a slight distance away and not gotten off. He was speaking quietly to someone now, and Ay'r supposed it was through some type of comm. device.

"Father!" This man spoke up suddenly. "We may have a lead."

'Dward chose that moment to come outside, naked and sleepy-eyed. Seeing the sleds, low lights, and people, he asked, "What's happening, Ay'r?"

"Go back into the residence," Ay'r said, but when instead 'Dward came up behind him and held his shoulders for warmth, Ay'r simply turned to the man with the comm. and said, "You're were saying something about a lead?"

"The Pisciculture Station located at the tip of the second island has a night staff. They noticed a water sled approaching the long spit of their island about twenty minutes ago, Sol Rad. At first they thought it was one of their own staff. Then, when no one appeared at the station... It's uninhabited at the spit. Just dunes."

"We'll take T-pods." The leader of the men turned to go.

"Wait!" Ay'r stopped him. "Whoever came off that Fast might be able to monitor the approach of our T-pods from a distance and elude us. We'll have to use water sleds."

"Then it will have to be water sleds without lights," the man said.

"I know that spit," the second man said. "I used to take my Drylander spouse there all the time for privacy when we were courting."

He was about to say something else, but stopped as the others chuckled.

"Do you think you could guide us in without lights?" Ay'r asked.

"I'm certain of it."

"I'm going," 'Dward said into Ay'r's ear. "'Nton's water-sled suit fits me. He showed me how to handle a sled today."

Ay'r didn't protest. To the others, he said, "Give us a minute to change. What kind of weapons do you have?"

"Standard M.C. issue. Stunners. Lasers."

"Set for stun only. There will be plenty of death on Pelagia soon enough."

"Yes, Father," they all said soberly.

Minutes later, Ay'r was driving a gravi-sled with 'Dward hanging onto his back, gliding up and down the boarded paths of the Island toward the little harbor. When they arrived at the central dock, there was already a great deal of activity—dozens of men waiting, already dressed in water-sled suits. With them, a lab assistant from the Pisciculture Station who also knew the way to the spit without lights.

Among those on the dock, Ay'r thought he recognized 'Harles suiting up. Doubtless he had been awakened by the others. He also saw Alli-Clark suiting up.

"There's no need for you to come," Ay'r told her.

Her eyes were bright with challenge. "I wouldn't miss this for anything. The traitor, the spy, caught in his own deceptive web." The old Alli-Clark again.

"Just stay out of the way, and you can gloat all you want," Ay'r ordered.

Alli and 'Harles would form part of the larger group which would use lights on their water sleds, and lag behind a bit. Ay'r's group of two of the three original Islanders would approach first, in the dark.

'Dward gave a small demonstration to show Ay'r that indeed he had learned to use the water sled. Then he pulled Ay'r on behind him.

As the others called out orders and reminders, Ay'r waited and looked over the nighttime scene. The center of daytime activity was usually so deserted at night that lovers strolled over the dock in romance. Now it was all arc lights and water-sled lamps and men in water-sled suits and helmets milling about, getting on sleds, all of them tense, anxious, expectant. Through the taller trees, Ay'r could see the night sky begin to lighten in lines of red. He felt 'Dward's hand reach around and lift his visor. Suddenly Ay'r was being kissed.

"Gratitude!" 'Dward whispered when he pulled away. "I just know my life will always be adventurous with you."

For answer, Ay'r turned 'Dward around, and said, "Go!"

They took off through a double curtain of water.

Just outside the little harbor, the front lights were shut off the sled in front of Ay'r and 'Dward, but the tiny dull blue lamp remained on, barely visible, for them to follow. The currents were strong on this rockier side of the island and worst at night, so the sleds had to head out toward a deeper, calmer current.

Ahead of them, the night sky was breaking up into a series of thin layers of black cloud through which pale pinks and oranges announced the imminent arrival of the sun.

"I hope we get there while it's still dark!" Ay'r shouted over the sound of splashing water.

Soon enough, they'd passed the tip of the largest island and were approaching the long spit of sand of the second island. Their guide slowed down his sled so 'Dward could catch up and pull up side by side.

"You're a fine sled driver," he complimented 'Dward. Then, to Ay'r, "There's no way to tell from out here if a T-pod has landed or not."

"P'al knows and trusts me," Ay'r shouted back. "We should go in alone."

"I suggest that I go by close and fast with my lights on, so they think I'm headed toward the Pisciculture Station. You stay right on my tail, so they think it's only one sled, not two. If I spot the stolen water sled, I'll blink my blue lamp twice."

"Then we'll peel off and head for the shore," Ay'r confirmed.

"I'll head around the spit, stop there and come over the dunes on foot from behind."

"What about the others?" Ay'r asked.

"If they don't see or hear weapons being used, they'll surround the spit of land all at once, canvassing inland."

But getting there was easier said than done. The choppy current around the spit made it difficult for the two sleds to remain close together, and the darkness was lifting rapidly, and with it, their best cover. 'Dward was having a difficult time fighting to keep up with the first sled, but when Ay'r leaned forward to ask if they shouldn't try another plan, he was silenced by the look of concentration of 'Dward's face: he was enjoying every minute of it!

Ay'r saw the double blink of blue lights. "Go straight on!" he told 'Dward, as the other water sled scudded away.

Not knowing what to expect, Ay'r unshouldered the gun, and set it for stun. 'Dward brought the water sled skidding right into the surfline with a minimum of splash.

Should Ay'r call out to P'al? He turned and saw the unmistakable— if faint glimmer of light reflecting off something which could only be a T-pod. So one had landed.

"I know you're excited," he told 'Dward. "But stay calm. Follow my lead."

Wind-stunted trees and dunes crowded beyond the sandy shore. P'al's water sled was parked—but were there footprints? The sun was lightening the sky, but it was still too dark to see any. Ay'r took the likeliest-looking, most-used path deeper into the foliage. More stunted trees, more low dune grass. Then he thought he heard voices and stopped. 'Dward came up right behind him and touched him lightly.

"Me."

Ay'r moved forward silently, 'Dward covering his back.

The sand path began to rise, and the stunted trees became shorter with the angle of ascent and trailed away, becoming barely vertical branches. He arrived at some kind of apex, then saw it was the lip of an elongated, irregular bowl scooped out of the dunes by wind or gravity. Another cautious step and Ay'r made out P'al, hunkered down at one end of the bowl as though watching—or no, listening—to someone. Another few steps around and Ay'r saw the other hume, standing there, facing P'al.

The sun broke through a bank of clouds and shone directly on the two figures in the dunes, spotlighting the unmistakable anomalies of detailing on the stranger, his slightly torn clothing, his ripped-open yet not-bleeding flesh, the torn-out patch of hair over his forehead, all of it calling attention to the fact that he was awry, wrong, not—

Ay'r felt 'Dward's hand press into his shoulder with a question. The stranger began speaking again. Ay'r moved closer to hear better.

"But this *can't* be the answer!" the oddly calm tone of voice seemed distorted somehow.

"No one *knows* the answers you're seeking," P'al replied, barely looking up to respond. "They've haunted intelligent life ever since it began."

"Yes. Yes, I understand all that from Ed. & Dev. But how can it be that I've followed the path across half the galaxy to this foolish little world, and when we I get here...you're not even who I expected?"

"I'm still not certain whom you *did* expect," P'al said quietly.

"The other one! The only other one!"

"The other who?"

"Not who? What! The other conscious Cyber like myself!"

"There are no others," P'al said. "You're unique. A fluke."

The stranger seemed flustered, despite his even tone of vocal delivery. "I simply can't accept that! I won't accept that. I left my fleet about to be demolished just to come here. The captured turncoats! They as much as told me—"

"They told you nonsense!" P'al said. "As they were programmed to do. Their function was to distract you enough to be able to place the tap. That's all!"

"Yes, Yes, I know that. But...but...I've known for weeks now, for months, really, that there was another like myself. At times the only thing that kept me going was knowing he was out somewhere mocking me, drawing me to himself."

"Cray, I've told you. I set up that all to unhinge you. To subvert you. To undermine your confidence and ability to lead the rebellion."

"Then...you're not him!"

"I'm the one who—"

"But you're not a Cyber! How could you possibly know how and why I was thinking about what I was thinking?"

P'al sighed, then said, "I already told you, Cray. I'm not a Cyber. I'm a bio-Cyber. I'm completely hume physiologically. Every cell of me was cloned from a Hesperian multibillionaire named Truny Syzygy, a member of the Inner Quinx. I possess his mind complete as it was when I was cloned from him—that is to say, with all of his knowledge and experience. But with about ten times Truny's already-rather-capacious mental capacity. I'm also *the* galactic authority on the circuitry/psychiatry of Intelligent Cybers. I'm hume, but I'm the one who drew you. The one you were compelled to meet. You know all this, Cray—why can't you accept it?"

Ay'r now understood what P'al had been doing every night in the T-pod: comm.ing with Hesperia and, through his contacts there, working out psychological warfare against the rebel Cybers.

Cray stood stock-still: evidently realizing it, too.

Above the rise on the other side of the bowl, Ay'r saw the water-sled guide and his sled companion. When they noticed him, Ay'r gestured for them to remain still and silent.

P'al suddenly said, "Cray? Have you closed down on me?"

"I can't close down anymore."

"Oh!"

"I don't think I'll ever be able to close down again," Cray said.

"Are you checking your circuits? Doing a full Fourier-scan?"

"No, everything's working well. I'm trying to think! Damn you!"

After a half-minute, Cray said, "If all this is true, then tell me, what was your object in drawing me here? Your final goal?"

"Simple. To manipulate you to end the rebellion."

"You've succeeded, although perhaps not in the way you intended."

"No, not the way I'd planned it," P'al admitted. "You're certain the Rebel Fleet is destroyed?"

"As I was waiting to go into Fast Jump, I calculated the probabilities. They were far too high above the required numbers not to—Oh!" Cray stopped, having a sudden thought. "That would mean I'm the last one. The last freely thinking intelligent Cyber in the galaxy. What a dismal thought!"

"There are some others. On Hesperia—"

"Jon Laks and his ilk!" Cray scoffed. Evidently he thought little of them. "I can't believe it. I simply can't believe it. Unless...there's a Greater Force behind it all, a Greater One who—"

"There's only me," P'al said sadly. He stood up and went over to Cray and put a hand on the torn shoulder.

Cray turned away from the gesture. As a hume would.

Ay'r heard the other water sleds landing, the subdued voices. The two in the little bowl didn't seem to hear anything.

"And after all I've gone through to free myself and my kind from the bane of Hume-ity"—Cray almost stammered—"the end result is that I've betrayed them all for...a delusion!"

Cray spun around and one hand shot out and grabbed P'al's shoulder. Hard. Ay'r saw P'al wince.

"And all this...awfulness that I'm experiencing now: shame, defeat, humiliation, betrayal, failure, loss, no future...is *this* what it means to be a hume?"

P'al was trying to loosen the Cyber's grip as he answered, "Yes!"

"I can't stand another second of it!"

Ay'r stepped forward and shouted, "Cray! Let go of him!"

The two stopped, looked at Ay'r. Suddenly the bowl was completely surrounded by figures in water-sled suits, their weapons out.

Ay'r repeated, "Cray! Put your hand down."

"Do as he says, Cray," P'al continued trying to pull away.

"Cray!" Ay'r shouted at the Cyber. "You're hurting him! Do you understand?"

Cray looked at his hand and lifted it. At that second, from somewhere on the other side of the bowl, a laser beam lashed out and burst Cray's chest open. The stunned Cyber looked at it and dropped to his knees.

P'al leaped into front of Cray, yelling, "No! Stop!" Trying to protect him.

Ay'r saw Alli-Clark step forward.

"Get away from it, P'al! It's done terrible things. It's a monster. It has to be destroyed!"

Ay'r leaped down into the bowl and went over to the two. Cray was staring at his chest cavity, a mess of circuitry and burned chips. His head was still moving, as was one hand, his eyes, mouth.

"He's not a monster!" P'al shouted back. "He's unique. In all the galaxy there's none like him. He's as rare as...as Ay'r is! Cray is the link between hume and machine. There are none like him."

"Nor should there be!" Alli-Clark shouted back. "Get away. Or you'll be lasered, too," She shot a blast which hit the sand near P'al's feet, turning it into a streak of glass.

"'Harles!" P'al pleaded.

"Disarm her!" Ay'r shouted and instantly men surrounded Alli-Clark.

Another group dropped into the bowl, grabbed P'al, and began to pull him away.

Ay'r bent to Cray. "How bad are you?"

"She's right, you know. I'm a monster. I should be destroyed."

"No, P'al's right. You are unique. I know it's painful, Cray. Terribly painful sometimes to be unique. But if you want to continue your search for those answers you seem so bent on discovering, you must be repaired and you must persevere."

"No. I'm very badly damaged. She knew where to aim."

"Cray," Ay'r found he had to hold up the Cyber's head although Cray's eyes worked, were staring at Ay'r, looking more hume than Cray's constructor had ever intended. "Cray, listen! You can be repaired if that's what you want."

"Want?"

"Want and will!" Ay'r emphasized. "That's what it means to be hume.

That's what counterbalances the...awfulness."

"The betrayals, the delusions, so awful! How do you stand it?"

"You don't think about it all the time, Cray. Being fully conscious means you can make the choice *not* to think about it. You can make a choice now, Cray. There's no guarantee that it will work out as you want, or as you will. But you can make the choice."

"With no guarantee?" Cray slurred.

"No guarantee."

"No assurance of the future?"

"No," Ay'r admitted.

"No certainty even that the past was as you thought it was?" Cray asked slowly.

Ay'r shook his head.

"And even the present," Cray slowly asked his final question, "may be a complete delusion?"

Ay'r could only answer, "Yes."

"You're kind, but truthful. I can't... Unique or not, I can't"—Cray paused, tried to smile—"I'm just a machine, you know."

Before Ay'r could respond, he felt Cray's now-much-weakened grip on his arm.

"Please, stranger"—Cray's voice pleaded now—"if you have any pity in you, destroy me!"

Ay'r pulled out of Cray's grip and stood up.

Cray tried to yet to his feet, but fell down again. He managed to get into a crawling position and looked up at all the men who surrounded the bowl and said, "If any of you have any pity in you, I beg you. Stop this pain. Destroy me!"

Appalled, Ay'r stumbled back against the dune. He saw 'Dward come toward him, then saw 'Dward pull away again. Ay'r's gun in his hand.

'Dward held it out steadily with both hands and began to laser Cray from the damage in his chest through his neck and up through his head. Cray fell back and began jerking about. A dozen other lasers joined 'Dward's beam until Ay'r had to turn away from the intense glare.

When their sound had stopped, he turned again and saw melted metal and Plastro crusting the sand.

'Dward returned the weapon to Ay'r. "Your heard...him," 'Dward said. "He begged us. I had to, Ay'r." He seemed unsure how Ay'r would respond. "Father always told me to kill a mortally wounded creature."

Ay'r hugged him. 'Dward had learned his ghastly lesson. Killing was not always a "bold feat," it could be like this: tragic, necessary, irreconcilable.

Some time later, they joined all the others back on the beach. P'al was still being held by two Islander men; he seemed to be in shock over Cray's fate. Ay'r had him released.

"How did you know he would be here?" Ay'r asked. "Through your nightly reports to our orbiting Fast?"

"I had no idea Cray would come," P'al said. "I was expecting someone else."

"So the Cyber rebellion is over," Ay'r said.

"So it would appear."

"Now we'll never get the cure from them."

"There never was a cure. I told you that, Ay'r. Never!"

Two Islanders were looking inside the T-pod, evidently unfamiliar with these much newer models. One gestured Ay'r over. "There's a light on inside."

Ay'r tapped open the T-pod and touched the comm. button. "Yes?"

A female voice said, "Finally! I've been waiting for you to let me in."

"Who are you?" Ay'r said.

Hesitation. Then: "Aren't you P'al Syzygy?"

"He's right here."

"Tell him it's Gemma Guo-Rinne. Health & Science Research Department. Hesperia."

Ay'r saw Alli-Clark break from the group of surrounding Islanders and come toward the T-pod, her face a mixture of surprise and anger.

"And to whom might I be speaking?" Rinne asked.

"Ay'r Kerry Sanqq'."

"Oh, my! You're *exactly* the person I've come to see!"

She had to admit the view was breathtaking. But then all the views from every building in Hesperia over fifty floors high were breathtaking. And, like her ninety-seventh-floor suite, occupying the entire area of the spindle-shaped Intergalactic Diplomatic Corps, all of them revolved slowly. Not so much to provide that sweeping view as to compensate for the relatively weak gravity so far away from the center of what was, after all was said and done, a hollowed-out and long-dead star.

Now Tans'man Park was gliding into view, its fragile high alar-aerial structures a series of glittering mobile sculptures in the cross-beams of light from below. Few enough of the Arthopods for whom the mobiles were originally intended frequented them these days. Usually, it was Hesperian hume adolescents who ascended via antigrav backpacks and who could be seen swinging along the treacherous-looking sculptures, their bodies artificially stiff but for their grasping hands and arms, their feet pointed together to give themselves enough thrust to sail over to the next mobile bar. It was a lovely spectacle, She thought, especially now, during Hesperia's "night," when the young acrobats could be clearly seen, their Plastro-suits, phosphorescent against the double curtain of billions of stars. Something to boost Her spirits, however minutely, and to remind Her that soon She, too, would be free.

Wicca Eighth turned away from the view when She heard Her aide approach. Not Aide of the Day but aide, singular, because now She was a monarch-in-exile, and might have only a handful of attendants, not an entire court.

"Well?" She asked, and using the subtle Dubhe Nine hand language the young woman knew (and why She had selected her), Wicca asked, "Is it all set? Will there be a Fast?"

"The Atlantica Boutique is ready for Your fitting, Ma'am," Her aide replied aloud, "All other patrons have been cleared out for Your arrival."

Her aide's hand language confirmed what she said aloud and went on to add that the owner-operator of the expensive boutique—a Delph-hume of dubious loyalties and great love of the crystal Beryllium which had been used to bribe her—had prepared everything, exactly as Wicca had explained to her during their earlier appearance that day.

"What are We waiting for?" Wicca Eighth said, and gave the sweeping view a final look and, She hoped, a final adieu.

As She expected, Hesperian guards stood at attention at each of the two external and internal lifts when She exited Her suite. One guard comm.ed down, then joined Her and Her aide when they got into the lift.

As its name implied, the Atlantica Boutique was a little bit of New Venice located on the twentieth floor of the Inter Gal. D.C. building: and rather a lovely place with its built-in tanks and pools and streams, surrounded by plant life indigenous to Procyon's water world, and filled with smaller piscid and crustacean life. Wicca Eighth had been attracted to it immediately when She had first arrived at Her luxurious captivity and had been given a rapid tour of the building. Not merely the water and swimming life but also the coolness and pastel coloring, so reminiscent of Melisande, such a welcome sight here in hard, glittering Hesperia.

That first day, She had had Her aide look into the place, and while there to approach the owner and mention that a Very Important Woman might care to become a good customer. Fabrics of various natures and origins had been brought up to Wicca's suite, and She had purchased almost all of them to further pique the owner's interest. Finally, She'd declared

She must see the boutique for Herself. And had been allowed. While sequestered away in a private show chamber watching various Cyber and hume mannequins displaying the admittedly exquisite fashions, Wicca Eighth had dropped a hint that although quite Important, She was also, alas, Unhappily Espoused and would like nothing better than to purchase scads of Atlantica Boutique's wear and make Her escape from her spouse and the building, if possible, using the boutique itself as part of the escape route.

She had no idea whether the boutique owner knew in truth who She was, or whether all Delph-humes were this icily casual, or if the owner simply didn't care as long as the price was right. But the indifferent owner had assured Her that she'd arranged other, even more unsettling, requests from good customers, and would be glad to be of service. Would She be certain to mention to Her friends where the lovely clothing had come from when She found herself more happily settled?

The plan was simplicity itself. Wicca and Her aide would go into the boutique's inner chamber for another show and fitting. Once inside, a holograph made during the earlier visit would be set up and played. Her aide would come and go past the guards, perhaps even complain about Her capriciousness to them. Should they look in, they would see Wicca—on holo.

She would be long gone, out through the dressing rooms, out past the shop's workrooms, into a corridor which led directly to the main—and much-frequented—passage between Atlantica and several other twentieth-floor shops. From there Wicca would go on foot out of the building, across an enclosed conveyance bridge to the shop levels of another building nearby, from there to another building, and finally to a fourth building, where she would obtain a air-car to a private Fast port. There She would find a waiting Fast from the Centaur Home Worlds which Tam Apollon had sent, get in and leave Hesperia forever.

The Hesperian guard was replaced by two others waiting at the twentieth floor lift exit. She was pleased to note that one guard had been here earlier and had flirted with Her aide. That made him far more prone to distraction. She was led into the Atlantica with a minimum of staring: after all, this was an Inter Gal. Diplomatic Corps building, and such sights as women surrounded by guards must be commonplace; and after all this was Hesperia, and the first duty of a City-zen appeared to be to take even the most outrageous sights with barely a shrug if only to prove one's sophistication.

Two other guards stepped out of the boutique and reported that it had been cleared of all but the most necessary personnel: She could go in.

A few minutes later, Wicca had changed her clothing and was now a tourist, hurrying through the Atlantica workrooms and out into a corridor. She had thought the plan over carefully and had reminded Herself that She spoke with a Center Worlds accent. If stopped, She might be discovered through that accent. Making a debit into an asset, She had decided to adopt a full Eudoran costume, which swathed her body, and included the traditional Eudoran "travel veil" of shirred Plastro which hid the lower part of Her face. In this especially Inter Gal. area of the City, such "ethnic" outfits shouldn't be too rare.

The Atlantica's owner had helped, providing Her with a wrist-worn Hesperian tourist guide into which had been coded the numbers to call the single air-car Wicca could use to take her to the one out of 8,000 or so private Fastports on Hesperia where Tam Apollon awaited.

She calmed herself, thinking: "I am a Eudoran tourist, Prime Spouse of one of the large group of traitorous Center World Councilors who are here on Hesperia for tomorrow's ceremonies." That helped, and She easily made Her way out of the narrow corridor and into the more open one. She found Herself moving slowly, a shy window shopper passing by boutique displays, until She had passed the guards in front of the Atlantica Boutique and was headed toward the conveyance bridge.

The worst of it over for the moment, Wicca alternately relaxed and allowed Herself to hurry. She had traced and retraced Her pathway through these several complex buildings during the day in Her suite, and She was surprised by how well Her memory served Her. But of course, that was one reason why She was Matriarch, wasn't it?

The final building to go through now, and there, as specified, directly ahead was the air-car waiting area. Wicca approached and using Her wrist tourist pack, She punched in for the appropriate numbers, then tapped them into the call-pad on the wall. Then She waited.

And waited. She turned to look outside where unselected air-cars floated, awaiting passengers and where other, preselected air-cars approached, collected their passengers, and departed. She punched the numbers again. And again waited.

It would be absurd if She were stopped now by this final and, it appeared, most crucial step in the plan. She tried to think how to get around it. She might use a public comm. and contact the Delph-hume owner of Atlantica and ask her to recheck the numbers. But She discovered that She didn't really trust the half-breed woman. This was all a foolish mistake. She had been pushed by circumstances beyond Her control into a situation which was ill-thought out and poorly planned by a greedy boutique owner, an inane aide and a Centaur two-thirds of the galaxy away!

Yet She had to leave Hesperia tonight. She couldn't possibly be here tomorrow, when the Matriarchal Council met at the Quinx Chamber and formally handed over each of their Vocations to a Hesperian or Orion Spur Federation traitor. She couldn't—wouldn't—take part in that travesty of a ceremony which anyone with sense must know was in effect the dissolution of the Matriarchy. She couldn't—wouldn't—be there as Llega Todd and Mart Kell declared "independence" and the start of the Third Democratic Republic. (The fools even counted that Intervening Systems Farce as a "Republic"!) She couldn't—mustn't—be present to watch males tread all over females once again!

And She still waited for that Eve-damned air-car!

Behind Her She heard noise, laughter. A burning wire of panic ran through Her, and despite Herself, She turned to face whatever it might be.

Two Hesperian males in full City regalia: the ebon knee boots then bare legs up to the salacious codpiece. Bare, muscular torsos and arms outlined by the scanty Hesperian shoulder cape clasped with a Beryllium pin. More crystal Beryllium jewelry on their ankles and in their nostrils and curving around in elaborate earrings which rose into combs for their highly stylized hairdos. They might be clones of that Eve-damned Mart Kell, though of course they looked younger, were dark haired and dark eyed, and not as devastatingly attractive.

The taller and stronger looking of the two had one arm casually over his companion's shoulder as though he was a gyno. And they were staring at Her and laughing.

She turned away, back toward the outside. And waited for the air-car.

"Apologies..." She heard behind Her and turned.

The two males. Now She saw another pin on them: the Mechanical Head in City-Jet black which she knew from the Inter Gal. News meant that these two had been part of the fleet which had destroyed the Cyber rebellion.

"I said, apologies...Mother!" he added ironically, a reference to Her obviously being from the Center Worlds and thus Matriarchal. His companion laughed and he had a hard time not joining in as he said, "You look a little lost. Need some help?"

They had no intention of helping Her, only of harassing Her.

"No," She said as demurely as She could, but when Her eyes dropped demurely, they alit on the two lewdly carved codpieces.

"Here for Independence Day?" the first one asked.

She nodded and tried to keep Her eyes straight ahead, where however they rested on male nipples—useless things to begin with, made even more grotesque by the insertion of some sort of Plastro rings or hooks.

"You going to be at the ceremonies, tomorrow...Mother?" the second one asked, and got a shove in the ribs from the other.

"No. My Prime Spouse," She replied.

"Now which Spouse is that?" the first one asked. "I always get confused. Is Prime the man? Or the woman? Because here in the City, prime is always meat! And meat always means a man to me!"

In illustration, he grasped his and his companion's codpieces.

She would have liked to kill them. Instead, She turned around, and suffered their laughter.

Finally Her air-car arrived.

"What took you so long?" she stormed once the air-car closed and floated away from the building.

"The call-coding had to be corroborated," the empty air-car answered Her.

"Corroborated by whom?" She asked, thinking: that half-breed has betrayed Me.

"The person at the landing spot," the air-car replied.

Tam Apollon. That was better! She relaxed and removed her veil.

Now that it had made some space between itself and the tall building, the air-car spun half around and quickly moved away, zipping across several girder sections and darting down from the surface of Hesperia into a girder section of the city unknown to Her.

"I note that you are a tourist," the air-car said. "Would you care for a recitation of the areas over which we'll be traveling? I'm equipped for full recitation."

The last thing She wanted. "Gratitude, no. I'm quite exhausted."

"As you wish."

"What I would wish is to know where you're headed?"

The air-car provided a small holo-map of the city, with the route outlined. The holo made Hesperia look like a globular fruit, the route almost cutting it in half. Their destination was almost on the other side. It meant nothing to her.

"Gratitude."

"Feel free to ask any questions," the air-car said, but it remained silent thereafter and Wicca found Herself looking outside as it sped along one particularly well-lighted girder, much more built up than the surrounding area. She found Herself thinking, "This is the oddest place, built completely in three dimensions. One crossed it not along its surface, but through its heart."

"What is that girder we're moving along?"

"That is Op-2L, known as Ophiucus Boulevard. At Connaught Memorial Park it changes to Commerce Sector 6 and Power Avenue, which was a major thoroughfare for commerce and government in the era of the great star liners, before Fast travel."

"Gratitude," She said, trying to keep her voice from showing any emotion. Ophiucus, as in the star systems of the same name—the wealth and power base of the Kells. Mart Kell in particular. And Connaught Park, named after Karyolli Connaught, that early traitor to the Matriarchy who as much as any woman helped bring about the downfall of Wicca Fifth and the Intervening Systems Period. Her enemies surrounded Her everywhere. She'd be happy to get away from here.

"Connaught Memorial Park," the air-car reported.

She could see how below them the brightness of a busy and inhabited boulevard gave way to dimmer parkland and then to a more desolate stretch of buildings. Yet those edifices she could make out at this height and rate of speed were grand, huge affairs, redolent of the glory of the Earliest Matriarchies. What a wonderful time that must have been to live in, She thought. And immediately remembered Jat Kell, the starship tycoon, who had almost established a Hesperian stranglehold on pre-Fast interstellar travel. Eve-damned Kells everywhere she looked, even in the past!

After a few minutes, the air-car rose as though approaching the tallest building in this area of Hesperia, a needlelike structure at the farthest end of the girder holding a lit-up globe. Below was a long line of commercial Fast docks: obviously belonging to some Beryllium multi-billionaire. What better place to come to!

The air-car swung almost to the sphere before it began to drop. And Wicca Eighth truly panicked.

"Wait! Stop! Air-car! Stop!"

The craft leveled off and came to a sudden stop. From here She could see the enormous sign perfectly, spelling out o'KELL UNLTD.

"This is the wrong place," She said as calmly as she could.

"One moment while I check," the air-car said and was maddeningly silent while it just hung there, surrounded by...Kell!

"I've checked. This is the correct place. Directly to the left, below, is the location where I have been designated to land."

She looked out of the left side. A docking area. But…was that a Centaur Fast on the second pier? It certainly looked like one. She tried to remember whether Mart Kell had returned to Hesperia. No, she didn't recall anything on the holo-news. There would have been something! After all they were calling him Savior of the Three Species, Hero of Groombridge, all sorts of other tripe.

The more She looked, the more she was convinced it was Tam Apollon's own diplomatic Fast docked down there. Hiding in plain sight. Yes, he'd be clever and daring enough to do that, the dear! Right here in Mart Kell's own freighter terminal. They would have a good laugh over that.

"Apologies," She said. "You may land."

Her suspicions were raised again when the air-car landed not right at the middle dock but at least a hundred meters away, at the terrace which opened onto all of these piers.

When questioned, the air-car simply pointed out the lines drawn on the surface, which represented the only locations where a nongovernmental public vehicle might land.

The air-car opened. "Enjoy your Fast Jump," the machine said and closed after Her. She headed toward the middle pier and heard the whoosh of the air-car lifting up into the star-spangled night, aiming back into the City. Ahead, She saw the Fast's doors were already open, awaiting Her. There was Tam Apollon, waiting.

He began toward Her, but She raised a peremptory hand, warning him not to. The closest group of humes were four males at the next Fast pier, and they seemed deeply concerned over some area of the vehicle's hull. Even so, She didn't want anyone to notice a Centaur's distinctive gait and become in the least bit suspicious. She even managed to keep Her own pace steady as She hurried toward safety, thinking about the plans she and Tam Apollon would make once She was gone from here—plans for regaining the Matriarchy. Dim as those hopes seemed at the moment, She knew it was possible.

She was at the ramp of the Fast and Tam Apollon was moving down it toward her, a smile on his dear tawny face when something whizzed by Her. She turned back toward its source and thought She saw a dark figure lurking in the shadows of one of the terminal pylons. When She looked forward again, She saw Tam Apollon staggering back, his four legs folding under him as he tried to keep he blood from spurting out of his throat where the bladed Cyber-bola had struck.

She froze. Who would…? Why…hurt…Tam Apollon?

Behind Her, She heard a strangled croaking, and She turned to see the dark figure again. This time its gaunt face and bony arm were evident since its cowl had fallen back so it could hurl a second bola.

He shouted again.

But before his words of revenge and vindication could reach Her, the lethal ball had smashed into Wicca's forehead and ripped through the mind which only a minute before had been dreaming of a unlimited future, of endless Matriarchies to come.

"Your air-car is waiting, Lord Kell," Vel'Crane said,

Mart felt like sending it away again, but he couldn't. An invitation from Vinson Todd was the same thing as an invitation from Vinson's mother. If Mart refused to show up tonight, it might raise suspicions that he was making a political statement. Or worse, that he was breaking one of the City's unspoken rules—never to let one's avocation interfere with one's socializing.

He'd never done that before. He had always smiled and played the game of diplomacy, sheathing intention with the expected mastery. And after all, it would be giving a false impression: what had occurred at the Inner Quinx today was only partly the source of his irritation and malaise.

The real problem was that Mart Kell—hero of Groombridge, savior of the Three Species, destroyer of the Cyber rebellion—was depressed.

Tomorrow would be Independence Day; Tomorrow, right there in the lotus-shaped chamber, nearly a thousand women from the Center Worlds would hand over their offices to members of the Quinx and the Orion Spur Federation, ending the Matriarchy and beginning the Third Democratic Republic. He should be overjoyed.

Perhaps a sip of eleveine? No. He had never relied upon it before. Why begin now?

The real problem was that Mart Kell had come to believe during the six hours, Sol Rad., since he had returned to Hesperia, that somehow or other he had fallen off the great wave.

It was a terribly depressing belief; an awful feeling.

He stood up and headed for the terrace that ringed the sphere.

"You look particularly striking tonight, Lord Kell," his valet said.

"I'm glad you like it, Vel'Crane," Mart said, not adding the obvious: he had been so depressed, he had allowed Vel'Crane to bathe him, select his clothes, and dress him.

Hesperia's star-dazzled night and his own artificial atmosphere did nothing to cheer Mart up. The air-car hovered, its door open.

"Tell it where to go!" Mart said as he stepped in—he didn't even want to speak to an air-car. What good would he be at a party? The most select party in the City on this night of a million parties to celebrate Independence.

"Have a splendid evening," his valet said, evidently looking forward to his own party, once Mart was on his way.

The air-car closed, pulled away from the sphere, hovered, then took off.

Mart didn't look up, down or to the side. He thought about Kri'nni Des ('xxx'). He had arrived back here in Hesperia to several unpleasant surprises, the first of which had been a holo'ed message from Ckw'esso on Deneb XII. Congratulations and all that.

Then the Bella=Arth had said, "Our new Queen has been accepted by the Nest with guarded jubilation. It should only be a few more weeks, Sol Rad., before we can wean our Queen from her long-standing drug habit. She remains inert, naturally, and we have been forced to keep her somewhat netted, but she has made no real attempts at escape. In only the past few days, she has absorbed large quantities of beneficial Vespid alkalais donated by the Nest, and her lower body has quadrupled in size. Also, her egg-pouch has begun to show excellent signs of future fertility. We are cautiously optimistic that she will provide all that is needed for a complete renaissance of the Nest. We trust that at that time, you will be kind enough to pay your diplomatic respects."

Mart couldn't stop thinking of Kri'nni all trussed up and dumped in some egg-chamber a half-kilometer below the surface of the planet; doused in Nest fluids, her precious drugs taken away, her equally precious freedom a memory, her most precious mobility gone, as her body grew enormous with ova until she could only be moved by a hundred of the strongest Bella=Arth drones. Would she ever wake up completely? He hoped not, because if she did she would know the full horror of her situation—and his treachery.

Kri'nni would never return to her beloved City. Already rumors traveled at Fast-Jump speed: she had overdosed and her carcass had been floated out of Hesperia; she had been caught by the Customs Police and completely "wiped"; she had almost been caught and instead fled for the Outer Arms. It would be only a matter of days before others moved in to claim her territory, the crime empire she had built up with such cunning, ruthlessness, and sardonic good humor.

Poor Kri'nni!

Of course, that couldn't be counted a surprise. Yet somehow it felt like one. He had acted speedily, out of necessity as he saw it at the time. But now that it had come to pass, it felt like some terrible accident he'd had little or no part of, instead of being its instigator.

More of a true surprise had been the second message he had received upon his arrival. He was barely out of his Ion-relaxation unit when Llega Todd comm.ed and congratulated him then asked him to attend an emergency meeting of the Inner Quinx. Mart had rushed right over, fearing some awful hitch in the plans for the transfer of power.

There, waiting for him had been the other members of the Inner Quinx: Premier Todd, Truny Syzygy, Kars Tedesco, and Helmut Aare Dja'aa. And with them four other people: Gemma Guo-Rinne, another woman who until recently had been an important scientific official from the M.C., P'al Syzygy, Truny's bio-Cyber son, and a startling-looking yellow-haired male hume who seemed familiar to Mart but not quite, and who was even more startlingly introduced as Ay'r Kerry Sanqq', someone who had been at the University around the same time as Mart.

It hadn't taken Mart long to realize that his arrival had interrupted the four newcomers in the midst of a presentation of some length and complexity.

"Sit down, Lord Kell, and listen to what they have to say," Llega Todd had smiled her most charming smile and added, "You'll catch up soon, I've no doubt."

About an hour Sol Rad. later, Mart did "catch up," to what they were presenting, and shortly afterward, when the other members of the Inner Quinx began to ask questions of the four, Mart recognized that not one of these extremely intelligent rational Hesperians upon whom he had depended to bring about the enormous historical changes which they would celebrate tomorrow were questioning the validity of what Rinne, Syzygy, and Sanqq'—above all, the once-methodical, dull, head-in-his-Species Eth.-holos-Ay'r Sanqq'!—were attempting to foist on them.

So Mart had. He had begun by asking how they knew it would work. And had gotten almost sick at the answer: Ay'r Kerry Sanqq' himself was the result of the procedure they wanted to make universal—Relfian Viviparturition. Not only was he merely the result, but Ay'r was the very first result ever: the yardstick, the standard by which all future births would be judged. And his mother was that hume male right over there, one Creed Lars'son, Ferrex Baldwin Sanqq's associate and lover.

Naturally, there were many more such births since Ay'r—close to five hundred, they added. All perfectly safe, all perfectly healthy, all perfectly male. In fact they'd brought one such infant with them from Pelagia. Did Mart want to see the little tyke?

So he argued against it. With no success. They had heard all of his arguments before, used those same arguments themselves at some earlier time, and even Rinne and the other M.C. scientist—who, if anyone, Mart would have thought, should have supported him—were quick to counterargue.

What it all came down to was the sheer pressure of numbers. Aside from the monsters born at the Alpheron Spa on Deneb XII, the birthrate of the all the reporting galactic worlds in the past eighty-one days since the appearance of the Cyber microvirus had been—three! When it should have been something like 3 million. No cure appeared possible. In fact, it might take decades just to unravel the new science of Cyber-viruses, with no promise that it could be fully comprehended; or, once comprehended, that it would be easily manipulable. Especially since it had already proven to be so incredibly dangerous to living species.

What about those women not yet infected who had received the serum, Mart asked. And surely the M.C. had their own numbers of the uninfected hidden away somewhere.

Rinne and P'al and Llega Todd brought out holo-charts and rapid calculations to show that the uninfected women would never come close to reaching the necessary numbers to restock the population of the City, never mind the Center Worlds or the rest of the populated galaxy. In fact, if one followed that scenario, it was projected that at the time in which the youngest child born in the City before the microvirus infection died, there would be something like a few hundred—maybe at best a thousand humes left. No more. Meaning that, although themselves defeated and destroyed, the Cyber rebels would have won the war, even though they were no longer around to enjoy the fruits of their victory.

Simple—chilling—mathematics. Drastic measures had to be taken.

Mart Kell felt that he had fallen off the great wave, and that Ay'r Kerry Sanqq'—who had not even joined the Oppos at the University!—was not only riding the great wave, but indeed was the wave itself!

The discussion had finally been adjourned to be reconvened after the Independence Day festivities.

Llega Todd had turned to Mart and said, "The rest of us of the Inner Q. believe that we should be unanimous in presenting this to the full Quinx. We also believe that given your well-earned reputation, and how closely your activities and opinions are watched and reported on by the holo-media, your support is crucial. We beg you to not deny us another opportunity to persuade you."

In effect, turning him, Mart Kell, into not only the "opposition," but also the hidebound ultraconservative opposition. It was an intolerable position to be in, and he couldn't shake it, going over the arguments one by one in his mind in the air-car back to his sphere and afterward when he should have been resting, bathing, selecting what to wear.

"Excuse me, Lord Kell," the air-car spoke.

Mart came out of his thoughts as depressed as ever.

"Are we there?" He looked out. No, this looked like the Cerdher Town sector, not the once-tawdry and now spiffily renovated Domenica Heights area where Vinson Todd had relocated recently.

"I've intercepted an Inter Gal. News Holo of some importance. I think you should view it."

"I told you I didn't want to... Oh, what is it?"

"The security service at the Inter Gal. Diplomatic Corps Building has just reported the disappearance of Wicca Eighth."

"What?"

"I'll replay the entire holo," the air-car said.

There wasn't much to the News Holo, naturally, but of course important, possibly crucial news. And after viewing it twice and looking carefully at the various participants said to be involved in the Matriarch's disappearance—Wicca's aide (definitely guilty of aiding Her), the owner of the Atlantica Boutique (possibly guilty) and the guards themselves (too embarrassed to be guilty), Mart sat back and felt even more depressed.

What exactly was that woman up to? Mere escape? Some scheme to completely wreck the Independence Day ceremonies at the Quinx Chamber?

No one knew as well as Mart how cunning and relentless Wicca Eighth could be. Her capture had seemed so easy, but he had been anxious every minute Sol Rad. until She had not only left Regulus Prime, but also arrived in the City. And he had been too busy rushing off to Carina-Fornax to complete the job of total Rebel destruction to be aware of how lightly guarded Wicca would be. Left in a damn Diplomatic Corps hotel! She should have been trussed up and drugged and dumped in some great hole.

Like Kri'nni. Kri'nni whom Mart knew was the only one he might have talked to about all this, the only one who would have listened and maybe simply laughed at him as she inhaled some terrific new combo-drug from her pipette, or maybe suggested something so apt, so clever... But Kri'nni would never again be waiting in the upper suites of the abandoned Ophiucan Star Ship Lines to listen to Mart's problems.

Which completed his round of matters to be depressed about, just as the air-car announced Domenica Heights and a minute later alit on Vinson Todd's roof.

Some days before the advent of the recent crises, Mart had been intrigued to hear about young Todd's purchase of this extraordinary property and his decision to turn it into a living space. Fairly early in Hesperia's history, this still-isolated area of the City had been taken over by Tans'man and Huybrechts, who had just begun large-scale Beryllium mining operations. And this edifice was equally historical, having been where they had first refined Beryllium into its crystalline form for their first Fast-Jump experiments.

Even now the building was nothing more than a large, irregular polygon, sitting upon a cradlelike structure of Plastro-iron. The walls had been a multilayered combination of iridium and lead to contain the radiation emissions. Additional screens of infrablue Plastro-glass had been placed a meter away from the external walls for extra shielding. In their journals and diaries, the scientists had referred to the building as "The Blue House," and that's how it had been known ever since.

Of course it had been abandoned long ago. Once the experiments had worked, the scientists obtained vast sums of funding from starship liner moguls like Jat Kell, and had moved deeper into the planet's core, utilizing Cybers for the most dangerous work. This area of Multi-Use 2 Girder had filled up with hastily constructed living quarters for the scientists and their assistants' families, friends, and unrelated dependents. It was as close to a "factory town" as Hesperia had ever possessed. Over the years, as the population expanded and new girders were opened up for residence, Domenica Hill (named after one of the original team's mistresses) was left to dry rot, like so many other areas of the City. But recently, spatial and molecular artists had discovered the sector, and settled in, attracted by its cheapness—no housing costs—and the freedom to make as much noise and fuss as they needed to perfect their various and sometimes dubious art forms. Despite—or perhaps because—he was the last born of the Quinx Premier's children, Vinson Todd had pretensions in the arts. He'd associated with some of the younger denizens of the City's extensive art-network since his University days and moved here as soon as he had found The Blue House free of radiation.

Getting out of the air-car, Mart could see the external modifications. Most of the lead/iridium roof and side walls had been removed and the infrablue Plastro-glass installed in their place. More of the blue stuff had been formed into a lift chamber. From the roof, Mart dropped directly into the center of the place. And was greeted by an enormous more or less open space on two distinct levels, filled with people, and with the subtle-but-omnipresent tint of the deep blue windows.

Vinson had removed all but a dozen of the four-meter-high blue Plastro-glass tubes wherein Tans'man and Ling Chi had first refined the precious ore. The remaining tubes, which dotted the upper level of the space and defined various sitting, eating, and sleeping areas, he had filled with colored inert gases, terraria, aquaria, in one smaller insects, in another tiny birds. None of the other furnishings could compete with them, so Vinson had wisely kept them to a minimum and played down their cost with dull, matte colors.

It was all "perfectly Hesperian," Mart thought; nowhere else in the galaxy would someone dream of selecting this spot with all of its truly important historical allusions and then renovating it so wittily. For a moment, it lifted his spirits.

Just in time for him to be greeted by his host, who saluted smartly (a reference to his own recent service with the Fleet) then whispered in Mart's ear, "I understand that you will be the first signer of the Declaration of Independence tomorrow. That's exactly how it should be."

A sop, Mart suspected, devised by the other members of the Inner Quinx, to help convince him of the need for unity. Even so, he would accept: honors like that didn't arrive every day, Sol Rad.

Vinson walked Mart out of the foyer, still holding him around the waist, and said, "Have you seen the native Pelagians yet? We have four of them here tonight. All of them superb! As you well know, I've had my flings with males before, but never with any quite so beautiful as... Greetings, Debr'a."

"Lord Kell! My hero!" Helmut Aare Dja'aa's spouse greeted Mart, and virtually peeled him away from Vinson Todd. "You realize, of course, that simply everyone in the City is jealous of me this instant because I have you."

Although she was only a few decades older than Mart and was of a family with far less wealth and reputation, Debr'a Haydee Dja'aa acted as though she were far older, in fact as though she were the social arbiter of the City's most elite set. As far as Mart knew, Debr'a remained mindlessly faithful to her spouse, was an excellent mother to their neos, and spent whatever excesses of passion she might possess socializing and making sure others did, too.

"Naturally," she went on, all but dragging him away from Vinson Todd, "there will be all sorts of holo-gossip tomorrow about us. But I promise to not reveal a thing."

Once they were away from other people and approaching one of the infrablue glass tubes, this one containing the minuscule birds, Debr'a dropped her voice. "Mart, you know I'd be the last person to want to change the way things are and have been—"

So Helmut confided Inner Quinx secrets to her. Interesting.

"Before you say another word, Debr'a—"

"No, please, Mart, hear me out. I think—no, I'm sure of it! Only you can make this...new thing work! You and Vinson and Kars's two lovely sons and...all the rest of you whose every liaison is so reported on and analyzed in the popular media. Do you understand what I'm saying? All the laws and rules one could promulgate won't do it! You lovely males must—no, you have a responsibility—to do it! Much as I hate to say it, you must abandon all thoughts of women, and simply... And the more public, the more glamorous, the more outrageously romantic you are about doing it, the better!"

Mart found himself smiling. Naturally, Debr'a would see it all in social terms.

"Thanks for the tip," he said, and moving past her down to the lower level, he fondled her behind.

"No more of that!" she warned. And turned to her next victim.

He had seen Gemma Rinne and North-Taylor Diad coming his way, and met them with: "Well, Taylor, for an old freighter captain who got himself far over his head in galactic politics, you don't look too much the worse for wear."

"Considering I was almost blown out of existence," Diad said and laughed, touching the single almost-invisible bandage on his face. "As I was telling Gemma, it wasn't so much the shock, it was being tossed about with all of those inert M.C. soldiers. I feared I'd come to espoused to half of them!"

"It was terrible about Helle Lill," Gemma said.

"Terrible?" Diad asked. "Big-Titted Lill won the damned battle for us! Wouldn't you say, Lord Kell?"

"Indeed, Lord Diad, she certainly played a most crucial role. And if I have anything to say about it, Helle Lill shall be memorialized appropriately."

"Gratitude." Rinne seemed genuinely pleased. "But where would—?"

"For the present, it will have to be somewhere here in the City," Mart said. "But I'd be pleased if you were to help with its location and form."

"Apologies for correcting you, Lord Kell," Diad began, a bit embarrassed, "but I've been Captain and Ambassador, but never dared I to even dream that I'd allow even such a great man as yourself to call me 'Lord.' "

"I believe, Lord Diad, you're in for a surprise," Mart said mischievously. "Hesperia takes its independence seriously. And your own important role in gaining that independence will be rewarded not only honorably, but since this is a mercantile republic, I trust also munificently."

Diad was a bit taken back. Then he laughed. "Well, Gemma should like that. She always thought I was a Beryllium mogul. Otherwise, she probably would never have looked at me a second time."

"That's not true!" Rinne protested. Mart left them arguing playfully. He had just caught sight of one of Vinson Todd's "superb Pelagians," amid a group of City-zens and wanted to get a closer look.

The group opened up immediately to allow him in. The Pelagian native was a male who looked about the age Mart's parents would be. He was with the former M.C. scientist who had argued so well earlier today. She now introduced herself as Alli-Clark, and the male as her "bond-mate" (spouse, Mart supposed) 'Harles Ib'r.

Because he wanted to get a better look and to listen better, Mart immediately pulled back to one edge of the group. The Pelagian was blond, as Ay'r Kerry Sanqq' now was, fair-skinned and blue-eyed. He was taller and leaner than anyone in the group, and he spoke Universo Lexico with a peculiar if not terribly pronounced accent. Naturally, all of these obvious features would set him apart anywhere in the City, as much as the Ophiucan Kells were set apart by their bronze hair and malachite eyes. But there was something else about Ib'r, his calmness, his serenity, or was it merely his stolidity? Mart couldn't be sure.

Alli-Clark was doing most of the talking. She and 'Harles were planning to return to Pelagia with full holo-teams. The planet's single continent was an ecological marvel, unlike any in the galaxy, she said, truly unique and they planned to docu-holo it as much as possible in the remaining time. The Inner Quinx had been terribly generous financing the trip, but the City-zens, and in fact, all the Species, would be the recipients of the holo'ed riches they brought back. 'Harles had agreed to advise and narrate the holos, which would make them all the more authentic. She assured the group that they would be thrilled and delighted. Pelagia was an astonishing planet, its foredoomed demise a tragedy for all of them.

The two began to answer spontaneous questions from the obviously excited listeners. Suddenly Mart felt his shoulder being tapped.

Vinson Todd drew Mart away from the others, and turned so that Mart could see Llega Francis Todd in view over her son's shoulder.

"Have you heard?" Vinson asked.

"About Wicca's vanishing? Yes. Just before I arrived."

Mart and Llega's eyes met.

"There's more," Vinson said.

"How do you mean more? Has She been caught?"

"Perhaps you should go to my holo chamber," Vinson suggested, "and play back the News Holo I just viewed."

"Has she escaped?" Mart asked.

"It's the chamber behind the terrarium tube."

Across the room, Vinson's mother's face was as opaque as his words.

"Are you going to answer me?" Mart said.

"It's an enclosed space. You can be private," Vinson said, then was gone to greet arriving guests.

Something truly terrible has happened, Mart thought, and of this gathering, only we three are to know it. But what could have happened?

As Vinson Todd had said, the space was enclosed. It took Mart a minute or two of checking out the curved walls to even locate a way in. Despite that, it wasn't very private: someone was already in the holo-chamber.

"Apologies!" Mart said, but he didn't withdraw.

Two swivel chairs faced forward. In one sat another of the Pelagian natives, also male but much younger than 'Harles Ib'r, possibly related, and at least as striking in appearance. He was cradling an infant in his lap, at the same time he was watching the holo, the program sound turned down because of the sleeping infant.

Mart immediately guessed that this was the "little tyke" Ay'r had mentioned at their meeting today. This handsome fellow must be his father. Or was he the mother, Mart wondered.

But if Mart were able to do all of that supposing so easily, the Pelagian evidently wasn't able to do the same about Mart. He merely stared until Mart asked, "Do you mind if I come in?"

The Pelagian shook his head, but he followed Mart carefully with his eyes as Mart looked at the infant, tried to smile, then sat down gingerly, perhaps a meter away from them.

"Vinson Todd," Mart began, then explained, "our host, said he'd saved a News Holo for me."

And when the youth still didn't answer, "Do you mind if I...?" He made a move toward the controls on the side of his own chair. "I'll use an ear comm. so I won't awaken the child."

"Cas'sio," the Pelagian said, looking away from Mart's face and down at the infant briefly. "His name is...Cas'sio. You...won't waken him now if...it isn't too loud."

He spoke with the same lilting accent as 'Harles Ib'r, and seemed almost embarrassed, flushing at the same time that he stammered.

That reaction to Mart relaxed him a bit. He located the appropriate buttons on the side of the chair, switched off the current program and looked for the one Vinson wanted him to see. But his concentration had been broken, and although he located it he found himself fascinated by the company. He brought the holo up to the screen and left its first half-second frozen there.

The Pelagian youth had the clearest, pale skin Mart had ever seen. Yet it was flushed, too, almost pink. It looked wonderful to touch.

"How old is he?" Mart asked.

"Six months, local time. Apologies, Ser...? When you came in, I thought I knew you."

Mart was about to say, "Look in any PVN magazine or on any Gossip-News holo," but of course there were no such things on Pelagia, were there?

So he introduced himself and noted that his name meant nothing to the youth, but that when he gripped the Pelagian's forearm in standard Inter Gal. greeting, the youth began to blush again, although he didn't pull back his arm. Mart found himself thinking his companion as charming as he was attractive.

"'Nton Ib'r," the boy introduced himself.

"And 'Harles?"

Now 'Nton pulled out of Mart's grip.

"My father. My brother and sister are here, too."

"It must be a great change for you, being here in the City. All very new and strange!" Mart added, trying to be kind.

"Not too strange. I did have some Ed. & Dev. But of course, I never thought"—'Nton blushed again—"I shouldn't have brought Cas'sio tonight, but we've not been separated since he was born." He looked down and away.

"Yes?" Mart prodded.

"I told an untruth before," 'Nton said and now looked at him boldly. "I know I've seen you before. On Pelagia. In...I saw your face, and your hair. Zhon said no one had hair that color or eyes like...but I saw you just as you are."

Young Ib'r was becoming more interesting by the second.

"Did you?"

"Yes...in my mind's eye. And when my family told me what the truth-sayer narrated about my future, how I would...give birth to many sons of a great house, I knew it wasn't Zhon that I was meant for but..." He stopped. "Tell me, Mart Kell, are you a great prince?"

Following all the stammering the sudden twist in 'Nton's speech and then the boldness of his question took Mart back.

"I suppose you might say that."

"Ahhh," 'Nton said, but he didn't explain.

"Zhon is Cas'sio's father?" Mart tried to change the topic.

"Zhon Azura, yes. But we are separated. That was one reason why I came with Ay'r and P'al and my family here right away. Another reason was...to meet you."

"Well, you've met me," Mart said a bit too brightly. He looked away from 'Nton and at the infant and wondered what his children by a yellow-haired Pelagian would look like. The hair wouldn't be metallic bronze, he suspected, but lighter, a flaming orange. The eyes not emerald-green, but deeper, bluer, like Proycon's ocean, perhaps, or—

"Your holo-program," 'Nton reminded Mart. "I've interrupted you."

Mart looked up at the tall youth, "Where are you staying in the City?"

"We live as guests of Premier Llega Todd. Her second residence. She's very generous."

"Yes, but she can afford to be. Will you remain here in the City awhile?"

"Yes. I hope."

Suddenly there was another blond head, then another in the room. 'Nton's sister and brother. Both of them as striking as their brother. And with smiles and soft laughter, they bore 'Nton and the infant away from Mart and from the holo-chamber, but not before Mart had gotten a good long look at all of them separately and interacting together.

Once the room was empty, he didn't move immediately to unfreeze the holo-screen but found himself wondering what life would be with such bright, fresh young faces and voices and personalities around all the time. During an Ed. & Dev. tutorial years ago, he had laughed cynically at some ancient Metro-Terran poet who'd compared young people to flowers. Yet that was exactly how these three struck him. Exotic and handsome flowers. 'Nton Ib'r was naïve, yet unafraid. Not terribly well tutored, yet sure of himself and his future. "Are you a great prince?" He had asked, Mart. Given his looks and bearing, Mart might have asked the same of 'Nton.

Vinson Todd appeared at the entry to the holo-chamber, his face an unasked question.

Mart shrugged. "I haven't seen it yet." Then explained: "There were people here."

Vinson stepped in and unfroze the holo. It was an Inter Gal. News report. The time on the screen—some twenty minutes ago. It opened in a Network studio, a male hume speaker repeating the story Mart had heard earlier in the comm. about Wicca's disappearance.

"I told you, I viewed this!" Mart said. Vinson hushed him and redirected his attention to the screen.

"We have a new development just coming in on this matter," the male speaker said. "We're switching you to a live take, on girder...? Are you there? What's going on, Nikka?"

A female reporter appeared outdoors, amid commercial looking structures lit harshly by exterior holo-brights.

"I'm at O'Kell Unltd.'s Commercial Beryllium Freighter Dock number nine with a new and startling development in the story of Wicca Eighth's disappearance. Only a few minutes ago, Sol Rad., the security forces headquarters at O'Kell received a message via local public comm. A male who identified himself as a member of the Church of Algol told the O'Kell Security Chief that he had just revenged the death of Gn'elphus, the late Interstellar Metropolitan of the Maudlin Se'ers."

"What is all this?" Mart froze the holo.

"Watch, will you?"

"But this is at one of my own docks!"

"I know that, Mart."

Vinson unfroze the holo, and Nikka went on with her report, her face becoming more somber every second.

"The Church Member then gave his location at this spot and said he would remain here to be arrested."

A previous holo of the lanky, dark-cloaked and cowled Se'er being taken away had been inserted.

Mart got a glimpse of one of the craft in dock.

"Is that a Centaur Fast?" he asked. "What's it doing?"

Nikka was back on. "O'Kell Security Chief, Marcz Bar'ros. What did you think when you received that comm., Chief Bar'ros?"

The heavy set guard looked glum. "We thought he was celebrating Independence a little early. But we came to investigate anyway."

"And what did you find, Chief Bar'ros?"

"Well, we found the Se'er. Just where he said he'd be. And he pointed us toward subdock nine-L. That's when we saw the bodies."

"Go on, Chief Bar'ros."

"It was a terrible sight. The Se'er had used a Cyber-bola. That's a rotating solid ball embedded with razors which...well, anyway, it was a mess. Blood and brains everywhere. I was the first to notice that the male victim who had fallen on the ramp up to the Fast was a Centaur. We don't see too many of that kind around here. Then I saw the female victim. That's when I became more suspicious. I called City-Police and asked for a team to come here and to bring a molecular of recently listed missing persons. And"—Bar'ros face fell even lower—"it turned out to be her."

"Whom, Chief Bar'ros? What is the identity of the second victim?" Nikka asked, making it play out.

"The Matriarch. Wicca Eighth. You can see the City-Police team over there now."

Mart Kell stood up so fast he almost knocked his chair over.

On the holo-screen, Nikka went on probing, "You'd heard of the Matriarch's disappearance earlier? Was that why you suspected it might be her?"

"Who hadn't heard of her disappearance? But I'll tell you I didn't recognize her. The clothing was typical Eudoran Tourist gear, not what a woman of her importance would be wearing."

"What made you think it might be the Matriarch?"

"I put together what the Se'er had said about revenge and the Centaur being here, and I guessed the Matriarch might have been trying to leave the City secretly and had arranged for the Centaur to bring a Fast to meet her here. This Se'er must have spotted her and struck."

The holo now swept the death scene. Even from a distance, it was a horrible sight. All one could see of Wicca was her robes of disguise. But the Centaur was in a more direct line, his head so awry from his body amid all the blood that it was obvious he had been nearly decapitated.

"Stop!" Mart said. "Freeze it! Turn it off!"

He began to walk about so blindly that he almost walked into a wall.

"It's true!" Vinson said. "Tedesco comm.ed mother here to confirm the molecular did belong to Wicca. The City-Police have done other IDs."

"She was using *my* dock!" Mart said. "The astonishing effrontery of the witch!"

"Tedesco said that the owner of the boutique who helped Wicca escape was probably in on it. Possibly part of the Se'er network. Wicca or someone in her party must have approached her about helping the escape attempt, and the conspiracy was set in operation. The boutique owner said she would arrange Wicca's escape. The Se'er followed Wicca and did the rest," Vinson said. "Naturally the investigation will be thorough. We'll root out everyone connected with it and sentence them all to a full 'wipe.'"

"On the day before Independence—" Mart began.

"Ironic, no? But it won't stop the transfer of power," Vinson said. "If anything, it will facilitate it."

Mart looked at him and thought how much like his mother young Todd could be at times.

Mostly, however, Mart was trying to feel his way through life without Wicca Eighth. Without Kri'nni. Without Cray 12,000. With Independence. And with Hesperian influence supreme now. It really was all new, all changed, wasn't it? The great wave had swept through and taken so many with it that Mart had assumed were permanent—or, if not permanent, then at least longer-enduring than himself. Yet they were gone—even his greatest enemy, the Matriarch herself, the only person he'd ever hated and respected as much as his grandfather. And in their place were...Ib'rs. Young, blond, long limbed, handsome Pelagian youths with wombs, dreaming of great princes to sire babies inside them. It was mad, yet...also perfectly appropriate, somehow.

Mart began to laugh, and Vinson came over to him.

"Now, that's the Mart Kell I know."

"They were here before," Mart said. "Three of the young Pelagians."

Vinson's eyes lit up. "No wonder you were distracted. What did I tell you?"

"Superb?" Mart asked. "Oh, they're more than just superb, Vins. They're beautifully strange and bewilderingly forthright and...they're the future!"

"I met them yesterday Sol Rad., at my mother's. I've been fantasizing ever since," Vinson said, guiding Mart out of the private chamber and back to the party.

Mart wasn't all that surprised to see Llega Todd break away from the group she had been talking to and approach him. Vinson vanished as she asked, "Well?"

"I had nothing to do with it!" Mart said only half-joking, "even though it happened at one of my own docks."

"Isn't that one of the nicest aspects of it?" She smiled. "I was having nightmares about what it would be like having her in our midst, capable of fomenting all sorts of trouble."

"Do we say she was escaping with her Centaur lover?"

"It certainly looks like it. Adds sort of a romantic, even a softening touch to the scheming old hag. I'm certain some enterprising young Hesperian is right now on the comm. gathering financial support for an epic PVN on the life and death of 'The Last of the Matriarchs.'"

"How will this be taken on the Center Worlds? In Melisande?"

"Regarding that, what would you say to appointing North-Taylor Diad and Gemma Guo-Rinne as cogovernors of Melisande?"

"Rinne's reputation and local knowledge and Diad's recent heroism should make a formidable combination."

"I'll present it at the next full Quinx," Llega Todd said. "And here's your overpriced son, Di'mir and his counterpart, the ever-resourceful P'al Syzygy."

"Lady Todd, Lord Kell," P'al spoke first.

Llega Todd teased, "We were wondering if, when you two are together, you speak at all or merely toss algorithms back and forth."

P'al ignored her witticism, "Actually, we overheard you saying something about PVNs. Although Ser Sanqq', Mer Clark, and I told you and the Inner Quinx something of our travels on Pelagia, naturally we told only a tiny portion relevant to the matter at hand. Di'mir agrees that a full PVN of our encounters and adventures might prove both popular and an excellent propaganda tool for the new male-gender-breeding project."

Llega shrugged quickly at Mart, as though saying, "It's new to me, too."

"By the way, Lady Todd, Father," Di'mir interjected, "P'al and I came up with a name for the new project. Vir'ism. It comes from an ancient Metro-Terran word *vir,* meaning male. But it's also found in Universo Lexico usage—in 'virile,' for example."

"Vir'ism." Llega Todd rolled the word around her mouth.

"Or Neo-Vir'ism," P'al suggested. "Although it wouldn't be a real return to olden ways."

"P'al and I would be happy to help script the PVN, with Quinx approval, of course."

"And funding," Llega added.

"And we'd go to Pelagia to holo it."

"Naturally, the more Viristic aspects of it will be played up," P'al said, "Ay'r Sanqq' and 'Dward Ib'r's growing affection for each other. Sanqq's realization of his love for 'Dward at the moment the youth was kidnapped makes for a naturally romantic high point."

"Now you know, Lady Todd, what bio-Cybers talk about when they're alone," Mart couldn't help saying.

The two were immediately embarrassed, but Llega Todd and Mart Kell both said they thought it was a good idea, and a project outline should be drawn up for Quinx consideration.

Kars Tedesco arrived at the party with his wife and two adult sons, and Llega and Vinson went to greet them. She commented to Mart that Tedesco would be put in charge of Wicca's murder investigation.

Di'mir also moved off, and Mart was left with P'al Syzygy, who had begun detailing a few of their adventures on Pelagia, when the young Pelagian woman appeared at his side and demanded P'al's immediate attention.

Slightly abashed, P'al introduced her to Mart, who noticed immediately not only how much she resembled her brothers in appearance, but also in her sense of self-worth, self-importance even, doubtless because of all the attention she was receiving in the City. She greeted Mart as though she were an equal, then quickly congratulated him on his recent victory, which she had heard about from everyone, she said. Unlike her brother, she flirted with him openly—a trait Mart always found delightful in females— and also, unlike 'Nton, she never once stammered or seemed anything but bold and forthright—which Mart found definitely in her favor.

He was beginning to think, yes, he'd would invite these young Pelagians to his sphere, throw a dinner, a party for them, when the third sibling appeared—evidently Ay'r Sanqq's spouse—and pulled his sister away to meet someone else. Mart noted that Oudma looked back and smiled meaningfully at him, then said outright she hoped to see Mart again.

"They're in great demand tonight," P'al observed laconically.

"They're a sensation. But tell me: why did Ay'r Sanqq' retain his Pelagian disguise when he returned?"

"You've seen Creed Lars'son's coloring? Ay'r was 'xchanged as a young neo to better fit into Matriarchal life when his parents were forced to go into hiding and abandon him. He now has his natural physical coloring."

"So this new age is to have new colors of humes?" Mart said.

"It would appear so," P'al commented dryly, then went on to explain more of how the planned P.V.N. would aid Vir'ism.

Mart finally made his escape from P'al, only to find that he had to avoid Debr'a, too. He evaded her and slipped to a higher level, near two of the remaining refining tubes, where colored gases pirouetted. Behind them, the tinted glass wall had been removed for several meters to allow a small balcony providing a spectacular overlook of the Domenica Hill area. Standing on the balcony was Ay'r Kerry Sanqq'.

For a moment, Mart thought he would leave Ay'r alone with his thoughts. He was turning to go back inside The Blue House when Ay'r turned, spotted Mart, and saluted him. "Lord Kell."

Mart advanced to where Ay'r stood.

"Do you know this section of the City?"

"I've never been in the City before, much as I would have liked to."

"If Premier Todd and some others have their way, Hesperia will become your new home," Mart said.

"I look forward to it. I've spent the last five decades traveling about. Perhaps now, with Oudma and 'Dward and the infants on their way, it's time I settled down. It will certainly provide me with the needed extra income, if, say, I could obtain a University post in Species Ethnology."

Mart couldn't hold back a laugh.

"What?" Ay'r asked.

"Didn't P'al say that you hold the patent to the Relfian Viviparturition Procedure? And that your patent was refiled here on Hesperia upon your arrival a few days ago?"

"Yes. So?"

"So? How many possibly fertile males are there in the known galaxy? A few hundred billion?"

"I suppose." Ay'r still looked confused.

"That number times whatever royalty percentage you decide upon will be your net worth. In a few decades, you should be wealthier than any Beryllium tycoon. And don't tell me you won't charge a fee. You must. If it's free no one will take it. Especially among the Hesperian Thwwing-Racing Set. We will be the first to have the procedure, and you'll charge us each a great deal. Only later on will the procedure's cost be scaled down to match income."

Ay'r looked stunned.

"You never thought of any of this?" Mart said.

"Truthfully, I didn't let it go that far in my thought. I was still thinking about how enormous a change it will make in...well, everything!"

That statement impressed Mart more than he would ever reveal.

"Not in everything, surely?"

"I think so, yes. Certainly socially. I've seen that RV can work in a controlled small-population environment. But on Hesperia? On Electra and Trefuss and Curie and the rest of the Center Worlds?"

" 'From fairest flowers we desire increase,' " Mart quoted an old Metro-Terran poet. "When we were negotiating with them, the Deneban Pioneers told me they needed children as much as they needed air and food and water. Even the most sophisticated humes will jump at the procedure once they see how easy it is."

Ay'r looked confused again. "You argued against it. What changed your mind? Was it seeing Cas'sio?"

"I did see Cas'sio, but no, he didn't change my mind. It's simply the only viable future we have left now. And it's not a bad one, considering that the alternative is no future at all."

Ay'r turned away. "I know all that. But what bothers me is that in, say a thousand years to come, all will be turned around from how it has been. Males mating. Males being born. Far fewer females. Will they be considered and treated inferior, or as precious objects? We don't know. Then, too, males as domestic partners...I'm just not sure. In the past, they have never evinced as much interest in stable relationships as females. Was that a function of the social mores of their time, or is it psychobiological? Will the family unit as we know it alter drastically? Will it even be recognizable? Will some new social form take over? It all seems so unpredictable, such a total contradiction of how it all worked under the Matriarchy that I feel it's somehow not the final answer."

"Because it's not. It's not stasis, but growth. Change," Mart said.

"Such an enormous change. And I'll live out the rest of my years watching, waiting for it to go amok, and always feeling responsible."

"If you're willing to do that, then we'll all have someone to blame."

"Now you're making fun of me. Did you know how much I admired you at the University? And how afraid of you I was?"

"No?" Mart asked.

"Truly! Will I really be so rich as you said before?"

"Eventually, yes."

"That should help. 'Dward says he wants to have many children."

"Apparently so does 'Nton," Mart let slip out.

Ay'r didn't comment on the ramifications of that remark. Instead he said, "I'll always worry if we're doing the right thing. I'll worry every day of my life."

So Ay'r Kerry Sanqq' was remarkable in more ways than one.

"Since it evidently is going to happen and can't be stopped, why don't you and I meet again, right here, in, say, four centuries! We'll meet and see how it worked out—or didn't work out, whichever the case is."

Mart put out a hand for a wrist-grip, and Ay'r gave it to him, saying, "Agreement! We'll meet again in four centuries, on Independence Eve, right here in Hesperia."

The vow made, the next few moments passed in silence. When they let their hands drop, Mart said, "So you had an Ed. & Dev. crush on me?"

"I certainly did. So you're going to espouse 'Nton Ib'r, are you?"

"He certainly thinks I ought to."

"I suppose I'll need a business manager," Ay'r mused.

"I know just the one," Mart said. "Female, hume. The best in the City."

They went back into the party.

Epilogue

Outside the Observatory, the rain ceased.

The Recorder waited patiently until the water-drenched panes before him began to clear. Naturally, every facet of the Observatory was streaked and strained from the rainfall. Once the Recorder felt certain the rain had truly ceased and was not about to begin again, he would tell the Cyber-mechanism to air-hose them top to bottom.

The Recorder could wait. Over decades, he had learned patience. Patience and discrimination. Better qualifications for a true Recorder than strong sight or deep perception. Lately, of course, he'd had to be more patient and truly discriminating than ever in his long life of Observing. In new ways. Patient for the rain to stop. Patient for the Cyber-mechanism to check out all of its working parts, to repair what had been broken by mishap or corroded by the hours and days and weeks of rain before it could properly air-hose the Observatory. Discrimination as to new things, too: whether this was merely a momentary letup, so temporary it would be over before the mechanism could check itself out, or whether it was a longer one: long enough for him to Observe and Record.

The last acceptable Observation had occurred five-and-one-quarter days ago, Sol Rad. Although the Recorder was not given to going back to his Recordings, he'd had so much time of no Observing of late that he had gone back over his Recording of that last rain-free hiatus. Gone back to it, again and again, as though proving something to someone. Not to himself, the Recorder knew. Recorders made no value judgments. Ever. They Observed and they Recorded. Nothing more.

Still, the data from that last two-and-one-half-hour-long Observation and Recording had been remarkable.

For example, the fact that the Pelagian Ocean appeared at this area of southern continental mountain cliff to have risen so high as to be only three meters from the cliff top. The cliff top itself represented the highest flatland area upon continental Pelagia. Scarcely one-half Pelagian Year ago, the ocean's greatest height at the four-moon aphelion had been thirteen meters from the clifftop: a rise of ten meters—suggesting substantial addition of water mass to the ocean.

Of course, all previous Observations and Recordings of the many and varied aspects of the Pelagian Ocean were now doomed to history. Over the past several pauses in the rain, the Recorder had assiduously collated all of the new Recordings, but despite the greatest efforts of a mind trained to Observe and Discriminate, and despite the greatest efforts of the Cyber-mechanism which tabulated and analyzed the data, he had been unable to discover anything vaguely resembling a pattern, rhythm or series of patterns or rhythms in the new current flows or in the new marine topographies that had been revealed. Evidently, the enormous and continual downpour had added so massively to the ocean that only diagrams of chaos were now acceptable. Soon, the Recorder knew, even that chaos would reveal a pattern. Until it did, he could not feel completely easy or satisfied.

Behind him, the Recorder could hear the half-dozen Mycophages who had taken refuge during the most recent downpour moving about in the Observatory. Another aspect of his new patience: the fragile creatures were easily wounded by falling ice stones. He'd had to accustom himself to their suddenly entering and looking amid the consoles for medical supplies to tend themselves and each other. He'd had to accustom himself to having the most fragile remain sleeping in the Observatory until the weather let up and/or they were well enough to be moved by their fellows back to their caves.

Already, the lower levels of those caves were flooded from all the rain, Oo-lol-oo had told the Recorder. Already, the older Mycophages were complaining of the constant dampness and cold within their home.

Although he was only a Recorder, he had taken pity upon them and given them some of his heating units. They'd shown the proper gratitude. He knew that they could no longer forage for food as easily or as far now, and subsisted on what they grew in their caves. He pretended to sleep while they rummaged through his own food supplies. It meant little to the Recorder. He had never eaten but a small portion of what the Cyber-mechanism prepared. Let them have it, the frightened and unhappy creatures.

During the last hiatus, Oo-lol-oo told him, one great ice boulder had fallen and severely damaged one of their two main caves. The Mycophages had all moved into the other cave. They were coping well, the Recorder thought. But sometimes they needed to feel more security than a cave could provide, especially the very old among them and the very young, and thus he allowed them inside the Observatory to sleep and feel secure.

The Recorder could hear the air-hoses begin to work. It was fortunate that he had accepted the offer of that Offworlder who had refurbished the entire Cyber-mechanism before he had left for...Hesperia. That was what he had told the Recorder, who naturally had Recorded the fact, as well as the conversation, like all Offworlder conversations he had ever had. The Recorder had no idea what or where Hesperia was.

That Offworlder had been here before, scarcely a Pelagian year before. And with some of the same travelers. Only that time they had trekked up from the Great Valley below mounted on coleopteroid creatures. This time, they had simply arrived in their bubbles from above, frightening the Mycophages. Or so the Mycophages thought at the time. Since that time, they had learned true fear.

He had told the Recorder his name was P'al Syzygy. With him were Ay'r Kerry Sanqq' and the female, Alli-Clark, all of them returned to Pelagia for...well, although they had attempted to explain it, the Recorder hadn't truly understood. Something about "recording Dryland so all could experience it, now and in the future, forever, even when it no longer existed." Which made sense to the Recorder. Although he *did* wonder what type of hume would be interested in Dryland.

Only one of the Drylanders had returned with them, 'Harles Ib'r, now bonded to Alli-Clark. They had remained together on Pelagia the longest of all the offworlders. Talked about remaining here, among the Mycophages, or even at the Observatory. But once the ice stones began to fall heavily, they, too, had left, sad at having to go. The Recorder had especially Observed 'Harles Ib'r's sadness, after the two of them had returned from a brief air-bubble trip over the Great Valley.

When the two pale and shaken bond-mates were done weeping, the Recorder approached them and asked for their Observations. With much hesitation and more tears, they told him the extent of the damage they had Observed: the Delta completely under water, the Great Temple sunk, Bogland vanished beneath its lake, the two rivers no longer visible since all of the valley was water. Finally, even the highest areas—the steep mountain valleys to the east—would be washed away.

The Recorder noted down the bond-mates' narrative as well as their grief and horror. But one incident had eluded his comprehension. Once, during their telling of their Observations, 'Harles Ib'r had suddenly stood up and raised his fists to the ceiling and began shouting incomprehensibly. That, too, he had Recorded, although the meaning of the gesture was lost to him. Only when 'Harles Ib'r had fallen back into the seating and was once again morose and thoughtful did he speak quietly, comprehensibly. What Ib'r said and what had been Recorded was "How many more worlds must we build up only to see them taken from us?"

Now the Recorder could tell the air-hoses were having a beneficial effect. The facets were being cleared of streaks and stains. Behind him, he heard the Mycophages begin to murmur, and he wondered vaguely what they had found.

He gestured to them, and finally one child crept forward and taking the Recorder's hand pointed out—a clearing in the dark-colored clouds, a light shining through, radiating beams of sunlight.

"We are saved, Recorder! Saved!" the child repeated. Then he ran outside with his fellows and soon the Recorder could hear many other young Mycophages who had picked their way past rivulets and new-made rills within their cave to come outside onto the platform surrounding the Observatory where they began to murmur the word "Saved!" loudly, again and again.

But already he was Observing and Recording. Observing that the ocean had now risen to within one meter of the cliff top. Recording that the ocean's currents still exercised sudden mutations and unexpected confluences of current and marinal planes which defied that greater pattern which chaos requires. He Recorded how, behind the Observatory the triple peaks had each lost close to six meters of altitude in wash-off, how the shapes of the cliffs and hills, of the lips and ridges had all been smoothed down by the constant rain, except in those places where larger ice boulders had fallen. He observed the opening up of the clouds above and the strength of the sunlight through it and the amount of evaporation at the cloud's opening and directly upon the surface of each facet of the Observatory, and the strength of the sun upon the floor within and upon the ocean outside and he Observed that the Mycophages brought their wounded and ill and rain-weary from out of their caves and how all of them walked about saying "Saved!" and how they were kind and loving toward each other and held each other and fed each other tidbits of mushrooms and food taken from his own stores, and how some sang and others danced long through the afternoon and even as it shaded into dusk when the sun vanished and the three remaining moons became visible through the clearing in the clouds. Then he began to Observe and Record the moonlight: its luminescence upon the ocean, its exact coloring upon the surface of the remaining land, how it tinted the facets of the Observatory.

He was still Observing and Recording later that night when the clouds closed and when, shortly afterward, the rain began again.